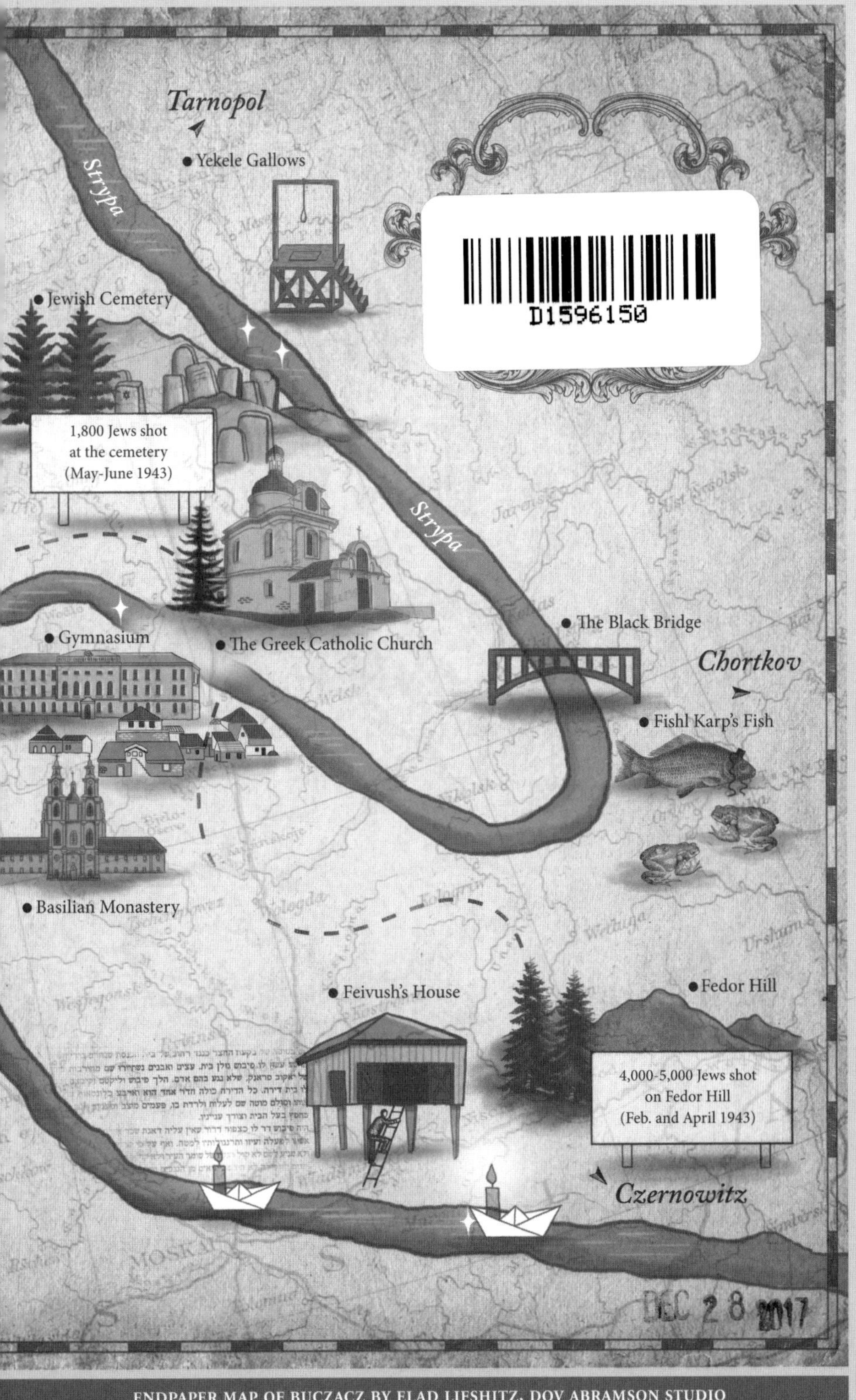

ENDPAPER MAP OF BUCZACZ BY ELAD LIFSHITZ, DOV ABRAMSON STUDIO

The **Toby Press S.Y. Agnon Library**
Jeffrey Saks, Series Editor

Books from this series

A Book That Was Lost: Thirty-Five Stories

To This Day

Shira

A Simple Story

Two Scholars That Were in Our Town and Other Novellas

Two Tales: Betrothed & Edo and Enam

A Guest for the Night

The Bridal Canopy

The Orange Peel and Other Satires

A City in Its Fullness

In Mr. Lublin's Store (forthcoming)

Forevermore & Other Stories of the Old World and the New (forthcoming)

And the Crooked Shall Be Made Straight (forthcoming)

Illustrated:
From Foe to Friend & Other Stories by S.Y. Agnon
A Graphic Novel by Shay Charka

A City in Its Fullness

S.Y. AGNON

TRANSLATED FROM THE HEBREW

EDITED BY
ALAN MINTZ AND JEFFREY SAKS

The Toby Press

A City in Its Fullness
by S.Y. Agnon
Edited by Alan Mintz and Jeffrey Saks

מוקדש בברכה ובכבוד לגרשון יעקב בן יוסף וחנה למשפחת קקסט

The Toby Press LLC
POB 8531, New Milford, CT 06776-8531, USA
& POB 2455, London W1A 5WY, England
www.tobypress.com

ISBN 978-1-59264-450-6

Printed and bound in the United States

In memory of

James S. Diamond ז"ל

Genial Master

A City in Its Fullness

This is the chronicle of the city of Buczacz, which I have written in my pain and anguish so that our descendants should know that our city was full of Torah, wisdom, love, piety, life, grace, kindness and charity from the time of its founding until the arrival of the blighted abomination and their befouled and deranged accomplices who wrought destruction upon it. May God avenge the blood of His servants and visit vengeance upon His enemies and deliver Israel from its sorrows.

Contents

STORIES FROM BOOK III: LATTER GENERATIONS

List of Illustrations

Foreword

"I Am Building a City": On Agnon's Buczacz Tales

In the mid-1950s, the great Hebrew writer S.Y. Agnon began to publish a series of stories about Buczacz, the Galician town in which he grew up and lived until he left for Palestine in 1908 at the age of nineteen. These were not reminiscences of childhood but rather tales set beyond the reach of modern memory, from the middle of the seventeenth century to the middle of the nineteenth. Many of the stories appeared in the literary pages of the newspaper *Haaretz,* and he was working on his Buczacz project through the period of excitement surrounding his 1966 receipt of the Nobel Prize for literature right up until his death in 1970. He left editorial guidelines for his daughter Emunah Yaron for shaping of the stories into an orchestrated sequence. She executed his plans, and in 1973 *'Ir u-Melo'ah* (*A City in Its Fullness*) appeared. It contained over 140 stories and ran to 724 pages.

Few readers or critics realized how powerfully the Buczacz project had preoccupied Agnon during the last period of his life. And few had paid much attention to the stories when they were appearing in newspapers and literary supplements. The 1950s and 1960s were a time of intense institution building for the young State of Israel, and there was little ready interest in stories about the lives of Jews in the Diaspora long ago. Zionist culture persisted in viewing East European Jewish life as weak and compromised, and literary accounts of those times were chiefly of interest as a way of understanding the "corrupt" milieu from which the new Hebrew nation had broken away. Those readers who did notice the Buczacz stories tended to regard them as the over-ripe fruit, the products of the aging master's nostalgia for his origins.

From our vantage point, over a half century later, things look very different. With the gift of hindsight, we can now discern in this late phase of Agnon's life the contours of an enterprise that is ambitious, innovative and challenging. Rather than winding down into a wistful, elegiac homage to the cradle of his youth, Agnon was girding his loins to undertake a major revision of the perception of East European Jewry. He was seeking to rescue its memory from a series of unfortunate fates. In earlier Hebrew literature, the shtetl had been figured as a place of spiritual exhaustion and communal venality. The vector of judgment was reversed after the Holocaust in the abundance of memorial volumes for destroyed communities, which tended to present an idealized picture of a vanished way of life. And certainly the emergence of Holocaust literature itself, which focused on the ways Jews perished, portrayed pre-war Jewish life as existing always under the sign of persecution and extermination.

But it was not only balance and accuracy that Agnon was after in his grand revision. The deeper truth about Polish Jewry, he argued, could be grasped only by leaping backward in time to the period before modernization had eroded the authority that the Torah and the community exerted on the everyday lives of Jews. What he saw in this "classic" period was not a dour allegiance to rabbinic discipline but rather a variegated vitality bubbling up from an organically Jewish life. As the title *A City in Its Fullness* indicates, Agnon's project has epic ambitions. And indeed the book succeeds in conjuring up a vast canvas that stretches horizontally over two centuries and vertically from the wealthiest merchants and most distinguished rabbis down to the poorest artisans and most piteous scoundrels. Yet even as Agnon aspired for totality, he recognized the need for selectivity and organization – not only to give shape to his sprawling evocation but also to impose on it a normative vision.

By the term normative I mean the relationship of an experience or an activity to a set of privileged values. Both Agnon the author and the narrator he created to tell these stories held the study of Torah and the worship of God in the synagogue service to be supremely important values in Jewish society. The difference between the world depicted in *A City in Its Fullness* and East European Jewish life in the period of modernity hinges on the force and plausibility of these values. Most all the stories in this collection attest to the difficulty in making Torah and worship preeminent and authoritative even in this so-called classic period. The human heart is what it is; grandiosity, cupidity, and resentment are constant obstacles, leaving a gap between the real and the ideal. The interests and animosities of the gentile rulers exert a corrosive effect on the community's ability or desire to live according to its true priorities. Yet amidst all the crowded instances of deviation and deficiencies, the narrator never lets us forget the force of the values against which these failures are found to be wanting. Thus *A City in Its Fullness* is distinguished both by its honesty in aspiring to represent all of Jewish life and by its insistence on viewing that fullness through a normative grid.

A key example is the novella-length story "In Search of a Rabbi, *or* The Governor's Whim." As a city with a long tradition of Torah scholarship, Buczacz considers itself deserving of a distinguished scholar as its rabbi. But many real-world forces frustrate this ambition. Richer cities lure away Buczacz-born scholars and even "kidnap" rabbis on their way to Buczacz to take up a rabbinical post. The Polish nobles who own the city mix in the internal affairs of the Jewish community, and their interference puts off high-minded scholars from settling there. The community itself is dividing among quarrelsome factions. The story begins when all parties agree upon the candidacy of the Rabbi of Zabno, and an embassy is dispatched to his faraway town. After a long and fascinating tale-within-a-tale told by the rabbi, the representatives are informed that, to their amazement, the greatest scholar of the generation, one Rabbi Mordechai, is actually a tinsmith living unacknowledged within their very midst, within Buczacz itself. The representatives bring their report back home, and the leaders of Buczacz pride themselves on their willingness to set aside a bias against artisans and to appoint Rabbi Mordechai their rabbi, and they are further encouraged to discover that the appointment is looked on favorably by the Polish ruler of the city. But once Rabbi Mordechai learns of the ruler's involvement, he peremptorily turns down the appointment and moves away from Buczacz, leaving the city once again without spiritual leadership and with nothing to show for its considerable troubles.

Although seemingly capricious, Rabbi Mordechai's rejection in fact comes at the end of a long series of telescoping narratives that demonstrate the treacherous influence of gentile rulers on the disinterested pursuit of Torah study. The proof that the noble pursuit of Torah study is not in fact an unobtainable ideal is provided by the story the Rabbi of Zabno tells the Buczacz representatives about his private study sessions with Rabbi Mordechai, which are both deeply passionate and bracingly competitive. To be sure, the norm of true Torah study is only fleetingly realized, but its truth serves to locate and organize the array of human experiences represented in the story. This same constellation applies in the other hallmark area of normative value: synagogue worship. A series of stories about ḥazzanim, synagogue prayer leaders, valorizes purity and selflessness in the pursuit of this vocation and at the same time presents them as ideals that ordinary human nature can fulfill only rarely and with extreme difficulty.

To be sure, study and worship are transcendental values that provide the keys to the iconography of *A City in Its Fullness*. Yet the vivid liveliness of the stories depends on Agnon's grounding these values in the concreteness of geography and history. Agnon chose to re-imagine the inner life of Polish Jewry by focusing exclusively on one city, a city of some ten thousand Jewish souls that was certainly not among the first tier of Galician cities, despite its scholarly *amour-propre*. The choice of Buczacz is of course an homage of a son of Buczacz to his hometown, and it is the place whose stories and legends he knew best. But the choice is far cannier than nostalgia and convenience. Like James Joyce's Dublin and William Faulkner's Yoknapatawpha County, Agnon was expressing the modernist's aesthetic preference for the particular over the universal. Anatomizing this one, modest community gave Agnon a greater chance of saying something true about the larger picture of Polish Jewry.

A City in Its Fullness is conceived in part as a "Baedeker" to Buczacz. In the larger Hebrew original from which these stories are taken, the reader is accompanied on a guided tour of the city that begins with its sacred center (the study houses and synagogues), proceeds to its civil spaces (marketplace, fountain, Town Hall), and eventually leads to the liminal areas on its fringes and beyond the River Strypa that runs through it. Each of these places serves as an impetus to storytelling. Sometimes the purpose of the story is straightforwardly etiological. On his tour of the Great Synagogue, the narrator comes across a chandelier made of Italian glass and tells the story of the Buczacz merchant who brought it back from Trieste as a gift from a Jewish apostate ("The Brilliant Chandelier"); the fate of the synagogue's seven-branch candelabrum provides an occasion for reviewing the uneasy relationship between the Jewish community and the successive regimes of gentile rulers ("The Tale of the Menorah"). At other times, the place, be it as grand as the magnificent Town Hall, is only the occasion for a "back story" that becomes a fictional exploration on its own terms. Such is the case with the story "The Partners," which, in the guise of explaining why a family of Jewish yeast merchants has occupied the basement of the Town Hall for far more than a century, provocatively imagines an intimate encounter between a humble Jewish charcoal maker and Count Potocki, the owner of Buczacz.

The vivid realization of time and place might appear to be simply good literary practice. But if this takes place in Hebrew within the Zionist imagination and if the place is located in the Diaspora, then the matter is not so simple. Even before the emergence of political Zionism at the end of the nineteenth century, Hebrew literature represented Jewish life in Eastern Europe as riddled with corruption and obscurantism; and once a viable Jewish settlement in Palestine was established in the 1920s, the disintegrating life of European Jewry was constantly compared to the promise of the new society being created in the Hebrew homeland. The impatient and scant reception given to the stories of *A City in Its Fullness* when they were published already after the establishment of Israel is further evidence of a general turning away from the European past and a suspicion of large-scale investment in imagining its inner workings. The exception to this distemper was of course Agnon's own writings, beginning from *And the Crooked Shall Be Made Straight* in 1912 through *A Guest for the Night* in 1939. But the epic and sustained nature of the Buczacz stories, coming as they did after the establishment of the state, made a claim that was especially provocative. While David Ben-Gurion, Israel's Prime Minister during the country's first two decades, was engaged in the process of building a state, S.Y. Agnon was engaged in another kind construction project. "I am building a city," he wrote to the literary critic Baruch Kurzweil. That city was Buczacz, and it was located very far from Zion in both time and place.

Agnon was a deeply professing religious Zionist whose commitment was manifest in his life choices and at all levels of his writings. How then to reconcile the old city with the new state? The prompt to solving this puzzle is found in the very first story in *A City in Its Fullness*, titled, simply, "Buczacz." Many Jewish communities in Eastern Europe have stories about how they were founded, so-called origin myths, and this inaugural story is the one Agnon tells about Buczacz. In this telling, the city was founded by Jews from an ancient community in the Rhineland Valley who undertook "to ascend" and settle in the Land of Israel. Setting off with no practical direction and only their faith in hand, their eastward march was overcome by winter, and they are forced to wait out the cold season deep in the forests. Their encampment was discovered by Polish nobles on a hunting party. The Poles had recently colonized what is now western Ukraine, and they invited the Jews to survive the winter by returning to their estates. They found the Jews brought them economic benefit by helping to manage their vast holdings and by introducing commerce into these primitive regions. When the next winter came, the Jews calculated that the elderly and the pregnant could not withstand the rigors of a renewed journey to the Holy Land, and it was decided to stay put for the time being. Their affairs prospered, and eventually they were able to create a centralized Jewish settlement with all the appurtenance of a *Kehilah Kedoshah,* a full Jewish community with its synagogues, study houses, law courts, and schools; the dream of continuing on to Zion was quietly put aside.

In Agnon's rendering of its origins, then, Buczacz is a way station on the path to the Land of Israel, the result of an arrested journey. The Rhineland Jews did not reach their objective because they were deficient in the practical worldliness necessary to accomplish such a journey and because of the very real geographical and historical difficulties that stood in their way. But their motivation was unimpeachable, and the fact that the Holy Community of Buczacz came into existence was the result of their readiness to move forward and upward. Buczacz is thus a compromise, a millennium-long act of temporizing between the (old) Exile and Zion. As such, it is a community that is aspiring rather than fallen. It is as much of a sovereign Jewish polity that can exist *short* of the return of the people to its homeland. In the best of times, the covenants granted by the Polish nobility allowed the Jews a substantial degree of self-government, which was implemented by rabbinic law and communal cohesion. The stories of *A City in Its Fullness* recount tales not only of rabbi-sages but also of non-rabbinic communal leaders like R. Moshe Aharon, a mead merchant who is presented as being nothing less than a statesman ("R. Moshe Aharon the Mead Merchant"). Buczacz is but one constituent city-state within the larger commonwealth of the Council of the Four Lands, which, until it was abolished in 1764, served as a kind of legislative body for the Jewish communities of Eastern Europe.

The relationship between Buczacz and Zion is deeply dialectical. On the one hand, as we have seen, Buczacz is presented as a link in the movement toward Zion. This takes up a position against early Zionist historiography, which viewed the intense religious culture of Diaspora communities as a sublimation of the worldly national impulse; inscribing daily life within the world of Torah was taken merely as a way of surviving the abnormal conditions of Exile. Agnon's Buczacz, by contrast, is a fully-functioning organism engaging life at all levels possible, and as such it is a true anticipation of the Jewish state to come. On the other hand, Buczacz, in its capacity as a representative of the classical civilization of Polish Jewry, presents a critique of the State of Israel, the culmination of Zionism in Agnon's time. Because of their subjugation to gentile rule, to be sure, the Jews of Buczacz could never attain to the sovereignty enjoyed by the modern Jewish state. But that modern state is hobbled by a radical secularity that produced as a reaction an obscurantist Orthodoxy. The organic integration of Torah and life, the particular with the universal, is an example of what would be necessary to make the Zionist reality whole.

The factors that prevent Buczacz from being whole are evident in nearly every story in this collection. Agnon displays a nuanced awareness of how the lives of the Jews were affected by the changing history of the region. When the Jews were brought to the area by Polish landowners in the sixteenth and seventeenth centuries, the local population was made up of Ruthenian (Ukrainian) peasants, who became serfs to the Polish nobles. The Jews served the interests of the Poles as a managerial and commercial class. The Jews were mostly town dwellers who stimulated the market economy by buying the peasants' surplus production and selling them manufactured goods they could not produce themselves. They practiced such handicrafts as tanning, butchering, candle making, haberdashery, and shoe making. They leased the rights to fish the rivers, harvest the forests and manufacture salt. A significant number of Jews made a living from operating rural taverns, where they dispensed to the peasantry liquor distilled from the lord's surplus grain. Situated thus between the Polish landowners and the Ruthenian peasants, the Jews were often perceived by the latter as agents of the former. In the great cataclysm of the mid-seventeenth century, the Khmelnitski Massacres, in which hundreds of Jewish communities were decimated, Cossacks from east of the Dnieper River joined with Tatar bands to exploit the resentment of the Ruthenians against their Polish oppressors and their Jewish agents. After the Cossacks withdrew, the Jewish communities slowly rebuilt and a relatively stable commercial life was reestablished.

Ruthenian-Jewish relations do not receive much treatment in *A City in Its Fullness*, and when they are represented—see "The Partners" and "In a Single Moment"—the Jews are portrayed as displaying far more humanity than the Poles. It is rather the transactions between the Jews and their Polish overlords that compel Agnon's attention. Some of these noble families were fabulously wealthy and owned outright dozens of cities and hundreds of villages and trackless forests. Relations between these princes, dukes and counts and great Jewish merchants are portrayed in a number of stories, especially in "In Search of a Rabbi, *or* The Governor's Whim" with its intricate patterning of power relations. The moral of this epic tale is the baleful impact of the rulers' intervention in communal affairs on the disinterestedness of Torah study and rabbinic leadership. Other stories are concerned with staging encounters between unusual Jews and high nobles, meetings that are as revelatory as they are unlikely to have taken place in real life. A great prince of the realm, sick with a wasting disease brought on by the commission of a terrible sin, ends up on the doorstep of the eponymous hero of "R. Moshe Aharon the Mead Merchant," who not only cures him but becomes his friend. In "The Partners" a humble Jewish charcoal maker incurs the gratitude of the great Count Potocki for saving his life after he was separated from his hunting party in the forest. In these tales Agnon is concerned less with plot than with character. The Poles looked down upon the Jews for being merchants and tradesmen, for being town dwellers, for not being Catholics, and for simply being Jews. The social distance between the two groups, at least perceived by the Poles, was enormous. Through the freedom afforded by fictional reimagining, Agnon reveals the inner thoughts of both parties and evens the playing field.

In the 1770s, the Polish-Lithuanian Commonwealth ceased to exist, and its lands were divided among Russia, Prussia and Austria. The southeastern borderlands, formerly called Rus, fell to the Austrian Empire, which renamed them the province of Galicia. This was a hybrid entity: A German-speaking administration dispatched from Vienna ruled over Poles, Jews and Ruthenians, three groups with distinct cultures and languages. The Polish nobility retained ownership of most of their estates but ceased to be a law unto themselves; they were now subject to a bureaucracy administered from afar. For the Jews, the changes were far reaching, and in the eyes of traditionalists, like the narrator of the stories in *A City in Its Fullness*, a great misfortune.

The *modus vivendi* worked out over generations between Jewish leaders and the Polish magnates who owned the towns in which they lived had left Jewish communities a substantial degree of autonomy. Deviance and disputes, whether religious or civil, were largely handled by Jewish courts, and this allowed rabbinic and community authority to maintain its sway. The shift from being inhabitants of privately owned towns and estates to being subjects of a multi-national empire was enormous, and Agnon's stories attend closely to these changes. The enlightened absolutism of the Hapsburgs dictated that army service should be incumbent on all imperial subjects, the Jews being no exception. Despite objections to young men being ripped from their homes and placed for prolonged periods in situations in which traditional observance could not be maintained, especially Shabbat and kashrut, each community was given a quota it had to fulfill. This turned out to be an invitation to communal corruption; the town's elders would pay the itinerant poor to fill the quotas or they would forcibly offer up young tradesmen in order to avoid the induction of Torah scholars or the sons of householders. The powerful and heart-rending story "Disappeared" gives an account of a tailor's apprentice who is subjected to this fate; ironically, the boy's army experience turns out to be much less damaging than the turpitude of the Buczacz community and the grotesque fate that awaits him afterward. Centralized taxation was another temptation to corruption. Encouraged by rapacious Jewish tax contractors, Vienna levied a punishing tax on the use of every single candle used on Sabbaths and at weddings. "Feivush Gazlan" is the affecting story of a local Jewish enforcer who is employed to stomp into homes on Friday evenings to ensure the tax has been paid and take action if not. Another, crucial change introduced by the Austrians is depicted in the two stories, alternate accounts of the same event, carrying the title "Yekele." The imposition of a centralized judicial system took away from the Jewish community its authority to adjudicate all but ritual matters. Yekele is a deviant youth falsely accused of theft, but because he has publically insulted the autocratic leader of the Buczacz Jewish community, his case is handed over to the authorities, and he ends up swinging from the gallows in a shameful public execution.

Over time, the axis between Buczacz and Vienna turned into a grand avenue for modernization for those who sought it. Polish Jews living under the Russian Czar in the nineteenth century experienced mounting persecution and xenophobia on many fronts, but Jews living under the Hapsburgs gained rights as citizens of a liberal empire. The Austro-Hungarian form of Serfdom was abolished in 1848, and the Jews of Galicia were emancipated and given the vote in 1867. For a young man from Buczacz there was no bar to taking up residence in Vienna and attending university. The availability of these freedoms, along with the rise of socialism and modern nationalism in various forms, had a significant impact on Jewish life in Buczacz. But this is precisely the territory that *A City in Its Fullness* declines to explore. By ending the scope of the stories just as these changes were arriving, Agnon underscored his desire to focus on the era before the eclipse and erosion of rabbinic and communal authority. He had already devoted two novels to what came afterward. *A Simple Story* (1935) takes place in Buczacz at the beginning of the twentieth century, and *A Guest for the Night* (1939) is set, also in Buczacz, in 1930. The difference between those two works and *A City in Its Fullness* lies not only in the time period represented. Although each is written in a different mode, both are novels, the quintessentially modern prose form, whereas *A City in Its Fullness* is a cycle of stories told after the manner of more traditional storytelling.

One of the seeming paradoxes of these stories is the pervasive mention of the Holocaust. If the stories are set in the premodern period, how can they know about the terrible fate of European Jewry in the twentieth century? The beginnings of an answer can be found in "The Sign," a major story Agnon published in 1962. The story is told from the point of view of an Agnon-like narrator living in Jerusalem who hears about the final destruction of Buczacz's Jews by the Nazis and their Ukrainian helpers on the eve of the Shavuot holiday in June 1943. The narrator puts off his grieving in deference to the holiday, but later that night alone in the synagogue he experiences a mystical visitation from the great medieval sacred poet Solomon Ibn Gabirol. In his presence, the narrator finally breaks down and expresses his anguish, and as a consolation the ghostly poet composes an acrostic hymn that will memorialize the name of the destroyed community. "The Sign" is a consecration story that dramatizes Agnon's decision to devote himself to re-imagining the world of Buczacz. *A City in Its Fullness* is indeed a major response to the murder of European Jewry; but it charts a mode of response that is substantively different from what has come to be known as the literature of the Holocaust. Rather than seeking to represent the atrocities themselves and their effects on survivors and their children, Agnon's Buczacz stories make the claim that the truest response to the Holocaust is to recreate literarily the fullness of Jewish life *before* that dark shadow was cast. So, while the terrible occasion for the telling is recurrently and explicitly marked in stories, it itself is not part of the narrative. The Holocaust is typically mentioned in the closing lines of a story as a kind of tragic coda that lies outside its narrative framework.

(Because of its importance as a "consecration story," calling forth the author-narrator to be the scribe dedicated to the literary immortalization of Buczacz, we have chosen to open this collection with "The Sign." In the Hebrew edition Agnon's daughter opted to include the story—which had already appeared in a previous volume—as an appendix.)

The determination of what is in any given story and what is out necessarily draws our attention to the question of who is doing the telling. It is a truth worth recalling that every story is not just told, but is told by someone and from some point of view. Agnon, the historical personage who lived in the Talpiyot neighborhood of Jerusalem and whose likeness formerly appeared on the fifty-shekel bill, is such an indelible presence that readers are tempted to imagine him as the narrator of his stories. But it is a temptation to be resisted, and not just because the real Agnon would have relished having his readers fall into the trap. Over the course of his long writing career, Agnon had occasion to fashion a number of different kinds of narrators, although his favorite is admittedly close to himself. One of Agnon's greatest achievements is taking the autobiographical persona of a middle-aged religious writer and submitting it to a corrosive irony. But when it came to *A City in Its Fullness,* Agnon had to invent a new narrator. Having determined that the stories would be set centuries ago, he could not make do with a narrator whose recall, even when extended by tales transmitted by parents and grandparents, could not journey back beyond the edge of modern memory.

More importantly, Agnon needed a narrator who did not condescend to this long-ago way of life but shared its mental world. He therefore created a kind of amalgam. The narrator would be a man of Buczacz whose attitudes and knowledge would ally him with the rabbinic classes of the age. He is a man, for example, who, despite his wariness of things mystical or ḥasidic, has no problem in describing how the Maharam Schiff, an eminent German Talmudist who died in 1644, could materialize at a circumcision feast in Galicia more than a century later. This narrator—a general construct who voice takes on slightly different colorations in different stories—would not be an identifiable person with a name, and he would not be involved in the action of the stories. Despite being more of a device than a character, the narrator's voice would nevertheless not be devoid of personality. His tics and digressions indeed remind us of some of the habits of the autobiographically-infused narrators in Agnon's earlier fiction, although we should not be drawn to conflate the two. The new narrator's outstanding endowment is his omniscience. The action of *A City in Its Fullness* ranges over two centuries, and not only is the narrator at home in each of these periods but he knows all within them. He knows the exact fare paid by a scholar for a wagon ride between Buczacz and a neighboring town in the same way as he knows the thoughts of a charcoal maker as he tramps through the forest on his way to pray with the community in the Great Synagogue. And to preserve his reliability in the eyes of his readers, the narrator will make a big show of *not* knowing some inconsequential detail as if the admission of this lapse guarantees his status as a trusted chronicler. This is in fact not so different from the omniscience taken for granted by the great nineteenth-century novelists in the realist tradition; Flaubert takes for granted that he can tell us what is in Emma Bovary's heart. Yet because Agnon's narrator is speaking from an earlier time and from within a more traditional community, the sanction for his omniscience had to come from something more than "literature" or "fiction." Agnon found it in the precedent of the *pinkas*, the register or minute book kept by every Jewish community. Although this was usually a dry document tersely recording births and deaths, tax obligations, rabbinic appointments, and the like, it also included anomalous incidents worthy of note. This gave Agnon leave to appropriate the communal authority of the *pinkas* to create a credible position from which his narrator could speak.

To whom the narrator is speaking in *A City in Its Fullness* turns out to be not a simple matter. There are two transactions taking place simultaneously in these stories. On one level, the level dramatized within the stories themselves, the narrator speaks as if conversing with a like-minded audience contemporary to him in time. Just as he is a learned, believing Jew—with the *hauteur* and skepticisms of the scholarly class—he addresses listeners who share the basic assumptions of his worldview. On the second level, the level of the stories as published in *Haaretz* and elsewhere during the first two decades of the State of Israel, Agnon, who is what literary theorists call the implied author, is sending messages via his stories to a modern readership, one contemporary to *his* time. This creates the conditions for ramifying ironies and intriguing complexities. Take, for example, Miriam Devorah, the musically gifted wife of a ḥazzan in the story "The Ḥazzanim," set in the early eighteenth century. She has a dream in which she sees herself dressed in white vestments leading the congregation in prayer on Yom Kippur. From her dream she deduces that she must have been a man in a previous life and because of a sin unknown to her she has been reborn in the body of a woman. This thought throws her into a spiral of melancholy that leads to her early death. In the narrator's telling of the story, set squarely in its time and place, it needs hardly be said that there is no awareness of psychoanalysis or gender theory. The narrator understands the hapless Miriam Devorah's condition through the kabbalistic concepts of demons and transmigration of souls that were widely held among Polish Jews at the time. And he, the narrator, assumes these ideas are shared by his readers even as he elaborates their nuances. But Agnon's readers reading the story in the second half of the twentieth century in modern Hebrew surely possess a different set of explanatory frameworks within which to make sense of Miriam Devorah's plight. This kind of dual patterning is one of the enriching features of *A City in Its Fullness* and must have been counted by Agnon as a compensation for having to give up the autobiographical persona he had earlier used to such good effect.

This volume is a selection of twenty-seven representative stories from the 140-plus Hebrew stories in *A City in Its Fullness*. Indeed, many of the selections in this volume are more properly considered as novellas. But lest that seem like a paltry number, it is worth explaining that a number of the stories in the Hebrew volume are very short, and many of them are less stories in the sense of fiction as we now use the term than ethnographic reports about the practices and customs of Jewish life in Buczacz. It is in fact the size of the volume (724 pages) and the presence of this historically informative material, although fascinating in its own right, that put off earlier Hebrew readers from exploring it in depth and discovering the full-fledged stories that are as brilliant as anything Agnon ever wrote. The present collection includes those stories, and although they are relatively few in number, they have greater heft than many of the shorter units and actually represent slightly less than half of the original volume. There is a major absence worth noting.

One of the great stories of *A City in Its Fullness* is "The Parable and Its Lesson," which tells the story of a descent into the Underworld to free a young bride from abandonment. A translation of the story by James S. Diamond, accompanied by a critical essay by myself, was recently published by Stanford University Press as a separate volume. It should be thought of as part and parcel of the current project.

James S. Diamond, the translator of "A Parable and Its Lesson," was supposed to continue on to translate all the stories in the current volume. Sadly, in April 2013 he was killed by a car while standing near the home of a friend in Princeton, New Jersey. He had prepared draft translations of several of the stories, and those have been completed and edited by Jeffrey Saks. Other translators were invited to step in to complete the task. *A City in Its Fullness* is dedicated to Jim's memory.

The stories here are presented in the order in which they appear in the Hebrew edition of *A City in Its Fullness* (with the exception of "The Sign," discussed above). Agnon's principles of organization are several, including following a general chronology of historical events in which the tales unfold. The stories depicting life under the Polish nobles before the partitions of Poland come before the stories of life under the Austrian rulers. The early sections of the book are devoted to a guided tour of the main sites of Jewish life in Buczacz. That tour also extends to a taxonomy of occupations connected to the community: rabbis, ḥazzanim, gabbaim (lay heads of the communal apparatus), lomdim (full-time scholars), and shamashim (synagogue assistants).

Listing those occupations provides an opportunity to state an editorial preference visible in the texts of these stories: the scarcity of italicized terms. In the case of the present volume, the convention of placing foreign-language terms in italics would result in distracting and unsightly pages studded with words in special fonts. This would undermine the goal pursued here of naturalizing Agnon into English. Take, for example, the terms ḥazzan and shamash. Rendering these terms as "cantor" or "sexton" or "beadle" provides no solution because such words are already strange in English and produce no yield in understanding. The choice made in these pages has been to generally use unique Hebrew terms and not to set them apart graphically. The terms are explained in a glossary at the end of the volume, and after first consulting it for an unfamiliar term, the reader will see each term gaining contextual meaning the more it is used.

A similar approach has been followed when it comes to annotation. Because Agnon has created a Judaically erudite narrator who addresses a similarly erudite audience, most references go unlabeled or unexplained in the text. Either the identity of their origin is taken for granted or the contemporary reader/listener would have not experienced a need for a precise identification. It goes without saying that most English readers—and for that matter most Israeli readers nowadays—do not catch these references. The aspiration here has been to even the playing field for the English reader without peppering the pages with footnotes. Major references are indeed supplied but they appear in a special section of annotations at the end of the volume. Terms or quotations that are candidates for glossing or explication are not flagged by special markings in the body of the text. They can be found referenced by page number in the section at the end, and it is the reader's choice in any given instance whether or not to seek them there. Generally, when quoted as such, biblical verses appear in italics; which is not the case when a biblical phrase makes its way into the speech of the narrator or a character in a story. In addition, we have appended a chart with historical information on the rabbis that served in Buczacz overly nearly four centuries, many of whom are featured throughout the stories in this volume, as well as some population statistics of the town.

One editorial choice requires explanation. The names of many characters in these stories are preceded by "R." This convention, corresponding to the Hebrew letter *reish* with an apostrophe, indicates an honorific title that could include one of the following: *rabi, rav, rabeinu, rebbe, reb.* Some of these titles refer to a man with rabbinic ordination or scholarly status, while the simple *reb* can at times denote any male adult. Rather than trying to parse out each occurrence, the decision was made to gather them all under the sign of "R." and—with the exception of instances where the specific title is significant to the story—let the context suggest its inflection.

When it comes to the spelling of place names, readers and editors have to be tolerant of a certain degree of chaos. For every town in Galicia there are at least three names: Jewish/Yiddish, Polish and Ukrainian, and sometimes a separate German spelling. The classic example is the great city of eastern Galicia that is variously named Lviv (Ukrainian), Lvov (Yiddish), Liwow (Polish), and Lemberg (German). The general preference here has been for the name as used by Jews among themselves. The problem is that because Yiddish is written in Hebrew characters and pronounced differently according to regional dialects, there is no agreed-upon spelling of the Jewish place names in Roman characters. The most that can be hoped is that the spelling of these villages, towns, and cities will approximate Agnon's intent. (The spelling and pronunciation of the eponymous town that is the subject of these stories is similarly embroiled. Buczacz is the Polish spelling and the most widely used.)

Finally, there is the perennial challenge of translation itself. The differing approaches to rendering Agnon's unique Hebrew were discussed in the introduction to *The Parable and Its Lesson* and will not be repeated here. James Diamond devised a stylistic register that privileged a high modernist idiom while preserving a trace of Agnon's distinct lyricism, and that is the model that has been followed here. There was the added challenge of accommodating the voices of a number of different translators. It is to be hoped that both Agnon and his English readers will be well served by the care taken to make this collection as seamless as possible.

Alan Mintz
New York City
Rosh Ḥodesh Shevat 5776
January 2016

The Sign

1

In the year when the news reached us that all the Jews in my town had been killed, I was living in a certain section of Jerusalem, in a house I had built for myself after the disturbances of 1929 (5629 which numerically is equal to "The Eternity of Israel"). On the night when the Arabs destroyed my home, I vowed that if God would save me from the hands of the enemy and I should live, I would build a house in this particular neighborhood which the Arabs had tried to destroy. By the grace of God, I was saved from the hands of our despoilers and my wife and children and I remained alive in Jerusalem. Thus I fulfilled my vow and there built a house and made a garden. I planted a tree, and lived in that place with my wife and children, by the will of our Rock and Creator. Sometimes we dwelt in quiet and rest, and sometimes in fear and trembling because of the desert sword that waved in fuming anger over all the inhabitants of our holy land. And even though many troubles and evils passed over my head, I accepted all with good humor and without complaint. On the contrary, with every sorrow I used to say how much better it was to live in the Land of Israel than outside the land, for the Land of Israel has given us the strength to stand up for our lives, while outside the land we went to meet the enemy like sheep to the slaughter. Myriads of thousands of Israel, none of whom the enemy was worthy even to touch, were killed and strangled and drowned and buried alive; among them my brothers and friends and family, who went through all kinds of great sufferings in their lives and in their deaths, by the wickedness of our blasphemers and our desecrators, a filthy people, blasphemers of God, whose wickedness had not been matched since man was placed upon the earth.

2

I made no lament for my city and did not call for tears or for mourning over the congregation of God whom the enemy had wiped out. The day when we heard the news of the city and its dead was the afternoon before Shavuot, so I put aside my mourning for the dead because of the joy of the season when our Torah was given. It seemed to me that the two things came together to show me that in God's love for His people He still gives us some of that same power that He gave us as we stood before Sinai and received the Torah and commandments; it was that power which stood up within me so that I could exchange my sorrow over the dead of my city for the happiness of the holiday of Shavuot, when the Torah was given to us, and not to our blasphemers and desecrators who kill us because of it.

3

Our house was ready for the holiday. Everything about the house said: Shavuot.

The sun shone down on the outside of the house; inside, on the walls, we had hung cypress, pine, and laurel branches, and flowers. Every beautiful flower and everything with a sweet smell had been brought in to decorate the house for the holiday of Shavuot. In all the days I had lived in the Land of Israel, our house had never been decorated as nicely as it was that day. All the flaws in the house had vanished, and not a crack was to be seen, either in the ceiling or in the walls. From the places where the cracks in the house used to gape with open mouths and laugh at the builders, there came instead the pleasant smell of branches and shrubs, and especially of the flowers we had brought from our garden. These humble creatures, which because of their great modesty don't raise themselves high above the ground except to give off their good smell, made the eye rejoice because of the many colors with which the Holy

One, blessed be He, has decorated them, to glorify His land, which, in His lovingkindness, He has given to us.

4

Dressed in a new summer suit and new light shoes, I went to the house of prayer. Thus my mother, may she rest in peace, taught me: if a man gets new clothes or new shoes, he wears them first to honor the holiday, and goes to the synagogue in them. I am thankful to my body, which waited for me, and did not tempt me into wearing the new clothes and shoes before the holiday, even though the old ones were heavy, and hot desert winds ran through the country. And—if I haven't reached the heights of all my forefathers' deeds—in these matters I can do as well as my forefathers, for my body stands ready to fulfill most of those customs which depend upon it.

5

I walked to the house of prayer. The two stores in the neighborhood were shut, and even the bus, which usually violates the Sabbath, was gone from the neighborhood. Not a man was seen in the streets, except for little errand boys delivering flowers. They too, by the time you could look at them, had disappeared. Nothing remained of them except the smell of the flowers they had brought, and this smell merged with the aroma of the gardens in our neighborhood.

The neighborhood was quietly at rest. No one stopped me on the street, and no one asked me for news of the world. Even if they had asked, I wouldn't have told them what had happened to my city. The days have come when every man keeps his sorrows to himself. What would it help if I told someone else what happened to my city? His city surely had also suffered that same fate.

6

I arrived at the house of prayer and sat down in my place. I kept the events in my city, as they appeared to me, hidden in my heart. A few days later, when the true stories reached me, I saw that the deeds of the enemy were evil beyond the power of the imagination. The power of the imagination is stronger than the power of deeds, except for the evil of the nations, which goes beyond all imagination.

I opened a maḥzor and looked at the evening prayers for the first night of Shavuot. People outside the Land of Israel generally add many liturgical poems, especially in those ancient communities that follow the customs of their forefathers. Although I think of myself as a resident of the Land of Israel in every sense, I like these piyyutim, which prepare the soul for the theme of the day. Our teachers, the holy writers of the piyyutim, are good intermediaries between the hearts of Israel and their Father in heaven. They knew what we need to ask of God and what He demands of us, and they wrote hymns to open our lips before our Father in heaven.

The people who come to the house of prayer began to gather. Even those whom one usually doesn't see in the synagogue came, to bring their children. As long as a child is a child, he is drawn after his father and draws his father with him. That is, he is drawn after his Father in heaven and draws with him the father who gave him birth. In my town, all the synagogues used to be filled with babes like these. They were good and sweet and healthy; now they are all dead. The hand of the enemy has finished them all. There is no remnant, no one left. And if a few of them do remain, they've been captured by Gentiles and are being educated by Gentiles. Let's hope that they too will not be added to our enemies. Those about whom it is written "I shall bear you on the wings of eagles and bring you unto Me" are given over to others and are trampled under the feet of human filth.

7

Although on the Sabbath and festivals one says the evening prayers early, on Shavuot we wait to say Maariv until the stars are out. For if we were to pray early and receive the holiness of the festival, we would be shortening the days of the Omer, and the Torah said: "There shall be seven full weeks."

Since they had already finished Minḥah and it was not yet time for Maariv, most of the congregation sat talking with one another, except for the children, who stood about in wonder. I know that if I say this people will smile at me, but I'll say it anyway: The same thing happened to those children at this season of the giving of our Torah as happened to them when their souls stood before Mount Sinai, ready to receive the Torah the following day.

While the adults were sitting and talking, and the children were standing about in amazement, the time came for the evening prayer. The gabbai pounded on the table and the leader of the prayers went down before the ark. After a short order of prayers, including neither piyyutim nor "And Moses declared the festivals of the Lord," they greeted one another and went home in peace.

8

I came home and greeted my wife and children with the blessing of the holiday. I stood amazed to think that here I was celebrating our holiday in my home, in my land, with my wife and children, at a time when tens of thousands of Israel were being killed and slaughtered and burned and buried alive, and those who were still alive were running about as though lost in the fields and forests, or were hidden in holes in the earth.

I bowed my head toward the earth, this earth of the Land of Israel upon which my house is built, and in which my garden grows with trees and flowers, and I said over it the verse "Because of you, the soul liveth." Afterward I said kiddush and the blessing "Who has given us life," and I took a sip of wine and passed my glass to my wife and children. I didn't even dilute the wine with tears. This says a lot for a man; his city is wiped out of the world, and he doesn't even dilute his drink with tears.

I washed my hands and recited the blessing over the bread, giving everyone a piece of the fine ḥallot that were formed in the shape of the Tablets, to remember the two tablets of the Covenant that Moses brought down from heaven. The custom of Israel is Torah: if the bread comes from the earth, its shape is from the heavens.

We sat down to the festive meal of the first night of Shavuot. Part of the meal was the fruit of our soil, which we had turned over with our own hands and watered with our own lips. When we came here we found parched earth, for hands had not touched the land since her children had left her. But now she is a fruitful land, thankful to her masters, and giving us of her goodness.

The meal was good. All that was eaten was of the fruits of the land. Even the dairy dishes were from the milk of cows who grazed about our house. It is good when a man's food comes from close to him and not from far away, for that which is close to a man is close to his tastes. Yet Solomon, in praising the woman of valor, praises her because she "brings her bread from afar." But the days of Solomon were different, for Solomon ruled over all the lands and every man in Israel was a hero. And as a man's wife is like her husband, the women of valor in Israel left it for the weak to bring their bread from nearby, while they would go to the trouble of bringing it from afar. In these times, when the land has shrunk and we all have trouble making a living, bread from nearby is better than that which comes from afar.

9

The meal which the land had given us was good, and good too is the land itself, which gives life to its inhabitants. As the holiday began, Jerusalem was freed from the rough desert winds, which rule from Passover to Shavuot, and a soft breeze blew from the desert and the sea. Two winds blow in our neighborhood, one from the sea and one from the desert, and between them blows another wind, from the little gardens that the people of the neighborhood have planted around their houses. Our house too stands in the midst of a garden where there grow cypresses and pines, and, at their feet, lilies, dahlias, carnations, snapdragons, dandelions, chrysanthemums, and violets. It is the way of pines and cypresses not to let even grass grow between them, but the trees in our garden looked with favor upon our flowers and lived side by side with them, for they remembered how hard we had worked when they were first beginning to grow. We were stingy with our own bread and bought saplings; we drank less water in order to water the gentle young trees, and we guarded them against the wicked herdsmen who used to send their cattle into our garden. Now they have become big trees, which shade us from the sun, giving us their branches as covering for the sukkah, and greens for the holiday of Shavuot, to cover our walls in memory of the event at Sinai. They used to do the same in my town when I was a child, except that in my town most of the greens came from the gardens of the Gentiles, while here I took from my own garden, from the branches of my trees and from the flowers between my trees. They gave off a good aroma and added flavor to our meal.

10

I sat inside my house with my wife and little children. The house and everything in it said: Holiday. So too we and our garments, for we were dressed in the new clothes we had made for the festival. The festival is for God and for us; we honor it in whatever way we can, with pleasant goods and new clothing. God in heaven also honors the holiday and gives us the strength to rejoice.

I looked around at my family, and I felt in the mood to tell them about what we used to do in my city. It was true that my city was dead, and those who were not dead were like the dead, but before the enemy had come and killed them all, my city used to be full of life and good and blessing. If I start telling tales of my city I never have enough. But let's tell just a few of the deeds of the town. And since we are in the midst of the holiday of Shavuot, I'll tell a little concerning this day.

11

From the Sabbath when we blessed the new month of Sivan, we emerged from the mourning of the days of the Omer, and a spirit of rest passed through the town: especially on the New Moon, and especially with the saying of Hallel. When the leader of prayer said, "The heavens are the heavens of God, but the earth hath He given to the children of men," we saw that the earth and even the river were smiling at us. I don't know whether we or the river first said, "It's all right to swim." But even the heavens agreed that the river was good for bathing, for the sun had already begun to break through its coldness; not only through the coldness of the river, but of the entire world. A man could now open his window without fear of the cold. Some people turned their ears toward the sound of a bird, for the birds had already returned to their nests and were making themselves heard. In the houses arose the aroma of dairy foods being prepared for Shavuot, and the smell of the fresh-woven clothes of the brides and grooms who would enter under the bridal canopy after the holiday. The sound of the barber's scissors could be heard in the town, and every face was renewed. All were ready to welcome the holiday on which we received the Torah and commandments. See how the holiday on which we received the Torah and commandments is happier and easier than all the other holidays. On Passover we can't eat *whatever* we want; on Sukkot we can't eat *wherever* we want. But on Shavuot we can eat anything we want, wherever we want to eat it.

The world is also glad and rejoices with us. The lids of the skies are as bright as the sun, and glory and beauty cover the earth.

12

Now, children, listen to me. I'll tell you something of my youth. Now your father is old, and if he let his beard grow as did Abraham, you'd see white hair in his beard. But I too was once a little boy who used to do the things children do. While the old men sat in the house of study preparing themselves for the time of the giving of the Torah the following morning, my friends and I would stand outside looking upward, hoping to catch the moment when the sky splits open and everything you ask for (even supernatural things!) is immediately given you by God—if you are worthy and you catch the right moment. In that case, why do I feel as though none of my wishes has ever been granted? Because I had so many things to ask for that before I decided what to wish first, sleep came upon me and I dozed off. When a man is young, his wishes are many; before he gets around to asking for anything, he is overcome by sleep. When a man is old, he has no desires; if he asks for anything, he asks for a little sleep.

Now let me remove the sleep from my eyes, and I'll tell a little bit about this day.

Nowadays a man is found outdoors more than in his house. In former times, if a man's business didn't bring him out, he sat either in his house or in the house of study. But on the first day of Shavuot everybody would go to the gardens and forests outside the town in honor of the Torah, which was given outdoors. The trees and bushes and shrubs and flowers that I know from those walks on the first day of Shavuot, I know well. The animals and beasts and birds that I know from those walks on the first day of Shavuot, I know well. How so? While we were walking, my father, of blessed memory, would show me a tree or a bush or a flower and say, "This is its name in the holy tongue." He would show me an animal or a beast or a bird and say to me, "This is its name in the holy tongue." For if they were worthy to have the Torah write their names, surely we must recognize them and know their names. In that case, why don't I list their names? Because of those who have turned upon the Torah and wrought havoc with the language.

13

I saw that my wife and children enjoyed the tales of my town. So I went on and told them more, especially about the Great Synagogue—the glory of the town—the beauty of which was mentioned even by the gentile princes. Not a Shavuot went by that Count Potocki didn't send a wagon full of greens for the synagogue. There was one family in the town that had the special rights in arranging these branches.

I also told them about our little kloyz, our prayer room. People know me as one of the regulars in the old house of study, but before I pitched my tent in the old house of study, I was one of the young men of the kloyz. I have so very, very much to tell about those times but here I'll tell only things that concern this day.

On the day before Shavuot eve, I used to go out to the woods near town with a group of friends to gather green boughs. I would take a ball of cord from my mother, may she rest in peace, and I would string it up from the roof of our house in the shape of a Star of David, and on the cord I would hang the leaves we had pulled off the branches, one by one. I don't like to boast, but something like this it's all right for me to tell. Even the old men of the kloyz used to say, "Fine, fine. The work of an artist, the work of an artist." These men were careful about what they said, and their mouth uttered no word that did not come from their heart. I purposely didn't tell my wife and children about the poems I used to write after the festival—sad songs. When I saw the faded leaves falling from the Star of David I would be overcome by sadness, and I would compose sad poems.

Once my heart was aroused, my soul remembered other things about Shavuot. Among them were the paper roses that were stuck to the windowpanes. This was done by the simple folk at the edge of town. The respected heads of families in town did not do this, for they clung carefully to the customs of their fathers, while the others did not. But since the enemy has destroyed them all together, I shall not distinguish between them here.

I told my wife and children many more things about the town and about the day. And to everything I said, I added, "This was in former days, when the town stood in peace." Nevertheless, I was able to tell the things calmly and not in sorrow, and one would not have known from my voice what had happened to my town—that all the Jews in it had been killed. The Holy One, blessed be He, has been gracious to Israel: even when we remember the greatness and glory of bygone days, our soul does not leave us out of sorrow and longing. Thus a man like me can talk about the past, and his soul doesn't pass out of him as he speaks.

14

Following the Blessing after Meals I said to my wife and children, "You go to sleep, and I'll go to the synagogue for the vigil of Shavuot night." Now I was born in Buczacz and grew up in the old house of study, where the spirit of the great men of Israel pervaded. But I shall admit freely that I don't follow them in all their ways. They read the Order of Study for Shavuot night and I read the book of hymns that Rabbi Solomon Ibn Gabirol, may his soul rest, composed on the six hundred thirteen commandments.

There have arisen many poets in Israel, who have graced the order of prayers with their poems and strengthened the hearts of Israel with their piyyutim, serving as good intermediaries between the hearts of Israel and their Father in heaven. And even I, when I humbly come to plead for my soul before my Rock and Creator, find expression in the words of our holy poets—especially in the poems of Rabbi Solomon Ibn Gabirol, may his soul rest.

I have already told elsewhere how, when I was a small child, my father, of blessed memory, would bring me a new prayer book every year from the fair. Once Father brought me a prayer book and I opened it to a plea of Rabbi Solomon Ibn Gabirol. I read and was amazed: Was it possible that such a righteous man as this, whose name was written in the prayer book, did not find God before him at all times and in every hour, so that he had to write "At the dawn I seek Thee, my rock and tower"? Not only did God make him seek Him, but even when the poet found Him, fear fell upon him and he stood confused. Thus he says, "Before Thy greatness I stand and am confounded."

As I lie down at night I see this saint rising from his bed on a stormy windblown night. The cold engulfs him and enters into his bones, and a cold wind slaps at his face, ripping his cloak and struggling with its fringes. The tzaddik strengthens himself to call for God. When he finds Him, terror falls upon him out of the fear of God and the majesty of His presence.

For many days that saint wouldn't leave my sight. Sometimes he seemed to me like a baby asking for his father, and sometimes like a grownup, exhausted from so much chasing after God. And when he finally does find Him, he's confused because of God's greatness.

After a time, sorrow came and added to sorrow.

15

Once, on the Sabbath after Passover, I got up and went to the great house of study. I found the old cantor raising his voice in song. There were men in Buczacz who would not allow the interruption of the prayers between the Blessing of Redemption and the Amidah for additional hymns. Thus the cantor would go up to the platform after Musaf and recite the hymns of redemption. I turned my ear and listened to him intone: "O poor captive in a foreign land." I felt sorry for the poor captive girl, who must have been in great trouble, judging from the tone of the cantor. It was a little hard for me to understand why God didn't hurry and take her out of captivity, or why He didn't have mercy on the poor old man who stood, his head bowed, begging and praying for her. I also wondered at the men of my city, who were doing nothing to redeem her from captivity.

One day I was turning the pages of the big prayer book in my grandfather's house, and I found those same words written in the prayer book. I noticed that every line started with a large letter. I joined the letters together, and they formed the name "Solomon." My heart leaped for joy, for I knew it was Rabbi Solomon from my prayer book. But I felt sorry for that Tzaddik. As though he didn't have enough troubles himself, searching for God and standing in confusion before Him, he also had to feel the sorrow of this captive girl who was taken as a slave to a foreign country. A few days later I came back and leafed through the prayer book, checking the first letters of the lines of every hymn. Whenever I found a hymn with the name Solomon Ibn Gabirol written in it, I didn't put it down until I had read it through.

16

I don't remember when I started the custom of reading the hymns of Rabbi Solomon Ibn Gabirol on Shavuot eve, but since I started this custom, I haven't skipped a year. It goes without saying that I did it while I lived in Germany, where they like piyyutim, but even here in the Land of Israel, where they don't say many of these poems, I haven't done away with my custom. Even in times of danger, when the Arabs were besieging Jerusalem and machine-gun fire was flying over our heads, I didn't keep myself from the house of study, where I spent most of the night, as has been done everywhere, in all generations, in remembrance of our fathers who stood trembling all night in the third month after going out of Egypt, waiting to receive the Torah from God Himself.

17

My home is near the house of prayer; it takes only a little while to get there. You walk down the narrow street on which my house stands, and you turn down the wide street at the end, till you come to a little wooden shack which serves as a house of prayer. That night the way made itself longer. Or maybe it didn't make itself longer, but I made it longer. My thoughts had tired out my soul, and my soul my feet. I stopped and stood more than I walked.

18

The world and all within it rested in a kind of pleasant silence: the houses, the gardens, the woods; and above them the heavens, the moon and the stars. Heaven and earth know that if it weren't for Israel, who accepted the Torah, they would not be standing. They stand and fulfill their tasks: the earth to bring forth bread, and the heavens to give light to the earth and those who dwell upon it. Could it be that even in my hometown the heavens are giving light and the earth bringing forth its produce? In the Land of Israel, the Holy One, blessed be He, judges the land Himself, whereas outside the land He has handed this supervision over to angels. The angels' first task is to turn their eyes aside from the deeds of the Gentiles who do evil to Israel, and therefore the heavens there give their light and the earth its produce—perhaps twice as much as in the Land of Israel.

19

I stood among the little houses, each of which was surrounded by a garden. Since the time we were exiled from our land, this area had given forth thorns and briers; now that we have returned, it is rebuilt with houses, trees, shrubs, and flowers.

Because I love the little houses and their blossoming gardens, I'll tell their story.

A young veterinarian from Constantinople was appointed to watch over the animals of the sultan. One day he was working in a village in the midst of the desert sands. On his way home, he stopped to rest. He looked up and saw the Dead Sea on one side and the Temple Mount on the other. A fresh breeze was blowing, and the air was better and more pleasant than any place in the land. He got down from his donkey and began to stroll about, until he found himself making a path among the thorn bushes, briers, and rocks. If only I could live here with my wife and children, he thought. But to live here is impossible, as the place is far from any settlement, and there's no sign that anyone lives here, nor is there any form of life, except for the birds of the sky and various creeping things. The doctor remained until it began to get dark and the time came to return to the city. He mounted his ass and went back to the city. A few days later he came again. A few days after that he came once more. Thus he did several times.

It happened that a certain Arab's cow became sick. He brought her to the doctor. The doctor prepared some medicine for her, and she got well. After a while, another one got sick. She too was brought to the doctor. Again he prepared some medicine and she became well. The Arab heard that the doctor wanted to build a summer house outside of town. The Arab said to him, "I have a piece of land near the town. If you like it, it's yours." It turned out to be just the spot the doctor had wanted. He bought thirty dunams of land from the Arab, built a summer house, dug a well, and planted a garden and an almond grove. All the clever people in Jerusalem laughed at him and said, "He's buried his money in the desert." But he himself was happy with his lot, and whenever he was free from work he would ride out there on his ass and busy himself with planting. Sometimes he would take along his young wife and small children to share in his happiness.

The word got around. There was a group of people that worked for the settlement of the land. They went and bought a piece of land near his. They divided their section up into lots and sent messengers to other lands to offer Zionists the purchase of a share in the inheritance of the Land of Israel. A few among them bought.

The Great War came, bringing death on all sides and destroying in one hour that which had been built up over many generations. If one was not hurt bodily by the war, it hurt one financially. And if neither one's body nor one's money was hurt, it damaged one's soul. The war was harder for the Jews than for anyone else, as it affected their bodies, their money, and their souls. Thus it was in the place we are discussing. Turkey, which also entered the war, sent her legions to wherever she ruled. One legion came to Jerusalem and camped there, in this place, on the land of the doctor. The soldiers ripped out the almond trees to make fires to cook their food and to warm their bodies and turned the garden into a lair for cannons.

From out of the storm of war and the thunder of cannons, a kind of heralding voice was heard—a voice that, if we interpreted it according to our wishes and desires, heralded the end of troubles and the beginning of good, salvation, and comfort. The war, however, was still going strong. Neither the end of the troubles nor the beginning of salvation could yet be seen.

Slowly the strength of those who had started the fighting wore out, the hands of war were broken, and they could fight no more. The bravery of the heroes had been drained, so they left the battlefronts. Behind them they left destruction and desolation, wailing and tears, forever.

20

After the war, Jerusalem awoke bit by bit from her destruction. A few people began to think of expanding the city, for even if there were a few places left that had not been damaged by the war, they were crowded and overpopulated. Even before the war, when Jerusalem lay in peace and her inhabitants were satisfied with little, the air had become stifling. How much more so after the war. Even before the war there was little room left in Jerusalem; after the war, when the city was filled with new immigrants, how much more so.

People formed little societies to buy land in and around Jerusalem, and began to build new neighborhoods. These were small and far from town, and the sums owed were always great. People ran from bank to bank, borrowing in one place to pay off in another, paying in one place and borrowing in another. If it weren't for the bit of peace a man finds in his home and garden, they would have fallen by the way.

21

That stretch of barren desert also had its turn. They remembered the lands the doctor had bought and asked him to sell them part of his holdings. He liked the idea, sold them a section of his land, and helped them to buy from others. The news got around, and people began to flock. They bought twenty-one thousand dunams, each dunam equaling a thousand six hundred Turkish pik, at the price of a grush and a half a pik. Some bought in order to build, and some bought in order to sell.

Now I shall leave the real-estate agents who held back the building of Jerusalem. If a man wanted to build a house, they asked so much money that he was taken aback and went away. And if he agreed to come the next day to sign away his wealth, it would happen that overnight the lot had been sold to someone else, who had more than doubled his bid. The agents used to conspire together. Someone would ask to have a house built, and either they wouldn't build it for him or they'd build it in the wrong place. So his lot stood empty, without a house, along with the rest of the fields to which the same thing had happened.

The neighborhood was finally built, but its residents were not able to open a school or a post office branch or a pharmacy or any of the institutions that people from the city needed, except for two or three stores, each of which was superfluous because of the others. During the disturbances it was even worse. Since the population was small, they could not hold out against the enemy, either in the disturbance of 1929 or in the War of Independence. And between 1929 and the War of Independence, in the days of the riots and horrors that began in 1936 and lasted until World War II began, they were given over to the hands of the enemy, and a man wouldn't dare to go out alone.

Of the Zionists outside the land who had bought plots before the war, some died in the war and others wound up in various other places. When those who were fortunate enough to come to the Land saw what had happened to the section, they sold their lots and built homes in other places. Of those who bought them, perhaps one or two built houses, and the rest left them until a buyer would come their way, to fill their palms with money.

22

Now I shall leave those who did not build the neighborhood and shall tell only about those who did build it.

Four men went out into the dusts of the desert, an hour's walking distance from the city, and built themselves houses, each in one spot, according to lots. The whole area was still a wilderness; there were neither roads nor any signs of habitation. They would go to work in the city every morning and come back an hour or two before dark, bringing with them all that they needed. Then they would eat something and rush out to their gardens to kill snakes and scorpions, weed out thorns, level off holes in the ground, prepare the soil, and plant and water the gentle saplings, in the hope that these saplings would grow into great trees and give their shade. As yet there were neither trees nor shrubs in the neighborhood, but only parched earth which gave rise to thorns and briers. When the desert storms came, they sometimes lasted as long as nine days, burning our skin and flesh, and drying out our bones. Even at night there was no rest. But when the storms passed, the land was like paradise once again. A man would go out to his garden, water his gentle young trees, dig holes, and add two or three shrubs or flowers to his garden.

From the very beginning, one of the four founders took it upon himself to attend to community business: to see that the Arabs didn't send their beasts into the gardens and that the garbage collector took the garbage from the houses; to speak with the Governor and those in charge of the water so that water wouldn't be lacking in the pipes, and to see that the bus would come and go on schedule, four times a day. What would he do if he had to consult his neighbors? There was no telephone as yet. He would take a shofar and go up on his roof and blow. His neighbors would hear him and come.

After a while, more people came and built homes and planted gardens. During the day they would work in the city, and an hour or two before dark they would come home to break earth, weed, pull up thorns, plant trees and gardens, and clear the place of snakes and scorpions. Soon more people came, and then still more. They too built houses and made gardens. Some of them would rent out a room or two to a young couple who wanted to raise their child in the clear air. Some of them rented out their whole houses and continued to live in the city until they paid off their mortgage. After a time I too came to live here, fleeing from the tremors of 1927, which shook the walls of the house where I was living and forced me to leave my home. I came to this neighborhood with my wife and two children, and we rented an apartment. Roads had already been built, and the buses would come and go at regular times. We felt as though this place, which had been barren since the day of our exile from our land, was being built again.

23

Automobiles still came, but rarely, and a man could walk in the streets without fear of being hit. At night there was a restful quiet. If you didn't hear the dew fall, it was because you were sleeping a good, sweet sleep. The Dead Sea would smile at us almost every day, its blue waters shining in graceful peace between the gray and blue hills of Moab. The site of the Temple would look upon us. I don't know who longed for whom more; we for the Temple Mount, or the Temple Mount for us. The king of the winds, who dwelt in a mountain not far from us, used to stroll about the neighborhood, and his servants and slaves—the winds—would follow at his feet, brushing through the area. Fresh air filled the neighborhood.

People from far and near would come to walk, saying, "No man knoweth its value." Old men used to come and say, "Here we would find length of days." Sick people came and said, "Here we would be free from our illnesses." Arabs would pass through and say, "Shalom"; they came to our doctor, who cured them of their ills. The doctor's wife would help their wives when they had difficulty in childbirth. The Arab women would come from their villages around us, bringing the fruits of their gardens and the eggs of their hens, giving praises to Allah, who, in His mercy upon them, had given the Jews the idea of building houses here, so that they would not have to bring their wares all the way into the city. As an Arab would go to work in the city, taking a shortcut through these streets, he would stand in wonder at the deeds of Allah, who had given the Jewish lords wisdom to build roads, mend the ways, and so forth. Suddenly, one Sabbath after Tishah b'Av, our neighbors rose up against us to make trouble for us. The people of the neighborhood could not believe that this was possible. Our neighbors, for whom we had provided help at every chance, for whom we had made life so much easier—buying their produce, having our doctor heal their sick, building roads to shorten the way for them—came upon these same roads to destroy us.

24

By the grace of God upon us, we rose up and were strong. As I said in the beginning, I built a house and planted a garden. In this place from which the enemy tried to rout us, I built my home. I built it facing the Temple Mount, always to keep upon my heart our beloved dwelling which was destroyed and has not yet been rebuilt. If "we cannot go up and be seen there, because of the hand which has cast itself into our Temple," we direct our hearts there in prayer.

Now I'll say something about the house of prayer in our neighborhood.

Our forefathers, who saw their dwelling in this world as temporary but the dwelling in the synagogue and the house of study as permanent, built great structures for prayer and study. We, whose minds are given over mainly to things of this world, build great and beautiful houses for ourselves, and suffice with little buildings and shacks for prayer. Thus our house of prayer in this neighborhood is a wooden shack. This is one reason. Aside from this, they didn't get around to finishing the synagogue before the first disturbance, the riots, or the War of Independence, and at each of those times the residents had to leave the neighborhood. It was also not completed because of the changes in its congregants, who changed after each disturbance. That's why, as I've explained, our place of prayer is a shack and not a stone building.

Now I shall tell what happened in this shack on that Shavuot night when the rumor reached us that all the Jews in my town had been killed.

25

I entered the house of prayer. No one else was in the place. Light and rest and a good smell filled the room. All kinds of shrubs and flowers with which our land is blessed gave off their aroma. Already at Maariv I had taken note of the smell, and now every blossom and flower gave off the aroma with which God had blessed it. A young man, one who had come from a town where all the Jews had been killed, went out to the fields of the neighborhood with his wife, and picked and gathered every blossoming plant and decorated the synagogue for the holiday of Shavuot, the time of the giving of our Torah, just as they used to do in their town, before all the Jews there had been killed. In addition to all the wildflowers they gathered in the nearby fields, they brought roses and zinnias and laurel boughs from their own garden.

26

I shall choose among the words of our holy tongue to make a crown of glory for our prayer room, its candelabra, and its ornaments.

The eternal light hangs down from the ceiling, facing the holy ark and the two tablets of the Law above it. The light is wrapped in capers and thistles and bluebells, and it shines and gives off its light from between the green leaves of the capers' thorns and from its white flowers, from between the blue hues in the thistles, and from the gray leaves and purple flowers around it. All the wildflowers that grow in the fields of our neighborhood gather together in this month to beautify our house of prayer for the holiday of Shavuot, along with the garden flowers that the gardens in our neighborhood give us. To the right of the holy ark stands the reader's table, and on the table a lamp with red roses around it. Six candles shine from among the roses. The candles have almost burned down to the end, yet they still give off light, for so long as the oil is not finished they gather their strength to light the way for the prayers of Israel until they reach the gates of heaven. A time of trouble has come to Jacob, and we need much strength. Opposite them, to the south, stand the memorial candles, without number and without end. Six million Jews have been killed by the Gentiles; because of them a third of us are dead and two-thirds of us are orphans. You won't find a man in Israel who hasn't lost ten of his people. The memorial candles light them all up for us, and their light is equal, so that you can't tell the difference between the candle of a man who lived out his days and one who was killed. But in heaven they certainly distinguish between the candles, just as they distinguish between one soul and another. The Eternal had a great thought in mind when He chose us from all peoples and gave us His Torah of life. Nevertheless, it's a bit difficult to see why He created, as opposed to us, the kinds of people who take away our lives because we keep His Torah.

27

By the grace of God upon me, those thoughts left me. But the thought of my city did not take itself away from me. Is it possible that a city full of Torah and life is suddenly uprooted from the world, and all its people—old and young; men, women, and children— killed, that now the city is silent, with not a soul of Israel left in it?

I stood facing the candles, and my eyes shone like them, except that those candles were surrounded with flowers, and my eyes had thorns upon them. I closed my eyes so that I would not see the deaths of my brothers, the people of my town. It pains me to see my town and its slain, how they are tortured in the hands of their tormentors, the cruel and harsh deaths they suffer. And I closed my eyes for yet another reason. When I close my eyes I become, as it were, master of the world, and I see only that which I desire to see. So I closed my eyes and asked my city to rise before me, with all its inhabitants, and with all its houses of prayer. I put every man in the place where he used to sit and where he studied, along with his sons, sons-in-law, and grandsons—for in my town everyone came to prayer. The only difference was in the places. Some fixed their places for prayer in the old house of study and some in the other synagogues and houses of study, but every man had his fixed place in his own house of prayer.

28

After I had arranged all the people in the old beit midrash, with which I was more familiar than the other places in town, I turned to the other houses of prayer. As I had done with the old house of study, so I did with them. I brought up every man before me. If he had sons or sons-in-law or grandsons, I brought them into view along with him. I didn't skip a single holy place in our town, or a single man. I did this not by the power of memory but by the power of the synagogues and the houses of study. For once the synagogues and houses of study stood before me, all their worshippers also came and stood before me. The places of prayer brought life to the people of my city in their deaths as in their lives. I too stood in the midst of the city among my people, as though the time of the resurrection of the dead had arrived. The day of the resurrection will indeed be great; I felt a taste of it that day as I stood among my brothers and townspeople who have gone to another world, and they stood about me, along with all the synagogues and houses of study in my town. And were it not difficult for me to speak, I would have asked them what Abraham, Isaac, and Jacob say, and what Moses says, about all that has happened in this generation.

I stood in wonder, looking at my townspeople. They too looked at me, and there was not a trace of condemnation in their glances, that I was thus and they were thus. They just seemed covered with sadness, a great and frightening sadness, except for one old man who had a kind of smile on his lips, and seemed to say, *Ariber geshprungen*—that is, We have "jumped over" and left the world of sorrows. In the Conversations of Rabbi Naḥman of Breslov, of blessed memory, something like that can be found. He heard about a certain preacher in Lemberg who, in the hour of his death, snapped his fingers and said that he would show them a trick. At that moment he passed from the world of sorrows. And the Tzaddik enjoyed those words.

29

Bit by bit the people of my town began to disappear and go away. I didn't try to run after them, for I knew that a man's thoughts cannot reach the place where they were going. And even if I could reach there, why should I prevent them from going, and why should I confuse them with my thoughts?

I was left alone, and I wandered back to former days when my town was alive and all those who were now dead were alive and singing the praise of God in the synagogues and the houses of prayer, and the old cantor served in the Great Synagogue, while I, a small child, saw him standing on the platform intoning "O Poor Captive," with the old prayer book containing all the prayers and hymns open before him. He didn't turn the pages, for the print had been wiped out by the age of the book and the tears of former cantors, and not a letter could be made out. But he, may God give light to his lot in the world to come, knew all the hymns by heart, and the praise of God together with the sorrow of Israel would rise from his lip hymns and in prayer.

30

Let me describe him. He was tall and straight-backed; his beard was white, and his eyes looked like the prayer books published in Slavita, which were printed on blue-tinged paper. His voice was sweet and his clothes were clean. Only his talit was covered with tears. He never took his talit down from his head during the prayers. But after every prayer of love or redemption he would take it down a little and look about, to see if there was yet a sign of the redemption. For forty years he was our city's messenger before God. After forty years he went to see his relatives in Russia. The border patrol caught him and threw him into prison. He lamented and begged God to take him out of captivity and return him to his place. God did not let the warden sleep. The warden knew that as long as the voice of the Jew was to be heard in his prison, sleep would not return to him. He commanded that the cantor be set free and returned home. They released him and sent him to our town. He came bringing with him a new melody to which he would sing "O Poor Captive."

31

The first time I heard that hymn was the Sabbath after Passover when I was still a little boy. I woke up in the middle of the night, and there was a light shining into the house. I got out of bed and opened the window, so that the light could come in. I stood by the window, trying to see from where the light was coming. I washed my hands and face, put on my Sabbath clothes, and went outside. Nobody in the house saw or heard me go out. Even my mother and father, who never took their eyes off me, didn't see me go out. I went outside and there was no one there. The birds, singing the song of morning, alone were outside.

I stood still until the birds had finished their song. Then I walked to the well, for I heard the sound of the well's waters, and I said, "I'll go hear the water talking." For I had not yet seen the waters as they talked.

I came to the well and saw that the water was running, but there was no one there to drink. I filled my palms, recited the blessing, and drank. Then I went to walk wherever my legs would carry me. My legs took me to the Great Synagogue, and the place was filled with men at prayer. The old cantor stood on the platform and raised his voice in the hymn "O Poor Captive." Now that hymn of redemption began to rise from my lips and sing itself in the way I had heard it from the lips of the old cantor. The city then stood yet in peace, and all the many and honored Jews who have been killed by the enemy were still alive.

32

The candles that had given light for the prayers had gone out; only their smoke remained to be seen. But the light of the memorial candles still shone, in memory of our brothers and sisters who were killed and slaughtered and drowned and burned and strangled and buried alive by the evil of our blasphemers, cursed of God, the Nazis and their helpers. I walked by the light of the candles until I came to my city, which my soul longed to see.

I came to my city and entered the old beit midrash, as I used to do when I came home to visit—I would enter the old beit midrash first.

I found Ḥayyim the Shamash standing on the platform and rolling a Torah scroll, for it was the eve of the New Moon, and he was rolling the scroll to the reading for that day. Below him, in an alcove near the window, sat Shalom the Shoemaker, his pipe in his mouth, reading the Shevet Yehudah, exactly as he did when I was a child; he used to sit there reading the Shevet Yehudah, pipe in mouth, puffing away like one who is breathing smoke. The pipe was burnt out and empty, and there wasn't a leaf of tobacco in it, but they said that just as long as he held it in his mouth it tasted as though he were smoking.

I said to him, "I hear that you now fast on the eve of the New Moon (something they didn't do before I left for the Land of Israel; they would say the prayers for the "Small Yom Kippur" but not fast). Ḥayyim said to Shalom, "Answer him." Shalom took his pipe out of his mouth and said, "So it is. Formerly we would pray and not fast, now we fast but don't say the prayers. Why? Because we don't have a minyan; there aren't ten men to pray left in the city." I said to Ḥayyim and Shalom, "You say there's not a minyan left for prayer. Does this mean that those who used to pray are not left, or that those who are left don't pray? In either case, why haven't I seen a living soul in the whole town?" They both answered me together and said, "That was the first destruction, and this is the last destruction. After the first destruction a few Jews were left; after the last destruction not a man of Israel remained." I said to them, "Permit me to ask you one more thing. You say that in the last destruction not a man from Israel was left in the whole city. Then how is it that you are alive?" Ḥayyim smiled at me the way the dead smile when they see that you think they're alive. I picked myself up and went elsewhere.

33

I saw a group of the sick and afflicted running by. I asked a man at the end of the line, "Where are you running?" He placed his hand on an oozing sore and answered, "We run to greet the rebbe." "Who is he?" I asked. He moved his hand from one affliction to another and, smiling, said, "A man has only two hands, and twice as many afflictions." Then he told me the name of his rebbe. It was a little difficult for me to understand. Was it possible that this rebbe who had left for the Land of Israel six or seven generations ago, and had been buried in the soil of the holy city of Safed, had returned? I decided to go and see. I ran along and reached the Tzaddik together with them. They began to cry out before him how they were stricken with afflictions and persecuted by the rulers and driven from one exile to another, with no sign of redemption in view. The Tzaddik sighed and said, "What can I tell you, my children? 'May God give strength to His people; may God bless His people with peace.'" Why did he quote that particular verse? He said it only about this generation: before God will bless His people with peace He must give strength to His people, so that the Gentiles will be afraid of them, and not make any more war upon them because of that fear.

I said, "Let me go and make this known to the world." I walked over to the sink and dabbed some water onto my eyes. I awoke and saw that the book lay open before me, and I hadn't yet finished reciting the order of the commandments of the Lord. I went back and read the commandments of the Lord as composed by Rabbi Solomon Ibn Gabirol, may his soul rest.

34

There was nobody in the shack; I sat in the shack alone. It was pleasant and nicely fixed up. All kinds of flowers which the soil of our neighborhood gives us were hung from the wall between branches of pine and laurel; roses and zinnias crowned the ark and the reader's table, the prayer stand, and the eternal light. A wind blew through the shack and caused the leaves and flowers and blossoms to sway, and the house was filled with a goodly smell; the memorial candles gave their light to the building. I sat there and read the holy words God put into the hands of the poet, to glorify the commandments He gave to His people Israel. How great is the love of the holy poets before God! He gives power to their lips to glorify the laws and commandments that He gave to us in His great love.

35

The doors of the holy ark opened, and I saw a likeness of the form of a man standing there, his head resting between the scrolls of the Torah, and I heard a voice come forth from the ark, from between the trees of life. I bowed my head and closed my eyes, for I feared to look at the holy ark. I looked into my prayer book and saw that the letters that the voice from among the scrolls was reciting were at the same time being written into my book. The letters were the letters of the commandments of the Lord, in the order set for them by Rabbi Solomon Ibn Gabirol, may his soul rest. Now the man whom I had first seen between the scrolls of the Torah stood before me, and his appearance was like the appearance of a king.

I made myself small, until I was as though I were not, so that he should not feel the presence of a man in the place. Is it right that a king enter one of his provinces, and he not find any of his officers and servants, except for one little servant?

But my tricks didn't help any. I made myself small, and nevertheless he saw me. How do I know he saw me? Because he spoke to me. And how do I know that it was to me he spoke? Because I was alone in the house of prayer; there was no one there with me. He did not speak to me by word of mouth, but his thought was engraved into mine, his holy thought into mine. Every word he said was carved into the forms of letters, and the letters joined together into words, and the words formed what he had to say. These are the things as I remember them, word for word.

36

I shall put down the things he said to me, the things he asked me, and the things I answered him, as I took my life in my own hands, daring to speak before him. (But before I say them, I must tell you that he did not speak to me with words. Only the thoughts that he thought were engraved before me, and these created the words.)

And now I shall tell you all he asked me, and everything I answered him. He asked me, "What are you doing here alone at night?" And I answered, "My lord must know that this is the eve of Shavuot, when one stays awake all night reading the Order of Shavuot night. I too do this, except that I read the hymns of Rabbi Solomon Ibn Gabirol, may his soul rest."

He turned his head toward me and toward the book that stood before me on the table. He looked at the book and said, "It is Solomon's." I heard him and was astonished that he mentioned Rabbi Solomon Ibn Gabirol and did not affix some title of honor before his name. For I did not yet know that the man speaking to me was Rabbi Solomon Ibn Gabirol himself.

37

Now I shall tell the things that transpired after these former things. The memorial candles lit up the shack, the thronged flowers that crowned the eternal light before the holy ark and the other flowers gave off their aromas, and one smell was mixed with another—the aroma of the house of prayer with that of the roses and zinnias from the gardens. A restful quiet was felt on the earth below and in the heavens above. Neither the call of the heart's pleas on earth nor the sound of the heavens as they opened could be heard.

I rested my head in my arm, and sat and thought about what was happening to me. It couldn't have been in a dream, because he specifically asked me what I was doing here alone at night, and I answered him, "Doesn't my lord know that this night is the eve of Shavuot, when we stay awake all night and read the Order of Shavuot eve?" In any case, it seems a little difficult. Rabbi Solomon Ibn Gabirol is the greatest of the holy poets. Why did he see fit to descend from the Palace of Song to this shack in this neighborhood to talk with a man like me?

38

I took my life into my own hands and raised my head to see where I was, for it was a little hard to explain the things as they had happened, though their happening itself was witness to them, and there was no doubt that he was here. Not only did he speak to me, but I answered him. Maybe the thing happened when the heavens were open. But for how long do the heavens open? Only for a moment. Is it possible that so great a thing as this could happen in one brief moment?

I don't know just how long it was, but certainly not much time passed before he spoke to me again. He didn't speak with his voice, but his thought was impressed upon mine and created words. And God gave my heart the wisdom to understand. But to copy the things down—I could not. I just know this: that he spoke to me, for I was sitting alone in the house of prayer, reading the commandments of the Lord as composed by Rabbi Solomon Ibn Gabirol. For ever since I was old enough to do so, I follow the custom, every Shavuot eve, of reading the commandments of the Lord by Rabbi Solomon Ibn Gabirol, may his soul rest.

39

I was reminded of the sorrow I had felt for Rabbi Solomon Ibn Gabirol because God made him search for Him, as he says, "At the dawn I seek Thee, my rock and my fortress," and when he finally found Him, awe fell upon him and he stood confused, as he says, "Before Thy greatness I stand and am confounded." And as if he didn't have enough troubles himself, he had to add the sorrow of that poor captive girl. I put my finger to my throat, as the old cantor used to do, and raised my voice to sing "O Poor Captive" in the melody he had written. I saw that Rabbi Solomon, may his soul rest, turned his ear and listened to the pleasant sound of this hymn of redemption. I got up my courage and said to him, "In our town, wherever they prayed in the Ashkenazic rite, they used to say a lot of piyyutim. The beauty of each piyyut has stayed in my heart, and especially this 'O Poor Captive,' which was the first hymn of redemption I heard in my youth." I remembered that Sabbath morning when I had stood in the Great Synagogue in our city, which was now laid waste. My throat became stopped up and my voice choked, and I broke out in tears.

Rabbi Solomon saw this and asked me, "Why are you crying?" I answered, "I cry for my city and all the Jews in it who have been killed." His eyes closed, and I saw that the sorrow of my city had drawn itself to him. I thought to myself, since the rabbi doesn't know all of the people of my town, he'll weigh the glory of all of them by the likes of me. I bowed my head and lowered my eyes and said to him, "In my sorrow and in my humility, I am not worthy. I am not the man in whom the greatness of our city can be seen."

40

Rabbi Solomon saw my sorrow and my affliction and the lowness of my spirit, for my spirit was indeed very low. He came close to me, until I found myself standing next to him, and there was no distance between us except that created by the lowness of my spirit. I raised my eyes and saw his lips moving. I turned my ear and heard him mention the name of my city. I looked and saw him move his lips again. I heard him say, "I shall make a sign so that I won't forget the name." My heart melted and I stood trembling, because he had mentioned the name of my city and had drawn mercy to it, saying he would make a sign, so as not to forget its name.

I began to think about what sign Rabbi Solomon could make for my city. With ink? It was a holiday, so he wouldn't have his writer's inkwell in his pocket. With his clothes? The clothes with which the Holy One, blessed be He, clothes His holy ones have no folds and don't take to any imprint made upon them from outside.

Once more he moved his lips. I turned my ear and heard him recite a poem, each line of which began with one of the letters of the name of my town. And so I knew that the sign the poet made for my town was in beautiful and rhymed verse, in the holy tongue.

41

The hairs of my flesh stood on end and my heart melted as I left my own being, and I was as though I was not. Were it not for remembering the poem, I would have been like all my townsfolk, who were lost, who had died at the hand of a despicable people, those who trampled my people until they were no longer a nation. But it was because of the power of the poem that my soul went out of me. And if my town has been wiped out of the world, it remains alive in the poem that the poet wrote as a sign for my city. And if I don't remember the words of the poem, for my soul left me because of its greatness, the poem sings itself in the heavens above, among the poems of the holy poets, the beloved of God.

42

Now to whom shall I turn who can tell me the words of the song? To the old cantor who knew all the hymns of the holy poets? I alone remain to shed their tears. The old cantor rests in the shadow of the holy poets, who recite their hymns in the Great Synagogue of our city. And if he answers me, his voice will be as pleasant as it was when our city was yet alive and all of its people were also still in life. But here—here there is only a song of mourning, lamentation, and wailing, for the city and its dead.

Translated by Arthur Green

1900 postcard: "Greetings from Buczacz"

Buczacz

When was our city founded, and who was its founder? Long have all the chroniclers labored to find this out in vain. But some few facts have been revealed to us, and I am herewith setting down a faithful record of all I know.

There once was a band of Jews who were moved by their own pure hearts to go up to the Land of Israel, together with their wives and their sons and their daughters. They sold their fields, their vineyards, their male and female servants, their houses, and all their property that could not be transported. They obtained permission from the authorities to leave their city. They purchased provisions and set forth on the road.

They did not know the road to the Land of Israel, nor did anyone they met along the way know where the Land of Israel was. They only knew that it was in the East; so they turned their faces eastward, and that was the way they went. Whoever had a mount to ride rode his mount; whoever had no mount went by foot, leaning on his staff.

They passed by many towns and villages and castles and Jewish settlements and long stretches of forest and places inhabited by packs of wild animals and bandits. But since the Lord loves to see His children in His home, He made the gentiles look upon them favorably, so that they let them pass unharmed. Even the brigands who lie in wait for wayfarers and ambush passersby and seize their lives and goods did them no harm; they were content with tribute in the form of money or a silver goblet or a ring or such jewelry as the pilgrims gave them.

They set out at the beginning of the month of Iyar, when the highways are merry and the fields and vineyards full of people, but as they proceeded, people became scarce, vineyards and fields vanished, and all the roads led through forests that never seemed to end, with birds and beasts. If they came upon a person, he would not know their language or they his. Even had they understood his tongue, the gentiles in those lands could not show them the way, for they were ignorant; they had no idea of any town or province other than their birthplace, certainly not of the Land of Israel. If anybody there had heard of it, he thought it must be in the heavens above.

In this way, they passed the summer and reached the end of August. They made a halt and set up camp for the month of holidays: Rosh Hashanah, Yom Kippur, and Sukkot.

They made their camp in a place of forests and rivers, with no sign of habitation for several days' march in any direction, and they fashioned booths from the forest's trees. They celebrated the Days of Awe in prayer and supplication, and the Days of Joy in feasting and delight, trusting in the faithful mercy of God that in the year to come, they would observe these days before Him in the holy city of Jerusalem. For the rites of Sukkot, they used the old palm branches, citrons, and myrtles that they had brought with them upon setting out; the fourth species, willows, they gathered new each day of the festival. These willows were the best that they had ever seen, for the place where they had made their camp was well watered, with many rivers, ponds, and streams.

In those regions, as in most of the lands of the Slavs, winter comes on early. They were already suffering from the cold when they arrived, but particularly so during Sukkot, when they could hardly observe the ritual of dwelling in booths. At the holiday's end, when they ought to have set forth, the snow began to fall, fitfully at first, and then nonstop, until the roads were blotted out and they could not distinguish land from water or tell where it was solid and where it was river or pond. Like it or not, the pilgrims had to linger in their camp.

They brought wood from the forest and fixed up their booths into something more like cabins, and in them they set up various kinds of ovens for cooking their meals and for keeping themselves warm during the cold season. Out of the bark of trees they made themselves shoes, for their leather shoes were all tattered from their march. They also made new walking staffs and waited for the time when the Lord would restore the sun's strength and the roads would be clear of snow and they could set forth again. Huddled they sat in their booths in the snow, snug and secure from storm winds and bears and other wild beasts that would come alone or in packs right up to their doors and let out their awesome roar.

One day, when they were sitting as usual in their booths, some reading the Psalms, others doing their work, one of them cocked his head, perked up his ears, and said, I think I hear a trumpet's call. Another said, No, it is the sound of horses. A third said, No, it is the sound of people.

So they sat arguing about the sounds so suddenly heard in the forest. At length, they all yielded: the one who had called it the sound of a trumpet agreed that it was the sound of a dog, and the one who had called it the sound of a dog agreed that it was the sound of people. At last, they realized that there were actually three different sounds: the sound of a trumpet, the sound of a dog, and the sound of people. Then they found themselves surrounded by strange people who seemed to them like animals, with huge and fearsome dogs at their heels and great trumpets at their lips. But these people had not come to them with evil intent but only to hunt animals. They were great and distinguished noblemen, and it is the way of noblemen to go to the forests to hunt game.

One of the noblemen asked them in Latin, Who are you and what are you doing here? They told him their whole story, how they had purposed to go up to the Holy Land and had been overtaken by winter and had made camp there until the winter should be over and the cold should pass. The noblemen began to ask them what they had seen along the way and what was the news of the day and who were the rulers who governed those lands, and the pilgrims answered all their questions in such detail that the noblemen were struck by their cleverness and eloquence. So enchanted were they that they forgot the game and gave up the hunt and began to urge them to come with them and to live with them, arguing that winter is very hard in that land, that many people fall sick from the great cold, that not everyone is built to bear it, and that these Rhinelanders would certainly never survive a winter in the forest. The pilgrims saw that the noblemen's counsel was right. They agreed to go and live with them until the end of the winter season; then, with winter gone and the snow cleared, they would reassemble and set out on the road again. Each nobleman took with him an individual or a family and brought them home, treating them with every courtesy. The pilgrims stayed with the noblemen throughout the winter.

The noblemen who had taken the Jews into their homes enjoyed prosperity in whatever they did. They realized that their success was due to the Jews. Each one began to worry and fret, What shall I do when the Jews leave us? They will certainly take their blessing with them, or the blessing will go away of its own accord. They began to urge them to stay, saying, The whole land is yours; make your home wherever you like. If you want to engage in commerce in the land, better yet, for no one here knows anything about commerce. Some of the pilgrims paid no attention to them and wanted to be on their way; but others let themselves be won over by the noblemen, for they were weary, and many were sick and fearful of the rigors of the road. And because they were not of one mind, even those who wanted to go did not, for they were but few, and the roads were presumed too dangerous to be traversed by any but a large band.

In the meanwhile, the Days of Awe returned. The entire band gathered in a certain place for communal prayer, and there they remained until after Sukkot. They did the same the following year and for several years thereafter: throughout the year, each one would live in his own place by his nobleman, and on the Days of Awe and the three festivals they would assemble to observe the holidays by holding prayers, Torah reading, and performing all the other mitzvot.

One year, at Simḥat Torah, when they were all in good spirits because of the joy of the Torah and the great feast that they had made to celebrate its completion, one of them said, with a sigh, Now we are content, for we are together, worshiping as a community and reading the Torah; but what about tomorrow and the next day and the next? Winter is here, and again we shall go without the reading of the Torah and without communal prayer.

They thought about it and began to discuss what to do. To leave where they were and go to the Land of Israel was out of the question; for by now, they had acquired property in the land and built houses and were in favor with the nobility. As for the women, some were pregnant, some were nursing, some were worn out and weak. And the elders were even older than before, so that traveling would have been hard on them. But to stay where they were, without Torah or communal prayer, was certainly not acceptable as a permanent arrangement. It would have been better if they had not given in to the noblemen and had gone their way right after the snow had cleared and were now settled before the Lord in Jerusalem; but having yielded and not made the pilgrimage, they now had to take active steps to enable themselves to perform all the rites of God that we are commanded to perform. After much discussion, they agreed unanimously to establish a permanent house of prayer and to hold services on every weekday when the Torah is read, and, of course, on the Sabbath and New Moon and Ḥanukkah and Purim. Whoever was able to attend the services would attend, and whoever was not able on account of illness or some other impediment would try to have someone attend in his stead. The building in which they had been holding services on the festivals they designated as the synagogue.

When word reached the local nobleman, it so pleased him that he gave them the building and everything in it as an outright and perpetual gift. Before he died, he ordered his sons to treat the Jews with benevolence, for God had granted him prosperity on account of the Jews, and from the Jews had come whatever he was leaving them.

They turned the building into a synagogue, and there they would come to pray on all the days when the Torah is read, including especially the Sabbaths and festivals and other days of distinction. Occasionally, they would hold communal prayer even on days when the Torah is not read; for if someone happened to be in the vicinity, he would say, I think I will go to see if enough Jews happen to be there to hold services, so that I can hear Barekhu and Kedushah. Thus, with one coming from one way and one coming from another, they would come together and hold a service. The place came to be a favorite, for whoever was hungry for the word of the Lord or whoever yearned to see his fellow Jews would turn to it. And whoever could afford to do so built himself a house nearby, so that, living near the place of prayer, he would be able to participate in communal prayer.

Little by little, the entire place came to be settled by Jews. They built themselves a ritual bath and whatever else a community needs. Whenever they needed a rabbi to answer a ritual question, or a teacher for their children, or tzitzit, or to have their tefilin examined, they would turn to that place. Even the noblemen and their servants would come there for advice or business, knowing that they would find Jews there. The place acquired a reputation; people began to come from far and wide on the days of their festivals, both to see and to be seen. Noblemen and noblewomen came, too, riding on their horses. Then the local nobleman built himself a stone house; eventually, he built a castle up on the mountain facing the River Strypa, a great castle befitting one of the great princes of the land. This castle was for many years the defense and refuge of the lord of the town and his retainers, until the Tatars attacked it, and, on defeating him, compelled him to destroy it. The ruins are there to this day.

That is how Buczacz began. Formerly, it was not called Buczacz but Biczacz; and at the very first, it was called something very like.

As to the name and its meaning, there are many opinions and conjectures, some of which, though plausible, remain conjectures nonetheless. I am setting aside the *ifs* and *maybes* and writing only the truth as it actually is.

Eventually, the holy community of Buczacz was joined by a number of Jews from other places, especially from Germany. Disaster had overtaken the people of God, the holy communities of Worms, Mainz, Speyer, and other distinguished communities in Germany, because of the filthy infidels whose arrogance moved them to go up to the Holy Land to fight the king of Ishmael and to conquer the land. Wherever they encountered Jews along the way, they murdered them, killing them in cruel and unusual ways. Many of the people of God valiantly sanctified His Name; they were killed and slaughtered as martyrs to the unity of God's awe-inspiring, unique Name. Most of the communities in the land of Germany were destroyed; the few survivors wandered from one nation to another until they reached the lands of the Slavs, and of them, some reached our town. In our town, they dwelled in safety and in peace. On minor ritual matters, they consulted their own sages; and on major ritual matters, they consulted our sages in Germany until from among the townspeople emerged some great and authoritative masters of the Torah who illuminated the world with their learning. Now they were completely supplied with religious wisdom and knowledge of God. They were secure in their wealth and dignity, their piety and righteousness, until, struck by divine justice, they nearly all perished in God's rage through the persecution of Khmelnitski's thugs.

When some quiet was restored after the riots and rebellions and killing and breakdown, some of those who survived the sword returned to their towns and their settlements. So did those who had been dispersed from Buczacz. They built themselves houses and shops; but first, they built houses for study and prayer. There they dwelled for many generations in security and tranquility, except in years of war and revolution. Their first protector was the kingdom of Poland, and later Austria; then Poland reestablished its kingdom and engaged in conquest and destruction, until the Enemy came and eradicated them all.

May God return the remnants of His people from wherever they are; may He assemble our Diaspora from among the nations; may He bring them to Zion, His city, in song, and to Jerusalem, His temple, in lasting joy; may no enemy or foe enter the gates of Jerusalem from this day forth. Amen.

Translated by Raymond P. Scheindlin

The Great Synagogue

As THE CITY AND ITS POPULATION GREW, some Jews having come on their own, others brought by the city's lord from other places and from his estates, the beit midrash filled up. People would contract themselves and crowd together, which would occasionally cause them to waste the time they had for studying Torah. Those who lived nearby would take their time praying, some repeating every word two or three times. For during the days of upheaval they had been chased like wild animals of the forest and had forgotten their prayers. So when they came to the city and were fortunate to pray in community, they doubled and trebled every word. For if the first was not exact, perhaps the second or third time it would be right in God's eyes.

The town elders decided to build a new structure dedicated only to prayer so that everyone could find a place to pray and so that the students of Torah would have more space in the beit midrash. Those who took a long time praying could pray in the synagogue, and those who both prayed and studied could pray in the beit midrash. The synagogue would be devoted to prayer and the beit midrash to both prayer and study.

They put their thoughts into action, notified the whole town and went from house to house and from person to person so that each could take part in building the city's synagogue. Everyone opened his hand and gave his gift, the rich from his riches and the poor from his poverty.

There was no one in the city who did not part with some of his wealth, according to his capacity and the strength of his faith; for everyone who honors God with his monetary resources, God makes up what he lacks. Even the poor person, who has only his poverty, brought his offering. Moreover, we should recall with praise those generous-hearted people who were the first to give and, during the time of the building, gave again, not to mention the reserved seats that they bought for themselves and for their descendants until the coming of the Redeemer, especially those seats that were near the holy ark and the prayer stand. The seats they purchased were all around the bimah, for there you were near the reading desk and could hear the reading of the Torah without losing a single word.

Each action led to the next and they began to build. With God's help, the work did not cease either on account of death or the acts of gentiles. Even the royal authorities looked favorably on the building of a synagogue and helped to design it as a kind of fortress of strength and protection against the Ottoman Turks, their frequent enemies. Therefore openings were made underneath the roof from which they could shoot at the enemy in time of war. The head of the monastery also did not stand in the way, for the Jews rented their houses and shops from him and helped greatly to increase his income.

The early chronicles say that it was first built of wood. So, too, were the beit midrash and the homes of the Jews. After some time, the city's lord gave permission to build the synagogue from stone. Even the head priest agreed, with the condition that the Jews give him each year so many basketfuls of tallow to make candles for their church. Before thirteen years were up, a beautiful building was built. This is the great synagogue, to which Jews come to pray that trouble should not be visited upon them. God hears the prayer of His people Israel, and saves us from all oppressors and enemies. For not one time alone did our enemies seek to destroy us, the Cossacks on the one side and the monastery students on the other, both city and village folk.

Translated by Herbert Levine and Reena Spicehandler

The Brilliant Chandelier

HERE IT IS FITTING TO TELL THE STORY of the brilliant chandelier that hung in our town's Great Synagogue, just as it is fitting to recall R. Shalom, of the curly hair, who brought it to our city.

There was a great chandelier that hung in the Great Synagogue in our city. It hung from the ceiling above the reader's desk. It was all shining, polished glass, with hanging chains, and a lily below. When the chandelier was lit up, it would project the light in a variety of hues. R. Shalom of the curly hair brought it from the city of Trieste in Italy.

R. Shalom of the curly hair was a great merchant. In pursuit of his business, he would travel to great commercial centers even beyond the borders of Poland. Once, he traveled to the city of Trieste. There was a leading merchant there with whom he had connections and with whom he concluded a major piece of business. When he arrived in Trieste and met the merchant face-to-face, they became fast friends.

When it came time for R. Shalom to return to his city, the merchant invited him to his house for a repast of fruit. R. Shalom went willingly. The merchant sat him down in a large room full of pleasant objects, including furnishings and lamps, the most pleasing of which was the huge chandelier that hung unlit from the ceiling. R. Shalom looked at it and was amazed; he had never seen such a house or such furnishings or lights like these. Above all, he was amazed by the brilliant chandelier, for even though it stood idle, it appeared that all the other lights received their light from it. R. Shalom gazed and could not take his eyes off it.

The merchant observed this and said, What do you see in it? Said R. Shalom, What is there to say? I have never seen anything as beautiful. The merchant nodded his head and said, I also think that it is very comely. R. Shalom continued and said, If it shines so brightly when it is not lit, then how radiant it must be when it is lit. How many candles does it have? I count twenty-six. It is difficult for the imagination to grasp the joy that the chandelier brings to those who see it when all twenty-six candles are burning.

The merchant said, I have not yet seen it lit. R. Shalom replied, Is it not in working order? The merchant said, It is fine and works as well as on the day that it stopped being used.

Whenever he heard an astonishing thing, R. Shalom would keep to himself because, when he had a chance to examine it and determine that it was truly astonishing, he probed the matter until the reason for it became clear. And so it was concerning the chandelier. However, why am I speaking in such theoretical terms? It is better to describe things whose explicit meaning teaches us about what is concealed.

Said R. Shalom to the merchant, With your permission, my dear sir, may I ask how it is possible that this chandelier, which was created for light, stands idle? The merchant replied, Now it is idle, but in the past, in the days of my great-grandfather, it was alight on Sabbath eves and on the eves of the Jewish festivals. Said R. Shalom, Sir, now I am even more amazed. What did you mean by saying, "in the days of your great-grandfather"? What is the meaning of "on Sabbath eves and on the eves of Jewish festivals?"—surely you are Christians, you and your ancestors?

The merchant said, But my great-grandfather was a Jew, a Jew who became a Christian.

R. Shalom bent his head. The merchant elaborated: Because of a mistake in his business caused by one of his Christian workers, he was forced to convert. But inwardly, he repented his action, and when matters subsided, he planned to go to another country such as Holland, where there was freedom for Jews, and return to his Judaism. But a plague then broke out; he caught it and died. His sons and daughters, however, were still small and remained true to the Christian faith that their father had taken upon himself.

R. Shalom sat and was sad for the old man who had brought an end to himself and to his seed and to his descendants thereafter. Said the merchant, From the day the old man became a Christian, he did not light the chandelier; neither did his children, and neither did I. Has this made you sad?

R. Shalom replied wisely, Alas for the great and splendid chandelier that remains in darkness. The merchant said, About this, I, too, am sad. And then he added, I do not want to sell it, for it is an heirloom, and I do not want to leave it to my children, for fear they will depart from the tradition that has been established by their forefathers.

R. Shalom sat and was quiet, and the merchant sat and was quiet, and both of them sat quietly. R. Shalom saw that it was time to go. As he stood to go, the merchant stirred himself and said to him, Are you going? R. Shalom said, With God's help, at this time tomorrow, I am setting off; and if God grants me a peaceful journey to my city, I shall celebrate the Sabbath there in ten days' time.

The merchant asked R. Shalom, How many Jews are in your city, and how do they earn a living, and does the governor of the city behave toward them with a mean spirit? And he asked further, How many synagogues are there in the city, and is there a Great Synagogue in which all the Jews of the city can gather?

R. Shalom answered each question in turn. As far as the synagogue was concerned, he told him some of the things that are generally told about the Great Synagogue in our city, and told him that he had had the honor of being appointed the synagogue's gabbai.

The merchant said to him, When I saw you looking at the chandelier, a thought was sparked in me that perhaps it was time to restore light to the chandelier as it was in the time of my Jewish great-grandfather.

R. Shalom heard and kept quiet.

R. Shalom was about to depart from Trieste when one of the merchant's servants brought him a crate in which the chandelier lay wrapped and protected in a swath of wool. A card affixed to it showed that it was addressed to the Great Synagogue of the Jews of the city of Buczacz.

R. Shalom reached our city in peace. He took the chandelier out of the crate and hung it in our synagogue. It was shining on Sabbath eves and on the eves of the festivals and on the eves when we recited Seliḥot, petitionary prayers.

That is the tale of the brilliant chandelier that was shrouded in darkness. Once it came into our city, the chandelier shone again ever more brightly, until the arrival of the depraved and reviled one, with his cursed and polluted gang, and then its light went out.

Translated by Pnina and Mordechai Beck

The Tale of the Menorah

1

R. Naḥman, keeper of the roal seal, was a man of great importance in the eyes of the king. Whenever he came to the royal court, the palace attendants gave him an audience with the king, for they knew how beloved Naḥman the Jew was to the king.

It happened one day that R. Naḥman came to the royal court, for he had a matter about which he had to speak to the king. The king, too, had a certain matter that he had concealed from his closest counselors, his company of advisers. The moment he saw R. Naḥman, the king said, This is the man I shall consult.

So the king related to R. Naḥman the matter that he had not wished to tell a single one of his counselors. But he did tell it to R. Naḥman, the keeper of the royal seal.

The Almighty bestowed wisdom upon R. Naḥman, and he responded with intelligent advice. The king listened and did as R. Naḥman had advised. And it turned out to be a blessing for the king. Then he knew how excellent was the advice Naḥman had given him.

After this, R. Naḥman was summoned to the palace court. When the king heard that Naḥman was in the royal courtyard, he commanded, Bring him to me.

R. Naḥman entered the king's chamber. The king said to him, The advice you gave me was excellent. Ask of me now whatever you desire, and I will grant it to you.

R. Naḥman replied, Blessed be the Lord who has shared His wonderful counsel with the king.

But for himself, R. Naḥman did not ask for a single thing. He said to the king, I am unworthy of the least of all your kindnesses.

These were the very words that Jacob our forefather spoke to Esau, and R. Naḥman said them to the king. The king replied, Because you have not asked for a single thing for yourself, I will make a holy donation to your God.

R. Naḥman did not ask the king what it was he promised to give. And the king did not tell him.

2

It came to pass in those days that Buczacz built itself a Great Synagogue. Its community of Jews had grown to nearly 250 householders, in addition to the women and the children and all the servants of the wealthy who had come from other towns and now lived in the city. So the people of Buczacz built themselves a large synagogue in which to worship. That is the same building that the gentiles living in the city made into a church for their gods after the city fell into the hands of Khmelnitski and he had slain every Jew who had not fled in haste from the sword of his wrath.

The king commanded his metalworkers to make him a great brass menorah to place in the synagogue in Buczacz in honor of Naḥman, the keeper of the royal seal and the leader of the community of Israel in Buczacz.

The king's metalworkers made a great menorah out of brass. There were seven branches in the candelabrum, the same number of branches that we had in ancient days in the holy candelabrum in the Temple, the house of our glory. The artisans did not know that it is forbidden to make a vessel identical to one that had been in the Temple.

When they brought the menorah, which was a gift from the king, to the synagogue, the Jews saw it and beheld its seven branches. They said, We cannot place this menorah in the synagogue. If we do, they said to themselves, we will sin against God; on the other hand, if we do not set it in the synagogue, we will insult the king and his gift.

They did not know what counsel to take for themselves. Even Naḥman, the counselor to the king, had no solution. He said, This has all befallen us because I frequented the court of the king.

But God saw their distress, and He set the idea in their heads to remove one branch from the menorah and thus make it into an ordinary candelabrum. Then if they placed the menorah in the synagogue, there would be no sin for them in doing so. And if someone mentioned it to the king, they could say, From the day that our Temple was destroyed, we make nothing without marking upon it a sign in remembrance of the destruction.

So they removed the middle branch. Then they brought the menorah into the house of God and placed it on the ark and lit its candles.

The menorah stood in the synagogue. The six candles in the six branches of the menorah lit up the building on the eve of every Sabbath and holiday. And on Yom Kippur and on those holidays when the memorial prayer for the departed is recited in synagogue to remember the souls of the departed, they shone during the day as well. A gentile watched the candles lest one fall out.

So the menorah stood there, and so it shone for the entire time that this house of God was indeed a house *for* God, until the day Israel was driven out by Khmelnitski and the town's gentiles made the house of God into a church for their gods. Then the gentile who watched the candles, who was a millworker, took the menorah and hid it in the River Strypa, which was near the mill. The menorah lay at the bottom of the Strypa's waters, and no one knew where it was. As for the millworker, he died after his body got caught in the millstone's wheel; he was ground up and cast away, and his flesh became food for the fish in the River Strypa.

3

After some years, those who had survived Khmelnitski's sword returned to their homeland and towns. The few survivors from Buczacz also returned to the town, and there they built themselves a small sanctuary in place of the Great Synagogue, which the gentiles had plundered and made into a house for their gods.

That year, on a Saturday night at the close of the Sabbath, on the night that was also the first night for reciting the Seliḥot, the penitential hymns, the young children were shining candles over the surface of the Strypa. They were doing this in order to make light for the slain martyrs who had drowned in rivers, streams, and lakes. On the first night of Seliḥot, all the dead whom our enemies have drowned come to pray to the eternal God in the same synagogue in which they prayed during their lifetimes. The other nights of Seliḥot are dedicated to those martyrs who died by fire, to those who were stabbed to death, to the ones who were strangled, and to those who were murdered. For on account of their numbers, the building could not contain all the slain at once. As a result, they divided up the nights among them, one congregation of martyrs for each night of prayer.

Now while the children were on the banks of the Strypa shining their candles, a great menorah such as they had never seen before suddenly shone forth from beneath the water. They said, That must be the menorah of the dead; for the dead bring with them their own menorot when they come to pray. Their hearts quaked in fear, and the children fled.

Some grown-ups heard the story about the menorah that the children had told, and they said, Let us go and see for ourselves! They went and came to the Strypa. Indeed, there was a menorah in the Strypa. The story is true, they said. It is a menorah.

But not a person knew that it was the menorah that the king of Poland had given to the old Great Synagogue before the gentiles of the city took it over and made it into a church for their gods.

The Jews retrieved the menorah from the waters of the Strypa and brought it to the synagogue. There they placed it upon the reading table, for another menorah already stood on the stand before the ark, and they had promised the donor of that menorah that no one would ever replace it. Besides, the stand before the ark was too small to hold the large menorah. And so they placed the menorah they had drawn from the waters on the reading table.

The menorah illuminated the house of God with the six candles that stood in its six branches. And for a long time, the menorah lit up the house of God on the evenings of the Sabbath and the holidays. The candles of the menorah shone on the holidays during the daytime as well, and on the twentieth of Sivan, when the souls of the departed are remembered in the service. And when the sun came out in all its strength and reached into the house of God, then the menorah shone with the luster of burnished brass in sunlight.

4

Many days later, after that entire generation had died, a new generation arose that did not know all that had happened to their forefathers. After looking at the menorah day after day, one of them said, We should repair the menorah; it should not look like a vessel that is missing something. And they did not realize that their forefathers had already repaired the menorah when they cut off one of its branches to avoid sinning against God or the king.

They made an eagle of glittering brass and placed a large amount of lead in the brass so that it would appear to be a white eagle, for a white eagle is the national insignia of Poland. They placed the eagle beneath the spot where their forefathers had removed the branch. Originally, it had been a menorah with seven branches, but our forefathers had repaired the menorah when they removed one of its branches. But the members of the next generation, those who brought the national insignia of Poland into our synagogue, said to one another, Now we will let Poland know how truly attached we are to our country and homeland, the land of Poland. Out of our love for the homeland, we have even placed the national insignia of Poland in our house of worship!

So the menorah stood on the holy reading table on which they used to read from the Torah of God. And the eagle—the Polish eagle—lay between the branches of the menorah. So stood the menorah: three branches on one side, three branches on the other, with the candles in the menorah shining on one side toward the reader's stand and on the other side toward the holy Torah ark. And in the center, the white eagle, the national insignia of the Polish kingdom, stood between the candles. So stood the eagle in the menorah in the synagogue for all the time Poland was a sovereign state ruling over the entire land of Poland.

5

Sometime later, Poland was conquered. The country was divided up among its neighbors, each neighbor taking for itself all that it could, and Buczacz fell to the lot of Austria. The Austrian forces camped across the city—the soldiers, their officers, the entire army that had conquered the territory of Buczacz.

After summoning the town's rulers, the army generals ordered them to make a holiday now that the city had come under the rule of the Austrian emperor. They commanded the Jews to gather in their Great Synagogue to praise and glorify their Lord, the God of Israel, who had bestowed upon them the emperor of Austria to be their ruler. The heads of the city and of the Jewish community listened and did just as the generals said, for no one disobeys the orders of an army general; whoever does, disobeys at the risk of his life.

And so everyone in the city came to make a holiday that God had given them the Austrian emperor to protect them beneath the wings of his kindness. Many of the Jews offered their gratitude innocently and sincerely, for God had indeed liberated them from the oppressiveness of Poland and from the priests who handed Israel over to despoilment through the libels and plots they had devised against them, so as to persecute the Jews and take their money and lead them astray from God's statutes. Not a year had passed that righteous and innocent men were not murdered because of blood libels and every other type of false accusation.

And so all the Jews of Buczacz came and filled the synagogue, even its women's section. Many of the city's leaders who were not Jews also attended, and at their head came the generals of the Austrian army.

The synagogue's cantor and his choir chanted from the psalms of David, from those psalms that David, king of Israel, had sung to the God of Israel when the people of Israel lived in their land and when David, our king, reigned in the city of God, in Israel's holy Zion. The generals and the city's rulers sat there and gazed at the synagogue building and its walls and the ceiling and the candelabra that hung from the ceiling. All of them were of burnished brass, the handiwork of artisans. They gazed at the holy curtain covering the holy ark of the Torah, and at the covering over the holy curtain, and at the lectern, and at the cantor and his choir standing in front of the lectern. They gazed at the raised platform made of hewn stone that stood at the center of the synagogue, and at the steps leading up to the platform, and at the table on the platform. Then they saw the great menorah that stood on the table with its branches and flower-shaped cups. And they saw how beautiful it was.

And as they were looking, the officers suddenly saw the Polish eagle on the menorah. They immediately became incensed at the Jews. The synagogue president rushed off, grabbed the gavel that the synagogue's shamash used to rouse the congregants for morning services, and smashed the white eagle with the gavel. He hit the eagle with the gavel and knocked it off the synagogue menorah. And thus he removed the national insignia of Poland from the house of worship. The officers said to him, You acted well. If you had not done this, we would have imprisoned you and the elders of the community, and we would have fined the Jewish community as punishment.

Then the army officers ordered that a two-headed eagle be set on the menorah in place of the eagle they had removed. For the two-headed eagle is the Austrian eagle. They immediately sent for Yisrael the Metalworker, summoning him to come. This was the same Yisrael the Metalworker whose wife received seven copper pennies every Friday, so that she could buy herself sustenance for the Sabbath during the period that the Austrian emperor imprisoned her husband and she had literally nothing with which to celebrate the Sabbath, as I related in my tale "My Sabbath."

Yisrael the Metalworker made a brass eagle with two heads, and they set that two-headed eagle on the menorah in place of the one-headed eagle. The young boys took the eagle that Yisrael the Metalworker had discarded, and they brought it to him to make dreidels for them to play with during Ḥanukkah. And those are the very same dreidels that our grandfathers told us about—the dreidels of burnished brass that Yisrael the Metalworker made for the children of Buczacz.

The menorah stood in the Great Synagogue for many days. With its six candles in its six branches, the menorah lit up the synagogue. On Sabbath nights and the nights of the holidays, the menorah's candles were lit, as they also were on the Austrian emperor's birthday, which the country celebrated as a holiday because he was a beneficent ruler. And so the two-headed eagle vanquished the menorah and its branches.

But the Polish people never reconciled themselves to the Austrian rulers who had stolen their land. They prepared war against them. They came out of every town and village to wage a war on behalf of their nation and homeland.

6

Buczacz, like the other towns and villages, supported the uprising. Many Jews were also among those fighting on behalf of Poland. They held a heavy hand over their own brethren; indeed, they were particularly hard upon all those who sought peace and quiet and upon all who remained loyal to Austria.

Certain Jews passed through the land of Galicia to rouse their brethren in every town and make them come to the rescue of Poland. They spoke of all the wonderful things Poland had done for the Jews but did not recall the wicked things. One of these men came to Buczacz. He was wearing a hammer on his belt just like those that firemen wear when they go out to fight a fire. On the Sabbath morning, he came to the Great Synagogue. The Jews there paid him much honor; they seated him next to the eastern wall of the synagogue and called him up to the Torah.

And so it happened, as he was standing before the Torah, that the man saw the two-headed eagle. He began to scream, This is an abomination! An abomination! Then he grabbed the hammer from around his waist and struck at the two-headed eagle. He paid no attention to the other worshipers, not even when they pleaded with him to stop and not desecrate the Sabbath. He did not listen to them until he had broken the Austrian eagle from off the menorah and cast it to the ground.

The young boys took the eagle that had been removed from the menorah and brought it to one of the metalworkers to make into dreidels for Ḥanukkah, for they had heard that their forefathers had made dreidels for themselves from brass. But the metalworker did not make dreidels for them because it is very difficult to make dreidels from brass. But he did make them dice, which children also play with on Ḥanukkah.

And all the days of the uprising, the menorah stood there with the eagle cut off.

7

Eventually, the uprising was put down, and Austria returned to ruling over the country. Now, though, its rulers cast a wary eye upon every matter, large and small, in enforcing the law of the land and its ordinances.

It was then that the synagogue treasurers hastened to make for themselves an eagle with two heads, which they set on the menorah in place of the eagle that had been cut off and discarded.

The eagle stood there between the six branches of the menorah, its one head turned to the three branches to the right, and its second head toward the three branches to the left. All the years until the Great War broke out, until Austria and Russia became enemies, the eagle stood there on the menorah, and the menorah stood on the holy reading table, the table on which the Torah was read.

8

As conditions in the war grew more difficult, it became harder for the soldiers to find weapons to shoot. So they took metal utensils, large and fine utensils, and they melted them down in order to make out of them weapons with which to destroy the country. These soldiers came as well to the Great Synagogue in Buczacz. They took the brass basin in which every man who entered the sanctuary washed his hands. They took the brass pitcher that the Levites used to pour water over the hands of the priests before they went up before the congregation on holidays to bless them with the priestly blessing. They took every utensil made of brass and lead. They took the charity box that was made of gold, the box in which people made secret contributions to charity. And the officers also fixed their eyes upon the great menorah. A certain metalworker was with them. For they had brought a metalworker in order to take the utensils from the synagogue and melt them down into weapons.

But just as they were about to seize the menorah, the sound of Russian tanks was heard. The Austrian forces immediately fled for their lives, and left behind all they had taken. But the metalworker, the one who had come with the army officers when they came to take the brass utensils: he did not flee. He took the menorah and hid it in a place that only he knew. No one else knew its place. And no one gave a thought to the menorah, for all anyone cared about was saving his own life from the Great War and from the heavy shellfire that fell continuously through the war until its conclusion.

Then the war ended, and the land of Poland that had been fought over came under Polish rule. And the town of Buczacz was also given over to Poland.

9

A number of the former inhabitants of Buczacz returned to the town. Many villagers from around Buczacz also settled in the town, for their houses had been stolen by their neighbors with whom they had fought on behalf of their homeland. They all came to worship in the Great Synagogue for, of all the prayer houses, the Great Synagogue alone survived the war.

And so it happened, when they could not find a single lamp to light up the house of worship at night, that they took some stones from the place, they bored holes in them, and then they set the stones on the lectern in order to place candles in them to make light for themselves when they stood in prayer before the Lord. Later, they made for themselves menorot out of tin and wood because they were very poor, for they had been unable to recover anything of all they had owned. Whatever the war had spared, the enemy had taken; and whatever the enemy had spared, the Poles took. So it was not within their means to make for themselves menorot from brass or from lead, as they once had.

10

One man who had been born in Buczacz came home after being a captive in Russia. And it happened that, when he came to the Great Synagogue on Friday night and saw the menorot of tin and wood that were without any beauty, he remembered how he happened to be in the trenches with a metalworker, and how that metalworker had told him that, when the Russians advanced upon Buczacz, he had hidden the town's great menorah to keep it from falling into the Russians' hands. But before the metalworker was able to tell him where he had hidden the menorah, a cannon hit the trench and the two never saw each other again. And now, when the man saw the synagogue, he remembered the metalworker and the trench that the cannon had blown up. For if the cannon had not blown up the trench, he would now have known the place where the metalworker had hidden the menorah.

The next morning, on the Sabbath day, the man was called to the Torah, for it was the first Sabbath since he had returned to his hometown. The Torah reading for that Sabbath was the portion called *Terumah,* which begins with Exodus 25. As the Torah reader read aloud the section in Scripture describing the making of the menorah that was used in the tabernacle, he came to the verse "Note well, and follow the patterns for them that are being shown you on the mountain." At that instant, the man knew that the menorah was hidden on a mountain!

The town of Buczacz is surrounded by mountains; it sits on a mountaintop itself. And the man had no idea which mountain it was that held the menorah.

The man began to wander the mountains. There was not a mountain of all the mountains around Buczacz that he did not search. The man did not reveal to anyone that he was searching for the menorah, for he feared the riffraff that had joined the town and that, if they heard about the menorah, they would take it away. Every day, the man went in search of the menorah, through cold and heat, until summer and winter had both passed. But he still had not found the menorah.

Now the days of cold, the winter season, returned, and the man did not return from his daily labors in the mountains. At the end of several days, after wandering in the mountains, he said to himself, Let me return home and no longer search for the menorah. For I am not able to find it.

And it came to pass that, as the man was returning home, another man was standing on the road, a man crippled in his legs and missing an arm. The two of them stood there. They looked at each other in astonishment and exclaimed, Blessed be He who resurrects the dead!

Then the man who had been searching for the menorah said, I told myself that you were blown up in the trench, and now I see you are alive!

The metalworker said to him, I, too, thought that you were among the dead. Blessed be the Lord who has saved us from the Russian cannons and who has left us alive after the horrible Great War.

The man who had been searching for the menorah asked him, Did you not tell me that when the Russians first came to Buczacz, you hid the great menorah? Well, where did you hide it?

The metalworker replied, That is why I have come.

Where is it? the other asked.

It is hidden in the ground beneath my house, he answered.

Where is your house?

It is destroyed, the metalworker said. It no longer exists. But the place is still there. It is beneath a pile of snow. If I only had a shovel in my hand, I could already have cleared away the snow and the earth beneath it and dug the menorah out.

The two of them went off. They brought a shovel and worked there all day and all night and all the next day, for a huge amount of snow covered the mountains, until, finally, they had cleared the snow and the earth, and they found the menorah.

They removed the menorah and brought it to the Great Synagogue, where they stood it on the reading table where the menorah had once stood. And so the menorah stood on the reading table as it had in earlier days, in the days when there was peace in the land. The metalworker said, Now I will cut off that bird with two heads, for Austria has ceased to rule over Buczacz. And if there are young boys in town, I will make dreidels from the brass eagle for them to play with during Ḥanukkah, just as our grandfathers did for our fathers.

He added, Let us also not make a one-headed eagle, like the eagle that is the national insignia of Poland. I have heard that the Ruthenians have revolted against Poland. If they see the eagle of Poland in our synagogue, they will say that we have prepared to go to war against the Ruthenian nation.

The two men said to each other, One kingdom comes and another kingdom passes away. But Israel remains forever. And they said, O Lord!

Have pity on Your people. Let not Your possession become a mockery, to be taunted by nations! How long shall they direct us however they wish? You, our God, are our rock and refuge forever. You alone we have desired; let us never be ashamed.

Translated by David Stern

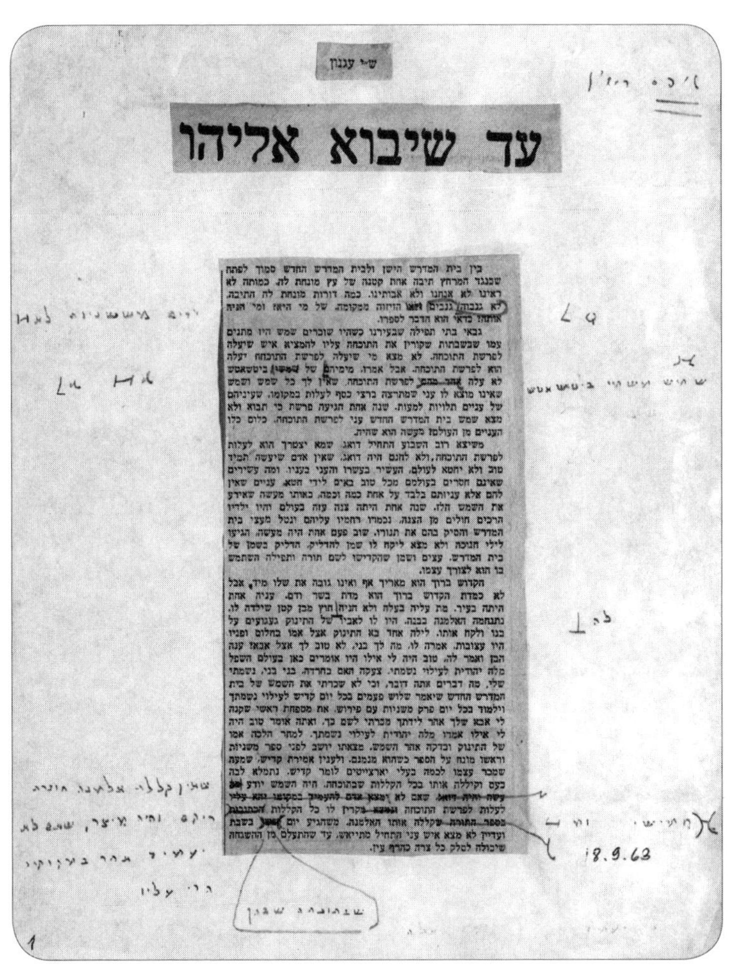

ש"י עגנון

עד שיבוא אליהו

בין בית המדרש הישן ולבית המדרש החדש סמוך לפתח שבנגד המרחץ תיבה אחת קטנה של עץ מונחת לה, כמותה לא ראינו לא אנחנו ולא אבותינו. כמה דורות מונחת לה התיבה, לא גנבוה גנבים [illegible] הזיזוה ממקומה. של מי היא? ומי הניח אותה? כדאי הוא הדבר לספרו.

גבאי בתי תפילה שבעירנו כשהיו שוכרים שמש היו מתנים עמו שבשבתות שקורין את התוכחה עליו להמציא איש שיעלה לפרשת התוכחה. לא מצא מי שיעלה לפרשת התוכחה יעלה הוא לפרשת התוכחה. אבל אמרו, מימיהם של [illegible] ביטשאטש לא עלה אחד מהם לפרשת התוכחה. שאין לך כל שמש ושמש שאינו מוצא לו עני שמתרצה ברצי כסף לעלות במקומו, שעיניהם של עניים תלויות למעות. שנה אחת הגיעה פרשת כי תבוא ולא מצא שמש בית המדרש החדש עני לפרשת התוכחה. כלום כלו העניים מן העולם? מעשה הוא שהיה.

משיצא רוב השבוע התחיל דואג, שמא יצטרך הוא לעלות לפרשת התוכחה, ולא לחנם היה דואג, שאין אדם שיעשה תמיד טוב ולא יחטא לעולם, העשיר בעשרו והעני בעניו. ומה עשירים שאינם חסרים בעולמם מכל טוב באים לידי חטא, עניים שאין להם אלא עניותם בלבד על אחת כמה וכמה. כאותו מעשה שאירע את השמש הלז. שנה אחת היתה צנה עזה בעולם והיו ילדיו הרכים חולים מן הצנה. נכמרו רחמיו עליהם ונטל מעצי בית המדרש והסיק בהם את תנורו. שוב פעם אחת היה מעשה, הגיעו לילי חנוכה ולא מצא ליקח לו שמן להדליק, הדליק בשמן של בית המדרש. עצים ושמן שהקדישו לשם תורה ותפילה השתמש בו הוא לצורך עצמו.

הקדוש ברוך הוא מאריך אף ואינו גובה את שלו מיד, אבל לא כמדת הקדוש ברוך הוא מדת בשר ודם. ענייה אחת היתה בעיר. מת עליה בעלה ולא הניח חוץ מבן קטן שילדה לו. נתנחמה האלמנה בבנה. היו לו לאביו של התינוק געגועים על בנו ולקח אותו. לילה אחד בא התינוק אצל אמו בחלום ופניו היו עצובות. אמרה לו, מה לך בני, לא טוב לך אצל אבא? ענה הבן ואמר לה, טוב היה לי אילו היו אומרים כאן בעולם השפל מלה יהודית לעילוי נשמתי. צעקה האם בחרדה, בני בני, נשמתי שלי, מה דברים אתה דובר, וכי לא שכרתי את השמש של בית המדרש החדש שיאמר שלוש פעמים בכל יום קדיש לעילוי נשמתך וילמוד בכל יום פרק משניות עם פירוש. את מטפחת ראשי שקנה לי אבא שלך אחר לידתך מכרתי לשם כך. ואתה אומר טוב היה לי אילו אמרו מלה יהודית לעילוי נשמתך. למחר הלכה אמו של התינוק ובדקה אחר השמש. מצאתו יושב לפני ספר משניות וראשו מונח על הספר כשהוא מנמנם. ולענין אמירת קדיש, שמעה שמכר עצמו לכמה בעלי יארצייטים לומר קדיש. נתמלא לבה כעס וקיללה אותו בכל הקללות שבתוכחה. היה השמש יודע [illegible] שאם לא ימצא אדם להעמיד במקומו הוא עליו לעלות לפרשת התוכחה [illegible] מקרין לו כל הקללות [illegible] שקללה אותו האלמנה. משהגיע יום [illegible] בשבת ועדיין לא מצא איש עני התחיל מתיאש, עד שהתעלם בן והשגחה שיכולה לסלק כל צרה כהרף עין.

Agnon's handwritten revisions to the opening page of the 1963 *Haaretz* edition of "Until Elijah Comes"
(Courtesy of Agnon Archive, AC4025, The National Library of Israel, Jerusalem, and Schocken Publishing House, Tel Aviv.)

Until Elijah Comes

1

Between the old beit midrash and the new beit midrash, next to an opening opposite the bathhouse, rests a small wooden trunk. Neither we nor our ancestors have ever seen its equal. The trunk has been sitting there for generations. Thieves have not stolen it; grasping hands have not moved it from its spot. To whom does it belong? Who deposited it there? The tale is worth telling.

Synagogue leaders in our town, upon hiring a shamash, made it clear that he was responsible for selecting the person to chant the Torah blessings for the section known as the Curses. If he could not find someone to recite the blessings, he himself would be responsible for doing so. But, they continued, never in the history of Buczacz had a shamash actually been obliged to say the blessings himself. For there had not been a single shamash who had failed to find a poor man happy to replace him for a bit of cash, for the poor are always concerned about money. One year, the Torah portion of Ki Tavo arrived, and the shamash of the new beit midrash, Yoel Yonah, could not a find a poor person for the Curses. Had all the poor people vanished from the world? This is what happened.

When most of the week had passed, the shamash began to worry that he would have to say the blessings for the Curses himself. His worries were not unfounded, for there is no one in this world who always does good and never sins, the rich according to their wealth and the poor according to their poverty. And if the wealthy, who lack for nothing in their world come to sin, how much more so do the poor, who have only their poverty. So it happened with this shamash.

One year, it was bitterly cold, and the young children of the shamash sickened from the cold. Overwhelmed with compassion for them, he took some wood from the beit midrash to heat his stove. Another time, Ḥanukkah arrived, and he had no oil with which to fulfill the commandment, so he lit some of the oil belonging to the beit midrash. He used wood and oil, which had been donated to sanctify Torah and prayer, for his personal needs.

The blessed Holy One refrains from wrath and does not immediately claim what is due. But human nature is not the equal of divine nature. There was a certain poor woman in our city. Her husband died, bequeathing her nothing but a young son. The widow took comfort in her son. But the father pined for his son and took him. One night, the young boy appeared to his mother in a dream, sadness on his face. She said to him, What ails you, my son? Does being with father not suit you? He said to her, Things would be fine for me if only someone in the world below would say a Jewish word for the ascent of my soul.

The woman cried out in fear and trembling, My son, my son, my own soul, what are you saying? Did I not hire the shamash of the new beit midrash to say kaddish three times a day, so that your soul could ascend, and also to study daily a chapter of Mishnah with commentaries? I sold the kerchief that your father bought me in honor of your birth for that very purpose and you tell me that it would be fine if someone would say a Jewish word for the ascent of your soul?

The next day, the child's mother went to check up on the shamash. She found him sitting before a Mishnah, dozing with his head on the book. As for his saying kaddish, she discovered that he had hired himself out to several people. Her heart filled with fury, and she cursed him with all the maledictions in the Curses. The shamash knew that the curses of a widow are never ineffectual. He foresaw that if someone did not replace him, he would be obligated to recite the blessings for the Curses' portion, and all the curses with which the widow had cursed him would fall upon him. When Thursday arrived and he still had not found a poor man, he began to despair, so that he lost sight of the providential care that could have removed all his sorrow in the blink of an eye.

2

After the last of the worshipers had left the beit midrash, the shamash opened a volume of the Mishnah, for many widows and orphans had hired him to learn Mishnah in order to elevate the souls of their deceased relatives. Whoever could manage it would add another coin so that he would study the Mishnah's commentary as well; the person who could not manage it relied on the mercy of the blessed Holy One to benefit the deceased on the strength of a chapter of Mishnah alone, even without commentary.

A Torah scholar the shamash was not, let alone an adept of Mishnah, which requires added discernment to be able to clarify its obscurities. Yet is it possible for one who spends all his years in the beit midrash never to open a book? Such a person sits before the book, its letters rising from the page, floating up and reaching his eyes. If God helps him, he combines letters into words and words into subjects. So it was with this shamash. Because he was always in the beit midrash, he accustomed himself to sit with a volume of the Mishnah, for Mishnah suits the soul, as the Hebrew letters of the two words—"mishnah" and "neshamah"—are the same. He arranged twenty-two chapters according to the number of letters in the Hebrew alphabet; and from them, he would combine various chapters to recite according to the names of the dead for whom he had received recompense. For example, if the deceased had been called Abraham, he would study chapters beginning with each letter of his name. So he would do for the letters in the name of the deceased's father, for the letters in the word, soul, neshamah, and similarly for a deceased woman. Thus, he would sit every day, reviewing so many chapters according to the names of the dead for whom he had received payment. On this particular day, he had not read a chapter—not even a single sentence—as if the resurrection of the dead had come and all those who sleep in the dust had stood up from their graves, no longer needing a chapter of Mishnah to help their souls ascend.

The shamash sat and internally weighed his deeds. He regarded his deliberate sins as unwitting ones and the unwitting ones as nothing at all. What he had done deliberately, he saw as accidental. And what had been accidental, he saw as a man who was surprised to open his eyes and see what he had just done. Nonetheless, regrets broke his heart.

3

The door opened, and a vagrant entered. His hat was torn, his clothes were but threads, and his shoes were slung over his arm. He was the poorest of the poor, possessing only his poverty. Had the shamash not personally known the father of the deceased child, he might have thought that it was he. In truth, one was not much like the other; one's poverty hid itself in his clothes, while the poverty of the other cried out from every thread. But the shamash, with the curse of the widow still ringing in his ears, remembered her deceased husband, and because he remembered him, it seemed that the man before him was he.

The vagrant tapped the shamash on his shoulders, in the manner of those lacking everything who show their affection through their touch, tapping a shoulder or patting a person's belly. In this manner, he said to him, Why, my beloved Jew, are you distressed? We are Jews, blessed be God, and it is good for a Jew to be happy at all seasons, having merited to be a Jew. But you, my beloved Jew, show a darkened countenance. God forbid that you have forgotten that you are a Jew!

The shamash looked angrily at the vagrant. He wanted to grab him by the neck and throw him bodily out of the beit midrash. But his heart said to him, Slow down; sometimes, deliverance can come from a person such as this.

The shamash made his angry face vanish and stretched out his right hand to greet him, as one greets a guest. In answer to the vagrant's question, he replied, You want to know why I am sad, so I will tell you. But, first, sit. Why should you stand? You must be tired from the road, as I assume that you did not come by a bounding chariot. Sit, my friend, sit. Here is a bench. Ai, ai, ai—this bench that I seat you upon is a bench for those who have means, for the esteemed rich, who have hundreds of gold coins hidden in their cellar cupboards. You and I, my friend, would be happy if we only had as many pickled cucumbers! Now that you are sitting, I will answer your question.

You ask why I am distressed. I will reveal to you my heart's sorrows, as one does to a friend. Even though I am only seeing you now for the first time, it seems as if we came forth from one womb, as twins. I will not make an elaborate introduction, but proceed to the heart of the matter. This Sabbath, we will read the portion, Ki Tavo, which includes the section of the Curses. Today is already Thursday, and I have not yet found someone to say the Torah blessing for the Curses. If there is no one else to say the Torah blessing for the Curses, then I must do it. Now I am certain, my friend, that you have penetrated to the depth of the matter.

The vagrant fixed him in his gaze and said, My beloved Jew, what nonsense are you speaking? Can there be a Jew who is distressed to be given the honor of blessing the Torah? Everyone who merits such an honor should be glad and, what's more, give charity. But you, my beloved Jew, are afraid lest you be called up to bless the Torah? Please do not toy with me. Do you think me such a fool to believe that? If your beard and your side-locks did not testify that you are a man of standing, I might think you a professional jester.

The shamash's face showed surprise. He thought, I am talking about the Curses and he says it is an honor to bless the Torah. What is this? It is like the yokel who swings a rooster over his head on the eve of Yom Kippur and then, by mistake, makes the blessing for going to the toilet!

The shamash regretted every word he had wasted on the vagrant. If it were not for his good heart and the kind words already spoken, he would have turned away and left him alone. But his heart prompted him with words from the Mishnah that were worth repeating: There is no person who does not have his hour; there is no thing that does not have its place.

The shamash said to the vagrant, I see that you have not studied much Torah; not every person merits doing so. Therefore, you do not distinguish between the Curses and all other sections of the Torah.

The vagrant looked at him with laughing eyes and said, What do you think of me, my beloved Jew, that I am empty of Torah learning? At this very moment, I will read both sections of curses from the Torah, the one from Leviticus and the other from Deuteronomy, and you will see that I am not a complete ignoramus.

The shamash snorted with anger and shouted, Close your mouth and be quiet!

The vagrant said to him, My beloved Jew, why are you covering your ears—are you afraid a mosquito will enter them? I offer to recite words of the living God for you, and you, my beloved Jew, are severe with me. If it were not forbidden to suspect a fellow Jew, I would say that you are attempting to avoid hearing words of Torah. All Torah is good. It brings blessings and life. Yet you are distressed, lest you be called up to recite the blessing over the Curses. Moreover, it should be a joy to you that you can stand next to the reader and hear word for word what he recites in an undertone. If we were not standing in a holy place, I would say that you mock me when you say that you are afraid of being called to the Torah for the Curses, which the blessed Holy One spoke through the mouth of Moses.

The shamash concluded inwardly that this vagrant was not too bright, though good-natured: If I were to ask him, perhaps he would take my place. It is too bad that I regretted wasting my time on him. From now on, I have only to regret that I regretted earlier. It is difficult to understand: he is an expert on these two passages from the Torah, yet he has no idea what they mean.

4

He began to chat with the vagrant, You put it well, my friend. All the Torah portions are holy, and there is no distinguishing among them in that regard, but not all tastes are the same. There are those who prefer to go up for the third Torah honor, since our father Abraham does so in the heavenly Garden of Eden, while Aaron, as the high priest, takes the first and Moses, a Levite, the second. Then there are those who prefer the haftarah, the prophetic reading, some for the sake of the special blessings and some to show off their voices. And there are even some, among those who call themselves ḥasidim, who insist on the sixth Torah honor. Therefore, do not be surprised, my friend, that a man such as I chooses to appoint someone else to take his place to recite the blessings for the Curses. But tell me, my friend, where do you stand with respect to the Torah blessings? I know some who shout their brilliance from the rooftops, but when they come up to say the Torah blessings, they mumble half the blessing and stutter the other half because they do not know how to bless properly. Some are budding scholars, and others are ignoramuses. I do not mean to offend your honor; I am only asking a question. An unnecessary question is not a transgression. Tell me, my friend, do you know how to recite the Torah blessings?

The vagrant fixed him with his eyes and said, Does a Jew exist who does not know how to bless the Torah? For if one knows the blessings for food and drink, which are only matters of temporal life, then how much more should one concern oneself with blessings of the Torah, our eternal life? If you would like me to do so, I will recite the Torah blessings for you now.

The shamash replied, To recite them in vain is not worthwhile. They contain holy names of God, which should not be pronounced without purpose. In any case, I see that you know how to recite the blessings. Due to the multitude of our sins, many ordinary Jews do not know how to recite a single blessing properly. One time, a bridegroom was called to the Torah during the festive week following his wedding, and if it were not for the fact that I, as shamash, drummed on the table as if to quiet a chattering congregation, all would have heard that he did not know how to recite the blessing.

The vagrant sighed and said, Doubtless he was the son of poor people, and his parents did not have the means to educate him.

The shamash replied, Who said anything about being poor? You and I would be delighted to have on Sabbath and holidays what he stuffs himself with and imbibes every Monday and Thursday! There are those who do not study Torah because of poverty, and there are those who do not study Torah because of wealth. That particular bridegroom came from a wealthy family. And if it were not for my saving the groom from public ridicule, they would not be able to hold their heads up in public. And what reward did they give me—a few worn, copper coins.

As he was speaking to the vagrant, the shamash silently had a heart-to-heart talk with himself: This is not the time to be telling old stories; it is time for action.

He touched the vagrant's arm affectionately and said, Now, my friend, let us head to my house and have a little breakfast. I have a feeling that we will find some radishes and onions and cucumbers, maybe even some fermented milk. "Fermented milk does the heart renew, as for a wolf the taste of ewe." Or to put it simply, Fermented milk feeds the soul, preventing pain its worthy goal.

The vagrant replied, That is not necessary.

The shamash responded, What do you mean, it is not necessary? Eating is not necessary? What fairy tales are you feeding me?

He replied, It is not worth it.

What do you mean, it is not worth it? Eating is not worth it? What does the verse say: "I was a youth, and now am an old man and have never known a righteous man who did not want to eat?" The vagrant replied, At a time when one's basket contains bread, why should he impose upon others?

He responded, Where is the basket and where is the bread?

He replied, I deposited them in the trunk.

What trunk? Where do you have a trunk? Did you not arrive here empty-handed? Where is there a trunk here? There is no trunk.

He replied, I placed it in the courtyard.

The shamash thought, Why should I quibble with him? I should be satisfied that I have found someone just in time to recite the blessings for the Curses. Just so it does not turn out as it did for that other shamash who hosted and fattened up a poor man for a week, intending to call him to the Torah to say the blessings for the Curses, only to have him disappear two or three verses prior to the reading.

He began speaking to the vagrant to win him over, telling him about the important men of the synagogue—how much this one was worth and how much that one; how much this one donated for his daughter's dowry and how much that one squandered buying legal permission from a hundred rabbis for his son to marry. The vagrant said, Were I not in such haste to be on my way, I would perforate my ears like sieves in order to hear more.

The shamash responded, Where do you intend to go?

To Pribiluk.

Why Pribiluk?

A son was born to a Jew there.

So a son was born there, so what?

I want to attend the circumcision ceremony.

If you are looking for brandy, you'll find a full container at my house, and if you desire things to eat, the delicacies of Buczacz surpass any baked goods in the world. Once, R. Zechariah, son of the community head, R. Leibush, may they both find rest in the Garden of Eden, went to visit his in-laws in Pidayets. When he returned, his esteemed mother asked him, What did your in-laws give you to eat? He said to her, The whole time I was there, nothing was spared to load my table with delicacies, but all of it was not equal to a single baked good from our shamash's wife.

Do you know who that was, my friend? It was my grandmother. And my mother, of blessed memory, received the recipes from her, and my wife received them from her. Come to my house, and we will say the appropriate blessings together.

The vagrant replied, Your words are dearer to me than all the pleasures of this world, but I am in a rush. I want to reach Pribiluk before dark to hear the children recite the Shema for the new mother.

The shamash laughed: You found a real miracle, village children reciting the Shema! If it is children reading the Shema that you wish to hear, wait until the children arrive at the beit midrash for the evening prayer, and you will get to hear not only the Shema but even the mourners' kaddish! On account of our generation's sins, many die young and leave behind small orphans. What makes you sigh—the fact that Jews die? That really is a cause for sighing, but you should conclude from this not to weary your feet traipsing to villages just to hear a Jewish word. I will not lie to you: villagers are like rams and young bulls; half of them are foolish and illiterate, and half of them are complete gentiles. So what if a son was born? You will not come upon Elijah there.

The vagrant smiled and remained silent. The shamash continued, I doubt that even those shoes hanging over your arm could make it to the village. Take up your trunk, and come with me. Why should you leave it outside if you can deposit it at my house? God forbid that there should be thieves here, but there are those accustomed to touching everything; when they see an object, they immediately need to finger it. If it is heavy, I will surely help you.

The vagrant laughed and replied, It is as light as a poor person's garment at the start of the rainy season. If it gets touched or handled by others, so be it.

The shamash felt around in his clothing and extracted a small coin from his pocket, saying, Here you go.

He replied, What is this?

Pocket money.

What do I need pocket money for?

If you want to get yourself a glass of liquor or a piece of fruit, you will have something to pay with.

He replied, The people of Israel are merciful. If I get hungry, I'll find a Jew who will feed me for free, and if I become thirsty, I'll find a spring or a well.

Holding a coin in your grip guarantees that you will never trip.

In that case, I would need to grasp the coins in my hand; in that case, I would need to walk with a clenched fist. In that case, people would suspect that I was a moneylender; in that case, I would be responsible for an evil deed for because of me, they would come to suspect a Jew.

The shamash realized that his words were getting him nowhere. He placed his confidence in the blessed Holy One. Just as He had sent him the vagrant today, He would return him on the Sabbath. Even so, the shamash preempted providence and asked the vagrant when he would be back. He replied, God willing, on the Sabbath.

The shamash realized that the vagrant's words were not deceitful. Yet he feared that he would turn up at the door of another beit midrash and end up reciting the blessings over the Curses there. Oh, for the good old days, when everyone in town prayed in one house of prayer! Now that there were five synagogues, there was cause for concern that someone else would snatch the vagrant from his hands. In reality, there were six houses of prayer in Buczacz at that time, but the sixth was ḥasidic and not deemed a house of prayer by Yoel Yonah, the shamash.

While the latter was lamenting the loss of the good old days, the former set off for the circumcision.

5

Friday arrived, and the vagrant did not return. Sundown arrived, and he still had not returned. The shamash began to be distressed but not to the point of despair. He said to himself, If he does not arrive by the time of the evening prayers, he will arrive afterward, for he learned from me that among our worshipers are distinguished men, and it is the manner of a poor man to hunger for the table of such men. The evening prayer was finished, and the poor and the destitute came to the shamash to request placement at a householder's table, but the vagrant was not among them.

The shamash saw this and was distressed but not to the point of utter despair. Yoel Yonah said to himself, Tomorrow, he will come; tomorrow, he will come.

In all his days, he had never so yearned for a person as on that night; in all his days, he had never been as angry with a person as on that night. All night, he continued arguing with him: So are you a man of your word? Did you not say that you would come?

When the congregation had prayed the morning service and risen to take out the Torah scroll and the vagrant still had not arrived, Yoel Yonah began to prepare himself for calamity. They took out the scroll and placed it on the reading table. As the gabbai prepared to assign the Torah honors, the shamash stood behind him, in case he was needed—for instance, if a person was called up not by his familiar name or if the gabbai forgot the name of the father of the person he intended to honor, he would send the shamash to inquire.

The shamash stood by and saw one man after another rise for his Torah honor. He stood in distress and saw that the fourth had already risen. His certainty fled, and he lost hope. He did not raise his eyes to the door lest, despite all, the vagrant were to arrive. The shamash stood ready to rise for the sixth section, in which the Curses are found, for all possibility that the vagrant would appear had vanished.

He suddenly felt the vagrant's presence. No sound of a door was heard, nor did the shamash glance at the door; nevertheless, he sensed the vagrant standing by the door. How does one explain such an event? If the shamash did not know, how should we know?

The shamash still had not raised his eyes to the door lest the vagrant evaporate, for he certainly would vanish. The vagrant was revealed to him face-to-face. He looked at him and saw his integrity and innocence. The shamash said to himself, His face testifies that he is not some worthless fellow. Certainly, he will fulfill his promise. In an instant, like the blink of an eye, the shamash reviewed what he had learned over many years about keeping one's word. Torah says, *The words of your mouth you must honor.* And if the Torah says it, then all Israel must remember and keep to it. So now, do not doubt, even in the slightest, for if a son of Israel says that he will do something, you can rely on his word. In this way, a person's faithfulness grows stronger, seeing that other people rely on him to stand by his word. And just as Israel behaves here below, so it is done for them in the world above; all the promises that have been made to us will be fulfilled.

The shamash went over to the vagrant with a bright countenance and asked him in a gentle voice, What is your name?

He told him his name. The shamash responded, And what is your father's name?

He told him his father's name. The shamash then said, You know, my dear friend, why I have asked your name and the name of your father. I intend to call you up to the Torah, to give you the honor of blessing the Torah, as one would give to an important visitor.

The vagrant replied to the shamash, It is too bad that so much time has passed. What happiness, what joy, what pleasure I would have had, had you come to me earlier.

Said the shamash, What difference is it to you, earlier or now?

Is not the fifth a good section? Is it not one of the seven designated readings?

Here, the shamash was deceptive about the section containing the Curses, for it is really the sixth, though he called it the fifth. The vagrant said to the shamash, You, my beloved Jew, are asking me to rise as the sixth in order, but I am descended from kohanim and priestly descendants rise only for the first reading.

The shamash grew so angry that his eyes filled with sparks of fury, which, had they been of fire, would have burned the vagrant up alive. The vagrant tugged at his belt, looked at the shamash with laughing eyes, and said to him, Remove anger from your heart, my beloved Jew; do not be distressed on your Sabbath day of rest. All sections of the Torah are beloved, all dear, all good, all blessed. Hurry, my beloved Jew, go up to the Torah. Do not let the Torah wait upon you. The gabbai is already furious that you are delaying the reading.

Yoel Yonah gave the vagrant a look that, had it been fire, would have instantly consumed him.

But the vagrant encouraged him with his eyes and surrounded him with the warmth of his love. This love surrounded and penetrated the heart of the shamash. His anger left him, and love entered. And as love entered, so did joy. He turned toward the scroll and joyously seized its wooden rollers, those trees of life, and he blessed the Torah with joy, as if he had been called up for the portion of the blessings read on Simḥat Torah.

From the power of his joy, the whole beit midrash was filled with joy, and from the joy of the congregation, the joy of Yoel Yonah was multiplied. This is the power of transcendent joy—joy that brings joy that brings more joy.

6

After the prayer service, Yoel Yonah went over to the bench reserved for the poor in order to invite the vagrant to Sabbath lunch, but did not find him. Yoel Yonah was certain that someone else had already claimed him since there are wealthy men who fear that they will be left without a guest at their table and hasten over to the poor, grabbing hold of one and saying, You are dining with me!

Yoel Yonah realized that there was nothing he could do. He spoke to himself in the words of the vagrant: Do not bring distress to your Sabbath rest, my beloved Jew.

What's done is done! He returned to his home, blessed the wine, ritually washed his hands, blessed the ḥallah, and began to sing Sabbath hymns. He recalled that the vagrant had a pleasant voice. Yoel Yonah said, If he were here, we would certainly hear a new melody.

Thinking of him, Yoel Yonah began to speak. He said to his wife, A vagabond visitor has arrived and transformed my spirit. You remember, Brachah Gitl, all the trouble I put myself through, year after year, to find someone to recite the blessings for the Curses' portion. Now I regret all the years I wasted trying to avoid reciting the blessings myself. With age comes wisdom! Yet there are still young men who are convinced that they are wiser than their fathers. They are not wise men; they are fools. And, as for the guest, since I did not succeed in hosting him for lunch, I will invite him for the third Sabbath meal.

He tried to find consolation in the idea of the afternoon meal but was not consoled. For the third meal cannot be compared with Sabbath lunch, when people are really hungry and when there is a special blessing over wine and when delicious dishes are served in addition to kugel, of which it is said, "the quality of the kugel matches that of the guests." None of this pertains to the third meal, which is eaten when sated. In fact, one eats simply to fulfill the obligation of taking a meal and only enough to justify reciting the blessing over bread and the recitation of grace after meals.

Yoel Yonah sat in wonderment: A vagrant, possessed only of his poverty, yet my heart is drawn to him. And even if it is in human nature to sometimes yearn for one another, we do not know the cause of such yearning. If it is because of the man himself, why did I not yearn for him earlier? Now that I know him, I see that the change resides in me, not in him. If this is so, why did it happen now and not earlier? In any case, it makes no sense to waste time in such musings when Sabbath delicacies lie before you.

Yoel Yonah turned his attention away from his thoughts and sat down to the Sabbath feast, which included ḥallah and brandy and agreeable dishes. Yoel Yonah was not lacking in gratitude toward his wife, and he sang the praises of every one of the dishes that she served. But he continued and said, If only the guest were dining with us, I would have said "very good."

Brachah Gitl said, If that is the case, let us put aside a portion for the guest from every good dish and have him come sup with you for the third meal.

Yoel Yonah said, That is a good suggestion, but I am surprised that I did not think of it earlier. In fact, I, too, thought of this, but my sorrow distracted me. Indeed, I will invite him for the third meal. Great are the deeds of God, who continuously provides opportunities for man to repair his actions. Now let us sing some hymns and whatever we do not do at Sabbath lunch, we will fulfill at the third meal.

They finished their meal, and Yoel Yonah recited the grace after meals while Brachah Gitl sat and watched every word that came out of his mouth, responding amen after each blessing. Following the grace after meals, Yoel Yonah rose from the table and stretched out on his bed in order to celebrate the Sabbath with an afternoon nap. Those who attribute meaning to abbreviations say that the letters that form the word "Sabbath" are those that begin the words, *sleep on Shabbat is a pleasure*. Indeed, it is so, for when one lies in bed during the week, one's mind is distracted by business worries, which is hardly the case on the Sabbath, whose business is sleep. Indeed, sleep is the means of fulfilling the commandment of Sabbath rest.

Yoel Yonah lay on his bed and conjured up the image of the vagrant dining at his table—eating and drinking and enjoying himself—for a poor person hosting a poor person does not resemble a rich person who does so. A rich person, who eats until sated on a daily basis, tends to eat less, and so he thinks that the poor man should as well. What happens to a poor person at a rich person's table? He ends up hungry. But a poor person understands the soul of another poor person who goes hungry every day. And a poor person who hosts another poor person tries to fill him with every good thing that satisfies the body and, more than that, even brings pleasure to the soul.

Yoel Yonah lay on his bed and imagined the vagrant sitting next to him, eating at his table that was filled with all the dishes that Brachah Gitl had prepared. Six days a week, the shamash's bowl was empty; but on the Sabbath, his bowl was always full, sometimes because of the grace of God, who sent some coins his way and sometimes because of the resourcefulness of Brachah Gitl, who could transform a pile of bones into a meaty dish. Even this derives from the most Wise One. Here is a woman who does not know how to recite blessings and only knows the short Yiddish prayer "Creator of all created beings, You alone do I want to worship in truth." But the blessed Holy One endows such a woman with the wisdom to make pleasing dishes with which to regale a man.

The master of dreams came to Yoel Yonah and outdid even Brachah Gitl. Brachah Gitl had prepared a poor person's meal; the master of dreams transformed it into a royal banquet. A bone that did not hold even an olive-size morsel of meat became roasted doves. Yoel Yonah licked his lips as he murmured, Doves, doves.

And if it were not for the fact that he awakened to the sound of doves cooing on his window sill, it is possible that the dish of kasha in gravy that his wife had served on Friday night would have turned itself into noodles in turkey sauce. The master of dreams moves in miraculous ways: even Pharaoh's master chef, who knew how to infuse a single dish with sixty flavors, was a beginner compared to the master of dreams!

And so Yoel Yonah awoke with a start from his afternoon nap, washed his hands, and rose from his bed. His wife brought him a jug of fruit juice that she had cooled overnight in a container of cold water. He recited the blessing and drank, drank and recited a blessing, and left for the beit midrash. As he left, he said to his wife, So, Brachah Gitl, immediately after the afternoon service, I'll return with the guest.

Brachah Gitl replied, Do not worry. I guarantee you that he will not leave our house hungry, and even you will be satisfied.

7

The shamash came into the beit midrash, sat in his place near the furnace, and reviewed a chapter from *Ethics of the Fathers*. A person who is self-aware makes it a priority to fulfill his daily study obligation with a chapter of Mishnah. Then if he has enough time, he also reads a chapter or two to uplift the souls of those for whom he had received some recompense. Since the day on which the deceased child had announced to his mother that no Jewish word was being heard in this world for his soul's ascent, Yoel Yonah had tried not to let a day pass without studying Mishnah.

So he sat and studied. He recited merely with his lips, for more than he looked in the book, he looked at the door, lest he miss the vagrant. But the vagrant did not come. Yoel Yonah said to himself, Do not be distressed on your day of Sabbath rest, my beloved Jew.

The words that the vagrant had said to Yoel Yonah with laughing eyes and a joyous voice, he now said to himself weakly, with a sad countenance.

Why draw out the story and prolong our spirit's distress? The time for the afternoon service arrived, and the vagrant did not come, not for the Torah reading, not for the prayer. Yoel Yonah reviewed the things that the vagrant had said to him. But whereas they came joyously from the vagrant's mouth, they came pitifully from the mouth of the shamash. Even so, he did not despair. Yoel Yonah said, If he does not come to the afternoon service, then he will surely come to the evening service. If he does not eat the third Sabbath meal with me, then he will eat the farewell feast for the Sabbath Queen. What gave Yoel Yonah the strength not to despair? If it were not the fine dishes that would be served for that feast, I do not know what it was.

When a person's good fortune flees, even a vagabond visitor bolts. The Sabbath was over. They had already prayed the weekday evening service, and still the vagrant did not appear. Where did he pray the evening service? Wherever he had prayed the afternoon service, he prayed the evening service. Buczacz was not lacking for houses of prayer. Once, all of Buczacz had assembled in a single synagogue. Now there were five, and, if you count the prayer room of the ḥasidim, you could even say six.

Yoel Yonah made his lonely way home, without the vagrant. Over wine, he made the blessing for separating the Sabbath from the week and sang the hymns appointed for that hour. Yoel Yonah never had a beautiful voice, but now, its tone sounded more suitable for laments than for hymns. Even when he mentioned Elijah, whom all Israel mentions joyously, with longing and with the hope that he will come quickly with Messiah, son of David, his voice did not change in the slightest because of his heart's sorrow that the vagrant had not returned. We will not delay ourselves mentioning each and every sigh that Yoel Yonah sighed. Whether or not everyone benefits from sighing, it was enough for Yoel Yonah that his sighs satisfied him. Therefore, I give him the benefit of the doubt and say something about which there can be no doubt. If a person intended to fulfill a commandment but was prevented from doing so, it is accounted to him as if he had done it. To what do I refer? He had determined to fulfill the commandment of hospitality to a guest for its own sake, but in this instance, his motive was compromised. How so? His heart had been drawn to the vagrant, like a person who has longings of love.

Before daybreak, Yoel Yonah got out of bed and went to the beit midrash to do his work. The things he had not done the evening before because of his distress, he now did at sunrise.

He took off the tablecloths that had been spread since Sabbath eve. He changed the Sabbath curtain on the ark to the weekday curtain. He trimmed the candlewicks and added oil to the eternal light. So, too, he added oil to the lamps lit for those recently deceased and for those on whose behalf memorial prayers were being said. He suddenly desired a candle so bright that it could shut out the day, so that the person saying the memorial prayer would not suspect the shamash of failing to put in enough oil. After he had done his work, he reviewed it all, lest he had left something to do that he had not done. For the world is filled with controversy. No matter how careful you are, you still may not have fulfilled your duty. The day brightened, and the worshipers entered the beit midrash for prayer. After the closing prayer, the orphans and the reciters of memorial prayers surrounded the ark on three sides to recite kaddish, and in their midst was Yoel Yonah—the orphans because they were in mourning, the reciters of memorial prayers because it was the anniversary of a death, and Yoel Yonah because he had been hired to say kaddish. After these prayers, he was surprised to find his mind suddenly return to the vagrant. There is no one who recognizes the character of vagabond visitors so well as the shamash of a beit midrash. In the blink of an eye, he can recognize it. But regarding this vagrant, the mind of the shamash was stymied; it was hard for Yoel Yonah to pigeonhole him. He wandered about the country like the other vagabond visitors but was different from them; everything about him showed his difference from other loiterers. Yoel Yonah said, I will go see what is in the trunk that the vagrant deposited. He closed the book, stood up, and started on his way.

He left the beit midrash and turned to the opening across from the bathhouse, where the vagrant had deposited the trunk. Just as the shamash was going out, the vagrant approached his trunk. Yoel Yonah looked at him and was sorry to see that the shoes that had been hanging from his arms were no longer there. Yoel Yonah was convinced that he must have pawned them for something to eat or that the vagrant had been accosted by a ruffian who had grabbed the shoes by force. He did not know that he had given them to a poor man, for there is no poor person who cannot find someone poorer than he. As the saying goes, "A person may sell whatever he has, but never his shoes." But here was one who had only his poverty and, what is more, nothing to sell.

They stood opposite each other, the vagrant next to his trunk and the shamash silently waiting to see what the other would do. In the end, Yoel Yonah could not contain himself and prepared to speak with him. As he was about to open his mouth, the vagrant opened the trunk, took out one possession and hid it in his cloak, near his heart, closed the trunk, looked at him with a pleasant gaze and departed.

Yoel Yonah was startled like a person waking from a dream. He rubbed his eyes and looked after the vagrant, who was simply walking along. Yoel Yonah uprooted himself from where he stood and went after him.

He came near the vagrant and stood close by him. The vagrant cocked his head and took him in his gaze, as if to say, My beloved Jew, you desire to say something to me? Speak up, beloved Jew, speak up. Yoel Yonah wanted to say something but was tongue-tied and said nothing.

Yoel Yonah thought to himself, If I do not speak to him now, he will depart, and all the efforts I have made will have been for naught. But what can I do if I cannot get a word out of my mouth? He raised his eyes and thought that if God does not save me, then all my effort will have been in vain.

The blessed Holy One saw his distress and had mercy on him. He restored his power of speech, as it is written, *Who gives utterance to the mute.* Yoel Yonah said to the vagrant, You left your trunk.

The vagrant waved to him with his right hand and said, Let it rest where it is.

The shamash replied, For how long?

The vagrant took him in his gaze, smiled, and said to him, Until Elijah comes.

The eyes of Yoel Yonah were opened, and he shouted, But you are Elijah!

The vagrant smiled and vanished.

Come and see the power of Buczacz. The shamash of the new beit midrash was worthy to see in waking what great righteous men seek to see only in dreams and which few of them merit. You might think that it would have been the shamash of the old beit midrash who merited the sight, on account of all the Torah that is learned there. But no, it was the shamash of the new beit midrash, where the congregation are mostly householders whose business dealings exceed their Torah learning. But they conducted their business faithfully.

Here we have reached the end of the story, whose beginning is included in its end, namely: Who is the owner of the trunk sitting in the courtyard of the beit midrash? You might ask, What need did this vagrant have with a trunk, and if he needed it, why did he leave it? To such a question, we can only say what the Talmud said: In the future, Elijah the Tishbite will decide unanswered questions and problems. And what was the possession that the vagrant took from the trunk? A believer will believe that it was a shofar, for before the Messiah, our redeemer, is revealed, Elijah will climb the Mount of Olives and blow the shofar, which will be heard from one end of the world to the other, from the heights to the depths of the earth, all Israel hearing it wherever they may be, and all the exiles will assemble and go up to Jerusalem. May it be speedily and in our days, Amen.

Translated by Herbert Levine and Reena Spicehandler

The Ḥazzanim

THE FIRST OF THE ḤAZZANIM to serve in the Great Synagogue of our town just after it was built was R. Yitzḥak Shatz. He was a fourth-generation descendant of R. Yitzḥak Wernick, who, eighty years before 1648, served as the loyal representative of his congregants in their prayers, delighting brides and bridegrooms underneath the bridal canopy with his pleasant voice.

Just like his grandfather, this R. Yitzḥak delighted the hearts of his brethren with his pleasant voice on the Sabbaths before the New Moon, Sabbaths when yotzrot were recited, the eves of holidays and on holiday mornings, on the eve of Rosh Hashanah and on the day of Rosh Hashanah, on the eve of Yom Kippur and on the day of Yom Kippur, both Musaf and Neilah, and on days when Seliḥot were recited. The melody we use for the memorial prayer on the twentieth of Sivan is his composition. Before R. Yitzḥak, the prayer was recited to the tune of the Yizkor service; R. Yitzḥak recited it as one who prays with his dead laid out before him.

R. Yitzḥak served as the ḥazzan in the Great Synagogue of our town for twenty-two years, warming the hearts of his brethren with his prayers and delighting brides and bridegrooms under the bridal canopy. And when a bridegroom was present in the synagogue or when a circumcision ceremony was taking place, he would lead the prayers; in honor of the bridegroom, he would sing the psalm *The heavens declare the glory of Lord,* especially for the verse *Which is as a bridegroom coming out of his chamber.* He would also take charge of assigning the aliyot; there was none better than he at deciding who came before whom for an aliyah, calling each with a melody appropriate to his relationship to the bride or the bridegroom and, it goes without saying, with a special melody for the bridegroom himself, as is customary in all congregations.

From the day the Great Synagogue opened its doors with the psalm *A Song of Ascents: I was glad when they said unto me: Let us go into the house of the Lord* and until the day he died, R. Yitzḥak did not miss a single day in the synagogue, even during the days of rioting by the students of the monastery. When the danger had passed, people said to him, It was because of your great merit that the rabble didn't see you. He responded, It is not on my account but on account of the holy ark—it knows that I never in my life had an extraneous thought while praying. It hid me from their eyes and saved me from certain death.

When they answered that this was what they had meant, he replied, The rabble did not see me because the ark is sunk halfway into the floor.

R. Yitzḥak passed away with a good name and passed his voice on to his sons. As I have already told the story in too much detail, I will cut this short and continue.

After R. Yitzḥak's death, his eldest son, R. Yekutiel, was chosen to be the ḥazzan. He honored God with the pleasant melodies that he had learned from his father and from his father's father, who learned them from R. Yitzḥak Wernick, who learned them from his ancestors, who learned them from the exiles of Ashkenaz upon whose piety Buczacz had been founded. In his entire life, R. Yekutiel did not change a single melody and composed no new melodies of his own.

He served in the synagogue for three years; in the fourth year, his throat became hoarse, and his younger brother R. Elyah became the ḥazzan in his place.

Once R. Elyah accepted the position, he remained in it. R. Yekutiel himself renounced his tenure and never again led the congregation in prayer. R. Yekutiel explained, It is a bad sign to send to Israel's enemies when their representative's throat becomes hoarse on Yom Kippur.

There are those who say that R. Yekutiel himself was the cause of his voice's ruin. Once, on the eve of Yom Kippur, an important gentile lord came to the synagogue to hear the singing and the prayers, and R. Yekutiel sweetened his voice especially for him. The next day, when he led the Musaf service and the recital of the Hineni prayer, his throat closed up and he lost his voice. Elyah, his younger brother, was then instructed to continue in his place.

R. Elyah was only fifteen or sixteen years old at the time and only in the third year of his marriage. The Great Synagogue of our city had never seen a prayer leader as young as R. Elyah. Why was he chosen instead of his older brothers? Because each of them was officiating at a different synagogue on that day, though it must be admitted that they chose well. Even before he gave R. Elyah his daughter in marriage, R. Nisan, the ḥazzan of Monasterzyska, had already declared that he had heard many fine voices in his life but had never heard a voice like Elyah's.

R. Elyah was a tall, handsome man; his voice was like the combination of a bell and a violin. He sang many prayers differently from his ancestors. It is said that the melody for "Soon in our days, may You dwell among us forever" was composed by his wife, Miriam Devorah (though the matter needs to be looked into, since "Soon in our days, may You dwell among us forever" belongs to the Kedushah of Shaḥarit, and R. Elyah, like all other ḥazzanim, would have led only the Musaf service).

Miriam Devorah, R. Elyah's wife, was the daughter of R. Nisan, the ḥazzan of Monasterzyska, who was famous for the melody he composed for the piyyut "Those who dwell in earthen houses," which we would sing in our part of the country on evenings when the Omer was counted. It was said about R. Nisan that he would change his voice according to the season: during the summer, a summer voice; and during the winter, a winter voice. Since this is a matter that I am unable to explain, I will cut this short and continue.

The daughter's voice resembled the father's. Miriam Devorah was his only surviving child from many sons and daughters who died in infancy. She composed new melodies for prayers and piyyutim—in particular, for the kerovah recited on the Sabbath just before the month of Nisan. Her melodies were not used in the synagogue because it was said that a woman's voice could be discerned in them. But women, while working or sitting and plucking feathers or sewing and weaving, would sweeten their labor with her songs. She taught her neighbors' daughters to read the siddur, and all her children learned how to chant Torah from her. Miriam Devorah was very much beloved by her neighbors, even by the wealthier women of the town, who would especially invite her to their homes when they celebrated happy occasions. When a woman came to visit her, it was as if she had already been waiting for her. But it was said that many times, she was found sitting alone and appeared sad. When she saw that her sadness had been noticed, she would quickly change her expression from despair to joy. When they would press her to find out why she had been sad, she would answer, I was reminded of the Psalm 91, the song of sorrows, and I became melancholy.

She also composed poems about the troubles that befell our ancestors in 1648 and the riots of the monastery students and set them to music. I remember one autumn day, when I was a young man, I was sitting by the window in the old beit midrash reading the book *Yeven Metzulah*, when an old man said to me, I had a grandmother by the name of Miriam Devorah. She wrote songs about the events that you are reading about. I will sing you one of her songs.

She wrote other songs to entertain her small children. I include one such song here that I think I have reproduced accurately:

To the forest ventures a maiden
To collect berries for a pie,
When upon a horse there comes a rider
To rob her high and dry.

"Hear O Israel" calls the maiden,
And the rider catches fright.
The horse too grows wary
And rides away into the night.

A little boy is off to ḥeder
With his prayer book in hand

When the wind summons a priest
From a distant foreign land.

"Here's an apple for your troubles,"
Says the priest to the little boy,
And he pats him on his gentle head
With the grubby hand of a goy.

But the little boy looks up confused,
Saying, "Reb Priest please do explain:
What's the blessing for this delight?"
And no answer could he feign.

Three years before her death, her melancholy intensified, and she became dispirited. The neighbors came to visit her. She warned them, Don't come close to me. Melancholy can pass from one person to another.

Still, they came, but she would not open the door for them. In the end, she barred the door to every visitor, save for pious Leah Rachel, to whom she still showed goodwill. From that pious woman, we heard some of what Miriam Devorah told her.

R. Elyah sent for her father in Monasterzyska, and he came immediately. He went in to see her and talk with her, trying several tricks to get her to open up her heart. He held his cane as if it were a violin and made his voice sound like a string instrument. He then changed his voice to that of an old woman chasing goats from her garden and then a boy riding the town's billy goat. He mimicked Miriam Devorah's own voice from when she was a young child collecting mushrooms in the forest, singing songs to herself. R. Nisan did many other things to gladden his daughter's heart. At times, a smile would appear on her lips, and it seemed that R. Nisan had driven her sadness away. But in the end, her smile vanished and her sadness returned.

Her father implored, Tell me, my daughter, why are you sad? Are you sad about the world? Did you think that the world was created for rejoicing? Now that you see that there is no happiness in the world, you are distraught at your mistake. In this, I am different from you, my daughter. I have not made this mistake, and even if I have, I say to myself that I shall not respond in sadness to the world so that I will not be ridiculed for deceiving myself.

R. Nisan solicited advice from wise men, who counseled him to send for R. Mikhl the wonder worker in Oziran. Even Leah Rachel agreed. R. Mikhl was sent for, and, even though the wonder worker was busy preparing for Passover, he did not delay.

R. Mikhl arrived with a pipe in his hand and with his talit and tefilin bag under his arm. He put down the talit and tefilin bag and demanded that he be brought a burning coal to light his pipe. The coal was brought to him. He lit his pipe and took a puff of smoke, closing his eyes as if suddenly struck by sleepiness. He had yet to ask a single question about Miriam Devorah or say anything at all. Finally, he opened his eyes and asked, What was it you were telling me?

Just as they began to explain, he stopped them, saying, Shah, shah, I know, I know. When they had quieted down, he asked again, What did you say? Just as they started speaking again, he interrupted, You don't need to explain, I already know. If I did not know, I wouldn't have come.

In the end, he stood up from his chair and said, Bring me to her room.

He opened the door and stood as tall as he could with his cane in his hand and his pipe in his mouth. He exhaled a cloud of smoke and looked at Miriam Devorah as if from within the smoke. He exclaimed loudly and with joy, R. Elyah's wife, we have come to bring you a cure from the heavens.

Miriam Devorah stared back at him, stood up from her chair, and left. R. Mikhl smiled and said to her father, We are familiar with such impudence, we are *quite* familiar with such impudence. She will come back, she will certainly come back, and we will, in God's name, be successful.

Miriam Devorah heard what R. Mikhl said and turned around. She stood on the threshold with her hand on the doorknob. She again stared at R. Mikhl and said to him, You know what the future holds for every living being, and yet you don't know what the future holds for your own beard.

I will pause now from this story and say a few things about R. Mikhl's beard. What I should tell you now I will leave to the end, since that seems to me its proper place.

R. Mikhl the wonder worker had a long beard, its length the same as its width. The beard's color was like the rich amber of the cleft of his pipe, and each strand grew without touching the others. One small tuft of hair stood out, hanging down like a beard within a beard. Jokesters would remark about R. Mikhl saying, R. Mikhl, may he live long, appointed a shamash just to take care of his beard.

On the contrary, R. Mikhl would not even put a comb through his beard. Instead, on Friday afternoons before the Sabbath, after taking a bath, R. Mikhl would take a small washbasin and fill it with liquor. He would then dunk his beard in it to soak for a half-hour or longer.

In those days, R. Mikhl became a widower and then took a new wife. She was an orphan and was half R. Mikhl's age. There was a song that was sung in our part of the country about a poor Jew who would run to the synagogue to welcome the Sabbath just as the sun was setting. Once, Count Potocki saw him running; in that moment, Potocki had nothing better to do, so he stopped the poor man and ordered him to dance before him. The poor man begged Potocki to let him go to the synagogue, but Potocki would not let him go until he danced. The poor man refused. Potocki struck him in the knees with his whip until the poor man's legs gave way. This song was based on what happened to the father of Mindl, R. Mikhl the wonder worker's new wife.

Here is one stanza from the song that I have translated from Polish, even though I am no poet. This is the stanza in which the poor man begs the nobleman to let him go to the synagogue:

Show mercy, enlightened lord,
And let me go to my house of prayer
To welcome in the Sabbath's holiness
The beloved of my soul, the light of my deliverance.

Mindl, R. Mikhl's new wife, was a good woman and a good housekeeper. She adored her husband, who provided for all her needs after years of hunger in her father's house. When her father died and her mother remarried, there was almost no room for her to remain with them in their little hut. Now she had become the mistress of a household and lacked for nothing with her new husband. But she did complain about how her husband would offer his help to the entire world but not to her. In the two months between his first wife's death and his marriage to Mindl, when the house was left without a woman to take care of it, bedbugs had taken over Mindl's bed, a fact that now afflicted her greatly.

In truth, R. Mikhl had already done everything he could, both by reciting incantations and through natural methods. He stuffed the seams of the bed with candle wax that had been sprinkled with a green dust that was known to be effective even by non-Jewish doctors. But the bedbugs not only did not disappear from the house, but grew in number.

One Friday afternoon before the Sabbath, after he had returned from the public bath, R. Mikhl filled his cup with brandy and his washbasin with liquor. After he soaked and treated his beard, he stretched out on his bed and watched his wife as she prepared fish for the Sabbath dinner. Suddenly, a bedbug bit him. He tried to ignore it. The bedbug bit him again. He crushed the bug with his finger and tried to take his mind off bedbugs. Another bedbug bit him and still another. He thought, too, of his wife's suffering and decided that something needed to be done. He jumped up from the bed and took a candle that he had prepared for the search for ḥametz. He lit the candle and started to check the seams of the bed; as soon as he found a bedbug, he burned it with the flame. As he pointed the candle in different directions, the flame struck his beard. The fire consumed nearly all the hair on his face, leaving only the small tuft of hair that was nothing, compared with the rest of his beard.

Now I will say what I should have said at the beginning: sometimes, what slips out of the mouth unintentionally causes something to happen. It just so happened that R. Mikhl went to Miriam Devorah to cure her and she said to him, You are R. Mikhl the wonder worker about whom it is said that you know what the future holds for every living being, and yet you do not know what the future holds for your own beard.

When Miriam Devorah was told what happened to R. Mikhl the wonder worker's beard, she replied, It was not me who caused his beard to burn off. It was the brandy and the liquor that he drinks heavily that caused it. When Miriam Devorah's words were relayed to R. Mikhl, he responded that he knew who was the cause of all this but that he himself would not take vengeance upon her because demons and spirits had already exacted his revenge upon her.

This is how we should interpret R. Mikhl's statement about demons: the spirits that haunt a person who has sinned can be male or female. Not in every instance does a male spirit haunt a female, nor does a female spirit always haunt a male. Sometimes female demons encircle another female, and these are the most difficult because it is accepted that a man courts a woman, and it is not generally accepted that a woman do the courting. R. Mikhl the wonder worker, who was an expert in demons and knew which demons cause man's suffering, immediately saw that the spirit that had attached itself to Miriam Devorah was female, as he said that he himself would not take vengeance upon her since demons and spirits had already exacted his revenge upon her. However, this deserves more reflection. If R. Mikhl thought that a demoness was at work in this instance, why did he also say "spirits"? Perhaps it was just a figure of speech to include spirits as well as female demons. Since this is not necessarily relevant to the story, we will not linger on it any longer.

After they appeased R. Mikhl with kind words and payment, the whole problem returned to its beginning: something still needed to be done to cure Miriam Devorah of her sickness. Melancholy is a difficult disease because once it attaches itself to a person, it will not let go until it reduces the person to dust. First, it takes away your happiness, then it puts you in a gloomy mood, then it dries up your bones, and finally, it takes your life and leads you to death.

Because Passover was approaching, R. Nisan returned to Monasterzyska. His congregation would not agree to miss the ḥazzan's prayer on the holidays, especially on Passover, when there is the prayer for dew, and especially R. Nisan's prayer for dew, in which he was able to make his voice sound like dew. But on the first day of the intermediate days of Passover, he returned to his daughter, this time with his wife, Miriam Devorah's mother.

Puah, Miriam Devorah's mother, was a wise woman. She knew that no problem can be solved without action. Already in Monasterzyska, she had heard of R. Menele, who was called the good Jew of Buczacz, and of the many people who had been saved by his amulets. She was dismayed at her son-in-law and at the entire community: A Jewish woman is suffering wretchedly but no one is doing anything to alleviate her suffering! Is it so hard to get to R. Menele's? Does he live beyond the Sambatyon River? He only lives on the other side of the Strypa, and the Strypa of Buczacz, the Lord should not punish me for what I am about to say, may be just enough of a stream to make it proper for Tashlikh and the writing of writs of divorce, but its meager size does not prevent one from crossing over to visit someone on the other side.

Within a couple of days, she took R. Nisan and R. Elyah with her and went to R. Menele. R. Menele lived on the other side of the Strypa in a ramshackle house near the river that he had inherited from his ancestors. There was a minyan of men who resided there as well, who clung to him on account of his righteousness. Even though he would lengthen his prayers, and most of the residents of the area were laborers who did not have time for such long worship, every day there was at least one full service. And it goes without saying that there was quorum for worship on the Sabbath and holidays, when R. Menele would further lengthen his prayers out of joy for the day.

Now we will describe some of R. Menele's habits, those that have been revealed to us and those that are hidden away and known only by the Lord our God.

Every day before sunrise, in summer and in winter, R. Menele would wake up and go down to the Strypa to immerse himself a certain number of times according to the day's status, meaning according to the day's level in the mystical hierarchy, since every day exists on a different spiritual level and no two days are alike. This is one of the mysteries of creation, one of the Blessed One's secrets that He has revealed only to those who fear Him, to the spiritual seekers whom He has tested, purified, acknowledged, and affirmed that they act only for the glory of His name. You should know that the terms "status," "level," and "influence" do not conform to a single concept even though there are those who combine them into one. Rather, one's status and level in the mystical hierarchy are related, while one's influence is separate. Anyone who has done all he can with his affairs can bring great blessing to the upper worlds as well as the lower ones. Enough has been said.

After he would immerse himself, he would immediately put on his clothes without drying himself beforehand, for what good is immersing yourself if you immediately wipe away from your body, with your own hands, the purified water? And do not deflect my argument with the example of the holy priests in the Jerusalem Temple about whom we learned that they would immerse themselves and then dry off. The priests are different; their bodies are pure from birth. So R. Menele's side curls and beard would drip with water. He would enter his home and welcome the day with the psalms appropriate for that day, as specified by King David. He would sit and recite the psalms until the time for the morning service arrived, at which point he would lead the congregation in prayer with all his might, inspiring love and awe in all those who prayed with him. After prayer, he would study one or two passages of Mishnah and then have a bite or two of food before turning to the holy task of being a scribe. He would sit and write tefilin and mezuzot but would not write very much because of the great intensity of thought that he devoted to each stroke of his quill. He would sell his tefilin and mezuzot only to those few who knew how to protect their tefilin and had built homes founded on righteousness. He would sell very few tefilin and mezuzot also so that he would not threaten the income of other scribes who needed money more than he because he made do with very little, and the very little he did earn he would share with others. His wife and children did not complain about his supporting other poor people instead of his own family because he had instilled in them from a young age the belief that the one who limits his needs in this world will receive tens of hundreds of thousands times more reward in the world to come. Out of his love for his fellow human beings, he would agree to write amulets for those suffering but would not accept payment for them, even for the price of the parchment upon which he wrote the incantation. He would even bestow his blessing upon any non-Jew who would come to seek salvation from him. If a non-Jew would request an amulet, he would write one for him, although because the non-Jew has no obligation to adhere to words that are written in Hebrew letters—after all, the non-Jew eats pig and all other impure foods—he would write amulets for them with letters that he would invent from his own imagination. Because of the pure intention that he infused in the letters, they would still have the power to complete their intended purpose.

If someone would come to request an amulet, he would not write one immediately. Instead, he would tell the person to come again tomorrow or the day after, or even two days later, in order to better understand the reason behind the sickness and to determine which amulet would best eradicate it. Sometimes, he would not even give the person an amulet. Instead, he would tell the person to take a blade of a particular kind of grass and put it under the sick person's pillow or take a particular object and tie it around the sick person's neck.

When Miriam Devorah's parents, along with the pious Leah Rachel, came to R. Menele the good Jew's home to ask for an amulet for the sick Miriam Devorah, he said to them, First of all, do not call her sick, so that you do not spur the angels who control sickness. Also, I will not write an amulet for her; rather, I will give you some advice. I examined the causes and saw that everything that happened to her was because of the evil eye that was put upon her. Because of our great sins, there are women who look askance at their neighbors and set the evil eye upon them. The woman on whose behalf you have come to me has had the evil eye placed upon her because of her voice, a gift that God gave her. There is nothing better to fend off the evil eye than the fin of a fish. So take the fin of a fish and tie it around her neck, and I assure you that with God's help, she will soon be well. If you are bewildered by my advice, do not be. Numerologically, the Hebrew word for fin, *snapir,* is equal to 400 just as the Hebrew words for evil eye, *ayin har'a,* are equal to 400. The 400 of the fin will cancel out the 400 of the evil eye. Just as the 400 soldiers of Esau's camp could do no harm to Jacob, so the 400 of the evil eye will do no harm to Miriam Devorah.

They listened to R. Menele's advice and bought a big fish so that they could use its fin for the patient. One of the members of the household figured that R. Menele must have meant that the fin should come from a fish that was cooked for the Sabbath. There was no sense in going back to R. Menele to ask him, since nothing good comes from questions after the fact. So they waited until Sabbath eve. In any case, the fin of a fish cooked for the Sabbath meal is better than a fish cooked during the rest of the week. However, they were wrong to wait until the

Sabbath because by then, Miriam Devorah's sadness had intensified so much that they began to fear for her life.

Where did this sadness come from? Pious Leah Rachel explained that Miriam Devorah told her at the onset of her illness that the sadness started with a dream. One year on the eve of Yom Kippur, she saw herself in a dream wearing a kittel and a big talit, leading the prayer service in a synagogue full of worshipers. When she woke from sleep, she was pleased with her dream. But her happiness was incomplete because of the different ways she began to interpret the dream. In the end she understood her dream as meaning that in a previous incarnation she had been male instead of female. She then began to examine her life and everything she had done as a thinking person, and she started to wonder what she had done wrong or what sin she had committed in her previous life that she should be reincarnated in the lower world as a woman. She became melancholy and wandered about despondently until she came to the gates of death.

In her last moments, she said, Until now, I lived in a world that was not my own. Now I am going to my world.

When she died, they found that she was wearing tzitzit. It is said that she also wore tefilin, and her husband allowed it. Her husband ordered that they engrave these words on her headstone: "A woman that feareth the Lord, she shall be praised, her strength in prayer and piyyutim was like that of a man." He also expressed his sorrow in an acrostic. All that remains of the poem is the lines beginning with the name "Devorah" and the first letter of "daughter." The lines for "Miriam" and her parents' names have not survived. It is shame that they have been lost. Here are the surviving lines of the acrostic:

*D*espondent and hollow
*E*nsconced in shadow
*V*eiled and neglected
Orphaned and rejected—
*R*oam alone, six poor daughters and sons.
*A*nguished and crushed
*H*er glory hushed
Drink, parents, the sorrow of your lost one.

From the acrostic, we learn that she left behind six children. Which among them were boys and which were girls is impossible to tell from these lines, and I have not been able to determine the number from other sources.

R. Elyah lived longer than all his brothers. He was close to ninety-seven years old when he passed away, and he continued to lead the congregation until the day he died. That is, except for the year after Miriam Devorah's death, when he had to tend to the children who were still quite young. They had been born one after another, following several years in which R. Elyah and his wife did not have children. Miriam Devorah was very young when she entered the bridal canopy and was very attached to her parents and so would spend much of her time in Monasterzyska. Whenever she saw that a wagon was traveling to Monasterzyska, she would catch a ride to visit her mother and father. After several years, she reconciled herself to the fact that a woman was meant to be with her husband. She returned to R. Elyah and did not leave him, giving birth to daughters and sons. When she died, some of them were still young. The children could not find what they wanted in a house without their mother in it. They would try to flee to their grandparents in Monasterzyska. Their father would go to look for them and find them lost in the streets. This scenario would repeat itself often. R. Elyah's family and friends suggested to him that a home needs a woman's touch, that the children need a mother, and that a ḥazzan needs a wife. They searched for a wife for him and found one. He arranged a wedding and brought her into his home.

A man's first wife is decreed for him in the heavens forty days before he is conceived. The choice of a second wife depends on the luck of the stars. R. Elyah and his new wife did not have the same sign, and she was a stranger to him from the moment she entered his home on account of the way she spoke, her voice, the words she used, and several other things that were difficult to explain. When a sigh would escape from his mouth, she would put her hands on her hips and look at him with scorn as she berated him, You miss Miriam Devorah. You seem to have forgotten that she left you and married the angel of death.

Worse than her words was the unrest she stirred up among the children. R. Elyah suffered with her for a year and half and then gave her a divorce and due compensation.

After he had parted from this woman, people began again to encourage him to marry, saying that his home needed a woman's touch and that the children needed a mother and that a stepmother was better than nothing. The elders of the Great Synagogue added that a ḥazzan needs a wife. Every day they implored him, and every day he would listen but not respond. When they forced him to answer, he would say, A man is only content with his first wife.

They would counter, It is not your contentment that we care about but the needs of your household. He would respond, He who is burned by boiling water is afraid of lukewarm water.

Rivkah Henya, the daughter of R. Yekutiel, R. Elyah's brother, was older than R. Elyah by five or six years. But her age was not discernible in her face, as she was a descendant of R. Yitzḥak Wernick, whose offspring was blessed with height, beauty, and health.

From a young age, Rivkah Henya harbored affections for R. Elyah. When he was five or six years old and she was nineteen years old, she would play with him so often that her friends would poke fun at her and call them bride and groom. She would answer, When Elyah grows up, I will ask grandfather and grandmother to give him to me as my husband.

What she did not get in her first match, she got in her second. Here, too, we can see what the unintentionally spoken word can accomplish, but first let us go back to the days when they were still young.

Four or five years later, Rivkah Henya was married to Natan Leib, the son of Mendel from the village of Trybuchowce, not far from Buczacz. Four or five years later, R. Elyah married Miriam Devorah, daughter of R. Nisan the ḥazzan of Monasterzyska.

Rivkah Henya had sons and daughters through her husband, and R. Elyah had sons and daughters through Miriam Devorah. After Rivkah Henya and Natan Leib had used up their years of boarding at R. Yekutiel's table, they moved to the village for some years of boarding at Mendel's table, as had been decided in the marriage contract. When that period of boarding was up, they returned to Buczacz with four children, one from their stay in the city and three from their stay in the village. In Buczacz, Natan Leib opened a store and made a living from the villagers of Trybuchowce who would buy their provisions from him, the Jews as well as the non-Jews (forgive the comparison). They led a good life until Natan Leib became ill and died after suffering an injury. There was bad blood between two clans of non-Jews, and one of each happened to come into Natan Leib's store at the same time. A fight broke out, and Natan Leib tried to intercede. He was struck with a kick from one of the non-Jews and then fell ill. He did not recover and passed away. This happened the same year that R. Elyah divorced his second wife.

Since Rivkah Henya was now a widow and since R. Elyah had rid himself of a wife he never wanted in the first place, people began to hint to R. Elyah that he should act before someone else did. R. Elyah did not say yes or no. His relatives got involved, and soon the two were married.

Rivkah Henya brought with her to R. Elyah's home three small children from her first marriage while her two older children went with her mother, as Rivkah Henya had five children during her first marriage. The children she brought with her were the same age as R. Elyah's eldest children. The children all knew one another from school and so were friendly with one another. They quarreled and reconciled, quarreled and reconciled. Rivkah did not favor her own children nor did she favor Miriam Devorah's children, even though at times she wanted to get in her husband's good graces by being easier on her stepchildren.

Rivkah Henya raised the orphans and showed them affection according to their own deeds. She also made sure they kept up with their studies. R. Elyah had taken his attentions away from his children at that time because he had begun to study the book *Ḥemdat Yamim*, into which he poured his heart and soul. If it were not for his wife, he would have abandoned the world to wear sackcloth and to fast. He received further warning from Rivkah Henya's father, R. Yekutiel, who taught: "Any addition is balanced by whatever is made absent by it. Just as the Lord holds humans accountable for breaking his commandments, so, too, does he hold accountable those who perform over and above what was commanded. The Lord knows what is good for man and gave us the Torah to lead us to the good, as explained by our rabbis of blessed memory. All those who seek to do more act as if they doubt their wisdom, as if our rabbis, heaven forbid, did not know the depths of the Torah."

The words of R. Yekutiel eased R. Elyah's mind, and he returned to acting like any other faithful Jew. He performed the mitzvot as commanded by all the generations of rabbis, though he still continued to read *Ḥemdat Yamim*. Before he had found this book, R. Elyah would sit in the beit midrash and study a page of Talmud every day after the morning service. After he discovered *Ḥemdat Yamim,* he would go to the small prayer house near the old market (which was afterward called the prayer house of R. Ephraim) and sit and study *Ḥemdat Yamim* most of the day. I, too, in my youth read from the same copy of the book, which was the only one in our town. But this was not the copy read by our great and righteous rabbi, the Da'at Kedoshim; R. Avraham David received his copy from another great rabbi who brought it with him to our city. This copy was already around in the days of R. Elyah, who preceded R. Avraham David by two generations or more. There is an important rule in Buczacz that one never removes a book from a holy place, even for the sake of a great man.

I will tell one more story about Rivkah Henya. Rivkah Henya was of a mind with her first husband, who was a child of village life. When he lived in the village, he worked with his father in the field and got his daily bread from the land and from trade. He had a store in his house with provisions that the villagers needed. It was the same in the city, where he opened a store and made a living from the sweat of his own brow and did not receive charity from the community or handouts from the wealthy householders. He himself was considered a householder but did not pay attention to the wealthy, to the synagogue managers, or to others that instigated quarreling and competition. Such people would start a war with anyone who did not conform to their demands. There was once a great rabbi in Buczacz, the most honored and respected rabbi of the time, and all the surrounding communities were jealous of our town because of him. One family went before the rabbi for a rabbinic ruling. The rabbi rendered his decision according to the law, finding the family responsible and their rivals innocent. The family swore to take their revenge on the rabbi, and so they began to humiliate him in a number of ways. Their desire for revenge was not slaked until they denounced him to the authorities. The rabbi was in great trouble because he faced the threat of both monetary and physical punishments. The heavens took pity on him, and God softened the hearts of another community to accept him as their rabbi. Their leaders lobbied ministers and took it upon themselves to pay the fines as long as the rabbi was spared from bodily harm. The authorities granted their request. The rabbi was saved from harm, but Buczacz lost its beloved rabbi.

From the day she married R. Elyah, Rivkah Henya tried to banish the thought of her first husband from her mind. Sometimes she was successful, and sometimes she was not. There was one thing that she would recall willingly that continued to amaze her. One Purim after his business was well established in the city, Natan Leib was sitting at the head of the table upon which a big plate of coins was placed that he had prepared in order to give to anyone who asked for Purim donations. In between seeing one person and another, he called out to Rivkah Henya, Let us put together a package to send to the rabbi, the rabbinical judge, and the ḥazzan. Rivkah Henya put together several pastries for each one according to his position, and Natan Leib wrapped a certain number of coins in sugar paper to add to each package. You know who the ḥazzan was—it was R. Elyah, now her husband.

So Rivkah Henya encouraged the children to seek out their living from the same place that everyone else made a living and instructed them not to set their sights on religious vocations that depend on the community: "He who has a pleasant voice should honor God with his singing but should not ask for payment. God favors man's prayers when they are of pure intention without any benefit for man himself. The community too appreciates someone who is not entirely dependent on the community."

She endeavored to put her words into action. She married the children to families that were merchants and shopkeepers. She married the sons to the daughters of merchants and shopkeepers, and she married the daughters to the sons of merchants and shopkeepers. But whenever she heard one of Miriam Devorah's sons read from the Torah, she was happy, for the terrible custom of paying someone to read Torah had not yet spread to Buczacz. Miriam Devorah's sons taught Rivkah Henya's sons (and many others sons of the town) the melodies for chanting the Torah. What Miriam Devorah was not able to do with prayers and piyyutim, she was able to do with Torah chanting. Any Torah reader in our city, and, of course, anyone chanting the Book of Esther, endeavored to use the melodies taught to them by Miriam Devorah's sons, who learned them from her. That was the custom until the ḥasidic movement arrived and introduced a new style of prayer and changed many of the customs that had been performed in Buczacz for many generations, all the way back to the exiles from Ashkenaz, among which were many righteous and holy people.

There is much more to tell about R. Elyah's sons, especially the youngest, Elḥanan, who was very similar to his mother. He, too, had a beautiful voice and composed songs, though Miriam Devorah's songs were in Yiddish while Elḥanan's were in the holy tongue with melodies that were like kisses on one's lips. It is told that when he was absorbed in his songs, he would not be able to tell where he was or where he was going. Once, he left his house in the morning to go to the beit midrash. A day passed and then another, and he did not return home. A search was organized and he was found in a clearing in the forest wearing his tefilin, sitting and staring at the swelling waves of the Strypa. In another story, at his wedding, when the bride stretched out her finger for the ring, he placed the ring on her finger but instead of reciting, "Behold, you are consecrated to me with this ring," he said, "I found it!" It was assumed that he was referring to the verse *Whoever finds a wife finds a great good,* but he really meant that he had found a rhyme for the bride's name. It may be that this story is only partially true or even that the whole thing was made up by people who deride composers of poetry. Still, a similar thing happened to him as a shopkeeper. Often, a customer would be talking to him but he would be unable to answer because of his preoccupation with his poetry. There are also many stories about the rest of R. Elyah's sons, who became great merchants, bringing merchandise from abroad and shipping Polish goods to other countries. Because of their upstanding practices and their honesty, they found favor in the eyes of the authorities and were often able to intercede on behalf of the community. R. Elyah's sons-in-law achieved the same successes.

However, since I intended only to report on the ḥazzanim of our town, and since they were not ḥazzanim, I will leave them behind and continue only with stories of ḥazzanim.

Translated by Saul Zaritt

The Man Dressed in Linen

1

After R. Elyah died, the teivah stood without a regular ḥazzan. Because the community had dwindled, because of the taxes and duties imposed by the government and because of the need to redeem captives and to pay bribes, the community was unable to pay a ḥazzan's salary. They made use of the congregants. Whoever was willing stood before the teivah: one Sabbath, Reuven; Simon the next; then Levi and Judah. When a year had gone by and then another and no ḥazzan had been appointed, people began to complain. They were accustomed to a good singer, someone who made the prayers tuneful with his beautiful voice, but once anyone was permitted to stand before the teivah, people who were not compatible with the teivah pushed their way toward the teivah—one because he had yahrzeit, another because he thought that everyone else found his voice as beautiful as he did. In the end, everyone with a usable larynx used his larynx, which was a nuisance for the community. Where were the sons of R. Elyah, may he rest in peace? And what about the grandsons of R. Elyah's brother, who had passed on to them the voice of their grandfather R. Yitzḥak—where were they? The grandsons of R. Elyah's brother had gone off to different towns and were serving as ḥazzanim in various other communities. As for R. Elyah's sons, their father's wife, who had raised them as a mother, charged them before her death never to approach the teivah, saying that whoever once passes before the teivah grips and is gripped by the teivah, and there he stands until his voice gives out and the community becomes sick and tired of him; yet he never lets go of the teivah and the teivah never lets go of him. R. Elyah's sons kept their stepmother's behest. They hardly even permitted themselves to go before the teivah on their father's yahrzeit if it fell on a weekday; but if it fell on a Sabbath, they ceded it. And, as always happens, wherever the great give way, the lowest of the low push themselves forward to take their places. If not for the gabbai and his skillful management of the synagogue, the teivah would have become a free-for-all.

2

Every year around the days of Seliḥot, a certain linen dealer would come to our town. Because his business was in linen and because he dressed in linen, he was known in Yiddish as *dos laynen yidl,* that is, the "Linen Jew," to the point that his nickname supplanted his real name, which was Gavriel. Because he was a man of integrity and had good merchandise, he would sell it off in two or three days, return to his home village, collect what his wife and daughters had woven, and go somewhere else. Because part of the sainted R. Gavriel, his grandfather, whose name he bore, was buried in the soil of our town, he used to come to our town during the month of Elul, when it is customary to visit ancestors' graves, to pray at his grave. One year, the Man Dressed in Linen came to our town, as he did every year, but God brought it about that he was detained in our town longer than usual, and he did not manage to get back to his home before Friday. And as he would not go on a journey on the eve of the Sabbath, he passed the Sabbath in the home of a tailor, using his own wine and bread and a dish of vegetables and other greens that he had prepared for himself shortly before midday.

3

On Sabbath morning, on his way to the synagogue, the tailor met up with the synagogue gabbai. The tailor said to the gabbai, "The Man Dressed in Linen dined with me, and if I live a thousand years, I will never forget how beautifully he sang the zemirot at my table." The gabbai listened and said nothing. There were elders in bygone days who would not speak before prayers, and if anyone spoke to them, they would not let it reach their ears, and if it reached their ears, they would not answer.

Before maftir, the gabbai indicated to the shamash that he should call the Man in Linen to go up as maftir. After the Man in Linen had recited the haftarah and the concluding blessings, the gabbai said to him, "Go up!" meaning, "go before the teivah." So he went ahead and recited Yekum Purkan and the blessing for the congregation, and the blessing for all who refrain from conversing during the service, for there was a custom in our town that on the Sabbath and festivals and the Days of Awe, the ḥazzan would offer a separate blessing for all who refrain from conversation during the service, which in truth was not even necessary, for people did not yet feel free to converse in the synagogues and the study houses. Then he took the Torah and recited the prayer for the dead on behalf of his grandfather, the sainted R. Gavriel, and Av Haraḥamim, Ashrei, Yehalelu, and so on, and returned the Torah to the ark. Then he went to the teivah, and recited the half-kaddish and the Musaf prayer.

4

When they left the synagogue, no one spoke at all. When they began to separate to go home, one said to the other, "The man who recited Musaf gave me a real taste of prayer. I haven't heard davening like that since the voice of R. Elyah, peace be upon him, went silent; but when R. Elyah davened, I would hear R. Elyah's voice, and when the Linen Man prayed, I heard the prayer alone." And the other replied, "I know that you don't know what you are talking about, but I have to agree with you. It wasn't a voice we heard; it was prayer. Such a prayer leader would make our davening on Rosh Hashanah and Yom Kippur real prayer. I hope that our gabbai can arrange for the man who led the prayers today to daven with us on the Days of Awe." Yet another said, "I was looking at the gabbai when the Linen Man said Av Haraḥamim, and he was wiping his eyes with the corner of his talit."

That was the Sabbath before Rosh Hashanah. In the morning, when they came early to recite Seliḥot, the gabbai handed the Man in Linen a talit and a copy of the Seliḥot and said, "Go up!" meaning, "Go before the teivah and recite the Seliḥot." He put on the talit and recited Seliḥot and led the morning service in accordance with the local custom that whoever recites Seliḥot leads the morning service.

After the service, the gabbai took the Man in Linen and left the synagogue with him. When they were outside, the gabbai said to him, "I see that the congregation likes you, so get ready to be our messenger to God on Rosh Hashanah." He said, "The people of my own town have long been used to my going before the teivah." The gabbai said, "And what about Yom Kippur?" The Man in Linen was silent. The gabbai said, "What is your answer?" He said, "I have never in my life gone before the teivah on Yom Kippur." He said, "Why don't you go before the teivah on Yom Kippur?" He said, "On Yom Kippur, I pray by myself." "By yourself? How can a person pray on Yom Kippur apart from the community?" He said, "I do pray with the community, but silently." "What do you mean by 'silently'?" He said, "I pray by moving my lips but without making a sound." The gabbai said, "A prayer leader who pleases the congregation is pleasing to God, so please do not refuse me. The Man in Linen consented.

On the day before Yom Kippur, three hours before evening, he arrived in town and went to the tailor's house. He left there a jug and a cup and some food for the end of Yom Kippur and spent the time reciting Psalms until they went to the synagogue.

He came to the synagogue and put on the kittel and talit and recited Kol Nidre with a very sweet melody; then he went before the teivah and recited the evening service and Musaf and Neilah with pious awe and reverence and with beautiful melodies that no ear had ever heard before.

5

When Yom Kippur was over, the gabbai wanted to invite the prayer leader for dinner but could not find him. He asked around and was told that, most likely, he had gone to the tailor's. The gabbai was angry at the tailor for snatching the guest away from him but stifled his anger because it was through him that such a prayer leader had come his way.

After the meal, the gabbai's relatives and some townspeople gathered at his house to wish him a good year. They sat around and spoke of the events of Yom Kippur and of the prayer leader whose davening was real prayer and about the moon, which was due for the sanctification ritual. Then they brought up the Man Dressed in Linen again, and since they had brought him up again, they again talked about him and his davening. One of the group said, "The kind of davening that the Linen Man did stirs the heart to repentance." Another said, "You say that it stirs the heart to repentance. I say that we rely on His mercy, may He be blessed, to accept our repentance, and there is no further reason to speak of sin."

One of the group said, "When the ḥazzan said the Avodah and recited the words 'And this is what the high priest would say,' I thought, If my heart feels as if it is about to leap out of my body at the mere recitation of the story, how did our ancestors, who actually saw the Temple in its splendor and the high priest performing the service, keep their souls in their bodies? And how do I know that their souls did not leave their bodies? Because the Mishnah tells us that all the people would follow the high priest when he left the Temple." Another said, "But what about the rest of the passage, where it says that he would make a feast for his friends when he left the Holy Place unharmed; the words 'When he left the Holy Place unharmed' imply that not every year *did* the high priest leave the Holy Place unharmed, either because he collapsed with emotion or the people collapsed with emotion. But I tell you that there is no comparing what you hear with what you see; sometimes simply telling the story can arouse such emotion in the listener that he collapses. What can I tell you? When the Linen Man was davening, there were moments when I thought I was seeing the hand extended to accept our repentance."

6

The gabbai took a jug of raisin wine and said to the late-born child of his eldest son, R. Samuel, "Take the jug and go to the tailor's and give it to the prayer leader, and tell the prayer leader that he is requested to come to my house in the morning, God willing, right after the morning service. And now," the gabbai said, "let us go to greet the rabbi."

They were still getting ready to go when the gabbai's grandson returned and said, "The Linen Man was not at the tailor's, and the tailor doesn't know where he went or why he went, since he brought his own food and wine." The gabbai stood there wondering: "After a fast, a person needs to eat, and since he did not eat at the tailor's, he must have eaten at someone else's, so whom did he dine with? And it is out of the question that he went back to his own village without eating, since it is a walk of several hours from here to the village where he lives. Did anyone here see him at the sanctification of the moon?" No one had seen him at the sanctification of the moon.

R. Joseph, the gabbai's brother-in-law, was a man who enjoyed a joke, and if one fell into his mouth, he did not keep it to himself. So when someone asked whether anyone had seen the prayer leader at the sanctification of the moon, he said in jest, "Well, he certainly did not jump into the moon!"

R. Samuel, the gabbai's eldest son, who was several years older than R. Joseph, hated jokes, especially about religious matters. R. Samuel used to say, "A single joke undoes a hundred good deeds." When he heard what R. Joseph said, he said to him, "You say that he certainly did not jump into the moon. I say that it isn't out of the question, for I read in a book that a man was confronted by highwaymen and they were about to kill him and he begged them to let him perform one mitzvah before he died and they said he might. It was just the time of the new moon. He performed the sanctification of the moon with great devotion, and a miracle occurred: When he hopped three times in accordance with the custom, the wind lifted him up and saved him from the highwaymen." The gabbai's brother-in-law said, "But here no highwaymen accosted him and he stood amid an assembly of Jews and there was no wind and even if there were a wind, it would have had no reason to lift him up." The gabbai said, "Let's get going before the rabbi goes to bed." So they rose and went to the rabbi's house.

7

The rabbi heard their footsteps and rose, for it was the custom of our rabbi, R. Zvi, may the memory of the righteous be a blessing, that if he heard footsteps, he would rise from his chair before the visitor entered, so that if the visitor was beneath him in learning and years, he would not be rising in his honor. Once he adopted this practice, he ceased to distinguish between individuals and groups.

They entered and greeted the rabbi, and he greeted them all and he praised the etrog that the community had sent him. The rabbi said,

"If the prayers on Yom Kippur go well, the etrog is good." Once they were speaking about the day's prayers, they spoke of the Man Dressed in Linen, who had davened so beautifully. They spoke also of the davening of the men who had led the morning service and the afternoon service, who had been inspired to daven beautifully by the davening of the Man Dressed in Linen. They began to laud the Linen Man. One lauded his voice and another his pronunciation, for every word out of his mouth had been so clear and exact that they could almost see the vowel points. The rabbi said, "From his voice, you can tell that he is a God-fearing man."

They sat speaking about the Yom Kippur that was just past and about the festival of Sukkot that was about to begin. They spoke of the good years when they observed the festival punctiliously all seven days, and they spoke about the years that were not so good, years when a person barely managed to say the benediction over dwelling in the sukkah—sometimes because the rain wouldn't stop, sometimes because the snow came early, sometimes because the cold was so severe that no garment could withstand it. One year, they did not fulfill the commandment of dwelling in the sukkah for the first three days of the festival—not because of the rain and not because of the cold and not because of harsh winds that sometimes blow away the sukkah's covering, but because of the raids of the seminarians from the Basilian monastery. What was the story? When the whole town was assembled in the synagogue on the first night of the festival reciting the poems that accompany the evening prayer, the seminarians emerged from their residence and descended upon the Jewish street together with some of the townspeople and overturned all the sukkot. They did not leave a single sukkah whole enough to permit the blessing "to dwell in the sukkah" to be recited over it.

As long as they were sitting with the rabbi, the gabbai did not tell the rabbi that the Man in Linen had vanished, and since the gabbai did not tell him, neither did the people who were with him. One kept quiet out of good manners, and the other kept quiet thinking that if R. Abele was silent, he must have a good reason for keeping silent, and even if you don't know the reason, that's no reason for speaking in his place. But when the gabbai asked the rabbi if it would be all right to make the Man in Linen the permanent ḥazzan, they forgot their manners, and before the rabbi could open his mouth, they all said, "If only!," meaning, "If only the Man in Linen were made the permanent ḥazzan." By the time they left the rabbi, they were unanimous about appointing the Man in Linen as the permanent ḥazzan.

When they left the rabbi's house, the gabbai said, "You must be wondering that I did not tell the rabbi that the prayer leader has disappeared." One spoke up and said, "Not at all. On the contrary, I would have been surprised if your honor *had* told the rabbi, for why bother the rabbi after the long Yom Kippur service?" R. Abele said, "That, too, would have been a good reason, but I will tell you my reason. In these times, when we have no Temple and no altar and no high priest, every rabbi in his own town is a kind of high priest. If something goes wrong in his community on Yom Kippur, it is as if it went wrong because his prayer was not successful. If I had told the rabbi what happened, it would have seemed as if I were implying that it happened on his account. That's why I did not tell him. Now, gentlemen, it is nighttime, and at night there's nothing we can do. We'll see what to do in the morning, God willing."

8

In days gone by, there were old men who would get to the synagogue earlier on the day after Yom Kippur than on other days. Satan might come and say, "Look at Your beloved children: no sooner have they received their writ of life from You yesterday than they have become negligent about their prayers." To forestall this, those old men would cleverly get to the synagogue two or three hours before the actual time of the service.

Thus, when these old men entered the synagogue, they found the Man Dressed in Linen wrapped in his talit, robed in the shrouds of the dead, and standing barefoot with a maḥzor before him, open to the prayers of Yom Kippur, his lips moving but his voice unheard. They realized that he was observing a second day of Yom Kippur.

All night and all day, he stood there fasting and praying. When the day was over and the stars appeared and they had recited the evening prayers, they brought him wine for havdalah and some slices of cake. He said, "If you don't mind, I will just go to the tailor's, for I left my wine and food there." The tailor came with the Linen Man's kit and his food.

He said havdalah over apple wine and ate a small piece of cinder cake, that is, a cake baked on coals that his wife had baked for him on Yom Kippur eve. After saying the appropriate blessing, he got up and said, "If you don't mind, I will go home now, and may God give you and all Israel and the whole world a good and blessed year."

The shamash grabbed him by the arm and said, "How can you go, when the gabbai is waiting for you? They've made a feast for you—such a feast as I hope to see at my daughter's wedding!" So the Man in Linen went to the gabbai's house.

9

The gabbai set him down in front of him, opened the desk compartment, handed him a purse full of gold coins and said, "Here's the fee for your davening." He said, "What does davening have to do with a fee? I would have prayed anyway." He said, "This money is enough for you to buy a new talit or a maḥzor or a Ḥumash with commentaries. R. Joseph, the gabbai's brother-in-law, was present. R. Joseph said, "Everyone else runs after money, and this one doesn't want to touch it! Take it, friend, take it." The Man Dressed in Linen sat silent.

R. Samuel, the gabbai's firstborn son, said to him, "Perhaps you don't want to benefit from money that has been vowed and offered in the presence of the Torah scroll, but I tell you that this money comes from my father's own pocket. And if you are in doubt as to whether it is clean money, I tell you that it is clean. When the angel asks my father, 'Did you conduct your business honestly?' I have no doubt that he—long life to him—will not have to hem and haw, for never in his life has my father benefited from a single unclean penny." The Man Dressed in Linen said to R. Samuel, "A man like your father is a gift from heaven." They responded, "In that case, why do you refuse to take the fee for your davening?" He responded and said, "My name is Gavriel, and I am named after R. Gavriel, my sainted grandfather." They said to him, "What does that have to do with a fee for davening?" He sat silent. R. Samuel said, "So what do you answer to this?" He replied, "It is hard to answer, but since you are asking, I will answer." He paused a while, murmuring. They said to him, "What were you murmuring?" He said to them, "I was praying that what I say might please Him Who gives a mouth to those who lack speech." The host said, "Did you hear the prayer that this man offered?" They nodded and said, "A beautiful prayer." The host said, "Now let's hear what he has to say."

The Man in Linen said, "I have examined the world in my heart and observed that every good or bad event that befalls us is an event wrapped up in another event and that they all come from the will of the blessed God, Who is their author and cause. If a person learns one thing from another thing and this leads him to do or avoid something, that is a good thing for him." They said to him, "You spoke of your sainted grandfather and said that you are named for him. You certainly had a reason to mention that, and it must be on good authority, so tell us about your sainted grandfather. To speak the praise of the righteous is meritorious, especially of a holy man of God who had the good fortune to give his life for the sanctity of God's name." The Man in Linen said, "To speak in praise of the righteous is meritorious, if telling their praises leads to action, so that men behave like them. I, to my sorrow, have never attained to such behavior. All I have is the tale of my sainted grandfather, for whom I am named. I have often told his story to myself. Now that you are saying to me, 'Tell us the story of your sainted grandfather,' the words are coming up to my lips and demanding to be let out. So with your permission, dear Jews, I will try to help them to come out." He paused and murmured, and they knew that he was praying that his words be pleasing to the Master of All Deeds.

10

By this time, the housewife was worried about the prayer leader, who had not yet come in to eat. She sent for him time and again, but he did not come, so she went herself to see why he hadn't come.

When she came, she saw that they were all staring at his mouth, and she guessed that he had told them something important and that they were wanting to hear more, and she realized why the maid had come back without him.

She thought, "A man goes two days in a row fasting and praying and hasn't yet eaten. If I don't call him to eat, no one will tell him to get up and eat." She whispered to her husband, "Abele, the table is set and the soup is ready. Tell the prayer leader to come and wash his hands." R. Abele said to the prayer leader, "Your dinner is calling you. Come and wash your hands." He said, "I have already eaten." They all looked at him in astonishment, for they knew that all he had eaten after the two-day fast was a cup of apple wine and a slice of cake. He said to them, "I only eat once a day, except on Sabbath and festivals." They said, "Is an olive-size piece of cake a meal?" He said, "If a person makes do with little and doesn't ask for more, he is granted as much satisfaction as if he had eaten a lot. With your permission, I will just go home to my wife and daughters."

They said to him, "A person should always depart in an auspicious moment, that is, in the morning. Stay here overnight, and go on your way first thing in the morning, right after the morning service, God willing." He said to them, "Please don't detain me. I want to hammer in the first peg of the sukkah." They said, "Aren't you afraid to walk alone at night?" He said, "I exchange my fear for fear of Him of Whom it is said, 'Your God alone should you fear.' " They said, "But before you go, won't you tell us the story of your sainted grandfather?" He nodded and began his tale.

11

"My sainted grandfather had a beautiful voice. People who understood music would say that such a voice is born once in a hundred years. When he began to study Ḥumash, the cantor attached him to his choir. My grandfather would help the cantor in his davening, giving joy to God and man. And because my grandfather was very modest, people liked him, as did the old ḥazzan, and whenever my grandfather had a break from his studies, the cantor would chat with him about the old melodies that were dear to our ancestors and to God. Some of them could be heard two or three generations ago, and some of them even I have heard. And how do I know that these melodies were the old ones? Because the soul takes pleasure in them. For the soul has a yearning for whatever it heard before descending into the body, and when something reaches it that it heard before descending into the body, it experiences pleasure. When our righteous Messiah arrives—soon and in our time!—we will hear and rejoice, all of us.

"One day, the ḥazzan developed an ailment in his feet. A few days passed, then a few weeks, and he was not even able to drag himself about. When the Days of Awe were approaching and they saw that the ḥazzan was not able to stand before the teivah, they began to ask who would go before the teivah on Rosh Hashanah and Yom Kippur. The ḥazzan heard and said, 'Gavriel will go before the teivah. His voice is beautiful and his heart is devoted to heaven and he is a good messenger before the Lord.' My grandfather R. Gavriel was still a youth, married less than three years.

"My grandfather began to prepare his heart for the Days of Awe, and he asked the ḥazzan which tunes to use for this prayer and that prayer, and which melodies to sing slowly and which melodies quickly. My grandfather applied to himself the proverb *He who listens to advice is wise*, for though people are not normally jealous of their disciples, a disciple is well advised to take counsel with his master and to ask his advice; for he thereby gives the master the pleasure of showing that he still needs him.

"On the eve of Rosh Hashanah, the old man forced himself to sit up in bed, and said to those around him, 'Bring me my festival garments. I wish to receive the new year in the synagogue with all the other people of my town.' They said to him, 'How can you go, when you are sick?' He answered and said to them, 'The merit of the community's davening will support me and renew my strength.' They dressed him in festival clothes and brought him to the synagogue. They literally carried him in their arms, and he cried as they went, *Those who hope in the Lord will renew their strength; they will rise up on eagles' wings.* They brought him to the synagogue and set him in his place. He said to them, 'Set me a chair by the teivah and I will listen to my dear Gavriel's davening.' They brought him a chair and set him down next to the teivah.

"The time for the evening service arrived. My grandfather R. Gavriel wrapped himself in his talit and approached the teivah. The ḥazzan whispered to him and said, 'Gavriel, my son, I was the congregation's messenger one year short of forty years, and now that the fortieth year has arrived, I want to receive it in prayer by the teivah. Stand me up on my feet, my boy, and support me and stand by my right side and help me with your voice, and may He Who hears Israel's prayer in mercy accept our prayer with pleasure.' My grandfather answered amen and gave the talit to him. He wrapped himself in it and recited Barekhu and the Shema with its benedictions, and recited the Amidah at length. From the intensity of his worship, which he performed in fear and trembling, the talit was soaked with sweat.

"Before the full kaddish, the ḥazzan held out his arms and spread his two palms and began to chant, *The earth is the Lord's and the fullness thereof.* This was not customary in our congregations, but there are places where this psalm is recited on the evenings of the Days of Awe between the Amidah and the full kaddish; and in some places, it is recited with the ark open. The reason is that when Rosh Hashanah and Yom Kippur arrive and the Jews assemble in the synagogues and houses of study and stand in prayer, Satan comes to make accusations, saying, 'Do you think they mean all this for the glory of His great name? All they are after is children, life, and food.' So some sages found a way to counter the accuser of Israel by instituting the recitation of the psalm 'The earth is the Lord's' after the Amidah of the evening service. When the accuser sees that the Jews have finished the Amidah, he goes away, not knowing that this psalm has the power to ensure sustenance; and He Who bestows sustenance also bestows children and life. Thus the accuser cannot open his mouth or utter a peep against the Jews, and God fulfills all their hearts' wishes favorably, for the sake of His servant David, who had already begged God, in the preceding psalm, *Set a table before me in the presence of my enemies.*

"So the old man stood before the teivah and repeated King David's words in trembling and trepidation until the teivah and the synagogue itself began to tremble. Forgetting that his legs no longer could hold him up, forgetting that he was leaning on the teivah, the old man again spread out his palms and cried, *Who shall ascend unto the mountain of the Lord, and who shall stand in His Holy Place?* His legs collapsed. And since his legs collapsed, he fell.

"For Musaf, they set my grandfather before the teivah. My grandfather passed before the teivah on Rosh Hashanah and Yom Kippur, on Sukkot and Shemini Atzeret and Simḥat Torah, and his davening was effective. How did they know that his davening was effective? Because no one's attention wandered from his davening. And now, I will tell you something in praise of this man of simple piety. When the ḥazzan's sons returned from the synagogue, their father asked them, 'How was Gavriel's davening?' They thought that if their father heard that his davening was beautiful, it would upset him, so what did they do? They answered him evasively. The old man realized this and said, 'You are foolish to think that I envy Gavriel. It is you I envy, because Gavriel is your messenger to God.'

12

"A week or so after the holiday, the shamash came to my grandfather's house and set a little bag full of money down before him. Right on the Talmud volume that my grandfather was studying, he put down the bag. My grandfather whisked the bag off the book and asked, 'What is this?' The shamash answered and said to him, 'I have brought you the fee for your davening.' My grandfather's face turned white with embarrassment, and he said to the shamash, 'Quick, take the money and return it to whoever sent it. I don't need the community's money, thank God.' The shamash stood there in astonishment and said, 'In that case, so be it.' He took the money and left. He had entered with a certain pomp; he left deflated. My grandfather called him back, opened the desk compartment, scraped a few coins out of it, and said in a low voice, I repay my vow to the Lord. To the shamash, he said, 'Here's what I vowed, and here's something for your trouble.'

"After the evening service, when his father-in-law returned from the synagogue and his mother-in-law from the shop, he told them the whole story. His father-in-law said, 'You did well to return the money to them, and you spoke well to tell them that you don't need the community's money. As long as I am alive and God gives me the means, my table is at your disposal—you and your wife and your children that are to be.' His wife chimed in and went further, saying, 'Thank God, your Rivkah Devorah can cook you a hot meal without the community adding a single stick onto the fire.' My grandfather said, 'Maybe I should have taken the money and sent it to the old ḥazzan.' My grandmother said, 'A person should always make an effort to keep his hands clean of community funds. If God prospers us, let's give him some of our own.'

Her father and mother said to my sainted grandfather, 'Gavriel, what do you say about your wife? We thought she was just a little chick who did not even know how to chirp, but she speaks with wisdom.'

"My grandfather gave thanks and praise to His blessed name for allotting him a place among good folk who made it possible for him to fulfill God's commands with no expectation of reward in this world. He went back to his books and studied most of the night, and no one told him to spare the oil or to spare the wick. Quite the contrary: his father-in-law—my great-grandfather, who was the father of my grandmother, may they all rest in peace—would say, 'May the light of his Torah studies shine in my grave as it shines in my house.' And his mother-in-law, who was my grandmother's mother, may she rest in peace, said almost the same thing in slightly different words: 'May I wake up at the Resurrection to the sound of such a melody.'

"The following year, the gabbai again sent my grandfather a fee for his davening. Why did he send it when he knew that he did not want a fee? The gabbai said, 'I do my part, and the ḥazzan will do his. If he wants it, he will take it, and if not, he can return it.' My grandfather took the money and held it a while and chatted with the shamash about synagogue affairs and the like and then he returned the money to him and said, 'I held the money out of respect for the community and I am returning the money to the community out of gratitude for God's favor in not putting me in need of the community's gift.' He opened the desk compartment and took out a few coins and divided the coins into two parts. One part he gave to the shamash for his trouble and the other part to the synagogue for his vows and offerings.

"The next year, the gabbai again sent him the fee for his davening. The gabbai said, 'Last year, it was easy for his father-in-law to support him; but this year, when his wife has given birth to a boy, it is uncomfortable for Gavriel to depend on his father-in-law for his support.' My grandfather did the same that year as he had done the two preceding years: he took the money and chatted with the shamash and then returned the money to him and gave him some for his trouble and some for his vows to the synagogue.

13

"The old cantor passed away, and my sainted grandfather was no longer called the new cantor. The Torah scholars called him 'R. Gavriel, the prayer leader,' and the townspeople called him 'R. Gavriel, the ḥazzan.' Visitors who passed through the town and heard his davening would say, 'How God will punish us for pursuing our livelihoods if, after hearing such davening, we are still obsessed with them.' If a visitor from a great city happened to be in our town and heard my sainted grandfather daven, he would say, 'We would shower such a cantor with gold coins.' Someone from a great city once happened to come to our town and heard my sainted grandfather daven and tried to lure him to his city by saying to him something like what the tribesmen of Dan said to the young priest in the story of Micah's idol, altering the language slightly: 'Are you better off being the ḥazzan in a town of two hundred Jews or being a cantor in a huge community with—no evil eye!—more than two thousand Jews, many of them wealthy?'

"My sainted grandfather was not tempted by money or glory; he desired nothing but God's Torah, and that through his davening, the name of God should come to be loved; for whoever davened with my sainted grandfather would be stirred to love God's name and to cling to Him. In addition, my sainted grandfather began to teach Mishnah to a group of ordinary people every day after the evening service. But his father-in-law and mother-in-law deserve credit for supporting him so that he did not have to make use of money from the community or gifts from the gentry, for God had allotted him a place among good and honest folk who relieved him of the burden of making a living and enabled him to serve God in all His ways.

14

"When my grandfather entered his father-in-law's house, only he and his wife and his father-in-law and his wife were living there. In time, the house filled up with children of both sexes. In time, the boys came to the age of responsibility for the commandments, and the girls came to the age of marriage, and there was never a meal without a quorum of three for grace, and there was often a quorum of ten, so that they blessed

God by name, as when a marriage broker was present, or an in-law or a young husband or some other person who had been sent to make sure that the bride wasn't lame or blind. When my grandmother was married to my grandfather, she was her father and mother's only daughter. Later, her mother had other sons and daughters, and my grandmother felt bad that she was crowding her sisters. She went and rented a room, where she made a home and opened a shop and earned a living.

"My grandmother Rivkah Devorah, who must have entered paradise without suffering the torments of the grave because she lived to see the fourth generation of her descendants with her own eyes, was a great woman. She had expert knowledge of merchandise and could tell whether a person could be trusted and whether he could be extended credit or not. She would do her business in her shop, and she had dealings with the gentile village women who made linens and brought their handiwork to her to sell. Those she knew from her mother's shop she sent back to her mother's shop, but she bought the goods of those she did not know from her mother's shop, such as girls who had meanwhile grown up or women from distant villages who had followed their husbands or girls whom the proprietors of the villages had brought to their villages. In addition, she did everything a woman does for her husband: she cooked and baked and sewed and laundered his shirt for Sabbath and brought the children to ḥeder and did not bother my sainted grandfather about anything that might interrupt his Torah study, except that once a week she would lay before him all the money she had brought in so that he could tally it and set aside a tithe to distribute to poor Torah scholars. For there are Torah scholars who study Torah in poverty, and God opens the eyes of the pious and opens their hands to give to them so that they not die of hunger. The accounts of her dealings with the gentile women who brought her their homemade goods my grandmother did on her own.

15

"One year, a book dealer appeared in my grandfather's town. On his way to the fair where the great rabbis were to convene with the leaders of the Council of the Four Lands, a book dealer passed through my grandfather's town. In the middle of the market there was a kind of stone with a figure that the local gentiles would venerate. The wagon hit the stone, and a barrel fell from the wagon; the barrel broke open, and the books in the barrel were scattered.

"Word got around in town that a book dealer had appeared. Some of the Torah scholars went out to see what books he had brought. The time for the afternoon prayers arrived. He took the books out of their hands and put them on the wagon and turned the wagon and the horses over to a man who rented horses to travelers and ran to the beit midrash to say the afternoon and evening prayers. The people of the beit midrash crowded around him and said to him, 'You've left your books with the horses. Wouldn't it be better if they were here in the beit midrash? Here's a table, and here are learned people; lay your books out on the table so that we can look at them.' He went and got the books that were in the broken barrel and laid them out on the table that they had cleared for him. Some were books that no one had ever seen; others were by authors whose names had reached us but not their books.

"Books were dear in those days, and not everyone had the wherewithal. If a coin found its way into a person's hand, it was needed for many things on which the body depends. But they said, 'It isn't every day that a traveler like this happens by.' While the workman was fixing the wagon and binding the barrels in new hoops, the book dealer sold most of the books from the broken barrel. The books that found no buyer he placed in a bag and got ready to resume his journey.

"Among the precious books that the book dealer put on the table in the beit midrash, my sainted grandfather saw the book *Torat HaOlah,* by the great scholar and kabbalist R. Moshe of Kraków, author of the commentary on the Turim titled *Darkhe Moshe.* He was a universal scholar who was versed in the seven sciences, by means of which he explained the esoteric meaning of the dimensions, weights, and measures used in the Temple in connection with sacrifices and festivals and a number of God's other commandments, as well as many sayings of the ancient rabbinical sages. I mention all this on account of things that happened to my sainted grandfather. From this point on, I deal with both: my sainted grandfather and the book *Torat HaOlah* together. But first, I will say a few things about my sainted grandfather.

16

"From the time that my grandfather reached the age of judgment, he was constantly studying the Talmud with the commentaries of Rashi and Tosafot. When asked to teach the Mishnah to a group of ordinary people, he would go over the lesson before expounding it to others. On Fridays, he would read the weekly portion twice in the original and once in Aramaic; and on Sabbath, he would recite the Mishnah of Tractate Shabbat, and if he did not finish the entire tractate on the Sabbath, he would finish it on Saturday night or on Sunday. When he was appointed cantor, he would look over the commentaries on the maḥzor before every festival and before the Days of Awe. If he found a satisfactory explanation, he would be pleased; if he did not find one, he would apply to himself the maxim in Ben Sira, quoted in the Talmud, 'Do not seek out that which is too far from you, and do not examine that which is hidden from you; contemplate what has been permitted to you and have no business with mysteries.'

"As a holy man whose soul was bound up in the Torah, my grandfather was shown in dreams things that can be known only by those who have been purified by the study of Torah. One time, the mystery of the Temple's plan was revealed to him in a dream, along with the ways in which it was analogous to the plan of the cosmos. Also revealed to him was what the ancient sages meant when they said that David's harp had seven strings but that in the Messianic era, it will have eight, and in the World to Come, ten. This, too, was revealed to him.

"Now that my grandfather had examined *Torat HaOlah* and found in it things similar to those that he himself had seen in his dream, besides other marvels that he had avoided thinking about because of the maxim 'Do not seek out that which is too far from you'—now that he had found them stated explicitly and plainly and explained by a great scholar, a righteous man, and a kabbalist, one whose rulings were considered authoritative nearly everywhere, he passionately desired that precious book so that he might give delight to his pure soul.

17

"The book was expensive because it was printed on fine paper in big letters and had various diagrams, and, in addition, the boards it was bound in were decorated in many colors with gold shimmering over them. How could he buy such a book when he led an ordinary life, studying Torah while his wife kept shop to support him and the family? It would be unseemly for a man to ask his wife for something so remote from her concerns. My sainted grandfather said, 'Why should I be any better than my forefathers? My father's grandfather wanted to go the yeshivah of R. Shakhna in Lublin but did not go because he had no shoes for his feet and my grandfather wanted to buy a copy of the *Mordechai* but did not buy it because he had no money.'

"A righteous man can control his desires. When it came into his mind to take some of the tithe money, he paid no heed. When his thoughts said to him, 'There are wealthy men who use tithe money to pay the vows and offerings they make in the presence of the Torah,' he paid no heed. His thoughts persisted, saying, 'That isn't all; the beautiful talit on their shoulders and the tefilin on their heads, the Ḥumashim and siddurim in their hands have been bought with tithe money.' My grandfather was sad that his Evil Inclination still thought him so frivolous as to try to try to catch him with such words.

"My pious grandmother, may she rest in peace, observed everything that went on in her household and knew whatever was happening deep in the heart of everyone in the house. She saw my grandfather's face and said to him, 'I can see that something has happened to you and that you are keeping it from me.' So he told her the whole story. She sat silent. At last, she opened the desk compartment and said, 'Look and see if there's enough there for you to buy the book.' My grandfather was shocked and said, 'How can I take money that you have put aside to buy new merchandise?' My pious grandmother said, 'Well, we haven't yet counted all the money in the compartment. If God has put it into your heart to buy yourself a book, maybe He put in enough money to buy both merchandise and the book. Hurry up and take it, and go to the book dealer because I hear that he is getting ready to leave.'

"My grandfather took the money and went to the book dealer. He found him packing up his things for departure. My grandfather put the money for the book down before him. The book merchant said, 'I have already sold it.' 'Who bought the book?' 'I did not ask him who he was, and he did not tell me his name.' My grandfather returned to my grandmother and told her that the book was already sold to someone else. My grandmother said, 'This means that the book wasn't meant for you but for the one who bought it.' Here, that pious grandmother of mine was both wrong and not so very wrong. But before I get to the main point of my story, I will tell you this. After my grandfather returned all the money to my grandmother, his spirits reverted to their usual tranquility, and he went back to his regular studies and studied with great passion, as if the flavor of the Torah had been restored to him. The content of his dreams also changed. But on Rosh Hashanah—by day and not by night, awake and not sleeping—R. Amnon, author of the piyyut "Let us declare the majestic sanctity of the day," appeared to him, and my sainted grandfather chanted the piyyut with the same tune as that with which R. Amnon chanted the piyyut after the bishop of Mainz cut off his hands and feet. And how can this be proved? By the fact that the next day, when he tried to recall it, he could not bring it back. For this is the way of the tunes that you see in a vision: at the moment you see them, you can repeat them; but when you want to bring them back, you cannot bring them back.

"On the night of Simḥat Torah, one of the synagogue people said to my grandfather, 'R. Gavriel, when you recited Geshem, you added pleasure to my pleasure in the festival. If you still desire the book *Torat HaOlah*, it is yours.' My grandfather nodded affirmatively, as if to say that he still wanted the book. Because of the sanctity of the festival and the sanctity of the synagogue, where one does not speak of anything but synagogue matters, my grandfather did not ask about the price.

"When my grandfather approached the teivah for Musaf, a fatigue descended upon him. He thought that this fatigue was caused by mere tiredness, but it was not that. The *Torat HaOlah* distracted him; and it wasn't the book that distracted him but worry about the money that distracted him. Where would he get the money to pay the price?

"That day, people who used to say that R. Gavriel's davening put the pleasure of the Sabbath into their hearts on the Sabbath and the pleasure of the festival on festivals said, 'What's the matter with our cantor? His davening seemed as if it hadn't tasted the flavor of a festival.' Some said that perhaps there was trouble in his household; others said that perhaps something was worrying him. Some said that he was tired, that he was overcome with exhaustion after all the davening he had done from Rosh Hashanah till that moment. But those who knew my sainted grandfather said, 'Don't call it exhaustion. If we, who get our strength from his davening, still have our strength, how much more he, whose strength comes from Him Whose might and power fill the universe.' 'Then what's happened to him?' 'It is a question.'

"Among them was a clever man who knew how to explain every little thing that happened in town. He said to them, 'Quiet, while I tell you. His livelihood depends on the shop, and the shop depends on his wife, and his wife depends on the customers, and the customers—some of them want to buy but don't have what to buy with, and others have what to buy with but don't want to buy. The boys and the girls are growing up, and their needs are growing with them. And winter is on the way but doesn't bring winter's necessaries with it, and R. Gavriel's father-in-law, who used to provide whatever he lacked, has died. And after all that, are you surprised that his prayer gave you no pleasure? If he has no pleasure, how can he give you pleasure?'

"My grandmother saw indoors what people were saying outdoors: he ate but did not know what he was eating, drank but did not know what he was drinking, recited grace after the meal but not in the festival melody. Has something, God forbid, happened to him? She was silent but asked nothing because a guest was dining at their table and because of the children. What she saw, the children also saw, but because of the guest and because she was silent, they, too, kept silent.

18

"R. Eliezer Simḥah the elder, the gabbai of the synagogue in my sainted grandfather's time, was a quick, sharp man. The wise men of the day who knew him well said that if he had devoted himself to Torah the way he devoted himself to worldly affairs, he could have been like R. Heschel of Lublin, with whom he claimed a family connection. He devised a compromise between two very rich men, the sons-in-law of Mendtzi the tax collector, who had quarreled continually for twenty years, ever since the day they came to divide their father-in-law's estate. A great deal of the inheritance money simply vanished in the process. Had R. Eliezer Simḥah not gotten involved, nothing would have been left of all the vast wealth that Mendtzi had left his daughters but enough to buy them a beggars' bag so that they might go from house to house begging. He also made peace between two great families who stirred up discord in the Jewish community over the rabbinic position in their town, when each claimed that the rabbinic position in that town belonged by right to a relative of their own. One claimed that the right to the position descended from his scholarly grandfather who had once occupied it, and the other claimed that the right to the position descended from the stepfather of a relative of theirs who had been deposed from it by means of a bribe that his opponent had given to the government officials. A lot of money was thrown into this dispute, and many persons wound up impoverished, since each of the families found supporters among government officials and the leading Christian clergy. If R. Eliezer Simḥah hadn't mediated between the two sides, nearly all of them would have ended their days in prison, for whenever the Jews submit their legal disputes to non-Jews, they are really handing over their lives. I do not mention their names out of respect for two families who produced rabbis and out of consideration of the fact that they have received their punishment in this world.

"But credit is due to R. Eliezer Simḥah for promoting peace among Jews. Great communities begged him to settle among them, but he was satisfied to dwell in a small town of two hundred Jews. In his time, there were no quarrels in the town, and even after he died, there was peace in the community. They say that before he died, he said to the people of his community, 'The reason you have lived in ease is not because the government is benevolent or because the town's owner is a worthy gentile but because you are easygoing with one another and not quarrelsome. Take this to heart, and you will live in ease till the end of time.' He was so beloved that the minstrels set his Last Will to a tune in language that we were accustomed to use. I don't remember all of it, but I do remember the end: 'Listen to my pious speech, and you will be secure from all sorrow.'

R. Gavriel, the Man Dressed in Linen, said further, "I have dwelled on him at length because it is good to speak the praises of good men. And I will add one point in connection with our subject. He respected and loved my sainted grandfather. Because my sainted grandfather refused a fee for his davening and did not want to benefit even from money that the community had raised by a communal directive that whoever had the means should give festival money and Purim money to the rabbi and the cantor, the only way R. Eliezer Simḥah could find to give him pleasure was to treat him with respect. When word of the things that people were saying on Simḥat Torah reached him, he said to himself, 'Now I will reward him as he deserves.'

19

"On the day after the holiday, R. Eliezer Simḥah went by my sainted grandfather's house. He saw a child playing in front of the house. He looked at him and said to him, 'Aren't you the one who tore a loop from the rabbi's lulav?' The child said, 'No, no, that was my sister's boy.' He was the one who had snatched the wax that had dripped from the gabbai's candle right out of the shamash's hand when Yom Kippur was over. R. Eliezer Simḥah pinched the boy's cheek and said to him, 'In that case, you come from a family of quick folks, so go quick and see if the ḥazzan is at home and come out and tell me. But first straighten your side-locks. Side-locks mark the difference between Jew and gentile, so they ought to be neat.' At that moment, my sainted grandfather was changing the water in the cup in which he had been soaking his etrog to leech out its bitterness so that it could be made into preserves, and he was setting the cup in the window so that the etrog would absorb some of the sun's light.

"And where did my grandfather get a etrog? Here's how it came about. My grandfather's town was one of the communities that received a etrog and the other species, besides the etrog that the chief rabbinic judge would receive from his son's father-in-law, which was one of the three etrogs in the district. The whole town would get up early and go to the gabbai's house to say the blessing over it, the rabbi first, for the rabbi's etrog was valid for waving during the synagogue service but not for the blessing. After the holiday, the gabbai would give the myrtles to the synagogue to be used for the blessing over fragrance after every Sabbath, and he would put aside the palm frond for the future—for there were years when etrog and myrtles would arrive but no palm fronds—and he would give the etrog to his wife so that she could make it into preserves as a curative.

"That year, an additional etrog reached the town. A fire had broken out in the next town over on the Friday night of the intermediate days of the festival, and all the houses in the Jewish street burned down. Half the town scattered, and the rest of the people came to my grandfather's town, bringing their etrog with them. My pious grandmother knew that my grandfather was very fond of saying the blessing 'Who has kept us alive' on the Fifteenth of Shevat over the fruit of a tree, so she went and bought their etrog from them in order to cook it whole for the Fifteenth of Shevat so that he could recite the blessing for the fruit of a tree and 'Who has kept us alive' over it. When my sainted grandfather set his etrog in the window and saw R. Eliezer Simḥah and heard that he was asking for him, he went out and brought him in.

20

"R. Eliezer Simḥah said to my grandfather, 'I haven't been here since your daughter's wedding, long life to her. I see that nothing has changed, except that the ceiling needs to be mended. The walls, too, wouldn't mind some repairs.'

"My grandfather said to himself, 'Not only doesn't he do anything for the house, but he takes away from the house. After Simḥat Torah, my grandmother bought him an etrog, and now he wants to buy a book, when the ceiling might fall in any day now.' My pious grandmother would relate that when she visited my sainted grandfather in prison before he was executed, he told her that if it were not for Rashi's commentary, which explains the verse in Ecclesiastes *Through sloth the ceiling sags; through lazy hands the house caves in* as meaning 'when the Jews neglect the Torah, they waste away, and their splendid and mighty house falls into waste,' he would not be able to bear his sorrow.

"R. Eliezer Simḥah saw that he had upset my grandfather, so he turned to happier subjects. He began to talk about synagogue matters and went on from there to town matters and went on from there to praising the town because its householders were on good terms with one another and did not quarrel with one another or with the head of the community and the head of the community did not quarrel with the rabbi and the rabbi did not quarrel with the shoḥet and the shoḥet did not quarrel with the butchers and the rabbi did not begrudge the ḥazzan the praise that everyone gave him for his voice and the cantor wasn't insolent to the rabbi; for there are communities where if the ḥazzan is a bit of a scholar, he pays no attention to anything that the rabbi says, and if he is not learned, he treats him with insolence and arrogance. From criticizing ḥazzanim of that sort, R. Eliezer went on to praise my sainted grandfather.

"My sainted grandfather sat silent. Prayer leaders' speech comes mostly from the prayer book, so that even when they want to have a friendly conversation, their tongues do not obey them. But rather than tell you about them, I will say something about myself. I was not there with them. I did not know R. Eliezer Simḥah, not to mention my sainted grandfather, for whom I am named, so how can I be telling all these details? But I tell you that I am relating them as my grandmother related them to me, for when she would speak about the things that happened to my sainted grandfather, she did not speak only about the events; she spoke about even the innermost thoughts of the heart. The old men of that generation who knew my sainted grandfather would say that when that pious woman would speak about her sainted husband, they heard not just what he said but his inner thoughts, as if his thoughts acquired a voice and spoke through her throat. To what my pious grandmother said, I am adding what I have heard in the name of R. Eliezer Simḥah, may he rest in peace, for he was constantly speaking about everything that happened on that day in connection with my sainted grandfather. Now that I have accounted for everything that you were wondering, I will return to my story.

21

"So my sainted grandfather and R. Eliezer Simḥah sat together, and R. Eliezer turned to public affairs. R. Eliezer Simḥah said, 'I have no complaint about all the money they collect from us in the form of taxes and imposts and gifts for the noblemen and noblewomen and priests and informers. This is God's decree, praise be to Him, *Because you did not serve the Lord your God in joy and generosity amid your wealth; therefore you will serve your enemies.* That is the meaning of the midrash that says,

'Had you deserved it, you would have been sitting in Jerusalem, drinking the pure, sweet waters of Shiloaḥ brook, but since you did not deserve it, you have been exiled to Babylonia to drink the murky, smelly waters of the Euphrates.' My complaint is with the councils. The king is dead and no new king has been chosen, and the queen, the king's wife, was already dead; so what call do they have to impose a pin-money tax on us for the queen's jewels? It is only because the council chiefs want to make themselves look good to the new king who will come to the throne, as if to say to him, 'Look, lord king, how fine and diligent we are to be already bringing a gift to the queen.' I have heard from old men who heard from their ancestors who heard from their ancestors that there are kinds of tax that never occurred to the gentiles to impose on us but that were imposed on us by community leaders who wanted to show the lords and nobles how much we love the king, and once they brought us under this obligation, the gentiles demand it of us and we pay; this is certainly the case of the pin-money tax. So what did we do? We took a vote and decided that as long as there is no king or queen, we are not obliged pay the pin-money tax. Wasn't that right, R. Gavriel?'

"My sainted grandfather responded and said, 'If the whole body is of one accord, it can only mean that heaven is in agreement.' R. Eliezer Simḥah said, 'Wonderful, R. Gavriel. Now I will tell you what the community wants to do with the money. It is giving the money to someone who makes his prayers into lovely ornaments for the King, for God who lives forever.' My sainted grandfather understood and did not understand who was meant by these words. R. Eliezer Simḥah took my sainted grandfather's hand and put his other hand on it and said, 'You are the community's messenger, and I am the community's messenger. You are their messenger to God, and I am their messenger to you. On the authority of the community and on the authority of its leading householders, I am bringing this money to you, for who is it who makes lovely ornaments for the crown of the King, to God Who lives forever?—It is you, with your davening.'

"R. Eliezer Simḥah took out a roll of money—silver coins wrapped up and rolled—and set it in front of my sainted grandfather and waited in silence to see how my sainted grandfather would respond. My sainted grandfather stood up and went to the window and took the etrog and said, 'My wife, long life to her, bought this etrog from the people whose houses were burned down all of a sudden. I am amazed at you, R. Eliezer Simḥah, who is said to be the wisest man of the district. You should have said to the leading householders, "There are Jews who have no roof to their heads, yet you want to give your money to someone who sits in his own home and lacks for nothing!" ' My sainted grandfather wasn't a talkative man, but out of pity for the people who had been burned out, he made the effort to find the words.

"R. Eliezer Simḥah said, 'He who caused the fire will duly pay.' The fire was not caused by the Sabbath candles that some housewife blessed on the Friday night of the intermediate days in the sukkah but by the envy of the town's proprietor. Let me explain. The proprietor saw that the town belonging to Mikołaj Potocki was made up of stone houses, so he set fire to the houses of the Jews in his own town, which were made of wood. But he said that for every house that was rotten with age, he would build a good house of stone. It follows that if he finds out that we ourselves are offering to help the people who were burned out, he will not only be angry at us for mixing in with his affairs, but he will abandon those who were burned out, with the result that we will be causing them so much harm that even if we all sold the clothing on our backs, there would not be enough to build houses for them.'

"My sainted grandfather sat there, sunk in his own thoughts. 'If the proprietor had set fire to the houses of the Jews because he intended to rebuild his town out of stone houses, and he specially chose a Friday night to do it because the Jews were prohibited from extinguishing a fire on the Sabbath, he ought to have considered that the fire might catch on to the houses of their gentile neighbors, and the gentiles would come and extinguish it. Anyway, he could have ordered the Jews of his town to build stone houses at his own expense in place of their rotted-out houses, and then he wouldn't have had to cause them suffering; he could even have paid for their damages. On the other hand, even if R. Eliezer Simḥah is exaggerating, he is not a man to tell a lie.'

"R. Eliezer Simḥah stood up from his place and went away. Absorbed in his own thoughts, my sainted grandfather did not notice that R. Eliezer Simḥah had left and did not see him out and had no idea that he would never see him again in this world. In this world, they did not see each other; but in the next world, they did see each other. The one was sitting among the martyrs who sanctified God's name with their deaths, and the other died of old age at nearly ninety-seven; yet because the latter had expended all his wealth and endangered himself repeatedly to alleviate my sainted grandfather's sufferings in this world, he was shown my sainted grandfather's glory in the upper world. How do I know this? R. Eliezer Simḥah had a daughter born in his old age from his second wife, who was a descendant of the author of *Terumat Hadeshen*. On the day the stone was erected over his grave, she cried out and said, '*Ikh zeh*,' meaning 'I see.' They asked her, 'What did you see?' She replied, 'I saw Father pushing his way in to see R. Gavriel, and I heard R. Gavriel saying, 'Let R. Eliezer Simḥah in to see the glory of those who sanctify the Name.'

22

"Now I will come back to my sainted grandfather as he was two or three hours before the calamity that God brought upon him in order that he might enter the next world in a state of perfection.

"He lived in his home in tranquility, quietly fulfilling God's commands. His pious wife, my grandmother Rivkah Devorah, may she rest in peace, dealt in merchandise and provided for the household and left him alone so that he could devote himself entirely to God, Torah, and prayer. Alongside my pious grandmother was her eldest daughter, Rachel Leah, my aunt who was married to a Torah scholar from a distinguished family. Her husband (my uncle) sat in the beit midrash with the sons of his father-in-law (my sainted grandfather) and expanded God's world for Him; for the Holy One, blessed be He, has nothing in this world but the four cubits of the law, and when a man sits and devotes himself to the Torah, that person, in a manner of speaking, makes His world more expansive. My father and teacher, blessed be the memory of that righteous man, stood apart from them between the teivah and the window, for he would study the Torah standing. It was said of him that from the time his intellect shone brightly enough to understand a page of the Talmud, he would stand studying sixteen hours every day; and on Thursday nights, he would stay awake all night to review his studies. This is what made it possible for him to know most of the tractates of the Talmud by heart when he was not yet twelve years old. It was said of him that the Torah made his face shine like a man who was constantly engaged in his love for it.

"My father was so eager to study the Torah that my sainted grandfather agreed to defer his marriage until he would be thirteen years old, paying no heed to the bride's mother, who stormed and raged to get him to advance the wedding date, for she was anxious to live to see children from her daughter, the only one left her of her thirteen children.

"I was born of a different marriage because everyone was preoccupied with what happened to my sainted grandfather. My pious grandmother gave no thought to arranging a wedding for her son, the bride's father canceled the match, revoked the marriage agreement, and married off his daughter to someone else. Several years passed before my father and teacher, blessed be the memory of that righteous man, took a wife, namely, my mother, may she rest in peace in paradise. This is why the sages of the age would say, 'One should never postpone the marriage of his son nor should one revoke a marriage agreement': for because my sainted grandfather postponed his son's marriage by a year, it was postponed for many years, and because the bride's father revoked the marriage settlement, he did not live to see his daughter's wedding. It is related that when she was being led to the ḥuppah, a rider came by, saw her, and was smitten with love for her. He got down from the horse and grabbed her and ran away with her while the whole town looked on.

"I will mention a few things that I have already spoken of. That day was the day after Simḥat Torah. My sainted grandfather stood at the window tending the etrog that my pious grandmother had bought so that he could say the blessing of the fruit of trees and 'Who has kept us alive' over it on the Fifteenth of Shevat, for from the time he reached the age of awareness, he loved to recite the blessing on the fruit of trees on the New Year of the trees. And though a person like myself does not know the mind of the righteous, and certainly not of such a righteous man as this one, a man who became a sacrifice to God, I see him as if in a vision, changing the water in the cup in which the etrog was soaking, standing there as if God were already putting in his mouth the taste of the blessing that he was going to recite over the etrog on its New Year.

"I am going into all this detail to show you what a goodly atmosphere prevailed in the house of my sainted grandfather; yet when the calamity came over him, he accepted his suffering with love. How far did this go? After R. Eliezer Simḥah prevailed upon the sons-in-law of Mendtzi the tax collector and got them to bring bags of gold coins to the priests so that they opened the doors of the prison to my pious grandmother, and she found my sainted grandfather fettered in iron chains attached to the wall, his body full of wounds and visible through clothing that had rotted on him, she let out such a wail that the walls of the prison shook and the prison guards were staggered. My sainted grandfather said to her, *Why are you weeping, and why is your heart bitter?* Is it for my own honor that I am lying here? No, I am lying here for the honor of Him Who spoke and the world came into being. Perhaps you are thinking that it is impossible to fulfill God's commands in a place of filth; but our ancient sages of blessed memory said, 'God exempts from the commandments one who is unable to perform them.' I am certain that He, may He be blessed, of whom it is said that *His mercy extends to all His creatures,* will regard my stay here as if I were sitting in the synagogue or the beit midrash.'

"And so on that day, a few hours before the calamity, R. Eliezer Simḥah visited my sainted grandfather and followed the practice of pious people, of not beginning with a financial matter first, if one had to be dealt with, but first speaking of God's mercies. So we find that when our father Abraham, peace be upon him, came to the Hittites to ask for a burial ground in which to bury Sarah, what did he say to the Hittite?—*I am a stranger and sojourner among you,* and though the land is promised to us, as long as it is in the hands of the nations of the world and we are strangers and sojourners among you, none of our needs, even a burial ground, can be supplied except through purchase.' That is why R. Eliezer Simḥah began by speaking of taxes before getting to the pin-money tax, or *szpilowka* tax, as it is called in their language. And when he got to that particular tax, he said, 'Now that there is no king and no queen, and no one knows who will become king and who that king's wife will be, the community regards itself as not liable for the pin-money tax. And so the community is taking all the money that was set aside for the queen's ornaments and giving it to him who makes ornaments for the crown of God, Who lives forever.' Before R. Eliezer Simḥah left my sainted grandfather, he left him with a roll of silver coins. My sainted grandfather, who never in all his days looked at a coin other than the tithe coins that my grandmother would set aside for indigent Torah scholars, did not open the roll and did not look to see how much was in it; but in his holy heart, he reckoned that God had brought the roll of silver coins his way for no other reason than for the sake of the *Torat HaOlah*.

23

"My sainted grandfather sat and brooded on R. Eliezer Simḥah's words. After a while, he stood up and kissed the mezuzah and left the house and went to the place where he wanted to go. His heart was heavy, and his feet were heavy. My sainted grandfather said, 'The Talmud says, "A person's feet carry him to the place where he is supposed to be," yet that person's feet feel so heavy that he can barely move them.' He was speaking of himself, but he referred to himself as 'that person' so as not to arouse the power of divine judgment against himself for contradicting the express words of the Talmud.

"The way of the righteous is that if they have trouble grasping something in the words of the ancient sages, they apply themselves to finding a solution, and that is what my sainted grandfather did now. My sainted grandfather said, 'It is no surprise that my feet are heavy. I have made them forget how to walk. Since Tashlikh, I have not walked anywhere but from home to the synagogue and from the synagogue to home. It is only thanks to God's mercy that my feet carry themselves at all.'

"He recalled the old ḥazzan who developed an ailment in his legs and was not able to stand before the teivah. On the first night of Rosh Hashanah, he wanted to receive the new year with the community. His sons brought him to the synagogue. Before the evening service, he said to my sainted grandfather, 'Hold me up so that I can go before the teivah just this once more and pray for the people of Israel.' After the Amidah, he recited the 'The earth is the Lord's,' and when he reached the verse *Who shall ascend unto the mountain of the Lord, and who shall stand in His Holy Place,* his feet collapsed and he died.

"My sainted grandfather recalled the story of R. Amnon, whose hands and feet were cut off by the bishop. On the first day of Rosh

Hashanah, R. Amnon asked his family to bring him to the synagogue with his hands and feet and to lay him down beside the ḥazzan. They brought him to the synagogue. When the ḥazzan reached the moment to recite the Kedushah, R. Amnon raised his voice and recited the poem 'Let us declare the majestic sanctity of the day.' And when he came to the end of this silluk prayer, he departed from the world in the presence of everyone, *for God had taken him*.

"My pious grandmother said, 'When I visited my sainted husband in prison, my sainted husband said to me, "All my life, I kept before my eyes the saints who sanctify the name of heaven in their deaths. The day I went to buy the book *Torat HaOlah*, I could barely stand upright, so great was my desire to sacrifice myself as a whole-offering to God." ' My pious grandmother said, 'My heart tells me that on that day, he had a vision of R. Amnon.' And my pious grandmother further said, 'On what grounds do I say so? Because when he spoke to me, he spoke in a singsong that sounded like the melody of "Let us declare the majestic sanctity" on the first day of Rosh Hashanah.' And my pious grandmother said further, 'Even though it was obvious that he no longer had a connection with this world, he remembered every thought that was passing through his mind as he was going to buy the book.' And my pious grandmother said further, 'On what grounds do I say so? He told me that when he felt in his clothing and did not find the roll of silver, he was not sad; and when he felt in his clothing again and found the silver, he was not happy.' And my pious grandmother said further, 'This was nothing new, for never in his whole life did money mean anything to him, except for the money that he used to fulfill the commandments.'

24

"A river runs through the middle of my sainted grandfather's town and makes it seem like two towns. On one side of the river was the Jewish street and on the other side was the town court, and behind it was a place for pasturing animals and behind that the houses of the gentiles. My sainted grandfather lived on one side of the river, on the Jews' street, near the synagogue; and Gershon Wolf, to whose house my grandfather went on account of the book *Torat HaOlah*, lived on the other side, near the town court, above the pasture. Formerly, Jews were not permitted to cross over, and certainly not to live there; in my sainted grandfather's time, a few Jews did live there. The first of them was Gershon Wolf, who was brought in from somewhere else by the town's proprietor to establish a factory for making paper. I have heard from old people that it was not the gentiles who prohibited the Jews from living there but that the Jews had undertaken on their own not to live there. When I was a child, I once went there with my friends to collect willow boughs for Hoshana Rabba. My father, whose memory is a blessing along with the righteous, said, 'They are kosher, but the place they come from is not proper.' Much later, when I heard the story of what had happened, I recalled what my father, whose memory is a blessing along with the righteous, had said. It is nearly time for the morning service. With your permission, gentlemen, I will stop here."

They said to him, "It is not yet time for the morning service." He replied, "It is not yet time for the morning service, but it is time for the hour before the morning service." R. Samuel, the eldest son of R. Abele, whispered to his father, R. Abele, "The Mishnah teaches that the early pietists used to put aside an hour before saying their prayers. I have not seen the early pietists, but now I am seeing someone who resembles them." R. Abele looked over at the Man Dressed in Linen and said, "My heart tells me the same."

R. Joseph, R. Abele's brother-in-law, said to the Man in Linen, "You stopped in the middle of the story." The Man in Linen replied, "If God spares me till after the service, I will take up where I left off." R. Samuel, the firstborn of R. Abele, whispered to his father, R. Abele, "Did you hear him say, 'If God spares me till after the service'?" R. Abele said, "I heard." R. Samuel said, "I wonder if he is one of those who offer their lives when they pray." R. Abele looked over at the Man in Linen and said to R. Samuel, "The rabbi spoke well when he said that he appears to be a pious man."

The Man in Linen remained seated, but by the manner of his sitting, he tore himself away from his place and planted himself elsewhere. This is really only a figure of speech, but if you had been there, you would not have called it a figure of speech.

25

(I don't know when he resumed telling the story or when he finished telling the story. Right after the morning service? Can a person go two days fasting and praying, taking nothing to eat or drink afterward but a cinder cake and a little apple wine, and then sit through the night from beginning to end, telling this story—and then resume telling it? And if I say that he resumed telling the story after that night, the question of when this could have been still stands: The same day? The next? Can a person clear his mind for storytelling when he ought to be making preparations for the festival? During the intermediate days of Sukkot?—One doesn't leave the sukkah except in case of great need. On the day after the festival?—He would not have had the opportunity because of what happened to him on the day after the festival. In such a case as this, I say that there are problems in this world that we cannot resolve, so I will let the problems stand and return to the story. But I have to preface it with this remark: up to this point, I have been telling the story on the authority of the Man Dressed in Linen, that is, from those who heard from their ancestors and their ancestors from their ancestors back to the original people who heard it from his mouth and were very careful not to change a word of what he said. From this point on, I speak on the indirect authority of the Man in Linen, that is, from others, less scrupulous, who were stimulated by the Man in Linen to look into the story of the things that befell the sainted R. Gavriel.)

So R. Gavriel the prayer leader, the grandfather of R. Gavriel the Man in Linen, came to the home of Gershon Wolf, who had been invited by the town's proprietor to oversee the factory for the manufacture of paper. R. Gavriel placed the roll of silver coins before him and said to him, "Count the money and see if it is enough to cover the cost of the book." Gershon Wolf looked at the roll of silver coins and said, "Whether it is enough to cover the cost of the book or not, the book is yours."

R. Gavriel the prayer leader took the book and kissed it and got up to go. Gershon Wolf said to him, "Sit, R. Gavriel, and let me give you a little drink so that you can say the blessing and leave a blessing on my house." R. Gavriel said, "Please don't insist. From the first day of Seliḥot until today, I have not looked at the Mishnah, and today I return to teaching the daily Mishnah chapter, and I want to review it and plan my lesson." Gershon Wolf said, "I have not yet counted the money that you gave me." R. Gavriel said, "If it contains enough to pay for the book, fine, and if it contains more, let it be for the poor." Gershon Wolf said, "And if it doesn't contain enough to pay for the book?" R. Gavriel said, "Then I give the book back to you." Gershon Wolf said, "The moment I looked at it, I knew that the roll of silver contained more than the value of the book, and everything I have just said has been because how can I let a man like you come to my house and go off without eating or drinking anything? Take possession of your property, R. Gavriel, take the book, but can't you sit a while and have a taste of something?" R. Gavriel said, "As I have already told you, I want to go over the lesson that I will be teaching in public between the afternoon and evening service." Gershon Wolf said, "God forbid that I should keep you from the study of Torah."

R. Gavriel left Gershon Wolf's house and went his way. His feet were heavy, and his heart was heavier. He went back the way he had originally walked. When he got to the judge's house he saw a crowd. He stepped to one side and stood waiting for the crowd to pass. Suddenly, he heard a voice crying, "That's him! That's him!" R. Gavriel was just realizing that it was he whom they meant when he received a blow on his face. Before he could cover his face, he was knocked down. Before he could pick himself up, they begin kicking him, one with a wooden shoe and one with a hobnailed boot. In the meanwhile, they grabbed the book from him, crying, "This is the book that he uses to cast his magic spells! Everything that he does is with the figures in this book!"

Now I will tell you what it was all about. The wife of the sacristan of their church used to prepare the sacramental bread, as his first wife, who had died, had done. One day, the number of loaves came out short. She knew that she hadn't used less than the full amount of flour and so was puzzled. When the same thing happened again two or three times, she told her husband. Her husband said, "Be quiet, and I will find the thief."

The sacristan knew that his first wife's mother was a thief, and a greedy one at that, who never held back from taking anything edible that she came across. He thought to himself, "She's the only one who could have made off with the holy bread." He kept it in mind and watched her. Before a few days had passed, he caught her in the act of stealing. He began to quarrel with her, and she replied in her fashion. His wife heard and came out and added to what her husband had said. The old woman became furious that the woman who had taken over her daughter's place was speaking so insolently to her. She raised her hand and slapped her on the face. The young woman paid her back double. The old woman raised a hue and a cry. The neighbors came and heard the kinds of things that were being said, and it was not a moment before they dragged her into court, beating her as they went. She was shouting and saying, "Don't do anything to me! I did not do anything on my own. I did it all under the influence of a certain Jew who cast a spell on me. He bewitched me into bringing him the holy bread to feed the cats that help him with his witchcraft." They said to her, "Who would dare to do such a thing?" She saw R. Gavriel the prayer leader standing aside waiting for the crowd to pass. She pointed a finger at him and raised a cry, shouting, "That's him! That's him! That's the Jew who bewitched me into stealing the bread of God to feed his cats!"

The gentiles crowded around him and beat him severely and cruelly until he had no strength left. They lifted him off the ground and chained him with iron chains and threw him into the prison where highwaymen and other murderous types are locked up, before being taken out for execution.

The affair was heard of in the town, and it reached the Jews, and the cry was all around the town. The principal men of the town and the townspeople assembled and discussed what was to be done. What did they do, and what did they not do to relieve him of his suffering?

But this has to be said: from the moment that he was brought into the prison, he did not utter a single groan, so that the gentiles thought that he was relieving his pains by sorcery. They did not know that he was enduring suffering lovingly, like the truly righteous, who bear every kind of suffering and declare God's justice.

At that time, there was no king in Poland, so the enemies of Israel were ascendant, especially the priests, for the land was in their power.

All the great men of Israel in that district—the leaders, committee heads, not to mention the rich and the powerful—did their best to save the tormented man from his tormentors, especially R. Eliezer Simḥah, who spent all his money and mortgaged his house to raise money for bribes and to pay his way to go from nobleman to nobleman and from priest to priest, but this did not help, nor did his wisdom do him any good, and the bribes served no purpose but to whet the appetite of the noblemen and their agents to demand more, as it is written, *Wealth is no help on a day of anger*. When God is angry at a person, money does not help to save him from death.

Two and a half years that righteous man lay in prison; and every single day, a priest came and spoke to him about their faith and told him of all the rewards that are available in this world to those who profess it; and every day, the officers of their court came after the priest and tortured R. Gavriel with severe, terrible torments. He withstood them all, and no change was evident in his face, which went on glowing brighter and brighter every day, as if he had joy on top of joy. About him and those like him, David said, *Light is scattered over the righteous, and joy to those pure of heart.* And what did the priests say?—"This is just sorcery!—for how can a person endure such torments and even rejoice in them?" They did not know or grasp that this was God's doing, that He, may He be blessed, gives His friends strength to overcome all the torments of this world and to accept what befalls them with joy and a generous spirit, for His name's sake, in love.

The priests had begun to fear that R. Gavriel's behavior might turn their own people from their faith, for word had already gotten around that some of the prisoners had said that if they ever left the prison, they would abandon their faith and cling to the God of Israel, Who gives His people Israel might and strength.

Among the townspeople, too, rumors that were not pleasing to the priests were heard. The townspeople said, "We are aware that the lady is a thief. It is well known that she made off with the church's sacred vessels, and we have never heard of any traffic with sorcery on the part of the Jew whom she accused of bewitching her to steal the church's sacred vessels and the sacred bread to feed to his cats." They were coming to doubt that the judgment of the priests was correct. The villagers were shocked and amazed that a righteous and innocent man had been taken and tortured when he had done no wrong, for the villagers used to hear from their wives and daughters that the shopkeeper who bought their cloth from them treated them with the utmost fairness, and surely the woman's husband was like her. The priests gradually became weary of talking and the torturers of using their fists, and they stopped torturing him. But they sentenced him to be quartered and thrown to the dogs.

They took him from the prison and tied him to a horse's tail and drove the horse all around the town with the nobles and ladies looking on, as well as all the gentiles who had gathered to witness the execution of the Jew who had lured them with witchcraft away from their faith so as to steal the church's sacred vessels and the bread of their god to feed the cats that assisted him in his sorcery. But their god had stood by them, so that he did not succeed in putting the sacred bread into the church's sacred vessels; for had he managed to put the sacred bread into the church's sacred vessels and to feed it to his cats, his crimes would never have come out.

While that saint was being dragged about the town's streets tied to a horse's tail, the artisans were at the town's outskirts building a great scaffold and benches of wood and stone as seats for the noblemen and ladies who came to see the judgment and execution of that Jew. When the horse was tired of running and dragging and the noblemen and ladies were tired of waiting for the judgment and execution of the Jew, R. Gavriel was released from the horse's tail and brought up to the scaffold. The chief priest stood on one side of R. Gavriel and the executioner with his ax on the other. The priest was attempting to speak to R. Gavriel's heart, saying things that do not deserve to be mentioned, and at each point that the priest made, the executioner flourished his ax to intimidate him. Thanks to the grace of God to those who fear Him, R. Gavriel paid no attention to the priest's prating and did not see the ax as it was being flourished, for his soul was already ranging about the worlds in which there is no fear of flesh and blood but only love of God and God's love for those who fear Him.

By now, the noblemen and ladies were beginning to mutter that the priest was speaking too long and that the executioner was taking too much time and procrastinating. Observing this, the head of the ecclesiastical court made a sign to the executioner. The executioner flourished the ax in his hand and struck down the sainted R. Gavriel. Then he cut him into four pieces. Then he took the pieces and threw each one to a different place as food for the birds of heaven and the beasts of the earth. A certain unclean gentile—the son of the gentile woman on whose account R. Gavriel was killed—picked up one of the four pieces of the holy body and brought it to our town. It was on account of the piece that was buried in our town's cemetery that the Man in Linen used to come to our town during the month of Elul, when it is customary to visit ancestral graves. It was what brought it about that the Man in Linen happened to lead the prayers in the synagogue in our town on Yom Kippur.

"My grandfather, who was a faithful messenger of the community to Him Who hears the prayers of His people Israel, who studied and taught others—why was it that he underwent such extreme suffering, and why was his body destined not even to be buried whole? All the sages of the age struggled with this question until they finally came to the opinion that Satan resented him because by his davening he brought thoughts of repentance into the hearts of the worshipers. For anyone who does a mitzvah in complete sincerity and does not expect a reward is given the strength through that mitzvah to induce others to perform mitzvot and good deeds. And in order to blind Satan's eyes and prevent him from denouncing him, my sainted grandfather was induced to accept a worldly reward for the mitzvah in the form of taking a fee for his davening. And because it was known that nothing in the world would induce him to take a fee for davening, the Lord brought it about that a book dealer happened to come through the town and put into my grandfather's heart a desire to buy the book *Torat HaOlah*. And because God's trials are numerous, it came about that the book dealer sold the book and my grandfather thought that the object of his desire was lost, and it came about that the man who bought the book agreed to sell it to him, and he went and bought the book with the fee for his davening. And because the Holy One, blessed be He, wanted (if such a word is appropriate) that this righteous man should come to Him unblemished, he was enabled to die as a martyr."

"This is the story of my sainted grandfather, R. Gavriel; but I will add this one item. That righteous man, who was steadfast in his righteousness all his days and who enhanced the prayers of Israel with his voice and who taught the Mishnah every night—why was he sentenced to such cruel and extreme torments? And when he withstood them all and did not deny the God of Israel, why was he killed for the sanctity of His name, may He be blessed, and did not even attain burial for his whole body? In a world that is all problems and conundrums, this is a great question, but in the world in which there are no problems and conundrums, it is not a question at all."

The Man in Linen said, "I have seen my sainted grandfather, R. Gavriel, in a vision." They said to him, "Your grandfather appeared to you? How did he appear to you—his whole body, or only the part that had a Jewish burial?" (For there are books in which it is written that anyone who dies as a martyr and does not receive a Jewish burial has a grudge against this world and does not show himself to anyone in it.) The Man in Linen hung his head in silence.

The gabbai said, "You still haven't told us why you refused the money that the congregation is offering you." The Man in Linen said, "I saw my grandfather and remembered what happened to him." The gabbai said, "In any case, I beg you to come to us for Sukkot, and if that is impossible, come for Shemini Atzeret for the prayer for rain." The Man in Linen was silent and did not answer one way or the other.

Sukkot passed and Simḥat Torah came, but the Man in Linen did not come. Two days after the holiday, someone from our town happened to be traveling somewhere. On the way, at a certain town, the wagon driver said, "This town is where my home is. Let me go and look in on my family." He said to him, "What is the name of this town?" He told him. He said, "It seems to me that this is the town where Gavriel the linen dealer lives." He said, "You call him Gavriel the linen dealer, and we call him the friend of God." He said to him, "Can you bring me to his house?" He said, "Why not?"

He came to his house and found him wrapped in a talit and tefilin and reciting the deathbed confession. After he finished the confession, he said to the people of his house, "Get together a minyan for me, for I want to return my soul to the Master of Souls among a minyan of Jews."

They cried in horror, "What are you saying? Thank God you are healthy, with no symptoms of illness." He showed them a beaming face and said to them, "It has come to be God's will to take me to Him today." All the Jews of the village gathered and came as one person. The Man in Linen looked at each individual and said to them, "Thank you for coming. I won't keep you long." He stood and untied his tefilin and drew his talit down over his face, which was burning as if on fire. After a little while, he said, "Open the windows and make room for me." He lay down on the floor of the house and began to murmur verses of the Song of Songs. When he reached the verse *Many waters cannot extinguish love,* he passed his hand over his forehead and spread his hand in front of his eyes and stared at it. Again he passed his hand over his eyes and closed his eyes and left the world.

He was given a Jewish burial.

People spoke about this event for a long time, but none of the wise men could find out what it meant. Someone said, "I heard his davening and realized that he was a true master of prayer. Now that I heard what happened to him, I say that it is very likely that he was called to serve in the celestial choir, either to help the cantor or to be appointed himself as cantor."

Only He who hears the prayers of Israel knows.

Translated by Raymond P. Scheindlin

The Ḥazzanim, Continued

At last, a ḥazzan came to our city, and his name, too, was Gavriel. If I am not mistaken, he was a kohen, and he was appointed ḥazzan.

I shall relate the matter as it transpired.

Between Passover and Shavuot, ḥazzanim are exempt from leading prayers in their own communities. Instead, they travel from place to place and are remunerated for leading prayers. In some places, there is a fixed fee for their performance. In others, a delegation of three or four makes the rounds of the households after the conclusion of the Sabbath, and each gives according to his means or according to his desire to call attention to himself. One day, Gavriel the ḥazzan happened upon our city. In his youth, he had assisted the ḥazzan of Lublin; after that, he was appointed second ḥazzan in the synagogue of the Maharsha in Ostrow, and after that, first ḥazzan in the community of Kamenetz-Podolsk. He put together a choir and made a name for himself, circulating among the large and small cities between Passover and Shavuot, as was the wont of ḥazzanim, performing here one Sabbath and there another. He arrived in Buczacz for one of these Sabbaths and led the congregation in prayer on Sabbath and stayed for another Sabbath. His prayers touched the hearts of the men of the Great Synagogue and even the hearts of those from other study houses who came to hear his prayers.

At the conclusion of the Sabbath, R. Gavriel and all his choir singers went to the home of the rabbi and sang hymns for the conclusion of the Sabbath, and when the time arrived to sing "There Once Was a Ḥasid," he sang in such a way that all could feel just how poor this ḥasid was, subsisting without food and without sustenance and without clothes to wear, and all could see how he lived with his dignified wife and their five sons. When he mentioned those five sons, the voices of his singers sounded just like the voices of children begging for bread. So, too, with the voice of the wife imploring him, What shall we eat now? and hurrying him to the market with the hope that the Merciful One would take pity on them. The ḥasid accepted her advice and said, You have advised me well, but how can appear in the market without proper clothes to wear or a penny to my name? So she borrowed proper clothes from his neighbors. To make a long story short: when the ḥazzan concluded the hymn with Elijah's sudden disappearance, all the listeners looked about to see just where he had flown off to.

To make a long story short, no one would leave the rabbi's house until R. Gavriel was appointed the ḥazzan of the synagogue.

I now need to relate the crux of the matter.

But when R. Gavriel heard that the community could not afford to pay for the choir, he refused the appointment. The next day, he sent his bass singer to hire a carriage so that they could leave the city. All the carriage drivers declared that even if all their carriages were filled with gold and silver, they would not transport the ḥazzan from Buczacz. When he attempted to hire a carriage from a gentile, the carriage owners told the gentile that they could not be held responsible for the lives of his horses. That is what they said to every gentile whom the bass tried to hire. R. Gavriel and his choir were compelled to stay in Buczacz another day and yet another. He himself had no interest in speaking ever again with anyone in Buczacz.

Meanwhile, the prominent men of the city got together and said, Just because Buczacz wants a ḥazzan, should his choir singers starve to death? These men would not budge until they found those willing to commit themselves to pay for the choir out of their own pockets until such time as each singer could find a situation with another ḥazzan. They then went to R. Gavriel and asked him whether he would agree to these terms. R. Gavriel screamed out in anger, I certainly will not agree!

At the time of this dispute, the eminent R. Kehat was sojourning in our city, having come to settle the matter of the ḥalitzah of his sister, who had been waiting approximately ten years for the brother of her deceased husband to reach bar mitzvah age, so that he could perform the ḥalitzah ceremony and exempt his sister-in-law from levirate marriage. That same year, R. Kehat had assumed the position of head of the community of Podheitz. R. Kehat took a look at the bass, and fancied him for his sister. He began talking to the bass, asking him, Is it better for you to be under the thumb of a ḥazzan or to be a ḥazzan in your own right? Come with me to Podheitz, and I will make you the ḥazzan of the synagogue there.

The idea seemed good to the bass, so he went and told R. Gavriel. R. Gavriel said, So how did you reply to the man making you this offer? The bass said, I told him I would go and speak about it with the ḥazzan. R. Gavriel said, What did you expect the ḥazzan to say to you? He said, That's what I came here to find out. R. Gavriel said, And what do you expect to hear? The bass said, I expect the ḥazzan not to be angry with me if I choose to go to Podheitz.

The ḥazzan put his foot out and pushed the bass away, screaming in anger, Get lost, and let me never see your face again!

The bass went with R. Kehat to Podheitz and took with him the youngest of the choir singers, as he was his guardian.

When R. Gavriel's anger subsided, he went to the rabbi for the purpose of bringing a legal claim in the rabbinical court against the community. R. Tzadok, the son of R. Shlomo the salt merchant, who had been advising R. Gavriel from the time he had arrived in the city, heard about all this and went out to meet him, saying, I hear you intend to bring a case against the community. What do you hope to gain from this? Even I have no idea whether it is you or they who will be found liable. But I will tell you, never once have I heard that an individual who sues the entire community ends up deriving any benefit whatsoever from the court's ruling, even if the entire matter were ruled in his favor.

R. Gavriel screamed out in anger, If that is the case, there is no law and no justice in this world! R. Tzadok said, The world is as it is.

There is law and there is justice. But what can a poor community do, if it cannot afford to maintain a choir? It is enough for Buczacz to take on the salary of a ḥazzan. R. Gavriel said, What would you have me do? R. Tzadok said, I have two pieces of contradictory advice for you.

And what are these pieces of advice?

The first is that you assume the post of ḥazzan and lead the services here in Buczacz, and that over the course of the year you disband your choir. The other is that you say farewell to Buczacz and leave in peace.

R. Gavriel kept silent and returned to his lodgings. There he called together his choir and told them to gather their things together, saying, We are leaving this place today.

It wasn't more than an hour before they were all ready to leave. R. Gavriel departed from the lodgings, together with his choir singers. The people of Buczacz saw them and told R. Gavriel not to leave. As for R. Gavriel, he said nothing. After considerable pleading on their part, R. Gavriel sat down on a rock, tore off his shoes, and threw them down in anger, screaming, These shoes that have tread upon the dust of Buczacz, I don't want them on my feet.

After that, he stood up on his bare feet and walked at the head of his choir, his talit and tefilin on his arm, his walking stick in hand.

Women came out of their houses and screamed, Compassion has ceased in Buczacz! Jews are walking barefoot in the mud and muck, carrying their belongings in their hands, and no one takes pity on them enough to give them a horse and carriage.

One of the carriage drivers said, He's a stubborn one, that ḥazzan. Even so, it's not right to let him walk barefoot through the rocky and hilly streets of Buczacz.

His comrades said, Ḥazzan, climb aboard, choose whichever carriage most appeals to you, and be on your way.

R. Gavriel looked at them said, You are mocking me. They said, Heaven forfend. R. Gavriel said, Are there men of kindness left in this town whose name is not worth uttering? They said, Do not speak so harshly, ḥazzan. Even the horses in Buczacz prefer gentle talk.

The ḥazzan said, How much? How much is this trip going to cost me? They told him, Do not worry, we will get you on your way. In any case, we will not charge you a gold coin for each and every footstep of the horses.

The ḥazzan sat together with his choir singers in the carriage and was silent. The carriage driver began to sing. The ḥazzan listened and noticed that he was singing his tune for Veshamru in a lovely voice. Suddenly, the carriage driver stopped singing. R. Gavriel asked, Why did you stop? He said, To tell you the truth, while I was singing Veshamru to the ḥazzan's melody, it suddenly seemed as if it were Sabbath today. I was frightened at the thought of violating the Sabbath, and so I stopped. R. Gavriel said, If so, sing another tune.

The carriage driver began singing another one of R. Gavriel's melodies. R. Gavriel said to his choir singers, Why does Buczacz need a ḥazzan if its carriage drivers know how to sing so well? The melodies soothed R. Gavriel's anger at the people of Buczacz such that he began to chat with the carriage driver. He told the ḥazzan the story of the Man Dressed in Linen. R. Gavriel was astonished two times over: first, that he did not want to accept a salary for leading prayers; and second, that he followed his wife's advice and did not accept the position as ḥazzan. R. Gavriel said to his choir, Now I know why they say that all ḥazzanim are idiots. For was it not idiotic for him not to accept a position as ḥazzan on account of his wife?

The carriage driver also told him about R. Elyah, of blessed memory, who led the congregation's prayers for some seventy years. And about Miriam Devorah, the wife of R. Elyah the ḥazzan, who composed such lovely melodies that they say that R. Elyah included some of them when he led prayers for the community. He spoke about the ancestors of R. Elyah who were ḥazzanim in Buczacz in generations past, one hundred, two hundred, three hundred years ago.

R. Gavriel sat and listened. In the end, he said about himself, And this idiot was appointed ḥazzan in Buczacz, and left there on bad terms. After that, R. Gavriel asked the carriage driver, Why don't you sing us one of the melodies of the Linen Man? The carriage driver said, It would not be good manners for me to sing one of these melodies before the ḥazzan of Kamenetz-Podolsk. R. Gavriel said to his choir, Have you ever in your life seen people as well-mannered as the people of Buczacz, who refuse to sing the melody of another ḥazzan in my presence?

They traveled for as long as they traveled, until night fell and they reached their inn. The next day, the carriage driver passed the ḥazzan and his choir onto another driver, and then took his leave and returned to Buczacz. I do not know how much he asked for his services. From the sound of R. Gavriel's blessings, it could not have been a lot.

From the time R. Gavriel left Buczacz, he fell outside the history of the ḥazzanim in Buczacz. But I will return to him later. How so, you will just have to see.

Two years passed, and no ḥazzan was appointed in Buczacz. Perhaps it was because of the dwindling of the community, or perhaps because R. Gavriel had slandered the community, saying that it did not treat its ḥazzanim well, such that no ḥazzan was willing to come to Buczacz. So it was that two years passed without a ḥazzan being appointed in Buczacz, and no appointment seemed likely in the near future, either.

Then one day, around Rosh Hashanah, a guest arrived in Buczacz, who looked like R. Gavriel but did not act like him. R. Gavriel was demanding, ill-tempered, and irascible, whereas this man spoke peaceably and amiably to everyone. In the end, it became clear that it was R. Gavriel after all and that he had come to town on account of a marriage prospect because during the intervening two years since he had last been in Buczacz, his wife had passed away. There are those who say that while he did not anticipate this, his mazal did, which is why he took off his shoes and walked around in his stocking feet. In any case, after two years without a wife, he made up his mind to marry a woman who happened to live in our city, and so R. Gavriel came to town to propose to and marry this woman. She did not want to move with him back to Kamenetz-Podolsk, and so R. Gavriel stayed with his wife in Buczacz. You may remember my mentioning those women who came out of their houses and screamed over the fact that people were letting the ḥazzan walk barefoot and were not giving him a horse and carriage. It is worth mentioning now that at the head of this group was the very woman who married R. Gavriel.

So it was that R. Gavriel found a wife and a great good, for she was an honest, God-fearing woman of impeccable manners and an expert in the Holy Scriptures. People began asking her whether perhaps her husband would agree to lead services for the High Holidays. She laughed and said, You remind me of those who said to Samson's wife, *Entice thy husband.* My husband is right here before you. You speak with him as you see fit.

R. Tzadok the son of R. Shlomo the salt merchant and a few other men came to their house and began speaking with R. Gavriel about whether he would be willing to lead the prayers on the High Holidays. R. Gavriel said, I will be praying on the High Holidays in any case. I can simply raise my voice a bit and, in that way, serve as your ḥazzan for the High Holidays.

So it was that R. Gavriel passed led the prayers on the first day of Seliḥot and the evening and Musaf services on Rosh Hashanah, on Yom Kippur eve, Musaf and Neilah, and his davening was accepted below as well as on high. Below, that is, in the hearts of those in the Buczacz synagogue. On high, that is, before He Who mercifully hears prayers from the mouths of all His people Israel. As on the High Holidays, so, too, he led prayers on Sukkot, Shemini Atzeret, and Simḥat Torah. It is worth mentioning that on Sukkot eve, when he added the ma'aravot hymn "Those Who Carry Plantings Have Their Fill of Joy," joy indeed filled the hearts of those in the synagogue and increased each day of the holiday even beyond Simḥat Torah. This is what I shall say about those communities that do not say piyyutim: I know their reasons, but when I am reminded of the taste of the piyyutim and how much joy they added to the holiday, I pity those who deprive themselves of the piyyutim.

Gavriel served as ḥazzan for five years and the community was pleased with him, for they knew that he was God-fearing, and surely heaven was pleased with him, too. But on several occasions, he caused pain to certain householders for shortening the number of melodies under the ḥuppah at weddings or at circumcision ceremonies. He did this even to the wealthy folk. *Riches profit not on a day of wrath* if it was wrath he felt for that individual. But in all other respects, his deeds were righteous. You might even say that R. Gavriel assumed the manners of Buczacz.

R. Gavriel served as ḥazzan for five years and then left the position because of a dream. For eight days in a row, he had the same dream.

What was this dream? He was leading the prayers on Yom Kippur and was reciting Ahavah Rabbah when he reached "And our hearts will cleave to your mitzvot," his hands gathered the fringes of his tzitzit, but the fringes escaped his fingers, once, twice, three times, up to eight times, and when he finally managed to gather the fringes, his talit slipped off. They said to him, But the Shema and its blessings are recited during the morning service on Yom Kippur, and you lead the Musaf service, which does not include the Shema with its blessings, and on festival or High Holiday evenings, when the fringes are not gathered.

The ḥazzan's distress was soothed by their words, and he was just about to resume his post as ḥazzan when another dream came to him such that he left town for good. What was this dream? He was singing in the choir of the ḥazzan of Lublin on Yom Kippur eve, accompanying the ḥazzan with his tender voice. Suddenly, the ḥazzan looked at him, struck him on the head, and screamed, Wicked one: where are your tefilin?

The people of Buczacz said to R. Gavriel, One doesn't wear tefilin on Yom Kippur. Moreover, when you were in the choir of the ḥazzan of Lublin, you were but a boy, around eight or nine years old, and so you weren't obligated to wear tefilin. These words soothed the ḥazzan's anguish, and he was just about to return to his position as ḥazzan, when another dream came to him that changed his mind once again.

R. Gavriel did not tell his dream to anyone; but from his pain, the people could see that it was indeed a bad dream, even worse than the previous ones. From then on, he did not go near the prayer-stand nor did he lead any of the prayers, even on his mother's or father's yahrzeit. Rather, he would sit for hours every day in the synagogue in his talit and tefilin, even beyond the time of the afternoon service, and he would fast many fasts and remained miserable all the time. On occasion, he would ask one of the singers in the community to sing him one of his melodies, but just as they would begin, he would interrupt them and say, Pardon me, I must go to the scribe to have him check my tefilah. Tefilah, he would say, in the singular, rather than in the plural, as in a pair of tefilin. By the same token, he would change the fringes on his prayer shawl several times a year or even pay for an entirely new prayer shawl.

His close kin found out the substance of his dream when he was near death. When he served as the associate ḥazzan in the Jewish community of Ostrow in the great synagogue and stood at the prayer-stand during the morning service on the first day of Rosh Hashanah, a cannon that had been suspended in the synagogue from the days of Khmelnitski fell on his maḥzor and on the stand, which sunk into the ground from the force of the impact. He heard a kind of voice speaking, saying, All this is the result of your actions.

When he died, they found that he had several pairs of tefilin and several bundles of tzitzit and several prayer shawls.

(When he was nearing his end, he asked to have sung to him his melody for "The Lord Is My Shepherd." And then he sang in a weakened voice "Accept the Utterances of My Mouth" from the prayer for rain, and repeated it several times until his soul departed.)

During that time, Menasheh Kravitz, who had been appointed ḥazzan in Podheitz after marrying the widowed sister of the head of the community of Podheitz, arrived in our city. He went to visit R. Gavriel because years ago, he had been in his choir. When Menasheh came to the house, R. Gavriel did not recognize him because back then, he was a young man and, like other young men, had been clean-shaven, whereas now he had a full beard. When R. Gavriel finally recognized him, he welcomed him warmly and made no mention of his prior sin of leaving his choir without a bass. They sat for a while and spoke about where life had taken them and recalled those early days when their greatest happiness was to hear a beautiful melody. And since they were talking about those early days and the melodies most beloved to the people, R. Gavriel starting singing a melody, and Menasheh accompanied him. Then R. Gavriel said to Menasheh, Why don't you sing one of the melodies that you learned after you left my choir? Menasheh sang one of those melodies. And then R. Gavriel sang some of the melodies that he composed after leaving his post as ḥazzan. When R. Gavriel observed that Menasheh was very moved by these melodies, he placed his hand on Menasheh's shoulder and said, I see that you like them. Menasheh said, I have never heard melodies more beautiful than these. R. Gavriel said, I must make you swear that you will not sing them, not in public and not in private. If in heaven, my prayers are not wanted, I do not want to bother the world with them. R. Gavriel wept, Menasheh wept, the two of them wept together.

After that, R. Gavriel said, If I could only go to the Land of Israel, all would change for me for the good, but the Land of Israel is there and I am here, and I see no way to go to the Land of Israel other than to wait for the coming of the messiah and to go with along with the rest of the people of Israel.

R. Gavriel then turned quiet, as if he were cut off from the world. Finally, he said to Menasheh, You are going, I see. Go and come back after the evening service, and we will eat the evening meal together. Menasheh got up and left.

After the evening service, Menasheh came back. R. Gavriel's wife set the table, they sat down, and ate and drank. R. Gavriel did not speak much with Menasheh during dinner. After the final washing of the hands, R. Gavriel sang "By the Rivers of Babylon." Tears streamed down Menasheh's face. R. Gavriel's wife wept as she did on Yom Kippur upon the recitation of "These [martyrs] I remember." R. Gavriel sang it once and then again another time. After he completed the last verse, they had to prop him up so that he would not fall off his chair. He managed with great difficulty to say the grace after meals, and after that, they put him to bed. Menasheh said, Ḥazzan, are you feeling better? R. Gavriel smiled and said, Gavriel is not going to subject the world any longer to his vain utterances.

He pointed to the prayer book on the table and said, Read me the Confession.

R. Gavriel's wife heard this and began to scream, Gavriel, Gavriel, you shall live yet, and for many more years. He said, Close the windows, and summon some men so that I can die in the presence of a minyan. An hour had not passed before the room was filled and the house was so surrounded that the windows were darkened. None of them heard his voice as it was already circulating in the realms where only true voices are heard.

So long as R. Gavriel was alive, even though he did not pass before the teivah, the teivah did not complain about the prayer leaders because no one without a pleasant voice dared approach the teivah. For if he sang a melody incorrectly or mispronounced a word, R. Gavriel would turn up his nose and say, Hmm, causing the prayer leader to quake unto his very bones.

When R. Gavriel passed away, the prayer leaders stopped being as meticulous. There were men who burst upon the teivah who were not competent when it came to knowledge of the proper melodies or how to sing. Things got to the point that the prayer leaders were mispronouncing words in the prayers. Men observing a yahrzeit began claiming that it was their due to lead prayers on that day. Thus the teivah was held hostage by anyone who wanted to hear his own voice, no matter what it sounded like. But what could be done? When a ḥazzan with proper training and proper Hebrew presented himself, the synagogue did not have enough to pay him. He made clear that he was willing to make do with what they could offer, but then people began to say that he was not like R. Elyah or like the Gavriels. Thus they never reached an agreement, and no ḥazzan was appointed.

One clever man said, Let us do what the Polish nobles did with respect to crowning a king.

What did the Polish nobles do when they could not decide among them who to crown? They decided that whoever came to the city first the next morning would be their king. Given that this story is told in the annals of Poland, there is no need to go over it again.

One day, a Russian Jew came to our city. This was at a time when people were not so accustomed to traveling from country to country on account of the difficulty of traveling and the ease of staying put. If one could stay where he was, that was what he would do rather than seek other places to live. What caused this man, then, to leave his former place? It was because of something that happened to him.

In that generation, troubles beset the Jews of Russia, as the evil czarist empire imposed one evil decree after another upon the Jews in order to doom them and, heaven forbid, lead them to deny the God of Israel.

Among these evil decrees was that of conscripting Jews into the czar's army. This is what the government would do: it would announce to the communities that they would have to produce such and such number of conscripts, a number that could not be met. The government would soften the decree in its typical fashion, permitting the communities to take boys from age seven and up and, in that way, fulfill the required amount. Because boys of this age are not soldiers, the government would train them for war. How so? They would send them to places within

Russia where there were no Jews in order to accustom them to the religions of the gentiles until the boys grew old enough to serve in the army. They would offer the boys all kinds of gifts in order to win their hearts. A few were won over. Most were not. Those who were not won over were beaten. Those who died from the beatings, died. Those who survived were handed over to the czar's army. There is no suffering on the part of the Jewish people in which Jews themselves are not involved. There were those evil sinners who presented themselves to the government for the purpose of producing Jewish children for the czar's army. If they saw a boy walking to ḥeder, they would kidnap him and hand him over to the czar's officers. Kidnappers prowled the streets of every city where Jews lived, snatching little children from their mothers and handing them over to czar's officers, who would, in turn, hand them over to gentiles far away, who would beat them cruelly on account of their Jewishness. The gentiles justified this by saying that the beatings beat the Jewishness out of them.

At this point, I shall note the exceptions to the rule, namely, those Jews in Russia who would save their children from the kidnappers by hanging a little pouch form their necks in which they would write down the child's lineage and then smuggling him over the Russian border into Galicia. I was acquainted with two elderly bothers in Buczacz, one of whom became a great Torah scholar and who, at age seven, had been smuggled over the Podvolochisk border together with his younger brother and brought to our city.

We now return to the subject of the guest who arrived in our city from Russia. On one occasion, he witnessed two kidnappers snatching a child. He put himself in danger and grabbed the child from the kidnappers and fled with him to Galicia. At the same time, he heard that in Buczacz they were looking for a prayer leader, and so he went to Buczacz. They tested him on the various prayers, hymns, and yotzrot that ḥazzanim usually struggle with on account of their difficult language, and he succeeded in every case. They said to him, Your voice is pleasant and your pronunciation is correct, but you come from a faraway place and no one knows you here. He told them, the Tzaddik of Ruzhin knows me, and he lives in Sadigura. You can write and ask him about me.

They heard this and trembled. Given the fact that Buczacz does not even allow ḥasidic leaders to stay overnight in the town, is it likely that they will accept a prayer leader who is vouched for by such a rabbi? Nevertheless, because he led prayers so pleasantly and he was respectable and polite in every way and everyone in the community was so pleased with him, they agreed to write to the rebbe from Ruzhin. The rebbe responded, The person about whom you are inquiring is beloved in this place by everyone.

And so they accepted him as ḥazzan. Because I do not like repeating what I have written elsewhere and because I already spoke of most of his deeds in my story "The Sign," I will skip this material and move on. I will simply add that the ḥazzan lived long, like the previous ḥazzanim in Buczacz, who lived long and led the prayers up until their very last days. I will also add, and I do not know whether I have already mentioned this elsewhere, that many times during the recitation of hymns, it seemed as if he no longer had the strength to utter another word; but in the end, he overcame this, and his voice grew ever stronger, like a man who has something particular to say and strives with all his strength to make this thing heard.

And now I have arrived at the last of the ḥazzanim who served in Buczacz before the First World War, which was also the beginning of the Second World War, which brought calamity to the entire world, with us at the head, for the Holy One, blessed be He, knows us better than any of the other peoples on earth, and it is for this reason that he visits all their sins upon us. So long as the Temple was standing and the people of Israel dwelled in their own land, God held us accountable only for our own sins, as it is written, *You alone have I singled out of all the families of the earth—that is why I will call you to account for all your iniquities.* When our city was destroyed and we were exiled and dispersed among all the nations, God began holding us accountable not only for our own sins but also for the sins of the nations in whose midst we dwelled.

The last ḥazzan to serve in Buczacz was a man of pleasant manners and voice. Every day after praying in the Great Synagogue, he would sit in the old beit midrash before a volume of the Talmud or another work of scholarship. In those days, my own father was one of the denizens of the house of study, so I had the opportunity to speak with the ḥazzan every so often and even to show him some of my poems. He composed melodies for two of them, in fact. Because I have no training in playing music or singing, these melodies did not last with me; in fact both the poems and the melodies have been lost.

Translated by Wendy Zierler

R. Moshe Aharon the Mead Merchant

After R. Zvi left the position of gabbai, R. Moshe Aharon was prevailed upon to accept the responsibility of filling that position, thereby adding to the other tasks that the community had set for him, as well as the tasks that he had taken upon himself. R. Moshe Aharon was one of the most formidable inhabitants our city. He was the son of R. Neḥemiah, the son of the prodigy R. Aharon, who died during the lifetime of his own father, R. Shaul, who had given him the added name of Moshe during his illness. When the Turks attacked the city and Sobieski and all his troops joined in that battle, R. Shaul came to the aid of the city, sword in hand, bringing along a host of warriors to stand at the side of R. Yeraḥmiel, who had been appointed by the city officials to defend the Street of the Jews. During the battle, a Turk leaped up and with his sword wounded R. Shaul, who took ill from his wounds. So they added the name Moshe to his own name because Moshe was always added to the name of an ailing Torah scholar, and R. Shaul was renowned in his generation as an outstanding Torah scholar.

R. Moshe Aharon was not counted among the lomdim, those who were constantly immersed in study, but he was considered learned in the Torah. While he was still a youth, his father had sent him to study with his kinsman, the rabbi of Yaslowitz, who gave him as a wedding gift the *Tzemaḥ David,* a work composed by the outstanding rabbi of his generation, R. David Ganz. In that work, one finds all the events affecting the Jews and the entire world from the time of the first man to the generation of the author, which preceded R. Moshe Shaul by two generations. (The rabbi of Yaslowitz also gave R. Moshe Aharon the manuscript of *Sefer Neḥmad veNa'im.* This manuscript lacked none of the many diagrams that were included in the book, which contained information about the shape of the four basic elements, the nine galaxies, the height of the sun, and the height of every star beyond the horizon, and about many other wondrous phenomena.)

R. Moshe Aharon learned a great deal from the *Tzemaḥ David,* but after he read from the book about the greatness of kings and emperors he learned even more. Yet the more he learned, the more he felt saddened that the glory of the Jews had been taken from them and given to the nations of the world. How could this have happened? All the nations of the world have emperors and kings, princes, officials, and rulers, whereas we, the holy people Israel, are mired in exile without a king or a ruler or a sovereign.

(He also meditated on the *Sefer Neḥmad veNa'im.* From that volume, he learned about the affairs of the world and about the stars. About the North Pole he learned that those who live there have daylight for six months followed by six months of nighttime. This, too, he found in that book: the existence of a new world called Amorico, which had been discovered in the year 1492 and the existence of a land called Peru, which some say is the land of Ophir, where King Solomon, may he rest in peace, sent his ships. That book did not remain long in R. Moshe Aharon's possession. For when R. Moshe Aharon told the noble who owned the city about the discovery of the new land of Amorico, he was told that this was just another of the fabrications that the Jews fill their books with. R. Moshe Aharon responded, I am not an expert in all the languages of the world, and I do not know what is written in all their books, but you will discover that everything I have told you can be found written in Latin. Then R. Moshe Aharon took out *Sefer Neḥmad veNa'im* and showed it to the ruler, together with a copy of that work written in Latin, which almost certainly included the material written about in the holy tongue of Hebrew. The ruler borrowed the book from him but never returned it. This led R. Moshe Aharon to declare that a Jew should never tell a gentile anything that the gentile knows nothing about and that a Jew should never take into his home any book written in the language of the gentiles.)

R. Moshe Aharon was tall and handsome, with a full beard and sharp eyes. His long sidelocks fell beneath his ears. He walked with measured steps, and his voice was robust and resonant. From the time he came of age, he never uttered an extraneous word, and he paid no heed to people's talk. When people spoke to him, it was never clear whether he had heard them. When he did respond, however, he spoke with the authority of a judge rendering a ruling or a rabbi declaring that something is kosher or treif.

He wore an old coat lined with cotton and a gray hat, wide at the bottom and narrowed in a circle to the top. It appeared to be woven, although, in fact, it was not. He never wore anything woven after once discovering that the threads in a garment he had purchased had been woven like the shape of a cross. Wearing these garments, he would go about his work, and wearing the same garments, he would receive princes and lords visiting who had come to taste his mead. Whenever he recited the blessings after meals or walked to the synagogue or set out to circumcise an infant, he would wear a coat over these garments, with a lambskin hat in place of his regular one. On Sabbaths and holidays, he would wear a satin coat and a silk hat. On Sabbaths in the winter, he would wear a marten-fur coat and a goatskin hat of such deep and lustrous blackness that it seemed to give off sparks of blue light. This hat was his most valued possession, not because of its beauty and not because there was none like it in the entire city.

It was because it had been given to him as a gift from his teacher, the rabbi of Yaslowitz, after he had saved the rabbi's life. It happened that after his wedding, the rabbi took him along with him to a meeting of the Council of the Four Lands. During their journey, an armed bandit jumped up and seized their carriage. He told the rabbi, Get down from the carriage, take off your clothes, and hand over your hat and your money! The rabbi was very well dressed, wearing an expensive hat worth about ten gold coins, and his valise contained several compartments filled with gold coins. R. Moshe Aharon jumped down from the carriage, surprised the thief from behind, threw him down, and thrashed him vigorously until he was unable to get up. Then R. Moshe Aharon jumped up onto the carriage, grabbed the reins from the driver, and drove the carriage to the city that was the seat of the council. A great fair was being held there, and many varieties of expensive merchandise usually unavailable in our land were offered for sale. It was there that the rabbi bought the hat for R. Moshe Aharon.

For himself, R. Moshe Aharon purchased some Talmud tractates as well as a book containing the commentaries of the Maharsha. It has been said that when learned people inspect the Maharsha's work, some ask, Why did the author take the trouble to write down his commentaries and publish them in a book when they are really self-evident? Then when they reexamine them, they admit, It is not so much that they are self-evident, but because they coincide with the true law, we would have come to the same conclusion by ourselves, even though we did not reach our conclusion until after we looked at them.

It was for this reason in Buczacz that when someone responded to a talmudic insight by saying, Yes, yes, I know, I know, it was said of him that he had the mind of the Maharsha.

As long as his father, R. Neḥemiah Shaul, was alive, he ate at his table and assisted him in his mead trade, an enterprise in which his family had always been involved. When R. Neḥemiah departed for his eternal home, leaving no children other than R. Moshe Aharon, the son inherited the house as well as the cellar, which was filled with valuable casks of mead. Among them were round casks filled with mead from the days of the early lords who ruled Buczacz and its environs from the time before the horrors of Khmelnitski, may his name be cursed. R. Moshe Aharon's beverages were much sought after by lords and princes; priests and abbots licked their fingers from the touch of it on their lips. No important banquet took place in which the host did not turn to his guests and say, And now, honored lords, now we shall drink a small drop from the cellar of the Mishiarin. Now, because they could not properly pronounce the name of Moshe Aharon, they would mumble Mishiarin. The priests would sing that all the Jews' houses should burn like stubble except for the cellar of the Jew who makes mead.

While his father was still alive, R. Moshe Aharon led the community, and all its affairs were conducted according to his instructions. For R. Neḥemiah Shaul was among those for whom the entire world was not worth as much as one hour studying Torah. Had he not accepted the responsibility of leading the community from his own father (as his father had accepted it from his father before him), he would have abandoned it to devote all his time to Torah. Once R. Moshe Aharon had grown up, the father gave up his involvement in all community matters, thus fulfilling the traditional teaching to make Torah study the equal of everything else.

After R. Neḥemiah had departed to his eternal home, there was no change in the management of communal affairs, with the one exception that where R. Neḥemiah used to sign his name in the city's pinkas, now it was R. Moshe Aharon who placed his signature. He also made decisions as he willed, and when he assembled the city leaders, it was only for the purpose of telling them, This I have done. If they said, You have done well, he would nod his head in agreement, but if they said, You need not have done that, or if they said, You should have done such and such, he would close his eyes as if he were asleep, and no one could know whether he had heard.

He conducted his affairs as leader autocratically, showing favor to no one and treating slanderers as they deserved. Once, in need of funds, the community levied a tax on its members. One individual requested to be excused from that tax because of his connections to the authorities. R. Moshe Aharon declared, The money will remain in your possession until the day when you are brought to your grave. At that time, several times the value of the debt will be collected from your heirs.

What he meant was that when that person dies and they take his body for burial, he would not be buried until they collect from his heirs the total amount that the head of the community obliges them to pay. While R. Moshe Aharon was alive, the insolent did not dare to complain, and the quarrelsome bit their tongues. And whenever they came to tell him, So-and-so said such-and-such about you, he told them, As long as he does not come and tell me that *you* have said the same about me, he is not someone with whom I would deign to speak.

A distinguished householder once complained that a community representative had not treated him with the respect that he deserved. Here is R. Moshe Aharon's reply: Wait until Yom Kippur eve, when he will want to appease you, and if it is difficult for you to wait, forgive him right now. Someone else once said, My father, may he rest in peace, told me that your father, of blessed memory, spoke with everyone gently. R. Moshe Aharon replied, Why do you compare me with my father? My father saw that he was dealing with men of understanding like your father, but I see that I am dealing with troublemakers and malcontents like you.

Where did R. Moshe Aharon find the courage to act in that way? Many people have struggled with that question. The elders who knew him from his youth say that such a well-mannered young man was not to be found among all the students in the beit midrash. Those who had grown up with him and who had studied with him in ḥeder would say that he was good to his friends, that he would never do anything disagreeable to them, and that he never showed the slightest sign of aggressiveness, with one exception, and that was the time when he grabbed the teacher's strap out of his hands. The story goes that once a melamed was about to hit him, and if they had not taken the strap out of Moshe Aharon's hands, the melamed would have been struck by him. So we return once again to the question about the source of his aggressiveness. This remains a question without an answer.

I have already related that R. Moshe Aharon was a mead merchant. Now I wish to tell you that, in addition to providing him with an honorable living, his business activities were a source of blessing for the entire community. This can be seen from what happened to him with a great prince of the land, who ruled over a domain so enormous that a horse could not traverse it in a single day. That prince committed a sin so egregious that it was considered to be a great sin even among the gentiles; he sinned against his sister and her husband. Jealousy took hold of him and he became exceedingly jealous of them both, each one because of the other. His jealousy became unbearable. Before they were married, they had obeyed him; but afterward, they refused to do so. He hired assassins, who killed both of them at the same time.

After the deed was done, his conscience began to weigh heavily upon him. He could not undo what had been done and was unable to stop thinking about it. To divert himself from his anguish, he held banquets with songsters and clowns and storytellers. As long as was drinking wine and feasting and the singers were singing and the clowns entertaining and the storytellers reciting tales from ages past, his torment was assuaged. However, once the effects of the wine wore off and the music ended and the storytellers' tales ceased and the clowns' jokes ran out, his conscience came back to afflict him.

He went out hunting. He sighted an animal and was about to take aim when suddenly the animal spoke up: Do you intend to kill me as you killed your sister and her husband?

That the prince understood what the animal was saying should not surprise you because wild animals and birds are able to speak Hebrew, as we know from the incident of Balaam's talking ass. Now, the prince did not know Hebrew. However, animals, beasts, and birds do not waste a word, and they were not party to the sin of the generation of the Tower of Babel and remained unaffected by its punishment. They therefore retained their unitary language from the time when the entire world had one tongue. So when the animal opened its mouth to speak, the prince understood what it was saying. He threw away all his weapons and began to run.

He came upon a church and went inside. He bowed down before the statue they worshiped, walked around it, and heaped gold coins around it and around the statue of their worship's mother. He felt that these figures were considering him benevolently, for such indeed had been the intent of the artists who made them. He removed the gold rings from his fingers and gave them to the priests for tallow to make candles. He also sent the priests fat rendered from goats and lambs in a weight equivalent to that of his sister and her husband. He returned after a few days. By the light of the candles, he could make out the forms of a man and a woman. At first, he thought that they were visitors to the church; but suddenly, he realized that they were his sister and her husband. He first thought that they were alive, but when he looked again, he realized that they were dead. They followed him. He hid his face from them, but they would not let him go and made certain that he would be able to see them. Sometimes they appeared to be happy because death had united them, and sometimes they appeared to be sad because their lives had been taken away just when they had begun to enjoy life with each other.

It is not only Jews who are tormented by their sins, heaven forbid. Gentiles are tormented as well. But the trivial sins that torment a Jew are of almost no account to a gentile. There are sins, and there are sins. I have already dealt with this distinction in my book *Days of Awe* in connection with the confession, "For the sin that we have sinned against You with the evil impulse." All sins, of course, have their source in the counsels of the evil impulse, but there are some sins so terrible that even the evil impulse is embarrassed by them. And there are sins for which a man is not seduced by the impulse to evil but the other way around. He seduces his evil impulse and later blames it for his transgression. It is all the same for the sin, although it is not so for the thoughts that one has after the sin has been committed.

The prince realized that no matter how much he donated to the Church, it would not avail him. On the contrary, he was shown his sin from many different angles. To you, my friend, I need not explain that the Church is not equipped to help its worshipers or to teach those who have sinned about their sins. I am only relating you the thoughts of the prince after he had wasted large sums of money on the Church, including coins mixed with precious jewels and pearls. It was only afterward that he went to the priest to confess his sins.

The great priests, who know the lords and the princes and are familiar with their deeds, hear their confessions and search on their behalf for openings to penance. This was the case with the priest who heard what the prince had done and considered which path of repentance to recommend to him. He could hardly ask him to distribute more silver and gold to the Church. Charity for the poor? Who can determine the amount of charity needed to sustain a poor man? Whatever is adequate for a poor man who is starving will be less than adequate when he is starving no longer, and he will not be satisfied with the usual amount that had been given to him.

There is a grave in a certain place where a great miracle worker is buried, the priest told the prince. Go there, for surely he will favor you and plead for the forgiveness of your sins. But you must not be pompous, arriving in a horse-drawn carriage. Rather, travel there on foot like other penitents, and change into plainer garb because sometimes they want to show the people that they take no account of princes and lords.

The prince followed the advice of his father confessor. He sent away his horses and carriage, changed into plain clothes, and proceeded on foot. When he arrived there he did what is done when visiting the graves of their saints. He spread his arms straight out on both sides, forming the shape of a cross. After standing there for some time, he spread himself out in the shape of a cross on the length and width of the grave and proceeded to do the other things done by gentiles when they make pilgrimages to holy sites. I do not need to tell you, my friend, that all his efforts accomplished nothing for him, just as they accomplished nothing for the other sinners and ruffians who came to seek atonement.

On the contrary: one trouble followed another when he learned about a land known as Egypt—*Mitzrayim* in the holy tongue—where many caves had been carved into a mountain. The caves were dug out by holy men who lived their lives in them, this one on his knees, another fallen prostrate on the ground, and yet another spreading arms out to the right or to the left, one in silence and another calling out, this one laughing and that one groaning, this one sobbing and that one deep in thought. Now, among those caves was one in which a very holy man was buried, a man who had been an extravagant sinner in his youth. When he grew old, he regretted his misdeeds, ignored all worldly matters and lustful desires, and went into the wilderness, far, far away from any human habitation. There he hewed out a cave half his height; he kneeled there, not eating or drinking or bathing. Sores broke out on his body and exuded puss. Worms crept beneath his skin, licking his blood, and yet he paid no attention to them; it seemed that he did not even feel them, for his mouth was filled with praise to their savior for having shown him the way of repentance. Word spread, and people began coming to see him, for seeing him provoked thoughts of repentance. When the chief priest became aware of this, he had a monastery built near the cave so that the monks would learn not to follow their desires. Not long after, the holy man died, and they buried him in the cave that he himself had hewn.

It was the custom of one monk to visit the cave for solitary mediation. On a visit there one day, he heard a voice issuing forth from the cave. Although he listened attentively, he could not understand the language in which the voice spoke because he was not learned in languages. He informed the abbot, who came to the cave, together with his assistant and several elder monks, several of whom were experts in all the books of the Church. Greater than all of them was the abbot himself, who, in addition to his expertise in the books of their religion, knew languages unknown to most, as we soon shall see.

They listened carefully and heard the voice but could not understand the language that it was speaking. The abbot asked, Did you hear that? They all answered, We heard.

And what did you hear?

They were all in agreement, saying, We heard the voice but we did not understand a word. Their teacher said, Since that is so, I will tell you what the voice is saying. They all responded, Please, master, tell us!

He told them, I heard the worms that were rustling about in his body, saying, one to another, Now that he has died, who will feed us flesh, who will give us blood? Then I heard one worm saying, Instead of worrying about the food and drink that you lack, you should be happy that you are together with him in this cave because I have heard that it has been decreed from on high that a person who stays in our cave for three nights will be forgiven all his sins, even if he has committed sins for which there is no atonement.

When the monks heard this, they declared that because nowadays there are so many sinners, this is something that should be heard by everyone alive. So they went forth to spread the word throughout the world. (Truth to tell, many of the priests said that this was an exaggeration. They said that the worms were not speaking, but the *birds* were speaking, because during that holy man's life, he would share his food with the birds. Since he had died, they were weeping over what they now lacked. There was one exception to this, a bird that considered its soul to be more important than its body.) Be that as it may, there is no difference of opinion concerning the heart of the matter: every sinner who spent the night in that holy cave felt that he had been absolved of all his sins in the morning.

When word about this spread, all manner of sinners, men and women, came to spend two or three nights in the cave, each according to the gravity of his or her sin. I do not need to tell you, my friend, that their sins were *not* forgiven. Let it be hoped that they at least did not add more sins to those already committed.

When the prince heard about the power of the cave, he realized that he could not do better than make his way there as quickly as possible because his sins were driving him to the point of madness. Nevertheless, he succeeded in persevering and maintaining his sanity. It need not even be mentioned that this was due not to any merit of his own but to the merit of R. Moshe Aharon, the leader of the Jewish community of Buczacz. Now, what does R. Moshe Aharon have to do with that prince? We shall have to wait and see.

So the prince left the grave of the wonder worker, whose wonders were hardly wonders at all during his lifetime, not to mention after his death. The prince already had been astonished by the priest confessor's having advised him to wear his legs out, walking to a grave that held no hope as a source of salvation, when there was another grave that everyone claimed was a source of healing for every sinner. Because the prince was astonished by that priest confessor's advice, he came to doubt the depth of his learning. Nevertheless, he did not change his mind about going on foot because all sinners who had visited the grave of the miracle worker had gone on foot.

On the road, he was joined by men and women who were eager to reach the land of Egypt in order to stay at the holy cave where they would be eased of their afflictions, for their sins were afflicting them unceasingly. This was even truer for the prince, whose dead sister and brother-in-law harassed him constantly, whether he was awake or dreaming. I have already described how this happened when he was awake. Regarding his dreams, I must explain that from the day he first heard about the cave, he constantly thought about the prospect of staying there; and while in this state of anticipation, he would fall asleep. While he was in a deep slumber, his sister and her husband would appear to him and blast him with their accusations, venting their outrage that he had killed them while they were taking pleasure in each other.

The sinners walked along, group by group, one after the other. At times the prince walked with them, and at times he walked alone. When they noticed that he was walking alone, they would say to him, You had the strength to commit a sin, but you do not have the courage to repent. Pick up your feet and come along, you hunk of putrid flesh, for if you do not, we will leave you and you will never be able to find the way.

He struggled to keep up with them, but he could not. He had been able to sin, but to repent was beyond him. Realizing that he had no strength, they took pity on him and began to hold him up to make the difficult journey easier for him. Sometimes a man would support him, and sometimes a woman. The prince closed his eyes as he dragged his feet because he feared it might be his sister or her husband who was supporting him.

Suddenly, one of those supporting him said, It is hard enough for me to drag along my own sins; I do not want the burden of dragging along *this* one's sins as well.

So he let him go and walked away. The prince was left alone with another one of the sinners, who, to make the way seem shorter, began telling him about some of the sins that he had committed. The prince was astonished not by the sins that the man had committed but by his voice, the voice of a man who clearly was enjoying the recollection of his sins. The prince began to look around, this way and that. Many of the people already had begun to take their leave, yet he could still see them clearly. They all looked alike. The women looked like his sister, and the men like his sister's husband. Logically, this was impossible because his sister was just one person, and here there were many women. Furthermore, his sister had been killed by a murderer whom he himself had hired, whereas all these women were alive. The same with the men. Logically, it could not be, but when he saw them all, reason was obliterated. If he had already not gone crazy, he was sure that he would lose his mind before he reached the cave. But he did not lose his mind, neither on the way to the cave nor upon his return from the cave, as I alluded to earlier, alluding to the reason for it as well.

The sinners walked along, group by group, one after the other, men and women. The road was long, endless. But anyone who has not lost his sense knows how to make a journey shorter with intimate conversation or with conversations about times gone by. While moving from one conversation to another, a person comes to talk about himself and, in his own words, reveals the reason that he had decided to undertake such a long journey. Because he is already talking, he does not try to hide his transgressions, thus shortening the journey even more.

Sin is a heavy burden. For a person who is going to sin, there is so much care given and so much trouble taken. When a man recalls a sin from the past, he begins yearning for it. You may not hear as much from his words, but you can hear it in his voice. Each sin creates its own musical inflection, and when a sinner speaks about the sin in that special melody, he is speaking about the goodness that is associated with it. Each and every sin is associated with a saint, and the very mention of the saint's name leads to penance for that sin. Since we have no business with saints, not to mention their sins, we shall put them and their transgressions aside and return to the prince.

After many wanderings and endless struggles, he arrived in the land of Egypt. There he found a group that was going out into the desert to the cave of the saint. His own group, with which he had set out, had left him along the way. Some left because it was too hard for them to watch his struggles, and some left because they themselves left the road to repentance. Sometimes sin crouches at the site of repentance. To speak in allusions, I will only hint at the fact that along the way, a man found a woman in whose company he took pleasure, and they went on together without giving further thought to reaching the saint's cave and seeking his prayers on their behalf. Because I have taken so long to reach this point, I shall now be brief.

In short, the prince reached the desert near the city and approached the cave. He stayed there one night. On the following day, he was like a new man. His two wrathful companions, namely, his sister and her husband, disappeared and never showed themselves to him again. However, he was seized by a severe fever that rattled and convulsed him. I am not learned in medical tomes and know not whether already in the prince's time they called this affliction "cave fever," but he showed all the signs of that malady. His illness was so severe that he forgot about his sister and her husband, whom he had hired assassins to kill. Even though his illness was not contagious, his sister and her husband kept their distance from him; and even in his dreams, they no longer terrified him.

One day, a great lord arrived who was on a tour of the country. After he had visited all the sites that such a man is usually shown, he asked to see the sites that he had not been shown. In the manner of great lords who pay scant attention to the dwellings of the poor and needy in their own land, here in another land, he insisted on being shown the poor in their misery. Over and over again, they warned him that he would not be able to stand their stench and that he would be startled and stunned by their distressing appearance. However, no one could refuse him when he insisted upon seeing the poor and the needy in their hovels. It was during his tour that the lord came to the hospice where the prince lay. When the official took a second look at the prince, he realized that he was nothing at all like the other paupers. He told his companions something flattering about the ailing man, speaking in French so that the latter would not understand. The prince heard and responded in French. This startled the lord, who said, From the way that you speak, I realize that you are not like the other beggars. Who are you, and what brought you here?

The prince identified himself and explained that because of a certain matter, he had attached himself to the pilgrims who were journeying to the cave of the saint, that he had spent the night with them there, and that ever since, he had been seized with fever. The lord immediately seated him in his carriage and took him to his place of lodging, where he removed his soiled clothes and replaced them with fine garments befitting his rank, arranged for a bed, and brought him a doctor and medications. When the prince had begun to recover from his illness, the official hired a carriage and horses to carry him back to his land and gave him as a loan purses filled with gold coins.

Thus the prince began the journey back to his own land. In every city where he stopped, he consulted doctors. He found physicians of great repute, and the fees they charged were more costly than gold, as were the medications they prescribed. Yet their medicines not only yielded no improvement; they made him weaker than ever. This seems to be the way it is with such rarified elixirs—the greater their expense, the less effective their curative power. It was as if these medicines were saying to him, If you think you are so important that you can trouble us to take care of you, you are very much mistaken.

He heard that in a certain land, there was a great doctor named Charlatagne, who had cured kings and emperors. He traveled there and had to wait for quite some time before the doctor could see him because he was occupied treating the emperor's mistress. Finally, the prince was seen by the doctor. The doctor examined him and said, You were, in fact, not ill; it was all the doctors and their cures that made you ill. Had you come to me immediately, you would not have had to spend your money acquiring a serious illness brought on by those who were supposed to cure you. Nevertheless, I shall try to do everything in my power to cure you.

The doctor kept him there for many days, trying all sorts of medications. He did this first to counteract the effects of the drugs given him by the doctors and then to prepare his body for salubrious medications that would heal him and restore him to health. The prince began to recover, for he had obeyed the doctor and drank all the medications that the doctor had given him. The doctor was extremely busy, however, for after the emperor's mistress fell ill, the archbishop was afflicted by that same illness, to be followed by the children of the archbishop's sister and a number of prominent officials, men and women, for that is the way with contagious diseases. Not even the servants could escape the illness, and the doctors were exceedingly occupied with attending to the ill and their servants, who could endanger the entire land with their contagion, including the emperor and the empress.

The prince came to realize that many days would pass before he could be received by the doctor. So he said to himself, In the meantime I will take a trip to my own land and my own city to see what is happening there.

To tell the truth, when he had been in his land and in his city in the past, he paid no attention to what was happening there because he was immersed in his own pleasures. But now that he was far away from home, he felt obliged to return to his land and give some thought to what was taking place there. So he left the doctor's city and traveled to his native land and to his estates. His fever took his mind away from thinking about his sister and her husband, who had caused him such anguish; for if it were not for them, he would not have had to stay in the saint's cave and contract fever. Oh, that fever! Before he fell ill from it, he had believed that there is no affliction like the affliction of the soul. After it, he recognized that the suffering of the body can be as terrible as the suffering of the soul.

The prince had not even reached the region of his estates before he was seized by the fever and tormented by harsh and bitter pains. It was the end of the world! If only the whole world would end, along with that man! The prince had only himself in mind when he said that. The carriage driver saw the immensity of his master's suffering. With compassion for his master, he said, With your permission, my lord, if he wishes, we could stop at the nearest town, where my lord could rest and regain strength before continuing on to our destination. I can see that there is a town not far from here. If it pleases my lord, I could bring him to that town, where he could he could consult a doctor who might ease his suffering.

So they continued and reached the city. That city was Buczacz. Now it just so happened that the carriage stopped near the house of R. Moshe Aharon the mead maker, head of the community of Buczacz. His house was located at a site between the Serpent Bridge and the cemetery, but at the time, there was neither a bridge nor a cemetery there but only pasture. There, riders on horseback and passengers on carts would let their animals rest and drink from the stream.

Hearing the wheels of a carriage, R. Moshe Aharon peered out the window and saw a carriage with four horses harnessed to it. He reasoned that there must be an important lord sitting in the carriage. So he walked out and said to the prince, Please come into to my home, sir, and rest while the driver gives the horses water and feed. The prince stepped down from the carriage and entered the house of R. Moshe Aharon. I smell the aroma of mead, said the prince. Pour me a cup. So R. Moshe poured him a cup. Before the prince could bring the cup to his mouth, the fever took hold of him, and he was seized by terrible convulsions. Seeing his ordeal, R. Moshe Aharon said to the prince, My ancestors teach that there is no illness without a cure, and sometimes the Holy One creates the cure before the illness strikes. Lie down, sir, on the bed, and I will give you a cup to drink and, God willing, it will heal you.

R. Moshe Aharon removed the prince's clothes and laid him down on his bed, near the stove. Then he went down into the cellar and searched here and there among the barrels until he found a barrel of mead that his father, R. Neḥemiah, had purchased fifty years earlier from a nobleman, after the barrel had lain in *his* cellar nearly two hundred years. R. Moshe Aharon poured out a beaker so large that it could be carried only with great difficulty. He brought it up from the cellar, took a large cup, poured the drink into it, walked into his bedroom, and said to the prince, Drink, sir. And if it is too little for you, I will give you another cup. For I am convinced that once you taste this drink, you will be healed and will forget your illness and all the worthless doctors who have bothered you with their drugs.

The prince drank one large cup and asked for another. Before the second cup even touched his lips, he fell into a deep slumber. R. Moshe Aharon covered the prince with many blankets and sent the carriage away to the prince's city so that preparations could be made for his arrival; for in three days, he would be returning to his city and his home. The carriage continued on its way, while the prince lay sleeping upon R. Moshe Aharon's bed, sweating so profusely that all the blankets and pillows that R. Moshe Aharon had provided for him were soaked through and through.

Two days later, the prince awoke and opened his eyes and then closed them again. By the next day, the prince seemed to have regained his health. Looking at R. Moshe Aharon, the prince said, I think I have seen you before. But where have I seen you? Not in the land of Egypt. Maybe it was in Rome, or perhaps in France or in Germany. The prince went on to mention a number of other countries, cities and villages. Finally, slapping his forehead, he cried out in joy, You are the one who healed me!

At once, the prince took all the purses of gold that he had in the pockets of his garments and handed them to R. Moshe Aharon. This is what the prince told R. Moshe Aharon: Take this, my friend, take it, and when I reach home, I will send you more.... What's this? It looks like you are afraid to touch money! R. Moshe Aharon said, And because of the small cup that I poured for my master the prince, I should take all this gold? If my master the prince indeed has been cured, it is not because of any wisdom of mine but it because of His will, may He be blessed, who put the power of healing into this old drink to cure the prince.

The prince was astounded to hear this. All the physicians who were unable to cure him had taken huge sums from him, while this Jew who had healed him asked no reward.

News spread throughout the city and its environs that the great prince, who owned one-fifth of the land of Poland, had returned. All the important nobles of the land came to pay their respects to the prince, some by carriage and some by horse, for everyone had been asking where the prince had disappeared to. Some had assumed that he had gone for pleasure to the splendid city of Paris, and others had assumed that he had visited Rome to seek forgiveness for his sins, for who in this generation is so righteous that he has not sinned? Blessed is he who has enough silver and gold to journey great distances, even to the pope in Rome, the supreme head of all the priests, who can absolve any sinner of his sins. In brief, all the leading lords came to appear before the prince to share his great joy, and each one invited the prince to his palace for a day or two before he returned to his residence his own city. The prince told all of them, As long as my dear friend Mishiarin (that is, Moshe Aharon, namely, R. Moshe Aharon, leader of the Jewish community of Buczacz) gives me a place to stay in his home, I am not moving from here.

When these lords realized that R. Moshe Aharon was so beloved by the prince, they, too, began to speak to him with all sorts of terms of endearment, in the manner of officials who arrange their words appropriately when speaking to those who exceed them in importance, and each one told R. Moshe Aharon, I will do whatever you ask of me.

Yet the prince surpassed them all when he said, in the presence of all the officials and lords, Henceforth, the Israelite Moshe Aharon is under my personal protection; whoever harms him will pay with his life, and whoever pleases him pleases me as well. R. Moshe Aharon, pleased to hear their words, said, Distinguished, honored lords and his majesty the prince: I will do as you wish, and, with your permission, whenever I am in need of something that requires your help, I will ask you to trouble yourselves with it, secure in the knowledge that you indeed honor me and will never forget what you have promised.

When the prince heard this, he said, Woe to anyone who does not fulfill that promise, anyone who will not do whatever my dear friend Mishiarin asks of him. But you, my dear friend Mishiarin, turn not to them, but turn to me. Whatever you ask has already been granted.

While those words were being spoken, the leaders of the prince's city came to restore the prince to his city and his home. The prince asked them to wait "until I take leave of my dear friend, my beloved Mishiarin." He took leave of him with a hug and a kiss, saying, Do not forget that I shall protect you from every enemy and adversary; I shall always be your help.

When the officials saw how important the Israelite Mishiarin was in the eyes of the prince, they, too, showed him respect and affection. Then each one asked to buy several barrels of mead from him. And if the prince had not told R. Moshe Aharon to save some barrels for him, they would have emptied out the cellar without leaving even a small cask of mead for the last day of Passover. R. Moshe Aharon took note of this.

And so, year after year, the prince himself would come to visit R. Moshe Aharon. Sometimes he would stay for a day, and sometimes he would stay for two; and they would talk about worldly matters, the prince based upon what he had seen with his own eyes and R. Moshe Aharon from what he had read in the *Tzemaḥ David* or in the *Sefer Neḥmad veNa'im*. Not only was R. Moshe Aharon conversant with world history from the days of the first man, Adam. He knew how to speak Polish like the Polish elders who were true to their people and their land and who were content to be dwelling among their own people and not wander in other lands where people snatch a man's own language away from his very lips and replace it with a jumble of tongues. Because of the care they took, their language remained intact.

R. Moshe Aharon renewed the force of an old decree that forbade minyanim in villages on Rosh Hashanah and Yom Kippur. All village Jews, without exception, were required to spend those holy days in a synagogue in the city. For "the King is honored in the presence of great numbers of people" and those who live among the gentiles all year are likely to forget that they are Jews. You have no idea how miserable were those who lived in villages; most were illiterate, and most of their wives did not even know the blessings for the Sabbath candles. And he did not allow them to make a minyan in their homes. He would say, If I could find a legal support for it, I would establish a rule that required mourners to observe shiva in the synagogue courtyard, and not at home, so that we would never be short of worshipers in the synagogue.

Before his death, he divided his property into thirds: a third for his wife, a third for communal needs, and a third for the synagogue; for R. Moshe Aharon had no children, may the Merciful One have mercy. This will of his caused many arguments, for his brothers and all his other relatives came to claim their share of the inheritance; and they were poor.

A great funeral was arranged for him, with an impressive eulogy given by the rabbi. When the mourners returned from the funeral, the monastery students went on one of their rampages. Everyone who had accompanied the coffin fled this way and that and did not emerge from their hiding places until morning. Thus there was no minyan held in the house of the deceased. Many people said that this was a punishment, for what R. Moshe Aharon had visited upon others was done to him. He had planned to forbid mourners to have a minyan in the home of the deceased; therefore there was no minyan in his home. How blind people are! As if there never had been student rampages in Buczacz!

On the next day, the Holy One showed them that their thoughts are not the same as His. Before sunrise, people began coming from all the surrounding villages to comfort the widow. Not one village from the region surrounding Buczacz was not represented. Some came on the first day of mourning, some came on the second day, and so it went for the entire seven days. Of course, they came from villages that were near the city, but they also came from faraway villages. Many people thought very well of R. Moshe Aharon because of the ordinance he promulgated and enforced that require village dwellers to come to the city on Rosh Hashanah and on Yom Kippur. For in that way, the essential Jewishness of the village Jews could undergo a process of cleansing on those three sacred days when they prayed with other Jews and ate at their tables.

Thus we come to learn that anyone who tends to the needs of the community for the sake of heaven should have no fear of those who those who murmur against them. If you see the need to promulgate a new ordinance or to renew an ancient one for the sake of the many, then do it, and blessing will eventually come to you. As long as a man is alive, he is beset by many tribulations, and there are many people who say that there was no need for him to do what he did. After he dies, it is shown from heaven that everything he did was done for good reason.

With this, I conclude my narrative of a small portion of the deeds of R. Moshe Aharon, may he rest in peace; and to conclude, I shall relate part of what befell him during his lifetime. Three things occurred during R. Moshe Aharon's lifetime. The city's owner arranged a banquet for the wedding of his wife's daughter. High lords and officials attended the banquet, and each brought a gift. Those gifts included a monkey and a dwarf. The owners of those creatures happened to meet on their way to the courtyard of the mayor's home. They stepped out of their carriages to show one another what they were bringing, and thus everyone in the city saw the monkey and the dwarf. Upon seeing the monkey, they made the appropriate blessing. Upon seeing the dwarf, however, they did not because an idolatrous image had been drawn upon his forehead. And what is the third thing that occurred during R. Moshe Aharon's lifetime? On that day, a Negro appeared in the city. Everyone came out of their homes to see him and to say the blessing praising God "who creates a variety of creatures." It was later revealed that this really was not a Negro; it was the son of a noble who had blackened his face and his hands for the purpose of mocking God's creatures. In the end, he succeeded in mocking only himself. The color with which he had dyed his hands and face adhered to his skin and could not be removed with any known cleanser. He became an object of miserable derision to everyone who caught sight of him.

Translated by Jules Harlow

The Rabbi Turei Zahav and the Two Porters of Buczacz

After our rabbi, the author of *Turei Zahav,* published his book of commentaries, he began to have qualms lest he had presented something that did not agree with the law, and teachers relying on his work would be drawn, God forbid, into error. He carefully reviewed his teachings. As soon as he emerged safely from one law, another came and seized him. He acquitted himself from that one only to encounter one more difficult. Once he explained it, another appeared with its doubts. He despaired, thinking to himself, if this is what it is like for me, how must it be for others? Yet several great masters had praised his halakhic insights. Indeed, many praise a scholar as long as he remains in his own town. If he really wants to hear the truth, he should go someplace where no one knows him, for there the strength of his words will have to stand on their own unaided by reputation.

Our Rabbi examined his treatise. The book had already passed out of his hands and he could not have it back, nor could he chase after every person who had acquired it, saying, Do not base your decisions on the teachings in my book. He tore his eyes from the book, thinking, It seems to me that these thoughts have come only to distract me from my studies. Not long afterwards he took upon himself the pain of exile. Our Rabbi said, Exile brings atonement.

Our Rabbi took up the trappings of exile and left his house and his city. Only the mezuzah noticed that the town's rabbi had departed. He left his house and his city and began wandering from place to place, like wandering beggars and itinerant guests, except that, unlike those who stay in one place as long as possible, he never stayed the night in the same place he had spent the day, nor did he spend the day in the place he had stayed the night. During all those days of wandering, he never revealed who he was. If someone wished to speak with him, he took flight, but he always haunted the places where Torah was studied and drew close to Torah scholars.

After a year, ill from bodily fatigue and the hardships of the road, he reached a certain village. He put down his staff and knapsack and sat down to rest. As he sat himself down, he began to review what had happened since he had left his home, his house of study, and his city. He had suffered many hardships, seen many communities, and attended many houses of study. He had heard many words of Torah but had never heard his own commentaries mentioned. He had included in his book only matters that had been carefully investigated and only for the purpose of clarifying the law for students of the Torah. He gazed up to heaven, for if they don't know on earth, they know in heaven.

The heavens passed from phase to phase, from day to evening, shifting their light from one place to another. Even the trees of the field were changed. Formerly, they had been encompassed by light, and now they were steeped in darkness. A kind of darkness seeped out of them, as happens to trees on sunny days close to the hour of the afternoon prayer. For the day had already passed and minḥah time had arrived. He roused himself and went over to a spring in the field, washed his hands, determined the correct direction, stood up and prayed. Once he had prayed, he took something to eat from his knapsack and broke off a small piece in order to recite the blessing. After he ate, drank, and recited the final blessing, he filled up a jug at the well, took up his staff and knapsack and set off for the city. That city was Buczacz.

It was nighttime when he entered the city, but the night was as bright as day, illuminated by the light of Torah radiating from the homes of the people of Buczacz. They knew that Torah was man's foundation and spent their days and nights studying it.

Our Rabbi entered one of the buildings and lay down behind the stove. He didn't have time to determine where he was before he was overtaken by sleep and dozed off. He was stretched out behind the stove and hidden from all eyes until he awoke to words of Torah. He opened his eyes, saw a house filled with books, and knew he was in a holy space. And what place was it? It was the kloyz of Buczacz that is next to the pond formed from a cloud, for the cloud had once broken open and poured out an ocean of water, creating the pond. The kloyz was crammed with great scholars, enlightened and secure in their learning, who did not cease from Torah study day and night.

Entering the synagogue cast a great sense of awe upon our Rabbi, as is evident in his commentary in section 151. ("As for me, during my younger days I lived with my family in my study house, which was above the synagogue of the holy community of Cracow. On account of this I was greatly punished by the death of some of my children.") The rabbi arose in great fear, washed his hands with the water from the jug in his knapsack and sat down.

He saw two men, one old and one young, dressed in torn, patched clothing, belted with braided ropes, wearing oval hats, made like hats padded with small cushions, like those worn by porters shouldering heavy burdens. They were doing battle over Torah, vigorously exchanging insights. One asked, the other answered; one constructed, the other demolished; one built mountains of logic, the other crushed them with hair-splitting arguments. Our Rabbi said to himself, I'll sit and listen. He sat and listened.

He realized from their conversations that they were experts in Torah, mighty in argumentation, divided in their opinions, sharp and expert in Talmud, understanding the logic of Mishnah, knowing all the talmudic passages, having the additional variant texts and commentaries on the tips of their tongues. They spoke fluently, with heartfelt understanding. Every word that came out of their mouths was supported by a legal decree according to the truth of Torah. They came to one among those halakhot that our rabbi had toiled to clarify, explicate and organize in his treatise. But they had apparently never heard of our rabbi and knew nothing of his book. Our rabbi said to himself, I'll sit and listen.

He heard the old man say to the young one, You have come up with a wonderful insight, my son, something beautiful and persuasive, but I don't see any support for it in the sacred books. The youth said to the old man, Is all of Torah commentary contained in the collection of books found in our town? There are many books in the world. If we can't find support in the ones we have here, perhaps we will find it elsewhere. Torah's extent is longer than the earth is its measure, and wider than the sea. The old man replied, I am amazed at you, my son. You hold a precious pearl in your hands and have hidden if from me until now. The boy answered, Father, this insight came to me just now, and if you had not taught me never to deal in mystical matters, I would say that someone else has arrived at this interpretation before me. Why do I say that someone else has made this interpretation before me? Because I feel its author standing beside me and telling it to me. The old man responded, Praised be the One who gives intelligence to human beings! We'll search the holy books for support.

The boy attended to the candle and wiped his fingers on the rope around his waist. He said to his father, Isn't it astonishing that an interpretation as straightforward as this one was never dealt with by others, and if they did, why wouldn't they have written it down in a book? Maybe it was so obvious that they had no need to record it. The old man said, Not so, my son. For you have made a truly great and original observation. If it has not yet been written down, it must be recorded. What are you holding? A book of the later rabbis, a useless volume. The boy responded, It is clear that many have consulted it. The old man said, Just because it is tattered, you say that many have consulted it. They did not read it carefully, they glanced through it. One sees an old book and pages through it as you are doing. If you mean to examine it carefully—what a waste of time! The young man said to the old, Father, haven't you taught me that if something falls into your hands it is a sign that it hold some usefulness for you? The father replied, A thing, yes, but not a book! Everything is in the hands of heaven, except for those modern books about which it is written, *Of the making of many books there is no end*. There is no end to the making of books that serve only to lead one into error. If only the authors themselves erred, I would say they are punished for their burning desire to produce new insights and interpretations. But how much greater the sin if others have been led astray by these books? Their sin lies in abandoning the works of our first rabbis for those of the later ones. I see that I have not convinced you and that you are studying that book. What are you gaping at? The boy bestirred himself and said, Father, let me read you something. He immediately began to read. His father nodded his head and said, Very nice. This is the very subject we were debating and this is the interpretation that you discovered. What is the name of the book? The boy said, the title page has been torn from much use and I do not know the name, but I think it is Turei Zahav. The father replied, It would have sufficed if you had said, I don't know, my son. It is better to say that you don't know than to make conjectures. Just because you don't know the name, you chose the first one that popped into your head. The young man said, Father, it is because I found things in this book that I have heard quoted in the name of the author of Turei Zahav that I am certain that it is his book. The old man replied, In any case, his is an elegant and persuasive interpretation. The Holy One, blessed be He, brought this halakhah to our attention only so that you could offer your beautiful explanation, and He placed this book into your hands only so that you should find your interpretation within it. I see that it is already very late. Let us return home and sleep a little before rising for the day's work. The Rabbi Turei Zahav followed them with his eyes as they walked away and whispered, Blessed are You who gave Torah to the people Israel and blessed are You who have shown me that I did not labor in vain. He roused himself, rinsed his hands and prayed the evening service. He took up his staff and his knapsack, kissed the ark's curtain, the ark itself and the mezuzah, and went out to return to his city and his place.

This is one of the stories that people used to tell in Buczacz in the time when Buczacz was full of Torah study and all of its sons were surrounded by Torah. And who were these two Torah students? A father and his son. We don't know their names, but we know their trade. They were porters, porters from among the porters of Buczacz, who during the day bend their backs under burdens and at night study Torah.

Behold the wisdom of Buczacz! Poor porters whose bodies are bent from hard work take upon themselves the yoke of Torah. If you are astonished, don't be. The body's toil increases the power of thought and gives strength to the weary.

Translated by Herbert Levine and Reena Spicehandler

A Single Commandment

THE GAON RABBI ISRAEL, may his memory be for a blessing, was the head of the beit din in the city of Svirz and half of the district of Lvov during the days of the Turei Zahav, who had also served there in the rabbinate. In Svirz, a fair is held right after Passover. The brewers would brew up a large batch of beer and would sell it before the holiday to a gentile through a bill of sale so that they would have good beer ready for the fair after Passover. Rabbi Israel heard about this and ruled that the brewers were violating the laws of Passover, because the whole sale was a mere deceit, inasmuch as the leavened beer had been brewed solely to be used by the Jewish brewers for their economic benefit after Passover. He declared in the synagogue that no one was allowed to brew beer close to the Passover holiday and that anyone found violating this prohibition would be excommunicated. The brewers heeded the ban and chose to avoid the sin. That is all except one householder, who made light of the rabbi's interdiction because other great rabbis – the author of *Bayit Ḥadash*, and Rabbi Aryeh Leib of Cracow, and the Turei Zahav himself, who held great sway in Svirz – had not decreed such a ban. So he went and brewed beer in secret.

This same householder loaned money out at interest to the local villagers. On the first of the intermediate days of Passover, he took the notebook in which he recorded his loans, and some matzot as provision for the journey, mounted his horse and made his way to the villages. On the road, some farmers attacked him, and he sensed that they wanted to kill him. But he had a good horse which he spurred on and he was able to escape from them.

When it came to mealtime, he was seized by hunger, but he did not have water for the purpose of ritually washing his hands before eating, and he did not want to eat without discharging that ritual. So he kept riding until he no longer had strength to ride. He recalled a mountain spring that was close to the road. He said to himself, If I go down to the spring, the murderers will catch up with me and kill me, and if I don't stop at the spring, I will die of hunger, because I have no water for hand-washing and I won't transgress against the command of the Sages by eating without first ritually washing my hands. He concluded, What will be will be, because I need to eat. He went off toward the spring, alighted and washed his hands. The murderers came upon him there and killed him.

It was the custom of the Gaon, Rabbi Israel, that his best student would sleep near him in his room. He awoke from his sleep two or three times a night, each time washed his hands, instructing his student to wash hands as well and reviewed with him the intricacies of the laws of hand-washing. That night, the student was Rabbi Nathan, who later acquired fame as a great preacher and settled in the holy community of Buczacz, where he was called Rabbi Nathan Teacher.

At midnight, a voice was heard at the door. The Gaon asked, Who is here? A voice was heard behind the door, I am the householder So-and-So. This was very surprising to the Gaon. Why had he come in the middle of the night? He ordered his student, our teacher Rabbi Nathan, to open the door for him.

The householder came in and stood in the doorway. They could not tell that he had been killed. The Gaon said to him, Why are you standing in the doorway? Come in. He replied, You think that I am alive, but I was killed. And he told them the whole story.

The Gaon said to him, What are you asking for? The murdered man told him that a decree had gone forth in the upper world that they would not hold him to a strict accounting of his deeds, for the Holy Blessed One had already forgiven him his sins, because he had sanctified the name of God by dying on behalf of a non-biblical commandment ordained only by the Sages. They would allow his soul to return to the place of its origin deterred neither by an impure spirit or a hostile angel. But when he reached the gates of the Garden of Eden, an angel told him, Stand by and wait till I ask, for you are under the ban of the rabbi, Rabbi Israel. The angel brought back the answer that he was not to be admitted until a note from that rabbi released him from the excommunication. So he had come to ask the rabbi to free him from the bonds of the ban and grant him the permission he needed.

The rabbi asked the murdered man, Could I be so important in that world? I am neither rich nor a rabbi from a great city. The murdered man told him, Not everyone merits two tables in that world. How do you know to reply in that way? the Rabbi asked, for this householder was an ignorant man. He replied, "Now, my Rabbi, you can ask me about anything in the Torah and I will explain it for you. And what's more, when they told me to bring a note from the rabbi, they said it with two R's, "the rabbi, Rabbi Israel." The Gaon wrote out the release.

The rabbi asked the murdered man, Who killed you? So he told him, Three farmers from Such-and-Such killed me and these are their names. And my account book can be found in the barn of one of them where he stores the buckwheat, and his name is So-and-So. The rabbi sent the murdered man on to his eternal rest.

In the morning, the rabbi sent for the wife of the murdered man and told her, Your husband had an accident on the road in Such-and-Such, near the mountain spring, and he hurt his thigh. Send a wagon and two men to bring him back to the city. Weeping, the woman hastened to hire a wagon and two or three men to bring him back. They came to the spring and found him dead, picked him up, put him in the wagon and brought him back to town.

The widow of the murdered man cried a great and bitter cry and came with great lamentation to the rabbi: The rabbi said he was wounded in his thigh and behold he is dead! I knew, answered the rabbi, but I did not want to give you this terrible news, so I told you to hire a wagon and men to bring him to town. You should know that his murderers are three farmers from Such-and-Such, and your husband's notebook lies hidden by one of them in his buckwheat barn, and this is his name.

When the news came to the fortress, its commander ordered that the murdered man be set up in the middle of the market and to announce, as was their custom, that So-and-So has been murdered and anyone who knows anything about who killed him should come forward and testify. But there was no one who came forward to testify, so they buried him.

The murdered man's widow came to the commander and told him, I know who his murderers are. They live in Such-and-Such village and these are their names. His account book is hidden in the barn of one and this is his name. The commander immediately sent out cavalry, who caught the murderers and brought the account book. When the murderers saw that they had no way out, they confessed their deed. The commander passed judgment against them and they were hanged. So God takes revenge on our spilt blood.

Our great rabbi, the accomplished preacher, Rabbi Nathan of Buczacz, the student of the Gaon Rabbi Israel, in every congregation where he preached he would reproach those who made light of the ritual of hand-washing. At the end of every sermon, he would tell this story and say, If a man gives his life for a commandment ordained only by the Sages and thereby merits eternal life, how much more merit is accounted to those who observe all the commandments of the Torah?

Translated by Herbert Levine and Reena Spicehandler

The Blessing of the Moon

NEAR THE PLACE where the equipment for purifying the dead stood, there was a large pane of thick glass standing on wooden pillars. Upon this glass, the whole text for the sanctification of the moon ceremony was written in large, beautiful letters. A wooden frame enclosed the board, and a peg hung from it. Once a month, when the blessing of the new moon took place, a lamp was hung there, candles were lit, the board was brought outside the synagogue, and the worshipers would read the whole text of the ceremony. Originally, the text had been etched into the glass itself because there used to be craftsmen who knew how to write on glass. When the glass broke and no one could be found who still knew the craft of glass etching, they took thick paper and wrote the text on it. They dipped the paper in olive oil so that it would be bright, and then placed glass over it. And who broke the board first? It was the monastery students who broke it. Once, they came out of an inn and saw Jews standing outdoors before a shining glass board, and they took their sticks and broke it.

We never saw the original board, but we heard what happened to it. If you want to hear about it, I am willing to tell you.

A householder, a descendant of the Ba'al Halevushim, had an old Torah scholar staying with him as a guest. As was customary in those days, an important person did not travel alone; so his grandson, the son of his daughter, traveled with him. At night, the householder made dinner for the old man and for the boy who accompanied him. When water was brought for the ritual washing at the end of the meal, the old man looked up and saw a comely child standing before him, holding a cloth with which to wipe his hands. She was upright in his eyes, and he said to himself, She would be suitable for my grandson, my daughter's son.

But it is not the way for big money to combine with small money, for the father of the young girl was wealthy and counted his money in weighty coins, whereas the scholar's son-in-law counted his in pennies.

After a year or more, or perhaps less—why concern ourselves with exact calculations when we are not in a position to be exact?—it happened that the same old man, accompanied by his grandson, returned to Buczacz and stayed with the same householder. When it was time for dinner, the guest asked his host, Where is that young girl? You hadn't mentioned to me that she has married – has she?

The host groaned and was silent. The guest stared at him. The householder felt the stare and was afraid that the guest would bring up matters having to do with death, heaven forbid. He did not want to leave it in doubt, and so he said, You remind me of my sorrow. Married? Not married. I have no hope that she will find a marriage partner, unless I hide the truth from him, but if I hide the truth, the truth will not hide itself.

The old man said, Heaven forbid that His mercies be exhausted! For even if the doors to hope are closed, the Holy One, blessed be He, opens them and makes them wider. What is the sorrow to which you alluded?

The householder said, If others will not tell our guest, I will tell him. Each month when the moon is full, my daughter gets out of her bed and leaves her room. She wanders through the courtyards and streets, making a circuit of the town, and then walks from rooftop to rooftop until the moon has set in the sky. I have already brought the wonder worker, R. Moshe David of Pidayets, to fashion amulets and to surround her bed with good-luck charms and make spells to prevent the doors and the windows from opening before her. But nothing has availed.

The old man shook his hand and said in a mocking tone, If only all these charms and oaths do not harm her! Have you heard that her feet stood on the roof of the church?

He said to him, This I did not hear. If the gentiles have not accused us of plotting against their place of worship and have not said that so-and-so the daughter of so-and-so has been seen on the roof of their church, then I believe that my daughter's feet have not trodden there.

Said the old man, If that is so, there is still a remedy for that poor girl. My grandson is a ready scribe who knows how to write on glass. I will ask him for your sake to inscribe the order of the new moon ceremony on a glass plate, and his Excellency will donate it to the Great Synagogue, where many of the Jews pray. I am almost certain that if Jews bless the moon for twelve months using this board, the young girl will be revived and returned to health, and the powers that emanate from the moon's light will no longer have a hold over her.

The householder had a white glass brought to him and two types of color, red and black, and he placed the grandson in a special room where he would not be disturbed. The young man sat as long as he needed, and wrote the whole text of the blessing over the moon on the glass in large letters in a beautiful hand. He wrote the text of the blessings in red letters, as well as the beginning of each passage and also the exclamation "A good sign!, Good luck!," and also the verse *Hark! My beloved! Behold he cometh*. The rest of the text he wrote in ink that was black but bright.

The householder saw the writing on the board and was delighted. His delight did not fade before summoning a craftsman to his home, who made a base for the tablet to stand upon. He had it brought to the Great Synagogue and placed in the courtyard.

The same night happened to be the time for the blessing of the moon. The whole city gathered and looked at the board and read from it all the text. So it was on that month and every month thereafter.

After twelve months, the young man who had etched the letters wed the daughter of the householder. She was healthy and restored to herself. The moon did not strike her, and its rays could not harm her or dislodge her from her bed at night. She gave birth to boys and girls who were steeped in Torah and gave birth in turn to children beloved by both man and heaven. And so it was, generation after generation, up to our own time. If only they had not been murdered by the impure and accursed, they would have continued to glorify the world with their wisdom.

Translated by Pnina and Mordechai Beck

Buczacz Market

The Market Well

IN THE MIDDLE OF THE MARKET stands a well that has never run dry, not in the daytime, nor at night, not in summer, nor in winter. Even before the town was built the waters flowed. Animals and birds drank its waters and occasionally even passing travelers slaked their thirst there. But the pulley, the fence and the two pipes that form the subject of my tale have existed for about four or five generations.

The pious master, R. Ḥayyim, the author of Be'er Mayim Hayyim, came from the village of Pribiluk. Like all those seeking knowledge from the area surrounding Buczacz, he came to study Torah in our old study house here in Buczacz, where ḥidushim are produced on a daily basis. From the end of one Sabbath to the eve of the next, R. Ḥayyim did not budge from the beit midrash. He drank from the basin and ate food he had brought from his father's house in the village. Dining in inns or at others' tables could lead to wasting time; for the mistress of the house might not have the meal ready on time or the master of the house might be talkative and keep one away from words of Torah.

One noontime, R. Ḥayyim stood and left his Talmud in order to wash his hands and eat. He found an old man sitting there, a stranger in the town, and invited him to eat. The man did not accept. R. Ḥayyim urged him, but he wouldn't hear of it. He pressed him further, and the man said, "Do not implore me to eat, but I would drink fresh water."

Since he said “fresh water,” R. Ḥayyim realized that the old man was referring to water from a spring or a well rather than water that had already been drawn. For if he simply wanted water, there was some in the basin.

R. Ḥayyim ran to the well and brought him water. The man drank and said, “You have revived my soul.” The old man had been fasting from Sabbath to Sabbath and had become exhausted. He broke his fast with a little water. R. Ḥayyim said, “I’ll go and bring more.” He replied, “I’ll go and drink at the source.” They went together to the well.

The old man gazed at the water gushing from the well. He planted his staff in the loosened earth and rested his beard on it and watched the waters gushing forth and then returning into the ground. R. Ḥayyim saw the old man’s face illuminated like that of one of the righteous who discern God’s deeds and miracles in everything they see.

The old man raised his head and said, “A well of living waters!” He bent down and filled his hands, adding, “Pure water, pure.” He blessed once again and drank.

After he had prayed at the well, he took off. For he was among those who live out the verse, *I am a stranger in the land*. They never stay the night where they have spent the day, and never spend the day where they have stayed the night. Their main goal in exile is to seek a place for their souls where God’s presence is not as hidden. R. Ḥayyim told this tale of the old man and the well between the afternoon and evening services. Those who heard it began drawing their water from that well. One householder installed a pulley to make it easier to draw water; another paved the area in front so people wouldn’t become mired in mud. Someone else built a stone wall so that a person could lean on it while another filled his pitchers. Everyone in the city began to draw water from that well, Jews and non-Jews alike. When it came to water for making matzah, people drew from the King’s Well as they had always done. For one doesn’t change an established custom, and if there exists some other reason, I know nothing of it. Afterwards they attached two metal pipes. Once it became a public well, it began to be monitored and repaired as necessary. In the winter it was wrapped in burlap and buried in straw so that the water wouldn’t freeze.

In the beginning, the pious of Buczacz would collect enough water on the eve of Passover to last all eight days of the holiday for fear of consuming leaven. For if a grain of wheat or barley were found in the water, all the prepared food and all the utensils that were used in cooking it would come under the prohibition of eating leaven on Passover. For that reason, the God-fearing prepared a large barrel, like the ones used for storing honey, and filled it with water on Passover eve, covering it with a shawl and binding it up tightly with ropes. Even so, there remained a concern that a careless child could draw water from the barrel and a bird could come and drop a piece of grain into it. After two or three generations had passed and nothing bad happened on Passover, they finally understood the words of the old man who had said, "Pure waters." People stopped preparing water before Passover and instead brought fresh water daily from the well. With regard to water, they acted on Passover as they did on every other day of the year.

And what did they do with all those large barrels? Stingy people wanted to sell them, while the generous donated them for the public good to be placed, filled with water, in the city's four corners, so that if fire broke out, they would be prepared to douse it.

City dignitaries held a meeting and decided where to place the barrels. They set them up, each in its place. But before they could be filled with water, a fire broke out in the city. The whole city went up in flames and the barrels were burnt up.

Since the fire was a calamity, I will not dwell on it.

Translated by Herbert Levine and Reena Spicehandler

The Great Town Hall

1

Right next to the market well stands a magnificent building, perfect in its splendor, exceedingly beautiful. It is the great town hall in our city, for which we were envied by all the cities in Poland. Its great beauty even inspired a saying among us: if we saw someone who meticulously adorned his attire, we would say, Did you see him? He is trying to clothe himself in the great town hall of Buczacz!

Just as the building itself became legendary, so all the lovely engraved images with which the artist decorated the town hall inspired a byword. For if we saw a man silenced by amazement, we would say, He is astonished, struck dumb like the statues of the town hall of Buczacz. Now that Buczacz has been destroyed and our brothers and sisters have been murdered, all those people of Buczacz who embellished the city with their loveliness and their conversations with beautiful sayings, I have come to explain their expressions, so that you will not be astonished by good Jews who cleaved to the living God in their lives and in their deaths, yet referenced idols in their speech.

2

Mikołaj Potocki, Count of Buczacz, wanted to make a name for himself in the land of Poland. He set his heart on building the houses in his city of stone rather than of wood so that his city would not be destroyed by fire, as happened to most of Poland's cities whose houses were wooden. If fire occurred in one house, it would burst out and consume all the houses, and even if they rebuilt the city, fire would again escape from one of the houses and consume all the others so that nothing but heaps of ashes would remain. Thus the cities of Poland changed their appearances and sons did not see the same city as their fathers, just as their own sons, in turn, did not see the same city they had seen. So Mikołaj, count of Buczacz, took the initiative to construct the city's houses of stone so that his city would endure for many days and not be destroyed out from under him by fire.

3

Mikołaj Potocki brought in builders to construct houses of stone, and they built him many fine houses. They even built a church for the Roman Catholics and one for the Greek Catholics, since, with the passage of time, their wooden walls had rotted. He had them built of stone. For the Basilian priests, he built a monastery on the way to Fedor Hill, above the Strypa River. Then Potocki said, I will build such a town hall in the city that anyone who comes to Buczacz and sees it will never forget it or its maker.

Potocki traveled to Italy and brought back a craftsman to build him a town hall. The craftsman's name was Theodor. Yet all those who worked with Theodor called him Fedor, for they were Ruthenians; since they could not pronounce Theodor, they called him Fedor.

4

Buczacz is built amid hills. The only flat area in Buczacz is between the foothills, on the right bank of the Strypa. This was the only spot suitable for a city center. Yet that, too, is narrow rather than broad. The designer did not plan to situate the town center in the geometric center of the narrow plain, but in the west. He dug out a foundation on the hillside and spread out the soil, creating a flat area. He built a defensive wall to the west, for in the west the road was higher than the plain. He built the town hall about twenty or thirty meters away from the eastern corner, so that it would not sink, since the waters of the Strypa made the ground unstable in the west. They brought Trembowla stone to build the town hall, for Trembowla stone is strong, unlike the stones of Buczacz. Therefore anyone who wants to build a sturdy, substantial house or to construct a staircase for his home imports Trembowla stone.

5

This is the account of the building's construction. The building was rectangular and its style baroque. There were two lower stories, one above the other, and two towers above, one atop the other. The bottom tower was square, the upper one narrow. The building's length was about twenty meters on the northern side and twenty meters on the south; and its width was about fifteen meters on the eastern side and fifteen meters on the west. The building's height was about eleven meters on the eastern side and twelve meters on the west. On the lower level were shops. You descended to these shops by a stairway, for in the east the ground was lower. Above the stores were offices for the municipal workers.

6

The main building was topped by a tower, which was topped by another tower. The height of the lower tower was ten meters and the height of the upper tower about eight meters. The towers were square. The bottom section measured eight meters by eight meters and the upper, about six meters by six. The building was highest in this central section. You ascended from floor to floor on spiral staircases. The central column of the staircase was the trunk of a thick and mighty oak. The stairs were wooden, of fine, hard oak, encircling the central column. A large Buczacz forest was cut down to make the stairs for the great town hall. The height of each stair was about thirty centimeters. For this reason, you did not ascend or descend the staircase lightly.

7

Theodor made ornamental columns for the main building, six on the south and six on the north, four on the east and four on the west. Each of them was a work of artistry. And the capitals that crowned them were made of engraved wood that was a delight to behold. He made stone balustrades and a parapet for the lower roof. He fashioned a stone parapet around the lower section of the tower, like the one on the roof of the lower building.

He made eight more columns matching those of the main building on the facades of the towers, two on each side. He made a stone border for the tower. The center of each façade featured an arch to house the clock's face, for he had placed a clock high on the town hall.

This is the account of the town hall that Theodor made for Mikołaj Potocki, Count of Buczacz. For six years, Theodor built the town hall, its communal spaces, its offices and its corridors. Theodor crafted many stone statues for the corners of the lower section and for the southern facade. He gave all the statues names from Scripture. The features of their faces were Jewish features like those Theodor saw in the city of Buczacz and like those of the Jews he saw in dreams and nighttime visions. For, as a small boy, he was walking home from the synagogue with his young sister when priests accosted them. They snatched the boy from his sister's hands. They took her to a convent and brought him to the home of a sculptor, who adopted him and named him Theodor after himself. From the day that he arrived at the craftsman's home, he never again saw his mother or sister and never again spoke to Jews.

8

A day came when Theodor arose early to walk about the city. He came to the street of the Jews. He looked and behold, the street was empty, not a soul in sight. There was a building illuminated by many candles and people were filling the house. They were dressed in white, without shoes on their feet and with books in their hands. A man was standing in their midst, entirely wrapped up in a white garment and his voice was that of a man praying for his soul. Theodor did not know whether he saw what he saw in a waking state or in a dream.

9

Indeed, he was not dreaming when he saw what he saw, but was wide awake, having seen something similar while yet a child. For when he was a boy of about four, or at the most five years old, his mother had taken him to a house full of candles with many people all dressed in white, like the people that Theodor once more saw. An old man stood and raised his voice in song and the people responded aloud, while the boy sat at his mother's feet and slept. His sister took him to walk home with him. While they were walking, it came to pass that men dressed in black came and snatched him out of his sister's hands, so that he never again saw his sister or his mother. For they took his sister away and brought him to the home of a man who built buildings and carved statues, who called him by his own name, Theodor. Theodor lived in Theodor's house, and Theodor did all that Theodor did, just as Theodor did it.

He grew to be a man and as he grew, so did his reputation as one of the great artists who build buildings and sculpt statues.

10

Mikołaj Potocki heard of Theodor's reputation. He approached him and brought him back to his own land and to his own city in order to design the town hall that he wished to build. Theodor built him that town hall. He decorated it with beautiful figures, fashioned after the figures of the men and women whom he saw in the city and whom he saw in his dreams. For since he had seen God's house on Yom Kippur eve, the faces of the people he had seen there had been constantly in his dreams, along with the faces of those he saw while awake in the Jews' streets in the city of Buczacz. So Theodore fashioned with his hands what he saw with his eyes and what he saw with his heart.

11

Theodor finished all of his work. Potocki saw the town hall from without and from within and also the figures of people that he had fashioned. He said to Theodor: "You have surpassed yourself, Theodor."

He asked him, "Is there another building as beautiful as this?" Theodor answered Potocki, saying, "There is none in Poland, and there are not many buildings in other lands to equal it."

Potocki heard and said, "I will go and bring you an offering of thanksgiving." Potocki went out and Theodor remained to observe what he had made.

12

After much time passed and Potocki did not return, Theodor began to wonder, for Potocki had said to him, I will go and come back shortly.

A long time had passed, and he still had not returned. Theodor thought, I will go to meet him.

Theodor went to the door and found it closed, for Potocki had closed the door behind him. Theodor tried to open the door but could not. For Potocki had closed and locked it, taking the keys with him, so that the craftsman could not leave the building and could never design such a building for other patrons.

13

Theodor stood and thought to himself, Why did the Count treat me in this way after I dealt with him in good faith and built him this hall. It must be that he imprisoned me here so that I cannot build another like it.

Theodor raised his voice and cried out, Listen to me, all you people, come, open up for me. But no one heard his voice, because he was high above everyone else and a person's voice could not be heard on the earth below. Despite this, Theodor did not stop crying out until his throat was all parched.

14

Theodor knew that he was crying out in vain, that no one would hear him, and even if they heard, they could not open the doors for him, since the count had taken the keys with him.

Theodor knew that he was cut off from the land of the living; he would die of starvation and never again experience life. If he should die outside, ravens would pluck out his eyes, and if he should die inside, mice would nibble upon his flesh.

So he decided, I will jump, and if my bones should break and I die, I will at least be buried and not become food for birds of the sky or household mice.

15

He was about to throw himself to the earth, but it pained him to die. So he tried to think of a way to avoid doing so.

He went and gathered wood and ropes and cloth from what the workmen had left behind. He made himself wings in order to fly, not like the wings of the planes that fly today, not even like the wings of the first aeroplane that a Jew would make many years after him, first of all the aeroplanes ever made. When God makes something new in the world, it is not done by means of one individual or in a single generation. Something new comes about little by little, by means of many different individuals, until a generation is pleasing in God's sight, and God finds in it an individual who can bring it to pass.

Theodor took the wings that he had made and tied them to his shoulders, one wing to each shoulder. Off he flew until he came to the forested valley across the Strypa, on the way to the city of Yaslowitz. There, with no more strength left him, he fell to his death.

16

At the time of his flight, servants of the Count Potocki were at their work in the fields. They saw spread wings above their heads, attached to a man who was flying. They stood in wonder. Who had seen the like and who had heard that a person could be lifted high above the earth?

As the man plummeted and fell to earth, they saw that it was Theodor. They were dumbstruck, for they had heard from their lord that Theodor had returned to his own country. Now, here he was, falling dead before them, with wings attached to his shoulders. They were moved and trembled mightily. They began keening over him, for Theodor had been a good man and had done them many kindnesses all the time that they had worked with him. They called the hill where Theodor fell by his name. You will recall that they were Ruthenians who could not make the sound "th," so they called it the Hill of Fedor as a namesake for Theodor—that Theodor who had designed the town hall for the count of the city, who then entombed him in it, that Theodor who then made wings for himself and flew as far as this hill, where he fell to the ground and died. It is the very same hill on which five hundred Jews were buried alive, when the accursed, polluted ones, sent to the city by the abominable destroyer, commanded the Jews to dig a pit and be buried there alive. Five hundred Jews buried themselves alive in that pit. The last one to cover his brothers with dirt fell upon their corpses when the murderous commander felled with him with a fatal shot, so that he rolled, roiling in his blood, upon the corpses of his brothers.

17

And as to the rest of the people of my city, what did the accursed, polluted ones do to them? With clubs and revolvers they led them to the town hall, where they tied them together with metal wires, poured oil over them, lit the fire and burned them all alive. From the bowels of the earth and its deep pit to the heights of the heavens, the sound of the Jews' cry went up, partly from within the pit and partly from amidst the flames of holy fire. And the gentiles were laughing and saying, They are crying out, just as in their House of Prayer.

Translated by Herbert Levine and Reena Spicehandler

Buczacz Town Hall, built in Rococo style in 1751, depicted in an early 20th century postcard

The Partners

1

In the city hall there is a cellar, its length without measure, without end. It has been said that it goes on and on and on, all the way into another country, and that it was made this way because of the Tatars; if the city should fall, the city's leaders would not fall into their hands as captives. You descend on stone steps into the cellar, where four iron doors are set in place, two inside and two outside. The outer doors are closed and locked; the inner doors are left open. When the Tatars were no longer a threat to Poland, they stopped locking the cellar from inside.

The entrance to the cellar is lower than the height of a medium-size man, and it is open to the marketplace. At the top, a stone juts out from the threshold, and a high step leads up from the basement. On top of this step, which is as wide as a workbench, stands a statue of Naḥum Ber Wallach, the yeast merchant who inherited the cellar from his father, just as his father had received it from *his* father, going all the way back to their ancestor Naḥum Ze'ev the charcoal maker, who received it as a gift from Potocki the count of Buczacz, along with a commission for making and selling yeast.

This is exactly what galled the three brothers of the House of Potocki: not only had their ancestor brought in a partner to share the city hall, but that partner was a Jew. This was really too much to swallow. They had already offered Naḥum Ber Wallach an enormous sum—some say it amounted to thousands of gold dinars—to buy out his partnership and vacate the cellar. This is how he responded: If I have already gained the privilege of a partnership with the distinguished nobility of the House of Potocki in the city hall that is the glorious splendor of the city and an object of envy throughout Poland, could I possibly dissolve the partnership? I would not dissolve it for all the money in the world.

2

Why did the Potocki brothers' grandfather bring him in as a partner in the city hall, a man who was not only a Jew but a yeast merchant? Was it because he owed him money? Potocki was a wealthy man. Had he lost money at cards? He had many, many villages, forests, and farmlands with which he could pay his debts, aside from the city itself and its branches, and aside from distilleries that produced beer and brandy. No, Potocki *gave* the cellar to Naḥum Ze'ev the Jew, and Naḥum Ber Wallach was his descendant. And why did Potocki give such a generous gift to a Jew? He did so on account of a certain incident. And here is an accounting of that incident.

Potocki had gone out on a hunt in the forests around the city, forests that extended on and on, endlessly, beyond measure, for at that time, all the suburbs that now surround the city were still forests. Potocki was accompanied by his hounds and his servants, as well as by the minor lords who ate at his table and accompanied him wherever he went. When he caught sight of an animal, he took aim with his rifle and shot. He missed, however, and then ran after the animal. This brought him to a spot far removed from his companions. So, suddenly, he found himself alone, without his servants and companions, without food or water, and even without his faithful hounds. He tried to return to them but could not find the way. He began wandering here and there, and this went on and on until his legs gave out and he fell down. Having fallen, he just lay there. And, once he had fallen down, sleep overtook him; he dozed off into slumber, and slept.

In that city, there was a Jew who at one time had the lease on a tavern, like his ancestors, and like their ancestors before them. After a few years went by, he was no longer able to pay the lord what was due on the lease. The lord warned him that if he did not pay, he would throw him into a pit. As long as no other Jew came along to rent the tavern, the official was content to let him stay there. But one year, when another Jew came along and leased the tavern, the lord threw him out. He lacked the funds to lease a tavern elsewhere. So he began wandering around from one place to another, in search of a place where he could earn a living. But he found none.

One day, he came to one of the forests owned by Potocki. There was an old man there who knew him from better times and had often benefited from his largesse.

The old man asked him, Nuḥum Ze'yv, what are *you* doing here?

He responded, My sons and I are cutting down trees in the forest to make charcoal that we take to the city and sell to Jews.

How blessed you are, and how blessed your children, for you have something to do! So you certainly must have food to eat and a place to rest your heads. But I, my friend, have become homeless, a wanderer, and neither my wife nor I has anything to eat, or even a roof over our heads.

The old man said, Stay here with us, and the One who provides bread for all flesh will also provide for you and your wife. Hearing this, he stayed with the old man and his sons in the forest, passed the time with them, and learned how to cut down trees and make charcoal, which they sold in the city. Eventually, the old man died; one of his sons became a soldier, one indentured himself as a servant, and the other was arrested for brigandage. Naḥum Ze'ev was left to fell trees and make them into charcoal, which he sold in town.

At that time, he had already raised his sons and daughters and sent them out into the world. He was left alone with his wife, she busy with her goat and her chickens and her kettles and he with his trees and his charcoal. And so it went all week. But on Sabbaths and Holy Days, and on weekdays when the Torah is read, he would take leave of his trees and his charcoal and try to reach the synagogue before sunrise so that he could pray there at the proper hour. Nothing stopped him, neither rain in the summer nor snow and winds in the winter. During the week, he would walk along, carrying a bag of charcoal over his shoulder. He would sell the charcoal in order to buy those things that are sold in town but are not to be found in the village.

One day, he rose early, as was his wont, and went on his way. What occupied his thoughts at that hour? No one really knows what is on his neighbor's mind. One could assume, however, that he wanted what most villagers want, namely, to live in a city with other Jews so that he could pray every day with the community. This is especially so for the morning prayer, for at dawn, you can sense God's workings, restoring souls to lifeless bodies, and the heart seeks to acknowledge God in a house of prayer that has a holy ark and religious books and Jews.

And so Naḥum Ze'ev stepped along from wood to wood, and from thicket to thicket among the tall and lofty trees that cover the road with their thick branches, refusing to reveal even the hint of a path to anyone who spends most of his days in the city, hiding even a hint of a path from all except those who had spent most of their days in the woods. When rain in the summer and snow in the winter muddy up the path beyond recognition, the fragrance of the roadside trees serves to lead one along the right path, for every tree had its own fragrance. However, he also sensed a human smell, and that is the smell that drew him along, until he came to a thick oak tree. He saw a man lying there, beneath the oak. Was he drunk? Or was he just someone who had been walking along, decided to rest a bit, and fell asleep? Many, many people walk along that road, wandering from one place to another, and wherever they lie down they make the place their own. The moon rose, casting its light upon the man's clothes. Naḥum Ze'ev had the feeling that this was an important lord lying there. But if indeed he was so important, where were his servants and his bodyguards? How could they have left him alone in the forest in the dead of night in a place of danger?

When he bent over the man, he was amazed and astounded to realize that this man beneath the tree was none other than the lord of Buczacz. Why was the lord of Buczacz lying here in the forest? Naḥum Ze'ev actually had heard the sounds of carriages and the barking of hounds and the shouts of officials who had gone out with Potocki to hunt. If that is what he heard, where were his companions? And why had they left him alone in the forest in the dead of night? Had a wild animal attacked and bitten him? If that was so, he certainly must not be left alone there in the forest.

Looking closely, he saw no sign of a bruise, a discoloration, a fresh wound, or blood on his clothes. In any case, he could not leave him alone there because of the wild animals, and it was impossible to wait until he awoke, because it was already autumn and his blood could congeal.

He set down his bag of charcoal, placed his talit and tefilin on top of it, and tried to wake the man up. But he would not wake up. After some thought, he decided to carry him on his shoulders, and, taking his talit and tefilin in one hand, he returned to his hut with the man on his shoulders.

He took small steps so that he would not wake up before they reached the hut. Potocki was not a heavy man and not too much of a burden. However, he was a short-tempered man, and whenever he lost his temper, no one was able to bear it.

At dawn, the birds began to chirp, all the trees of the forest awoke, and each and every branch and leaf and shrub gave off its own fragrance, the fragrance of an autumn morning covered in dew.

3

When Naḥum Ze'ev brought Potocki to his hut, his wife, Ḥayyah Sarah, was about to set pots over the fire to boil. Even before he entered, she could hear the heavy tread of his feet. She was surprised that he was returning home, because it was impossible that he already had recited the entire service that morning, including the Torah reading and the long petitionary prayers for Monday or Thursday. When he entered, she saw that he was carrying on his shoulders one of the great lords, who appeared to be dead, and she thought that her soul would take flight. Naḥum Ze'ev lifted up his burden and put him down on his bed; then he took his sheepskin coat off its hook and covered him with it. His bed, near the wall, was made of stones, soil, and mud covered over with plaster. Spread over that was a straw mattress and a pillow stuffed with feathers. A wider bed jutted out from the opposite wall, with a straw mattress and a bundle of clothes. This wider bed was Ḥayyah Sarah's; the narrow one belonged to Naḥum Ze'ev.

When Ḥayyah Sarah recovered from the shock, she wanted to ask her husband what was going on but could not find the words. Standing there, she just stared ahead without any expression in her eyes. Finally, she leaned over her husband. Naḥum Ze'ev told her, Set your questions aside for a bit, add some logs to the fire, and heat up some water.

Ḥayyah Sarah shouted, Are you going to tell me what this is all about? The lord, shaken by the sound of her shouting, opened his eyes. His eyes did not reflect the slightest bit of amazement, but they glared with a kind of indignation that cannot be expressed in words. Perhaps this was because she had awakened him, or perhaps his anger had preceded his sleep. Whatever the reason, he closed his eyes again and fell asleep again.

Naḥum Ze'ev, who had seen the lord opening his eyes and was unaware that he had closed them again, raised his arms heavenward and said, Blessed be the One who has restored the breath of life to this exalted lord! I will not try to hide from my master my fear that his blood had congealed and that he would not regain consciousness again so quickly.

Potocki opened his eyes again and asked, What did you say? Then, almost at one and the same time, he shouted: Where am I and who are you?

Naḥum Ze'ev bowed down to him, in fear and trembling, and told him that at night, near dawn, he had gone out to walk to the city, to pray at the synagogue there. On the way, in the forest, he saw a man lying beneath one of the trees. As he drew near, he realized that this was the great lord of Buczacz, who had decided to take a rest on the ground in the forest beneath a tree. The Holy One's kindnesses had kept the cold at bay. Nevertheless, he was very concerned lest the exalted lord should suffer a chill because it was no longer summer and the forest was covered with dew. Therefore, he boldly took courage and lifted up the exalted lord in his arms, brought him to his hut, and laid him down on the bed. He added, And if the master so desires, we shall bring him something warm to drink.

When Ḥayyah Sarah heard this, she brought an earthen pot of water boiling with licorice root. Naḥum Ze'ev took the pot and brought it to Potocki's lips. Potocki was silent and amazed.

Naḥum Ze'ev said to Potocki, If the master would be kind enough to drink until he is no longer chilled.

Potocki took one swallow and asked, What have you given me to drink? Don't you have a little wine, or mead? Naḥum Ze'ev answered, There is neither wine nor mead in the house. If the master would like some brandy, I shall bring it to him.

He poured it into his kiddush cup, filling it to the brim. Potocki drank it, and asked for another. Naḥum Ze'ev said, Praise the living God! Indeed, my master lives, and thus may he continue forever!

Potocki said, Take me home.

I am at my master's command.

Said Potocki, So, what are you waiting for?

I cannot conceal from my master the fact that I have not yet prayed the morning service. So I will do so now while my wife goes to the village to bring back a horse and a carriage.

Said Potocki, Go, pray to your God, and pray for me, too.

The hut consisted of one room, with two beds of stone and soil jutting out from the walls; these beds faced each other and were used for sitting by day and for lying down at night. In the middle of the room, a barrel turned upside-down served as a table. Opposite the barrel, near the door, was a stove with an oven. Near the hut stood a sukkah for use during the Sukkot festival. Naḥum Ze'ev thought about praying in the sukkah, as was his custom in the summer. However, it would be awkward to leave the lord there by himself, since Ḥayyah Sarah had gone to the village to find horses and a carriage. So he made up his mind to pray in the hut. Then he rinsed his hands, wrapped himself in talit and tefilin, picked up a prayer book, and was ready to say his prayers.

Approximately eighteen hundred Jews lived on Count Potocki's estates. Among them were leaseholders of farmland and taverns, grain merchants, and businessmen who handled financial transactions, not to mention shopkeepers and artisans. But when it came to the customs of the Jews, he had not the least notion, and their prayers he had never heard, except for parodies of them by the banquet jesters who were a constant presence at his table. Now that fate had placed him in the home of a Jew who was preparing himself for prayer, he lay there with eyes wide open, waiting to see a Jew at prayer. But fatigue and the brandy overcame him, and he fell asleep.

Naḥum Ze'ev completed his prayers, wrapped up his talit and tefilin, put them into a bag with his prayer book, and hung it on a hook in the wall. The loud noise made by the carriage wheels woke up Potocki, who asked Naḥum Ze'ev, Why aren't you praying?

I have already prayed, he responded.

The lord replied in amazement, You prayed already?

Yes, my enlightened, generous, exalted, and distinguished lord. And now that my wife has brought up the horse and the carriage, if my lord so desires, I shall bring him to his city, to his castle. Listen! The horse is neighing in joy, just to hear that! Then, turning to Ḥayyah Sarah, Naḥum Ze'ev said, Take the mattresses and spread them out in the carriage. Then, with our lord's permission, we shall lift him up into the carriage for the trip to his city and his palace.

Potocki realized that there was no longer any sign of danger, but his strength had left him. He was just lying down and looking at the man and the woman as they took him down from the bed and out of the hut, lifted him up to the carriage, lay him down there, and covered him with the woolen cloak, placing a pillow beneath his back. Potocki realized that they were taking care of him, yet he was confused. *Who* was taking care of him, Potocki wanted to know. He did not understand what was happening. He was keenly aware of everything that was being done for him but did not recognize who was doing it.

4

Potocki was lying down in a carriage harnessed to a horse. He just lay there in amazement, for never in his life had he seen such an appalling sight. Is it possible that anyone could be making use of such broken-down things, like the ones this Jew and his wife were using to take care of him?

Naḥum Ze'ev rubbed his hands and said, Thank God, we are on our way!

The lord awoke and realized where he was, traveling with this Jew in that same carriage with that same horse. He went over the Jew's words in his mind and gave them some thought: We are on our way!

Then he continued, to himself, I really should offer a prayer, but what would a prayer do for us? When I went out to hunt, didn't the priest offer a prayer, and at the end… well, what about the end? What did I intend to say? Well, I really did not intend to say anything. But I will speak with the Jew.

Potocki asked Naḥum Ze'ev, Is this horse yours and is this carriage yours?

He replied, With your permission, esteemed lord of great compassion, I am a poor man, with neither a horse nor a carriage.

Potocki continued his questioning, So how do you come to have them?

He replied, My wife borrowed them from our neighbor in the village. The horse belongs to Nekiti, and I don't know who owns the carriage. Maybe it belongs to Nikolai and maybe it belongs to Nekiti. Both of them have been boasting that they were about to purchase a carriage, so it clearly belongs to one of them.

Potocki nodded in agreement, and then, resting his head on his shoulder, he dozed off.

Naḥum Ze'ev led Potocki along the same path that he used to bring his charcoal to town. He took the charcoal by horse, whereas he took Potocki by horse and carriage. When they reached the thickets of the forest, there was no way for a carriage to pass. He stopped the horse and looked at the lord.

Are we there?

He replied, We have not reached the city, but we have reached a place where the carriage cannot pass.

Potocki shouted in anger, Why?

Naḥum Ze'ev responded humbly, Because there is no road here.

Potocki said, Tell my servant to put me up on the carriage. Why are you silent?

While this one was thinking about how to answer, the other one reached a decision and said, I will give it a try, and maybe I will be able to ride on the horse.

Potocki came down from the carriage and tried to mount the horse. As soon as he got on, he felt dizzy and thought he would fall. Naḥum Ze'ev came to his aid and helped him to sit down on a fallen tree trunk. He then began talking to himself, Let's leave the carriage here in the forest, but let's hide it to keep it from thieves, and when we return safely from town we will give it back to Nikolai or Nekiti, but the horse we shall take along with us, we shall take the horse with us.

Potocki asked him, What was the prayer that you offered?

He replied, I was not praying. I was thinking about the path that I should take.

And what conclusion did you reach?

What conclusion did I reach? With the permission of my exalted lord, I reached the following conclusion: If my lord desires to go by foot, he will reach his castle at sunset. Should it be too difficult for him to proceed on foot, I will carry him on my shoulder, just as I did on the road from the forest to my house, when my lord showed us his kind favor by resting there.

Naḥum Ze'ev hid the carriage among the trees, whistled for the horse to follow him, took hold of Potocki by the arm, and they were on their way. At times, Naḥum Ze'ev stopped to give Potocki a rest; and at times, he stopped because Potocki was leaning so heavily against him.

It was close to sunset when they neared Buczacz.

5

The entire city was lit up with torches, and its streets hummed with the tumult of search parties gone out to look for their lord, who was lost in the forest. What was the cause of all this celebration? Potocki angrily asked Naḥum Ze'ev that question, and then demanded, Go and ask! Look! There is a reckless drunkard dancing around. Ask him.

Naḥum Ze'ev asked him, Why is the whole city lit up?

The drunkard answered him rudely with a vulgar word and said, Shut your mouth, Jew, and get out of the way of esteemed lords.

Potocki asked Naḥum Ze'ev, What did he say to you?

Naḥum Ze'ev said, I could not understand his language.

Potocki replied, You don't understand Polish? When will I get to my castle?

Naḥum Ze'ev said, We are not far from town. If the torch carriers don't cause us any delay, my lord will reach his castle in a short while.

Night had just begun when they neared the castle, with Naḥum Ze'ev holding Potocki by the arm, drawing the horse along behind him. Because of all the noise and the press of the crowd, no one noticed

Potocki or his companion or the horse that was being drawn along behind them.

As the horse and the lord and the Jew were being drawn along in the crowd, one of the torch carriers saw a Jew being pushed along. He kicked him in the legs. Naḥum Ze'ev faltered, and Potocki fell down with him. Startled, Naḥum Ze'ev asked Potocki, Have you been hurt?

Potocki asked angrily, What happened?

Naḥum Ze'ev lacked the strength to answer. The rope with which he had been holding the horse had been pulled out of his weakened hands and fell near the horse's hooves. Sensing that the rope had come loose, the horse picked up his hooves and went on his way. The two of them, Naḥum Ze'ev and the lord, lay down there, without any sense of time or of pain. But they were too weak to get up. Potocki lay there with eyes wide open. Looking around, he could see groups of people walking along, and he thought that he heard them mention his name. Little by little, he began to recognize them. Some were nobles who ate at his table. He knew who they were, but their names he could not recall.

Once again, he heard them mention his name. He recognized two of them. The names by which they were known were really indecent; so even now, when he was in such trouble, he had to laugh.

He said, Please hear me out, gentlemen. What are these torches all about?

One of those he asked did not respond, but one of them did respond, At this time tomorrow, I'll give you an answer.

There were so many torches that their faces were not recognizable. Naḥum Ze'ev, with great effort, managed to stand. He examined his legs and said, It's nothing.

Then he said to Potocki, Is our lord close to his castle? Then Naḥum Ze'ev let the lord lean against his shoulder, and the two of them walked along together. A little while later, they reached the castle. Everything was wide open. There was no one in the castle. All the lord's servants and all the other officials who had been with Potocki on the hunt had gone out to look for him. All the rooms in the castle were lit up, and the tables were laden with platters and dishes, cups and goblets, bottles and jars and remnants of food and drink as if there had been a great banquet there.

Potocki was weary and did not utter a word. He realized that the palace had been left unguarded. He looked at the remains of the meal, but his weariness outweighed his anger. He closed his eyes and said, Help me lie down on my bed.

Now, Naḥum Ze'ev had never been in Potocki's palace and did not know where Potocki's bed was located, and it was impossible to ask Potocki because he was asleep. He caught sight of a couch at the end of the hall and went over to it. Potocki thought that he had brought him to his bed and said, Put me down there.

The nobles returned and sat down at the table. They had dispatched their servants and the lesser nobles to look for their master. The food and drink that was left over from the big banquet was not enough to satisfy their appetite. They had been scouring the countryside in search of their lord and were starving. They clapped their hands and rattled the silverware to arouse the household servants. However, the servants who had already returned to the castle had not returned to their duties.

One of the lords saw the master of the house lying on the couch. He roused the others with the cry, Long may he live! The others arose and began to dance. Potocki paid no attention to them and did not say a word. They approached his couch, babbling in confusion, telling him how upset they had been when they realized that he had disappeared, and how they had left the catch from their hunt in order to scatter about looking for him, and finally, when they still had not found him, how they had gone out with torches in search of him.

Potocki asked derisively, And did you find him? Where is the Jew? Where is my rescuer?

The officials did not know whom Potocki was talking about, for Naḥum Ze'ev had already slipped away out of dread of being caught in the company of Potocki's men.

Potocki said, Go after him, and bring him here to me. And let no one do him any harm.

Potocki lay down with open eyes and waited impatiently for the Jew. The head of his household came to ask, What is my lord's desire, and what may I bring him?

Potocki shouted angrily, You can bring me my rescuer! Why are you just standing there? Why have you not brought him here?

The head of the household bowed and said, They have already gone out to look for him. They surely will bring him here very soon.

Potocki shouted, And you? Why did you let him go?

I? I did not see him.

Why *didn't* you see him? You didn't see him? What do you have eyes for? Anyway, here he is!

Naḥum Ze'ev was standing in front of Potocki, being held up by two of his men, one at each side.

Potocki shouted at them, Let him go! Take your hands off of him and get out of here!

And to Naḥum Ze'ev, he said, You have gone to a great deal of trouble for me, you and your wife. You gave me bread to eat and liquor to drink, a bed to lie down on, and you have looked after me all day, from nightfall to nightfall.

Everyone in Potocki's house stood there listening. Some who heard him imagined that Potocki was feverish, and some who heard him imagined that Potocki said what he said only to let the officials know that they had not acted as the Jew had acted, and still others did not understand what they heard.

Potocki spoke again, What can I give you as a reward for your trouble?

Naḥum Ze'ev was silent.

Potocki said, What is your answer to my question?

Naḥum Ze'ev said, What can I say? I had the opportunity to perform a mitzvah, so I am not asking for any reward.

One official said to Potocki, Give him *something*, give him whatever you want, so he won't have the opportunity to boast about doing you a favor.

Potocki continued speaking to Naḥum Ze'ev, If you want to return home, go there, and if you want to have two or three drops of wine, have a drink. And to his servants Potocki said, Two or three of you should see that he gets home.

Naḥum Ze'ev said, With my lord's kind permission, please allow me to go by myself.

By yourself ? Why?

Naḥum Ze'ev said, Since I find myself in town, I would like to go the synagogue for the evening prayer.

Potocki nodded his head, giving permission, and Naḥum Ze'ev went on his way.

6

Lying in his bed at night, Potocki recalled the day's events. In all his life, nothing like this had ever happened to him. Were it not for that Jew, Potocki thought to himself, I would be dead, and all the lords who had gone out on the hunt would be making decisions now about the funeral arrangements. They said that they had gone out to look for me. Undoubtedly, they indeed had gone out to look for me. And what was the result? They looked, and they did not find me. However, I am amazed about my dogs. They also went in search of me and did not find me. How could that have happened?

Potocki lay in his bed and thought about several of his dogs, each one by name, and also thought about each one's traits. One of them jumped up on him, and then another and another, each one expecting its master to pat its head, stroke its neck, say a kind word. Potocki did not move a hand or utter a word. At that moment, all his wonderful dogs were no more important to him than a pack of friends. He twisted his lips, stretched his hands out, and scattered the group of dogs that had gathered quietly around him as he shut his eyes tight to fall asleep. He already had fallen asleep about half an hour earlier, but in his dream he had imagined that he was awake, unable to sleep.

The next morning, when his elderly servant came to dress him, Potocki told him, I'm going to sleep all day, so do not let anyone bother me. And tell me now what I should give to the Jew who saved my life. Why are you silent? Why don't you answer me?

He said, I'm thinking about it.

What are your thoughts telling you?

With my lord's kind permission I will tell him what happened to me with that Jew.

Potocki said, Tell me.

He said, Several days ago, I was invited to that Jew's place. I was able to take note of his poverty and his labors, as well as what he had to eat, which could not have been satisfying. When I asked if he was being supported by charity, he replied, Thank God, I have enough to eat.

I asked him, What are your heart's desires?

He repeated my question: What are my heart's desires? One thing that I do ask for is to be worthy before God in His service.

I said, That really was not the purpose of my question. What do you need to have a chance to rest from your labors, to make life better for you?

He answered, What do I ask for? I ask that God will enable me to be satisfied with whatever He gives to me and my wife.

I told him, *Everyone* has something special to ask for, and that must apply to you as well. However, you prefer to hide that from me, and you don't want to tell me.

He said, I did have a special request, but I put it out of my mind.

Why?

Because I have seen that if a man asks for more than he has, they take away from what he has already.

I said, What did you have, and what did they take away? From what I can see, you had nothing that could be taken away from you.

He said, Don't say that. I had something, and I still have it. But it just is not the same now as it was before. All my life, I regretted that I could not pray every day with other Jews in a synagogue, for I lived in a village and the synagogue was in town. But I tried, and even now I try to go to town at fixed times. However, now that I am getting older, this has become difficult. Look, a man must be satisfied with what he has been given, and he should not ask for what he has not been given.

Potocki was lying down with his pipe between his lips, looking at his servant, who was waiting for the opportunity to say something to his master.

Potocki held out his pipe and said, Take it. But let me know why you've told me this whole story. I asked you for some advice, not for stories. Not only have you failed to give me advice; you stand there telling me things I know nothing about.

The servant said, With my lord's permission, I have something to add to what I have said already.

Potocki said, Well, what do you have to say? Are you looking for an excuse, you scoundrel? I ask you for advice and you try to get out of it by telling me stories.

The servant said, In my opinion, with my lord's kind permission, if he is allowed to pray daily at the synagogue in town, he could have no better reward.

Potocki shouted at him, And who is preventing him from praying in town? Did the Jew tell you that I prevent him from praying wherever he wants? Do you mean to say that if I, who gave my own architect to the Jews in my town to build their house of prayer, allowed him to pray in the synagogue in town that this would be a reward?

The servant said, In order to pray every day in town, he would have to *live* in town, and in order to live in town, he would have to rent a place in town, and in order to rent a place, he would have to pay rent. And even if he had the money, he would not be able to find a place because most of the Jews' houses have been destroyed since the days of the great fire, and anything that even resembles a house is filled with tenants.

Potocki said, So there is no place to live in the entire town?

The servant answered, With my lord's permission, there is not one available place in town.

Potocki said, In that event, I will be pleased to offer him the cellar of the city hall. Why are you silent? What is this? Does my gift not please you?

The servant said, I have been silent because I have been doing some thinking.

Potocki said, And what have you been thinking about?

He replied, Actually, I really have not been doing that much thinking, but I have been saying to myself that my lord's advice is quite good—very, very good. However, upon further consideration, I do not know how a Jew could support himself and his wife here. In the forest, there is always charcoal to be made. But what could he do in town? Nonetheless, my lord's advice is good, very, very good. If my lord would make the cellar available, there would then be a place where one could live. And God would also provide a livelihood, as people say: just as a master is good to his servants, so God the Master will be good to His creatures.

Potocki and his servant had no advice to offer. But a Jew who had dealings with Potocki's servant had some advice to give. What was it? To sell yeast.

I shall explain this is in some detail. Because most communities are small and unable to support their rabbis and because it has been said that one should not use the Torah "as a spade to dig with," the yeast concession was given to rabbis' wives. That is how it was in most small communities, and so it was in Buczacz as well. However, the rabbi's wife was ill and therefore unable to take on the business. It was announced that anyone who wants to have the concession to the yeast trade should come forward and take out a lease. Potocki contacted the town's leaders and purchased for himself the right to sell yeast in perpetuity.

Potocki arranged to meet Naḥum Ze'ev, to transfer the city-hall cellar to him with all its keys, and he gave him a bill of sale for the cellar stamped with his name and official seals. The document stated that from this time forth, the cellar is his in perpetuity and that Potocki's heirs, and *their* heirs, and anyone officially representing him or them for any reason whatsoever have no legal right to eject the Jew Naḥum Ze'ev from the cellar. And Potocki also transferred to him the communal document that grants the holder permission to sell yeast. This satisfies the amazement of people who wonder why the yeast trade in Buczacz is in the hands of a family of laymen rather than in the hands of the rabbi's wife.

7

Naḥum Ze'ev left his forest, his trees, his charcoal, and his hut to come with his wife to live in town. They set up house in the cellar of the Buczacz city hall that extended on and on into another country. But Naḥum Ze'ev and his wife made do with only a small part of the cellar, which was adequate for their needs. They cleared out their part of the cellar of rodents and insects that had been swarming there forever. Many people were envious of Naḥum Ze'ev, who had found a spacious place to live, for which he paid nothing, and because they were so jealous, they said to him, We are surprised that you can live in such a place, a place full of demons and evil spirits, a place where you can often hear weird noises coming up from the cellar because of the rats that are dancing around there.

Naḥum Ze'ev, however, had no fear of demons; indeed, he had no reason to fear them because before he took up residence in the cellar, he affixed a kosher mezuzah on each doorway that required one. So from then on, one heard no shrieks or mocking laughter coming from the cellar but only the sound of chapters of Psalms being recited, for it was Naḥum Ze'ev's practice to recite each day the psalm designated for that day.

David, king of Israel, has already expounded the matter in the Book of Psalms: *The wicked may lay it up, but the righteous will wear it.* When a ruthless person builds a house, he thinks that it is for himself and for his children and their children. In truth, however, he is building it for the righteous person who will appear in the future. This cellar, built by ruthless people out of fear of those who are even more ruthless, as a refuge in times of disaster, was given as an outright gift to that poor Jew for a place to live where he could serve his Creator and pray every day with all his fellow Jews.

We have something further to say about this matter. The Holy One makes use of everyone in order to accomplish His purposes. For example, a lord goes out on a hunt, and an animal crosses his path. The bullet that he shoots does not reach its target. He is drawn in pursuit of the animal and, after a time, finds that he is far away from his group and does not know how to get back. He begins to wander and then lies down and falls asleep. After he is discovered by a righteous person, he is returned to his castle. The point of all this is nothing other than to reward a Jew who yearns to pray together with others.

Thus, what that righteous man yearned for is given to him. Morning and evening, he would go to the synagogue and pray with the community. And between one service and another, he would sit in the cellar and sell yeast. Potocki had purchased this business for him from the community. Truth to tell, this is a story that we have told before. So why are we repeating it? We are repeating it in order to add the fact that the yeast made by Naḥum Ze'ev was of superior quality. The merchants therefore no longer had to purchase yeast from other locations to sell in Buczacz. Naḥum Ze'ev took pains to make his yeast so well that everyone could enjoy their daily bread and their Sabbath loaves. In this, he differed from other yeast sellers, whose only concern was profit and who caused anguish and shame for Jewish women when their bread did not rise and their ḥallot were not beautiful, but had collapsed, just like the flat noses of the gentile soldiers who had attacked Buczacz. For a man's wife is his equal and Ḥayyah Sarah was his true helpmate, just as Rashi had explained about Adam, first man: if he was deserving, she would be his helpmate.

From the first day that Naḥum Ze'ev and his wife had come to live in town, their sons and daughters would come to visit them, for the city of Buczacz was a metropolis, a center of trade. In addition to the market day that the founding fathers had established on Thursdays, Buczacz boasted a large fair every year. People came to it from a variety of places, some to sell and some to buy, including the sons and daughters of Naḥum Ze'ev and Ḥayyah Sarah, who were pleased to see that their children were following God's ways. To tell the truth, all Jews followed God's ways, but some do so out of habit because that is the custom, and some do so simply out of love of God, even though they had grown up in the forest without the good fortune of studying Torah. The integrity of their father and the modesty of their mother stood them in good stead.

8

It is customary for someone who owns a home or a courtyard to see that all of it is being utilized as a source of income. He rents out a room here or a large corner there or a bit of space elsewhere to store his merchandise according to his needs. This Naḥum Ze'ev did not do, but he kept the interests of others in mind. This was also the case for his children, and their children and *their* children, too. And this was true of Naḥum Ber, with whom I began this story.

What does it mean to be benevolent? There are small traders in town who do not have the money to rent a shop. They find small spots in the market where they spread out their merchandise. This takes a great deal of effort and entails the loss of a great deal of time because in the morning they bring their wares to the market, and at evening, they haul them back. There are certain kinds of merchandise too heavy for one man to handle. This necessitates an enormous amount of exhausting work. And if their merchandise is food, dogs and pigs can be an annoyance. And where do these small traders live? Far, far away from the market. It is only the wealthy who can afford to live nearby either because they inherited their homes or can afford the high rents. The poor and the needy are forced to live far from the market, far away from the source of their income.

Naḥum Ze'ev told them, There is space in my cellar for all the merchandise in Buczacz. Bring your merchandise to my cellar, and when you come for it in the morning, you will find it where you left it, and I am not asking for rent or for any kind of fee.

You can imagine the degree of help this afforded these small traders. He lightened the burden they bore in eking out their meager livelihood. This was truer still on Thursday, market day, when they were in a rush to set up in the morning and returned home late at night because of the people from villages who had come to town to purchase what they needed.

The traders, men and women alike, came every day between the afternoon and the evening prayers, or a little earlier or a little later, bringing their merchandise to the cellar, where it was safe from thieves, dogs and pigs, and fire. For the doors to the cellar were stronger than the doors of the stalls in the market, and this merchandise was safer than all the other merchandise in the market. How so? Because sometimes when the night watchman in the market would doze and the thieves heard his snores, they would open the doors and take out all the merchandise. Or perhaps the watchman and the thieves were in cahoots, and he let them make off with the merchandise. But the goods in the cellar were safe from thieves, for the cellar had double doors of iron so that if the inner doors were unlocked, the locked outer doors could be opened only by someone in possession of the key. This was the large key of the long cellar of the great city hall of Buczacz, given by the lord of Buczacz to that elder on the same day when he handed him the deed of title for the cellar. If you know how much the Poles feared the Tatars, you can imagine how fortified the cellar was, for it was there that the leaders of Buczacz sought protection from the Tatars. And if you know that this cellar is part of that great city hall that was the envy of all the cities of Poland, you can begin to imagine the pain that this caused the descendants of the noble house of Potocki, whose great-grandfather had brought them into partnership with none other than a Jew.

Those descendants had already made attempts to buy back the lease in perpetuity from Naḥum Ber Wallach, who had wisely responded, If I have attained the merit of being a partner to distinguished leaders from the House of Potocki, is it possible that I would withdraw my partnership?

Why am I repeating all of this since I have already told the entire story? It is to let you know how praiseworthy is Naḥum Ber, for he knew that the inheritance of a Jew, which was bequeathed to him by his ancestors, is more valuable than thousands and thousands of gold coins.

And so it was that Naḥum Ber Wallach did not sell his rights but continued to occupy the cellar and sell yeast, just like all his ancestors, in a chain of lineage stretching back to Naḥum Ze'ev the charcoal maker, who had received the cellar as a gift from Potocki.

At this point, I will leave the story of the generations between Naḥum Ze'ev and Naḥum Ber, to concentrate solely on Naḥum Ber.

Naḥum Ber was the last of his family to live in the cellar, for the Great War uprooted the people who lived in Buczacz and destroyed the town. When the war ended, and a few of the people of Buczacz were able to return, Buczacz was no longer ruled by Austria but by Poland, and Poland did not recall the kindnesses of ancestors, did not maintain the agreements forged by their predecessors with the Jews, and oppressed the Jews in every way possible. So the cellar was never returned to the heirs of Naḥum Ber, who was the last of those who had a stake in the cellar.

Naḥum Ber Wallach did not have the privilege of having sons, though he had two daughters. The name of the eldest I have forgotten; the name of the youngest was Nechi. The eldest did not have any good fortune. She was married to a difficult man who squandered her dowry and sent her away penniless. She returned to her father, bringing with her only the bad habits that she had learned from the man who had divorced her. She desecrated the Sabbath in public. One Sabbath, she was observed knitting while sitting on a bench near the River Strypa.

Neither the pleas of her father nor his promises to buy her a sweater lovelier than the one she was making were of any avail. People said that she had gone mad and that she wanted to irritate the God-fearing, who thought that the world should be governed by their standards. God-fearing people paid her no attention, but she caused her father pain when he saw his own daughter desecrating the Sabbath and leading a life that would lead her to Gehinnom.

People would ask, Why is Naḥum Ber being punished by having a daughter who transgresses Jewish law and religion? And they did not realize that in the future, their own children and grandchildren would be asking why *they* were being punished, being killed just because they were Jews.

We shall now set aside the questions that sages greater than we have asked without finding an answer, and we shall set aside Naḥum Ber's eldest daughter, who atoned for her sin through her suffering, and we shall say something about the youngest daughter Nechi, who was a source of comfort for her father all his life. I knew her when I was a youngster because my mother, my teacher of blessed memory, acted as her guardian after her mother died and left her without any relatives living in town.

It was because of changes in the nature of people and in the temperament of the generations that Nechi's mother died. People said that she died because of the unhealthy air in the cellar. Naḥum Ber left the home that he had made in the cellar and rented a place elsewhere. Because his Nechi was so attached to my mother, of blessed memory, he rented a place that was near our home. Thus Nechi could be close to her guardian and visit her whenever she wanted, rather than spend the entire day isolated and lonely. When Naḥum Ber was on his way home from evening prayers on winter evenings, he would visit us to drink a cup of tea. He did so for his health because people of that generation were not yet accustomed to drinking tea as a beverage. They considered it to be medicinal; in fact, in Polish, tea is called *herbata,* the name of a medicinal herb.

Nechi was married to a relative of ours, an upright man who was a grain merchant, Feivush Ringelblum by name. They lived together in contentment and had a brilliant son named Monyo. This was Menaḥem

Emanuel, who was Emanuel Ringelblum, murdered by the filthy, accursed agents of the wretched abomination, in the Warsaw Ghetto.

I do not know whether any of Naḥum Ber's family are still alive, or whether they shared the fate of most of the people in Buczacz, who were wiped out by the accursed filthy mobs. Whatever their fate was, I want to retain the memory of Naḥum Ber Wallach, the last of the family of Naḥum Ze'ev the charcoal maker, who received as a gift the large cellar in the great city hall of Buczacz because of his desire to pray with a congregation. And Naḥum Ber likewise would spend morning and evening in the study house, praying with the community.

Naḥum Ber was not among those who spent time in Torah studies; however, he had great esteem for those who studied Torah. In spite of all his troubles, he was a happy man who made other people happy as well. I remember that when I was studying Torah in the old study house with my father, my teacher, a righteous man whose memory is a blessing, the shop owners in the market would come to the study house in the winter several times a day to warm up and escape the cold because in the old study house there was a stove that was very well attended to; it was kept burning throughout the winter, day and night. And even Naḥum Ber Wallach would come to spend time there.

Whenever he came in, he would look around, with eyes that shone with joy, at the students sitting there in groups studying Torah. He would stand there and clap his hands while chanting one of the old melodies that inspire one with the love of Torah.

Many melodies have I heard and forgotten. But there is one that remains with me. When I remember days of the past, when our town was filled with Jews and our old study house was filled with the study of Torah, my mind goes back to that melody that Naḥum Ber would be humming as he came in to the study house. I am unable to repeat that melody, but its words were in Aramaic, and here is their translation:

God, who is exalted, unending and boundless,
The Torah, with favor, bestowed He upon us.

Translated by Jules Harlow

The Water Pit

THERE IS A STORY TO BE TOLD about the neighborhood behind the River Strypa. Once on Tishah b'Av after the fast, some schoolchildren were digging and found a pit full of water. The residents of the neighborhood rejoiced that they had found water, for they would no longer have to transport their water the distance from the well at the market.

There was one old woman there, who was visited nightly by the Master of Dreams, who would reveal things that were hidden from others. Some she would tell to her neighbors and some she would tell in the market and in the streets. There were those from Buczacz who saw her words as a kind of prophecy and acted accordingly, and there were others who mocked her and her dreams. On the following day when everyone was rejoicing over the water, the old woman came and stood over the mouth of the pit and declared, "It has been revealed to me in a dream that these waters have flowed here from the well of Ashmadai, King of the Demons; therefore take care and do not drink this water." There were those who heard her and laughed and there were others who became angry with her for turning their rejoicing into sorrow and mourning. When they went to draw water, the waters withdrew, and the pit became dry, without a drop of water in it.

A few days later, one of the walls of the Gymnasium burst and water began pouring out of it. There was no colder or more thirst-quenching water to be found anywhere in Buczacz. There were those who went to great lengths to quench their thirst there, while others refrained from drinking the waters or even cooling their hands in it in those hot days. They said that these were the very waters that had come from the well of Ashmadai, King of the Demons, as had been announced to the old woman through the Master of Dreams. In the end, even those who had made a regular practice of going there left off, because the Gymnasium's headmaster would no longer allow strangers into its courtyard. Those who could afford to paid a water carrier to haul their water from the market well, and those who could not had to rely on themselves or their daughters.

Such was the custom of the water-carrier. Every day after morning prayers, which he prayed at sunrise, he would take two large vessels and fill them from the market well; he would make his rounds of Jewish homes adding water to their barrels. There were some who would pay by the pitcher and others who fixed a monthly price and would pay him on the first of each month. One of his good qualities was to be precise in giving people their water at the same time each day and giving each household the amount it required. There were some who noticed his care and others who did not, until something happened that made everyone take notice.

There was a death in the neighborhood, so all the neighbors poured out their water. After the corpse was removed, the water carrier came by with his jugs and filled up their barrels. Someone said to him, "What is this? Every day you bring water in the morning and today you are bringing it only now? Are you a prophet? Did you know that all the water would have to be spilled out?" Another heard and said, "It must be that the deceased revealed to him in a dream that he would die today." Someone else added, "It's impossible that the Master of Dreams spoke with him, because I heard that the water carrier was up all night with a sick person." Still another said, "If so, it's truly a great question why on every other day he brings water in the morning, yet today he did so only after all the water had been poured out." The water carrier was silent. Because they pressed him so much, he said, "I did so because I was up all night. In the morning, I didn't have the strength to draw water. And now you must find another water carrier, for I see that I am weak and can no longer bring you your water." Two or three days later, he disappeared from the city without a trace.

There were many guesses, but they never guessed the truth. When it comes to a humble workman who lives by the labor of his hands and acts kindly to all, Buczacz is not sufficiently noble to regard him as a tzaddik, to say nothing of recognizing the hidden tzaddik whom no eye ever sees.

Translated by Herbert Levine and Reena Spicehandler

Feivush Gazlan

Prologue: Why I Call Feivush Feivush

Go four or five steps below the kosher slaughterhouse, and you will come to a level area that you might think is a valley. This valley lies between two waterways: the River Strypa, which the Holy One created with the primordial waters of Creation; and the Strypa canal, which was dug to power the wheel of the flour mill. The valley lies like a peaceful island surrounded by water. Willow branches overhang and proliferate densely day and night. Birds twitter in the gleaming silvery leaves. Because of those trees, the valley is called the Valley of the Willows. The elders of the Jewish community, however, call it the Courtyard Valley because that was where the courtyards of the Buczacz nobility once lay. The lords of Buczacz had built themselves houses there after the Tatars destroyed the castle and its fortifications, before Khmelnitski the Evildoer came and slaughtered the whole city. The courtyards face the demolished castle, the collapsed walls of which jut out from the protruding rocks that grind menacingly against one another.

Today nothing remains of that courtyard valley except those willows and the fragrant marsh grass and, if you will, this story itself that I am about to tell about a fire in Feivush Gazlan's house. Except that his name is not Feivush. For reasons that I will keep to myself I will not call him by his real name but rather will call him Feivush. Why Feivush and not another name? Because he served Feivush the tax collector and gave his life for Feivush the tax collector's money and was ready to jump into

Gehinnom for the sake of Feivush the tax collector. Therefore do I call him Feivush in the name of that other Feivush.

So that you not mistake one Feivush for the other, I will note some differences between them. Feivush the tax collector was corpulent, small and round, broad-shouldered and pot-bellied, as wide around as he was tall. His arms were short and thick, as were his hands and fingers. His face and nose were oval-shaped, like the pots in which the gentile women would carry pickled cabbage, and his chubby cheeks swallowed up his eyes, and his eyes swallowed up all that they beheld. A stubby beard encircled his cheeks and his earlocks were tucked behind his ears. His gait was unsteady; you didn't know if his feet thumped against the ground or the ground thumped against him. He had a kind of rattle in his throat. When he stood up his feet groped the ground until they brought him a chair to sit on.

On the other hand, Feivush Gazlan, that is, Feivush the enforcer, was tall. He had a long beard and his earlocks cascaded down his angular temples onto his sallow and sad cheeks like two perfectly curved slaughtering knives. His arms were long and one of his eyes was covered with a spleen-shaped scale. You couldn't tell if it was the right eye or the left one because no one looking up at Feivush could see past his mouth. You wouldn't hear him coming until he stood right in front of you. They used to call him "the stolen lulav" or "the withered lulav" because he was as thin as a withered lulav. When he became an enforcer they began to call him Feivush Gazlan. Some called him Feivish, and some called him Favish. Not everyone talks the same way and each place had its own way of pronouncing things.

1. A Song of Afflictions

There, at the far end of the courtyard valley, facing the street where the synagogue destroyed by Khmelnitski once stood, Feivush made a home for himself. Wood and stone debris from the demolished house of Jacob Frank lay there, untouched by human hands. Feivush collected it and built his home out of it. The whole house was one room supported on four poles, with a ladder leaning against it for entry and egress. Sometimes the ladder was set out and sometimes it was not, depending on the needs and desires of the owner.

Feivush dwelled there, free as a bird with no worries about rent. He and his wife Mamtchi lived above, his goat and chickens below. And even though they were far from town and could hear neither the footsteps of the town sentry nor the knocks of the shamash's mallet awakening slumberers to morning prayers, they had no fear of thieves or murderers, for at night they would pull up the ladder and no one could gain entry.

But Feivush could walk into any Jewish home. At any point during the night, as long as there was a candle burning inside, he was authorized to enter, for he was an inspector for the candle tax, which is to say, he was one of its enforcers. Candle tax inspectors were as intimidating as the royal constabulary: no door could be locked against them and they could walk into any place as if it were their own.

This is how they did it. On the Sabbath or a festival, on Ḥanukkah or any celebration in a Jewish home, the inspectors would enter and count up all the candles. If a candle was burning with no tag indicating that the tax on it had been paid, the inspectors were authorized to extinguish the candle and levy a fine on its owner. Why was that? Because the Crown had imposed a tax on all candles lit in honor of Sabbath, festivals, Ḥanukkah, and wedding feasts, and the householder had to place a tag on the candle to indicate that the tax on it had been paid. The candle tax darkened the lives of the Jews and brought their joyous occasions to a halt because at any moment an enforcer could walk in the door and blow out the candles and impose a fine. On the nights of Ḥanukkah and wedding feasts, Feivush would go in by himself, while on Sabbath and festival nights he would be accompanied by two gentiles, like the two angels who on Friday nights accompany every Jew home from synagogue. If he found a candle burning without the candle tax tag, he would instruct the gentiles to extinguish it, and they, on their own, would punish the innocent along with the guilty and extinguish even those candles that had the appropriate tag. Those who had the good fortune of finishing their meal by candlelight enhanced their Sabbath delight with a fish dinner, while those who did not were deprived of the pleasure of eating fish on the Sabbath for fear of having a bone lodged in their throat and thus endangering their life. As for the possibility that one of the gentiles might touch the wine and thus render it unfit, it was well established that once Esau would lay eyes on it, not a drop would remain. Moreover, in the countries in which we live the drink of choice is whisky and, as the Magen Avraham explains, one can make kiddush on Sabbath and holidays over whiskey.

But worse than the hardships of no fish or wine on Sabbath nights was the hardship of no Torah. On summer nights, one could make up for this deprivation by rising early and completing one's review of the weekly Torah portion in time. But in winter, when the nights are long, the problem was more acute because there was no light by which to read. Even if he knew twenty-four chapters by heart there were times when one wanted to look into the commentaries. The Jews of Buczacz in particular felt the sting of the candle decree because they studied the Bible regularly and their chief delight on the Sabbath was to savor the interpretations the commentators offered. If they were deprived of light at night they had no chance of consulting the commentaries and thus would miss out on the key pleasure of Sabbath. Summer and winter nights are, however, equal in regard to food, for it is one thing to see what you are eating and quite another not to know what is going into your mouth. But the hardest part of the whole decree was Feivush Gazlan. Feivush Gazlan was a creature of Buczacz, and the people of Buczacz are very precise about how they do things. They do nothing unscrupulously. But whereas they do good deeds, Feivush does evil. There was not a Sabbath or a festival or a wedding feast at which Feivush did not appear, even in houses that were falling apart. If he found a candle with no tax tag on it he would penalize the owner and blow it out. In those days in Buczacz they sang a dirge about this. I cite it here together with a paraphrase so that anyone who knows Yiddish can read it in the original, and whoever doesn't can read it in paraphrase. The lament went like this:

Der heyliker bashefer hot undz dem shabes koydesh gegebn
volt oykh avade, oy, keday geven tsu lebn
kumt ober plitslekh plitsem Favish gefloygn
un gazlt avek dos likht fun di oygn.

Got iz gerekht un zayne mishpotim zenen gerekht
s'iz ober undz prikre oyf aykh heylike lekht
far vos lozt ir aykh zogn fin Favishn deyes
farsarfet zol er vern mit bord un peyes.

For this our hearts faint, our eyes well with tears,
'Twixt man and the beast no difference appears.

This is what the words mean:

The Creator has given us the holy Sabbath
which makes life worth living.
But all of a sudden Feivush the Thief appears
and robs our eyes of their light.
You are righteous O God, and your precepts are right
But your holy lights are a bit hard on us
So why do you let Feivush be so impudent to You?
Let him be burned together with his beard and his earlocks.

2. The Troubles Jews Have

One Sabbath, which coincided with Tishah b'Av, the fast of the Ninth of Av, a small group of students were sitting in the old beit midrash and studying the chapter Hanizakin and the midrash on the Book of Lamentations. They began to enumerate the troubles that befell us from the day Jerusalem was destroyed and we were exiled from our land. Their spirits grew low and they became increasingly dejected. One of them, seeing how downcast his comrades were, opined that they should actually be grateful to Titus the Wicked for causing this day to come about because we use fewer candles and need fear neither the tax nor Feivush Gazlan. Since they mentioned the candle tax decree that was instituted in their time, they began to talk about it and came to make mention of Shlomo Kobler who was the reason it came about in the first place. Shlomo Kobler was born into a prosperous family in Nadvorna. He became well known throughout the country for his great Torah learning, his sharp mind, and his extensive knowledge of Talmud and codes of Jewish law.

Many of the great rabbis of the time cast their eyes on him as a potential match for their daughters. Our illustrious Master, author of *Sefer Neta Sha'ashuim* very nearly married off his daughter to him. But no harm befalls the righteous, for he did not take Shlomo as his son-in-law, taking instead his friend, who was better than he, our Master, the tzaddik who wrote the *Da'at Kedoshim,* who ruled as the rabbinic authority in Buczacz for fifty years after the *Neta Sha'ashuim*. Shlomo went to Vienna. While walking around the city he saw people eating and drinking and carousing. This is where I want to be, he thought to himself. Jews then were not yet allowed to live in Vienna except those who were needed by the royal court or who had dealings with it. Shlomo looked around and discovered that what the court needed were taxes. So he went to the ministers and proposed the idea of imposing a tax on candles lit on the nights of Sabbath, festivals, Ḥanukkah, and wedding feasts. The court looked into the matter and found that such a decree would be tolerated by most people in the country since it applied only to Jews. They then sent out tenders for the lease of the right to manage the collection of the tax. Some wealthy members of the Jewish community got wind of this and jumped at the opportunity. They bid up the price of the lease higher and higher until it rose far beyond what the ministers and clerks had estimated. The court, worrying that they might renege, awarded them the lease. The lessees promptly went back to their towns and hired intimidating individuals whom they appointed to collect the tax in all places where Jews lived, much like those who enforced the tax on the transportation of food and drink. Such overseers were known as *strasznhiks*; we call them enforcers. If my translation is imprecise, the general sense is not.

I now return to my subject. Whenever it came to be Sabbath or a festival or some celebratory feast, the enforcers would come and check to see if the candles were kosher, in other words if they were burning legally or illegally, in other words if the tax had been paid for every single candle. How did they determine this? A packet of tax certificate tags lay before the candles and the enforcers would count both candles and tags. If the numbers matched, all was well and good; if not, then woe to the candles and woe to the householder. That is how the decree worked.

But to this decree, the lessees added one decree of their own. They issued the tags only on Fridays and for that Sabbath alone. Each Sabbath had its own set of tags and they were given out just before nightfall. The same held for festivals and other nights when the candle tax had to be paid.

So the students in the beit midrash sat there pondering the troubles that the Holy One, blessed be He, had brought upon Israel. They reflected that there was no trouble that Israel suffered in which a Jew did not bear some responsibility. The hand may have been the hand of Esau, but the voice was the voice of Jacob. Jacob declares the harm to be done and Esau implements it. Had Jacob not whispered in Esau's ear, Esau would not have lifted his hand against the Jews; had a Jew not counseled the imposition of the candle tax, the court would never have instituted such a decree; had the wealthy Jews not secured the lease to collect the tax, the tax would not have been so onerous; and had Feivush not been the enforcer, the decree would have been softened by a small bribe, and these troubles would have been borne like all the others to which we are accustomed.

3. Old Men and Young

Among those sitting in the beit midrash was an old man, one of the learned men of earlier times. He was wont to search after the root cause of events, and he was not reluctant to express his opinions. Buczacz had its share of such elders who allowed their mouth to utter what was in their heart even if what came out was damaging, for sometimes words become deeds. This was the case with those tavern owners who paid heed to what the elders had said to them. They agreed not to inform on each other so they could serve drinks on which they paid no tax. The same thing happened with the young men who were detained under guard to be conscripted into the royal army, when the Jewish community had to supply a quota of men each year. Because no one wanted to give his son to the king's army where they would come to desecrate the Sabbath and eat forbidden foods and commit other transgressions, they would take young men from the lower ranks who were not Torah students or well born, and would send them to the army in place of those who were, soul for soul, as I have told elsewhere in detail.

The elders of the beit midrash bandied the matter about and opined that since all Israel are the children of Abraham, Isaac, and Jacob, and before God there is no difference between rich and poor, it followed that even if a man were rich or pedigreed, and his son knew how to make a display of his learning, he was not permitted to substitute him for another Jewish boy. What came out of all that talk? One morning they found the room where the detainees were kept with its door open and the guard drunk, and all the young men who were to be sent to the army had vanished. The clever elders of the beit midrash had the habit of finding in Scripture keys to moral conduct, and something tells me that they did so now, because they overdid their study of the biblical books. Some of them would learn twenty-four chapters every day; some would read through all the books of the prophets and the additional writings every month; some would ponder Scripture even while conducting business in the marketplace; and some would scrutinize their deeds and the deeds of others according to biblical verses that would occur to them. There is no language like that of the prophets to attune oneself to truth and righteousness and to express those qualities in words. This is why they became accustomed to saying what was in their heart even though it did not accord with the wishes of the powers in the community who held the leases on the beverage and other taxes. Now because young men are passionate about truth and fairness, the students were drawn to that old man. And he, too, was drawn to them because they were so attentive to his words. This is what he said to them:

I hear you saying that no trouble comes to Israel where a Jew is not behind it. This is especially true of the candle tax, especially in regard to its severity. It would be less severe were it not for the Jewish lessees. When a Jew purchases rights from the court he pays handsomely because he is afraid someone else will come and preempt him with a bribe. So he runs and bribes the officials, and highly placed officials can't be bought off cheaply. Such costs require income to offset them, and so a Jew who acquires the lease to some business will be very hard-nosed and will institute fines and penalties. And should you maintain that a person will always seek to make a profit, my answer is why exact it from Jewish blood? If you want to use your money to make a living, go and make it in a proper business and don't make money off Jewish blood. Nevertheless, I want to give Feivush Gazlan the benefit of the doubt. When a hungry person hires himself out in order to put bread on the table, it is not he who determines his actions but the work that he engages in. The task he is assigned to perform, whatever it is, will undo him. The very fact that he is assigned to do something will unhinge him. Even if his heart tells him to do this and not that, his unsettled state will disconcert him and subvert his actions. We see this in the cheerless way most of those charged with administering communal affairs walk around. Why are they cheerless? Because they are not at peace with themselves. What they do is not in line with what they believe. What I just said about every assignment undoing the one who is appointed to do it—well, that reminds me of a story I shall relate to you.

There was in the beit midrash this impoverished young man who groveled before every person he came in contact with. He made himself as nothing even before the least of the least. One day the shamash had to leave to go somewhere, and so he said to the penniless boy, here is the key to the cupboard, and if I do not return right after the evening service, open the closet and distribute the candles to the students. The time for giving out the candles arrived, and the shamash had not yet returned. So we said to that poor boy, Take out the candles. He raised himself up ponderously, as if he had put on a hundred pounds. He stuck the key in the lock, but the lock did not open. It was as if his hands had turned to wax. When he finally opened the cupboard, he took the candles, mounted the podium, and looked at us the way a parnas would look at the dolts he would deliver up to the army. At that precise moment, this formless entity was created anew. He acquired a discernible face, a nose and eyes, and even his hands regained their strength. He squashed the candles he had taken out to distribute thereby denying them to the outstretched hands of those waiting to receive them. He would also switch one candle with another even though they all were identical. This is what I meant when I said that authority of any kind undoes the one who exercises it. Indeed, as has been observed, love of greatness and power is a sickness. So it was with Feivush. It was not because the lessee cut him in for a penny on every guilder in fines he brought in that he became so exacting or so relentlessly wicked. Rather, it was because when a person is appointed to be an official or an officer of the law, another attitude takes hold in him and compels him to cause suffering.

The old man continued, Now that I have told you about that poor lad, perhaps you want to hear what he got in return for his elevation in status. I can tell you now that he was not happy with it. I will tell you why.

There was another time when the shamash had to leave and again he left it to the poor lad to distribute the candles. It happened that a burning candle fell and damaged his clothing, either because it fell or because someone tipped it. The fire took hold of his clothing and burned it and he too was singed. Heaven forfend that the intention was to cause him financial harm. Rather the idea was to frighten him, to let him know that he should not act maliciously even when he had the opportunity to do so. And so if you are ever given authority, restrain your impulses. If you don't, you will make people very angry at you.

4. Relaxation and Peace

At the very hour that the students cloistered in the beit midrash were commiserating about Israel's suffering, Feivush was getting up from his afternoon nap. His wife brought out a pitcher of chilled fruit juice. Feivush made the blessing over it, took a drink and then another. He affixed his spectacles and sat and read to his wife from the Tzenerena. No hour was more pleasant to Feivush than the one after his Sabbath afternoon nap when he would sit and read to his wife Mamtchi from the Tzenerena. Even though those Yiddish books were written expressly for women, Mamtchi did not know how to read them. Most of the women in Buczacz were learned, but Mamtchi came from another town. She was orphaned in her childhood and when her parents died they left her completely penniless. She hired herself out as a maid, and the women she worked for enslaved her as Pharaoh did in Egypt, and paid her a pittance. She did not have the means to hire a tutor nor did she even have the time to learn the alphabet. If Feivush did not read books to her on the Sabbath, she would be inferior to a cow. Except with a cow you can write a Torah scroll on its hide or make tefilin straps from it, whereas Mamtchi in this life was a mere mass of flesh, and in death would be dust and food for the worms.

Now it fell out that that Sabbath was Shabbat Ḥazon, the Sabbath of the Vision, as well as the Fast of the Ninth of Av, and so Feivush read to her the story of the destruction of Jerusalem. We must applaud the author of the Tzenerena, for Feivush's grief at recounting the destruction of Jerusalem was offset by his delight at the cleverness of those inestimable dwellers in Zion. That was topped by the story of the gnat that got into the evil Titus's nose and burrowed into his brain for seven years, and when he died they split open his skull and found there something like a bird weighing two *selas*, with a beak of brass and claws of iron. God initially allows the wicked to do whatever they wish, even to destroy the Temple, but in the end He exacts vengeance from them and brings upon them nasty and dire suffering. There was Pharaoh, and he was afflicted by ten plagues and wound up drowning in the sea. There was Sisera, and he was given over to the hands of a woman who crushed his head. There was Nebuchadnezzar, and he was turned into a bear and ate grass for seven years. There was Titus, and a gnat came and entered his nose and burrowed into his brain for seven years until he died of terrible and horrible suffering. That is the fate of all enemies of Israel, both those mentioned in the Torah and those not. So if you see a wicked oppressor eating and drinking and enjoying all kinds of pleasures and having a good time, the One who sits in Heaven is making a rope with which to hang him, for God does not countenance the wicked who bring distress to Israel. Why then does He allow them all those good things? In order to destroy them in the end, so that they should feel their sufferings to the fullest extent. One who has nothing has nothing to lose, one who has much has a lot to lose, and one who loses a lot suffers a lot.

Feivush looked at his wife to see if she had noticed his cleverness. Her excesses in food and drink had fattened her heart and shrunk her brain and she did not grasp the holy matters that he was relating to her. Feivush's expressive voice spiced up the telling but it meant nothing to her. Still, she sensed from it that the Holy One, Blessed be He, does not deny some benefit from the destruction of Jerusalem, for after Tishah b'Av come days of consolation when there are joyous occasions and many weddings. Feivush would go from one wedding ceremony to another, from one celebration to another, all the while imposing fines, because those joyous occasions required many candles. If you counted all the candles you would surely find some on which the tax had not been paid, and R. Feivush, that is, Feivush the tax collector, was generous with Feivush Gazlan. He gave him one percent of the fines he collected. It came out that he would make more from fines in one night in this season than he would normally have made in a week. Some nights, there would be more, some nights less; it all depended on how many weddings and celebrations took place. Mamtchi could sense all this because when she looked up from the edge of her shawl and gazed at him the way a wife looks at her loving husband, she saw in him a very astute man. Her love for his astuteness prompted her to tell him what she had prepared for him for the pre-fast meal. And what had she prepared? Chicken and some hot soup, a dish of groats, and a kugel stuffed with fresh plums encircled by puffs of flour roasted in goose fat. Feivush had been missing his meat dishes because of the Nine Days. Such dishes are usually eaten hot, but how could they retain their heat for the pre-fast meal when she had already opened the oven door at lunch time? In doing that she had not desecrated the Sabbath. If anyone had desecrated the Sabbath it was the Torah students cloistered in the beit midrash. They had not intended to do so, Heaven forfend, but the fact that the very holiness of the day requires that all words uttered on it must pertain to the Sabbath, can itself initiate its actual desecration.

But better I should tell of these matters as they happened and not be like those who excoriate loudly and theatrically and do not articulate what the eyes can plainly see.

5. A Sound of Burning is Heard

When the students had finished venting their opinions about that fatuous young man who got his comeuppance for the foolish authority he held for a few short moments, they resumed talking about Feivush Gazlan. There had been a Shalom Zakhor the night before and many people had gathered for a convivial feast. They were sitting and singing Sabbath songs such as "Rest and refreshment, a light to the Jews" when Feivush burst in together with two vicious agents. They found one candle without a tax tag and proceeded to put out all of them, and they slapped a fine on the man who had made the feast. At that moment the new mother was nursing her newborn, and her hold on him loosened and he fell from her hands. How appropriate for that wicked one, who extinguished the Jews' light, to discover that the punishment for one who acts as he had is meted out in this world.

And with that the old man got up and went on his way, and the young men resumed studying the opening passage of the midrash on the Book of Lamentations.

They sat and read with a chant, "King Solomon, peace be upon him, says in the Book of Proverbs, *When a wise man contends with a fool, there is anger and laughter but no rest*. This comes to teach us that whoever judges a fool is himself judged. When a wise man judges a fool, what is the result? Anger—even if there is laughter. Because that laughter will not spring from contentment. And so even if the fool makes you want to laugh, do not allow yourself to do so because it will be a laughter in which you will take no satisfaction." Thus did they read and interpret until they came to the section beginning with the verse *One who rebukes a buffoon will bring shame upon himself.*

Suddenly word was heard among them that Feivush Gazlan's house was on fire. At first they thought there was nothing to this report, that it was merely the result of an unspoken wish. Let the one who fed us with suffering taste a little bit of it himself. After all, he was worse than that fool whose clothes were burned by a candle. But when the report persisted they knew it was true.

They sat and pondered the judgments that the Holy One, blessed be He, ordains for the wicked: the very thing they prevent Israel from having, He ordains for them. That fool did not bestir himself to give scholars candles for illumination and withheld the light of Torah, and what was his punishment? Fire flared from a candle and burned his garments. Feivush Gazlan extinguished the light of the Jews, and what did he get for that? Fire broke out in his house. Moreover, because he dimmed the light of their eyes on the Sabbath, so was he punished on the Sabbath. And just as he disturbed the peace in their households, so was his own house stricken.

They began to deliberate whether they had an obligation to go to the rescue. If not to save him, then to save his wife, and if not his wife, then for the sake of the neighbors. They concluded that a woman can be presumed to save herself. As for the neighbors, well, Feivush's house was far from where people lived and there were no neighbors. And even if there were, the house stood on watery ground. In any case, they still had to clarify the laws dealing with such a fire on the Sabbath, what was permitted and what was forbidden and what was purposeful labor performed for its own sake where no danger was involved if left unextinguished.

They had not finished clarifying the legal rulings when they put their books back on the shelves and went out. Once outside they met up with many others. Some were going simply to have a look and some were motivated by a desire to fulfill the mitzvah of witnessing the downfall of the wicked. In doing do they were committing a whole host of transgressions. They were transgressing the prohibition of taking hurried steps on the Sabbath; they were transgressing the injunction not to walk on the Sabbath the way one walks during the week; they were transgressing the commandment *You shall not hate your brother in your heart*; they were transgressing the commandment *You shall not stand by the blood of your fellow man*; and they were transgressing several other commandments. There was no end to the commandments they were transgressing in the name of a mitzvah they had fabricated. But you should know that they repented for each and every one of them.

Presently they arrived at the bridge between the town and its outlying neighborhoods. Beyond the bridge was a wooded hill called Fedor, named for Theodor, whom the gentiles called Fedor. This is the Fedor or Theodor who built the city hall, which was the most magnificent building in all of Poland. To the left of the bridge, behind the Strypa, is an area with a cluster of small houses clapped together from boards and junk wood, like unlaid eggs recovered from within a slaughtered chicken. To the right of the bridge was the path leading to the kosher slaughterhouse, which I mentioned at the outset of the story. From there one came to the courtyard valley at the end of which Feivush had built the house where he and Mamtchi lived.

They crossed the bridge and turned right, in the direction of the Courtyard Valley, toward Feivush Gazlan's place, accompanied by those who lived behind the Strypa. They passed the slaughterhouse and entered the Courtyard Valley. They beheld the whole valley enveloped in tranquility. There was no fire or smoke other than a bluish haze that wafted up from the trees, and the shrubs and gave off a fragrance as pleasant as the havdalah spices. Birds flitted from tree to tree and from shrub to shrub chattering to one another. Or maybe they were conversing with the Holy One, blessed be He—who knows what they were saying? The waters of the Strypa rippled gently, the waves undulated in unison, and a light breeze blew from the two forests that surround the Strypa. Even the frogs, survivors of the Ten Plagues, put forth a kind of melody. Everyone stood there enraptured by that loveliness that was savored by no one other than Feivush Gazlan, whose house stood at the end of the courtyard valley. The ways of God are hidden, His thoughts must be very deep when He bestows serenity like that upon the wicked. Or maybe He bestows it upon them first in order to destroy them in the end, the case in point being that fire that was reported or had already been put out, or never happened.

They began to disperse, one going this way and one going that, one gazing at the trees and the shrubs and one at the water, one opening his shirt to the breeze and one looking down into the clear water and feeling sad. Was he sad out of mourning for Jerusalem? Not at all. He took pity on himself for not being able because of the Sabbath and Tishah b'Av to cast off his clothes and bathe, having not immersed in water for three weeks. While they were enjoying such pleasures they quite forgot about the destruction of Jerusalem and rejoiced at having come to such a pleasant and airy place. I am quite sure that there were some among them who were quite ready to conduct the afternoon service in the valley without a Torah scroll to read from, and to wait there until dark and enter into the chanting of the Tishah b'Av dirges with a joyful heart. Lest you think I exaggerate, know that everything is according to the deed. Whoever is worthy of praise, I praise; whoever is not worthy I do not—even if he is a fellow Buczaczer, and even if he is from earlier generations.

6. Goodwill and Grudges, Respectively

Feivush heard the clatter of feet and stood looking out the window. He saw a large crowd of Jews the likes of which was never seen in the valley except on Rosh Hashanah when they came to perform the Tashlikh ritual. They all came to that place because it faced what was known as the Street of the Synagogue. Before 1648 the Great Synagogue had stood there. The front end of the valley was directly across from the site of the destroyed synagogue but they did not hold the Tashlikh service there because a church had been erected on that spot.

Feivush began to contemplate the large crowd in the courtyard valley. The thought occurred to him that maybe the Messiah had arrived, for in the Tzenerena it is written that the Temple was destroyed on Tishah b'Av and we will be redeemed on Tishah b'Av. What Feivush didn't know was that the sources did not intend this to mean a Tishah b'Av that falls on the Sabbath. He began to wonder about himself: if the Messiah has come I should be happy, and I'm not happy. Heaven forbid that I am not like all the other Jews, but the Messiah has not yet come. So what is this large crowd doing here? I'll go and ask them.

He took hold of the ladder that stood to the left of the doorway. In his rush to go down and find out what was happening the ladder fell out of his hands. It was a miracle that it fell inside the house and not outside, for had it fallen outside it would have cracked open several heads looking up to catch sight of him. In short, he did not manage to lower the ladder before they all converged before him.

Feivush stood at the doorway of his house and cried, "Sabbath greetings, fellow Jews. Why are you all here, a big crowd like this? May the Lord increase you and your children. Hey, I'm getting the ladder and coming down to you. Come on Mamtchi, you cow, Jews are here to see us."

Feivush stood there looking around congenially, like a host welcoming guests. They all deserved something cold to drink but he hadn't prepared anything before the onset of Sabbath and what he had on hand was not enough for everyone.

So they stood below and he stood above. He looked at them and they looked at him. He was bewildered and they were bewildered. He wondered why they were there and they wondered why they were there. They came because they heard a rumor that fire had broken out in Feivush's house, and here was the house intact with no sign of any fire. So they had come on the basis of a false rumor. Who had misled them? Who had contrived this prank and put them through this needless bother?

Then began the accusations. This one said, You're the one who first yelled Fire in Feivush's house! And that one said, Not so. You're the one who first yelled, Fire has broken out in Feivush Gazlan's house! To which the first one retorted, You think I don't know the sound of your voice when you bellow like a cow? You think I don't remember that you hollered like a decapitated calf? To which the other replied, And you! You bellowed like an ox about to be stoned! The two began to mimic each other's voice when someone pushed someone else who was in the middle of quoting the verse *He who utters lies shall not stand firm before my eyes* and he banged into the poles on which the house stood. The poles quivered and the whole house started to shake. This should not be surprising because a house standing on old poles eaten away by termites cannot withstand the force of people quarrelling and pushing and shoving each other in anger. The house was now shaking and everything in it began to tremble, most of all Mamtchi. She began to scream, "Favish, the house is falling!" Hearing this Feivush reeled and his blood boiled. Furious, enraged, seething in anger, he began to swear and curse and blaspheme the Jews. There was not one profanity he did not utter about them, their homes, their belongings, even their ancestors. But their tongues did not sit quiet either as they in turn cursed and blasphemed him, and they didn't stop until they called him *gazlan,* the most hateful name they had for him. This redoubled his anger and made his blood boil to the point that his tongue got all twisted up from all the curses and profanities he wanted to spew. But now that he had exhausted his supply of curses and added a few more in the bargain, he waved his fist threateningly and warned them, "If I'm a *gazlan,* I'll show you what a *gazlan* can do!"

What Feivush did with words Mamtchi did with her hands. She opened the oven and took out a kettle of tea which was warming there for the pre-fast meal. The tea being still hot, she rushed over to the window, stood on tip toe, looked down on the heads of the people surrounding the house, and poured the hot liquid over them. Then she threw down the pitcher which shattered when it landed on their heads. Before they could even cry out she ran back to the oven and took out the pot of groats that was warming there for the pre-fast meal. Never had her agility served her so well as when she threw down the pot together with its contents over them. In short, Mamtchi did with the groats exactly what they had once done with pails of boiling millet when they poured them out over the invading Tatars.

Those who were scalded by the tea and the groats and the pottery shards clutched their heads and screamed in pain. Those who were unscathed but had gotten all spattered used their free hands to take hold of the poles supporting the house and shook them with all their might until they began to collapse. When they began to collapse, the whole house started to come apart, and when it came apart it fell, and when it fell everything in it tumbled down—beds, a table, a bench, pots, pans, bowls. Even Mamtchi and Feivush fell. And when the house and its contents fell, so did the oven with its fire. The fire caught hold of blankets and bedding and spread to the walls. The whole house started to burn and no one came to put it out. This was the origin of the saying, "There is a fire in Feivush Gazlan's house," which was uttered whenever something inflammatory resulted in suffering.

7. Suffering Individual and Collective

Feivush emerged completely bereft. He had only his crippled body. When the house collapsed with him inside it, a hand and a foot were broken among other bruises. Likewise his wife, whose hands and feet and whole body were hurt. She was, however, not injured as badly as Feivush. The Sabbath clothes she had on saved her, for having no light finery to wear on summer Sabbaths, she was in her thick winter garments. And if we are to believe what others said, she had put on extra clothes in honor of Tishah b'Av falling on the Sabbath.

When everyone saw them lying there in pain, their hearts went out to them and they began running in all directions. A few went back to town to avoid being implicated in what had happened. A few ran to the Strypa to bring water, since cold water is good for a person in shock. And a few followed the water carriers in order to show them where to best draw it from and what to carry it in. Mamtchi's utensils had all fallen and were strewn about and not a single one was unbroken.

Towards the end of the Sabbath, Elisha, the expert in medical matters, came, a satchel of medications in hand. He bent over and examined both Feivush and Mamtchi. He lingered over this limb and that, feeling and pressing, checking and rechecking, then shook his head and muttered, Hand and foot. Then, less tersely, he pronounced audibly and more fully, Broken arm and broken foot, both of them, and he opened his satchel and proceeded to bandage their injuries.

One of the bystanders remarked to Elisha, This shows us that the Holy One, blessed be He, does not let the wicked go unpunished but pays them back in kind. Feivush made your daughter lose her grip on her baby when he blew out her candles, and the Holy One, blessed be He, tossed him down right inside his own house and smashed him up. Elisha replied to that bystander, Your punishment is worse than Feivush's. Feivush was stricken in body, while you have been stricken in soul because you watched someone writhing in pain while rehearsing to him the sins he had committed.

Elisha the doctor was a member of a certain society whose members devised various strategies to cure themselves of moral afflictions, particularly the habit of answering too quickly without first thinking things over. When he realized what he had just said, he, who never walked four cubits without the writings of R. Mendel of Satanov in hand, berated himself for putting his mouth before his mind and not overcoming his bovine nature that allowed his tongue to gore other people the way an ox gores with its horns.

After the Book of Lamentations had been read, half the town arrived. They conferred among themselves and consulted with the expert, after which they brought Feivush and Mamtchi to an almshouse that served as a hospital. There they lay, like all the other poor and sick of Israel who had no roof over their heads, until their skin swelled and boils broke out. They were very nearly rotting alive, and it was Feivush's integrity in not leaving R. Feivush without any help that saved him and put him back on his feet.

Feivush gathered up his strength and left his bed limping on one leg, one arm in a sling. He went to show himself before Feivush the tax collector, to apologize to him, and to let him know that he was ready to return to work and serve him with a full heart as he did from the day he was appointed an enforcer.

So Feivush went to see R. Feivush. At that hour, R. Feivush was sitting down to eat. He ate, drank, and treated himself to all kinds of scrumptious delicacies, all in his customary leisurely way. When he finished his repast and recited grace, sleep overcame him. He dozed for a bit, then got up from his chair and went and stretched out on his bed, for nothing is as good for digestion as sleep after a meal. Maimonides explains this, and if you want to see how I can show you. Or, if you like, you can take instruction from the cow. Man, the pinnacle of Creation, of whom it is said *You have made him little less than divine,* can learn from the cow that just as it eats and drinks and hunches down and lies still until the food in its stomach is digested, so, too, should a person rest after a meal. Now how is it that I refer here to our Master Maimonides in connection with someone like Feivush the tax collector? Because I have seen too many pretentious scholars commandeer this towering giant of Torah, the light of our eyes, the pride of our people, to the exclusion of everything and everyone else in the tradition, so as to make you think they have discovered something new—and here you see that this is not so, for the tax collector already anticipated them.

While R. Feivush was getting his fill of sleep, Feivush stood the whole time propped up against the wall, holding on to his cane with his remaining strength lest he totter and fall, standing and waiting respectfully for R. Feivush to wake up and summon him in.

Feivush was hungry and weak. During his days in the almshouse that served as a hospital he had taken no nourishing food that would have strengthened his body. Now his body mutinied against him for making it move about. Taking its vengeance upon him, it toppled him. Feivush fell along with his cane, he in the place where he stood, the cane a short distance away. Yet even in his collapse Feivish was polite, not crying out in pain lest he interrupt his employer's slumber. But the thud of his fall was heard, and people ran outside to see what had caused the noise. They found Feivush splayed out like some nameless corpse with no next of kin. Had they not noticed him biting his lips in pain they would have declared him dead. Feivush sensed that the people standing over him were from R. Feivush's household. Gathering his remaining strength, he pulled himself together, reached out to grab his cane, and with a burst of energy stood up while straining to make himself as inconspicuous as possible to those around him.

But they noticed him nevertheless. They gazed upon him wondering whether this was the same Feivush whom the whole town feared. After they sated their eyes on him they said, Now we will see which eye has the spleeny scale on it, the one to the right of the left earlock or the one to the left of the right earlock. They began to debate the respective advantages of Feivush's fate, whether the leg he had broken required the use of this eye or that one. And as with the injured foot, so did they quibble over the broken arm.

While they were engaged in this verbal joust, a thug approached. Buczacz did not see the likes of him until the night he began to serve in place of Feivush, the Friday night of Shabbat Naḥamu, the Sabbath of Consolation. The thug took one look at Feivush and asked, Who is this sack of bones here? They replied, It's Feivush the enforcer, who served here in Buczacz until you came and took over from him. The thug crossed his arms over his chest, swayed back and forth, laughed, and said, You jokers, you're making fun of me, and then he spat in Feivush's face and said, Too bad for you Buczacz that you had to make do with this undernourished mouse. He then pursed his lips like a cat and let out a long "Meow!"

R. Feivush could hear all this and inquired as to what was going on out there.

Feivush has come, they told him.

He yawned and burped and asked jokingly, The hour of the Resurrection of the Dead must have come if Feivush has gotten up from the beating he took.

Well then, what shall we tell him? they asked.

Tell who?

Feivush Gazlan.

What should you tell him? There is nothing to tell him.

And they went and told him, Favish, R. Feivush says you can go home now. Feivush was baffled, like one whose mind does not grasp what he has just heard. When he finally understood the gravity of the situation, he began to brood about it. Where is the justice? Where is the conscience? I gave thirteen years to R. Feivush. There was not a Sabbath or a festival or a wedding when I did not bring in for him a goodly number of silver guilder, and now he throws me out like a rotten cadaver, and the Jews here leave me and Mamtchi with nothing to do but throw ourselves into the Strypa.

They said to him, Stop it, Feivush. You're talking nonsense. Why don't you admit that the job you had fits that bastard better than you? Or do you think that R. Feivush should have let the town just sit and wait till you gathered up your broken bones and returned to work? Admit it!

Feivush shook his head and went on brooding. Doesn't R. Feivush remember that my mother, may her memory be blessed, nursed him for two years, and when I would cry from hunger because she had no milk left to give me she would dip a rag in licorice water and stuff it in my mouth? At this memory of his mother's suffering he clutched his heart in pain, and his cane dropped out of his hand. As the cane fell away from him, his feet gave way; as his feet gave way, his whole body collapsed; as his body collapsed, he fell down.

The people from R. Feivush's house saw this and shook their heads. Look at this poor sick Jew. He has no livelihood. We need to give him some sustenance. He probably hasn't eaten today.

Who knows how long he would have lain there and distressed the onlookers had not the thug delivered him a kick. If you want to lie around, get yourself over to the bathhouse or to the place where the jokers pray. The courtyard of R. Feivush is no place for beggars. The kick brought Feivush to life. He cast an angry look at the thug as he took hold of the cane that had fallen from his hand. Pulling himself up on his feet again, he once more fixed his eye on the thug and said, Woe unto God that R. Feivush prefers Jews like this over me.

Feivush returned to his wife. Upon seeing him she burst out crying and screamed, My God, Favish! What have they done to you? Feivush let loose at her and yelled, You carcass of carrion! What do you want of me? Are these wounds I got at R. Feivush's house not enough for you that you come and pour salt on them? Oy, Mamtchi, they slaughtered me. They slaughtered me without a blessing, ate me up, devoured me. Mamtchi wailed and howled, Look, Jews! See if there is any pain like mine. God in heaven, I don't know what to say to you.

And as she cried and wept for her husband, he cried and wept for all his troubles: for his burned house, for his broken foot, for his broken arm, for his shattered body. Hardest of all was that his livelihood was taken away. And now, my friends, there was nothing for these two people to do but lie down in the street and die of hunger.

But Buczacz did not let Feivush and his wife die of hunger. The entire town felt their pain, some with words of consolation, some with curses for Feivush the tax collector who, after all the years that Feivush had worked for him, did not fulfill the commandment *You shall surely provide for him*. And as they did with words, so they did with actions. One gave them some coins, another some old clothes or shoes, another a bit of soup, and still another a hot dish with a drumstick on the side. Even better, there were people in Buczacz who invited them for dinner on Shabbat and holidays.

Here I could easily make fun of this hapless man as he sat anxiously in fear of the thug bastard who had taken over his job suddenly coming in and doing with the candles in his house what he himself in his heyday had done in others. He was particularly nervous when they brought fish to the table. Fish was his favorite food. Fish were his neighbors in the days when he lived in his house on the Strypa and he had established a relationship with them. But I do not make fun of the poor and the unfortunate. If the Holy One, blessed be He, settles his accounts with them in this world, they probably have accrued some merits. They atone for their sins through their sufferings so as to merit life in the world to come. Conversely, I do not glorify the powerful and the famous who prosper in all their undertakings. They enjoy their fill of this world without bothering to worry about the next one.

But this much I can say: everyone definitely preferred Feivush over Mamtchi, largely because she continually complained and lamented the loss of her goat and her hens. When they served her a cup of chicory with a drop of milk in it, she would declare, Let me tell you, good people, all cows are frauds. If you want to know what milk should taste like, I can tell you. I had this goat that was like no other. She gave me milk that would make even Count Potocki lick his lips. And just as she waxed exuberant about her goat, so did she sing the praises of her hens. When a chicken once jumped up onto the table and defecated on the bread, that immediately prompted Mamtchi to launch into a panegyric for her hens. Listen, good people, she would intone in the same singsong voice Feivush used when he read to her from the Tzenerena, did you see what this chicken did? My hens knew what respect was. Even their rooster knew how to act properly. He never would have dared to do something like this in front of me, much less in front of my hens. I remember, good people, the respect they showed me the year I was pregnant. I swung one of them around my head three times as my Favish stood beside me reciting the kapparot prayers. Would that all my hens could atone for the sins of all the Jews, most of all for those of that bastard who stole R. Feivush's heart and shoved my Favish aside.

From the day the Attribute of Divine Justice struck Feivush and all those troubles befell him—poverty, sickness and other calamities, may they never befall us or anyone of Israel!—Buczacz came to see that, compared to the enforcer who took his place, Feivush was a saintly man. His replacement tyrannized and extorted, while Feivush bore his suffering stolidly. As the saying goes, an old evildoer is better than a new one, and better than both is a broken one.

During the years when those troubles came upon Feivush, he would hold court with his Creator for what He did to him. There were those who argued that the purpose of his suffering in this world was to diminish his time in Gehinnom in the next one. Others proposed that his grievous sin was to build his house from the wood and stone left over from Jacob Frank. Frank was a sorcerer, and sorcerers live by illusions and chimeras. None of this satisfied Feivush. Were boards and rocks from the ruins of that dead evil one worse than the great and fine homes filched from orphans and widows? Why were the occupants of such houses dwelling in peace while he was cast out like a dog? As for suffering as atonement for sins, well, what suffering would be sent to the bastard who threw him out of his job? But there is a truth to be noted here. Feivush Gazlan spoke the truth, if not about his own tribulations, then about those that were visited upon Buczacz. The suffering that came about from that bastard the thug turned out to be worse than anything Feivush Gazlan had done.

As it always did, Buczacz accepted its vicissitudes and did not rise up against them. In fact, it lovingly embraced each and every calamity that befell it and repudiated none of them. The elders who were wont to search after the root causes of events as they unfolded and were never reluctant to make pronouncements about what they believed those causes to be, went to their eternal rest, and the conclusions they had put forth were distorted as they passed from person to person, until eventually they became mind boggling and ridiculous. The original pronouncements were thus been altered, and the elders who had made them were succeeded by others who themselves were quite different. Over time, Buczacz was transformed, and its inhabitants changed as well. For better or for worse, they lived at peace with their oppressors, Jewish and gentile alike.

Those who most rejoiced in their tribulations were the ones who had brought suffering upon Feivush. They actually went in search of hardships, embraced them, and prized them. They declared their hope that their suffering would atone for even a tiny part of the sins they had committed when they desecrated the Sabbath. Darkened by the distress of that desecration, they walked around mournfully, not a smile on their faces. They gave much to charity and took upon themselves many fasts, some as prescribed by the Shulḥan Arukh and some according to the numerical reckoning of the word Shabbat until their strength gave out and they died. At the hour of their death, some reproached themselves saying, Woe to one who leaves the world without his suffering having atoned for even half his sins. Should you ever see a person who studies much Torah, who fulfills the commandments of God which gladden the heart, and who observes the laws of the Sabbath punctiliously, in fear and in awe, and who nevertheless is sad—check to see if he is not descended from one of them.

I can say now that it all came down to this: the people of Buczacz bowed their heads and did not rise up against their tormentors. They put it astutely: We accept our fate not because we are so upright but because we live in fear that the new tormentors and oppressors will be worse than the old ones. You have seen that Feivush Gazlan's replacement was worse than he was. This is because evildoers grow progressively worse as the generations proceed. Each one is more fiendish than his predecessor. For evil feeds off those who do it; the wickeder they are, the more wickedness grows. I hope I am not proved wrong when I say that it will continue to grow and grow until that day comes when wickedness will vanish like smoke. When will that be? On the day when the Messiah will appear, may it happen speedily in our time, Amen.

Translated by James S. Diamond
with Jeffrey Saks

In Search of a Rabbi, *or* The Governor's Whim

After our rabbi, the gaon, R. Leibush Auerbach was summoned to the Yeshivah on High, Buczacz saw that all those ten years—while they had expected him to abandon the rabbinate of Stanislav and return to Buczacz—had been spent in vain. Now that he had passed away, and their hope was gone, the time had come to seek a rabbi for themselves.

Buczacz was divided into many factions, each of which wanted a different rabbi. Each sect split up, until every man became a sect for himself. No two people wanted the same thing. Because they saw that this was an impossible situation, they turned away from controversy. They settled upon three candidates and sent for them. One died on the way, and the parnas in the second one's city seized the letter that Buczacz had written to the rabbi and concealed it from him. Only one of the rabbis remained, and he was accused falsely to the lord of Buczacz, who said, If your rabbi comes to the city, I will have him lashed before your eyes. The rabbi heard of this and said, Why should I give my back to lashes? I had better not go. This was hard for Buczacz. Buczacz said, If we do not take action immediately, we will revert to controversy. They met in the council house with the intention of compromising with one another. The majority agreed to place the crown of the rabbinate on the head of the rabbi of Zabno. They said, As for his Torah learning, R. Moshe Avraham Abush has acquired a good name for his ḥidushim, which are said to be as deep as those of the

Maharam Schiff. As for his righteousness, while he was the rabbi, no fire fell upon the city, the eruv was never broken, not a crumb of ḥametz was found in the city well on Passover, and there was no need to ostracize a man for refusing to appear in court. As for his lineage, his father was the saintly R. Zvi of Yaslowitz, and his brothers are R. Ber, the head of the court of Yaslowitz, and R. Meir, the head of the court of Ostrow and the district of Lvov, and our R. Leibush Auerbach was his uncle.

The best men of the city selected three of the sharpest minds of Buczacz, R. Ber the Elder, "who merited two tables." Most of the rabbis of the country were related to him by marriage, and he was also worthy of serving as a rabbi himself. Second to him was R. Yeruḥam, whose comments on Torah were sharp and known as far off as Lvov. And third, equal to the first two, was R. Levi, the barley miller, who knew the Talmud by heart. They were all men who could evaluate a rabbi.

A letter of rabbinical appointment was placed in their hand to be delivered to the rabbi of Zabno, and they were given authority to make small changes if the rabbi asked for them. Men like them could be counted upon to pressure him until he came to Buczacz.

The selected men set out and, a month later, arrived in Zabno. They entered an inn to rest and dine. When the time came, they walked to the synagogue and prayed the afternoon and evening prayers with the rabbi. Between the afternoon and evening prayers, R. Ber said to his companions, It is impossible to say that his way of standing before his Creator is not fine. R. Yeruḥam said, His prayer is like his ḥidushim. R. Levi said, I do not know what R. Yeruḥam meant to say, but would that his way of standing with people be like his way of standing with his Creator.

2

After the evening prayer, the rabbi returned home because he was punctilious about rising for tikkun ḥatzot. It was his custom to have supper right after the evening prayer, then to sit and study until an hour before midnight, then to go to bed, recite the Shema, close his eyes, and open his heart to reflect on his deeds during the day. When a quarter of an hour before midnight came he would rise from his bed and recite the tikkun ḥatzot.

The emissaries from Buczacz followed the rabbi to the door of his house and stayed there for the time it would take to eat a slice of bread, read the psalm "By the Rivers of Babylon," and recite the grace after meals. Before the rabbi managed to open a volume of Gemara, they opened the door.

The rabbi greeted them and motioned to them to be seated. Once they were seated, he asked them from what place they had come and what brought them here. R. Yeruḥam said, If R. Ber gives me permission, I will answer. R. Ber said, It has been given to you.

R. Yeruḥam said, It is the custom in the world to answer the first question first and the last one last, but because the second question is answered by the Gemara, our explanation is not needed. Where is it explained? On the second side of folio thirty-three in tractate Niddah. The rabbi of Zabno said, I see that I am regarded in your eyes as a Torah scholar.

R. Ber sat and wondered what Yeruḥam had said and how the rabbi of Zabno knew that they regarded him as a scholar. In a moment, he nodded his head and said, Very nice, very nice. Certainly, you were referring to the passage in the Gemara where it says that when R. Papa came to a certain place, he said, There is a Torah sage here, I will go and greet him. R. Levi was silent. Words of the Gemara were given for study and understanding, not for mundane conversation.

The rabbi of Zabno said, You have answered the second question. What about the first question? R. Yeruḥam said, If you will, sir, it is already explained in the answer that I gave to the second one, and if you wish, sir, it is explained by this story: R. Yosei ben Kisma said, Once I was walking on the way, and a man met me, and so on. He said to me, From what place are you? I said to him, From a great city of sages and scribes am I, and since we are from a great city of sages and scribes, we have come to be acquainted with the rabbi of Zabno, of whom it is said that he discovers marvelous ḥidushim in the depths of Gemara, Rashi and Tosafot.

The rabbi of Zabno sighed and said to himself, This is the punishment of someone who believes that he is regarded as a Sage. People come and say things to him that could bring more pride into his heart than the bit that the Sages permit. R. Ber said, If Yeruḥam did not say explicitly from what city we come, from his general terms, the rabbi has certainly realized that we are from Buczacz.

The rabbi asked them whether the city was tranquil and about the new governor who had been placed in charge of Buczacz, whether he was oppressing the Jews so that they would give him large bribes or simply because his heart was evil. R. Ber said, The one depends on the other. Because his heart is evil, he oppresses the Jews, and because he oppresses the Jews, they pay him large bribes.

Are monetary bribes of any use?

R. Ber said, Verbal bribes are certainly of no use. R. Ber said, The Holy One, blessed be He, has done a great favor to our nation by placing desire for the Jews' wealth in the hearts of the nations. Were that not so, we would have no standing among them, perish the thought.

R. Yeruḥam said, You say that it was a favor, but it was a punishment. For if they were not placated with gifts of money, withdrawing one harsh decree today only to issue another tomorrow, the Holy One, blessed be He, would already have said that we have had enough troubles.

The rabbi asked R. Ber, What about the murderer who seized the wagon full of Jews in Buczacz and took them to Stanislav? Was he punished? The story is that a nobleman killed a Jew from Stanislav, and the governor of Stanislav was angry at him, so the murderer went to Buczacz seized a wagon full of Jews there, and brought them to the governor of Stanislav in place of the Jew he had killed. Some of the kidnapped people died of sorrow, and even though the murderer only intended to pay the governor with ten Jews for the one he had killed, the governor of Buczacz had to demand retribution for their blood. This was because the Jews only entered Poland after the rulers of Poland agreed to defend them from their persecutors. Finally, the rabbi of Zabno asked whether Buczacz had made up its mind to appoint a rabbi in place of his uncle R. Leibush, who had died, and whom had Buczacz made up its mind to install in his place. R. Yeruḥam answered, in the language of the *Two Tablets of the Covenant*: The question of a wise man is half the answer. For that reason, we have come. R. Ber took out the letter of appointment and placed it before the rabbi.

3

The rabbi examined the seals to see whether there was any symbol on them that the Torah had forbidden, because some wealthy Jews used to behave like the gentiles, who carve the figure of a person or of a large or small animal or a bird on their rings, which is entirely forbidden because of *You shall make no graven image*. R. Ber noticed this and was surprised that it could occur to the rabbi of Zabno that Buczacz might commit an act against the Torah. For there had been an incident involving a storekeeper in Buczacz who placed the image of a hand and foot over his door: a foot, so that feet would not cease entering his store, and a hand to hint to passersby that they should enter his store. This incident proves that such a thing is not done in Buczacz; he was fined fourteen groschen, and he was not called to the Torah until the next holiday had passed.

When the rabbi saw that there was no forbidden form on it, he spread out the writ of appointment and placed his hand on it and said to the emissaries, I can reply to your excellencies clearly even before reading it. However, my teachers have taught me that a document someone brings shows what his soul needs. Therefore, I will read what Buczacz has written to me.

R. Levi picked up a book from among those that lay on the table and read it where he opened it. R. Yeruḥam took a book and looked at it with one eye and at the rabbi of Zabno with the other eye, while he read the writ of appointment to the rabbinate. R. Ber did not take a book. Nor did he look at the man of the house. He sat and pondered: How was the rabbi of Zabno similar to the rabbis who were his sons-in-law, and in what way was he different? And how was he similar to his brother R. Meir and to his brother R. Ber and to their father R. Zvi, who had merited a long life? He had lived a hundred years, and, of those, he served as a rabbi for eighty-four. R. Ber sighed in his heart, Not every person merits such a long life and three such sons.

4

The rabbi read all the conditions. The first condition was that he had to lead the community in peace and moderation and not cause disputes, even if his intention was for the name of heaven. For example, he must not supervise the butchers by using stratagems against them to cause quarrels, so that one of them would report that his colleague had sold meat without removing the forbidden parts, so that the Jews would not be suspect, and so on. A second condition was that he had to decide every case according to the *Shulḥan Arukh* and the commentary of R. Moshe Isserles and not according to other books, so that one Torah should not be made into two. The third condition was that he had to take up every question of an agunah, a woman abandoned by her husband, that came before him, even from a distant land, and he may not say, What do I have to do with this problem, lest I might blunder, perish the thought, and free a married woman to remarry. Rather, he had to strive to improve the condition of daughters of Israel so that they would not be chained to absent husbands.

The fourth condition was that in his sermons on the Sabbaths before Yom Kippur and Passover and for the dedication of new Torah scrolls, he would end with a story for the simple people whose hearts were not open to clever words. Moreover, the rabbi would be obligated to observe the old customs practiced in Buczacz precisely, regarding the reciting of piyyutim and every other good custom that they clung to, and he may not replace them or alter them with new customs that have no grounding in halakhic rulings. He may not write amulets for pregnant women and nursing mothers and sick people, but he may pray for mercy for them. And he may not be lenient about the fast of the twentieth of Sivan for visitors who come from afar, from Germany or from Ottoman countries, who say that they were not included in that decree. Rather, he shall regard the fast of the twentieth of Sivan as one of the four fasts.

For their part, the congregation of the city promises to maintain the rabbi with honor both in the matter of a dwelling and in the matter of clothing, providing for his other needs as well and those of his household. If he keeps two or three young scholars at his table, the congregation takes it upon itself to provide their food and pay for new shoes every year at the Sukkot holiday. A chair is reserved for the rabbi in the old beit midrash to the left of the reading platform next to the holy ark, aside from the seat in the Great Synagogue to the right of the holy ark. The seat upon which the wife of the former rabbi sat is ready and waiting for the rabbi's wife, may she live. Other conditions were not written in the writ of appointment, such as serving as a godfather at circumcisions and attending ritual banquets. That is to say, the rabbi is not required to sit at those banquets that householders call ritual banquets, but they must invite the rabbi personally. However, they affirm that if there is a circumcision on Yom Kippur, the right to serve as godfather belongs to the rabbi, and when the boy grows up, the rabbi will watch over him and examine him in Ḥumash and Rashi, and, if he continues on in his studies, in Shas and Poskim. And as for the salary of the rabbinate, they will pay with the best coin, as they shall agree with him orally. In addition, he would be sent gifts of food baskets on Purim and gifts for the holidays such as chickens, vegetables, dried fruit, and blocks of cheese that the villagers give to the rabbi on Ḥanukkah.

5

The rabbi put down the letter of appointment and placed his hand over it, saying, I have read it. R. Ber looked at him sternly and said, What is the meaning of "I have read it," and what is to be deduced from it? The rabbi said, You did not need to take the trouble to come to me. In your city, you have a man more worthy of the rabbinate of Buczacz than I. They were surprised and said, There are many sages in our city, but we do not know which of them the rabbi of Zabno is referring to. He said to them, I refer to one special man, one of the geniuses of the generation. R. Ber said to him, Could there be a man like that in our city without my knowing him? R. Yeruḥam said, I will interpret the words of R. Ber. No scholar comes to our city without visiting R. Ber. Is that not so, R. Levi? The rabbi of Zabno repeated, That is his greatness: no one knows of him. But I was privileged to know him, and I must say that I have seen no one in this generation who knows as he does how to plumb the depths of each line spoken in the entire Talmud. Return to your home in peace, and may God enable you to receive him as the rabbi of your city, and may you enjoy the goodwill of God and men.

The three emissaries from Buczacz sat like people who had heard in a dream what cannot be conceived while awake. After they had somewhat recovered, R. Ber said to R. Yeruḥam and R. Levi, Do you know a man such as the one the rabbi of Zabno spoke of? R. Levi answered, I do not. R. Yeruḥam answered, It appears to me that the rabbi of Zabno did not hear that we are speaking of the rabbinate of Buczacz. The rabbi heard and said, I heard what you said. Indeed, I refer to the splendid community of Buczacz, which is one of the first nine congregations in Poland, and some say one of the three first communities of Poland, and I refer to my friend Rabbi Mordechai, who is greater than his praise. R. Ber said, After all, Buczacz is not Antioch or Alexandria, where if a man sits in one market, he does not know someone who sits in another market. Is it possible that such a great sage is present in Buczacz, and Buczacz does not know him? The rabbi said, You know him, but you do not know his greatness. As it is said of the Torah, *A man does not know its value,* so it is with his genius. Go in life and peace, and may God grant success to your journey. If Rabbi Mordechai accepts the rabbinate, Buczacz will raise its name until the coming of the redeemer.

R. Yeruḥam said, Perhaps the rabbi of Zabno could give us a teaching from the mouth of Rabbi Mordechai. R. Ber said, Or perhaps you could tell us some of this Rabbi Mordechai's deeds.

The rabbi began to ponder in his mind, Which was preferable, a teaching or the story of a deed? If you tell a teaching to a logic-chopper, he will chop away at it, and sometimes he gets as far as the Mountains of Darkness, and if you tell it to an expert, sometimes he will show you his own expertise by attaching it to a passage where it does not belong, and you need extra wisdom to restore the matter to its beginning. So the story of a deed is preferable, but if it was something that Rabbi Mordechai tried to conceal, had one the right to reveal it?

6

The door opened, and the rabbi's wife entered, bearing a metal tray with a kettle, cookies, and a thick, green glass bowl of fruit preserves with a rose engraved on it. The rabbi's wife placed it all in front of the rabbi and left. The rabbi uncovered the kettle and offered the preserves to his guests, saying, Say a blessing and taste. They started discussing the laws of blessings. Not because some doubt arose regarding the blessings, but so as not to enjoy food and drink without words of Torah.

Between tasting and grace, R. Ber asked the rabbi, This Rabbi Mordechai you spoke of, how did your Excellency come to know him? R. Yeruḥam looked at the rabbi in suspense, because the rabbi seemed hesitant as to whether he should answer R. Ber's question, even though it had been asked in all honesty. For the Torah, which loves modesty, as it is said, *With the humble is wisdom*, still lauds those who study it. A Torah scholar, ever the more so, must laud his comrade, to enhance his name in public.

The rabbi picked up the writ of appointment, held it in his hand, and looked at it with his eyes closed. He said, This writ of appointment only found its way to me for the sake of Rabbi Mordechai, for no one knows his greatness except me. I believe your Excellency's name is R. Ber? R. Ber nodded his head and said, Ber, Ber. The rabbi repeated, You asked me to tell how I know Rabbi Mordechai. Heaven privileged me to know Rabbi Mordechai. Things that I have concealed until now I am about to reveal today. This, too, is from what is said, *There is no man who has no hour, and there is no thing that has no place.* Rabbi Mordechai's hour has come for me to tell about him.

7

One day, I happened to be in a village near our city to serve as godfather at a circumcision. A man came in his wagon and took me and the mohel to the village. I did not yet know that the wagon driver was Rabbi Mordechai.

The baby's mother grew up in the home of my saintly mother-in-law, of blessed memory. She considered herself our relative, and that is how she was in our eyes. The baby's father also saw himself related to me because every year, when I go out to harvest wheat for shmurah matzah, I make a stop in his house. When he invited me to the banquet for his son's circumcision, I accepted, which is something I never do for anyone because I am stringent not to drink or eat outside of my own home and, it goes without saying, not to partake in strong drink, and the more so with villagers, whose wine is strong.

I saw a tall, thin man, whose years were between strength and wisdom. His dress was not like what people wear around here, and his hat was ridiculous. But his eyes showed that he was sharp and brilliant. It occurred to me that he was from Germany because once I had difficulty understanding a passage in the writings of one of the German sages, and that sage came to me in a dream and interpreted his words for me. His hat was like this man's because in Germany they force the Jews to cover their heads with a funny hat to make them a mockery and shame for the gentiles.

During the banquet, I said a few words of Torah on the controversy concerning the proper time for a circumcision, and I resolved the problem raised by Tosafot in Yevamot 72b, the comment that begins, "One is only circumcised by day." Along the way, I presented a great ḥidush about the story of Abraham and the issue of circumcision before the giving of the Torah and also about all the commandments which a father is obliged toward his son in which men are obligated and women exempt. I also mentioned the words of Rashi, of blessed memory, there at the end of the page. To save the Ari, whose words appear to contradict the Talmud in Yoma, I put forth a profound, sharp analysis. I adduced a challenge from the Maharsha, and I resolved his words from another place in the Gemara, in Zevaḥim, about which I heard that people find a difficulty. I saw that man was twisting his shoulders as though to turn his back on something he did not want to hear. What did I do? I took a matter I had once presented in the presence of great scholars, who acknowledged that it was exceedingly deep, like the ḥidushim of Maharam Schiff, and I recited it. I raised my eyes and saw that he was waving his hand in contempt like one who hears trivial things and dismisses them out of hand. I cut short and finished.

8

After grace, I rose from my place and said to him, I see that your mind is not at ease with what I said. He answered, saying to me, You are the one of whom everyone says that your ḥidushim are as deep as those of Maharam Schiff. Neither you nor anyone like you who claim to understand Maharam Schiff knows what you're talking about. I said to him, Sir, are you referring to a particular ḥidush? He waved his hand and said, What is a particular ḥidush to me? What are all your ḥidushim? *Pharaoh's dream is one.*

It occurred to me to present a ḥidush to him that I found on that subject while studying the Zohar. Sometimes dreams are visions, and sometimes they are visions of visions, and there is a difference between one kind of dream and another. The dreams of the wicked come from the wishes of their heart, and the dreams of the righteous come from the upper colors that emerge from the fireworks emitted by the mouths of the righteous when they debate fine points with one another in the Yeshivah on High. These are the ḥidushim that are revealed to the righteous in dreams. Before I could make up my mind to present my new idea to him, he posed a hard question, and a second, and a third, and a fourth. With each question, he contradicted one of my ḥidushim, until he had contradicted all the ḥidushim that are taught in my name in houses of study and yeshivot. With his sharp reasoning, he also contradicted the words of the Maharshal and the Rema and Beit Yosef, until my bones trembled, and my thoughts were in a panic. I was stunned and nodded my head to myself in dismay because I had caused someone to disagree with our great rabbis, from whose mouths we live. I said to him, Sir, return to the beginning of the chapter. I trusted in the mercy of heaven that it would help me respond to his words for the honor of our great rabbis. I noticed the man who had brought me in his wagon standing before me, and was astounded: What business does he have in a Torah debate such as this? He whispered to me, Rabbi of Zabno, you had better not try to answer, for *he is* Maharam Schiff. All my bones trembled, and I was alarmed. For he said, This is Maharam Schiff, who died in 1633 according to the *Tzemaḥ David*, over one hundred and twenty years earlier! I thought to myself, He has had one drink too many. But how had he even heard of the Maharam Schiff?

9

He turned away from me and said to Maharam Schiff, Rabbi, will you permit me to answer in place of the rabbi of Zabno? Maharam Schiff looked at him sternly like a man who says, Is there someone here who is worthy of answering my words? And I, too, looked at him harshly because he had persuaded me to keep quiet and had taken upon himself the honor of speaking in my place. Maharam Schiff said to him, Speak.

He began with sharp reasoning. I was amazed at his sharpness and expertise, but he did not touch on the matter, and, in any event, his words could not reconcile the words of our rabbis with which Maharam Schiff had disagreed. I was more surprised that Maharam Schiff was listening and did not interrupt him. Before I managed to free myself from that astonishment, I came to a new astonishment because I saw that every one of his words was intended to place the words of our rabbis on a firm foundation, until there was no way of challenging them anymore. In his fine logic, he mentioned some of my ḥidushim and supported a few of them. Maharam Schiff asked, Have you finished speaking? He said to him, If our rabbi intends to illuminate my eyes with an answer, I have finished. Maharam Schiff began to contradict his conclusions from end to beginning and from beginning to end without leaving a single argument uncontradicted. Rabbi Mordechai repeated, If the rabbi will permit me, I will ask something. Maharam Schiff answered, If you have something to ask, ask. But if you want to ask this, I will answer that, and if you wish to ask this, I will answer that. Rabbi Mordechai said, With a kiss to the floor beneath your feet, I will address another matter.

Rabbi Mordechai took up another passage, which they had not mentioned at first, and extracted three or four explanations for each of the problems raised by Maharam Schiff, who again contradicted what Rabbi Mordechai had resolved, and Rabbi Mordechai again resolved the problem with a mighty, witty display of logic, until my soul almost left my body because of the great sweetness of it all. Were it not for the crying of the circumcised baby, whose mother insisted on bringing him into the room to introduce words of Torah in his ears, I would have departed from the world because of the sweetness of the Torah. Thus Maharam Schiff and Rabbi Mordechai kept on debating until the time came for afternoon prayers.

Regarding Maharam Schiff, the question arose whether a curtain had to be put up, as one does when holding a prayer if there is a dead person in the room. I have a mighty logical argument about this that I have prepared to recite before the righteous in the Garden of Eden.

10

After the prayers, Rabbi Mordechai said to the Maharam Schiff, If we have been privileged to have your honor come to our place, perhaps you could tell us some of the ḥidushim that did not appear in your book. The Maharam Schiff answered, They were not included in my book, but they are in my writings, and they are deposited with Hinele, my daughter. But no one gives thought to print them because everyone is eager to publish their own ḥidushim rather than the true ḥidushim, which I discovered about the entire Talmud and the Four Turim, and also commentaries on the Torah and on the wisdom of the kabbalah.

Rabbi Mordechai sighed for the loss of the ḥidushim of the Maharam Schiff, of which there remains only a small part, that is, those that were printed and those that were published by others under their own name. All the rest were devoured by the fire in Frankfurt. Maharam Schiff did not know about this because they concealed it from him in heaven so as not to sadden him. What happened? When Maharam Schiff's hour came to leave the world, he called his righteous daughter Hinele, and delivered his writings to her. He ordered her to place them in a box and close the box with a lock. She did so and carried the box to the attic. Men came, opened the box, and took the writings. They published them in their own name without crediting Maharam Schiff. This is what was concealed from him in heaven.

Maharam Schiff said, I see that you are knowledgeable; therefore I will tell you some of the ḥidushim I left behind. He began to recite deep and marvelous insights and mighty, sharp, and witty logical arguments, the likes of which one does not hear in our generation. Indeed, we find some of them in the books of the new authors, but not everyone who copies understands what he copies.

11

With the cock's crow, our master the Maharam Schiff returned to the Yeshivah on High. I said to Rabbi Mordechai, I regard myself as if I were in the Garden of Eden in a dream. Rabbi Mordechai said, So do I. I said to him, I am grateful to you, sir, for acting on my behalf with Maharam Schiff. Rabbi Mordechai said to me, I am grateful to you, sir, that through you I had the privilege of standing in the company of Maharam Schiff and hearing Torah from his mouth. We began to review some of the ḥidushim we heard from Maharam Schiff, and we were surprised that each matter included many other matters, resolving issues with which the world has difficulty, refuting most of the explanations with which the world is satisfied, and raising difficulties and problems in places where we had never noticed any difficulty or problem.

We stood and reviewed every ḥidush we remembered. I remembered some of them, and Rabbi Mordechai remembered others. We took matters that we had heard from the mouth of Maharam Schiff and compared them with what was published in print. The mohel came and urged us to return to the city because he had another circumcision to perform. The wagon driver also pressed because mornings are good for traveling, since highway robbers are usually awake all night and sleep in the morning. I grasped Rabbi Mordechai with both hands and said to him, It is hard for me to part from you. Will you permit me to ask where you are from, who were your teachers, and why you are not the head of your own yeshivah, and why you are not a rabbi or the head of a court? How much benefit you would bring to the world if you sat in a yeshivah and taught Torah or if you sat in a seat of instruction and taught the law. If the world does not know you, you must say, I am a Torah scholar, so you not be mistaken as a mere wagon driver. Is it true, what I heard, that your Excellency is a tinsmith?

He answered modestly, May God's Name be praised that He has not required me to earn a livelihood from words of Torah and that He enabled me to earn a living from the work of my hands. I asked him again, Whom did you study with, sir, and from whom did you receive the majority of your Torah? He did not answer me. A tremor passed through my bones, that certainly he had learned from Elijah the Prophet, and because of his modesty, he did not answer me. He noticed that and told me the name of his teacher. In the end, he said, Time is short, and the matter is long, and the wagon driver is pressing, and I, too, must rush because I was called to the courtyard of the master of the village to do some work. If God so decrees, I will find my way to your house, sir, and I will answer all your questions.

I returned to my home and my studies, and every day I waited for him to come. But he did not come. I began to doubt what I had seen that night, lest it was a dream that came from the upper colors, which emanate from the sparks of fire when the righteous sit in the Yeshivah on High and interpret, and from them come the ḥidushim that are revealed in dreams to those who study Torah. One night, after I had despaired, he came.

12

We began with the new interpretations of Maharam Schiff that we had been privileged to hear from his mouth. After using them to clarify several obscure places in his published work, Rabbi Mordechai proposed a ḥidush that he himself had discovered, and I offered him some of what God enabled me to innovate in His holy Torah. Something miraculous happened with these ḥidushim, matters left by Rabbi Mordechai as unresolved and in need of further examination were resolved by my innovations, and that which I had marked as "needs examination" were resolved by his ḥidushim. Thus we sat after midnight, and the night shone like day with a joyous, smiling, and welcoming face. From the joy that I felt with Rabbi Mordechai, I was about to suggest the logical argument to him that I had prepared to present before the righteous in the Garden of Eden, for this is my portion in life from all my labor in the Torah.

But when we heard the footsteps of the shamash, who had gone out to rouse the sleepers to serve the Creator, Rabbi Mordechai's face changed. He threw off the spiritual form that the Torah gives to its masters and took on the form of a craftsman of the kind we call to our houses to do some job. I stood in a panic, lest all that I had seen was only one of those night visions that are shown to those who labor at the Torah in their sleep or one of those ḥidushim into the Torah that come from the colors that emerge from the sparks of fire that come from the mouths of the righteous in the upper world while they sit and interpret in the Yeshivah on High, as I explained at length in my ḥidushim on the Zohar.

Meanwhile, Rabbi Mordechai was about to part from me. I roused myself and said to him, You have a debt to me. Rabbi Mordechai said, Does the rabbi of Zabno refer to the matter he asked me about, who was my rabbi and from whom did I receive most of my Torah, and I said to him that I would conceal nothing from him and would tell him from the beginning to the end? I nodded my head yes to him. I did not have strength in my mouth to utter a word because of the excitement of my soul, because every single event that happened on that night was more surprising and miraculous than the next, and more so, because I was afraid lest in talking I might lose one of the ḥidushim we had found.

Rabbi Mordechai looked at me and said, If I were not in a hurry to get on my way, I would tell you immediately. Now that I am in a rush because of work, we will deposit the story of these things in the hands of the One Who lives eternally. God willing, another time I will tell everything about everything from beginning to end.

Rabbi Mordechai parted from me. My wife brought me a hot drink. I drank and prepared myself for prayer. The shamash of the synagogue came, took my talit and tefilin, placed my stick in my hands, and we walked to the synagogue.

13

Just four or five nights passed, and he returned. The lord of Zabno erected a wedding pavilion for his wife's son and wanted to illuminate the courtyard where his guests would eat and drink, aside from the torches that lined the roads. He summoned Rabbi Mordechai to prepare lanterns because Rabbi Mordechai was a marvelous craftsman in that art, and there was no minister or lord at a distance of several hundred leagues who did not call upon Rabbi Mordechai to do that work.

Rabbi Mordechai told me that these lanterns were of copper and made to resemble a room with a perforated dome bulging on top of it to let out the smoke. There was a socket inside for a thick candle that burns for several hours, and it was constructed in such a way that the wind does not extinguish it. Rabbi Mordechai told me that he had learned how to make the lanterns from the midrash on the verse *Arise, shine, for your light has come.* Since I have not managed to examine the midrash itself, I do not remember the exact words. Since I do not remember the exact words, I will not quote the matter because every word of our sages of the aggadah has great meaning, which cannot be grasped in our language. I heard a teaching in the name of the saintly gaon R. Zvi of Chortkov, of blessed memory, the father of the geonim R. Shmelke and R. Pinḥas, who said that the teachings of our sages of the aggadah are equivalent to the words of the Torah itself in the story of the Creation.

Rabbi Mordechai worked by day in the lord's court, and at night, after eating his supper, he would come to me. Why do I mention his supper? So that it would not seem wrong to you that I did not set a table for him and did not fill his cup. For even if I had offered him royal delicacies, he would not have tasted them. Rabbi Mordechai used to say that a traveler, here today and tomorrow elsewhere, must be scrupulous not to eat in other people's houses because not everyone is knowledgeable about foods that are forbidden according to certain strict halakhic authorities. In order not to insult the honor of Jews by distinguishing those whose practice is acceptable from those whose practice is not, he would eat nowhere other than his own home and partake of nothing except his own bread and food that he himself had prepared. How strict was he with himself? Even though there is no suspicion about brandy, he would not drink other people's. I questioned him, What does he do if he is given a cup of wine with which to perform a mitzvah, would not he drink? And in this matter I think my reasoning would have prevailed over his except in the case of a nazirite (who has vowed to drink no wine).

14

Thus Rabbi Mordechai came, and we sat together with marvelous ḥidushim and mighty analyses. He would recite a ḥidush, and I would say a ḥidush, and we would examine every ḥidush seven times, to see how well it could stand before the truth because sometimes, one builds up ḥidush upon ḥidush, up to seven or nine ḥidushim, and once you examine them, you see that the first ḥidush was shaky; so, of course, all the innovations that were built up on it have nothing to support them. Worse than that, out of love for ḥidushim, sometimes you trip up, heaven forfend, and you issue a new judgment that violates an explicit talmudic ruling, as happened to one famous rabbi, who innovated what he innovated, until a householder came along and challenged the ḥidush. The famous rabbi reprimanded him and stumbled, responding with words shameful to mention. The famous rabbi did not recall that the Gemara raised the same objection on the very page where he had found a ḥidush. Another thing worth mentioning is that if I said to Rabbi Mordechai, Let us take a book and see, he would say, No need. Why? Because everything was familiar to him, word for word. Students of the Torah have many virtues, sharp wit and knowledge, quick apprehension and a good memory, and, above all, common sense. Yet a man in whom all these virtues are found, and in addition, the entire Talmud and Tosafot and Alfasi and Maimonides and the Turim lie upon his tongue—I have found none other than Rabbi Mordechai.

But when the sound of the steps of the shamash were heard to rouse people for prayer, the glow of his face, which the Torah gives to those who study it, departed, and there was no difference between him and any artisan who does work. I flinched and was panicked and was amazed in my great astonishment, and I did not ask what I was eager to know. Rabbi Mordechai said, I assume that the rabbi of Zabno wishes me to tell him whom I studied with and from whom I received most of my learning, and so on, but the time for morning prayers has come, and I have to pray and go to the lord's court for my work. But if God wills it and my feet bring me back to the city, I will come and tell you, and I will not conceal a thing from all that happened to me, how I grew up in a village and herded geese and fished and laid traps for animals and birds, and how the Holy One, blessed be He, sent me a rabbi great in Torah, and how he taught me, and what methods he espoused. I will also tell what happened to my master and teacher because the events of my life belong to the events of his. The Torah brings together those who seek it, and by virtue of it, all the Jews hold and cleave to one another.

Rabbi Mordechai parted from me, and I prepared myself to go to the synagogue.

15

And thus it happened again and again. Once every few nights, after midnight, he would come because from the beginning of the night until after tikkun ḥatzot, he spoke with no one, lest he might hear things that tend toward pleasure and decrease his grief for Jerusalem. Upon entering, he would begin with a ḥidush that had come to him anew, and from it he would interpret an obscure passage and clarify the methods of the medieval rabbis and draw conclusions from their words. He would continue to correct matters that ignorant scribes had corrupted, until my eyes lit up with his emendations and I saw that all the words of the written Torah and the tradition are consistent and there is nothing twisted in them. They are still as pure as on the day they were given from the mouth of the Almighty and interpreted by our sages. I wrote down some of his corrections in the margins of books in my possession. I also debated with him. If I won, he admitted it and was not ashamed if the truth was with me. But while conceding, he would begin to quote proofs to contradict my words and go back to reinforce his ḥidush, and if he left anything under the category of "needs clarification," he would say, I depend on the rabbi of Zabno that in his studies, he will see that my words are not nonsense. Thus we would sit together until the sound of the shamash's hammer was heard, as he walked and knocked to wake men up for prayer.

All the time that Rabbi Mordechai sat with me, I distracted my mind from Rabbi Mordechai himself and from asking him where he came from and who were his ancestors, who was his rabbi, who had taught him Torah, and all the rest. I will give you an analogy: when a man reads from the Torah, does it cross his mind to ask how the scroll was written and from the skin of which animal the parchment was made, and from which merchant they bought the salt and the flour to cure the skin, and with what oils they mixed the soot to make ink from it, and how they kneaded it with the sap of trees and with honey, and made cakes of it, and how they brought gall water to soak the cakes in it, and so on? No, a man stands in fear and trembling and perspiration and gives his eyes and heart to every letter in the Torah. Thus I was in awe of Rabbi Mordechai's Torah and did not ask him where he came from and who his parents were and the like.

But he, when parting from me, would say to me, If God keeps me alive and I return, I will tell the rabbi of Zabno everything that happened to me. It was like, perish the thought, witchcraft. While he was far from my eyes, I wished to know where he came from and who his ancestors were and who his rabbi was. But when he sat before me, I did not ask him. Rather, the Torah says to those who study it, Why do you seek things that do not belong to the Torah while the Torah itself dances before you. I will repeat what I said, simply: Someone who has Torah before him is made to forget everything else, even things close to the Torah. So now it should not seem hard to understand why I did not ask Rabbi Mordechai what I always wanted to know. Out of love for Rabbi Mordechai, my soul was bound to his soul, and all day long he was in my thoughts, so that I turned away from my regular studies because of those passages we spoke about at night. Every night after tikkun ḥatzot, I would prick up my ears for the sound of his steps. Still, he had not told me where he was from and who his ancestors were and who his rabbi was, until things transpired so that he told me. After he told me, he never came back.

16

When he entered, he entered in secret, and he left in secret, and no one saw him in his going or his coming. I warned the people of my household that if they saw a man come to me at night, they should avert their eyes from him. It goes without saying that they should not try to look at him. They stood by the orders and observed my command, imagining that he was a penitent with whom I was awake all night long, teaching him the paths of repentance, and it was good for them to avert their eyes from him, so that he would not be embarrassed. Or else he was a convert, one of the great men of Poland, whom I was teaching Torah and the commandments, and care must be taken not to reveal it to the priests. When they heard the sound of the guest's feet, they would hide themselves so that he would not notice them.

My household and I kept the secret, but the secret did not keep itself. The first who helped it take wing was the shamash. While walking to rouse the men for prayers, the shamash used to come into my house for a hot drink. Since Rabbi Mordechai had stipulated with me that no one must be with me from his arrival to his departure, I told the shamash I was in the midst of a serious passage of the Talmud, and if someone was with me, I could not focus my thoughts and get to the bottom of things. The shamash accepted this and stopped coming to me at night. He did not think about what I had said. Once it happened close to morning that he saw a man leaving my house, a man he did not know, he began to follow him. I noticed and warned him severely not to do that. He heard me and did not disobey my order. He heeded me now as he had before not because of veneration for his rabbi but because of his daughter. He had a daughter born in his old age whom he married off to a traveler from another country. A few days after the marriage, the husband disappeared and the woman became an agunah and she was still a girl. I strove to rectify the situation and find a way to permit her to marry. The shamash was afraid that if he disobeyed my command, I would stop trying to free her. So weak is the opinion of many ignorant people that they believe the Torah depends on the rabbi's opinion, and they do not know that we are obliged by the Torah to strive to improve the plight of Jewish women so that they will not be chained to husbands who have abandoned them.

As long as no one else spoke to me about the visitor, he, too, did not speak. Once others began to speak about him, he also spoke. Once it happened very early in the morning that a pair of butchers returned from a village near our city, where they had taken an animal for slaughter. They passed by my house and heard the voice of Torah: not one voice but two voices. At that moment, the shamash passed by them. They asked him, With whom is the rabbi engaged in such sharp Torah study tonight? The shamash said to them, Do you think he just came tonight? No, he comes every night and sits with him all night and studies Torah with him. While the shamash was talking to the butchers, Rabbi Mordechai came out. They looked and saw a man dressed in work clothes leaving the rabbi's house, and they were astonished. In their great surprise, they stood without moving until Rabbi Mordechai was out of sight.

People in the city started whispering that the Prophet Elijah frequented their rabbi every night, and, nevertheless, their rabbi behaves like any teacher of the law. Is anyone as modest as their rabbi?

These matters came to me, and they were as hard for me as nails. Even if people praise a man for some virtue that he has, he should say, You are mistaken about me. For there is nothing so difficult as those praises that a man hears about himself, if he keeps quiet. If they are for something that are rightly his, it is deducted from his reward in the world to come, and if it is mistaken praise he is repaid for every single word with dreadful and horrible humiliations. In this world a man receives honor, and his body is not burned, in the next world there is no bone that is not burned.

17

I was afraid for my soul and did not know what to do. If I revealed the truth, I would be violating my promise to Rabbi Mordechai, who had stipulated with me that I was forbidden to mention his name before anyone and that I might say nothing in his name, so that his name would not be famous in the world. Yet here my praise was sung in everyone's mouth, and everyone exaggerated more than his fellow, and I was unable to reveal the truth.

I called my friends and told them, I heard what you are saying about me, and therefore I am obligated to tell you, that I was never privileged with a visitation from Elijah, and needless to say, I am not worthy to have Elijah come to me. As for the revelation of Elijah in general, I showed them in the book *Revealer of Depths* that Elijah has no free time, not even a single minute. At the time of prayer, he gives the Patriarchs water to wash their hands, and when a baby is circumcised, he is there, and if someone marries a woman who is forbidden to him, Elijah binds him up, and on the departure of the Sabbath, Elijah takes metes out judgment in defense of the righteous, who are not allowed to execute justice on their own. Furthermore, Elijah sits beneath the Tree of Life and writes down the merits of those who keep the Sabbath. Finally, I told them, we have learned in *The Great Order of the World* that Elijah is hidden and will not appear until the messiah comes, and now he is writing the deeds of all the generations.

What did the people of Zabno say? They said, If so, then it must be the holy Ari who comes to our rabbi to teach him kabbalah, and the appearance of the righteous is a higher level than the appearance of Elijah. I said to them, It is well known that every tzaddik who is privileged to dwell in the Land of Israel does not leave that place because the souls of those tzaddikim who have merited to breathe the air of the Land of Israel cannot bear the air outside the Land. They said, The tzaddikim of the Land of Israel can wrap themselves in the air of the Land of Israel and fly outside the Land, and the air of outside the Land does not harm their souls. I said to them, Who am I that the tzaddikim of the Land of Israel would take so much trouble for me, especially not the holy Ari, of blessed memory. For we have no conception at all as to the high place where he dwells.

In sum, the more I denied what was to be denied and lowered myself into dust to be trampled, the higher my name rose in the city and everywhere people of our city went. My heart was oppressed. I did not know what to do, but I knew that the truth could save me from my distress. If I asked Rabbi Mordechai's permission to reveal it, he would say to me, We have already stipulated that you will not tell anyone who I am. I acted wisely and offered him the rabbinate of Zabno, that is, he would sit on the seat of the rabbinate in my place and I would sit on his right as one of the judges in our court, and that way it would be revealed who he is, and people would no longer tell things about me that make my soul burn. But my wisdom did not help me. After Rabbi Mordechai heard what I was requesting from him, he answered me softly, If it is to make a living, I make a living, God be praised, with the work of my hands. And if it is for power and honor, the King of Honor has already granted me the merit of not wishing to taste honor and power.

18

Quite a few nights passed when I did not see Rabbi Mordechai. I began to wonder why he did not show himself to me. If he had finished his work and gone, would a man who regularly visits his friend go away without saying good-bye to him? Had I perhaps insulted his honor? In my whole life, I never even insulted the honor of a child, not to mention a Torah scholar. If so, I had to look for another reason. Perhaps he had gone to visit his wife in the village and fallen ill there because he used to spend the Sabbath with his wife in the village. In what village, I did not know.

I asked the people of my household whether the master of the city had already held the feast for his wife's son, and they said to me that people were still busy with building the wedding pavilion. I wanted to ask whether the lanterns were finished. Fatigue leaped upon me, and I lay my head on the table and dozed off. I saw Rabbi Mordechai turning his face away from me, and I knew that Rabbi Mordechai was displeased because I asked about him. I was careful not to ask about him. How careful? It happened that two partners came to me for judgment because the agent of the governor of the city had ordered sheets of tin to manufacture the lanterns and had not paid, and one of the partners claimed that the damage was the responsibility of his partner, who had extended credit to the agent, knowing that he did not pay debts. During their arguments, one partner mentioned Rabbi Mordechai; sometimes he called him Mordechai the tinsmith, and sometimes he called him the lantern man. I held my tongue and did not ask about him even with a hint.

One night, Rabbi Mordechai came to me. I told him about the trouble I was having because people were gossiping about me in the city. He sat and listened. I felt bitter and repeated the matter from beginning to end so that he would hear and know and understand that I could rid myself of all the sorrow if he gave me permission to reveal who it was who used to come to me at night. He heard and was silent. I hung my eyes upon him so that he would say something to me. He turned his face away from me and said nothing.

We sat for a long time, and I did not say another word. Rabbi Mordechai turned his face toward me and looked at me in sorrow. I saw that he was with me in my sorrow. I yearned for his words, and my yearning was disappointed. The lock that he had hung on his mouth did not open.

I heard a sound, and I thought that Rabbi Mordechai had risen from his place and was preparing to say something. I looked and saw that Rabbi Mordechai was about to leave because he had heard the sound of the shamash's footsteps as he woke people for prayers. After the shamash struck the door with his hammer, Rabbi Mordechai waited for the time it took for the shamash to walk away from the house. Then he stood and parted from me.

My wife came and brought me a hot drink. I put down the cup and prepared myself for prayers. The shamash of the synagogue came, took my talit and tefilin from me, placed my stick in my hand, and we walked to the synagogue.

19

That day, letters came from the Ukraine about a certain wanderer who had abandoned his wife for twenty years and who had now been found. He denied the whole thing and claimed that the woman was not his wife and that he was not her husband. The court of justice in that city had asked my opinion on the matter of this poor woman, for, according to the physical signs they found on the wayward husband, there was no doubt that he was her husband and that she was his wife. Now, according to the identifying signs they mentioned, I realized that he was the husband of the shamash's daughter, whom he had left empty and abandoned about a month after the wedding.

I cleared away all my business and set aside all the questions that did not demand an immediate answer, and, needless to say, those that were merely asked just for the sake of argument and ornamental erudition. I surrounded myself with many books, those that God had favored me with and those that I had found in the hands of Torah scholars in the city, and I immersed myself in the matter of the two miserable women that one cad had bound together in a single bundle. The elder of them had found the wayward husband, and he denied it. All the while, unbeknownst to the younger girl, her wayward husband had been found. But I knew, and I did not know what to do. Should I write to the rabbinical court and tell them to detain him until his wife from Zabno could come and testify against him and receive her bill of divorce, or should I ask the governor to have him brought here? If I asked the court, it was doubtful whether he would obey the court, and if he did not obey, it was doubtful whether the rabbinical court had the power to detain him until his wife came. But if it was done by the governor, the mercy of the wicked is cruel. Because he had mercy for the abandoned girl, who was prevented from marrying again by the wayward husband, he might be cruel to the husband and order his servants to flog him until his soul left his body, or his servants might beat him to death on their own initiative. So we would be the cause of a Jew's death. Thus a problem was given to me to solve and make me forget Rabbi Mordechai. But by way of forgetting him, I remembered him because if he were only here, I could discuss the issues with him and the two of us could enable a halakhic resolution.

Therefore I set aside all the local matters thrown upon a city rabbi and handed over every question that arose to the rabbinic judges, even the questions that came from the villagers, which I did not do at any other time. Usually, if a question comes from the village, I myself deal with it because sometimes a question to the rabbi brings out a new question that had not occurred to the questioner at first, and permission or prohibition depends on the unasked question. In short, I removed myself from everything and dealt only with the problem of the two miserable women so that malefactor would no longer torment them.

I spent day and night righting the wrong done to the daughters of Israel. I clarified the issues with myself as far as the ability of the intellect allowed, and I came to no new solution. The more I wearied myself, the more I reached the same conclusions. Today nothing was revealed to me that I did not know yesterday or the day before yesterday. What was dubious to me yesterday and the day before yesterday was not cleared up for me today.

When I saw that the matter had not moved even a hairbreadth and I was only repeating things that I knew by heart, I was troubled about myself lest I had committed a sin and the power of ḥidushim had been taken from me. For the Torah does not break the spirit of its students. On the contrary: it expands their minds and renews their spirits, and they find ḥidushim in the Torah. But in my case, a stupefying spirit surrounded me and stood before me like a wall. When I remembered the ḥidushim that I had discovered with Rabbi Mordechai, my spirit faltered. I began to fear that I had been deceived. So I passed them through the refining fire of scrutiny and saw that all of them were the truth of the Torah.

Nevertheless, I did not return to the question of the abandoned women but rather took myself to the very tractate that I had set aside on the day that I met Rabbi Mordechai. On the day that I met Rabbi Mordechai, I deferred my regular studies. I examined by day what I had innovated at night. Now I placed my hope in the Torah that it might renew my spirit for my regular studies, for I was taught that if a person studies every day in the order he has set for himself, an answer to every question that comes before him will be at hand. I, too, saw that in myself. Sometimes when I had wearied myself in some halakhic question, if I returned to my daily studies, I found a solution to it, as if a note had fallen from heaven with the answer to my question written on it.

But that day, I was like a man who returns home and the people of his household come and disturb him. When I returned to my regular study, a new difficulty popped up before me. In the second chapter of tractate Ḥullin there is a difficulty in the passage "He who wishes to eat an animal before its soul has departed." I had gone over that passage many times and never found a difficulty in it; but that day, it was very hard for me to understand, and I did not find anything in the commentators on the Talmud or in the commentators of the Rif to enlighten me. While I was seeking help in books I owned and in those borrowed from others, the letters began to fly away from me, and my eyes were as if sunken in sand. I closed the Gemara and opened the prayer book to recite the psalms before reciting the Shema in bed.

20

I heard the sound of steps and realized that Rabbi Mordechai had come. I rejected the notion but nevertheless, I waited expectantly for him. Before much time had passed, Rabbi Mordechai materialized.

Rabbi Mordechai saw that I was standing without an outer garment, and he stopped and said, If it were not that I am about to go somewhere else between today and tomorrow, I would not have come at an hour when people usually go to bed. I said to him, On the contrary, I am grateful to you, sir, for coming, but please tell me if you are pleased with the lord of Zabno, and tell me where you are going, sir.

Rabbi Mordechai said, Your two questions explain one another. Because my mind is not content with Esau, I am going to Jacob. As to the matter of where I am going, to a city of Jews I am going, to Buczacz, where I lived with my wife for a year after our marriage. He who provided my livelihood at the hands of Esau will provide me with livelihood at the hands of Jacob. Rabbi Mordechai said, The rabbi of Zabno asked a good question, whether I am pleased with the magnate, for if he had asked me whether the lord is pleased with me, I would not know how to answer. In my days, I have never put my mind to the opinion of the lords of the nations of the earth, because our exile persists only because we sin by depending on the opinion of the lords of the nations of the world. If they are not wicked, the mockery they make of the blood of the Jews is worse than wickedness. Harsher than they are their agents, sucking the blood of the poor man until nothing is left of him but the skin on his body. On this, Rabbi Mordechai quoted a midrash on the verse "you made men ride over our heads." Because I do not remember the words, I will not mention the matter, for it was my rabbis who taught me that one does not refer to an aggadah except in the language that it was written in because every word of the midrash has deep meaning, which is not conveyed in our language.

Rabbi Mordechai spoke again, saying, Our rabbis said, a person should not part from his companion except with words of halakhah. Now that I have come to part from you, I must part with a word of halakhah. But I have a debt to you to tell you from what place I am and who were my ancestors and from whom I learned Torah, and we are commanded to pay our debts. However, there is not enough time to fulfill both the teachings together because it is already after midnight, and I do not know whether I will manage to come back again. Of necessity, we must postpone one thing for another. If so, we must first choose what the sages preferred: payment of a debt or parting with a word of halakhah. Payment of a debt is always graver, for even death does not absolve a person from paying a debt. If Reuben owed Simon and died, Simon can delay his burial until he is repaid. To what does this refer? To a monetary debt. But whether saying things that a person has promised to say to his friend can be called a debt, the sages did not teach. If so, it is incumbent upon us to choose. But if we undertake to sort out the matter, the night will be over, and we will not reach a decision. If so, what good have we done with all our reasoning if it does not lead to a clear halakhah?

The power of ḥidush was aroused in me, and I considered entering into a learned debate about whether a story one promises to tell his fellow can legally be considered a debt. The two halakhot I had been studying came to my mind: one about two women whose husband had bound them in the shackles of abandonment; and one about a person who wishes to eat an animal before it has expired. These two halakhot said to me, When you sat and pondered over us, you used to say, if only Rabbi Mordechai were with you, you would present us to him. Now that Rabbi Mordechai is before you, you are not mentioning us to him.

I put them off and said to Rabbi Mordechai, Because time is short, I will not enlist your help on matters that are causing me difficulty. Rabbi Mordechai said, What are they? I told him, From the day they came before me, I used to say, if only Rabbi Mordechai were here, I would present them to him, and he would place me on the straight path. Now my mind is cloudy and my soul weary, and I do not have the strength to present them or, needless to say, to deliberate about them. All I ask for is some words to restore the soul. Please, sir, tell me where you come from and who your ancestors were, and from whom you learned Torah.

Rabbi Mordechai said, The rabbi of Zabno has given me timely advice. If I mention my teacher and rabbi, certainly I will repeat some halakhah that I heard from his mouth, and thus I will fulfill both the commandment, that a man must only part from his comrade with a word of halakhah, and also the commandment of paying a debt. In any event, please, sir, tell me the essence of the matters and what they are, and what words of ours, where we stand, will help you.

Despite Rabbi Mordechai's invitation to take up these matters, I did not present them to him. However, I did remind him that he wished to tell me his story. Rabbi Mordechai said, The rabbi of Zabno has trapped a debtor, and he is now entitled to his due. I will pay you directly.

21

Rabbi Mordechai sat down and began his story, but when the rabbi of Zabno came to relate that story to the visitors from Buczacz, the very same thing happened that had happened every night with Rabbi Mordechai when the shamash's approach had interrupted them and Rabbi Mordechai departed. Now, just when the rabbi of Zabno began to tell the story of Rabbi Mordechai, the sound of the footsteps of the shamash were heard and then his voice chanting, Wake up sleepers and rouse, rise to serve the Creator.

The rabbi of Zabno said, They are already waking us up to serve the Creator, and the heart is still asleep. Night, night, how did you leave us without Torah? R. Ber spoke with authority and said, The rabbi of Zabno's mind may be at ease. Once my three sons-in-law, all great rabbis, stayed with me, and all night long, they sat and discussed the troubles of Israel that came to them because of the persecutions of the evil Khmelnitski and at the hand of Shabbatai Zvi, and from that abominable Jacob Frank, may the name of the wicked rot. Not one of them said, How are we spending time without Torah? Here the rabbi of Zabno has spoken about the Maharam Schiff and about Rabbi Mordechai, from whose deeds it is evident that he is a great man, and in the end, you sigh, sir, for yourself because a night has passed without Torah? But are not the deeds of Israel Torah? If so, who prevented the rabbi of Zabno from telling us some of the things that he heard from the Maharam Schiff that night?

R. Yeruḥam answered and said, The rabbi of Zabno has done what the Maharsha did, who divided his ḥidushim into innovations in halakhah and innovations in aggadah. If we ask, you will tell us some of the excellent things that you heard from the mouth of the Maharam Schiff that night. R. Levi said, If so, you have to inform us first what tractate and what page so that we can refer to the Gemara.

R. Yeruḥam spoke again: Even someone who reads the history of the kings of the nations and their wars, so that he will have something to think about in a place where it is forbidden to think about the Torah, truly, when stories about the tribulations and adventures of the Jews come to his hand, will he stop? Rather, he will keep reading and will not worry about wasting time. Here, too, there is no fear of neglecting Torah – at least not after the fact. However, even from the outset, we are always permitted to do this. Moreover, a commandment is connected with it. We find that R. Ber spoke well when he said that the deeds of Israel are Torah. This is the meaning of the verse *Concerning this it is told in the book of the wars of the Lord,* which means most of the deeds of Israel are wars of the Lord, which we fight against our enemies, who wish to throw off the yoke of His kingdom, may He be blessed. We find that if we tell stories about the Jewish people, we are telling about the awesome deeds of the King of Kings, the Holy One, blessed be He, who stands by us in all our troubles. Not only that, but even the adventures of ordinary Jews are wars of the Lord, which they fight against their instincts, for the sake of His blessed Name. And not only that....

R. Yeruḥam did not manage to say "but also" before the rabbi's wife entered with a kettle full of tea and cups, and she said something to the rabbi in a whisper. The rabbi said to his guests, Do you know what she said? She said that you are all invited to breakfast. And she also said that I must add my request to her request. The guests nodded their heads in agreement, except for R. Ber. The rabbi noticed and asked, R. Ber, what does he say? R. Ber said, What can I say? I do not have my talit and tefilin with me.

What do you mean, you do not have your talit and tefilin with you? Can there be a man who goes on a journey without his talit and tefilin?

R. Yeruḥam said, I will explain the words of R. Ber, and I will solve the problem raised by the rabbi of Zabno. His talit and tefilin are in the wagon we came in, and the wagon is standing at the inn. R. Ber is scrupulous not to pray either in a borrowed talit or with borrowed tefilin. The rabbi's wife said, When you come to the house of prayer, each of you will find his talit and tefilin. How can that be? called out R. Ber in surprise. The rabbi said, I can resolve R. Ber's question in several different ways: either the rabbi's wife sent an agent, or the proprietor of the inn brought them himself. The rabbi's wife said, I sent the shamash.

R. Levi whispered to R. Yeruḥam, A fine understanding was given to the wife of the rabbi of Zabno. R. Yeruḥam said, Go and tell the people of Zabno. R. Levi said, How can we interpret your words? R. Yeruḥam said, What good does all her intelligence do if we leave her intelligence and her husband behind in Zabno?

22

From the day before Zabno had known that men had come to their rabbi, and it wanted to know why they had come. Some said that they had a legal dispute, and they had come to adjudicate it before their rabbi, and some said that they had come about a matter concerning all the Jews. And there were those who made all sorts of conjectures, not one of which was close to the truth. There was one whose opinion did touch the truth. They said to him, With all due respect to your honor, you are a fool, and you are talking the most foolish of foolishness. Because of the courtesy of the people of Zabno, no one dared to enter the rabbi's house at night and ask, Who are these people with you?

After morning prayers, several householders accompanied the rabbi and his guests. Before they managed to finish their meal, more people came, until the house was too small to hold everyone, since the house of the rabbi of Zabno is not like the house of the rabbi of Buczacz. Once R. Ber gave a wedding feast for his daughter, and his three sons-in-laws the rabbis came, and all the great men of Buczacz gathered to greet them, and the great men of Buczacz are greater in number than all the people of all Zabno.

They sat on two long benches to the right and left of the table, and also on the rabbi's bed, because at night it was a bed, and in the daytime it was a bench. And whoever did not find a place to sit, stood. But R. Ber, R. Yeruḥam, and R. Levi sat on chairs with a back, and the seat was made of a kind of cushion. Before R. Ber and R. Yeruḥam and R. Levi came, everyone in the rabbi's household refrained from sitting on those chairs, for fear that the cushions contained a forbidden mixture of linen and wool, lest they might have lamb's wool or goat's wool, and were sewn with linen thread. R. Levi said to the rabbi of Zabno, I was in the home of R. Ḥayyim Cohen Rapoport in Lvov, and I saw him sitting on a chair like this, and they said to me in the name of R. Ḥayyim that in the case of none of these cushions need one have a fear of mixture. It was the craftsmen's custom to use rabbit wool and join the cover of the pillow with iron buttons, and there was neither lamb's wool nor goat's wool and no linen threads. The rabbi of Zabno listened and said to R. Levi, Let R. Ber, who permitted it, sit on the chair. R. Ber came and sat on one chair, R. Yeruḥam came and sat on the second chair, R. Levi came and sat on the third chair. From then on, the chairs were permitted for use, and the rabbi of Zabno used to place them before important guests, and when there were no guests, he would put the books that he borrowed from other people on them because a person does not know his time, and it was better for the people of his household to know that the books were borrowed and return them to their owners.

The great men of Zabno sat with the great men of Buczacz, and the rabbi of Zabno said to the great men of Zabno, Do you remember that I and another man with me used to study Torah most nights, and you said things about me that are unworthy of me, and I did not reveal to you who he was because he had forbidden me to do so in order to prevent people from interrupting his learning with their questions? Today, my teachers and masters, it was revealed to me that the time has come to reveal to you who this person is, who is so beloved by heaven that he was allowed to conceal his actions from people. I am not telling you this from hearsay but from what I heard from the mouth of that genius, Rabbi Mordechai. But I will not mention either the name of the town in question, for it has already received its punishment in this world, nor will I call Rabbi Mordechai's teacher by name because his town and its leaders were punished because of him. You, my masters and teachers, do not press me to reveal what I must conceal. The Holy One, blessed be He, collects His debt from people who cause conflict, and since He has already exacted payment, and those who caused the conflict have been purged by their torments, they are innocent in my eyes, and far be it from us to mention their evil deeds. If we allow ourselves to mention their deeds, it is only for the sake of morality and edification that we permit ourselves. But we will not mention their names because avenging angels lie in wait for those who cause conflicts, even after their death and even if they have atoned for their transgressions with suffering.

The rabbi shut his eyes, but a light that appears only on the faces of the righteous when they relate the deeds of the righteous began to shine on his face. Everyone lowered his eyes and sat in awe. The rabbi began to tell about the deeds of Rabbi Mordechai. Sometimes he told them in detail, and sometimes briefly, sometimes with a hint, and sometimes he included a quotation from Gemara or from Tosefta or Maimonides, or an adage. But as for us, who possess neither the power of that genius nor his strength, we will tell the story in our simple language, according to our limited capacity and the sorrow of our soul. We have not been graced with the wisdom of the sages and the intelligence of the wise. If we tell stories about great Jews, beloved of God, our only merit is that we are enriched by them in their Torah. Be not surprised if already at the beginning, I call Rabbi Mordechai "Rabbi" Mordechai, though at first, he was only a young boy among the boys of the village, without Torah and without knowledge. Because of the respect I have for great Torah scholars I regard them already full of Torah while still in their cradles.

Rabbi Mordechai and His Teacher

1

Rabbi Mordechai was born by virtue of the commandment to redeem prisoners. His father redeemed a young woman from captivity and married her according to the religion of Moses and Israel. She bore a son to him, and they called him Mordechai, after her father who had passed away while fleeing the despot's fury.

We shall relate the matter in detail. Once there was a young fellow who worked for a merchant in the city. The young fellow went on an errand for his employer, and he was very pleased, because that day, for the first time, the merchant gave him a power of attorney for all his business. On the way, the young man came to a village. He was hungry and went to the tavern to dine. He found all the furnishings thrown about outside and the doors and windows broken, and there was no one in the place, which was a God-awful mess. The young fellow stood still in surprise. A place where travelers once stopped constantly, where they found a hot meal and a welcoming face, was now in ruins, and its furnishings smashed and tossed outside, and not a living soul was around.

The young fellow looked this way and that. He saw an old gentile standing in the mess and poking about. The young fellow asked the old man, Tell me what happened. Why is the door open and the windows smashed and all the furnishings thrown outside? Where is the tavern owner, and where is his daughter? The old man said to the young fellow, Do not ask, good man, do not ask, because you will not hear anything good from me. My heart is broken because of my neighbor's disaster. He has taken the road from which there is no return, following after his wife. But the daughter's sorrow is worse. They threw her in the dungeon, and who knows whether the bread that our most merciful lord, the lord of the village, has ordered his servants to give her actually reaches her mouth? Fire has come and burned the house, and strangers have set their hands on the remaining timbers, to cook their food. This is how things are. The bread that our lord has ordered to give to the girl is eaten by his servants. You, sir, you stand and look and do not know a thing, because how can a rich man know the heart of someone poor? The innkeeper could not pay our lord for the lease, until the debt grew to the height of the coach in which our lord rides to the Lord's house. Indeed our lord warned him by sending his chief servant, and this is what he said to him: If you do not pay by Saint Peter's Day, I will throw you and your daughter into the dungeon. Now the feast day came, and our neighbor did nothing to appease our lord. He brought him no money. Only the tears in his eyes did he bring. Our lord was merciful to him and gave him another month and a day, but when the time came to pay, the innkeeper did not do the lord's bidding. He brought no money to him. Then our lord was furious that a man would dare to defy him. The innkeeper knew that our lord was a man of truth and would carry out all his threats. Therefore he quickly fled with his daughter. Our lord sent people to seize them and throw them into the dungeon. But death came first and took the good innkeeper, leaving his daughter alive, doubly orphaned, for her mother died before the evil times was visited upon them. Our lord's servants found the girl standing in the field with her dead father. They dragged her away from the corpse and brought her to the village and put her in the dungeon. Now, good sir, the girl is lying in the dungeon. If our Lord God does not send an angel from on high to take the girl out of the dungeon, she, too, will die. Because the Lord God does not give everyone strength to bear the burden of suffering, even if he lives ninety or a hundred years like me today. Certainly not to a feeble springtime bird, struck by rain and hail.

2

The young fellow took this in, paid the debt and saved the maiden from the dungeon. He saw that she was young and charming. He said, She is the wife that God has approved for me. He went and betrothed her and took her as his wife. That young fellow was Yisrael Natan, Rabbi Mordechai's father, and that maiden was Sarah Rivkah, his mother.

Yisrael Natan left his master's table and rented lodgings and purchased furnishings. He and his wife moved into their lodgings. Before he married, he had eaten at his master's table and lived in an attic amid an abundance of goods, between sacks of rice or of raisins and almonds. Only on the Sabbath morning would he go to his sister Shaintshe, the wife of Nisan the tinsmith. There he would put on a clean shirt and leave the shirt he had taken off. He would sit and drink plum compote that Shaintshe took from the Sabbath oven, and discuss the news of the town with his brother-in-law. For his brother-in-law's shop opened onto the new market, between the tanners' quarter and the grain market, and he was as familiar with the doings of the townspeople as a parnas before he was appointed parnas.

3

Yisrael Natan brought his wife to town, but she was not happy there. She and her fathers and their fathers were country people from birth, and they only came to town on the High Holidays to pray with a congregation because their village was small and had no minyan. Needless to say this was so in earlier generations, when the parnasim of the congregations did not allow villagers to form congregations in their village on the High Holidays, because *the splendor of the king is in a great multitude*, and in order to increase the revenue of their community.

Yisrael Natan saw that it was hard for his wife to live in town. She walked in gloom under the pressure of her grief. He began to consult with his sister Shaintshe, who gave him all kinds of advice, though in her heart she said what she had said before the wedding: an orphaned woman is like a house with no wall. She was not pleased with Sarah Rivkah, because she had brought in no dowry. Anyone who marries a woman without a dowry is conniving with his own foolishness. Since Shaintshe's advice was ineffective, he began asking the wise women of the town. When their advice too proved ineffective, he went to the expert, who prescribed herbs whose liquid was good for the heart. Since that did not work, he started worrying more and more.

Once, an old woman came from the village and saw Sarah Rivkah. She shrieked and said, Oy, what has happened to you? I saw your mother at the time of her death, and her face was happier than yours. Yisrael Natan heard and said to her, Give me advice. She said to him, What good is correct advice if no one listens? There's no cure for your wife except to bring her back to the village, because she cannot stand the town. Yisrael Natan turned his face from the woman and said, How can I possibly leave my livelihood behind in town and dwell in a village unknown to my fathers and my fathers' fathers?

4

The village woman's words did not leave his heart. They rumbled inside him and pecked at his brain and made an impression on him. His master saw him and asked, What is the matter with you, Yisrael Natan? Are you in the world of chaos? Yisrael Natan told him what troubled his heart, without concealing what the village woman had said.

A few days later, after the departure of the Sabbath, his master invited him to his home and sat with him, saying, Let us make an accounting of how much you have invested with me and how much it will cost us to rent an inn in the village such that a decent living can be made from it.

They made the accounting and they found that all the money Yisrael Natan had invested with his master was not enough to rent an inn, and as for making a partnership with another Jew, that would be as if they intended from the start to make two Jews poor forever.

Yisrael Natan sat before his master as if his world was in ruins. His master looked at him and scolded him, saying, You are still a townsman but you are acting like a villager. Yisrael Natan raised his eyes to his master and said, *Whence will come my aid*? The merchant paced back and forth. Finally he stopped and said, I heard that the village magnate, to whom we sold a dozen sacks of rice last week, has built a new tavern with fine rooms for travelers attached to it. If no one else has beat you to it, we will go and feel the matter out to see whether it is worthwhile, and if it is worthwhile, we will lease it.

5

The next day the merchant happened to be in the village and chanced to meet the lord of the village. They began to talk about everything that was created in the first six days of creation and everything that would be created by the end of time, which is to say, about nothing that concerned either one of them. Finally they got to matters of the village. The lord told the merchant that he had built a new inn and added some spacious rooms for noblemen and wealthy merchants. The merchant yawned and put his hand over his mouth, saying, Pardon me, my lord, for yawning. I am exhausted from the trip to the village. What did you say? You built some rooms, for noblemen and merchants? I am not so well versed in the customs of noblemen, as to how much they like to drag their bones to country inns, but as for merchants, permit me to tell you that I would rather travel for an hour or two at night to avoid sleeping in a village. As for an inn, its profits will not weigh down your pockets. It is lucky for an innkeeper if his customers are satisfied with what is in the glass, without swallowing the glass.

The lord's spirits sagged, but he pulled himself together and asked the merchant to inspect the inn and the fine rooms for important guests.

6

The merchant looked at everything the village lord showed him. He said, Everything depends on the lessee. If the lessee is capable of running a business, he will be able to pay the rent. If he cannot pay the rent, the matter is not worthwhile. You cannot make a pot of soup from his tears. If he claims he has no money, you cannot do a thing to him. You cannot even throw him in the dungeon, because these days under His Highness, the Austrian Emperor, are not like former times. In the past, a lord could throw a lessee who failed to pay his rent in the dungeon, which is what happened to the father-in-law of one of my employees. However, surprisingly, after all their sorrows—for he died of sorrow, and his daughter was thrown into the dungeon—she is still so nostalgic for village life that her husband is prepared to exchange the good living he earns in town for a doubtful living in the village.

The lord of the village heard and asked the merchant to order his employee to lease the tavern with its fine rooms. The merchant said, Though nothing in the world is more valuable to me than doing your will, nevertheless I must tell you that I feel sorry for my faithful employee, who will lose his money in this business. But I can tell you that even if you lower the rent you set by a third, it is worth your while to rent to a man like that. Because many good people can guarantee that he will pay his rent on time. Perhaps others will promise you more, even double. But what is the importance of a promise with no security? In the end, because you are merciful, because your heart is soft and good, or, to put it differently, because of shame before the Austrian officials, you will have to give in. Anyway, I will send my employee to you, and you can speak with him. I can only be responsible for his paying the rent on time.

Yisrael Natan and Sarah Rivkah went down to the village, and with them came Nisan and Shaintshe. They saw what a member of the village magnate's household showed them and what their own eyes showed them, and they came to no agreement. But as soon as Sarah Rivkah saw the village, she said, Here will I dwell.

7

Yisrael Natan gathered his strength and left his master and the business he had grown up in. He left his livelihood behind and parted from his master and his home and from all his friends. He took his wife and moved to the village, placing his trust in God that He would not abandon them. He opened the tavern with the fine rooms and put mezuzot on the doors and added things that in his and his wife's opinion were needed for an inn, and he began to dispense drinks to the villagers and to travelers. Sarah Rivkah his wife stood by his side and helped him.

Villagers began to come individually and in groups, and they drank the wine that the Merchant Man served them, for that is what they called the new innkeeper, out of respect. Also poor travelers found a cup of milk or kvass there, a slice of bread, and a stretch of bench to sleep on at night. On the anniversary of her father's death, Sarah Rivkah went to town with a wagon full of bread for the poor and pitchers of soured milk, aside from coins for the poor and the shamash and the cemetery guard.

The innkeeper of the village earned a good name, aside from the good name that the tavern earned together with those fine rooms of the inn. If they were nearby, noblemen and ladies upon whom the sun set while they were on the road stayed in those fine rooms for a night and sometimes for several nights. Merchants as well, of whom R. Aaron, Yisrael Natan's master had said that they would rather travel for two hours at night so they could rest on their beds in their own houses and not in village inns, they, too, did not avoid staying in those rooms. They said they slept better there than on all their nights at home, and not because of fatigue from the road but because of the comfortable mattresses. This was because Sarah Rivkah refreshed the straw in the mattresses every year, not like most townspeople, who renew the straw once every few years.

Yisrael Natan prospered. What he earned from the tavern, he invested in the guest rooms, what he earned from the guest rooms, he invested in the tavern, and from the money that remained he began to pay back the money he had borrowed from moneylenders and what his master had lent him, and what he had borrowed from his sister's husband, Nisan the tinsmith. To prevent another Jew from coming and leasing the tavern on land belonging to the lord's sister at the other end of the village, Yisrael Natan rented it. To reduce the number of his employees, he left it locked. To conceal it from travelers, he planted a lot of poplars all around it, because they have many boughs

8

Yisrael Natan and Sarah Rivkah lived in the village, and their work brought them blessings. Yisrael Natan paid all his debts, even to his sister's husband. Very gradually Sarah Rivkah recovered, and her soul returned to her. A village woman once said that Sarah Rivkah's mother looked happier at the hour of her death than Sarah Rivkah, but if she could have seen Sarah Rivkah now, she would have been surprised. For Sarah Rivkah looked like a village girl whom the Holy One, blessed be He, had deprived of nothing in His world. But that village woman had already passed away, and in her place, by contrast, a Jewish person was born. Who bore him? Sarah Rivkah. After living for about eight years without children, she gave birth to a son. They named the son born to them Mordechai, after her father Mordechai, who had departed for life in the world to come when fleeing from the lord of the village. I will call the boy Rabbi Mordechai, for the reason I have explained: out of love and honor and affection for great Torah scholars, I see them as if they suckled from the breast of the Torah and wisdom from the hour of their birth.

9

The firstborn are beloved because of their birthright. Only sons are beloved because their parents devote all their love to them. Above all is a firstborn infant who is his parents' only child. After several more years passed, and Yisrael Natan and Sarah Rivkah were not blessed with other children, they add another term of affection to their son, beside "firstborn" and "only child": "child of old age." The new appellation did not squeeze out the first two nicknames. Sometimes they called him our firstborn son, and sometimes they called him our only child, and sometimes they called him our child of old age. But above all the fond names, the one his mother was fondest of was that given to him on his eighth day, when he was named after her father, who was sanctified in his suffering like the holy Jews who take suffering upon themselves in this world so they will enter the world to come refined and pure and cleaned of every sin.

10

Rabbi Mordechai grew up in the village and played with the village boys. He fished with them and trapped animals and birds, swam in the river and climbed trees. There was no tall tree that he did not climb, and there was no animal or bird whose call the boy could not imitate, so that the animals mistakenly thought one of their kind was calling them. If fish had a language, without doubt he would have known how to sound like them. Why do I tell this? Because he was expert in fish and the places they hide. Do not be surprised at his expertise in water creatures, because he was a great swimmer and could float on the water even on stormy days. The boy knew an abundance of such things. Since the only desire of our heart and the pleasure of our desire is to tell how Rabbi Mordechai learned Torah, I will not dwell on them, since inessential matters are of no interest to the Torah.

The boy's father and mother saw his doings and it pained them. Yisrael Natan was not Mar bar Rav Ashi, and Sarah Rivkah was not Sarah bat Tovim, but they were Jews, and they knew what the Lord our God demands of us. If not Gemara and Tosafot, the Blessed One certainly demands of us at least a verse of the Bible with Rashi. Yisrael Natan began to talk with the fathers of the boys his son's age, who were also growing up in the village without Torah. Together the parents scraped up enough to bring a poor fellow from the city, one of the teachers' assistants, and they made him the melamed of their sons. To avoid depriving any of the parents of merit, the melamed would eat in a different home every day, but they set aside a place for his Torah teaching in the home of a childless old woman, where they used to gather for prayer on the Sabbath and holidays.

The melamed taught Torah to the village children. He did not teach much, and less than what he taught was absorbed. But the true problem was in regard to Rabbi Mordechai, who in one hour would grasp what the others did not grasp in six days. But aside from the prayer book and chapters of the Bible and a few commandments, he learned nothing. If the melamed had not himself learned anything, from whom could the pupil learn? He would sit before this teacher, and boredom would drive him crazy. He would sneak out of the room and go to his friends in the village, the ones who did not have to bear the yoke of

Torah, and do as they did. Not only that, he thought up new things to do, grabbing an animal on the run or a bird in flight. The boy's father and mother saw their only child growing up like the non-Jewish village boys, and it caused them pain. But what could they do? It was impossible to live in the city, because city living was hard for Sarah Rivkah. Yisrael Natan, too, though he was a townsman, was afraid he could not make a living in town. He had already forgotten commerce. To send the boy to a teacher in the city, which was Nisan and Shaintshe's advice, was also impossible, because he was their only child, and their soul was bound up with his. They placed their hope in God, that He would save them.

11

One day Yisrael Natan's cow got lost. He went out to look for her and found an old man wandering in the field. Yisrael Natan called out in alarm, Rabbi, what are you doing here alone in the field? The rabbi said to him, If you have a secret place, hide me, because the duke is pursuing me.

Yisrael Natan turned his heart away from the cow to the rabbi's troubles. He led him through valleys and hills where no man's foot treads and brought him to his house. He brought a bowl full of warm water and washed his feet, which were swollen, and salved them with sheep fat and set a table for him and offered him a bed. He kept thinking, Where will I hide the rabbi? A tavern is open to passersby, and anyone who sees the rabbi will wonder about an old man whose countenance is like that of an angel of God, what is he doing in the village? Word would eventually get to the duke's ear, and the duke would send his servants to arrest the rabbi. Even though the duke had no authority over the village, the duke's arm was long, reaching wherever he wanted.

Sarah Rivkah saw her husband's worry. She picked up the keys of the tavern at the other end of the village. Yisrael Natan saw the keys and said, Now I know why I rented it and left it idle. I only leased it to house the rabbi there. From this we see that Yisrael Natan's heart reprimanded him for wasting his money so that another Jew would not profit. Now that he had to find a place for the rabbi, it seemed to him that heaven had enabled him to rent the tavern, to make a dwelling for the rabbi there. There was no better hiding place than the tavern on the other side of the village, because Yisrael Natan had made people forget the way to it. He brought a bed and a table and a chair there, and a barrel of water, and the night afterward he brought the rabbi there and placed Rabbi Mordechai at his service.

12

The lad's heart clung to the old man. So much so that he gave away to the village boys the traps for animals and birds made by his uncle the tinsmith and stood by the rabbi to serve him. With great ingenuity his uncle had also made him a hollow tin rod for shooting darts. This, too, he gave away to the local boys so that he could serve the rabbi. How did he serve him? Every day he brought him his meal and boiled a kettle for him, and he would bring his father's talit and tefilin, because the rabbi had not managed to take his own talit and tefilin when he fled.

13

The lad served the rabbi because it was a new interest for him, and because he regarded himself as chosen from all others, because his father and mother, who did not mention the rabbi to anyone, had chosen him to serve the rabbi. Because they had chosen him to serve the rabbi, he served him well. But he wondered why his father and mother were so concerned about the rabbi, and why, when they mentioned his name, they used all sorts of endearments. There are many delightful people in the world, like R. Aaron the merchant who lent father money without interest to rent the tavern and like Uncle Nisan, who had made the trap and the clever rod for him. Like those barefoot, naked people his mother fed and gave a bit of money. But father and mother are not as anxious about their welfare as they are anxious about the rabbi's.

Other people come to the tavern and are called hasidim, traveling in a group to meet their rebbe, dancing and clapping their hands while at prayer and praying for a long time. If the sun sets on them, they sleep in the tavern. They are in no hurry to lie down. They sit and tell stories about the deeds of the tzaddikim. His mother hears, and her eyes weep because of everything that happened to her and her father, and no tzaddik came to save them. In the morning when all the ḥasidim set out, Father gives each of them a coin, saying to him, If you become a rebbe, remember me for good. Even though they are important, father and mother are not concerned for them the way they are anxious about the rabbi's safety.

14

The lad began to observe the old man and found him full of surprises. He used to sit alone with his eyes closed and his hands lying on his knees, talking to himself. He would say, If so, according to Maimonides it comes out this way, but according to the method of Rabbenu Tam, and so on. Rabbenu Tam, he reasoned, must be connected to the second set of tefilin the ḥasidim put on. But what of Maimonides' position? Once he asked his father, who told him, The rabbi is murmuring words of Torah. Rabbi Mordechai said to himself, If the rabbi thinks about Torah even when the fear of a melamed was not upon him, then he must be thinking of a different Torah, one much finer than the one my melamed taught me. Once he rose early in the morning and heard the rabbi recite the benedictions of the Torah. The lad had never heard such a beautiful voice in his life. He understood from hearing the voice that the Torah was very lovely. If the Torah was lovely, why did people not study it? Aside from asking to be called to the Torah on the Sabbath and dancing with Torah on Simḥat Torah, nobody paid much attention to it.

15

From these puzzles his mind came to what men of science call awareness. He did not get there explicitly. He got there by way of unclear and unexplained thoughts. But according to the torments of his thoughts and his style, we would call this awareness.

One day, Rabbi Mordechai saw the rabbi while he recited the blessing before the Shema describing the Great Love. He saw from the voice and from the words and from the rabbi's joy, that we have a God who loves us greatly and has great and abundant compassion for us, because of our ancestors who trusted in Him, and He taught them the laws of life. The rabbi was asking that God have mercy on us and make our hearts understand and be wise and hear and learn and teach and keep and do and observe all the words of the Torah and its teachings with love. These were the laws of life that he had mentioned at the outset. And for this, too, he was asking, for illumination of the eyes and cleaving of the heart to the commandments of the Torah and unifying the heart in love and awe of the revered Name, that we may never be shamed, not in this world and not in the next. Yet this was not the end of all the requests, for the end of the requests was that He should bring us safely to our land. Why? Certainly because there was no fear of noblemen and dukes in our land, only closeness to God, who chooses His people Yisrael in love.

But when the rabbi came to reciting the Shema, and he called out, *God is our Lord, God is One,* the lad's thoughts ceased because of the fear that fell upon him, for he was alarmed and frightened lest the rabbi release his soul with the utterance of the word One, for it definitely appeared as if he was yielding up his soul in love and willingness and joy. Though no one dies except by the sword of the Angel of Death, who drips a bitter drop in him, it was clear that the rabbi was not yielding his soul to the Angel of Death but to the Lord our God, who is One. The lad was frightened lest the Lord our God might take the rabbi's soul, and he would be standing alone with a dead man. He remained in fear until the rabbi began to recite the passages following the Shema. When the rabbi called out the passage beginning "The help of our fathers…," the lad understood that if the rabbi did not die with uttering the word One, this was because the Holy One, blessed be He, is the help of our fathers. He defends and redeems them and their children after them in every generation.

After the rabbi had finished his prayer, Rabbi Mordechai brought him his meal. Rabbi Mordechai looked at him, and it seemed to him that even at the final meal before the beginning of Yom Kippur, his father and mother were not seized by holy trepidation as the rabbi was at his weekday meal.

16

From then on, Rabbi Mordechai did not part from the rabbi, and he spent a great deal of time observing him. If he saw him sitting with his eyes closed and his hands on his knees and his lips moving, Rabbi Mordechai would approach him and stand there listening to the names that the rabbi used to mention, Rambam, and Rashba, and the Rif, and the Rosh, and the other names. Little by little they began to take on the palpable form of great rabbis. Rabbi Mordechai wanted to know who they were and in what consisted their greatness. He also began to desire knowing how one achieves such greatness. If it was by the Torah, was there anyone greater in Torah than the rabbi? If it was by old age, he was even older than the wealthy R. Aaron. One way or another, he was more beloved than anyone else in the world.

Rabbi Mordechai loved his uncle Nisan, who produced marvelous objects. He loved his aunt Shaintshe, who knew how to recite proverbs in rhymes. Even though she and his mother did not love each other, he loved her. Rabbi Mordechai loved the wealthy R. Aaron, who had given his father a bag of money to rent the tavern. More than all he loved the rabbi. But he wondered why this lovely man had been forced to run away from the duke. Did the duke not see the rabbi's loveliness?

17

One night, the boy was bothered by the sound of weeping. He saw the rabbi sitting on a stool at the door, holding a lit candle, and mourning for Jerusalem. All day long Rabbi Mordechai considered what he had seen that night, and he said to himself, It is right for the rabbi to weep and mourn for the destruction of Jerusalem, because if we were in Jerusalem and not in exile, he would not have had to flee from the duke. Still it was hard to understand, and the duke was a fool for not loving the rabbi. All the troubles came from the exile, which deprived the gentiles of intelligence and gave them a wicked heart to do evil. Grandfather Mordechai had leased a tavern from the magnate, he did not earn enough with it to pay the rent, and the magnate had ordered his servants to throw grandfather Mordechai and Mother in the dungeon. The old rabbi had been the rabbi of a large city of merchants and wealthy men. The duke had ordered to put him in prison. The rabbi fled first. It is good to be a rabbi, because the rabbi knows the whole Torah, but if he has to hide from the duke, that is not good. So what is good? Nothing was good except to work at a craft. Uncle Nisan dwelled in the city, hammered tin flat, and produced useful vessels. Some things were easy to grasp in thought, but not the tinsmith's craft. A sheet of tin lies there. Uncle Nisan takes the sheet and flattens it the way a cobbler flattens a piece of leather, and he takes scissors that can cut metal, cuts a piece of the sheet, puts it on the anvil, and strikes it with the hammer, bending it here and there. While you are standing and looking, a lantern or a Ḥanukkah menorah or another vessel emerges. Father is very wealthy because he has three cows and a horse to ride, but all of Rabbi Mordechai's affection was given to the rabbi.

18

The rabbi found repose in the empty house at the end of the village, where no traveler ventured. It was neither noticed nor seen because of the tall poplars with their many boughs, which Yisrael Natan had planted to hide it from people's eyes, so that no one would approach the noblewoman and rent it and thus deprive him of part of his livelihood. Only the sun and the moon and the stars at night and Yisrael Natan's household knew about the house.

The rabbi's soul began to recover and began to seek its purpose. This already happened during the first days when he was living there, that is, before the event we have been relating at length.

The rabbi's soul recovered and sought its true purpose. He sent Rabbi Mordechai to bring him a volume of Maimonides. Yisrael Natan came and told him, Rabbi, Maimonides is not one of the fruits that grow on trees in the village. He said to him, But you have a Gemara. He said, We only see the Gemara on the eve of Passover.

What does that mean?

He said to him, On the eve of Passover in the morning, a fellow comes from the town with a Gemara in his hand, all the firstborn of the village gather, the fellow opens the Gemara and sits and reads three or four lines from the end of the Gemara, we fill glasses and drink brandy in honor of completing the tractate, and we are released from the fast of the firstborn. But if the rabbi can be satisfied with a Bible with Rashi's commentary, I will bring him one. The rabbi said, If I take a book from the town, tomorrow someone will look for the book and not find it, and people will say, certainly it is in the rabbi's possession. Then a dishonest person will hear it and report the words to the duke, and the duke will impose a boycott on the community until they reveal my hiding place.

It is better for me not to take books from the town and to be satisfied with the Bible with Rashi. But I do need my talit and tefilin, and I must report to my family that I am living among Jews and lack nothing.

Yisrael Natan heard and went off to the town. He sent someone to the rabbi's house to retrieve his talit and tefilin, and to bring a greeting from his house. From then on, whenever Yisrael Natan happened to be in the town, the rabbi sent a letter of greeting with him to his household, and Yisrael Natan would send it with a child. In every letter, the rabbi would warn them not to seek, inquire, or ask about his whereabouts. If they nevertheless sought after him, he threatened to stop writing to them. He told Rabbi Mordechai and his father and mother not to reveal his hiding place even to someone who was cautious in his speech, because of the eagerness to show they know more than others, people have a way of causing harm unintentionally. They listened and exercised care. They went so far that once when Nisan the tinsmith came to the village to spend several days with his brother-in-law, he did not discover that the rabbi was living in the village. But he reported on the welfare of the rabbi's family. So when Yisrael Natan happened to be in town, he would ask him about the welfare of the rabbi's family.

19

The rabbi studied the Bible with Rashi's commentary and was surprised. All his life he had believed that the studying the Bible with Rashi's commentary was a matter for the common folk and not for rabbis. Suddenly his eyes were opened and he saw all the goodness inherent in Rashi's commentary. The Shelah of blessed memory, said: Every single word of Rashi contains much matter, because Rashi, of blessed memory, wrote his work while infused with the holy spirit. Now that the rabbi examined Rashi's commentary, he saw the greatness of the Shelah's words. The genius, Ba'al Halevushim, wrote that all of Rashi's words in his commentary on the Torah contain both manifest and mystical matters, and both are true. The rabbi, in his righteous modesty, said, I have no interest in the mystical. With what is manifest, praised be the living God, I have some acquaintance, and I can say that all of Rashi's commentary is true and honest.

The rabbi dwelled in the house in the village, eating and drinking what Rabbi Mordechai brought him from his parents' house, and they, too, sometimes came to check of his welfare. When they came, they would bring him a clean shirt or some other thing he needed, and they thanked merciful God for placing the rabbi with them, because from the day the rabbi came to live with them, their son quit the pursuits of the village boys and set his mind to the Torah.

20

One day the rabbi said to Rabbi Mordechai, My son, if you want to study Torah, I will teach you. He opened the Bible before him and taught him Torah with Rashi's commentary, and the Aramaic translation, and the haftarot.

The rabbi saw that his pupil's mind was good and his thinking straight. He understood quickly and forgot little, he absorbed everything, and he loved studying. He was happy with every new teaching, and the new learning did not displace the old, so the rabbi doubled and redoubled what he taught him several times over. He began by teaching him a single weekly portion over seven days. Then he started teaching him two or three portions in two or three days, and he taught him Rashi and Onkelos's translation, and he started teaching him the Aramaic translation attributed to Yonatan, and the Jerusalem Aramaic translation, and the commentary on the haftarot. He would show him the several laws that were derived from each verse in the Torah, and this stood Rabbi Mordechai in good stead all his life. For if he remembered a verse, he remembered all the laws derived from that verse, and if he remembered a law, he remembered the place of that law in the Torah. This is a very great virtue among Torah scholars, which is not attained by all. Some great scholars are experts in the laws and know the opinion of the authorities. They even know the source of the law in the Gemara, and they sometimes derive a new ruling from it that is not mentioned by either the Medieval or latter-day authorities. But they do not know the divine quarry from which verse in the Torah the law was hewn. The rabbi also did something more. In the evening, when he went out to walk in the fields, leaning on his student, he would teach him general principles, and these too stood by Rabbi Mordechai in his Torah study.

21

One day a man in the village had his son circumcised. People came from the city, and one of them left behind a volume of the Gemara, but no one knew who had forgotten it. Yisrael Natan took it and brought it to the rabbi.

He saw the Gemara and laughed and wept. He wept for the days he had spent without a Gemara. He laughed because a Gemara had come into his possession. And which volume? The one he had been studying on the day that he fled from the duke's wrath. We, who do not wish to profit from a miracle even in a story, will reveal things as they truly happened. R. Birekh Shapira knew where his father-in-law was hiding. He brought the Gemara with him to that village and left it there, purposely choosing the volume that his father-in-law the rabbi had been studying.

The rabbi kissed the Gemara and said, It is pleasing for a man if his wealth enables people to observe a commandment. He opened the Gemara and began to study with a tear in his voice. Rabbi Mordechai sat on the threshold, dejected and disappointed, because the rabbi had turned his attention away from him on account of the Gemara. The rabbi noticed and said to him, Come, my son, and bring your soul alive by studying a page of Gemara.

22

Rabbi Mordechai came and sat before the Gemara, and he listened and heeded and learned the words of the living God, which Moses heard from the mouth of the Almighty during the forty days he was on Mount Sinai, along with the written Torah. Forty generations later, our holy rabbi, Judah Hanasi, set them down in the Mishnah, and afterward his students and their students, the tannaim and the amoraim came and interpreted the Mishnah and composed the Talmud, which sustained our ancestors and ourselves in every generation and land, and it will sustain us until the messiah is revealed to us, may it be soon in our days. He will show us all the places that were blocked from our intelligence because of the hardships of oppression and bitter exile. What we will learn from our righteous messiah are the obscure, marvelous, sublime things that the simple intelligence cannot attain, and they will be revealed by the king messiah.

The rabbi and his student sat and studied the Gemara together, with Rashi's commentary, and the Tosafot, and Piskei Tosafot, and the Rosh, and Maimonides' commentary on the Mishnah. In the daytime they reviewed what they had studied at night, and at night they reviewed what they had learned by day, and for every section in the Talmud the rabbi explained the matters that derived from it and matters from other tractates that related to that tractate. The dimensions of the Torah are greater than the earth, and all its commandments cannot be reduced to a single tractate. Hence the sages placed them in other tractates. R. Birekh, the rabbi's son-in-law, told a nice parable about this. He compared God to a king who has piles of silver and gold, precious stones, pearls, and fine vessels, so many that no house can contain them all. What does the king do? He divides them among many houses. R. Birekh also said, The king makes keys to his treasure houses and delivers them to his trusted servants. He gives the key to one house to one of them, and to someone else he gives the keys to two or three houses. To the most trusted man of all, he gives the keys to all his treasuries. Similarly, there are students of Torah to whom the key to one tractate was given, and some have the keys to two or three tractates. But all the keys to the Talmud have been given to my teacher, my father-in-law, may he live. This parable easily makes you understand how much Torah and how much benefit the student received from such a rabbi.

It is the way of authors of parables to compare the Holy One, blessed be He, to a king and the Torah to the treasures of fine vessels, and the sages of the Torah to the guardians of the keys. We, who are unable to compose new parables, take the ones composed by the ancients and apply them according to our needs, make use of the parable of R. Birekh the preacher here. However, because the parable does not correspond to its lesson in all its details and subtleties, we must add to it and say the following, From a single tractate, which happened to come into the rabbi's possession, the rabbi studied all the halakhot of the Torah with his student. Later on, when Rabbi Mordechai studied the whole Talmud from written texts, he already possessed everything contained there, because he had heard them from his rabbi.

Let us return to our story. No days of Torah for the rabbi and his student were like the days when they remained withdrawn and secluded, separated and distanced from the whole world, sitting and thinking about the Torah, which expands one's mind and strengthens one's soul and makes one forget all the vanities of the world. Hence you should not be surprised that Rabbi Mordechai abandoned the boys of the village and the river and the woods and the entire village, and he clung to his rabbi, and he and his teacher clung to the Torah, which is beyond compare to all the things of the world.

Now we will relate why the rabbi had to flee from his city and hide from the duke, and why the duke pursued the rabbi. If the matters turn out to be long and digress somewhat from the main subject, you should know that in the end everything comes back to the beginning, to the holy community of Buczacz, which was seeking a rabbi, and to Rabbi Mordechai, some of whose praises we have already heard.

Why the Rabbi Fled

1

Reuven and Shimon were leaseholders. Reuven had leased the river to trap fish, and Shimon had leased furnaces to manufacture salt. The noblewoman who owned the river had two large ponds that were standing idle. Reuven rented the ponds to grow fish. Shimon sent him a request to withdraw from that enterprise because if heavy rains came, the ponds would overflow their dikes and flood the furnaces. But Reuven did not heed Shimon's request, and he leased the ponds. One year, it was very snowy and rainy, and the water of the ponds flooded the furnaces. Shimon took the law into his own hands and seized several wagons full of fish that Reuven had sent to a certain lord who had ordered them for a banquet that he was holding for the king's army. Reuven sued Shimon for the great losses he incurred as a result, and Shimon sued Reuven, whose ponds had destroyed his furnaces, all his outbuildings, and his other property. Each appointed an advocate who, in turn, chose authority of a rabbi who was a great Torah scholar and a righteous man to arbitrate. They placed their arguments before him. The rabbi heard the arguments found the innocent party innocent and the guilty party guilty. The man who lost the case was close to the duke. The duke said to him, I heard that the rabbi in my city adjudicated your matter. He must certainly have found in your favor. The losing party answered the duke, The rabbi twisted his judgment toward my opponent, and now I can only hope he will not take all my property. The duke heard and said, Fear not. I will argue your case. The duke immediately ordered his servants to bring the rabbi before him. The rabbi knew the duke to be irascible and cruel, and no proof would be effective in proving the rabbi's judgment correct. He fled. Rabbi Mordechai's father found him and brought him to his home. The rabbi stayed as long as he had to and studied with Rabbi Mordechai until he became as great in the Torah as any of the great scholars in the land.

Such is the gist of the story. Now we will present the whole chain of events and the claims of the litigants. Although the additions may outweigh the essentials, there is certainly nothing superfluous about them because the details that fill out the matter turn the supplement into the main point.

2

Reuven had leased the river to trap fish. Now it is the way of fish to wander from place to place and not to stay still to be trapped, especially in mightily flowing rivers. Nor can one control the price of fish, because when they come in large schools, there is a surplus and this lowers the price, and when they come intermittently, the effort to catch them is great, and the profit small.

The noblewoman who owned the river also owned two large ponds where her ancestors once grew the fish that were the pride of her country. These ponds lay idle at the time, with neither water nor fish. Reuven approached the noblewoman and discussed the possibility of repairing them and the great profit that this would bring. Her advisers, agents, and those who ate at her table took note agreed that the ponds were worth repairing for there were none like them in all of Poland and there were no fish like those that the ponds would produce in abundance.

Some old people still used to tell what they had heard from their ancestors about the taste of the fish once raised in those ponds: Today's fish compares to the fish that once came from those ponds the way the taste of a fly compares to the loin of a bear.

The noblewoman was convinced and told Reuven, I agree to refurbish the ponds, if you will lease them. Reuven said to the lady, A man like myself has no joy greater than the joy of fulfilling your highness's wish. If your highness provides me with workers to scrape the earth and dig out the clogged wells, and lumber from her forests to make dams, I will be prepared to lease the ponds for as many years as your highness commands me.

The noblewoman ordered each of her villages to send her two or three energetic and strong young men to do the work. From every single one of her nine hundred and ninety-nine villages came vigorous, brawny young men. She sent them to Reuven. Reuven split them into two camps, one for each of the ponds. Their job was to clean them, to scrape up the earth, to remove the stones, to dig out the clogged wells, and the like.

Shimon heard and began to fear because he had furnaces to extract salt, the good salt that appears on people's tables, not the salt mixed into horse feed to make the horses thirsty so they will drink a lot and grow fat, which is mined from salt mountains. Those furnaces were near the ponds, not right next to them but not far. In rainy years, the ponds could overflow their dikes and flood the furnaces, all the salt stored in outbuildings, and the sheds in the field.

Shimon sent to Reuven, telling him that the ponds endangered his furnaces and that if the water harmed the furnaces, the water would destroy the houses and sheds and wash away the barrels, troughs, basins, and the molds, which had been fabricated at great expense by the kind of superior craftsmen who no longer exist. Now that the currency is debased and there are no more such craftsmen, vessels like these could not be fashioned even at several times the cost. Therefore he demanded Reuven withdraw from the business of the ponds and thereby prevent causing disaster to several Jewish families who supported themselves from the saltworks. If it was necessary to reconcile the noblewoman, his own lord, the owner of the furnaces, had already promised to take the matter up with the noblewoman, who had been gracious to him when her husband was alive. Reuven could not protest that if he did not lease the ponds, others would come along and do so because it was known that there was no one in the kingdom of Poland capable of investing the necessary capital. Furthermore, the arrangement he had made with the noblewoman was well known: if he leased the ponds, she was prepared to renovate them, and if not—not. It was proper for a Jew, both with respect to the law and also with respect to decency, to desist from a business that would damage the livelihood of several Jewish people.

Reuven shrugged his shoulders and said, What does Shimon want from me? Must I really withdraw from such a profitable arrangement because of his fears? He sent him an answer: A man has nothing but what his eyes see, and we have no business with what *might* happen. As far as my eyes see, the climate these days is regular, and the rivers and streams do not overflow their banks. On the contrary, half of them are dry. The earth is also dry, and the fields are thirsty, and all the owners of villages complain that this is a drought year, and the crops are burned. The priests are about to take out the statues of their gods to ask for rain. Thus all of Shimon's fears are groundless, and there is no reason to be worried about *might* and *perhaps*.

Shimon came to Reuven and showed him an ordinance from the old community register excommunicating any Jew who leased a business from the nobles that could harm others. This included the ponds, each of which was a quarter of a league in length and a quarter of a league in width, and if a lot of rain fell, the rivers would fill with water. They would overflow their banks and fill the ponds, which would overflow and flood the saltworks, the stockpiled salt, the outbuildings, and sheds, as well as the wagons, carriages, carts, horses, the molds, and other specialized equipment, the likes of which are not to be found throughout the land of Poland.

3

Reuven did not listen to Shimon's warnings. Reuven said, That ordinance applies only to its own time and cannot be taken to refer to my ponds, because I am building largc, strong dams for them, leaving sluices to let out the extra water. These ponds can withstand any stream of mighty water. Therefore there is no reason to be concerned with that ordinance, and so on.

Shimon saw that Reuven was not heeding him. He went and summoned him to judgment in a rabbinical court. Reuven agreed to go with him to any court he wished, even the court in Shimon's city. They chose a court in a city between the two cities in which they lived to prevent people from saying that such-and-such won his suit only because of the Purim gifts and holiday donations he gives to a judge in his city. Because of our many sorrows, alas, the judgment of ordinary people has deteriorated. When they see that a rabbi has judged in favor of their opponent, they automatically assume that the judge has been influenced by benefits he has received. They end up believing that what they said in anger is the absolute truth.

They placed their arguments before the judges. Shimon argued this and Reuven argued that. The judges repeated the arguments, sometimes word for word, and sometimes with additional verbiage. Reuven had no patience to hear what he already knew and said, I have a great deal of business, and my time is short. Why am I wasting time with people who, the more I explain matters to them, the more they get mixed up and just repeat what I said. Shimon, too, although he was the plaintiff and it was he who had summoned Reuven to judgment, also found it hard to waste time with the judges. Before a decision was reached, the litigants departed, each to his own place and business, after giving the judges a fee for their time.

Before they parted ways, Reuven said to Shimon, Rest easy, R. Shimon. I do not intend to damage even a hair on your head. On the contrary, you will benefit from my ponds because fish need salt. Also, the people who work with you at the saltworks have the advantage of enjoying the availability of inexpensive fish. With your permission, my good neighbor, on every holiday, including Purim, I will send you big, good fish for your enjoyment and health. Shimon was angry and said, Take your fish and throw them to the four winds. I do not need you or your favors. Reuven shrugged his shoulders and said, If that is the way it is, so be it.

4

The noblewoman's serfs came from the nine hundred and ninety-nine villages she inherited from her ancestors and her husband. They scraped the earth, removed the stones, and cleared the ponds from the detritus the river had thrown up and the winds had scattered and the rubble dumped by people and animals. After they removed all that, they dug up the clogged wells so they could supply the ponds, and they brought engineers from Italy to install the dams.

They built large, strong dams, marvelous in their strength. The dams were three and a half times the height of a person. Everyone who saw them was amazed at the feats that can be accomplished in our day. Also the experts whom Reuven brought from another country to examine the dams nodded their heads in agreement and pronounced that everything was proper and fit and there was neither danger nor the hint of a danger.

How did they construct the dams? The noblewoman possessed beams from the days of Popiel and Piast, when all those places were forested. They were as dry as pottery and as black as tar, and each of them was fourteen cubits in length, two cubits in breadth, and the same in width. They poured tar on them and surrounded them with soft twigs, coated the twigs with tar, and poured boiling lead on them. Then they brought in barrels, each one the height of a man and the same in diameter. They sank the beams in the barrels, each in its own barrel. Then they went to the forest and cut down two tall, thick trees, taller and thicker than any others in the estate's forests, some of which are half a day's journey in length.

They sank the tree trunks in the earth, one opposite the other, and tied a rope at the top. They fashioned a pulley for the rope like a balancing scale, so that if one pan is full, the second pan rises. They tied a barrel with a beam to it, and eight men on one side and eight men on the other pulled the rope. They pulled the rope with all their strength until the barrel reached the top of the tree trunks. When it reached the top, they released it all at once. The barrel with the beam in it plummeted down and plunged into the earth with the beam sticking out on top. The barrel was driven very deep into the earth with great force and a noise so huge it split the ground. Everyone who saw the barrels and the beams stuck into the ground said that they could never be dislodged even if all the winds in the world blew on them and therefore there was nothing to Shimon's apprehensions.

Reuven did another thing. He made sluices in the dams and placed supervisors over the ponds to inspect them, and if they were too full, they had instructions to remove the extra water through channels sunk beneath the ground. They did this every day, and needless to say, on rainy days. Before long Reuven filled the ponds with fish whose quality was soon to become famous. Little time passed before the neighbors began enjoying the fish, and they spoke well of the lessee of the ponds, who had made it possible for them to buy a bit of fish at a fair price.

5

But Shimon was not mollified and he sued Reuven again. Reuven said, How great is the power of obstinacy! Shimon has seen the wisdom and understanding of the judges and he is still in hot pursuit of them? If he insists, I am prepared to go with him to any court he wants, even to the court in his city, though usually one goes to the defendant's court. They chose judges whom they had heard were men of intelligence and laid their claims before them.

They argued their cases, and it was evident that the judges listened very carefully and understood everything. But when one of them began to ask or say something, he began with an irrelevant matter, and in each instance he would say, Let us imagine for example that the matter is this way, and if you wish, we can picture it differently. A man of sanguine humor, Reuven listened without being annoyed. Shimon, who was of melancholy humor, was angry at himself for choosing these judges and at the judges, who spoke profusely for no purpose and without getting to the heart of the matter, and who also said, After all, the ponds are working fine, and they do not harm the saltworks, so what is there to fear? They also said, Reuven spoke well in saying that Shimon would benefit from the fish ponds, because from the day that the ponds produced fish, the price of fish fell, and this was also good for the workers who were close to the fish ponds and bought fish for almost nothing. Once it happened that the workers complained to Shimon, that he was cutting their wages, and he scolded them, saying, What about the fish that you get almost for free, is that nothing? And when the owners of the carts that take the fish to market see a poor person, they throw a live fish to him. Truly, Reuven was very fortunate. The fish his ponds produced inclined people's hearts toward him, and even the judges, who have no law other than the *Shulḥan Arukh*, gave him credit for his ponds.

6

As long as the weather was average and the rains fell in moderation, or less than that, and the snow melted little by little, the water came down gently, and the river continued to flow for the pleasure of animals and people alike. In the summer people bathed in it, and fathers taught their sons to swim in it. And Women washed their sheets, and wagon drivers watered their horses, and all sorts of birds that are not found in our country came occasionally and flew above the river. Little boys threw stones into it, and the river made circle after circle. The Jews performed Tashlikh there, fishermen spread nets, and they all enjoyed the river in their own way.

In the winter, too, when the earth deprives people of its mercy because of the snow and cold, the Holy One, blessed be He, did not deprive people of enjoyment from the river. When the great cold began, the river began to be covered with ice, which got harder and harder until sleds and sleighs could pass over it. They were low and had no wheels, but they made their way very well with rejoicing and song. Lords came out with iron shoes and glided on the ice, and ladies minced along with shouts on the ice. One fell down and the other got up. One screamed with great pleasure, and another shouted for help. Jewish lads also came and did the same, showing their prowess on the ice until the lords and ladies were surprised and amazed.

But at the end of Adar, the sun draws a bit closer to the earth, and the world is divided and begins to wink an eye to the sun. The great river, too, which was as hard as stone and strong in its unified power, also begins to divide and split, and break itself into pieces. Every piece becomes its own master and turns to go its own way. As it goes, it collides with its fellow and shoves it, and so does its fellow with its fellow until the sound cracking and colliding can be heard from one end of the city to the other. Everyone who sees these ice floes says, Let us hope that we will get off with fear and dread of the sound of their thunder alone and that the ice does no harm to the houses and courtyards near the river. But there are brazen daredevils who go out and leap among the blocks of ice, each of which is twelve cubits by thirteen cubits, and some larger. The blocks of ice are angry at the men who climb on them. They roar and rumble, and as they rumble they split in two and threaten to crush the intrepid men. What do they do? They jump from block to block and clap their hands to celebrate their heroism. In the past, hidden tzaddikim used to come to the river at night, break the blocks of ice, and immerse themselves before reciting tikkun ḥatzot. Acts that the pious once performed secretly in the name of heaven are now done by their grandsons in a spirit of high jinks and bravado.

The ponds were even better than the river because marvelous fish could be taken from them at all times for the tables of lords and ladies. Jews too could now buy fresh fish for the Sabbath and not have to make do with salted fish or dried fish that tasted like the sole of a sandal, or fish salted with the bitter salt they mix with animal feed. Nor need they make do with those dead fish brought from Galati in Romania or to deal with a monger who claims that the bad odor comes from him and not from the fish. On winter days, when in most places people have forgotten what a living fish looks like, it was especially good to have fresh fish from the ponds. All the more so when they could buy fish in honor of the Sabbath at a fair price. This was also a boon for the ice cutters, who collect ice for summer days for sick people stricken by the sun or to keep food from spoiling. They could cut ice from the ponds and avoid the buffeting winds and storms on the great river. For if a storm suddenly arises out there on the river, a man's eyes are darkened and he cannot see where to flee and save himself.

7

In short, the river behaved properly, and the ponds behaved properly, and Reuven, the lessee of the river, behaved properly as well. He sent fish to the lords and ladies and priests, and he did not ask for money from them. Also the rabbi of the city, by contrast, never lacked for fish on his table for holiday meals, and if, on the eve of Yom Kippur, you saw a piece of fish on a poor man's table, it was a gift from Reuven's ponds.

I have mentioned his open hand. I will also mention his business affairs. No one benefits from most wealthy men when they are living. After they die, their heirs come and take what the dead man left, and the burial society also takes what is coming to it. But Reuven took care of things not only on time but even in advance. He treated the burial society the same way he conducted his business. Reuven used to say, Why should people sit and wait for my death and then begrudgingly pry money from my cold hands? I will show them a warm hand now. Therefore, every year, for the great banquet held by the burial society, he sent baskets of huge fish, without number or price. Were it not for the brandy they drank between fish and fish, they would have died from over-eating. While they drank, they blessed Reuven. I am not given to exaggeration but I can attest that Reuven was the only one in the kingdom of Poland whom the burial society blessed with the toast "To Life!" Thus it is easy to appreciate how well-liked Reuven was among the people if even the burial society wished him long life. Nevertheless, Shimon always spoke ill of this likable man and harassed him with lawsuits.

8

As long as the weather was average and the rainfall more or less moderate, the river behaved well, as did the ponds. The former did not overflow its banks and the latter did not break through its dikes and dams. The dams that Reuven made for his ponds were large, and each dam had fifty or sixty columns sunk into the earth in huge thick barrels full of iron and tin and lead and stones, and the diameter of each barrel was twice that of its column. Sometimes when they released some of the water from the ponds, the tops of the columns of the dams were visible, and people would be astonished and say, What a wonder! How great are the deeds of the workmen! Not even all the water in the world could break through a single dam.

9

One year changed its ways. Before summer departed, winter arrived. When winter came, snow began to fall. Once the snow began falling, it did not stop. All day and all night it kept falling, and as it fell it joined the snow that had already fallen. All the courtyards were full of snow, and all the houses were sunk in the snow over their windows. In the city, where there are a lot of people, the snow gets trampled and melts. But this light snow was stronger than any man or animal. If a man or an animal trod on the snow, new snow fell and covered it, erasing the traces of feet and hooves. The snow was piled up into drifts. Snow continued to fall, and snow covered snow. The whole world was snow upon snow. People stopped setting out on the roads because of the snow that kept falling and covered them, and the wagons, carriages, horses, and people, and because of the wolves, who went out looking for prey. Men could barely gather for prayer, and a woman could barely extract a drop of water from the barrel. Many times a day they had to break the ice on the barrel. Before they managed to draw water, it would freeze, and ice would grip the ladle.

We have described what happened in the city but we do not know what happened outside the city. It was said that because of the great snow, the mountains and all the hills rose up above their height. The valleys and vales also made mountains and hills of themselves, and there was no distinction between hill and dale, between woods and house, between village and village. Some people explain the heavy snows by saying that the world made up with snow for what had been lacking in rain. If so, it was likely that the following summer would have little rain, since the earth was supplied with moisture from the snow. This might be true when it comes to the science of nature, but when it comes to what we see with our own eyes, the matter requires further investigation. Even after the time came for reciting the blessing of dew on Passover, the whole world was still covered with snow upon snow.

10

The snow stopped falling but did not leave the earth. All the mountains were covered with snow, as were the hills. Also beneath them, on the sides of roads and elsewhere, the snow accumulated in heaps. Some of it froze, and some of it remained as it was when it fell from the sky. Suddenly, snowflakes would fly in the air. If this was not the work of the wind, then it was new snow. Experts in the seasons and those who make predictions said, We can only despair of summer.

Their prophecies were still on their lips when the sun began to shine. The snow was warmed and gave way to let the sun heat it. That is a parable. In fact, this is what happened: because the sun shone, the snow began to shrink and form pits. Also the great river, which was like a single lump of ice, was struck by the sun, and the thick ice opened up. No wagon could cross it anymore, and not even a cart would venture onto it. Travelers seldom went out on the roads because of the puddles and the mud and because of the water from the snow flowed everywhere without end.

The snow kept melting, and water gushed on all sides, in the trees, in the courtyards and houses, in the dairies and stables. The dreadful ice that had covered the river and the ponds broke up more and more. The earth shook from the sound of its roaring. Those daredevils who once displayed their prowess by jumping from one block of ice to the other did not show their faces outdoors, so that people would not say to them, If you are such big heroes, where is your heroism now? With fury and anger the chunks of ice in the river and the ponds floated about and harassed one another. Mighty, powerful sounds exploded increasingly with clap after clap of thunder. One block of ice struck another and tried to displace it. While they were pounding each other, a third one came and shoved the first two. Before it could occupy a place, yet another came to displace it, and as it went, it pounded and was pounded, and it, too, did not emerge whole. It seems there was no end, no surcease to the breaking of the ice. It would not rest until it had destroyed the walls of the ponds and demolished the dams and the water rushed out and flooded the world.

11

Shimon went out to inspect the furnaces, which began to bubble because of the snow water and the ice water that had undermined them. Shimon pressed his cloak to his heart and shouted, Now you see what that thief has done to me! Soon the chunks of ice in his accursed ponds will batter down all the dams and then descend and lay waste to all my labors. Oy, Master of the Universe, from what cursed breast did you bring forth such a murderer? Oy, what will become of me? Every thunderclap of the ice drives me crazy. How will I save the skin on my bones, and how will I preserve what I have built up? Oy, Master of the Universe, strike him with lightning and save me from that man, or remove him from the world in some other way, for the sake of Your great mercy.

At that very time Reuven was standing with all the inspectors of the ponds and all the men responsible for the dams and all the workers of the ponds and all the casters of nets, and with them a huge mass of more than a thousand of the noblewoman's serfs. Armed with picks, axes, hoes, and pitchforks, they pushed the chunks of ice to keep them from touching the walls of the ponds and breaching them. Nearby, on a stone platform, stood people from Reuven's household next to large kegs of brandy and pots and kettles full of hot pirogen stuffed with kasha and meat fried in goose fat. They poured brandy and dished food out to everyone, anyone who came from the ponds, and anyone who went to the ponds. The priest wandered among them, walking and saying, Be strong, people, be strong. Don't let the ice destroy the estate of our mistress, the lady, who gives you your bread and protects you from the Tatars.

12

But the blocks of ice did not intend to break through the dams. Rather, they conspired to overflow the ponds like their brothers on the river, which had overflowed its banks. The blocks of ice were already heaped in hillocks, piling up and rising. The inspectors had no idea what to do. They stood and stared with dead eyes at what the ice was scheming to do.

Reuven came and raised his face to the workers and said to them in his cordial voice, Children, what do you say about this story?

One of the workers leaped onto the dike of the pond and shouted, Brother! Hand me my pickax and my spade. His comrades leaped up after him, one after the other, with their tools in their hands and began chopping at the ice with their pickaxes and spades. While these men were pounding at one end, others climbed up in another place holding long spears that had been taken from the lady's armory, for her earliest ancestors had set out to battle against their enemies with them. For six or seven generations no one in all of Poland had seen such long lances, which could pierce the guts of an enemy from a distance and make him fall, never to rise again.

One group stood on the dikes of the pond at one end, and another group stood at the other end, chopping with their pickaxes and stabbing with their spears. The blocks of ice began to break up and sink back into the great water, and as they sank, some of the choppers and stabbers also sank. Some say they came up again. Their widows and orphans know the truth.

Fire, which heats what is below it and burns on all sides, is mightier than human strength. So they brought bales of hay and rags, dipped them in oil, and set them on fire. Then they threw them on the chunks of ice flows. Though the fire vanquished the lower water, which had hardened and become ice, it was vanquished in turn by the upper waters, for a hard rain began to fall and put out the fire. The workers could not abide before the smoke.

13

What ordinary fire could not do was done by the fire from above—the sweet sun, under which all the creatures that dwell on the earth warm themselves. Suddenly, the sun appeared on high. With all the ice, frost and snow, no one even remembered that such a thing as a pleasant and beneficent sun existed. It was still young, but the signs of its power were evident. When it winked its eyes, the chunks of ice submitted to it and they did not regain their strength. They no longer inspired fear and dread, and people began to watch the way they were floating and drifting. Everyone thought that they were headed here or there, but they were going neither here nor to there, but to a place no one had thought of. On their way, they go in each other's way and harassed each other, truly like people who wear themselves out and gradually fade away. There may be no moral here, but it makes for a nice story.

Little by little, the serfs were released to their villages. But if they were no longer needed here, they were needed elsewhere because the melting snow and the rain had destroyed the roads and ruined the fields and erased the gardens, and the water was still flowing. The whole land was sodden with it, and people could not sow wheat, barley, or oats, though the time for sowing had come.

14

Reuven reported back to the noblewoman and told her all about the vigor and intelligence of his workers and the supervisors of the dams, who had directed the serfs' work so the ice would not strike the dams and damage them. Although the dams were strong and could withstand any blow, it was preferable to shield them. After praising the craftsmen and supervisors, he praised the priest, who had come out on such a day and had not feared for his body. Rather he had walked about outside in the cold and the mud and urged the lady's serfs not to slack off and to do their work in good faith for the sake of the lady, who gives them their bread and defends them in all their troubles. After Reuven praised the priest, the priest praised Reuven, saying how many kegs of brandy he had provided for the lady's serfs, how many pans and pots of pirogen filled with fatty meat he had given to them. Who can count it all? Only a generous hand could do this.

The lady looked benevolently at Reuven and said to him, Could you explain to me what the Jew Shimon wanted, who sent lords to ask me to abandon the ponds. Please, tell me, dear sir, whom they harm and who loses because of them? Reuven lowered his shoulders modestly and said in his pleasant voice, It has pleased your highness to ask me a difficult question. In my opinion, there is no wise man in the world who can answer my gracious and puissant lady's question. Our neighbor Shimon is simply obstinate, and since he has come to think that your highness' ponds can harm the saltworks he has leased, he stubbornly vexes your highness with his obstinacy. The priest added, If your highness, the merciful and puissant lady permits, I, too, will say a word. These Jews are brothers in opposition to us Christians, but among themselves none can bear seeing another's profit. Reuven transferred his notebook from pocket to pocket, so that if he looked for his notebook, he would not find it in its place, and remember that something had to be done. What was that? To soften the priest with a fur coat or money, because you never know the depths of that man's heart. Today he bedevils Shimon, and tomorrow he will bedevil Reuven.

15

As you can see with your own eyes, everything went well. Neither Shimon's business nor the ponds were damaged. Now, as before the great melting, the two ponds held their own. We do not know whom to praise, the builders of the walls or the makers of the dams. Therefore we shall praise them all.

Reuven's gaze was friendly, and his hands were wide open. He gave presents to his men, who had worked with him during the crisis. But the favor that Reuven showed to his people caused sorrow to Shimon. Did Reuven scant Shimon in his presents? When Shimon's men heard about all the presents Reuven gave to his, they began to grumble about Shimon and complain that he did not recompense them for risking their lives for his saltworks. They had deprived their eyes of sleep and had not laid their heads on a pillow. They had stood day and night, scraping the snow and digging channels, bringing wood and stones and surrounding the outbuildings and sheds with them and plastering them with mud. They had stood up to their hips in salt water, until the salt ate at their skin and flesh. Thus they had guarded the furnaces and the vessels and the animals and all of Shimon's property, to protect them against flooding. After all that trouble, R. Shimon did not see fit to add even a worn penny to their wages? What did R. Shimon say? He told them, Did I not stand with you all day and all night? Did I sit idle? How are you better than I am, that you demand an increase in pay? One of them answered, I have been working for R. Shimon for thirteen years, and I cannot pay half of the eighteen pennies that I vowed in memory of the dead. Shimon said, King Solomon, may he rest in peace, said, *Better not to vow than to vow and not to pay*. The man sighed and nodded his head and said, I know that R. Shimon is a learned man and knows everything that is written in the Torah, but it would be better if R. Shimon knew that you should have a little mercy for a poor Jew. Shimon said, If you were not a fool, I would say you were stupid.

16

We will turn our eyes away from human stinginess and tell about the generosity of Creation. After the abundant snow, the earth flowed and flowed as it had never done. The earth was so saturated it was like a stream. The whole land was awash, and the fields full of water. Even more so, the trees in the forest. Some stood in snow that had not melted, and some stood in water. In regular years, the sun comes and melts the snow in the forest and dries up the puddles. This year the sun did not come out much. When it did try to come out, clouds stopped it.

Heavy clouds covered the sky and other clouds piled up upon them, these on top of those, and those on top of these. They kept spreading from one end of the sky to the other, and they did not move except to give some space for rain to fall. Once the rain started, it did not stop, except to give way for more rain.

Every day the inspectors opened the sluices and let out the extra water from the ponds, which already lapped the rim of the ponds. In response to the water from the sky they release twice as much from the ponds

The inspectors still had the upper hand, and when they were asked, they answered that everything was under control. The walls of the ponds were strong and holding up, and so were the dams. They were made of wood as strong as iron, which all the water in the world could not overwhelm. Who did not remember the black beams they brought from the noblewoman's forests, which had lain for generation after generation in the sun and rain, growing in strength and power in every generation? All remembered the tall barrels and the beams that were embedded in them. Each barrel was as wide as a house. The barrels were filled with iron, tin, lead and stones, on which tar was poured, and boiling lead was poured on them to block every hole and fill every space. Even if all the water in the world should come, it would not dislodge them.

17

The rain fell, and the inspectors inspected. Each day brought a rumor from somewhere else. A river overflowed its banks and the streams burst and flooded a whole region. Houses and sheds floated on the water, and in them were men and beasts. Many people stood and watched but were powerless to save them.

But there was no need to fear for Reuven's ponds. If the water was fierce, human ingenuity was fiercer. The dams built by the engineers and the sluices that removed the superfluous water could withstand all the water in the world. If Shimon did not grumble that the water Reuven let out of the ponds came to his furnaces and damaged the buildings, Reuven could have eaten his meals in tranquility, rested in his bed in peace, and been joyful because his wife had borne a daughter of their old age on the day of their fortieth wedding anniversary.

Truth is truth. They removed the extra water from the ponds, but before the earth could absorb it, new water came, and the earth spat out more than it could swallow. The water stood and went neither here nor there, because the earlier water had already conquered every location. They began to dig ditches. Before they could dig deep, the ditches filled up. The workers stood up to their waists in water and kept digging. They did not manage to dig much more before the water came up to their necks.

18

When the supervisor saw that all the water let out of the ponds did not diminish the ponds, he began to worry lest new springs had been opened up in the bottom of the ponds. For the moment he was merely conjecturing, but in any event he was not free of worry.

What the supervisor had only conjectured was confirmed by one of the workers, who discovered it. It seems to me, he said to his comrades, that I hear water flowing from underground. I do not know where the water comes from, but the sound of its flowing murmurs in my ears.

They went and told Reuven, Something strange is happening in the ponds. The ponds are flowing from within themselves. Before Reuven could understand what those words meant, some of the village elders entered and told him, We must ask the priest to come with all the clergymen and stop the disaster.

Reuven asked the supervisor, What are they talking about? What is happening inside the ponds? He answered him, I did not intend to tell you before we overcame the problem. Now that you have heard from others, I will tell you. I estimate that blocked wells on the bottom of the ponds have opened by themselves, and they are flowing with water.

What lies ahead of us?

The supervisor answered, We will ask God to spare us what is ahead of us. But I am worried about the earth, which has absorbed more water than it can hold, and there is danger that the water will return to the ponds, if not from above, it will return from below.

What can we do?

We have done what we were capable of doing, and we continue to labor at it, but the rain from above and the wells from below sabotage our work.

Reuven said, I will go and inform the noblewoman and she will call her serfs from all the villages, as she did when the snow melted.

He said to him, Can they drink all the extra water in the ponds? You, sir, go and think about what the river is doing. It is already up to its banks, and if it overflows, the water will come to our ponds, and they are already full to the brim.

19

On Sabbath morning, Reuven was called to the Torah. A gentile came to the synagogue bringing him a letter. Reuven shrugged his shoulders and recited the blessings before and after the reading, waited until the man called up after him had recited the blessing, and went back to sit in his seat.

Reuven was not learned in Torah, but he knew that the Sabbath was not given for secular business. If a Gentile had brought him a letter, it was surely about such business. He did not pick up the letter or touch it, because it was forbidden for use on the Sabbath. They told the gentile, Go to this man's house and deliver the letter there. The gentile went away, and Reuven raised his talit over his head, which he was not in the habit of doing during the Torah reading, when his talit usually lay on his shoulders. He stared at the Bible and found that his eyes were looking where they had been looking before he was called to the Torah, meaning that he had not turned the page. When he noticed that, he decided to turn the page, but he forgot and did not turn it. What is the matter? Reuven thought to himself, the reader was reading out loud. Did he not know that one reads the passage of the Curses in a soft voice? When he noticed they were already reading the haftarah, he was in doubt as to whether or not he had stood for the raising of the Torah.

After the service he lingered in the synagogue. Not because of the rains, but all the while he was in the synagogue, the matter of the letter did not disturb him. He looked for some subject to distract his mind from the letter, for his heart told him it did not augur well. A Torah scholar brings his mind to words of Torah, opens a Gemara and studies. What does a man do who has not studied Gemara? Reuven had already read the weekly portion twice and the Aramaic translation once, and he had already perused Rashi's commentary. He was not used to reciting psalms. He sat and looked at Rashi's commentary on the verses of the Curses, which he had skipped the night before.

He heard the sound of a quarrel. He turned his head and saw a poor man arguing with the shamash, who had sent him to the table of misers, who had left him hungry. Reuven told the poor man, Come with me. I promise you will not leave hungry. The shamash told the poor man, Your good luck exceeds your intelligence.

20

Reuven went home and put down his talit and Ḥumash and took up the large prayer book, in which were all the prayers and petitions and requests gathered from the early and late halakhic authorities. When he realized that the poor man was hungry, he put down the prayer book and said, I will skip reciting the verses, and may God forgive me. He poured a cup for himself and for the poor man. He recited the kiddush and gave wine to his wife and daughters, and he placed a platter full of fish and food before the poor man and said, Eat, my good Jew, eat. The poor man saw and wondered. From the day the Holy One, blessed be He, had oppressed him with poverty and forced him to beg at people's doors, he had never happened to come to such a house and such a table and such a generous host. But it was puzzling. A rich man with a good heart, why was he sad?

Between the soup and the meat, Reuven asked his wife, Was a gentile here bearing a letter? His wife answered and said, It is lying on the chest of drawers. He asked, Open? She answered, Open. He asked his young daughter, who was well versed in the gentiles' writing, What is written there? She answered, Father, I did not read it. He turned his face toward the guest and said to him, If you know a pretty melody, sing a song for us, only if it does not interfere with your eating. The poor man began to sing. His voice was not fine. Of such a voice, in our parts, they say it is like the sound of a saw on damp wood. But Reuven did not notice and began to join in. Once he joined in, the poor man was silent, and Reuven sang by himself. He sang, "Blessed be He, Who Gave Us Rest," and he sang, "This Day Is the Most Honored Among Days," and he sang, "Keep My Sabbaths," and he sang, "Today Is the Sabbath for the Lord," and he sang, "Because I Keep the Sabbath, God Will Keep Me."

His heart relaxed, and he began conversing with the guest. Reuven asked the guest, Where are you from, and what places have you seen? As he questioned him, he placed the food that was on the table before him.

The poor man had seen many places and trampled many cities with his heels, but he was not good at recounting his experiences. What could he say or tell? All the places were the same. The poor were many, and the rich were few. The poor taste the taste of poverty, and the rich do not know how to enjoy their wealth. Look, here was a wealthy house, and what did you see? The master of the house was sad. The poor man remembered the householder with whom he had eaten on the previous Sabbath. He sat and recounted, Last Sabbath I happened to eat with a very wealthy man who makes salt, and with every slice of bread and every spoonful of soup he would say angrily, If only the blessed Lord would destroy the Sabbaths of that murderer the way He destroys my Sabbaths! Because the poor man's eyes were drawn to the food, he did not notice that the people of the house were hinting to him to be silent. Since he was not much of a story teller, he fell silent on his own.

The master of the house turned his face to the guest and said to him: Concerning what we said in the table hymns today, Blessed be the High God Who Gave Rest to our Souls and Reprieve from Desolation and Sadness, I heard a fine thing. The word desolation comes from the verse in Lamentations that we recite on the eve of the Ninth of Av. You see, dear Jew, the author of the hymn saw there are Jews who destroy their Sabbaths for themselves. He sat and wrote that song to give praise and thanks to His blessed Name, who gave us rest to our souls and redemption from desolation and sadness. Certainly, you are hungry. Sarah Leah, have you any special food for the pleasure of our guest?

21

Before the Sabbath was over, Havrilo the stable boy came with two horses ready for travel. After havdalah, Reuven looked at the letter and prepared himself to ride out to see what the ponds were doing.

Sarah Leah pleaded with him not to go out on the road on such a stormy night. Reuven shrugged his shoulders and said to his wife, I was sure that you had learned that I do not like women who stick their noses into their husband's business. Sarah Leah heard him and walked away. His daughters came and said, Father, do not go. He shrugged his shoulders and said to them, My daughters, if a girl pushes her snout into grownups' business, her snout gets longer and longer, and a long snout is not nice for a girl. Anyway, ask your mother. Maybe she will tell you what I said to her before. Sarah Leah went and brought him the baby, daughter of their old age, whom she had borne forty years after they married. She stood and said to her husband, If not for our sake, do it for the baby's sake. Reuven said, Put the baby back in its cradle before it catches cold.

His neighbors came and said to him, R. Reuven, put off your journey until the morning. A person should always go out when God said, "*It is good.*" Your life is in danger outside. There has not been a storm like this in human memory. Reuven looked at them benevolently and said, I must go. The ponds need me. But I am sorry that tonight it is impossible for me to sit with you for the melaveh malkah meal, especially since I see ten men here, and we could have recited grace after meals with the name of God. Is David here, too? If so, let David recite the grace over a cup of wine. Have a good week, brothers. It is impossible to frustrate the horses. They have readied themselves for the road, and Havrilo is also waiting.

Reuven said to the stable boy, And you, my boy, what do you say? Havrilo answered, If my lord will allow me to say something. Reuven said, What would you say? The stable boy said, Let me ride to the ponds, and my lord will stay at home.

Because of the stormy tempest? What would your mother say? Havrilo answered, My mother had a dream.

What did your mother dream? Havrilo answered, A little dog bit her on two fingers of her left hand. Reuven laughed and said, Now Katrina is worried about her fingers? Havrilo answered, She is not worried, but she is angry at the brashness of the dog.

What did Katrina do to the dog?

She slapped it on the face and knocked out two of its teeth. Then she was sorry for it because without the teeth, it cannot chew and will die of hunger. Mother got up, took the teeth, and returned them to it. She saw they were round and thin and made like the silver coins that the lords give to babies to play with.

Reuven said, Marvelous. How did your mother interpret the dream?

Mother did not interpret the dream.

How is that? Katrina left a dream without an interpretation?

He said, Because lightning struck her little pig. When mother saw the little pig lying dead, she said, It is not good, my son, not good to go out on a night like this. Reuven said, Oy veh, veh. Katrina's little pig is dead. Now what will Katrina do? What do you think? If we give Karina a heifer, will she be consoled for the pig? What did your mother say? This night is not good for the road. Havrilo said, Mother said, It is not good, my son, not good to go out on a night like this. Reuven said, Is that what Katrina said? Havrilo said, Word for word. Reuven said, If so, we shall put off the trip and leave early in the morning. But early in the morning, did you hear me, Havrilo? Now I must attend to my business. David, For how much will you sell me your right to recite the grace over the cup of wine?

David said, Even if you gave me the whole world, I would not sell such a mitzvah. Reuven said, But if I give you a flagon of mead would you sell it to me? David said, Maybe for a flagon of mead it would be worthwhile.

Water Upon Water

1

Reuven never reached the ponds because on that Sabbath afternoon, the dams burst and flooded the roads, and the earth turned into a slurry. The horses' feet sank into it, and when they pulled them out and took a few more steps, they sank again into earth even softer than before. Although Reuven was in a rush to get to the ponds, he neither scolded his horse nor urged it on. Reuven knew that his horse knew he was in a hurry, and if the horse stood without moving, it was not from laziness but because he could not move.

Reuven sat on the horse and watched. Carriages, wagons, and carts were sunk above their wheels in the ground with their horses harnessed to them. Some were standing with their heads lowered in total despair; some made as if they had stopped on purpose and could go on if they wanted to. But in their hearts, they knew that this viscous swamp was plotting to swallow them alive.

From the heavy, moist clouds close to the ground rose dull sounds like bubbling water. The water was still far away, not nearby, but the bubbles that peeked out of the swamp looked with wicked eyes as if pleased at the imminent disaster.

Reuven pricked up his ears to determine whether the water was bubbling from the river or from the ponds. If it was from the ponds, they were already full and could contain no more water. Even if all the sluices were open, the ponds would not recede because new springs in the floor of the ponds had opened up and made up for what was drained off.

Suddenly, another sound was heard. Reuven listened and heard people calling for help. After that sound came a dreadful cry: Help! We are being buried alive! The horse tried to pull its feet out of the mud but could not.

Reuven said to the groom, Too bad for people like us who will find their death in such a swamp. Havrilo sat on his horse, all his limbs trembling. Everything that his master saw, Havrilo saw, too. Horses and wagons were sunk into the earth. Their owners were trying to extricate them and failing. But his heart told him, As long as Master Reuven was with him, nothing bad would befall him.

Havrilo inclined his head to his master. In the fog, his master looked like an effigy that protects those who worship it. Havrilo looked at his master's horse, which stood in the swamp, and two white patches above its thighs were shining at each other above the wet ground. Havrilo sat on his horse and looked at his master's horse, whose name was Bigtan. Havrilo thought to himself, Bigtan has stopped because our master stopped him, because our master wants to think things through, because our master has much business, because many people depend on our master, and our master has to put his mind to every one of them. As I said, so long as Master Reuven is with me, I have nothing to fear.

Reuven raised his right hand and said, I see a roof. If it is not the supervisor's office, then I do not know what it could be. If we turn our horses toward it, we will be out of danger. Bigtan tried to pull out his legs but sank in deeper. Reuven said, I see that we are fated to stay here and not to move. Let us look to see where help could come from. He looked and shrugged his shoulders and said, There is no help we can expect from there. He lowered his head to the horse's ears and said in a kind voice, Did you hear what I said? Help will not come from there.

The horse tried to remove his feet again and succeeded. But before it walked two steps, they sank in again. Oxen are what we need, Reuven thought to himself. Oxen would save me from danger. Though he knew that oxen were better than horses, he did not reveal his thought.

How could I have been so mistaken? Reuven was surprised at himself. I said it was the supervisor's office, but it is the Pink Palace. If so, that palace has also sunk into the water. It, and all its furnishings, its carpets, and its sculpture, and maybe the lady, too, and the owner of the saltworks. How great is the force of habit. Her husband is already dead, and he no longer threatens, but she still meets with her lover in that palace. What did I want to say? If the water has already reached the salt furnaces, Shimon will find an excuse to shout, Did I not say that those fish ponds endanger the salt furnaces? Havrilo, If you sleep, you will fall off your horse.

The groom roused himself and said, If it please your lord to let me speak, I will say that I was not asleep. Reuven said, Good, good Havrilo, that you are not asleep. My mind is not free to watch over you. Indeed, to delay my departure, Sarah Leah brought in Perele. She took the baby out of its cradle. Until a woman gives birth to children, she bends her husband's will through her own person. Once she has given birth, she bends her husband's will with the children. Between childbearing and old age, how does she do her husband's bidding? With good food and clean garments. It is good that I remembered my wife and daughters and that I am not wearying my soul with thoughts about the ponds and the salt boilers. If I get out of this alive, that angry man will sue me. If the salt furnaces really were damaged by my ponds, justice is on his side. Lucky for Shimon, he has someone to complain against. Whom will I complain against? But I will not object or complain. What do I ask of you, Master of the universe? Get me out of this swamp.

He remembered that he had set out on the road without reciting the traveler's prayer. Reuven said, My late father-in-law used to tell this story. Once he went out on important business. When he reached the palace gates, he remembered that he had not recited the traveler's prayer. He immediately turned back and withdrew from a deal that would have made him a lot of money. Later, he heard that the man who made the deal lost all his fortune. Reuven continued, A fine story. What is it about? It assumes that the one who lost all his money in the deal also forgot to recite the traveler's prayer. But if he recited the traveler's prayer and lost his money, the story has lost its moral. What did David say? Even if you give me the whole world, I will not sell my mitzvah. When I said to him, I will give you a flagon of mead, he agreed right away. A person can resist a great temptation but not a small one. Havrilo, do not fall asleep. But in his heart, Reuven said, He would be better off sleeping and dying in his sleep, because we cannot expect help. What, and you Bigtan, Reuven whispered to his horse, You are still standing in your place. The horse shook its head. Reuven laughed and said, King Solomon, in his wisdom, would have understood your answer. I do not understand. A dog bit Katrina, and its teeth were not teeth but toy coins. But the coins we accumulate are good money. You can acquire whatever can be sold with them. Now, if I gave all the money I have, I could not even buy one step of a horse. Money that is enough to buy a stable full of horses cannot buy a single step of a horse to deliver me from death to life. What did the Gentile woman say? It is not good to set out on a night like this. Now that it is day, is it better that I set out? Havrilo, are you asleep? If you sleep, in your dream you will see yourself falling from your horse, sinking into the earth, and being buried alive. Open your eyes, Havrilo. I would give you some brandy, but I am afraid it will put you to sleep. Gather your strength, boy, and do not fall asleep. I cannot watch over you.

From the place whence danger had come rescue came. A huge flood of water suddenly flowed from the ponds with great force and struck the horses. The horses were panicked, lifted their legs, and started to step and walk the way they walk in shallow water because the slurry turned into a bath of shallow water.

In a short time, Reuven and his groom reached a small island in the great water. Here, at this place, a few months earlier, Reuven had stood among his people, who were giving out hot pirogen and pouring brandy for the lads who had come from the nine hundred and ninety-nine villages to save the fish ponds from the dreadful ice.

2

The dams did not burst because of the upper water or because of any flaw in the dams but because of the lower water from the springs in the bottom of the ponds. When the earth above them became saturated, the springs opened. For there were many springs in the earth beneath the ponds, upon which heaps of earth had been piled, and they lay quietly and peacefully and did not plan to part with their water. Once the world filled with water, and it had nowhere to go, the water began to survey the earth and look for room. It reached those springs, which had been quiet and secure, having nothing to do with the ponds. It stood above them and surrounded them and dug under them. The earth that covered them dissolved, and they opened up. They began to flow, and the flood of their waters struck the barrels that stood on them, and with them the columns of the dams. Once the earth under the barrels was undermined, the barrels toppled and the columns fell. Once they collapsed and fell, the water from the ponds began to flow with no hindrance. Some flowed from above and some from below. The whole earth was full of water, and the earth itself became water. Nothing remained of dry land near the ponds except the stone platform they had made to supply food and drink to the workers.

3

Reuven stood on the stone platform that his people had made when the snow was melting to give food and brandy to all the workers who toiled to prevent the dreadful ice from destroying the dams. Before them, the land laid itself out like an endless marsh divided into puddle after shining puddle. This is what remained of the large ponds, each of which had been a quarter of a league in length and a quarter of a league in width. In the marsh lay the huge beams that had been used in the dams to stop the water from flooding the world. They lay where they had fallen, in their enormous, thick barrels. After the water had undermined them, they collapsed and fell, broken into pieces. People had been certain that they could never be budged. Now each of them lay like a golem, their power and splendor spent.

Reuven stood facing the two ponds, and with him were all the inspectors and the workers, who explained everything that had happened here the day before, on the Sabbath, while he was at home. Reuven listened attentively, shrugging his shoulders from time to time. His silence was harder for them than any reprimand. They repeated and interpreted and explained, and Reuven listened without stopping them. After hearing the whole story and hearing it again, he asked in a whisper, And what about the furnaces? They answered, The furnaces are still floating in the water. Reuven asked again, Did you hear any details? They answered, We heard no details, but we heard that all the buildings and equipment were flooded and with them the animals and all the stored salt. Reuven said, I see from your words that you have heard no details. So everything has sunk into the water. The buildings and the equipment and the animals, and all the salt that was stored and waiting. Very good. It seems to me that there is no need to ask for details. Is that not so, honored sirs? It seems to me, sirs, that all our words are finished. They nodded their heads with respect and agreement.

Reuven asked the inspectors and workers, Perhaps you have heard, honored sirs, about the whereabouts of the owner of the saltworks? One of them answered and said, I heard he was seen riding on his mare on the way to our mistress, the noblewoman.

4

Reuven looked at one of his men and said to him, Can you find a place where we can speak without anyone overhearing? The inspectors and workers left them alone.

When they were alone, Reuven said to him, I assume that the fish in the ponds are dead and the river will not provide us with many fish. I have obligated myself to the lord of the district to send him fish for a banquet he is holding for the king's army, which is camping in the city. Go to the Karshizshinovsky sisters and buy all the fish in their ponds. If they have already heard about my fish and raise their prices, tell them that you are willing to pay them with silver coins. If they hear that you are paying with silver coins, they will sell you their merchandise at a decent price.

5

We have told what happened to the ponds. Now we shall relate what happened to the furnaces.

When the water from the ponds flooded the world, it reached the furnaces. But having reached them, it stopped because Shimon's workers had anticipated the disaster and built a kind of dike around the furnaces. The water stood like a wall against it, without rushing things. Then a torrent of new water fell upon it, either to push it aside or to help it. One way or another, the water was torn from its place and leaped into the furnaces from north, south, east, and west. We do not know whether the water that fell upon the stones of the dikes ripped them from their place or whether it was the water that rose up and overflowed the walls of the salt furnaces, because the water mixed up everything, and the eye could see nothing but masses of water.

The furnaces filled with water, and after it came more water. Water came upon water, and water came after water. The furnaces stood like endless water, and water kept falling into them, and the water clung to the water in the water, and water to water. The water that had stood in the ponds where fish had grown became sick of its restraints and lusted after the furnaces.

The water flooded the furnaces, the outbuildings, the sheds, the animals stabled there, the carriages, wagons, and carts used to transport the salt. All Poland used to buy salt from those works, although the salt they mix into horse feed to make the horses thirsty and grow fat is brought from the salt mountains, where they mine bitter salt. On its way, the water inundated the good salt that had been collected in barrels and crates and troughs and in the shape of cones, both single and double. The molds used to shape the salt were also destroyed. Nothing remained of the salt furnaces except their mounts awash in water. Of all Shimon's assets nothing remained except the lease document itself.

6

Shimon took the law into his own hands. Reuven had committed himself to supply the district governor with a certain number of crates of fish for the banquet he planned to hold for the king's army, which was camped in the city. This was before the destruction of the ponds. When the ponds were destroyed and the fish killed, Reuven bought carp from the two old noblewomen. Their carp were fat because they were nourished from the worms born of dead animals. How is this done? A net is spread over the pond and the carcass of a horse or a heifer or a cow or a pig or a fowl is placed on it. The carcasses produce worms. The worms fall through the holes in the net into the water of the ponds. The carp catch them, eat them, and fatten up. As long as Reuven's ponds existed, everyone ran after his fish, which he sold generously, whereas no one bought the noblewomen's fish, which they sold stingily. So the noblewomen hated Reuven, aside from her general hatred of Jews. When Reuven's ponds were emptied, he sent to them to buy fish, their hearts exulted, and they swore by what they venerated they would sell him neither fin nor scale. What did Reuven do? He jingled coins at them. When they heard the sound of the silver coins, they forgot their oath and sold him their fish, from carp to sturgeon. The carp were the main thing in the pool, but the sturgeon were introduced to bite the indolent carp and keep them moving about. In conclusion, the noblewomen sold Reuven all the fish in their pond, without leaving even a single fish to breed.

7

Reuven sent a wagon full of fish to the district governor. Because fish cost him a lot of money, he made no profit from the transaction. Nevertheless, it was worth his while because it enabled him to keep his promise and prove his reliability to the district governor. Also, by doing so he would not have to worry about whether the district governor would return a precious object he had given as a pledge to guarantee the fish would be delivered on time.

Shimon got wind of Reuven's plans. He gathered his men and lay in wait for Reuven's crew who were transporting the fish. They seized the wagon and the fish, barely returning Reuven's horses.

Thus Shimon seized the wagon and impounded the fish that Reuven had sent to the district governor. Reuven recovered and dispatched other fish that he bought from the bishop. It was still worthwhile for him, although he had paid the bishop in gold for every fish. Reuven had to borrow money with a promissory note. (Merchants borrow sums, recording the capital and the interest together, and then they then issue a promissory note as if they had borrowed the total amount.) All this was still worthwhile for Reuven in order to avoid forfeiting the pledge, which was of exceeding value.

Shimon went and impounded those wagons, too. Now, not only had he shown Reuven to be a swindler and a man who did not keep his promises but he had also caused him serious financial harm, for even had the fish come from his own ponds, he would have lost a great deal of money. All the more so once he had bought them from others. He had bought the first ones from the noblewomen with coins of silver and then paid the bishop in gold pieces, not to mention bribes he had to pay to the bishop's men. Meanwhile, the army left the country before the appointed time, and in the end the governor did not make a banquet for them. Reuven claimed that if the fish had come in time, the governor would have paid him his fee. However, since Shimon impounded the fish, and they never reached the governor, the governor did not have to pay Reuven anything and refused to return the pledge. Until all this took place, Shimon had had a complaint against Reuven. Thenceforth Reuven had a complaint against Shimon. The circumstances had changed, and so had the parties.

Reuven charged that Shimon had made him lose a great deal of money and damaged his good name. Because Shimon impounded the fish and they did not reach the governor, he would not see a penny from them. Because the governor had not received any goods, he would pay nothing. Shimon had damaged the good name that Reuven had acquired throughout the kingdom of Poland as a man who never went back on his word, even if it caused him a great loss, and even if his excuses would be accepted without challenge. He was the one of whom the lords said, You cannot count on yourself, but you can count on Reuven. Now, after what Shimon had done, Reuven's good name was damaged.

8

This was Shimon's counterclaim: The damage I caused to Reuven is nothing compared to the damage he caused me, because his ponds destroyed my salt furnaces and did away with all the equipment and animals, and even the salt itself, which lost its taste and became insipid. As for Reuven's claim that he lost his good name because of me, he should have known long ago that neither good deeds nor good morals give a Jew a good name among the nations. It depends entirely on the profit they gain from him. He may take great pains to be highly regarded in their eyes, so they will say of him that he is *porządny człowiek* and *ładny Ẓyd,* but even if he rises and becomes Esau's minister and helper, I will have no respect for him. If he believes that because he is nicely dressed and he trims his beard, because he curls his side-locks, because he is a paid bootlicker, and because he teaches his daughters the foreign alphabet he is therefore well-liked by them, then I and the Blessed Name know that all of this is empty vanity. When I appear before a lord, I go in the clothes I work in, and if the lord is disgusted by my clothes, he is disgusted by my skin, and then I take my leave from him unscathed, whole in my body and whole in my skin. But first I read the Torah portion of Vayishlaḥ.

Shimon said, Reuven should not think that if I impounded two wagons full of fish, that I am finished with him. Let him know that in the future he must repay me for every pinch of salt that I lost because of him. And he should not depend on the noblewoman, because it is well known that she is in the hands of my lord, the owner of the saltworks, like a fish in a cook's hands. If he feels like it, he cooks it in sugar and honey, and if he feels like it, he cooks it in pepper and onions.

Shimon said, I only said this for Reuven's benefit, for if he is left with a penny in hand, he should not waste it on gifts to the lady's agents and her retainers. Rather, let him buy a slice of bread for his wife and daughters, because fish and meat are done with in his house. Shimon also said, I only said this for the benefit of his body. For the good of his soul, he still needs many entreaties to atone for his sin, for three sins that he occasioned: the sin of idolatry, the sin of fornication, and the sin of bloodshed. Idolatry, because on their holidays they used to make a large cross out of ice on his ponds, and they came there with statues of their gods. Fornication, because the lords and ladies used to skate on the ice there, and they would fondle each other with hugs and kisses. Bloodshed, because when the snow thawed and the ice broke, several lives were lost. But I promise you I will not be silent nor will I rest until I have done everything in my power to make Reuven atone for his sin by the poverty I will bring upon him until his teeth turn black from fasting and he cannot find a crust of bread to break his fast.

9

Goodhearted people heard everything that had happened to Reuven and they were grieved, because in a single day he, the notable son of a notable man, first contributor to charity projects, and well-liked and respected by the lords and ladies, had suddenly lost most of the wealth that his ancestors and parents-in-law had bequeathed him, as well as the wealth he had accrued with his own resourcefulness and integrity. After all the trouble that had come to him by the hand of heaven, Shimon had added grief upon grief by twice waylaying the merchandise promised to the governor.

Correspondingly, many were sorry about Shimon's fate. A learned Jew who sets aside time for Torah study and teaches lessons in the beit midrash had lost all his property in a single day because the flooding from Reuven's ponds inundated the furnaces and the outbuildings and all the equipment, and not even a pinch of salt was left to season a slice of bread for a blessing. Now several Jewish families were left truly without food for a single meal. All the workers were left without employment. As for Shimon, the lessee of the saltworks, if he had not married a rich woman in a second marriage, a woman who brought in great wealth, he would have had to hang a sack around his neck and beg at people's doors, because all his property had been swept away by the water.

But many wholehearted people deplored Shimon's action, because anyone who takes the law into his own hands makes a deceit of the Torah and brings harm and monetary loss to the Jews. Furthermore, because of the multitude of sorrows and malicious lawsuits, the sort of people who make themselves known to the authorities and lay blame upon their brethren appear among us, causing many evils: monetary loss, spiritual damage, sacrilege, and disgrace to the honor of the Jews in the eyes of the gentiles.

10

Good people in the country began to take counsel about what to do to avoid the evil impending because of Reuven and Shimon. Each of these grandees thought he was the righteous party and the other one wicked, and by cheating justice, they added ill upon ill. Each enlisted his master, this one the powerful lord who owned the saltworks and that one the power of the noblewoman who owned the river and the ponds. The lust for victory is harsh, and even more so when wealthy men who are assisted by princes of the nations. Our ancestors have told us what happened to the Jews in the state of Bohemia and cities of Ashkenaz, and we have seen it recorded in the books of latter-day rabbinic authorities. The wealthy Jews disputed with one another and brought their quarrels before the princes and dukes, and what transpired in the end? In the end the princes and dukes plundered their assets *and* their spirit. In the end these Jews were forced into exile and apostasy—first the poor Jews, afterward householders and the wealthy, and finally the grandees themselves and all their families. Because of the aggression of the wealthy Jews, householders lost their property and were torn from their homes and went from exile to exile, and the rich themselves were not released from the world before being driven from their homes with all their brethren of the house of Israel.

11

Prominent envoys of the Council of the Lands were dispatched to Reuven's city and to Shimon's city, to guard the gate and prevent them from placing their lawsuit before gentile officials, because anyone who falls into their hands will not soon rise again.

The notables of this one's city and those of the other's city chose four from among them, two from each city. Each city chose two men. All were prominent and influential, men of good lineage and impeccable manners, the first to take care of any problem in the community. In addition, they were wise and learned, knowing the proper time for everything and placing the desire of the Torah above all other desires. These men were R. Shmuel Veg Vaizer, R. Shaul the son of R. Moshe, R. Yosef Dov, and R. Shlomo the colleague of R. Yosef Dov, who had first been his teacher. They consulted with one another and went to Shimon first, because he was the last one to cause damage, and his hand was poised to do more damage.

Shimon received them in the new room that he added to his house after marrying a second time, for he had married a wealthy woman, who brought him assets and furnishings that she had inherited from her first husband, who died without children, without siblings, and without relatives with a claim to the estate. After seating them all, each according to his honor, Shimon began to deluge them with words, and he did not stop before telling them it was a great honor for him to give honor to such honorable, respected men as they, who were truly worthy of respect.

R. Shmuel, the eldest in the delegation, responded, saying, Great thanks are due you, R. Shimon, for all the honor you show us. But, since you have mentioned the matter of honor, I shall say to you, Give honor to the Lord your God and do not bring your suit before the princes and dukes. At first, they pretend that law and justice are the foundation of their heart, but then they do what their heart desires. Their heart desires nothing but their own benefit, and their own benefit consists only in causing damage to others. If you and your adversary cannot come to a compromise, there is law among the Jews. Bring your suit before a rabbinical court, and they will render a truthful judgment.

R. Shaul added, Perhaps you might protest that no rabbis are familiar enough with businesses as large as yours in order to understand them correctly, and you do not have a high enough opinion of them. If so, choose two merchants, and they will choose a third man to decide between you. But know that some great rabbis are wise in the wisdom of the Torah and have all the seven attributes that a panel of three judges must have: wisdom, modesty, fear of God, hatred of wealth, love of truth, love of humanity, and a good name. In addition to all of these, they also understand commerce and are familiar with the ways of the world. If you bring your case before them, we guarantee that they will adjudicate with true justice. You may choose: either a Torah court or a tribunal of Jewish merchants.

After R. Shaul finished speaking, he turned to his colleagues and said, Is that not so, my teachers and rabbis? His colleagues nodded their heads to him and said to Shimon, You, R. Shimon, what is your answer?

12

Shimon answered, I cannot bring a case against someone when everyone hopes he wins the suit because of the fins and scales they got from him. The judges will think of the fish Reuven sent them and lick their lips in remembrance of the pleasure they had from him, so they will incline the judgment toward him.

R. Shmuel said to Shimon, It is an insult to a talmid ḥakham for you to say that. Could Jewish judges, perish the thought, be suspected of perverting judgment?

Shimon said, Perish the thought. I did not intend to insult them. I meant to praise them. R. Shaul called out in surprise, In my life I have never heard such an explicit insult, and you interpret it as praise? Shimon said, If you allow me, I will explain my words. R. Shaul said, I wonder how you can explain it, and if there be an explanation, it is a twisted one. In any event, we are willing to listen. Shimon repeated, It is human nature that anyone who benefits from his fellow forgets the benefit, and if he is a hard man, he becomes his benefactor's enemy, because he was constrained to benefit from him. Thus, if he has an opportunity, he repays the good deed with a bad one in order to show that he is neither dependent on him nor subservient to him. But a good man remembers his benefactor, and if he has occasion, he returns a favor with a favor. Now, since all Jews are regarded as good, they will remember the tail of every fish they received from Reuven, and, as people say, If a judge has had some benefit in any matter, he must be recused. Therefore, I cannot try the case against Reuven before either a Torah court or before arbitrators. Hence, against my will, I must place my case before the owner of the saltworks, which Reuven's water flooded and destroyed.

R. Yosef Dov said to Shimon, Do you admit that the power of the noblewoman, Reuven's mistress, the owner of the ponds, is greater than that of your lord, the owner of the saltworks, because she is greater than he in wealth, honor, and lineage? If she stands by Reuven, your lord will necessarily be at a disadvantage. Shimon said to R. Yosef Dov, If you say so, you have said nothing. If when the lady's husband was living, the owner of the saltworks ruled her, now that her husband is dead, he rules her ever the more so.

13

R. Shmuel said to Shimon, We knew you would say that. Therefore, we will tell you something, which, if you heed it, perhaps you will not depend so much on the power of your lord, of which you are so confident.

Shimon said, What is the thing you know and I do not? He said to him, The lady's son has returned from the capital. Shimon said, And if a little shaygetz has returned, so what? R. Shmuel said to him, The shaygetz you spoke of has become a great goy, and he has come to transfer his father's estate from his mother's possession to his own hands.

Shimon mocked him and said, The very place where you are trying to tear me down is the place where you are building me up. Because gentiles, too, are conscientious in honoring their fathers. It can be expected of the son that he would not do a deed that his father would regret.

R. Shaul asked Shimon, What father are you talking about? His mother's husband or the lord she sinned with? If it is the lord she sinned with, you have said nothing. Because the son has already heard that people gossip about him, saying he is that man's son. Therefore he intends to offend him in order to shut people's mouths so they will know that he is the son of the man whose name he bears.

R. Shlomo added, Perhaps you would like to know who incited him to that? You should know that it is the duke. Perhaps you want to know why the duke went to all that trouble? You should know that it is because the duke hates your master. Nor do we have to explain the reason. For you know as well as we, it is because his coach preceded the duke's coach on the birthday of "that man" at the entrance to the courtyard of the house of the one they venerate. If someone's coach collides with the duke's coach and does not give way, the duke persecutes him, especially someone whose coach entered the courtyard of the house of the one they venerate in sight of all the ministers and the whole people.

14

Shimon's face darkened, because he knew the power of the duke and that all the lords count nothing before him. He had been relying on his wife to defend him. Her first husband had been esteemed by the duke because he had saved him from an evil spirit in the form of a murdered man, which had terrified the duke and tried to drive him from the world. This was because the duke had stolen the man's wife and killed him with a firearm. Now Shimon's wife's first husband had frequent dealings with the duke, and when he heard that the duke was terrified, he risked his own life to perform a kabbalistic rite so the murdered man would no longer harm or terrify the duke. The duke's soul was restored, and he said to him, Whatever request you make of me, I will fulfill. Before he could ask for something, he died. Indeed, he passed away right after the rite. After his widow married Shimon, he did well by the first husband. Before entering the marriage canopy with the widow, he studied a number of chapters of Mishnah, each beginning with a letter of his name, and he recited the kaddish on the merit of elevating his soul, so he would lie in his grave in peace. The dead man was grateful to Shimon, and Shimon had counted on him to act on his behalf with the duke. Now that the visiting notables had mentioned the story of the lords' coaches, Shimon's spirit flagged because he knew that the duke hated the lord of the saltworks and wanted to remove him from the world. When the duke's anger erupted, none of his promises meant anything. Why, then, had they mentioned the lady's power? Was it not so that he would mention the lord of the saltworks and they would mention the duke?

15

That very day, Shimon recited the widow's rite, which he had learned from a wise man from Jerusalem. How was it done? He assembled ten God-fearing scholars and sat them down in the beit midrash in a triangular pattern, five in the first row, three in the second row, and one in the third row, and one standing above them, facing the Holy Ark, all with their backs to the women's section. Then he recited the widow's rite, so that the spirit of her first husband, which remained in his wife, should leave his wife's body and join his soul, spirit, and vital principle in the place where he was lying and remove any bit of possession and control, and that he would have no more converse with him, not in this world and not in the world to come. This prayer had nothing to do with the prayer of Rashash, of blessed memory, because Rashash's prayer was for the benefit of the widow, and it is recited before she enters the marriage canopy. However, Shimon performed this ceremony for his own benefit, and he did it after he was already living with her, because Shimon knew that all the duke's promises to his wife's first husband were null and void in light of his hatred for the owner of the saltworks. Therefore it was better to have no connection or bond with him.

16

The notables parted from him and went to Reuven. Reuven said, Twice I have gone to court with Shimon, and each time I left before a decision was issued, and he did the same. It was a waste of time. The judges asked endless questions and nattered back and forth among themselves about every small issue and could not get to the bottom of difficult commercial matters until I lost all desire to sit and listen. Nevertheless, if Shimon is willing to go to a rabbinical court, I, too, will go. And if he wants a court of merchants, I agree to that, too.

Reuven also said, I have not studied a great deal of Torah, and what I have studied I have forgotten. But I know that our Torah is true, and the judgments of Torah are true and just. If the judges get to the bottom of the issue, they will issue a just decision. If it is a court of merchants, I have seen a lot of merchants who cannot make a single deal without cheating. By contrast, I know many honorable merchants who are scrupulous in their speech, who want the best for their fellows and do not thrust themselves into idle matters, and all their words are intelligent and honest. Let Shimon say whom he chooses, whether it is a religious court of a court of merchants. I am ready to go anywhere he summons me.

They returned to Shimon and said to him, Reuven agrees to go to any court you wish. They said to him, There is no need to review the law concerning a recalcitrant litigant. But we will tell you in brief, what happens if your adversary summons you to judgment. You, R. Shimon, who are a talmid ḥakham, certainly know how a litigant is summoned to judgment. A court sends him its emissary who tells him to come to court on the appointed day. If he does not come, he is summoned a second time. If he does not come, he is summoned a third time. If he does not come, they wait for him all that day. If he still does not come, they excommunicate him the next day. What does this refer to? To someone who lives in a village. But someone who lives in the city, they only set a date once, and if he does not come all that day, they excommunicate him the following day.

Shimon stood and raised his hands high, saying, Certainly that is how things are done, and that is the language of the *Shulḥan Arukh*, and if you require me to litigate before a Jewish court, I have no choice but to accept your words. In any event, I want to know before which kind of court, one of three rabbis or three laymen?

They said to him, That is in your hands. Which do you prefer: a rabbinic court or a panel of merchant arbitrators. But, R. Shmuel said to Shimon, If you want my advice, I advise that each of you should choose one judge, and those two will choose the third: two merchants, and the third, a rabbi. Why do I advise you do that? You can be sure that merchants will get to the bottom of your dispute, and a rabbi will decide between the mediators.

17

The notables of Reuven's city and those of Shimon's city sent out to the lords and masters and leaders of the country, saying that Reuven and Shimon had agreed to bring their case before a Jewish court, and this is what they had advised them.

The lords and masters took counsel among themselves and set their minds on two very great merchants, who were famous all over the country for their wealth and their honesty. They also set their eyes on a rabbi great and wise in the Torah whose name went before him throughout the land, and to whom difficult legal inquiries were addressed from lands far and wide.

The lords and masters went to the two merchants and said, The country has set its eyes upon you to sit in judgment on the case of Reuven and Shimon, and you have no recourse but to accept this assignment. But because your business makes great demands on your time, we have come to fix a time with you.

They examined their diaries and asked their assistants and set a time. Because of the honor of the rabbi, whom they appointed to be the third, they agreed to go to the rabbi's city.

They came to the rabbi's home and were immediately surprised. This rabbi, who was renowned in the whole land and even in other countries, lived in a poor dwelling with shabby furnishings, and he was dressed in old clothes beneath his dignity. Each of them thought to himself, God only brought me here to help this man collect the fee for his service and mitigate his poverty. The rabbi greeted them, seated them before him, and asked their names and occupations.

They told him they had been chosen by the lords of the country and on behalf of Reuven and Shimon to adjudicate between the litigants, and they were asking him to be the third judge.

The rabbi answered them, I am not willing to do it. Why? He said to them, Why should you ask why? I am telling you simply that I am not willing to sit in judgment with you.

They said to him, Do you have something against us? He said to them, Perish the thought. If only there were more people like you among the Jews. They said to him, Perhaps the rabbi is related to one of us or to the litigants? He said to them, I am no closer than any other Jew. But I cannot sit with you in judgment.

Why?

I have already asked you, Why are you asking why?

They said to him, Nevertheless, we wish to know. He said to them, If you insist, I will tell you. I know that you are wealthy merchants who have considerable business all over the country. You are experts in commercial negotiations, and you are well known as honest and intelligent men. You also boast distinguished lineages. But what about the study of Torah?

One of them nodded and said, I am burdened with business, and I am not free to set aside time for studying, but I keep a young Torah scholar in my home and feed him at my table, and I give him everything he needs, and sometimes when I can break away from business for a few minutes we study a page of Gemara and sometimes even with Tosafot.

His companion nodded and said, Nor can I claim praise for my studies, though in my youth I was regarded as a prodigy. But because of my business, I had to set aside my studies. In any case, when I find a free hour, I peruse a book.

The rabbi beamed at them and said, One studies more, one studies less, if only they direct their heart to heaven. But you know that the *Shulḥan Arukh* has four parts, and one part is called "The Breastplate of Justice," and that part begins with the laws of judges. The *Shulḥan Arukh* has several commentators, and one of them is *Sefer Me'irat Einayim*, the Book of the Enlightened Eye. Now I will show you what that book says about our matter.

He stood up and took out the Breastplate of Justice and opened it at section three of the laws of judges, and he showed them the words of the *Me'irat Einayim* there, which quotes a responsum of R. Yaakov Weil, which he wrote to the late Maharash: If you listen to my advice, you will not sit in the company in any judgment, since you know that the decisions of householders and the decisions of learned men are opposites.

In Poland, there are, thank God, rabbis who are familiar with the business of the world. Choose two rabbis for yourselves, each shall pick his own, and they will pick a third, and your judgment will come from them according to the laws of the Torah, or according to human reason as much as you wish.

They chose two great rabbis who were among the greatest in the generation. Both were sharp and clever and expert in the ways of commerce and the world and familiar with disputes among merchants, not to mention their preeminence in Torah and in all the branches of knowledge that extend from the Torah. As a third, these two chose a venerable rabbi who was famous all over the country as great in Torah and piety and a man of truth. The two rabbis sat before the old rabbi, and each of them presented their claims. Reuven's advocate stated that the governor of the city had ordered so many wagons of fish for him for such a time, and Reuven had given the governor a very precious object as a pledge, which, if the fish were not brought on time, would remain in the governor's hands.

In response, Shimon's advocate argued that the governor had not held the banquet and did not need the fish because the soldiers who had been camped in the city left before the date that had been set, and, because the banquet had been canceled, the need for the fish had been canceled.

Against this the rabbi on Reuven's side argued, It does not matter whether the governor gave the banquet or not. Rather, Reuven obligated himself to the governor to send him so and so many wagons of fish, which cost so and so many thousand gold coins, and Reuven gave him a pledge that would not be returned if the fish failed to arrive on time. Because Shimon seized the fish, Reuven lost the pledge, which he had bought for so many thousand gold coins, as well as all the money he would have received for his merchandise.

Against this the rabbi who represented Shimon argued that even if the fish had reached the governor, he would not have accepted them even if the soldiers had *not* left the country and the governor had given a banquet for them. For all the fish were bruised because they had been dragged out of the water of the ponds and in the process collided with the dams and stones and broken vessels. They were not worthy of being placed on a lord's table, especially not at a meal where the governor had intended to show his greatness and splendor before the generals of the army. So, not only had Shimon done Reuven a favor by seizing fish that were not worthy of eating, there was also reason to argue that Reuven must indemnify Shimon for the costs of disposing of the rotten fish through incineration. Shimon also argued that if the pledge had not been in the governor's possession, the government would have taken it away from Reuven, and, not only that, he would have been punished with a fine and corporal punishment because the pledge was war booty and belonged to the state. There was still reason to inquire whether Reuven could claim that he had bought it from a certain minister, because if he had said so, the minister would have denied it, and he would have placed himself in danger, appearing to testify falsely against a great prince, and they would have put him in prison in addition to confiscating his property.

Against this, the rabbi representing Reuven argued, Let us turn our attention away from the pledge and return to the matter of the fish. For if the governor had received them in time, he would have paid the price and returned the pledge to Reuven, and Reuven would have sold them elsewhere, and no one would have opened his mouth to object.

Against this, the rabbi who represented Shimon argued, Even if the governor had received the fish on time, and he had paid the price in full, it is still doubtful whether it would have been worth Reuven's while, because at that time the currency had been devalued. Now, since the governor did not have to pay, and Reuven was not forced to accept his devalued coins, his loss is offset by his gain. Furthermore, on account of this Reuven had become closely affiliated with the governor, who saw that Reuven had lost money because of him, and we have already heard that he offered him several business deals by which he could profit by more than he had lost with the fish.

Against this the rabbi representing Reuven argued that the governor was used to payment in gold coin for everything he bought or sold. Therefore, Reuven would not have lost because of the devaluation of the currency.

Against this the rabbi representing Shimon produced bunches of witnesses who had bought brandy from the governor, which he had made three years earlier, and paid with the local, devalued currency.

Against this the rabbi representing Reuven argued there was an essential difference between property owned by the governor and property over which he acted as a trustee. The brandy that he had sold came from liquor distilleries owned by his mother-in-law, and he was responsible for her business. It was well known that they were not on good terms because she had thought he would marry her, but instead he married her daughter. So she threatened to get back at both him and her daughter by bequeathing her estate to a convent.

Concerning these witnesses brought on behalf of Reuven the following questions were raised: If it is true that you bought brandy from the governor, it has to be clarified whether the brandy is to be considered as ḥametz that has been kept during Passover. For it was known that the governor's mother-in-law, the owner of the brandy, had meanwhile married a lord who was of Jewish descent, and every year before Passover the rabbinical court sold them the townsmen's ḥametz. Even if you say that marriage laws do not apply to idolaters, still whether it is permitted to buy three-year-old brandy that had not been sold as ḥametz is a question that should be put to a rabbi. Therefore it was doubtful whether people like that, who traded in ḥametz that had been kept during Passover and thus misled several Jews, were valid witnesses.

The rabbis sat and deliberated for a full five days. One of them argued on Reuven's behalf and the other on behalf of his opponent, and the old rabbi sat at the head of the table saying nothing, although from time to time he wrote something on a scrap of paper, and sometimes he closed his eyes and appeared to be dozing. The merchants began to regret that they had placed their suit in the hands of such an old man, whose silence indicated that he was not listening to what the rabbis were saying. They already began to complain to the rabbis for having appointed such an old man as the third judge. The rabbis, too, were wondering to themselves about the old man who sat in silence and who, when they came to speak to him in his quarters, did not answer with even half a word. Since the merchants had obligated themselves to accept the judgment that would be issued by this court, they could only wait for the judgment.

After several days the old rabbi asked the two advocates whether they had anything to add or whether the litigants had anything to add to their claims. The merchants repeated their arguments, and the rabbis presented their claims to the old rabbi again, but all of them knew there was nothing new in their words. Since that was the case, they proposed to the third rabbi that he should state which way the judgment should go.

The old rabbi sat and repeated all the arguments presented by each of the two other rabbis in the name of the one who had chosen him, and they were astonished at the old man's vigor, for he had forgotten nothing of what they said. The merchants were also surprised that someone could remember every single nuance and, after laying out all the details, he stopped and summarized them, and then he divided them into two matters. One concerned the claims made by the man called Reuven, and the other concerned the claims of the man called Shimon. The merchants were amazed at the rabbi's wisdom, and they said, Rabbi, whatever you say, we will do and hear. The rabbi turned his eyes away from them and did not look at them, as if they were not concerned with the judgment. Finally he issued his decision, clearing the innocent party and condemning the guilty one.

The two merchants went out. The one who had won the case was happy. The one who had lost was desolate. Finally he was seduced by his evil impulse and said that the rabbi had twisted his judgment. Why? If we do not know, certainly his evil impulse knows.

This grandee was close to great men of Poland and had thereby been able to intervene and prevent the passage of several harsh decrees against his Jewish brethren. He was therefore astonished that all his merits had not availed when it came to his court case. From thinking too much about the matter, his soul became gloomier from day to day.

Before long he happened to be in the home of the duke, in the city where the old rabbi lived. For this grandee did important business with the mighty men of Poland and especially with that duke. The duke asked him, What about that dispute you had with your partner concerning the saltworks? What did the rabbi of the city decree? The Jew responded, Since you ask, I must answer you truthfully. The rabbi did me an injustice. I do not know why he twisted the law against me, but one may hazard a guess at the reasons. The grandee immediately began to tell the duke one or two of those reasons, which he himself knew were foolish, but in his great distress he spoke them so plaintively that they entered the duke's heart. The duke heard and sent for the rabbi. The rabbi heard and fled. He came to the forest grove where Rabbi Mordechai's father found him and brought him to his home.

The rabbi lived in the village in the house that Rabbi Mordechai's father opened for him. He ate and drank what Rabbi Mordechai's father and mother gave him and lacked for nothing except books. He sat and studied with his pupil, linking the Written Torah to the Oral Law and the Oral Law to the Written Torah, as we have already related in detail, and not even a hairsbreadth more needs to be added. But just to make matters clear, I am constrained to add that because Rabbi Mordechai had no book beside the Torah with Rashi's commentary and the Aramaic translations, and one tractate of Talmud, he learned them all by heart, in addition to the principles and halakhot taught to him by the rabbi. Fortunate is he who knows the entire Torah by heart, and if you also add the commentaries and translations as well as a talmudic tractate to that, his good fortune is doubled and redoubled. If you wonder how he managed in a short time to learn so much Torah, do not be amazed. Anyone who does not turn his heart to idleness manages to accomplish a great deal. However, I must say that I might not have been precise about the time, and I might be mixing up later accomplishments with earlier ones. That is, I am combining the chapters he learned in the city with those he learned in the village. This does not change the main point very much.

One day, the rabbi and his student were sitting together and studying. Suddenly the sound of incessant weeping could be heard outside. The rabbi said to Rabbi Mordechai, Go and see what that sound is outside. He went out and saw a woman standing and crying and begging his father to show her the rabbi's house, and three young men were standing with her, and a girl. They all asked his father to have mercy on them and let them come before the rabbi. Rabbi Mordechai went back and told the rabbi what his eyes had seen and his ears had heard. The rabbi said, That means my hiding place has been discovered. I can depend only on our Father in heaven.

Just as he surrendered himself to the mercy of the Holy One, blessed be He, the woman pushed inside and prostrated herself at the rabbi's feet, breaking out in even more abandoned weeping and shouting, Rabbi, save me! The young men and the girl who accompanied her also wept. The rabbi said, Calm down, woman, and tell me why you came here and why you are crying. The woman gathered her strength and told him that her husband was lying sick with a severe illness and she implored the rabbi to forgive him because his suffering came to him only because of what he had done to the rabbi. The rabbi understood that she was the wife of the grandee, who had fallen ill, and they attributed his illness to the suffering he had caused the rabbi.

Just as the woman and her sons were weeping and asking forgiveness, an impressive coach hitched to two noble horses arrived. The duke's coachman was driving the coach. The people of Rabbi Mordechai's father's household nearly fainted because they believed the duke's men had come to arrest the rabbi. Hardly a minute passed before the coachman jumped down and opened the door of the coach, and three Jewish notables stepped out. They had come to bring their rabbi back to the city and restore him to the rabbinate. For the duke had already realized that the rabbi was a righteous man, and he had sent the carriage to bring him back.

The rabbi said to the grandee's wife and sons, I had already forgiven him when I first arrived here, and I hold nothing against him. Let us hope that God will also forgive him and send him a full recovery along with all other sick Jews.

The city notable heard and said, Rabbi, what answer will you give us? He said to them, I have not yet thought things through in my heart, and I do not know what answer I will give you. God willing, perhaps after the Sabbath I will know. Now, return to your homes safely, and have my wife and children bring me Sabbath clothes because all the time I have been living here in the village I have not worn my Sabbath clothes and the gentiles do not know that I am a rabbi. I also ask of you to send me a Gemara. They said to him, God willing, after the Sabbath our rabbi will return to the city and there he will find a full set of the Talmud and Maimonides and everything his soul desires. He said to them, I will tell you the truth. It is hard to move from place to place, especially from a place that is good and tranquil to a place that sated me with bitterness. Please do not pressure me. God willing, after the Sabbath I will know what to do.

One of the city notables asked the rabbi, Please tell us, rabbi, why you are putting us off until after the Sabbath? Why not come with us immediately? The whole city is already expecting our rabbi to come, and they speak about it all day. Even schoolchildren ask when will the rabbi come. The duke, too, extends his grace and has sent his carriage and his horses to bring our rabbi home, and in the end our rabbi puts us off until after the Sabbath. That which can be done after the Sabbath can already be done before the Sabbath. The rabbi said to the city notables, When the opportunity to perform a commandment comes your way, you should not miss out on it. But regarding the other things that have suddenly come to me, I prefer to wait to do them until after the Sabbath. For on the Sabbath some of the power that a Jew had upon receiving the Torah is restored to him, when he knows what is good and what God demands of him. If he is fortunate, he is told by an insight that suddenly comes to him. If he is very fortunate, the Torah itself reveals it to him by a verse in the portion of the week.

Seeing that the rabbi was resolute in his opinion and that no imploring or promises would change his mind, the notables asked his blessing and returned to the city.

On the Sabbath, before Minḥah, the rabbi and his student sat together and studied the Ethics of the Fathers. They came to the Mishnah, "Love work; hate dominion; and seek not undue intimacy with the government." The rabbi began to interpret it: Love work, even if a person has enough to live on, he must work at a trade and not say, I am great and it is a discredit to me to work at a trade, as Rav said to Rav Kahana, Better to skin carcasses in the marketplace and take payment, and do not say, I am a priest, I am a great man. And hate dominion, keep a distance from exercising power over the public because dominion buries those who have it. And seek not undue intimacy with the government in order to gain influence by means of it. Come and see how great are the words of the sages, who combined these three things together: anyone who has no trade necessarily seeks dominion to make a living from it, and in the end he is trapped in the net of the government, if not willingly, then against his will. Take the case of that grandee. He certainly feared heaven, and many good things came to the community because he was close to the duke. Because of his intimacy with the authorities, he succeeded in preventing the priests from imposing harsh decrees on the community. But because of that intimacy too he came to this sad end. He entered into a lawsuit in rabbinic court and lost, but instead of looking to the Torah, he went and laid false charges before the duke ended up where he is now.

The rabbi repeated the words of the Mishnah and told his student everything the sages said in praise of practicing a trade and everything they said in condemnation of the professional rabbinate. Finally he told his student things he had heard from his teachers about what had happened to them and their teachers because of involvement with the authorities, of which they taught in the Gemara, *Keep your way far from her*, that is idolatry and the authorities, and *Do not go near her doorway*, that is a whore. They said, *The leech has two daughters, 'Give,' 'Give.'* R. Ḥisda said, Mar Ukba said, The voice of two daughters shouting in hell, saying in this world, 'Give, give,' and who are these two? The skeptics and the authorities. Others say, R. Ḥisda said Mar Ukba said, The voice of Gehinnom shouts out, saying give me two daughters who say 'give, give' in this world. R. Yoḥanan said, I remember that they used to say in the beit midrash, He who concedes to them falls into their hands. He who depends on them is theirs. In the end, the rabbi returned to the Mishnah and said, When I was a young man, I wanted to be a rabbi, and when I entered the rabbinate, I neither loved the rabbinate, nor did I hate the rabbinate. Now, after everything that has happened to me, I am keeping the commandment to hate the rabbinate. But I cannot have the privilege of being able to practice a trade because I have no skill, and I can only hope I will not have to be intimate with a ruler, even one who wishes me well.

[The Rabbi of Zabno concluded, Rabbi Mordechai] told me he had been asked to go somewhere else. He did not tell me why, and he did not tell me the name of the place. Years later I heard that he was living in Buczacz, and his trade was tinsmithing. That is all I had to say about Rabbi Mordechai, may he live long. Now, gentlemen, emissaries of Buczacz, travel back to your homes in life and peace, and may God grant you that my teacher and friend, Rabbi Mordechai, will be willing to accept the rabbinate of your city, for it would be a glory to your city if that genius, that righteous man were your rabbi.

The emissaries saw that they could accomplish nothing here in the matter of the rabbinate, and they stood and asked permission of the rabbi to depart. The rabbi parted with them in peace and wished them a successful journey. They parted from the rabbi and from all the people of the household and went to the synagogue, because the time for morning prayers had already come.

The rabbi also rose and went to the synagogue to pray there with the emissaries from Buczacz, but he did not speak with them or look at them because during his prayer he was separate from all worldly matters, and some say even from matters of Torah, because he acted with the Holy One in such a way that his concentration would not be compromised. In this matter he was truly unique in his generation because most of the outstanding scholars required great effort during their prayer to keep from being disturbed by the multitude of scholarly puzzles and problems that had been occupying their minds, from simple textual glosses to complex interpretations of Maimonides and Tosafot. Nor did the emissaries from Buczacz try to speak further with the rabbi of Zabno because their hearts could not contain any more astonishing things.

They set out for home but their puzzlement did not abate. A brilliant and righteous man was to be found in their city and he was merely a tinsmith. Who was he, and what was he like? The rabbi of Zabno said explicitly that his name was Rabbi Mordechai, and that his trade was tinsmithing. If so, he was Mordechai the tinsmith, though perhaps he was a different Mordechai. Still it was a wonder.

One of them began to speak, saying, I remember something that is worth telling. I have a lantern in my house. It belongs to my little son. When he started studying on winter nights in his room, I had the lantern made. Now that my son has grown I sometimes use the lantern, especially on stormy, raging winter nights, when the wind blows and makes the light of the shavings in the fireplace flicker. One night after evening prayers I opened a Gemara and sat as studying, as is my custom. Suddenly the candle in the lantern fell down. I straightened the candle and sat down to study again. This happened once, twice, thrice. Finally the candle went out. I went to another room to light a candle and saw the members of my family sitting and playing cards. I scolded them and said, Do you already know the whole Torah, so you do not have to study anymore? Why are you sitting and engaged in idle matters? They looked at me in surprise. Finally my grandson stood up and said, Grandfather, it is Nittel-nacht tonight. Now, after the things that the rabbi of Zabno told us, I see that Rabbi Mordechai the tinsmith, that righteous man, did not want me to use the object he made to study Torah on Nittel-nacht.

Another of the men nodded and said, I heard your words and I remembered something. Near my house used to live an old gentile, a veteran of the king's army. Praise God, there was peace between him and me. But the trouble he caused me is great. See for yourself. On Sabbath eve, when I and my family were sitting at the meal and singing the hymn, "Everyone Who Sanctifies the Seventh Day," that old man came with his pipe and lit his pipe from our Sabbath candles and sat and filled the house with smoke. Who could tell an officer of the king's army what to do? I consulted wise and intelligent men, until one of them advised me to speak with Mordechai the tinsmith and ask him to make me an enclosure to put the Sabbath candles in. I went to him and asked him, Perhaps you can make me a device of that kind. He said to me, Why not? Before the Sabbath eve he brought me a fine enclosure. My wife stuck her candles in the enclosure, and blessed the candles. During the meal the warrior came in with his pipe in his mouth while we were sitting, and he also sat himself down. Meanwhile the fire went out in his pipe. He stood up to light it. The flame singed his mustache, and it almost caught fire. He quickly put out the fire and was saved from burning. We praised the Blessed Name for doing a miracle. If the officer had been burned, they would have accused the Jews of having a hand in it. He began to speak with us in our language, and this is what he said: I am astonished at the Holy One because the punishment for violating the Sabbath is stoning, not burning. I will not elaborate. In short, he did not leave until he told us that he was an apostate Jew.

How did he come to that? He was an agent for a nobleman. After the nobleman died, he began to deal with her widow. He came and went in her house and was alone with her, and sometimes their business continued until late at night, and sometimes he had to begin it early in the morning. He did not have time to go home and come back, and so he stayed in the castle. The lady used to invite him to her room, and he would sit and discuss business with her, and he also told her the news of the day and things like that. They became accustomed to one another, and they lost deference for one another. He forgot his people and his God and was seduced by his instincts. This happened once, twice, and thrice. He left behind his home and his Judaism and began to live in the lady's palace. He behaved like a nobleman in his eating and drinking, clothing, his dwelling, and in all their manners, which he knew and observed more punctiliously than all the other nobles, until they forgot his origins and regarded him as one of them. He began to notice that her sons were plotting to kill him. As long as the lady was alive, he did not fear them because she was a strict mistress and ruled over her sons. In any case, his heart was not easy because he knew that danger was lurking for him, if not from her sons then from their friends or servants. He avoided the imminent danger and left the lady, but he did not return to his wife or to the God of Israel. Rather he went and joined the king's army in a city distant from the one where the lady and her sons lived. Because he was familiar with their manners and an expert in horses, and a brave man, they made him a cavalry officer. All the time that he served the king, he cunningly kept his origins secret and prevented people from knowing that he once had business with a certain lady, especially since he heard that the lady was looking for him, and after she died he was even more afraid of her sons' revenge because they were ashamed that a Jew had been intimate with their mother the noblewoman. He forgot his wife and daughters and his body grew older, until he was dismissed from the king's service because of his age. He came to our city and settled there and made a decent living with the wealth he had acquired. He came and went in the courts of lords and ladies only as much as was necessary because his heart was not in truth drawn to them, and he was also afraid because when a person gets older, the signs of his origin are visible. If he was born a Jew, it would become evident in old age. During the six working days, he was at ease in his soul. He sat on the bench in front of his house, thought his thoughts, and conversed with passersby. That was on sunny days, and in the winter, too, he found ways to pass the time. But when the Sabbath came, his heart roiled like the River Sambatyon, which throws up stones during the six days of the week and rests on the Sabbath. Precisely at twilight, his soul would become agitated, and his heart would be drawn to a Jewish home. He could not calm the turmoil in his heart unless he entered a Jew's house, especially when the songs of the Sabbath eve came to his ears. So that people would not know he was a Jew, he came with his pipe in his mouth.

Thus the chosen men sat in the wagon and told stories until the horses smelled the city, raised their feet, and started to rush along. Within a short time, they arrived in the city. The driver gave his whip one last snap after the long journey. So, too, the horses, which trod the earth of Buczacz with power and joy. The chosen men saw they had reached Buczacz; they descended from the wagon, and each one went home. They ordered the wagon driver to announce their safe return from Zabno to the notables, and told him to bring them their luggage.

After evening prayers the notables and leaders gathered in the community hall, with all the good men of the city, and with them all the householders, and everyone with an opinion, to hear the outcome of the mission from the emissaries.

The chosen men related everything that had happened on their way and on their way back, leaving out no event. Finally, they spoke in praise of the rabbi of Zabno and his conduct. At last they came to the main point, the matter of the rabbinate of Buczacz. They conveyed what the rabbi of Zabno had answered them, and why he would not accept the rabbinate of Buczacz.

The notables and leaders, and with them all the people of Buczacz heard all this and were left speechless. When they were aroused from their first astonishment, they began to examine themselves. Perhaps they had sinned against that genius Rabbi Mordechai the tinsmith, who behaved like an ordinary person; for they had behaved toward him the way one behaves toward tradesmen, sometimes without respect, and sometimes with contempt. Later generations are not like the early ones, for in the early generations even the tannaim and amoraim were craftsmen. In later generations, however, who takes up a trade or a craft? An orphan with no one to teach him Torah or just a good-for-nothing whose skull is too thick to study. So that most craftsmen do not know any Torah, and they are not worthy of respect. I must say, however, that some of those gathered thought well of themselves, because they had already noticed that Rabbi Mordechai was a special man. But they admitted without shame that they did not know he was a mighty genius.

The notables and leaders, and with them the rest of the good men of the city, resolved to appoint Rabbi Mordechai as their rabbi and not to be concerned because he was not famous among the great scholars. As for his earning his living from a trade, Buczacz could allow itself such an action. You might say that Buczacz was not the first community to set a man over it who was not known to the outside world. It already happened in the time of the Maharshal of blessed memory, who, when his hour of death was near, was asked who should fill his place. He showed them a man, R. Avraham the vegetable seller, who lived in a dark cellar beneath the Maharshal's house and had been unknown in the city until it was revealed to the Maharshal that he was a great genius. But because he was sworn not to make him famous, he never revealed his nature to the world. Now that Lublin needed a great rabbi, the time had come for him to be famous in the world.

So as not to delay matters, they ordered the scribe to copy the writ of appointment word for word because there was not enough time to draft a new one. Wherever the name of the Gaon R. Moshe Avraham Abush was written, the scribe should write the Gaon Rabbi Mordechai, although he was free to add appropriate words with a verse such as *Light shone in the darkness for the righteous,* since Rabbi Mordechai hid his greatness and because he made lanterns for schoolboys to light them on winter nights. But no other changes were permitted, in order to avoid delay. That very day they decided unanimously that the three chosen men, R. Ber, R. Yeruḥam, and R. Levi should go to Rabbi Mordechai and offer him the rabbinate. They were the ones who had first heard of Rabbi Mordechai's greatness from the rabbi of Zabno, so they should bring him the writ of appointment. After them the parnasim and leaders would come, and with them the good men of the city, and also anyone in the city with an opinion, and the sooner the better, because no one could know the ways of craftsmen, who are suddenly summoned to a nobleman to repair a vessel in the palace, and they could tarry there for a week or more, while here Buczacz remained without a rabbi.

The emissaries hurried away immediately after breakfast with the writ of appointment. The scribe had not been indolent and had stayed awake all night writing it with a fine hand, as he was instructed. Nor were the notables and leaders who examined it after him indolent; they made sure everything was written correctly.

The chosen men went to the outskirts of the town and came to Rabbi Mordechai's door. They delayed for a while and stood there. They heard a voice in the house. They pricked up their ears and things that bring life to the soul. They heard a voice saying approximately this: According to the reading of the Sheiltot and the Bahag, it comes out this way; but according to the system of the Rif it is that way; and also the opinion of Maimonides, and his opinion is like that of Rabbenu Tam, and also the opinion of the Rosh, and that is how the Tur presents them. Thus they stood for a long while listening and more than they listened the more they yearned to enter the room. But they were afraid that if they went in, they would halt his studies or distract his students from the passage, for it was obvious to them that he was sitting with students around him and explaining the development of a halakhah from its earliest instance in the Mishnah to its later formulation in the *Arba'ah Turim*, and doing so with extraordinary sharpness of wit and expertise, the likes of which they had never heard even though they were from Buczacz. Finally their desire to see his face was too great and they could resist no longer. They opened the door and entered, and now their surprise exceeded their earlier astonishment. For they had been sure Rabbi Mordechai was teaching students and that the house was full of volumes of the Talmud and early and late halakhic decisions. But they found him sitting alone with only one book before him. Still, they were sure this must be some special work not known to them, perhaps from another country like Italy. They could not resist and lo and behold it was only a Ḥumash with Rashi and Onkelos. There were no other books in the house. In fact, there was nothing in the house except the tools of his trade and a talit and tefilin.

Rabbi Mordechai beheld the men who had come. He stood before them, and asked what had brought them there. They told him they had come on the orders of the community, which had agreed with the opinion of the rabbi of Zabno, who advised them to place him, that is Rabbi Mordechai, on the seat of the rabbinate. Rabbi Mordechai was silent for a while. Then he said, I am surprised that the rabbi of Zabno said to you what he did. But because we are commanded to heed the words of sages, I am not refusing immediately. However, I want to consider first. Wait for me for three days from now, and I will answer you.

But I must repeat what I said, I am surprised at R. Abush, for I did not see that it is written of me that I should be made a rabbi. The chosen men were pleased, because it was apparent to them from his words that he was willing to accept the rabbinate. Even though each of them yearned in their soul to speak with him and take his measure, they restrained themselves, because the whole city was waiting for them, to hear Rabbi Mordechai's answer.

Before parting from him, they said, Rabbi, would you allow us to ask you just one question? Before we entered, we stood at your door outside, and we heard some of your words, and it seemed to us that many books lay open before you because you mentioned the Babylonian and Jerusalem Talmuds, Sifri and Sifra, Mekhilta and Tosefta, Rif, Rambam, Rashi, and Tosafot, and other authorities. And here we see here only the Ḥumash. He answered them pleasantly, What is surprising here? Teachings delivered orally may be recited by heart. They said to him, That is not why we are surprised. We wonder how a mortal man can remember all the teachings precisely in the language in which they are recorded, especially when you have no book to consult. He said to them, Perish the thought, did I err in some halakhah or quote something without naming its source? They said to him, Far be it from us to think this of our rabbi. But we are wondering about the matter itself. Rabbi, how can you remember all of these things by heart? He said to them, I will tell you. I am a poor man and cannot afford to buy books. Therefore I became accustomed to learning by heart, and I study the Ḥumash with Rashi and Onkelos, and from every single word I propose to myself the halakhot that are derived from it, and God is my helper, who graced me with a good memory, and when I reach a place where there are books, I check to see whether I have made a mistake. God assists me, and I do not err. This is by virtue of the Torah, which is pure for those who study it without intending to register a victory or for purposes that are not relevant to the Torah. Now, gentlemen, after I have spoken too much, let everyone return to his work, and in three days, God willing, I will give you an answer.

The chosen men saw there was nothing to add to what they had said, and also because of their courtesy and because they were afraid to detain him, they said nothing further. They rose and parted from him and returned to those who had sent them, telling them everything they had seen and heard, and what he had told them.

The notables and leaders heard, as did the whole city, and they rejoiced greatly, because they were going to appoint such a great rabbi, one who knows how to link the entire Oral Law to the Written Torah without subtracting or adding, something that only the rabbis of the Mishnah and Talmud knew how to do, as well as a few of the greatest halakhic authorities. But no one in the world had heard that there was such a genius in recent generations. Everyone who knew him face to face regarded that as a privilege, and even more, everyone who had an object in his home made by Rabbi Mordechai took pleasure in that object as with an etrog before Sukkot.

At that time, Rabbi Mordechai's name was on everyone's lips. Buczacz spoke only about him. There was no one in the city who did not tell stories about him. Some told about something that had happened, and some made an event up and was sure that such a thing had happened. On account of our many sins, no righteous or pious man can stand before the multitude of the Jews, who imagine things that never happened about him. Even true things that they tell about them are full of exaggeration. Thus it was, and thus it will be, and nothing can be done about it. In any event, everyone must watch himself, so as not to be one of the tellers of tall tales. Needless to say, they should leave righteous and pious men alone and not hyperbolize about them. Of such things it should be recalled, Just as the dead are punished, so, too, eulogizers are punished.

While Buczacz was rejoicing, the news reached the governor of the city, the master of the city, who ruled the city. All the doings of the city were decreed by him, and everyone was subject to him, the Jews among them, needless to say. For since our city was destroyed, we have been in the hands of kings and ministers who do with us what their hearts desire. Especially in the land of Poland, where every duke ruled like a king, and when he spoke, no one opened his mouth to let out a peep. He sent for the notables and leaders. They obeyed and presented themselves. He said to them, I heard that you are about to appoint a new rabbi in place of Auerbach, who went to Stanislav. They said to him, With your permission, your lordship. He said to them, I know him. They said to him, That is an honor for him and for us. He said to them, You have chosen well. He is an honest man and expert in his craft. Every vessel and every thing he repaired in my palace remains in good condition, and I am pleased with his work, and with his manners. I give you permission to appoint him rabbi, and I warn you, that anyone who comes to me with accusations against him, the way they did with your former rabbi, Auerbach, I will have him placed in stocks and beaten until he forgets his flesh, and then I will throw him to the dogs. Therefore, return to your city and take Mordechai the tinsmith, and I give you authority to proclaim throughout the city that I have spoken thus, and if some rascally informer comes to inform against him, I will throw him to the dogs. Because you have already pestered me too much with your quarrels and disputes.

The notables and leaders heard and were ashamed because of the governor's words, especially because, in words that I did not quote, he praised those of the Christian faith, who dwell in peace with their priests and make no accusations against them, and they do not disturb the king and his ministers with quarrels. But the notables and leaders were happy because he agreed that Rabbi Mordechai should be appointed as their rabbi. They thanked the governor profusely for all the good things he said about the new rabbi, and they told the governor, We will obey your order wholeheartedly. The governor gave them permission to go. They parted from him and left. No sooner had they left, when he called them back and said to them, Tell your new rabbi that I give him power to judge and instruct and excommunicate and ban, and he need not fear informers and tale-bearers, because I am appointing him as rabbi. Now go and know that.

They left the governor and told the good men of the city what he had said. Within a short time everyone in the city knew everything the governor had said. The city rejoiced greatly. Some of them said, *When a man's ways are pleasing to the Lord, He makes even his enemies to be at peace with him.* Now we need not fear that informers and denouncers will make accusations to the governor, and others added, The mouse is not the thief, rather the hole is,that is, it is not the nobles who harm us but rather the informers and denouncers among us. As the prophet cried out, *Your destroyers and your ruiners come from you.* They remembered the

Gaon R. Leibush Auerbach, who sat honored by the world in Stanislav, and nobody opened his mouth to let out a peep against him, while in Buczacz, many people to whom he had done no harm hated him, and they made accusations against him to the government. At that time the status of the Jews was elevated, for everyone saw that the princes' hearts were in God's hand; *He turns them wherever He wishes,* not to tolerate defamation and informing, which had caused several holy communities to be uprooted from the world, and righteous and genius rabbis were forced to wander from town to town without finding rest for their feet until they died in the torments of hunger and were not properly eulogized, and their sons and daughters begged for bread at people's doorsteps.

Buczacz prepared itself to greet its new rabbi, and the entire city, both scholars and ordinary householders prepared themselves to greet the rabbi, the scholars, to hear the sermon he would give on the first Sabbath after his appointment, and ordinary householders, to be blessed by him, for everyone who is given greatness by heaven is given power in his blessings, and everyone whom he blesses is blessed.

The notables and leaders and good men of the city chose three of the most respectable men of the city to be the first to go to the new rabbi to deliver the writ of appointment to him.

Here are the names of the notables, the honored men of Buczacz, whom the holy community of Buczacz chose to go to Rabbi Mordechai first. The first in sanctity was the splendid lord Yissakhar Ber, of priestly lineage, whose family tree went back to the Holy Temple. He had the merit of blessing the sun three times in his life, and his strength was still as the sun at its height. He was not the same as the lord R. Yissakhar Ber, of whom it is said that the famous genius R. Ḥayyim Cohen, the head of the court of Lvov, wrote to him, instructing him to persecute our rabbi, the light of Israel, R. Yisrael Ba'al Shem Tov, whom he calls a witch doctor in his epistle, and other bad names, for it is known that the entire epistle is counterfeit from start to finish.

The second, similar to him, was the marvelous lord R. Mordechai Shainer, of the distinguished descendant of R. Mordechai Ba'al Halevushim, whose daughters married many of the geniuses of the generation, and many of the rabbis of the generation were related to him. This great man commissioned the making of a tablet upon which the whole service of sanctifying the new moon is written and which is taken outside to the courtyard of the Great Synagogue for sanctifying the new moon. It hangs on columns of wood in the form of crescents. If God helps me I will tell the whole story about this tablet in detail, for the story is worthy of being told. The third of the chosen was the splendid poet R. Shmuel, who versified all the laws for counting the Omer in metrical rhymes. Great men saw them and rabbis praised them, for they were surprised that a man in these later generations was capable of performing such a feat in the holy tongue, just as in ancient times when the entire House of Israel was fluent in our holy tongue. The gaon, the author of Meir Netivim, praised him especially, because he, too, tried his hand at poetry, and set some halakhot to rhyme. The three of them were highly learned and born and bred in Buczacz.

Immediately after breakfast, two of the notables, R. Mordechai and R. Shmuel, went to R. Yissakhar Ber Hacohen, who was the eldest of the group. They came to him and placed the writ of appointment in his hand so that he could deliver it to their new rabbi. The old man saw the writ and said, I have a family tradition according to which one may not deliver a document unless one has first examined it. He looked at it once and twice, nodded his head in agreement, and these are the words he said: I praise Shmuel the scribe, who is a master of the holy tongue. From the style of his language, it is evident that he is expert in the twenty-four books of the Bible. The crown of Torah that he drew is also fine. I saw a drawing like that seventy-five years ago in the hands of R. Moshe of Zlotshov, the son of the gaon R. Elazar of Kraków, which was sent by the community of Brody to R. Elazar, appointing him the rabbi of Brody, and I say that this crown is more lovely than the one that the scribe from Brody drew. Because the scribe of Brody made the crown with six arches, and our Shmuel made it with nine arches, which is the way of great kings, whose crown is nine spans. As for the crown of the Messiah, may he be revealed soon, in our day, no eye has seen it. Now, gentlemen, let us go to Rabbi Mordechai. I rely upon the rabbi of Zabno and also the three emissaries who spoke with Rabbi Mordechai may be depended upon.

They left R. Yissakhar Ber's house, which stood above the city on the way to Podheitz and traversed the entire city until they reached

Rabbi Mordechai's house, which stood below the city, close to the Strypa. The people of Buczacz saw the three notables walking to the new rabbi to offer him the writ of appointment, and they accompanied them. Before they reached Rabbi Mordechai's house, the banks of the Strypa were full of a multitude. Nothing like that was seen except on the first day of Rosh Hashanah, when people perform the Tashlikh rite.

They reached Rabbi Mordechai's house and knocked on the door. He came out and opened the door to them, ushering them into his room and inviting them to sit on the chairs he had prepared for them. R. Yissakhar Ber sat down, and R. Meir sat down, and R. Shmuel sat down. Rabbi Mordechai sat with them. R. Yissakhar Ber began by saying, Mazal tov, Rabbi. *Happy is the man whom You choose and bring near*. Happy is our city, which has chosen you as a rabbi, and happy is our rabbi, who will bring us close to the Torah. Rabbi Mordechai was silent, saying nothing. But from the expression on his face, it was evident that he had nothing against the words of R. Yissakhar Ber. Then R. Yissakhar Ber took out the writ of appointment and spread it before Rabbi Mordechai, repeating all the conditions orally because sometimes a scribe uses a verse or a quotation from the sages that can be severed from its literal meaning and interpreted in several ways. Therefore he told him all the matters orally, in the language of ordinary speech. The two colleagues, R. Meir and R. Shmuel, watched Rabbi Mordechai to see the impression the words made. Although they sensed in him that his heart was not drawn either to the money or to the honor that came with the rabbinate, their eyes did not leave him.

R. Meir added, If R. Ber permits, I will supplement his words with one thing that our rabbi should know. R. Ber nodded his head in agreement. R. Meir said, When it was known in the city that we had all agreed to appoint you as the rabbi of Buczacz, the governor of the city summoned the notables and magnates and spoke to them in the following words: I agree with the rabbi you are about to accept for yourself, and I give him permission to judge and instruct and excommunicate and ban, and I will not accept any defamation against him from any informer or denouncer. R. Ber nodded and said, No rabbi of Buczacz has ever received such assurance, and if I may rely upon my memory, not in any other city either. R. Shmuel said, If R. Ber will permit me to add to his words, from the days of the genius R. Shakhna of Lublin, the teacher of the Rema, such authority has not been given to any rabbi in any country.

Rabbi Mordechai's face turned as dark as the side of a pot. They were sure that he had been seized by weakness. But it was not weakness that fell upon him, but rather reservations. He said to them, Listen, gentlemen. When you came to me to offer me the rabbinate, I said I had to ponder first, because never in my life have I pursued the rabbinate, and it never occurred to me to accept a rabbinical position. But out of respect for the rabbi of Zabno, I did not refuse. I knocked on all the doors and received no answer. Since I received no answer, I concluded that the rabbinate did not suit me, and certainly it was not written of me in the book of Adam that I would be a rabbi. But it was a bit difficult for me because the rabbi of Zabno, who is a supreme holy man, set his eyes upon me to make me a rabbi. Now after the words of the governor, I know what the reason is that no one responded to all my inquiries.

They said to him, Did not the Rema write in his responsa that if a minister or king of the nations gave authority to a rabbi, this comes under the provision of "The law of the kingdom is law," on the condition that he is appointed with the agreement of the community? The Rema brings proof from Ezra and Neḥemiah son of Hacaliah, who ruled by command of Cyrus, the king of Persia, and from the other kings of Israel during the Second Temple period. We also find in chapter two of Tractate Shabbat that R. Yehudah is called the first speaker on all occasions. Why? Because he was appointed by the Roman emperor, and so it is also at the end of Tractate Menaḥot, where it says that he was the teacher of the house of the Nasi. They interpreted it there in the Tosafot to mean that the emperor appointed him to be the teacher in the house of the Nasi, the way he was appointed to be the first speaker. For the emperor is capable of appointing a teacher and rabbi, and so, too, wrote the Ribash and the Rashba, that authority from the king is valid, and it is included in the principle "The Law of the Kingdom Is Law," except he must be worthy of it, and it must be the wish of the congregation over which he is appointed.

The Rema concludes, as is also written in the Tur, Ḥoshen Mishpat, no. 2, as follows: And authority that the king gives, etc., etc.

Rabbi Mordechai answered them, I have not seen the responsa of the Rema, but according to the style of his language, I assume that our rabbi quoted there what was taught in Tractate Yoma on the verse *Fear of God increases days*—these are the priests of the First Temple—*And the years of the wicked will be shortened*—these are the priests of the Second Temple, and so on. In the Gemara, they interpreted this to mean that they were appointed by the king by giving a lot of money, as they said there, A pot of gold did Martha, the daughter of Boethus, give to King Jannai to nominate Joshua ben Gamla as one of the high priests.

R. Shmuel said, exactly so. Everything that our rabbi mentioned is cited in the responsum, for here there is no room for doubt as to whether to accept the rabbinate, because of the agreement of the city.

Rabbi Mordechai said, If regarding the law there may be no room for doubt. Nevertheless I will tell you what I heard from my teacher, who heard it from his teacher, and his teacher from his, as far back as our rabbis the Ḥasidim of Ashkenaz. Once it happened that the community of Cologne accepted a cantor who had all the virtues listed by the sages for a prayer leader. The duke heard and summoned him and said to him, I heard that the Jews have appointed you as cantor. I, too, agree that you should be the cantor. The cantor said to the duke, Since you appoint me, I am not worthy to be the emissary of the Jews before the Holy One, blessed be He. When he returned from the duke, he told the parnasim of the community, I am unworthy of being a prayer leader because it appears that I was appointed by a gentile. My teacher told me that all the arguments and reasoning of the parnasim of Cologne were invalid. That pious man withdrew from the post and did not wish to be the prayer leader, because he was acceptable to a gentile. Therefore, my teachers and masters, officers of Buczacz, since it was told to me that the governor of the city has given his agreement to appoint me rabbi of your city, I can no longer serve as a rabbi here, and I remove myself from the rabbinate.

And you, my masters and teachers, be not angry at me. This very day, after you leave my house, I will leave the city, and you will not see me anymore, and I bless you and your city, that you may have great and good rabbis, with the Torah of truth in their mouths, and no flaw found in them.

A few years later, our city was privileged to receive the genius R. Zvi Kara as its rabbi.

Translated by Jeffrey M. Green

Disappeared

1

At the time of this story, the Jews of Galicia were required to make men available for military service, each community according to a quota determined by the imperial authorities. Every year in each town, the local parnasim would gather in the communal meeting chamber to review who among the local populace had a son or a son-in-law who had reached the age of eligibility for military service. If he was from a prominent family or a Torah scholar, they would pass him over and in his place take some clod or numskull who would be no loss to the town. If they did not have enough men to fill the government's quota, they would recruit from itinerants in the region who sold themselves for military service.

Who were these itinerants? After the three kings divided up the Kingdom of Poland, the province of Galicia fell within the territory of Kaiser Joseph, emperor of Austria. He decreed that anyone who held no land or had an occupation of which the province had no need should be expelled. The imperial officials checked and found that there were many Jews who had neither land nor an occupation that served the emperor's interests. They were promptly expelled from their places of residence. They wandered from town to town in search of a place to settle. Those who found one prospered; those who did not hired themselves out to the imperial army, for the Emperor Joseph permitted Jews to serve in the military, which no emperor before him had ever done, nor was this the case in any other country.

Thus it was in former times in Israel that once each year, the imperial officials made known to the communal parnasim the exact number of men it had to present for military service. The parnasim would assemble in the communal meeting chamber to deliberate the matter. Not everyone wanted to go to the army because it involved desecrating the Sabbath and holidays, eating forbidden foods, and other transgressions common to soldiers. How did they deal with the problem? Those who had the means exempted themselves by buying off in their stead others who valued money over their bodies and their bodies over their souls, and were prepared to sell the latter to preserve the former. This included people who did not have the means to pay the exorbitant taxes that the new regime, in its oppressive stance toward the Jews, had levied on them, and were uprooted from their places of residence and wandered from town to town. Among these were villagers whom the regime had expelled. They were deemed to be harmful to the locals because they served them whiskey, which made them drunk and indolent to the point where the fields stood untended, the soil unplowed, and the crops unsown. The landowners consequently were unable to pay the taxes demanded by the regime.

After wandering around and finding no place to sustain them, some of these itinerants presented themselves to the community parnasim for service in the emperor's army. The parnasim picked out the younger men, whom they handed over to the army in place of those they were charged with delivering from their community for that year. If there were insufficient communal funds to pay off the conscripts, they took craftsmen whose skills were not absolutely necessary to the community's needs. If the quota set by the regime was still not met, they took from the ranks of the unlettered. Such was the practice in all the communities, and Buczacz was no different.

2

One year, Buczacz could not meet its quota. The regime regarded it as an important community and demanded from it the number of men commensurate with its reputation. They did not know that Buczacz's prominence lay in its Torah scholars and not in its general population.

After some investigation it was determined that that year's quota, which exceeded previous ones, could not be filled. All whom the community found to be suitable for conscription had already been taken, and those who were not were unfit.

Buczacz was in the grip of great anxiety. Anyone who had a son started worrying about him, as did anyone with a son-in-law. The upper crust of the town were worried that their servants on whom they were dependent would be taken from them. Once, when Buczacz did not meet its quota, a lottery was held, and the servant of one of the wealthy men of the community was taken. The rich man's world grew dark and his life became intolerable.

When the time came to send the recruits, the parnasim reconvened. All they could come up with was the verse *And your people are all of them righteous*. This was uttered in its most literal sense, for there could not be found in all Buczacz anyone who desecrated the Sabbath or committed adultery, nor were there any empty-headed good-for-nothings of whom any community would be happy to rid itself. Why, one could ask, did the community not retain those who offered themselves for army service for a fee? Because it had no money. When the plague struck, the community needed additional burial ground and acquired the portion of a field that belonged to a certain gentile. The parnasim had promised to give him his money by a certain date, but when the day came they could not do so. The many taxes and assessments that the regime imposed upon the Jews had impoverished the community and it was unable to repay the debt. No sooner did a little money come into their coffers then a new enactment came into force, each one requiring more and more Jewish money. The only way the impact of the new levies could be blunted was to bribe the court officials with hard currency. In the years of the Polish kingdom copper coins sufficed for this purpose, but now, in the new regime, silver ones were necessary. During the time of the Polish rule, officials regarded the Jews as a welcome source of the funds needed to make up the gap between the modest salaries they received from the government and what it cost to live. But now, in the new regime, officials took a more patronizing attitude; however much the Jews gave them, they always wanted more.

The community was therefore not able to repay its debt to the gentile from whom it had bought a portion of his field to use as a burial ground. The gentile proceeded to turn his pigs loose among the graves and there was a danger that the repose of the dead would be disturbed. He did in the end get his money, but to meet its obligation Buczacz had to empty its coffers and there was nothing left to recruit men for the army.

There was another reason why such men who offered themselves for army service for a fee were not available. It happened once that a certain number of them were retained by the community as recruits. They were given ample food and drink and whatever else they wanted. When the time came for them to be sent to the military authorities for induction, not one of them could be found. They had all bolted to search for another community to hire them.

3

When the parnasim saw that there was no one available, they cast their eyes on a young man who was the son of a widow, even though he was not yet old enough for military service. Some say they did this of their own accord. Others, however, maintain that a certain tailor was responsible. His daughter had cast her eyes on the boy and her father sought to break them up. He had a business, owned a home, and was the gabbai in the Tailors' Synagogue. His forbears of a few generations previous were related in some way to those of R. Leibush, who was serving his term as the monthly parnas. The girl's father hoped to marry her off to a family of substance when this fatherless son of a widow with nothing more than a shirt on his back worked his charms on the girl and stole her heart. Either way, these two possibilities are linked.

How so? That month, R. Leibush was serving as parnas. The young man's mother had come to him to receive her share of wheat money to buy Passover matzah. He gave it to her, but she demanded more. R. Leibush said to her, Look, this is what you are entitled to receive, this is what I gave you, now be gone and on your way. Whereupon she started screeching and hollering and recounting to him all her troubles. Her husband had died and left her with an only son and no visible means of support. Over the winter, they sustained themselves with whatever she could earn in her impoverished state. She would buy a chicken from a gentile woman and sell it at a small profit, she would salt the slaughtered chickens to remove the blood and render the meat kosher for the local women; she would prepare goose fat for them for Passover, or pluck feathers; she would prepare the chickens for the wedding feasts the wealthy families made for their daughters. Now that Passover was approaching she wanted to buy provisions for the festival so that she and her orphaned son would not go hungry as they had all winter, when there was nothing in their mouth but saliva. R. Leibush replied that there were many poor widows in town and many orphans too.

What makes you better than they? he asked. She grew angry at the way he compared her with the other poor widows and retorted fiercely, Whoever envies us, may his children be orphans and his wife a widow! Just at that moment, Godil the tailor came in. He wanted to measure R. Leibush for a garment. I am not sure if the garment was for him to wear on the approaching Passover holiday or to impress the officials of the provincial capital when he brought the recruits there to present them. When the widow saw Godil she exclaimed, Well now, here's Godil! He can say whether I deserve to be treated well or not. And if not on my own account, then on account of my son, who works with him.

Godil was silent. Said the widow, Godil, why are you silent? Why do you swallow your tongue? Say something. Let R. Leibush hear my son's praise. Said Godil, What can I say about your son? He works for me. The widow shrieked in anger, That is all? Nothing more? Godil continued, What more do you want me to say? That he is worthy of being a Landesrabbiner? He does his work, and I have nothing against him. The widow raised her voice at him and screamed, That is how you treat an orphan, the son of a widow? That is all you have to say about him?

Godil grew angry at the woman for addressing him that way, in the presence of R. Leibush. It might make him think that she was his, Godil's, equal. Sha! Sha!, said Godil to her, If you insist, I will praise your son to the skies. The widow replied, So open your mouth and say something. Godil turned to R. Leibush and said, He may be young but he is as strong as a grown man. He is as powerful as a mighty oak and taller than everyone his age. Twenty-year-olds, twenty-two-year-olds, men who sell themselves for the imperial army do not even come up to his shoulders.

Her love for her son prevented her from catching the import of what Godil had just said. Indeed, his earlier silence was better than the words he had now spoken. Triumphantly, she said to R. Leibush, So has R. Leibush heard what Godil has said about my son? I will add to his words. One Sabbath last summer, I took a walk with him. We came to a village and sat down in a park belonging to a Polish noblewoman from whom I buy chickens and fruit. The lady passed by and asked me who this young Jewish man was. I said to myself, May the eyes that this shiksa cannot take off my son wither away! She then said, A fellow like this, a fellow like this by us would be made a commissioned officer. And within two or three days, the widow's son was taken for the imperial army. The name of the boy was Dan; the name of the girl who had plighted her troth to him was Bilhah; and the name of Bilhah's father was Godil the tailor. The name of the widow, the boy's mother, I have forgotten. I do know the names they had for her husband because they called her by those names. (In our area, women are known by their husbands' names.) But her husband is dead, and one does not mention the unflattering names by which dead people were called.

4

They took Dan from his mother's arms. He was not yet old enough for military service, but they paid no attention to his age, just as they ignored his mother's tears that fell unremittingly.

Dan was sent far away from Buczacz, to a place where no one from Buczacz had ever been. He was given a surname, one that neither he nor his mother nor any of his father's or mother's families or anyone in Buczacz had ever heard of. No sooner had the name been given then the parnasim who gave it to him forgot it. At this point the name has no bearing on Dan's situation, but in time it would. They called him Hoffmann, which in German means "a man of hope," and in truth it must be said that even though their only intention was to add some luster to the name they had already given him, it was a nice one.

Dan was sent to a place far from Buczacz and left behind him four eyes streaming with tears. Bilhah cried secretly, behind closed doors, on her bed at night. His mother wept loudly, in public, in the streets.

Jews are supposed to be merciful, she screamed. So tell me: how right is it that the rich and the wealthy, who have sons and sons-in-law galore, and not one of them goes to the imperial army, and this poor widow's only son, who is all she has, is stolen from her? A stripling, barely wet behind the ears. A young boy whose tefilin are still new, who is barely eighteen. An orphan boy who needs his mother. Taken by force from his widowed mother's arms and sent to the remotest part of the country at the end of the world where there are no Jews. And now he will drift among the goyim for twelve years! Twelve years! And by the time he comes back half my flesh will have been eaten by the worms in the grave, and I will never get to hear my orphaned boy say even one mourners' kaddish. Among the goyim he will never find a minyan of Jews. O, Jews, Jews! What have you done to this miserable widow? What have you done to my little orphan? If what you knew didn't keep you from doing what you did, then the Judaism you all profess certainly should have.

Those who had sons or grandsons or sons-in-law who had reached the age of military service gave praises and thanks to the King of Kings, the Holy One, blessed be He, that it was that woman's son who was taken and not their son or grandson or son-in-law. Those who did not have sons or grandsons or sons-in-law were no less grateful to Divine Providence for selecting whoever was selected so that their relatives were spared from having to give their boys to the Emperor. But those who seek God selflessly and are faithful to His covenant, those people mourned for what happened to Dan as they would have mourned for any person. It is written that *a man can surely not redeem his brother, or give a ransom to God for him,* which means that a person cannot pay ransom with another person. And here they took a Jewish boy and gave him over in place of others. Our Teacher Moses, peace be upon him, who was equal in worth to the 600,000 Israelites, said to God, "Master of the universe, Let me perish and a hundred like me, but do not harm even a fingernail of one single Israelite," and here a holy community of

Israel has brought misery and suffering to two Jewish souls, a mother and her son, a widow and an orphan.

This is the place to tell of something that happened a generation before Dan. Our Master, the great and venerable R. Meshulam Igra, may the memory of the righteous be for a blessing, who was born in Buczacz, was the rabbi of the town of Tisminitz. He left Tisminitz to go to Pressburg in Hungary because in Hungary they did not take Jews for the army, while in Tisminitz, which was in Galicia, they did. In Tisminitz, they hired Jewish men for army service in exchange for others who were thus exempted. The matter did not go down well with the eminent rabbi. He went on record saying that if his only son, R. Yosef Eliyahu, were ever about to be conscripted, he, R. Meshulam, would let him go and would not redeem him with another Jewish man. The rabbi left Tisminitz, and Tisminitz continued this practice, as did Buczacz and all the other communities.

5

Great is the trauma of a mother whose only son has been taken from her and sent to some godforsaken place without her knowing when he would return and if indeed he would return. Great is the trauma of a girl whose beloved has vanished because others separated him from her. The widow's thoughts were all confused. Her distress and her agony muddled her mind. As in a nightmare, fantasies raged within her; she was totally discomfited. Her fantasies, though vague and shadowy, appeared before her as frighteningly real. Their actuality terrified her relentlessly and endlessly.

Bilhah, on the other hand, framed her thoughts quite clearly. She sat between the oven and the stove and reflected, I am eighteen and half now. If I add the twelve years that Dan will serve in the army, I will be thirty and half, a half year older than Mother is now. Will I be too old for Dan to still have feelings for me? As much as she envisioned how she would look on the day of Dan's return from the army, she could not imagine the changes the years would bring in his appearance, when he would come back and see her as an old lady. She could not imagine that he too would have aged, and on the day of his return would not look like he did when he left Buczacz.

The imagination is capable of showing us wondrous things, but sometimes its power weakens and it cannot make us see what is most obvious. What is more obvious than the fact that over the years all people age? Yet that girl could not visualize how Dan would look after many years, even as she was quite able to do this in regard to herself.

6

From the day Dan was taken from her arms and sent to the imperial army, his mother abandoned all her regular endeavors. She stopped going to the villages to buy chickens and vegetables; she no longer stationed herself at the crossroads in advance of her companions so as to solicit the gentile women who supplied chickens and vegetables to the town's peddlers; and she did not make her rounds of the homes of the wealthy to sell chickens or do housework. She walked the floors of her ramshackle hut, facing the four walls and lamenting her son as if the Angel of Death had snatched him away; and lamenting herself for being alone in the world with no one to rely on or to support her. Realizing that no one was listening to her, she went out into the streets and recited her laments to any man, woman, child or anyone who happened by. Sometimes she mistook a shadow for a real person and talked to it as if it were.

So what did that woman live on? What sustained her? If not her suffering, then it was only her saliva that kept her alive, as she had told R. Leibush the parnas before he took her son from her.

A few days later, Bilhah came to visit. As the two women sat, Bilhah began to talk about Dan. It is immaterial whether his mother knew that the couple had sworn to God that they would never ever forget or forsake one another; the important thing was that here was a living person sitting in front of her, and her ears were open to hear things about Dan, and it didn't matter if she heard them ten times or twenty times, or even fifty times. Before Bilhah came, Dan's mother had talked about her son, but the big difference was that then she spoke to the walls of her hut and now she was talking to a living human being. The walls of a hut listen in silence, but a living human being listens and sighs. No greater kindness can be done to those who suffer than listening to their sighs and sighing in sympathy with them. Moreover, the walls of her hut grew tired of hearing about Dan, not because they were old but because his mother's words were old, whereas in Bilhah's ears the same tired words spoken by his mother were new and delightful, and she could not stop listening.

Bilhah could see the mother's anguish and distress and began talking to her about her need to resume her regular activities. If not for her own sake, then for Dan's, for if she did not go back to work and support herself, it would be disastrous. Dan might inform her that he was coming back from the army and she would be lying ill and unable to go out and meet him, or, God forbid, she would be lying dead. She would thus cause Dan more pain and suffering than the parnasim of the town or the many years of Dan's absence ever had. Bilhah even depicted for her the day when Dan would come back from the army. Happy to see his mother again, he would come running and bounding into her hut and find it empty.

Bit by bit, Bilhah's words penetrated Dan's mother's mind. She began to return to her endeavors. She went out to the villages to buy chickens and vegetables; she stood at the crossroads in the middle of town to solicit the country women who supplied those things to the town; she made the rounds of the homes of the wealthy. Here she sold a plump chicken, there she prepared one for cooking. Here she paid out money, there she took in money. Here she swore to a gentile woman that the wares she was trying to sell were worthless, there she grabbed the hand of a thief who had taken a coin from her basket. Everywhere she displayed a great industriousness—in the marketplace, the middle of town, the homes of the wealthy. Wherever she went, she bottled up her pain and presented herself to her customers as a peddler whose livelihood depended solely on them. But the undeniable truth was that this public affectation only served to reveal her suffering. People soon took it as a clear reproach, as if she were saying, Look at what you have brought on me. Look at the pain and suffering you have caused me.

There were times when she did her work with one hand and with the other wiped away her tears. Were Buczacz not so full of merciful people, they would have abandoned her and bought their provisions from others. And it was not as though there were not enough peddlers in Buczacz. They used to say that for every one customer in Buczacz there were seven peddlers, and for every seven peddlers there was one chicken. The question has been asked by all who have studied Buczacz: when the cock crows, does it do so out of joy and pleasure or out of suffering and pain? Were such scholars to go out to the marketplace and observe seven peddlers selling one chicken, they would conclude that the cock there crows neither from joy and pleasure nor from suffering and pain but out of pride and privilege, for all Buczacz is eager to have him.

7

They brought the conscript Hoffmann, that is, Dan Hoffmann, to a town in upper Austria. Four or five hundred years ago Jews had lived there, owning land, homes and servants. They maintained their Judaism through Torah and worldly endeavors at home and at work in the fields, in their place of worship and wherever their affairs took them. Priests and other vilifiers observed them enviously and began to harass them by spreading libels against them. In one town the Jews were accused of enticing their maidservants to steal and desecrate the Host. In another it was said that the Jews kidnapped Christian children and killed them to use their blood in baking matzah. Libels, no matter how disgusting and abominable, find an audience. The town officials heard them and believed them. They took Jews and imprisoned them until they confessed to sins they had not committed or converted to the religion of their persecutors. Some were kept chained in dungeons until the flesh rotted off their bones. Some were killed in horrible ways. Amidst all these dire and cruel tortures, the Jews never lost their spiritual purity. They surrendered their souls in sanctity for the sake of the Divine Name. Any Jews who remained fled for their lives. Those who did not escape were caught, jeered, and driven from the town in humiliation. The towns were now completely empty of Jews; not a one remained. Their houses and all their possessions were plundered and their houses of worship turned into churches. The only trace of Jews was their cemeteries from which the despoilers took the gravestones to use as foundations for the houses they built. The only other vestiges of Jewish settlement in the area were the Jewish place names. Since then no Jew was ever seen in those parts and no Jew ever set foot there. All that people there knew of Jews were the fabrications they heard from their wet nurses and their priests, who hated and ostracized them.

And so there was Dan in that remote place, an army regular. His fellow soldiers were all tall and husky and spoke a German that could not be understood by anyone not born there, certainly not by this young Jewish boy who was born and raised in Buczacz, where everyone spoke Yiddish. If there was in Buczacz some enlightened person who knew German, it was the poetic German of Schiller and Shakespeare. The miracle was that this Jewish boy from Galicia who had no German, much less the literate German that even those who spoke it didn't know, was able to comprehend what his commanding officer wanted, and so he did not incur his wrath. Within that miracle was another: the commanding officer, who customarily reprimanded all who were of lower rank than he, did not do so with Dan.

There was Dan at the end of the world, with no other Jewish person in sight, just as his unhappy mother had said. Were it not for the fact that the gentiles' Sabbath fell each week one day after the Jewish one, Dan would have forgotten that God gave us the Sabbath day to make it holy. Woe to one who does not go to synagogue and does not participate in the communal prayers. All the more so on the Sabbath, when there are additional prayers. Woe to one for whom the Sabbath is no different from a regular day. All the more so to one who violates the day with forbidden labor. Woe to the person who performs purposeful labor on the Sabbath, all the more so when the Biblical punishment for that grave sin is stoning.

8

Having noted how the Sabbath was for Dan, let us now see what the other six days were like. He did not put on tefilin or wear tzitzit. The house he lived in had no mezuzah. He ate forbidden foods that shrivel the mind and deaden the soul. It is a wonder that he did not forget that he was a Jew.

At such times as he found himself alone with no one around, he would put his hand on his forehead, close his eyes, and stand and recite the one or two prayers he knew by heart. The prayer book that his father bought for him from which he learned the mourners' kaddish that he said after his father died was gone. He had guarded that prayer book carefully and took it with him wherever he went. It was near his pillow when he went to sleep at night. But then it was taken from him. Forty soldiers, all gentiles, lived with him in one room. They all smoked and were always in need of kindling paper to light their pipes. At one point they came upon a bundle of tattered pages. They took hold of it and divided it up among them without knowing that it was the prayer book of their fellow soldier Hoffmann. They had not taken it and torn it up and used its pages for kindling out of any malevolence but for their smoking needs. In any case, Dan's prayer book was gone. Through God's mercy Dan remembered a few prayers by heart and he would say them whenever he could, whenever he found himself alone. God's mercy also allowed him to recall his own personal Biblical verse: *Dan shall judge his people as one of the tribes of Israel.* One can find in some prayer books—and this was noted by the Shelah—a practical way not to forget one's name for the Day of Judgment, and that is to recite, at the very end of the silent Amidah prayer a biblical verse that begins with the first letter of one's name and ends with the last letter. Dan's biblical verse worked for him even in this world: the name Hoffmann was given to him by the parnasim of his town on the day they handed him over to the imperial army, and that name is so recorded in the army records.

One fine day, the soldier Dan was out in the barracks courtyard beating his clothes with a paddle to get the dust out of them. He considered that the clothes he was wearing contained shatnez, the forbidden mixture of wool and linen. He stopped in the middle of doing this when a disturbing memory came to mind. There was a family in Buczacz named Shatnez. They acquired that name when a rumor circulated that such forbidden mixtures were found in a garment that their grandfather had sewn. Once when Dan was a child and he and his friends were playing with stones, a member of that family passed by, and they threw stones at him yelling "Shatnez! Shatnez!" Now the hands that threw stones at a blameless person who happened to have a grandfather who had transgressed the shatnez commandment were busy with a garment that contained shatnez that he himself would wear.

What more can I say about Dan? That he was a soldier in the imperial army. The emperor had agreed to accept Jews in his legions and made no distinction between Jews and gentiles. The Jews ate the same food the gentiles ate, drank what they drank, wore the same uniforms, and did the same things. The only discernible difference between them was that the gentiles went to their churches and the Jews were not compelled to enter those houses of worships. Even so, there was one slight way in which Dan the Jewish soldier stood out from his fellow soldiers and that was in his great humility, which endeared him to all who had charge over him and made him very popular with most of his compatriots. Their fathers, however, were unhappy that a Jew was allowed to serve in the army together with their sons. They felt it an affront to Christian honor to have Jews serve alongside them.

9

Five or so months passed since Dan was sent away from his town and his mother, and she had not heard a word from him. He had, in fact, written her many letters, but not one of them had been sent. Neither he nor his friends knew how to get a letter to the town of Buczacz in Galicia. She too had no idea how to send any to him, nor did Bilhah or anyone with whom they consulted on the matter. Buczacz was small; it had only four thousand people, and even though there were some merchants who did a lot of business with several countries near and far, no one in town knew the name of the place where their native son was stationed. The officials of the imperial court also had no idea.

Dan's mother sits at home yearning to hear something from her only son. She runs from one person to another, getting advice. Each one gives her a different opinion, and they all make sense to her. She goes to Dovidl the scrivener to have a letter written to her son, and he tells her, I can write a thousand letters for you, but what would we do with them if we do not know where to send them? Not one idea that people have given you is right. Dovidl the scrivener is an honest man. He has no regard for the few pennies he could make for writing the letter; his only concern is not to deceive a poor widow. The unhappy woman screams, Oh, you clever people of Buczacz! You know who all the letter writers are and you cannot even tell me who could write a few lines for a poor widow! When Dovidl and his neighbors try to explain to her what the problem is, she yells in anger, Why do I need all your talk? All I want is to send two or three lines to my son. You took him away, so at least help his mother communicate to him her anguish.

They all nod and slink away, and she, too, slinks away and leaves. Seeing herself now desolate, alone and forsaken, she raises her arms heavenward and says, Master of the universe! You are the only One who sees my suffering. Help me! Help me! She beats her breast and says, How many more tears can this broken vessel hold? It is already overflowing. If You do not help me, God, Your children, the Jews You love so much, certainly won't.

A gentile man and woman pass by and see the woman standing in the street muttering things in a Jewish tongue. They ask her, Jewish woman, what are you saying? She answers them scornfully, If Jacob has no pity, why would Esau? They hear this and move on. She stands in the marketplaces of Buczacz and does not know where to turn. She starts walking toward the old beit midrash, which is always open. She goes in, opens the ark and rests her head on its base. She stands there and weeps for herself and for her son who has been forcibly wrested from her, and for this heartless world in which there is no one ready to come to the aid of a Jewish woman. Thus does she stand and cry, until her tears are exhausted and her voice fades into silence. She raises her head from the ark and leaves. But let us here commend the students in the beit midrash; they did not scold her but allowed her to pour out her words to God.

10

As much grief as his mother felt, Dan's was double. She longed only for her son; Dan longed for both his mother and for Bilhah. Though he and Bilhah had not written tenaim, they had pledged to marry.

So there is Dan, at the end of the world, far from his town and from everything he loved there—his mother, Bilhah, the houses, and the synagogue where he prayed on weekday mornings, and at all the services on Sabbath and festivals. He would have given all that he had for an hour in the beit midrash at the close of the Sabbath, just before the evening service at the start of the new week, when everyone was sitting and singing the psalm of David *Blessed be the Lord my Rock, who trains my hands for battle, my fingers for warfare*. Barely five months had passed and another eleven and a half years lay before him, on each day of which he would train his hands for battle and his fingers for warfare. Would he ever, after all those years, have the merit to sit again in that house of worship and sing that psalm? All the time he had lived in his town, he did not know how pleasant that was. Everywhere he turned, he saw Jews. Here, in this desolate wasteland, there were only gentiles. From the way he was living, he was half a goy himself.

Dan put aside his own grief and contemplated his mother's and Bilhah's. High mountains, deep valleys, flowing rivers and many streams separated them, but in his musings they were present to him constantly. Even at night they were near. Sometimes when he awoke he didn't know if he was with them there or they were with him here. But he clearly saw them together. This was quite wonderful because he had never told his mother that he and Bilhah had pledged to marry. Dreams bring near those who are far away. One night in a dream he saw Godil nodding his head—and Godil was the one who tried to get him away from Bilhah.

11

Hours become days, and days become weeks, and weeks become months, and months become a year. Each week has its Sabbath, and there are weeks when a festival also occurs. Dan made peace with the weekdays, when he never saw a single Jew. But a Sabbath without Jews is hard. There are Jews in Buczacz whose livelihood requires them to be among gentiles during the working week, but they come home for the Sabbath. For Dan, the weekdays and the Sabbath are all the same. Ensconced among the gentiles, he is for all intents and purposes one of them.

Dan looks around and sees only soldiers. They are all big husky gentile men none of whom had ever laid eyes on a Jew, just as Dan was not seeing any now. Dan shuts his eyes so as not to see his fellow soldiers and he strains to picture a Jew from his town in his mind's eye. But the oppression of the Jews by the nations impinges upon him and the hardships they impose on us cannot be removed. We can only hope that the yoke of those hardships will oppress us less in the present than they did in the past. So even though he got used to the drudgery and did whatever was asked of him, the whole idea of it ate at him. When it did not, he thought about R. Leibush who handed him over to the army officials, and about the officers to whom he was accountable and whose commands he was always ready to carry out.

Suddenly, panic seized him. He realized that he was going to be punished. No question, punishment was coming. Punishment was absolutely coming. Punishment was inescapable. He had committed a punishable offence. Not intentionally but inadvertently. It was only a mental lapse, but a mental lapse in the army is a serious offence. Whoever has a mental lapse while performing one's military duty forfeits his life. There is no reprieve. Certainly not in this case, when a sergeant stands before him and Dan fails to salute his own superior. Were the sergeant to pass by, he would be required to salute, regardless whether the sergeant looked at him or not. All the more so now, when the sergeant is standing directly in front of him.

Fearful and apprehensive though he is, the sergeant affectionately pats him on his shoulder and, in a German somewhat close to Yiddish, asks him, How are we doing today, Mr. Hoffmann? Have you gotten any letters from home?

Dan stood there before the sergeant, his right hand raised to his helmet. Flustered, he kept his hand there. He struggled to find his tongue to say something. Then the words came to him. He told the sergeant that he was the son of a widow. The sergeant had asked him if he had gotten any letters from his family, and he felt duty bound to tell him that he was the son a widow and had no father. Then, when the sergeant did not order him to march off to work, he repeated that his mother was a poor widow with no children other than he. He went on to relate that he worked for a tailor making clothes for women and that he had been taken while he was working on a dress and that he was pressed into service before he had reached the age of eligibility.

The sergeant took his pipe out of his pocket, filled it with tobacco, lit it, remained standing there and told Dan to go on. Dan thought it improper to stand before one's superior and natter on about things that surely would be of no interest to him. But the sergeant drew on his pipe, blew out some smoke, and told Dan to go on.

Dan related several things in a disjointed way, and then the sergeant exhorted him, You need to send more letters to your mother. Dan looked up at the sergeant and said dejectedly, I have written many letters to my mother but not one of them has been sent.

Why is that?

Because there is no one here who knows how you send a letter to Buczacz.

The sergeant laughed, There is no one here who knows how you send a letter to... to... Bud-chach. What is the name of your town?

Dan replied meekly, Buczacz. The sergeant repeated it. Buczacz. Dan nodded and replied respectfully, Yes, sir. Buczacz. The sergeant said to him, Tomorrow, Hoffmann, tomorrow you bring me all the letters you have written, and I will send them to your mother. You can be sure that if I send them, they will get to her. The sergeant then indicated that their conversation was over. He did not do this by ordering him to march off to work but rather the way a civilian would. The sergeant went on his way and Dan returned to his chores.

He was quite astounded. In all his time in the army, he had never seen a sergeant speak with a recruit that way. More than that, the sergeant asked him personal things about himself and his mother. And even more, the sergeant said that tomorrow he would send the letters Dan had written to his mother. Dan knew that there were Jews in the imperial army who had been promoted to the rank of sergeant. But the only sergeant he had ever seen was this one who had just happened to come to the town and was not part of the regular troops there.

The next day, Dan brought the sergeant a bundle containing all the letters he had written to his mother from the time he had settled in at the army base. He added one more about how it came about that God arranged for there to be a Jewish sergeant to accept and send the letters. Without him who knows if he ever could have sent her a letter.

The sergeant took the bundle and said to Dan, They will all get to their destination. All of them. Without fail. The sergeant sensed that Dan wanted to ask him about the chances of doing this in the future. He said to him, I will be returning here soon and we will see what we can do. I will in any case be talking with my colleagues about this. Be well now, Mr. Hoffmann.

12

One day, all Buczacz was in an uproar. A bundle of letters had arrived at the post office from a senior army officer stationed at the military base in Lemberg. On the bundle the following was written in clear script: *To the Honorable woman, The widow Mrs. Hoffmann in Buczacz.* People in Buczacz asked, Who is this honorable woman?

From the sound of her name, one could conclude that she was married to a man from Germany. From the fact that a ranking senior military officer wrote of "an honorable woman, etc." one could assume that this Hoffmann was a specific person. If he was someone appointed by the court, then the head of the post office would know of him, and if he was a wealthy man with property, then the local merchants would know him. But he was known to none of these. If Hoffmann's widow was a gentile woman, again, the head of the post office would know of her, and if she was Jewish, it was unheard of for a Jewish woman in Buczacz to be called by her family name, because if she were important and well known she would be called by her given name, and if she were important but not so well known she would be called by her husband's name. So who was this widow Mrs. Hoffmann? There were many conjectures. In the end all who offered them admitted that they were nothing but conjectures and the only thing to do was to wait until the matter resolved itself. The conjectures, however, continued, old ones giving way to new ones.

The head of the post office saw that there was no one who knew who this honorable widow was, and to return the bundle of letters to its sender would be difficult for him. He would be seen as negligent in his duties. He thought it over and decided that the only thing to do was to open the bundle and figure out from the letters to whom they were written. But when he opened the letters and saw the script, the mystery deepened. Could it be that a senior officer in the army would write something in Hebrew script, for it was clear that the writing in all the letters was in Hebrew characters.

He called in two leading members of the Jewish community and told them that letters written in your language had arrived in town. He said, I am giving them to you on condition that you deliver them to the person to whom they were sent. Search well. The sender is a senior officer in the army, and you are responsible to make sure that the letters reach the one for whom they are intended.

The two took the letters and promised the head of the post office that they would do as they were charged. Upon leaving him, they quoted to each other the words of the Taḥanun prayer, "As for us, we know not what to do." They went to the communal meeting chamber where all the other parnasim soon assembled. They opened the bundle of letters, and everyone saw that they were written by a Jewish boy to his mother. One parnas asked, What interest would an officer of the army have in a Jewish woman? To which another replied, What does a moth have to do with a flame?

What do you have to say? a third parnas asked a fourth.

What do I know that you do not? his colleague replied. What we need here is what Jacob said when he blessed his son Dan: *Dan shall be a serpent by the road.* The rabbis interpreted this verse to be referring to Samson. Jacob foresaw that Samson would one day stand between the pillars and pray to God to give him strength: "O God, remember me, be mindful of me and grant me strength." So here I pray that God will remember us and be mindful of us and give us the strength to find the widow, if not for her son's sake, then for the sake of the head of the post office who gave us the letters on the condition that we deliver them to the widow Hoffmann.

R. Leibush, serving as chief parnas that month, was not especially well versed in Torah, and whenever one of his colleagues would offer words of Torah at a meeting in the communal meeting chamber, R. Leibush would close his eyes and doze until the speaker finished, at which time he would open his eyes. And so it was on that day. When that parnas concluded his words of Torah, R. Leibush awoke and said, We need to send for Godil the tailor. Retorted another, The Talmud tells us that to settle a really difficult problem you need a scholar. It does not say you need a tailor.

Said R. Leibush, What is clear here is that the writer of the letters is an orphan. At the end of each letter, before he signs his name, he writes "your son who weeps with you in all your troubles and embraces you in pity." What is not clear is whether the boy we handed over to the court is named Dan. But I remember that he worked for Godil the tailor, and so I want to ask Godil if his name was Dan. But what are we to do about this widow named Hoffmann? It could be that when we handed over the boy to the imperial officers, one of us called him Hoffmann, and that's what they wrote in their files.

What are you talking about, R. Leibush? they said to him. Did you not hear that the bundle of letters was addressed "to the honorable woman"? Would an officer of the imperial army call a Jewish woman honorable and address her as "the honorable woman"? If the officer really had the mother of that poor orphan in mind, then who should we laugh at first, the officer or you, R. Leibush, for thinking he would do something like that?

Heavy sighs were heard. A few of the communal leaders in the chamber were uneasy about what they had done to the orphan boy and his widowed mother. Before adjourning, they sent Yonah the shamash to find Dan's mother and deliver her son's letters to her. He hurried to do this even though he knew that the widow was poor and he would get nothing for his efforts, not even a little shot of whiskey.

13

That very day, all Dan's letters were in his mother's hands. The One who brings deliverance to the downcast also dispenses tears to their eyes. The joy bestowed by the Holy One, blessed be He, on that widow made her eyes fill with tears. She wept out of happiness and rejoiced as her tears fell.

The human eye is small in volume, but the tears shed by that woman from the time her son was taken from her were uncountable. The wonder is that her eyes did not dry up and that she still had tears left to shed on that happy day when God had mercy on her and sent her a bundle of letters all written by her son. Amidst all her joyful weeping she forgot to ask what was in them. This is hard for people like us to understand, but life is stronger than logic. In the euphoria of receiving letters from her son she forgot to ask what he had written in them.

Bilhah, having heard from her father that letters from Dan had arrived, was very soon at Dan's mother's side. Had Bilhah not indicated to her that the letters should be opened, the whole night would have passed without knowing what Dan had written.

The two of them went to Dovidl the scrivener. He could read all kinds of writing. He was the one who taught the boys of Buczacz how to write, and also the one who read to the illiterate whatever they asked him to read.

They came to Dovidl in the evening just as he had returned from the evening service in the beit midrash and was getting ready to go to bed. He always went to bed early, unlike most people who come back from the evening service and sit down to supper and stuff themselves with radishes and onions and go to sleep on a full stomach. He would eat a heavy midday meal which sufficed for supper too, so that when he returned from the evening service in the beit midrash he did not have to bother making supper. The choice hours of the evening, when he was still wide awake, were thus available to him to do whatever he wished. Coarse people fill those hours with eating and drinking, talking, gossip and slander, but an astute person uses them wisely. Dovidl did not see himself as particularly astute but he was certainly no fool. He put on his greatcoat, lit the oil lantern, and sat down at the table to read. Before he became adept at writing letters he would pore over various epistolary collections. But when he became an expert at letter writing, he read more uplifting things, books that served to remind him that good people could do good things, and writings from which he could derive moral instruction that would bring joy to his heart and peace to his soul.

I will not elaborate on this edifying material. You can find it in the supplements to the annual almanacs that Joseph Perl put out. These supplements were called "The Almanac of the Heart," and anyone who reads them will gain much spiritual uplift from the lucid and instructive articles and stories they contain on Jewish law and lore.

So Dan's mother and Bilhah went to see Dovidl the scrivener. They explained to him why they had come. Dan's mother had received letters from her son and she wanted to know what was in them. Dovidl smiled knowingly and said, Yes, letters from Dan have indeed arrived.

Dovidl the scrivener had already heard about the letters and these silly women thought they were telling him something new. He called out to his wife, Ḥannah Hentsha, bring me my eyeglasses.

She went and got them. They were on the table inside R. Yossel's book *Faithful Messenger*, a book that was always before him because it was so full of wise and instructive sayings that feed the mind and replenish the soul.

Now even though there were many letters in the bundle, they were all the same. They were all written in the same style, only the dates were different. Dan was clearly more skilled with needle and thread than with pen and ink. All the letters were written to Dan's mother, none to Bilhah. It was not appropriate for a boy to write letters to a girl, and this couple, even though they had promised to marry one another, had not written tenaim. If you page through the Book of Hebrew Letters you will find the proper form missives should take with examples in Hebrew and German by Moshe Shmuel Neumann or the well-known poet Shalom Hakohen or by the renowned Meir Halevi Letteris, but you will not find even one facsimile of a letter from a Jewish boy to a Jewish girl who was not betrothed to him.

Dan did not write many letters. His hand was more skillful with needle and thread than with pen and ink. From the outset of his army service he was more adept at handling sword and spear than a scrivener's pen. Nevertheless he did not forget to write to his mother. He wrote to her before every festival and Rosh Hashanah, even at the Christian New Year, when he saw some of his fellow soldiers who knew how to write sending letters to their parents.

All Dan's letters were written in the same style, the way Dovidl the scrivener had taught him. Dovidl was the first to teach writing in Buczacz. He had studied at the school of Joseph Perl in Tarnopol and commended himself for that because Perl was believed to an expert in the art of writing. Some devoutly religious families sent their sons to Dovidl to learn how to write, but they stipulated that he not infuse them with heretical ideas. Dovidl is said to have answered them: "For teaching heretical ideas I charge an extra fee."

How were the letters written? The first line had the name of God in big letters in the center. On the second line was written: "To my revered, humble and beloved Mother, *most blessed of women in the tent*." The third line said: "I wish to inform her that her son, whom she reared and nurtured and brought him to this day, is well." The fourth line said: "May the beneficent God grant life and goodness and let us hear only good tidings." The fifth line said: "These are the words of your son who every day hopes for your well being and happiness." Following all that came his name, printed, because he was not a practiced writer and could not write in cursive script. Even so his mother remarked that though she was completely uneducated, if she saw a letter from her son in a dream she would recognize the letters of his name.

Within two or three years, Dan's mother got to know by heart the content of every single letter, not only those she had already received but the ones that continued to arrive. As noted, all of them were written in the same style. Yet in her eyes each one was new, as if there were things in it that none of its predecessors had. Even Bilhah, who Dan's mother permitted to read his letters to her, found something new in each letter that arrived and she read each one enthusiastically, as if she were reading something brand-new.

Dan's mother sits and caresses her son's letter. So many things has he put down on a sheet of paper no bigger than the page of a teḥinah book. She weeps for him like a woman saying teḥines. But a woman's eyes are large, and she wants to see more than what they take in. Since the field of her vision is limited, her ears do what her eyes cannot. She hands the letter to Bilhah saying, Here's Dan's letter. Read it to me again so I can hear what he writes.

Bilhah grabs the letter eagerly as if she had been waiting all her life for this moment. Dan's mother strokes the cat lying in her lap, fixes her eyes on Bilhah and listens attentively to every word coming out of Bilhah's mouth. She reflects in amazement, Here I am sitting in my house and my son Dan sits at the other end of the world. If he would want to talk to me, his voice, however loud, would not reach my ears. But if he takes a sheet of imperial stationery and a quill and dips the quill in ink and writes me a letter, then I can sit and listen to every single word that he wrote. Were I not so anxious to hear his voice I would say that writing is better than speaking. A letter that he writes I can listen to ten times, even a hundred times. As many times as I want.

Here I connect these thoughts of Dan's mother to things she did not say but which amplify her thoughts about this matter of writing. Consider the power of the letters of the alphabet as they appear on a page. They are tiny as peas, and in Dan's case as beans. Only a trained reader can tell one character from another. They all sit on the page immobile and mute. But when a girl like Bilhah looks at them, the letters immediately start talking and reveal to us what is happening in far off places. The letters form words that sometimes make us happy and sometimes make us sad. When we want to hear more we sit and stare at them. Then the letters become clever and pretend to be dumb. They follow the dictum that silence is golden. For his part, Dan serves the emperor and wants to tell about what he hears, what the emperor says to his subordinates and what his subordinates submissively reply, and so on. But the individual letters of the alphabet become humble and say to him, It is sufficient that you write what Dovidl the scrivener taught you to write.

Alas, poor Dan. Had he not been suddenly taken away to the army he would have studied for another year or two and learned how to write more and better letters to his mother.

Dan's mother says affectionately, That blasted Dovidl. He may be a skinny runt with chubby little cheeks. But when he gets his hands on a student, in a year or two he teaches him how to write, even how to write a letter that goes from one end of the earth to the other. I was foolish for trying to stop Dan when he began studying with Dovidl. I said to him, Stop doing what your forbears never did. For the good money you waste on tuition every month I could buy you every day a cup of milk with licorice and a bun with sesame seeds, and you would eat and drink and put on some weight and start looking like somebody successful. Tell me what pleasure you get from scribbling on a piece of paper. Even if you learned how to write and became a scrivener like Dovidl himself, what honor would you bring to yourself? Would the parnasim let you wear a shtreimel on the Sabbath? Would the shamash give you a seat in the synagogue on the eastern wall? Would the gabbai call you up for maftir? Look at Dovidl. On the Sabbath he wears a spodik, just like all the other ignoramuses. In the synagogue he stands by the door with all the undesirables in town. And if once or twice a year he gets called up to the Torah, why do they call him? For the pittance he will pledge to contribute. Now I see how smart Dan was to go and learn how to write and not listen to his mother. His letters keep me alive.

Dan's mother sits and strokes the cat lying in her lap and relates to Bilhah how Dovidl taught Dan how to write. She did not know that Dan had once told Bilhah all that, though Bilhah was very happy to hear anything at all about Dan, and she listened intently.

Dan's mother says, Sit down, Bilhah, and I will tell you some amazing things. You ask how Dan got to learn the art of writing. For three months, Dovidl taught him how to make ink and sharpen quills. I had a big fight with him about that because he took all the good feathers to Dovidl. After that Dovidl taught him how to hold the rule and mark off the lines with a stylus so the letters could all stand the way they like, in a row. After Dan acquired these skills Dovidl began to teach him the art of penmanship. How to hold the quill and dip it in the ink, and how much ink to draw, because if too much is drawn the paper will get spattered, and if too little, the quill will scratch. He continued teaching him until he knew how to write the letters of the alphabet and became adept at joining them together. Had he not been sent to the end of the earth he would be as good as Dovidl himself. But I am amazed at you, Bilhah. Who taught you how to write?

Bilhah replies that she never learned how to write, only how to read. But she never said who taught her. You and I know that it was Dan.

Dan's mother continues, I am also amazed that whenever a letter from Dan arrives, you are the first to know. Are you told this in a dream?

The truth was that there were times when Bilhah did dream that a letter from Dan had come, and it was so. But most of the dreams were wrong because then when Bilhah went to Dan's mother, she found no letter from him. So how did she know? She knew because there was a man in town named Mendel who was appointed by the head of the post office to be responsible for all letters sent to Jews there. Bilhah paid him for every letter he told her about. He did the same thing with the merchants in town: he would tell one that a letter had arrived for another or would give the letters for one to another, and so on, all for a fixed fee. The question is properly asked whether Bilhah was not concerned that Mendel would tell her father about the arrangement? After all, her father did not look kindly on her dealings with Dan's mother.

14

But there are times when there is no mail from Dan. When he goes out on training exercises, there is no postal service, and even if there were, a soldier has no time for personal matters. The emperor takes precedence. When training is over Dan returns to his barracks and again takes quill in hand to write to his mother. He writes things that Dovidl never taught him, like an explanation why he could not write to her because he was camped out in a field while they waged war on peace, that is, war games. Dan's mother sits with Bilhah beside her, and they both pore over the fresh contents of the letter. Bilhah holds the letter as Dan's mother sits stroking the cat lying on her lap and warming her cold chapped hands in its fur. The cat blinks and closes her green eyes as if to say that neither her mistress nor her neighbor nor Dan and the war he waged on peace are of any interest to her. Suddenly Dan's mother looks up at Bilhah and asks, Have you ever heard of a war on peace, what it is, and what was Dan doing camped out in a field? Does the emperor not have houses for his soldiers that Dan has to stay out in a field where there are all kinds of crawling things that no one wants to be near?

Bilhah answers, I think the army is playing at war the same way small children play. There are very many soldiers, because they take them from every town, and they spread out all over the field for their game.

Dan's mother hears this and fancies that she understands it all. But though her mind was put at rest, she was nevertheless still apprehensive. Today Dan emerges unscathed, but tomorrow who knows? Sometimes war starts out frivolously and ends badly. Bilhah has the same concerns as she gets up to take her leave. She needs to think things through, but not in the presence of others where her thoughts can be read on her face. Dan's mother also gets up and says to her, Bilhah, you're leaving? You just got here and now you're going?

She has no idea that two hours have gone by since Bilhah came. The cat lets out a loud "Meow," having been thrown off her mistress's lap when she got up.

It was good for Dan's mother to sit on that comfortable chair, her feet resting on a footstool, the cat in her lap. Were she one of the wealthy women in place of whose sons Dan was taken, she would like them be sitting with her husband in a house filled with all kinds of finery. She would have no worries about her son, who would be sitting all day in the beit midrash studying the holy Torah and attaining a good reward in the Hereafter for every word coming out of his mouth. Even in this world he would get along very well, eating and sleeping at regular times and getting married at the proper age. All this while Dan is out in the field under a blazing sun, living among the gentiles and not hearing a Jewish word, while his mother toils for the wealthy women. For one she prepares a chicken for cooking, for another she plucks feathers for the pillows and comforters that will be used by the very son who was substituted for Dan.

Alas, Master of the Universe, let me not speak rashly. You certainly know how to run the world, but with that woman and her son I am not sure You did well. Dan's mother is unschooled, dumb as an animal. But the thoughts in her head are not too different from what we sometimes hear from the philosophers, whose wisdom exceeds their piety. But the philosophers and their thoughts are not our concern here, so let us leave them and return to the telling of actual events as they proceeded to unfold.

I do not have a lot to tell, but this much I can relate. One day, Dovidl the scrivener came to Godil the tailor to discuss clothing. He wanted to know how much money a person of his means would need to have a handsome suit for Sabbath and festivals made for him. His old one was not fit even for weekdays and his wife was tired of mending it. The truth is Dovidl could not afford to have a new suit made for him and Godil did not repair old ones. Dovidl simply thought that a person needing a new suit should get a tailor's opinion.

What was Godil's counsel, and what came of it? Something quite significant, and not because of Godil but because of Dovidl. Dovidl would teach Godil's daughter how to write. When Godil first heard the idea he burst out laughing, and when he finally stopped laughing he called to his wife, Come over here and listen to something so funny that I cannot laugh anymore. But in the end he accepted it. By the time Dovidl left Godil had agreed.

This is how matters took their course. Dovidl said to Godil, Look, your daughter will one day be betrothed, and it could be to a boy from another town. A groom who lives in a different town than the bride would write letters to her. He would write to your daughter, and she would have to answer him, letter for letter. And so, who would write that letter? Would it be you, Godil? Why, you do not even know which end of the quill to dip in the ink. You would certainly need someone else. And who would that be? Someone who would have to impersonate on the page the authentic feelings of a pure maiden's heart. And even if such a person could do that, it would be apparent that it was a man's handwriting and not a woman's. But this Dovidl, who stands before you in a worn-out suit that can be replaced only with a shabbier one, this Dovidl has an idea.

Who would believe that this artful Dovidl succeeded in persuading a man as stubborn as Godil to make a suit for him at no cost if Bilhah could learn how to move the quill across the paper. The truth is Bilhah had no need to learn how to write. Her heart belonged to Dan and no other suitor would claim her attention, and she did not need letters. But she reasoned that if she would know how to write, Dan's mother would not have to ask Dovidl the scrivener to write to Dan. She could write him herself.

During all the years that Dan was in the army, no one ever found any fault with him. When it became known that he was a consummate tailor, the officers began to bring him to their homes to fix women's dresses and even to make new ones. We used to think that all fine apparel came from the big cities, but now we hear that high-ranking officers bring apprentices of Buczacz artisans to their homes to fashion garments for their wives and children. They wrote in his dossier that he was a master craftsman. This was made known by Dan in a letter to his mother, written for him by a friend. He further stated there that when he would be safely back in Buczacz, all the wealthy women there would have their dresses custom-made for them by him. The emphasis on "custom-made" was intentional on Dan's part because there were wealthy women in Buczacz who complained that Nushi the seamstress did not know how make dresses according to their specifications.

In short, Dan served in the army until his term of conscription was completed. Through God's mercy there was peace in the world and kings waged no wars. Before he entered the army Dan's hands had shed no blood and that was still true when he left.

In a letter, Dan informed his mother that his term of service in the imperial army was over and he would be coming home very soon. Each day he waited for the moment when he would see her once again face to face, hale and healthy. His mother, too, awaited the day when she would see him before her, and Bilhah likewise. Their anticipation and yearning were intense and were mitigated only by talk.

15

Dan laid down his arms and set forth with a heart full of hope and anticipation, along with letters testifying to his integrity and his talent. Anticipation and hope are commendable, especially for one who has a skill, but a bit of money also is no less helpful, especially to one who is about to be married. But money is something Dan did not have. His plan was to return home on foot, and on the way he inquired at the homes of the nobility to see if they needed an expert tailor to mend a garment or make a new dress. He did find clothes to mend and new dresses to make, but not the time required to write letters to his mother, nor pen and paper with which to write them. When there was no work, he was not inclined to stop and write letters, for letter writing is a laborious matter. It requires focused attention, writing instruments and a comfortable place to sit and write. A preoccupied traveler will not delay his journey for such things. Indeed, sometimes the person arrives before the letter.

I now leave off telling about the son who is not yet back with his mother and turn to the mother who is anticipating his arrival.

Dan's mother sits in her hut behind the river Strypa and gazes at the flowing water, thinking about her son. He should have arrived by now, yet he has not shown up. The whole time he served the emperor he wrote to his mother regularly, and now that the emperor has allowed him to return to her he has neither come back nor written. It is as if his mother has died and there is no need to keep sending her letters. In her suffering and pain the mother screams, "Dan, my son. Your mother is alive. She is dying to see you, my son, my Dan." Bilhah hears Dan's mother's cries and tries to calm her by talking to her. She says the same things the mother said but with different words and in a different tone of voice. Dan's mother howls and wails while

Bilhah's speech is soft and delicate. In both voices one can hear their respective bewilderment.

But not all moments in time are identical. There are days when Bilhah does not go to see Dan's mother. People who are not regular visitors at her parents' home have come over and sit for a long time over a glass or two of whisky and a plateful of onion and pepper crackers that her mother bakes. When they remark on how good the crackers are, Bilhah's mother gestures toward Bilhah to hint that they are her handiwork. This is, of course, an out-and-out lie, but her mother wants to show Bilhah in a good light, for these people are matchmakers and if they so desire, they could produce a good suitor for Bilhah. This would not be the suitor that Bilhah would want, but Bilhah is the quiet sort who does not like to provoke her parents. So she assists them in receiving the guests even as her heart is set on Dan. They could bring her all the prospective husbands in the world and her heart would not be swayed from Dan. Helping with guests is one reason why Bilhah does not visit Dan's mother. The other is because her parents often keep her from going. They do not consider it appropriate for an eligible young woman to keep visiting the mother of a soldier.

Dan's mother goes about among her neighbors and lays her troubles before them. The pessimists among them tell her that only something bad can account for Dan's delay. He must have done something for which he is being punished and that is why he is detained. The optimists tell her that any delay is due to something good. Dan has surely caught the eye of his superiors and they want to reward his talents with a promotion. He will come home this year or next bedecked with medals. Dan's mother listens to all this and replies to each group accordingly. The pessimists she mocks by telling them that Dan will give the lie to what they have said. "My son Dan is a good man, with a good heart, and he does good things. You can say any nasty things you want but his superiors love him. Why has he not come back? If I knew why, I would not be so broken hearted." To the optimists she replies, "You tell me that any delay is due to something good. What good is a delay if I die in the meantime?" Likewise Bilhah, who thinks to herself that even if they make him a sergeant it will not be good for her. And here Bilhah has said something significant. Just how significant she did not grasp, for she was emotionally bound to Dan and she was having a hard time because she missed him so much. Let us rely on God who guides the steps of man to guide Dan's steps and bring him back to where he belongs.

16

A month went by and then another, and Dan had not returned to his mother. No letter from him had come nor anything that could account for his delay. His mother started having nightmares, and even by day she saw terrifying visions. Bilhah too was ill at ease. Her heart told her that something bad had happened to Dan on the way even though she knew that the country was now at peace. The roads were free of robbers and murderers ever since Austria took control of the region, and even some of the forests where murderers hid out were now clear of them. A few murderers were still at large though, and hopefully Dan did not fall into the hands of one of them or of some robber.

Dan's mother goes about town with all kinds of horrendous tales that her dreams told, like the one in which her son fell into the hands of a she-demon in the guise of a noblewoman. But in Buczacz, belief in demons was thoroughly repudiated, and so there was no pity at all for the unfortunate woman. She was roundly rebuked and warned to talk no more of such things as defy reason. And yet the Talmud does speak of demons and spirits, like the story of Jonathan the demon or the one about the two spirits conversing in a cemetery. But talmudic times were different from ours. Then there were great rabbis who were like angels in their holiness, and demons were arrayed against them, as Scripture says, *God has made one no less than the other.* But we today are godforsaken and desolate, and our worthless deeds get done without the assistance of demonic powers.

The unhappy woman kept her visions to herself and spoke of them no more. Instead she began to knock on the doors of the homes of the parnasim to ask them why her son had not yet returned. They gave her answers that really were not answers. They were too busy dealing with governmental affairs and had no time for the woman and her appeals. She went back to them with the same question, and they gave her the same answers. She urged them to write to the Emperor and ask him what was keeping her son from coming back to his mother. The parnasim met her with laughter. We're sorry, they said, but actually we're too busy to laugh.

Understanding now that the parnasim would do nothing for her, the boy's mother began to entreat others. Those who had the time stood and listened patiently to her complaints, those in a hurry walked on by. Despairing of the townspeople, she went out and stood at the crossroads asking, Maybe you have seen my son? Maybe you know where he is? Maybe he told you when he would return to his mother?

She even went up to passing coaches and wagons and said to the passengers, I am the mother of Dan Hoffmann. Have you possibly come across him on the way? Perhaps he has given you a letter for his mother?

If the person she encountered was nice, he would listen, ask her for details, and offer her words of sympathy and encouragement: Your son is being detained for a good reason. He will almost certainly show up today or tomorrow.

If the person was callous, he would scold her: Look, if you've had too much to drink, go sleep it off and stop bothering people who need to get where they're going.

With gentiles, it depended. If he was a prankster, at the exact moment when she was up against the coach, he would whistle to his horses to move forward. When they started, the poor woman would fall, her hands and feet splayed out on the ground, the driver looking on in glee. If he were just plain cruel, he would lash her face with the whip in his hand. It is truly a miracle that she did not lose her mind. But Bilhah, to her credit, stood by Dan's mother throughout all her travails. She even took her to R. Abush to seek counsel from him. R. Abush was among the richest of the great merchants in the region and a clever man. One day when R. Abush was in town they came to him and Dan's mother told him her troubles. R. Abush listened to her and asked, Why have you come to me? I have given over the affairs of the town to those who think they are smarter than I. Go to them. They'll tell you what to do.

She replied, A letter from R. Abush to the emperor would get a quick response.

R. Abush heard this and was silent. R. Abush sat silent, and the woman stood there in her pain. Now R. Abush had a relative who had been an agunah for several years. All the great rabbis could find no legal remedy that would allow her to remarry. Upon hearing that R. Abush was in town, the woman came to him to ask him to get involved in her case. When she saw the boy's mother standing there motionless, she drove her away with harsh words.

Seeing that all avenues of appeal led nowhere, she went, accompanied by Bilhah, to the rabbi. She stationed herself between his house and the synagogue. That was where the rabbi walked daily to think through the answers he would give to the questions of halakhah that were put to him. Noticing two women standing in his way, he veered aside toward the wall. Whereupon the widow exclaimed, Rabbi! You see the misfortune of every unhappy woman. Why can you not see the misery of a desperate mother bereft of her only son, whom the heads of the town handed over to the imperial army in place of their sons?

And she continued, Let the good rabbi see the plight of this girl here who stands like a newlywed bride whose bridal canopy has been torn down. Had they not taken my son to the army she would already be married to him, and I would be favored with some wonderful grandchildren.

Pity for the mother overcame the rabbi, and he sent for the parnasim.

The parnasim arrived at the rabbi's house baffled. He was not wont to waste time on matters that did not pertain to Torah unless it was something truly important. Still, even if this was a Torah matter or something truly important—why all the haste?

The rabbi understood what they were thinking. He scrutinized them for a few moments and said, Look, you are busy and so am I. Let's cut out the talk and do something. From what that woman says, whose only son you took and handed over to the imperial army, I understand that his term of service is over, and he is free to go home, and he should have returned by now, and he hasn't. So you have to bring this to the attention of the court officials in this district, and they will bring the matter to the officers of the army.

The parnasim heard all this and were about to quibble with the rabbi for saying that they took an orphan boy, the only son of a widowed mother, and handed him over to the army in place of their own sons. The rabbi understood what they wanted to do, and he said to them, Listen, gentlemen. Now is not the time to debate fine points. Now is the time to do something. This woman is desperately anxious to see her only son. I am asking you gentlemen to please go back and write letters this very day. R. Moshe Alshikh, of blessed memory, when he would lament the destruction of Jerusalem, used to say, Gather round all you sons of Jacob and listen: because of your sins has your mother been cast away give honor to the Lord, your God. And we—how shall we lament the recent destruction? Because of our sins have our sons been cast away.

The parnasim were unnerved by the rabbi's insistence and they hurried to write the letter. Days passed and no answer came. The officials had their hands full and had no time for things that did not advance the state's interests or their own.

One day, two distinguished merchants from another town made a special trip to Buczacz to confer with the rabbi. From some things they said the rabbi deduced that they were held in some regard by certain government officials. He related to them the mother's predicament and asked them to bring it up to the officials. And this they did.

Some time later documents from the military administration arrived at the offices of the imperial court. The officials there sent them on to the head of the region. He in turn sent them to the official of the court in Buczacz, who then sent them to the parnasim and other leaders of the Jewish community. The court official who delivered the papers read to them their contents: one Dan Hoffmann, a native of the town of Buczacz in eastern Galicia, which belongs to such-and-such region, served in such-and-such regiment of the army from such-and-such day of such-and-such month of such-and-such year, and in such-and-such month, on such-and-such day of the month His Imperial and Royal Majesty the Emperor granted his officers permission to release him from the army. He then read from an additional document which stated that this Dan Hoffmann, whom His Imperial Majesty the Kaiser had consented to release from military service, declared to the imperial officials that he would be returning to his hometown Buczacz in eastern Galicia, which is part of such-and such region, and so on, and there is no doubt whatsoever that he has gone there, and it is attested in his file that he is en route to his hometown Buczacz.

The parnasim sent for his mother. She came and heard what the documents said. Her voice resounded through the communal chamber as she shrieked, If he has come back, why isn't he here? And if he is not here, then where is he? Every question has its own validity; her questions certainly did.

The mother went around among people and melted their hearts with her weeping. There was not a person in town before whom she did not weep for the son who went away and did not return. Bilhah too did not withhold her tears, at first privately, later in public. It was unheard of in Buczacz that a maiden would shed tears for a young man not related to her, to whom she was not betrothed and with whom she had not written prenuptial tenaim. All this notwithstanding, there were women among her neighbors who disregarded that fact and saw only her tears. Those good neighbors told Bilhah it was not good for her to sit and cry. If he hasn't come back, he will, they said. If not today, then tomorrow. He will suddenly show up and you will both be happy. Over against them were those mean-spirited neighbors who told her that if he did not come back it was because he didn't want to, and it was a known fact that whoever went to the army left not only his Judaism behind but his conscience, too. From now on, they said to her, the first man who comes to your father and tells him that he is ready to stand under the marriage canopy with his daughter, hurry and do it before people start talking. This is what is meant by the saying, May the Lord save us from the hands of Esau and the voice of Jacob. But Bilhah's integrity and her faith in Dan enabled her to reject this counsel. Her soul was bound to his, as his was to hers.

Around that time, her father arranged a match for her with a fine young man whose father was both an artisan and a householder. Her parents liked the young man but Bilhah dared to tell them that she did not. Neither he nor anyone else. I want only Dan, she declared. Her father's tirades and her mother's tears were of no avail in getting her to change her mind. Bilhah had spoken and there was nothing more to be said.

The story of the soldier who disappeared became a topic of conversation among people. Not because of the aching mother's constant weeping or the anguish of the girl who was so attached to him, but because of the boy himself. After all, it was known that he had set out for his hometown and several months had passed and he had not yet returned. Searches were made and inquiries conducted in all the localities surrounding Buczacz, in every town and every village. Even the imperial officials and the head of the district were on the alert for the missing soldier. A year went by and then another, and nothing turned up. There were, in fact, people who remembered that about a year or two ago they had run into a military man who said he was from Buczacz and was on his way there. If we knew he was being sought, they said, we would have paid more attention to him. Since we didn't know they were looking for him, we didn't give much thought to him. More specific details came from a textile merchant from Bohemia who made the rounds of the towns and the villages. He related that he had encountered a young tailor returning from the army. The boy bemoaned the fact that after all his years of army service he was not able to bring back a gift for his mother. The merchant had suggested that he go into the village and ask the mistress of the village if she needed a tailor, for she had bought fourteen cubits of blue velvet from him. What the name of that lady was and the village she lived in I cannot now remember.

This report of the merchant yielded more information than the documents of the imperial officials, but it added nothing to determining the whereabouts of the man who disappeared. It served only to intensify the mother's torment, for if there was indeed someone who saw her son on his way to Buczacz, then he was very nearly home. So why did he not arrive? And if he hasn't arrived, then where is he? Again, the same unanswered questions.

The urgency of the matter faded from the public mind. But in the mother's mind and in Bilhah's mind it was as sharply felt as ever, asserting itself anew every passing day. In earlier times, when the boy's mother would pour out her heart to people, they would stop and listen and say a word or two to her; now no one paid her any attention. This was not, God forbid, because there was no more pity in Buczacz; but new troubles came to claim people's attention; those of the unhappy woman were by now commonplace.

The unhappy woman now felt forlorn and abandoned. Not only by others but by her very self. She stopped cooking, stopped making her bed, mending her dress, and bringing her torn shoes to the cobbler. She did not even launder the kerchief on her head or change it for a fresh one. She began to decline, and declined so precipitously that she resembled a troll or one of the crones or demonesses that are found in Germany.

Her deterioration was not only physical but also emotional. One cannot gauge just how low a person can sink when God, heaven forbid, takes away His mind. Everyone began to ignore her, perfunctorily tossing a coin or two at her. Women discharged their obligation by bringing out to her the leftovers of their cooking or a bowl of soup, an old dress or a worn out shoe. Had Bilhah not protected her, children would have thrown stones and dirt at her and called her crazy, the way people treat those who are despondent and have descended into melancholia. Such individuals, when children throw stones at them and call them crazy, eventually lose their mind. They wander aimlessly through town in madness and come to a bad end.

Yet during the summer Bilhah would take her to the Strypa and bathe her, dress her in a clean frock and clean stockings, and put a clean kerchief on her head. She would also re-arrange the straw of her bed, and if it were rotting, would change it for fresh straw, thus keeping her free of filth and decay. The good things that Bilhah did for the unfortunate woman were seen by her parents as bad, for by taking care of her she was in effect proclaiming some kinship with her, and there was in fact no familial tie between them. So it was as if she were saying to the whole world that what she was doing for the madwoman was for the sake of her son.

17

Three years went by, and nothing came of all the searches and inquiries other than reams of paper, the voluminous correspondence sent from Buczacz to the head of the district and from the head of the district to various officials in several localities. All that paper became in time the pages we find in the bindings of the Talmud and other books. When the government offices became cluttered with old documents and space was needed for the new ones, the old ones were sold to storekeepers who resold them to bookbinders. The bookbinders would insert a sheet before the first and after the last pages of a book and then paste those sheets inside the front and back covers that bound the whole book together. There are elders in Buczacz whose excellent German was learned from those pages inside the binding. And there are elders in Buczacz whose proficiency at composing letters to the law courts was acquired from those pages.

Another year went by, and nothing turned up. If we count the time from when the letter arrived stating that Dan was released from army service and was returning to Buczacz, we would find that six years had passed. Why, then, had he not returned? Some suggested that he was eaten by a wild animal, or that he was murdered, or that he had fallen in with a band of robbers, since one who is accustomed to carrying arms, even if he has laid them down, will be easily attracted to such types. Some opined that priests had seized him and sent him to Rome where he became a priest. There were many conjectures and not a shred of truth to any of them.

18

But the truth was soon to be revealed, and from a source quite unexpected. There was a house in Buczacz set aside for the head of the officials dispatched there by the Crown to oversee the affairs of the town and the district. The Crown had just replaced the old head official with a new one, possibly because, as some said, he was suspected of having accepted bribes. This could hardly have been the reason, for if officials were replaced because they took bribes not one of them would be left anywhere in the country. Obviously, there was some other reason for the change. Since we are not conversant with the state's procedures we shall talk no more of them and return to our story.

The new district head arrived in Buczacz and was installed in the house set aside for him. He took one look at it and wrinkled up his nose in scorn to indicate his dissatisfaction with what he was given. It was probably not the district head who was unhappy but his wife. From the moment she entered the house she did not stop complaining. She found the floor crooked, the ceiling falling down, the walls cracked, and the oven venting its heat outside and its smoke into the house. The district head wrote to the owner of the house but got no reply. He wrote again with the same result. When he wrote still again, an answer came: on his next visit to town the owner would come and see what needed to be done. This owner was the Count Potocki.

Potocki arrived whip in hand and head bedecked, and with a tiny motion of his finger acknowledged the district head with a curt hello. In our eyes the district head is a man of some standing; in the eyes of Potocki he was nothing. After inspecting the rooms Potocki said, I am surprised that the district head is unhappy with his living quarters. My horses would be happy to live in a place like this. Stung by the Count's words, the district head announced that he was moving out. It was a statement he could not retract.

That was a serious error on his part. He thought he would find a nicer house without knowing that in Buczacz the houses were small and had few rooms and, besides, were completely occupied. There were homes in which several families lived; not everyone had the good fortune to have a private home for his family. Though it was difficult, the district head did succeed in finding a new house outside of town. It belonged to a man from Buczacz who had gotten rich from selling pigs to the army, and it was still being built. The district head and his wife moved in and the contractors were still busy working.

One day, the district head went in to one of the rooms where a Jewish craftsman was installing an oven. As he watched him work, the official nodded approvingly and with great satisfaction. He began to think to himself: most Jews find ways to go around the government's laws, and we would never catch them if it weren't for the few honest ones among them who turn in the cheaters. Now that I have here this Jew who looks like a trustworthy man, I will start a conversation with him and find out what is going on in town.

The district head began asking the oven maker if he was from the surrounding area and other such questions. After a while, he asked him what was new in town. The oven maker answered him shrewdly, What is new in town I do not know. But I do know what is new in the village.

I can see that you have something to tell me that's worth hearing, the district head said. The oven maker replied politely and respectfully, If my lord, the wise and powerful district head says so, it must be true.

Put your tools down and tell me what you saw.

Whatever my lord, the wise and powerful district head says, I will do.

My friend, stop with the words and start talking. What village are you referring to and what did you see there?

But I fear reprisal.

What did you see there that you fear reprisal?

Were not my lord the head of the town and the countryside around it, I would bite my tongue and not say a word about what I saw.

The district head looked at him sternly and saw that there were wounds on his face.

Why are there wounds on your face, and what is that scar on your cheek?

The oven maker rubbed his hand over his cheek once or twice and said, I did not know that the scar could still be seen. I got it from one quick peek that I took.

I can see, my friend, that you will do anything not to tell me what you saw there.

If I did not have this scar and my bones were not shaking, I would say that the thing that I saw was in a dream and that it was impossible that it was real.

Stop with the words. Put the tool down and start talking.

The oven maker looked around not once but twice and began to tremble. The district head said to him, Do not worry. I am the one demanding that you speak. The oven maker then said, Before the district head asked me to fix the oven, I was working in the house of a noblewoman in a certain village. By accident, I entered one of the rooms in her house that was always locked but on that day was open. I looked in and saw something that was clearly there but that I knew was logically impossible to see. What did I see? A human-like creature that was neither male nor female. I could not tell if it was a Jew or a gentile. It looked like a woman because it had long hair like a woman's, with braids and bows, and it had on a blue velvet dress. It looked like a man because there was hair on the cheeks like a beard, or maybe it was not a beard but long hair hanging down. It looked like a Jew because of the pain I could see in the eyes. And the person was tied to the wall with an iron chain. I stood aghast and trembling and could not move. The lady came and saw me standing and gaping. She raised the whip in her hand and gave me a lash across my face, crying, Jew, get out of here and be on your way! I fell backward and then started to leave. The lady locked the room, pulled me back, and said, You saw this, you got this whip. You speak about it, you die.

The district head asked, What village were you working in and what was the lady's name? The oven maker told him. The district head's eyes blazed like the fire of Gehinnom and he screamed, You lie, Jew, you lie! A very expensive flower pot stood in the window and the district head grabbed it and hurled it in anger. The pot shattered, the flower was ruined and the soil spilled out onto the floor, but the district official's anger did not abate. The oven maker wanted to leave but the official screamed at him to stop. The oven maker stood, awaiting his fate. The district official went back and forth, not quite knowing what he would do. Get back to work, he said to him.

The oven maker returned to work and began to ponder, What is it with these gentiles? If you watch what they do, they smack you. If you talk to them, they get angry. If you keep quiet, they tell you to speak. What are you supposed to do to get along with them?

That very day, the regional head came to town. The district head went to him and told him the whole story. The regional head heard it and was dumbfounded. The two men sat and looked at one another.

The regional head said to the district head, You know, we cannot leave this matter alone. We have to do something. But tell me, did you ever think that a woman who turned away bigwigs would keep a young man in her house? But why would she tie him to the wall with an iron chain? Is he some kind of stud horse? Or is this simply a matter of womanly jealousy? What did the Jew tell you? That he thought the young man looked like a Jew. In the name of all the saints, that is a lie, a complete lie.

The two officials sat together and recalled things that happened half a lifetime ago, when they were both young men and that lady was a young woman. Many important noblemen courted her, but she turned them all away and remained unmarried. Now she has gotten on in years and has lost all her holdings, except the little village in which she lives. Its fields yield more thorns than wheat or rye. The regional head said to the district head, You know, bad luck has brought me here. This is a matter I'd much rather have my enemies handle. But since it's been put in my hands, I cannot excuse myself and leave it alone.

The district head replied, True, you cannot leave it alone. There has to be an investigation.

Did we not say that the Jew who told you the story said that the person he saw tied to the wall was a Jew? Tell me, is it possible that she could actually have chosen a Jew?

I can already see how much anger and jealousy and hatred there will be when the noblemen, whom this woman rejected, find out that she has taken a Jew for herself.

Yes, and when I look at these Jews with their beards and side curls, I am amazed that a woman of her class would even get near one of them.

You know, I regret the conversation I had with that Jewish oven maker.

The head of the region laughed: You regret the conversation with the Jew. And the conversation with me you do not regret? Either way, we have to do something. I still do not know what that is, but it's clear that we have to get moving. Because she knows that a Jew witnessed her in her degradation, and she is already planning to cover it up. We had better get going before it's too late.

The regional head sat down and composed a letter to the chief of police in which he instructed him to take twelve of his best men and hurry to the village and to the house of that lady. There he should go through every room in the house and look in every nook and cranny. He gave the letter to a messenger and dispatched him. Hurry, he ordered, and do not let anything or anyone delay you. And do not tell anyone where you have come from or where you're going. And do not come back here until the chief of police has told you to. The messenger ran off and when he reached the chief of the police, gave him the letter. The chief read it and whistled loudly, the way one whistles when hearing something astounding. He promptly selected twelve policemen, each of whom had a record of distinguished service. Within forty-eight hours they arrived at their destination and surrounded the lady's courtyard. Upon seeing them, the lady went out and greeted them mincingly. To what do I owe the honor of this visit of the esteemed chief of the district police to the courtyard of my house? Would you and your boys pay me the honor of coming inside and enjoying something to eat and a glass of wine? To which the chief of police replied, If it would please the good and noble lady to remain standing just where she is, I will ask one of the boys here to bring her a chair, and if it would please the good lady to have a seat, let her do us the favor of giving me the keys to all the rooms of her mansion. For why would I want to ask the boys to break down the doors?

The lady's expression changed and she began speaking harshly: How dare you come into my courtyard without my permission? The chief of police answered, I already have permission from the emperor and his laws. We are here in the name of the emperor and the law.

The lady screamed, No! You are not officers of the emperor! You're a bunch of robbers, and you are so-and-so, the head of them. How dare you surround the house of a noblewoman living alone? If you do not know how to behave in front of a noblewoman, I will enter a complaint against you and then you will know how.

The chief of police replied, Give me the keys, please. All of them.

She threw a bundle of keys at him angrily.

Is there not one more key that you have to give me? he asked. She did not answer him. Well, we'll find a way to open any door for which I have no key.

The chief of police gave the keys to his men and told them to try all the doors, and if they found a room that had no key, they should break down the door: Do not stop until you find what we're looking for.

The policemen spread out over the courtyard and opened all the rooms. They found nothing untoward in any of them. They came back and reported this to the chief. The woman began to mock him. What are you looking for? she said. Maybe I can help you?

The chief of police gave her no answer, but to his men, he said, Are you sure you saw nothing?

Then one of the policemen said, We did notice a spike in a wall. But we didn't see any person chained to it.

It began to get dark. The chief of police told his men to get ready to spend the night there. He then told the messenger to run to town and bring food for the whole troop. He said to the policemen, Do not touch any food that they give you and do not drink anything you find here. I and this fine lady will sit here and I shall amuse myself in conversation with her.

The chief of police took out his little pipe and put some tobacco in it. One of the policemen got up to make a flame. As he was rubbing one stone against another, they looked and saw an old servant going into the stable and it appeared that he was leading some kind of creature, a bear or a dog. The chief of police told him to go and take a look.

The policeman went to the stable. He found there a young man with shaggy hair wearing a woman's dress tied to an iron chain, and the old servant holding the chain and straining to fasten it to a large stone resting on the stable floor. The policeman gave a whistle and let out a loud yell. The policemen heard this and came running. They asked the servant, Who is this boy and why is he tied up with this chain? The servant gave no answer. They asked again and he said nothing. They beat him several times, again and again, until they were exhausted. He opened his mouth and with his finger showed them that it was empty. They peered in and saw that he had no tongue. Who cut his tongue out and for what crime did they do that? Without a tongue, how could he answer? They asked the boy and he did not answer.

They went and informed the chief of police. He asked the lady about this. She did not answer him. He asked again, and she was silent. He then instructed the policemen to take the boy, the servant, and the lady with them and bring them to the town. They put the boy and the servant in one coach with a policeman on either side of them. The chief of police and the lady sat in a second coach with a policeman on either side of them. Three policemen went before the coaches and three behind, all of them with swords drawn. The messenger ran ahead to Buczacz to inform the district head that they were coming.

When the messenger arrived in town, people in the marketplace saw him sprinting. They understood that he was on no ordinary mission but surely had something urgent to report. By the time he got to the town hall a crowd had gathered in the streets. The whole area from the slaughter house behind the Strypa to the well in the marketplace and beyond was filled with people, all of them wondering why the runner was going so fast and speculating on what it was he had to report. When all theories were exhausted, people began trying to figure out where he came from. But what was the point of determining where he came from if they could not tell from which direction he was running.

The minutes passed as slowly as the sluggish waters of the Strypa in midsummer. Every theory that Buczacz developed fell apart. There was nothing to do but wait until events would take their course. Hope prolonged creates heartache.

They were about to despair when two policemen came into view. From the way they were walking you could see that they knew what happened. But at that moment the policemen, who had fattened themselves on payoffs from the townsmen, paid no heed to their inquiries and kept mum.

More and more people came, each one asking the other if he knew what happened, and no one was able to say. Usually when something occurs, there is someone who knows what it was; here not a soul knew. What had occurred was in fact known inside the town hall; in the streets people knew nothing.

Suddenly, a rumor spread that rocked the entire town. The fragment of truth that emerged from wherever it emerged made every heart tremble. No one in town yet knew what the lady's name was or the name of her village or who it was they had found tied to her bed. The room in which the oven maker said he saw a young man standing fastened to the wall by iron chains became in the popular mind the lady's bedroom, and if it was her bedroom, then it was to her bed that he was chained.

The whole town anxiously waited to hear further details, but they heard no more than what they had already picked up. Suddenly there was a rumor that they were bringing the lady and her lover into town. Upon hearing this, everyone started running in different directions since no one knew from which side they were coming. Those in the northern part of town charged to the south and those in the southern part of town charged to the north. Likewise, those in the eastern and western parts. Everyone pushed in the direction opposite from where he was even as no one really knew which way was which. It was hardest for those who could not move; they were shoved back and forth by the crowd, which swelled as new people kept arriving. Every man and woman, old and young, came out that day to hear and to watch in what became one huge throng, the biggest gathering of people Buczacz had ever seen. From the bridge under Fedor Hill to the area beyond the long bridge behind the cemetery, people stood packed in and squeezed together, pushing and shoving, in addition to all those who stood in the streets and alleyways and at the open windows of their houses.

Toward noon, the two coaches arrived in town. The lady and the chief of police were in one, the boy and the servant in the other. Armed policemen surrounded the coaches. The lady was wrapped in a brown mantle, her face covered by a shawl and invisible. I cannot say if she was shackled or not. The faces of the boy and the servant, however, were visible, but no one knew who they were or where they came from. What they did know was that the official sitting with the lady was the chief of police of the precinct to which Buczacz belonged.

Among the onlookers were Bilhah and her mother. Bilhah stood next to her mother, her mother shielding her. At times she was shoved aside by the force of the crowd, and at times she pushed herself forward without knowing whether she wanted to get a better look or to escape the pressure closing in on her. She felt exhausted and her head ached. She had no strong desire to see what everyone else was straining to behold, but suddenly she knew what she really wanted: to get out of that melee and go home and rest. Bilhah had gone through many difficult times. Her father had died after a long illness and she was left with her widowed mother. Worst of all, her head was still uncovered, that is, no man had covered it; in other words, she was still not married. Not because she had no dowry or because no one wanted to marry her, but because obstinacy had taken hold of her and she adamantly refused to marry. This caused her parents great pain, her mother because every mother wants to take pride in her daughter, her father for the same reason and for one other. His conscience bothered him for what he did to Dan, for it was because of Godil that the parnasim took Dan and sent him off to the imperial army. That is what hastened Godil's demise before he could bring his daughter to the marriage canopy, and that is what brought on the illness from which he died.

So the coaches were arriving in town carrying the lady, the boy in a woman's dress, and the servant with his tongue cut out. The clatter of the wheels and the neighing of the horses could be heard as the coaches approached, but it still was not clear where they were coming from and exactly who was in them. The chief of police, the policemen, the district head and the officials in the town hall all knew, but what good is it if others know and you do not.

God never lets down those who long to know something. Sometimes He lets them discover it for themselves, sometimes by having them learn of it through others. As everyone was standing and watching, a horrifying scream was heard that sent a chill through the crowd. That scream was even more shocking than the lady's story.

I have digressed a bit here, so let me return to the events themselves. The coaches were now entering the town carrying the lady, the servant with his tongue cut out, and the boy. The boy was dressed in woman's clothing, his hair done up like a woman's and his head bare. His face and eyes were lifeless. The chains had been removed from his body but his posture was that of one still bound.

Bilhah beheld the boy and emitted an ear-piercing scream. Another scream came from Dan as he looked at her. Dan is the boy dressed in woman's clothing, and from the way his eyes smiled at her everyone knew that this was the soldier who disappeared. But they were surprised to see no sign that this was the tailor's apprentice who had been taken for the imperial army. They overlooked the fact that ten years had passed since then, four of them in the army and six in the lady's room, not to mention that he was wearing a dress and had his hair done up like a woman. Everyone began shouting his name. Those who were not sure called out, Dan, is it you? Dan made no answer. He only shook his head as if to say no.

But there was no doubt that this was Dan, the widow's son who, because of the parnasim, was sent to the army. Everyone remembered his mother the widow, who went around town weeping for her son. Everyone remembered what she said and what they answered her. But not everyone always treats as they should a person whose spirits are crushed for whatever reason. Generally, when a suffering person groans and sighs, people react perfunctorily and walk away. Ironically, the greater a person's troubles, the less sympathy he gets. Soon people came to terms with how they had acted, and then they turned their thoughts back to Dan and his mother. Some lamented that his mother had died. She would have recognized him immediately. Some opined that it was a good thing that the unhappy woman did not live to see what had been done to her only son. But all were unanimous in wishing death upon the wanton woman whose depravity in taking a Jewish boy and using him for sinful purposes few could surpass. They turned again toward Dan and shouted out to him, Dan, why are you silent? Why don't you say something? Dan did not respond to their questions. He said nothing. But when they raised their voices or implored him to speak, he shook his head repeatedly, as if to say, No. No.

Suddenly, the chief of police started shouting, Enough already! Jews, go on home! Some, intimidated by this reprimand from the chief of police, recoiled and left. Others, undeterred, stood motionless, their gaze fixed on the one who disappeared sitting there in the coach. The lady and the servant were taken away by the police and hidden away from the town's fury.

Bilhah vanished. Did she disappear of her own accord or did her relatives take her somewhere? When the crowd had dispersed, some people who lived beyond the Strypa arrived. After talking with a few of the local officials they got permission to take Dan away with them. They brought him to Yukel the doctor, who was also a barber. Yukel took a razor and shaved Dan's head, leaving a beard and side curls. The blue dress had already been removed, replaced by Jewish clothes—a garment with tzitzit, trousers, a coat and hat of camel hair. In the meantime women in the neighborhood all came bringing plates of meat and bread they had prepared. They offered it to him and he ate, nodding his head and saying, Kosher. Kosher. Everyone thought he had regained his speech and they began peppering him with questions. But other than those two words, which were really one, nothing came out of his mouth. The questions were of no avail as were all the efforts to get him to talk. As before, neither a spoken word nor even some movement of his lips was forthcoming.

And so they cut his hair, leaving a beard and side curls, and they dressed him in a man's clothes and they fed him kosher food. His Jewish demeanor returned and he looked again like a normal person. Consultations began over what to do with him and where to house him. The hut his mother lived in had decayed and looked now more like a garbage dump than a dwelling place. The almshouse was filled with transients. As soon as one left, two more came to take his place. The bath house was a dangerous place for a person who did not have all his mental faculties; he could drown in the ritual bath or be scalded by the boiler. He needed to be in a place where people could watch over him. They found him a place in the home of a melamed whose students had disbanded when he developed an illness that left him paralyzed. In lodging him there, they fulfilled at one stroke two commandments: they provided Dan with a place to live and they assured the melamed's wife that they would pay her the costs of Dan's room and board. Some generous people came forward and took upon themselves to each contribute two thalers a week for Dan's support, and in weeks when festivals fell, three thalers. Every Thursday the melamed's wife went around to their houses and each one gave what he had pledged. But not everyone has the merit of always honoring his commitments. There were times when the benefactors were slack in their giving and the contributions decreased. The melamed's wife had to spend most of her Thursdays in town and she still did not collect enough to buy even half of what was needed for the Sabbath. But Bilhah, to her credit, would bring Dan food and drink two or three times a week, and on Fridays a clean shirt. When she came in there would be a glimmer in Dan's eyes and a faint smile would cross his face. It was clear from those signs that there was some improvement in his condition and that he recognized her. When she cried in his presence and begged him to say something, the look in his eyes reverted to what it was before she came in, and the smile on his face froze. When Bilhah noticed this, she would hold back from crying and suppress her tears. She was not always successful.

How long did this go on? Less than the number of years he was imprisoned by the noblewoman. At the noblewoman's house he was imprisoned for six years; here, in his hometown, in the house of the melamed, he lived for less than a year. The sorrow pent up within him brought on the illness from which he died.

The noblewoman, on the other hand, lived on for many years in the Mother of God convent. She was brought there of her own volition. She consecrated all her possessions to that convent, including her loyal tongueless servant. She was deeply devout in her faith, as can be seen from the diary she kept where, on every page, and for everything that she did or wanted to do, she mentions the Mother of God.

Thus ends the story of Dan Hoffmann. But the diary of the lady has come into my possession, and so I would add here that it is clear and apparent from what she writes that Dan was steadfast in his righteousness and his integrity and never submitted to transgression. He suffered much at the hands of that impure woman and never gave in to her seductions, served well by the merits of Joseph, the paragon of a virtuous man who did not succumb to the seductions of an alien woman.

In order not to commingle her words with those of the upright and virtuous people of Buczacz, I break off this telling of her diary. I will present it, in whole or in part, elsewhere.

The Lady's Diary

This is how it all began. A soldier newly released from the army came and knocked on the door of my palace. I asked him what he wanted. He said he was a tailor who knew how to make dresses for ladies and noblewomen. I looked him over and saw that he was good-looking and well built and charming. I asked him if there was anyone who could vouch for his ability to make dresses for ladies and noblewomen. He opened his handbag and pulled out a bundle of letters. But I did not look at them. I looked only at him, and said, Well, let's find out.

I sat him down in a private room and gave him the blue velvet that I bought a few days before from a textile merchant from Bohemia who came to my palace. When the boy started to unroll the blue velvet, my eyes were attracted to his. I could not tell which was bluer, the velvet or his eyes. I left the room to go lather myself in the bath, put on some perfume and change into a light dress. I came back into the room where the boy was sitting and told him to get out his tape and take my measurements. I knew he was a Jew but even so I had good feelings about him. I stood and showed off my figure so that the dress would not look baggy on me. I could see that he was being careful not to touch me, and I knew that it was out of great respect for me that he was not touching me.

I raised myself up to my full height so as to add to my stature. Let him see and know that such respect befits me.

I put aside all my affairs and told the mute that whoever comes to the door, I am not home. I even stopped writing in my diary in which I regularly record each night all the day's doings. I sat and watched the young tailor at work. His fingers were so delicate and all his movements were lovely. I have never ever seen such delicate fingers and I do not know anyone whose movements are so lovely. When it was time for a second measurement, I went and gave myself another bubbly bath, put on some perfume, and went and stood in front of him as tall as I could. Whenever I had to bend down or turn to one side or another and found myself up close with him, I noticed that he would move away. The truth is that I was wishing that the whole thing with the dress would be over. It does not befit the daughter of a nobleman to be so interested in a Jewish boy.

He measured me two more times, once because of the dress and once because I asked him to. Mother of God, I confess that I did not sin and did nothing that could be construed as foolish.

The dress turned out nicer than I expected. I knew it looked good on me and I could tell by the way all eyes were on me when I first wore it to church on Sunday. I gave the dressmaker what was coming to him for his work and added a tip, which I knew he would use to buy presents for his Jewish girlfriend. He used to tell me about that on the nights when I would sit and watch him at work. In any event, I must confess to the Mother of God that I thought that the boy would at some point go home and I would get back to my affairs and my household which I abandoned from the time he showed up at my house.

The next day, he came to take his leave of me. I extended my hand to him to say goodbye and wished him a safe journey. Jokingly, I asked him if he was ready to put off seeing his beloved for a few more days in order to make me another dress. I didn't know that I wanted another dress made for me or in what style I should have it made for me. In any case, the boy agreed to stay on for a few more days to make me another dress. It was all because he wanted to make a bit more money to buy a gift for his dearly beloved. And because I knew what his motivation was, I told him that I would pay him well, and that if this dress would be as nice as the first one, I would pay him more than he originally asked.

That was the week that I moved over to the small palace at the edge of the forest, as I do every year at the end of summer. The rooms in the big palace are large and even before winter sets in they are already too cold to live in. I must say that as a place to live the small palace is better than the big one. It has everything a woman needs. A person could spend a whole life there and no one on the outside would ever know he was there. That is why it was built. Father built it for the woman he brought from the royal city of Dresden in Saxony a year before Mother died. It is said that Mother did not die a natural death. She once went into that palace and happened to enter a room where there was a she-bear tied to the wall by a chain. The woman thought that Mother had come to spy on her and she locked the door on her from the outside. Mother died there from fright and hunger.

Three days went by, and I had not given him the fabric. I didn't even know from what fabric I should have the dress made for me. Once or twice I called him into my bedroom which has a big mirror, and told him to measure me. One time I told him to make me the dress in a certain style, another time I told him to make me one in a different style. I could see that he was standing there confused, but he did everything I told him to. When it became clear to me that I could no longer delay, I told him that I wanted him to make me a dress like the blue one he made for me and I gave him the rest of the blue velvet that I had left over. Good, he said, I have your measurements and do not need to take them for this dress, so I can do it quickly.

I told him that I had commanded the mute to go out and get him new dishes so he could cook Jewish food for himself every day and eat as much as he liked and did not have to rush. I also told him that I insisted that new measurements be taken and he should measure me again, as if my measurements had been lost and we had to start over. I asked myself why I had told him to make a dress like the first one, for which he had the measurements. I could have told him to make me a dress from different material and in a different style. But since I had already told him to go ahead, I let that idea go.

I called in the mute and sent him off to buy me a new razor. I wanted to remove the hair that was growing below my nose like a mustache. When he brought me the razor I changed my mind and did not remove the hair, because with hair the more you remove it, the more it grows back, until you cannot control it and eventually it spoils your appearance. I remember when I visited the Countess Molodovsky three days before she died. I found her lying in bed and I thought I had entered the bedroom of a man and not a woman. Shriveled red hairs drooped over her upper lip. She never shaved for fear that removal of the hair there would cause part of her lip to fall off.

To make the dressmaker's living conditions more comfortable, I sent my slave the mute to get him some new dishes so he could cook his own food. During the time he was making the first dress he ate no cooked food, only bread, eggs, and fruit.

The making of the dress took a long time, for reasons both external and internal. Whenever I was free I would go in and sit with him and watch his nimble fingers. I let him tell me about all the noblewomen for whom he made dresses. What amazed me most was that in all his stories he never once mentioned that he had gotten near a woman, and here was a good-looking boy with all his juices.

One night, he said that he had to hurry and finish the dress because the great holiday of Passover was coming and he needed to celebrate it among Jews. I saw that I could not detain him any longer so I agreed and told him to finish the job and go.

All that night, I tossed and turned restlessly. Many sinful ideas created havoc in my mind and I thought I was going crazy. I got out of bed and kneeled and prayed to the Holy Mother to stand by me in my hour of trial. She didn't answer me and I knew that she was angry at me for giving my heart to a Jewish man.

The dress did get finished, and it was many times nicer than the first one. I asked the dressmaker to wait one more day so I could, as

I told him, see the dress in daylight. He acceded to my request and said he would stay with me for one more day.

That night, I called my servant the mute and told him to take the dress and go into the dressmaker's room and leave it there and take in its place the boy's clothes, and that he should be careful that the boy not see him coming in or going out. The mute did just as I said, and the boy did not see him come in or go out.

In the morning, I mounted my dappled horse and rode around the whole day. When I got back home that night I heard nothing, for I had ordered the mute to guard the room where the Jew was staying and make sure that his voice not be heard on the outside.

The next morning, I thought about going to see what the boy was doing; but on the way, I decided instead to go that night.

On the way, I saw an amazing and wonderful sight. A gypsy was leading a little she-bear that was doing some things that were truly amazing. I asked him if he would sell it to me and how much he wanted for it, and very soon the she-bear was mine, right in my house.

I called the mute and told him to bang a spike into the wall so the gypsy could chain the she-bear to the wall. He did so, and the gypsy tied it up, and I stood there delighting in it and its antics. The she-bear did not enable me to forget about the Jew, but one good thing came of it: the sinful thoughts I had now faded and were not as wicked or as troubling as they had been before.

I do not know what it was with that she-bear but it suddenly stopped frolicking. A kind of sadness could be seen in its eyes. I called the mute to come and he began making gestures with his hands, but I did not understand what he was trying to communicate. He went out and came back with a rifle in his hand. I understood that he was indicating to me that the bear had to be shot. The thought of that pained me greatly. Here I had enjoyed her for three days and now I was to have it put to death.

The mute put a bullet into it and took the carcass outside and buried it in the ground. I understood from what he was doing that this was to prevent it from being eaten by birds or animals scavenging on its flesh and possibly contracting any sickness the she-bear had.

That night, I heard a commotion. I went out to see what it was and found the Hebrew boy struggling with the mute. I knew that he was trying to escape and the mute was trying to stop him. It did not make me happy but I told the mute to take him and tie him up with the chain to the spike in the wall where the she-bear was. I knew that the whole episode of the she-bear came about only for the sake of the Jew.

A few days went by, among them the days of the Jewish Passover. I restrained myself and did not ask the mute what the Jew was doing. I only ordered him to take care of him and see to it that he had his food that Jews eat and a clean bed, and that all his bodily needs were met.

One night, candle in hand, I opened the door to his room and went in. The dress looked good on him, but his eyes showed a deep sadness. That sadness in his eyes made him even more attractive, and the dress had its effects too.

I drew near him and started stroking the dress he was wearing. I never knew that a dress could change a man like this, if I didn't know you were a man I would have thought you disappeared into a young lady, but you really are a man. And as I spoke I stroked the hair on his cheeks.

I ordered the mute to shave his beard and be careful not to cut him and to give him a nice soapy bath with scented water. Whenever I knew he had been bathed and shaved I went in and put my hand on his face and stroked it. And I said to him, If I didn't know you were a man I would say you're a girl, your skin is so soft and smooth, like a virgin's, or maybe you really are a virgin. Sometimes I am not even sure you're a man. He never answered me, only the sorrow in his eyes grew deeper and deeper from week to week.

Many times, I wondered how long he was going to stay with me. But I could never find the strength to send him away. I even began to wonder if by sending him away I was placing myself in danger, because he could then tell everyone what I did to him.

Again I went in to him and spoke to him softly, but he gave no reply. I said to him, You have forgotten how to speak like a human being. You're just like the mute, except the mute had his tongue cut out and you still have yours, so say something.

For all that I spoke to him, he never ever answered.

I thought it would make him happy if I brought him a Jewish book. And I did. He looked at it and put it aside and never picked it up again. Later on, I learned that what I had given him was the New Testament, and the Jews do not like that book. Anything we Christians do, the Jews do not like.

I began to despair about the Jewish boy and tried to figure out how to rid myself of him. There was no one I could consult with on this other than the old slave, mute though he was. One time I told him that the time had come to send the Jewish boy packing. He slid his hand across his neck like one about to slaughter a chicken or a cow. That gesture distressed me and I scolded him and told him to be very, very careful to do no harm to this Jew.

This is the place for me to tell why the slave was mute and why he was so loyal and attached to me.

When I was a girl, a band of outlaws terrorized our whole region. Not a month went by when we were not horrified by the things they did. The area was then still in the hands of the Polish kings. They were unable to capture the outlaws nor could they weaken them.

When Poland was divided among the three empires and our area became part of Austria, Austria did what it could to rid the land of robbers and murderers. It did succeed in wiping out several gangs of murderers and capturing a few robbers. Some were executed, some were hanged in the streets and some were sentenced to life imprisonment. Among those captured and sentenced to be hanged was the servant, who at that point still had his tongue in his mouth. His comrades heard that he was going to be tortured until he would reveal where they were hiding out from the police. They knew that he would not withstand the torture and would doom them all to execution. They settled their score with him and cut out his tongue. Father found out about this and brought him home. I do not know under what conditions he was handed over to Father. What I do know is that Father saw to it that a doctor healed him and that he was taken care of and all his needs were provided, and that Father protected him from the officials and the police. He became very attached to Father and was extremely loyal to him, and to me especially, for he knew me from the time I was a girl. I heard that there was a close bond between Father and the mute going back to when he was a robber. There are those who say that on many occasions he was Father's agent in exacting vengeance on Father's enemies. The exact reason for that I do not know, nor will I ever know. Nor do I want to know.

Translated by James S. Diamond
with Jeffrey Saks

Yekele (I)

I WILL NOW TELL THE STORY OF YEKELE, the son of R. Moshe the Ḥasid.

R. Moshe the Ḥasid was part of a community of ḥasidim in Buczacz who served the Lord with all their might, every day, every hour, and every minute. In this, R. Moshe outdid them all. His friends claimed that the angels and the seraphs envied him the devoutness with which he served God, and according to those who know of such matters, there was no small measure of truth to this contention.

After having fulfilled the commandment to be fruitful and multiply, R. Moshe separated from his wife, left home, and abandoned all pursuits that normally occupy a person's days and years. His sole concern was to address the needs of heaven.

It would be nice if I could describe just what this entailed, but what do I or anyone else in this generation know of such matters? I shall, therefore, say no more about the father and will tell only about what happened with his son.

R. Moshe's son Yekele was a year old when his pious father left home to devote his every moment to the service of God. Two and a half years after he left home, he departed this world of travail, where the debasements of daily life eclipse the trials and temptations that dog a person's every step. Any confidence one has that he has escaped them is a dangerous illusion.

Yekele was left fatherless, his mother a disconsolate widow, impoverished, ailing, and laden with all the troubles penniless widows face. Such widows try to keep their troubles from the public, but by the time people take note of them they waste away in their poverty and die.

Yekele's mother did die, and he was left an orphan. His sister, who was a few years older than he, was taken in to the home of a relative in another town. But no one in the family was willing to take Yekele, for he was a difficult child. He bounced around among a few poor neighbors until eventually he left them all and ran wild, going wherever his inclinations took him. He studied no Torah or anything about the mitzvot, and took no instruction in how to behave properly. Out of pity for an offspring of R. Moshe the Ḥasid, he was dragged into a ḥeder. The first day there, he ran away. He did this not once or twice or thrice, but seven and even ten times, until all the well-meaning people let him go.

Yekele was thus left to his own devices, that is to say, to the whims of his infantile impulses. Totally lacking any self-control, his capacity for transgression was boundless. Because he was intimidated by neither the living nor the dead, the gravediggers accepted him into their ranks, and that became his occupation.

R. Yisrael Shlomo, the parnas of the town, got wind of all this and wrinkled up his nose at it. Yekele, in turn, got wind of that and understood that R. Yisrael Shlomo was not pleased with him, upon which he poured forth a series of rather insolent curses on R. Yisrael Shlomo. Jokingly he suggested that "even though Srul Shlomo doesn't think much of me, I hold him in such high regard that I am ready to bury him right now." It is not clear that these words of Yekele reached R. Yisrael Shlomo's ears, but logic dictates that no one in Buczacz would report such things to him.

One year, on the night of the seventh of Adar, the following happened. For a long time, R. Yisrael Avraham, the richest man in Buczacz, sought to be a member of the ḥevrah kadisha. Its ranks were restricted to eighteen members, eighteen being the numerical value of the word *ḥai*, and membership, once gained, was for life. Many God-fearing people wanted to be in the ḥevrah kadisha because attending to the dead and seeing a person's final state up close can bring one to the fear of heaven and, according to some, aids in meriting a long life.

That year R. Yisrael Avraham was finally successful and was accepted into the society. To mark the occasion, he made a sumptuous feast. There was white bread, wine, two meat dishes, baked fish, gefilte fish, turnips, goose necks stuffed with rice and raisins, and many other delicacies. In all the days of the ḥevrah kadisha in Buczacz, there had never been a feast like that, and it was savored by every member of the society.

While R. Yisrael Avraham was sitting with the heads of the society, eating and drinking and enjoying the wine and the food and a pleasant conversation with R. Yisrael Shlomo, not to mention the words of Torah that were offered between courses, robbers broke into his house. All the servants were already asleep, and R. Yisrael Avraham's wife, a woman of aristocratic bearing, had also dozed off. Even the little synagogue that the magnate had built for himself in his courtyard was empty, for it was now the middle of the night when everyone was in bed.

The robbers took everything they could find—silverware, copperware, clothing, bedding, pillows, and all the valuables they could get their hands on. Just as they were getting ready to leave, one of them remembered the lady of the house's jewelry, which was without compare in Buczacz. The robber figured out that it was hidden away in a little box under her head. Wasting no time, he approached her bed and began feeling around under her pillow. The woman awoke and let out a loud scream. Angered at this interruption of his labors, the robber scolded her and yelled at her in Polish, "*Cicho bestia!*," meaning, "Shut up, you animal!" Then, afraid that she would scream again before he could snatch the box of jewelry from under her pillow, he grabbed her by the throat and began choking her. It is not clear whether his intention was to strangle her or not, but, by the mercy of God, she was not killed.

When R. Yisrael Avraham returned from the banquet, happy at what he had finally attained and accompanied by a singing band of ḥevrah kadisha members, he entered his house and, understandably, was met with shrieks and wails and screams, for the robbers had cleaned the house out.

They ransacked the house but left no traces of their identity except for one thing: the voice of the robber who yelled at the lady of the house,

"*Cicho bestia!*," the meaning of which I have already explained as "Shut up, you animal!" These words were still ringing in her ears when she attested that the voice was the voice of Yekele.

Yekele was very hard for Buczacz to handle. There was no one in town who did not feel the sting of his gross impertinence or did not flinch at his strong language and his vulgar manners. He showed no respect even for the head of the community, R. Yisrael Shlomo, the town parnas, calling him Srul Shlomo, and not R. Yisrael Shlomo, as everyone else did because he was an important parnas, a wealthy man, and a leader with a large following on whom many depended. Besides which he came from an illustrious line of rabbinical eminences who ruled over many important communities and to whom many small-town rabbis were accountable. He was no less regarded and accepted by the government. Even the emperor's deputy, who hated Jews, paid heed to whatever he said.

The robbery and the strangling attempt convinced R. Yisrael Shlomo that the time had come to knock some sense into Yekele and to let him know that every hooligan winds up in jail. He summoned the chief of police who dispatched a pair of policemen to arrest Yekele. They went and bound his hands in iron chains and imprisoned him. Yekele declared to them, "Go and tell R. Yisrael Shlomo that when I get out of here I will kill him. And don't think this is just talk. You'd better know that when Yekele says he's going to do something, he means it." He repeated this warning to the warden of the prison and to all who came to visit him there, of which there were many. Some came out of pity for a Jewish boy whom the gentiles had locked up, and some came for the sake of his father, for in paradise R. Moshe was surely distressed at what was going on with his only son.

Yekele's words reached R. Yisrael Shlomo and he began to fear for his life. Esther Malkah, his wife, was even more afraid of what Yekele might do to her husband. R. Yisrael Shlomo cited the dictum that "if someone is coming to kill you, rise up and kill him first," but he had no thought of actually doing so.

A few days later, the deputy encountered R. Yisrael Shlomo as he was returning from a circumcision ceremony, where he had been the godfather. He met him with these words: "I am hearing some really nice things about all of you. Some lovely things are going on in your community. Break-ins, thefts, robberies, violence, killing."

R. Yisrael Shlomo replied, "You are exaggerating. I have not heard of anyone being killed."

The deputy angrily retorted, "Anyone who attacks a woman is trying to kill her. And if he doesn't actually kill her, he was ready to kill her."

R. Yisrael Shlomo sighed and said nothing.

The deputy said, "I would like to know what you think about what happened and what law we should apply to that hooligan. How should he be punished?"

Said R. Yisrael Shlomo, "I hear he has been put in jail."

The deputy laughed scornfully, "Yes, yes, they put him in jail. They put him in jail. From the day he was born he belonged in jail."

Then the deputy added, "How long can you keep a troublemaker locked up? A year, two years, three? Eventually he goes free. He goes free and returns to his old ways. So they lock him up again and he sits in prison for however long he's there. And then again they let him go. That's with a regular troublemaker. But what about one who tried to strangle a woman? For your Yekele a life sentence would be letting him off easy."

R. Yisrael Shlomo heard this and said nothing.

The deputy continued, "I do not know what the judges' verdict will be. In my opinion, that Yekele of yours deserves the death penalty. The gallows."

R. Yisrael Shlomo heard this and said nothing.

The deputy mused, Hmm, he says nothing when he should be agreeing with me.

R. Yisrael Shlomo left and went on his way, the deputy returned to his office. He went in and sat down; sat down and got up; got up and started pacing up and down. He looked at the wall, then at his desk, and began yelling at the clerk responsible for taking care of the office, berating him for not noticing that the caretaker had placed the inkwell on the left and the container of sand used for blotting the ink on the right, when every schoolchild knows that the sand goes on the left and the inkwell on the right.

After chewing out that clerk, he cast his eyes on another and did the same to him. Likewise with a third. Then he started screaming at the caretaker on whom the government had wasted its money in paying someone in its administrative office to supervise him to make sure he did his job properly. Here he had gone and put what belonged on the right on the left, and what belonged on the left on the right. Finally he cooled down and went back to his desk and sat down.

He sat and brooded about the Jews in the town and how they acted as if they were still living as wards of the Polish Commonwealth and could do whatever they liked. He was particularly angry at R. Yisrael Shlomo. Everyone obeyed him as if he were the head official, as if he were the one in charge, as if he were the judge. The deputy was no less upset with himself, for every time he talked with R. Yisrael Shlomo he softened his speech and spoke to him respectfully, as if R. Yisrael Shlomo were the emperor's deputy and not he. He did, however, take some comfort in having been able that day to tell him what should be done with the Jew Yekele.

The deputy inquired of the secretary if there was any new word about Yekele. There being none, he called for the judges and put the matter in their hands, and it turned out their opinion coincided with that of the deputy.

The town got wind of all this and was greatly upset. Fear enveloped it. Is Jewish blood a trifle? Is a person put to death on the strength of a woman's testimony? Even if Yekele had threatened to kill her, the fact is that he didn't. She was still wearing her jewelry and dazzling the gentiles. The word in town was that jewelry was the cause of all the Jews' troubles. The gentiles were seeing the Jewish women going about all decked out and they became jealous, and it is well known that jealousy leads to hate and hate leads to killing. Jealousy is not only a gentile matter; Jews are susceptible to it too. A poor man sees his wife and children wasting away from hunger because he cannot buy even a crust of bread, while the rich stuff themselves with all kinds of good things and adorn their bulging bellies with expensive ornaments. It was not for nothing that Solomon said, *Hold not a thief in contempt for stealing to appease his hunger*, to which the author of the *Metzudot* commented that a thief who steals because he is hungry should not be scorned too much; indeed, he is doing so almost out of compulsion. But those rich people could feed the poor with the value of their jewelry, and they are oblivious to their hunger, which could lead them to steal. But the case of Yekele is puzzling because the robbery took place while the sumptuous feast that R. Yisrael Avraham made for the ḥevrah kadisha was going on, and Yekele was at that feast.

At the trial the judges deliberated and sentenced Yekele to death. When news of the verdict reached town, there were still some people who felt that it was pronounced only to throw a scare into Yekele, for logic dictated that he did not deserve to die. But Yekele was not fated to die a normal death. When the judges sentenced him to death, the emperor's deputy sent to Czernowitz for the hangman. And still there were people in town who believed that he had done so only to break Yekele's impudent spirit.

The hangman arrived in Buczacz. He strolled through the streets, a short corpulent man with a mustache drooping over his lips on both sides, a small thick stick hanging on his arm by a braided strap. As he walked along he would curl his mustache or stop in to buy something at a store which he would then give to any young woman passing by. Every so often he would pull out the mirror he was carrying and glance into it. Buczacz was mystified by the hangman. It had never seen one before and so had no clear idea of what a hangman should look like. The consensus was that this one did not have the appearance of an executioner. Nevertheless, Buczacz was confident that the deputy knew about such things and if this was who he brought to hang someone, he knew what he was doing. Even so, it was clear to all that he was brought for the sole purpose of instilling fear into Yekele, and Yekele thought so too. But his insolence was unabated. "Tell Yisrael Shlomo to dig a grave and get some shrouds, because on the day I get out of jail I will take revenge on him," he said.

The hangman stayed with a woman whose husband had died and whose bed was empty. He ate what she cooked for him and drank the wine she bought at the winery. She was a devout Catholic and he a devout Protestant, and the antagonism between the two religions did not interfere with the love between the two of them. He even played with her children and gave them nuts, raisins and candies. When they asked to touch the sword with which he beheaded people, he let them, upon which he would sweep the sword through the air and bring it up against the neck of each of them, telling them that whoever touches an executioner's sword and the executioner does not sweep the sword though the air and lay it against their neck is destined to be beheaded. He also taught the children German songs. Nothing made him laugh more than to hear them sing in their Polish accents "Satilki Nakh, Heilie Nakh," which is "Stille Nacht, Heilige Nacht," meaning "silent night, holy night," the song that Christians sing in German on the night of Jesus' birth.

Meanwhile, the deputy went around the town and its surroundings looking for a suitable site for the gallows. He found an excellent place on the sloping hills of what is called the Basztę, fortress in Polish, because of the fortresses that were there several generations ago, when Poland ruled the area. The fortresses have since collapsed but the name remains, and the place is still called Basztę. Even when not even a stone of their structure is left standing, edifices and fortresses retain their names. Some of those fortresses were destroyed by the Tatars, and some were leveled by the Poles themselves at the order of the Ottomans, who demanded that they be knocked down lest the Poles hide out there during their invasion. Today, there is no trace of any fortress. It is a place where cattle graze and old horses that can no longer be ridden or hitched to a wagon are bought to be flayed.

The deputy liked those hills that cascade down to the Strypa in terraces, one below the other, as if the Creator of the world, when He was about to begin His work, foresaw the day they would set up row upon row of seats for those who would come from near and far to witness the downfall of the Jew Yekele, when the hangman would place the noose around his neck. The top rows, right near the gallows, were reserved for the noblemen and their wives, owners of the great estates. Below them were the lords and ladies of the emperor's court. Below them were the owners of the smaller estates, and below them were the gentlemen who dined with the nobles who owned the large estates. Below them were the townsfolk, and below them were those who worked in the fields and the peasant men and women. Below them were all those who flocked to any public event.

The time came and everything stood ready. On the seventh day of Adar they removed Yekele from prison and brought him outside the town to the gallows. Before he was placed on the gallows they asked him if there was anything he wanted, for it is customary to give the condemned whatever they desire before they die. Yekele asked for a horse to ride on. He said he needed to stretch his body which was stiff from sitting for so long. They gave him a horse and sent guards along to make sure he would not escape. He mounted the horse and off he rode. When he noticed noblemen and noblewomen rushing to witness a hanging, he called to them jokingly, "Good lords and ladies! No need to run. As long as I'm on this horse, you won't be late."

He rode around for a while and then dismounted. They took him and led him to the gallows. The hangman said to him in German, "Son, do honor to the Lord God of Israel and give thanks to Him, then tell me what you've done. Don't keep it from me." Yekele, who did not know German and did not understand what the hangman was saying, answered him cheekily, "If you are a human being, then speak to me like a human being." Those who knew German were moved by the hangman's words from Scripture. Those who knew the Jewish vernacular were delighted by the condemned man's impudence.

A few moments passed and then the hangman tied the rope around Yekele's neck. As he did this, the eyes of all the lords and ladies were transfixed. A few moments passed and Yekele's soul departed. At that very hour, not far from Buczacz, in the nearby village of Podlishi, all the Jews of Buczacz, led by the head of the rabbinic court, were offering prayers and supplications amidst much wailing. Suddenly the rabbi, together with all the devout, spread out their hands toward the town and declared, *Our hands did not shed this blood nor did our eyes see it done.*

And where was R. Yisrael Shlomo? I do not know. One can assume that he was not among those who witnessed Yekele's death. Nor was he among the community that declared *Our hands did not shed this blood.*

I must add here that just as they were taking Yekele's body down from the gallows, a runner arrived from the court in the town of Stanislav. In his hand was a letter from the court officials to the emperor's deputy. The letter stated that Yekele, the son of Moshe, was not to be given the death penalty.

I have related here the main outlines of the story. Later on I will elaborate on its various aspects. But let me add one note of behalf of Yekele's father, R. Moshe the Ḥasid.

There was in our town a distinguished Torah scholar whose teachings had wide authority. The halakhic queries he put to the greatest rabbis of his time were answered with utmost love and respect. In fact, when they published their books of responsa, his name appeared prominently and was cited with much admiration. That scholar was a descendant of R. Moshe the Ḥasid. Some say he was a grandson of Yekele, others that he was a grandson of Yekele's sister. Either way, R. Moshe the Ḥasid merited to be his forebear.

Translated by James S. Diamond
with Jeffrey Saks

Manuscript page from opening of "Yekele (II)"
(Courtesy of Agnon Archive, AC4025, The National Library of Israel, Jerusalem, and Schocken Publishing House, Tel Aviv.)

Yekele (II)

There was in our town a parnas who had no equal, neither among those who preceded him in that position nor among the provincial leaders. He was exceptional in every respect. He was wealthy, philanthropic, well bred, elegant, resolute, and unyielding. His name was R. Yisrael Shlomo, named after the pride of the family, the first Yisrael Shlomo, of blessed memory, who we have often mentioned. Whether it was the power of his pedigree or his own personal forcefulness, or the combination of the two, or because Buczacz was very accepting of authority, especially that of important people who have its interests at heart, everyone quailed before him. If he told someone "Do this" or "Don't do that," that person would nod and say "Certainly, certainly, your honor. Thank you for your good advice. I will always follow it." With such words or something approximating them, but always with the same compliance, did the townspeople, the gentry and the common folk alike, comport themselves with him. And so, before we get to the story we are about to tell, we can say with some certainty that there was no one in the town who did not accept R. Yisrael's authority unconditionally. And here I am pleased to note that he for his part treated them generously and graciously. If someone celebrated a brit milah and gave him the honor of being the sandek, he brought a gift for the infant. When the boy grew up and married, he would present him with a sum of money that was known as "the bridegroom's oration award." When a poor man's daughter came of age and the father was unable to provide her with a dowry, R. Yisrael Shlomo assisted him in making the wedding. Similarly, on unhappy occasions, he would send the meal of condolence to the house of mourning, and if they were poor, he would have food brought from his house to the mourners for the seven days of shiva.

Those who do good will always have people who are ungrateful to them. In fact, the latter will generally outnumber the former. By all rights, doing good should leave no room for ungratefulness. But the reality, hard as it is to come to terms with it, is otherwise. So it was with R. Yisrael Shlomo. After all the fine things he did for all kinds of people, there was one person in our town, Yekele his name, who scoffed at him, spoke ill of him, and did not even deign to address him as "Reb," a title of respect the whole town gave him even when he was not present. When R. Yisrael Shlomo first heard about this he was taken aback. Some say a smile crossed his face, for he was amused that there was someone in town who was at odds with the prevailing consensus. But when he heard it for a second and then a third time, it started to bother him. But the beginnings of the chain of events to be related here are trifling compared to what they led up to, and so we shall not dwell on them.

Too much time has passed for us to know exactly why this Yekele started up with the parnas. On the other hand, we can relate what we have heard from the elders of the town, who heard it from their forebears. It seems that on one occasion Yekele did something that angered R. Yisrael Shlomo well beyond what normally provoked him, and this caused him to express the wish that "that rascal reach the end of his days as everyone does." Some have it that what R. Yisrael Shlomo said was "I doubt if he will die the way other people do." Whatever they were, R. Yisrael Shlomo's words made an impression on Buczacz, and when the events, of which all I have thus far related is merely a prologue, reached their culmination, those words were clearly recalled.

Now having told about R. Yisrael Shlomo, of blessed memory, and the greatness of his doings, let us expend a few more drops of ink to say something about Yekele and his origins. We can begin with his father, for without fathers there are no sons.

Yekele's father, R. Moshe, was the youngest of the early ḥasidim in Buczacz. Those ḥasidim opened a prayer house there where they switched from the Ashkenazic to the Sephardic liturgy and followed the structure of the service as ordered by the Ari. R. Moshe lived with his wife for ten years after which, having produced no progeny, she accepted a bill of divorce from him without any rancor. That year was exceptionally cold. The many frosts made everything very expensive and those poor who did not freeze to death died of hunger.

When the Passover festival was approaching R. Moshe found himself without matzah or wine for the four cups or anything for the holiday. All he had was faith that the Holy One, blessed be He, would help him and save him from his plight. But he was heartsick at the fact that his divorced wife was completely destitute and alone in the world and would have to throw herself on her neighbors in order to sit at a seder. It's true, he thought to himself, I have nothing to make Pesaḥ with, but if I take my divorced wife back I can at least save her from having to throw herself at the mercy of others. He communicated this to her, and when she replied that "it is better to dwell as a duo than to live like a widow," a marriage ceremony was held, and they put all their trust in God to sustain them on the holy festival of Passover.

Now a bit more about R. Moshe and his wife. R. Moshe was physically weak. His was completely detached from business matters, his sole concern being Torah and ḥasidic practice. As we have noted, he was among the early ḥasidim who preceded the Ba'al Shem Tov, some whom opposed the Ba'al Shem Tov. He was wont to pray with the rising of the sun, yet in the manner of all God-fearing believers in Israel in those days, he did not remove his tefilin until after midday. In the winter, when the days are short, he kept them on until nightfall, for, like some of that group of ḥasidim, he would recite the afternoon prayer in talit and tefilin. Some hold that when they recited the Shema at the evening service, the tefilin were still on their heads. It is on the basis of that practice that I once explained to some scholars why it is that in all congregations the worshipers customarily pause between *emet,* the last word of the Shema, and *emunah,* the first word of the prayer that immediately follows. They wait so as to allow the rabbi to remove his tefilin. I shall not go into detail about that here.

But even in the summer time, when the days are long, R. Moshe would spend the whole day on Torah. He gave regular classes in the

Zohar and the writings of the Ari, of blessed memory, whose texts were hard to read because most books then were not yet printed and were written in very small script that had to be read very slowly. There was one printed book that was always at R. Moshe's side, and that was *Ḥemdat Yamim*, a book from which he took many good practices that were not followed in Buczacz.

R. Moshe had one other major routine. On Friday afternoons and the eve of festivals, he would run from one synagogue or beit midrash to another to check the Torah scrolls from which the weekly Torah portion would be read the next day. He even took the trouble to go to the place where the porters prayed, which was at the top of a hill and required a lot of stamina to reach. Since a person cannot in one day look through more than nine scrolls, he began his labors on Wednesdays, when the Sabbath comes into view and at the end of the morning service we add to the psalm for the day the first words of the psalm we say on Friday night, "Come let us sing unto God."

Because he devoted all his waking hours to holy activities, R. Moshe had no time for worldly matters. His wife, therefore, took upon herself the task of supporting the household. She did this by preparing chickens from the time they were slaughtered to the point when they were put into the oven. This was one of several domestic chores that some of the wealthy women in Buczacz found it worth their while to hand over to other women for a small fee.

Let us now return to R. Moshe after he took his divorced wife back. On the Friday evening before Passover, he returned from synagogue to find his wife sitting as if she were in mourning. He made himself oblivious to her distress, sang "Shalom Aleichem," and recited Kiddush over two loaves that were black as pitch. Then he dined on what his wife had prepared, which sufficed more to satisfy the minimum requirement of a Sabbath meal, that is, to keep one from fasting on the holy day, than it did to satisfy the body. This did not upset R. Moshe at all. He declared to his wife, "Well, now that the body has nothing to delight in, the true pleasure of the holy Sabbath is reserved for the soul, which is the way a Jewish person should feel the full joy of the day. And I am certain that God's grace will be with us even on the holy days of Passover." That very night his wife conceived and nine months later gave birth to a boy. But

R. Moshe was not to know of his good fortune. No sooner did his wife conceive when he died, and when the son was born, she too passed away. That son was Yekele. Why he was not named after his father is a story unto itself. When the eve of Passover was approaching and the couple still had no provisions for the holiday, a man from the country showed up in a wagon loaded down with all kinds of good things—meat, fish, vegetables, not to mention matzah and wine—all of which he gave them unstintingly, including even the parsley for the karpas. "Come help me get all this into your house," he said to the couple. When R. Moshe asked him his name, the man answered, "Wait, I have not finished what I'm doing," and as he said that he laid before R. Moshe a bag of coins. And then he vanished. R. Moshe stood there in astonishment. And as he stood there his wife counted out the money and found it to amount to 182 coins, which number she reported to her husband. R. Moshe calculated that the numerical equivalent of that sum is the name "Yaakov." But he had no idea what the man's intention was.

On the first night of Passover, after midnight, R. Moshe fell asleep while reclining after the seder. The Man of Truth appeared to him in a dream with a charming interpretation of the verse "You will show truth to Jacob." He said, "If you think that it was I who came to you in the form of a man from the villages and that it was I who brought you the Passover provisions, you are mistaken." And as he said this, he disappeared. The next day, R. Moshe's wife told him that there was a report in town about a man from the villages in a wagon on his way out of town who somehow drove his horses and wagon into a river and drowned. The man's name was Yaakov. R. Moshe then realized that this was the man from the villages who had brought him the Passover provisions, and he was greatly distressed at the idea that he might have been the cause of the man's death. Whereupon R. Moshe and his wife agreed that if they would have a son, he would be called Yaakov, named after that man from the country. And when the boy was born as she was dying, she instructed that he be named Yaakov. But because everyone loved him, they called him Yekele. He is the Yekele of our story.

We do not know just how Yekele spent his first few years. He was in all likelihood a neglected child like all orphans who have no mother or father to guide them on a straight path. But in one circumstance was he more privileged than most of the other townspeople: he was a registered member of the ḥevrah kadisha, the Jewish burial society. Before he even came into the world, his father, R. Moshe, donated to the ḥevrah kadisha the extra wine the man had brought him on the express condition that should he have a male child, the boy would be enrolled as a member of the ḥevrah kadisha. They kept their word, and while yet an infant Yekele was made a member. In time the ḥevrah kadisha and the gravediggers sent him on all kinds of errands and he served them admirably.

On the surface, it is strange that the ḥevrah kadisha would enroll as a member a child who had not yet been born when there were many older and more mature people who wanted to join and were not accepted. Nothing happens without a reason, of course, but why this was we do not know, and so we will have to be content only with the facts.

Now since we have mentioned the ḥevrah kadisha and its prestige, let us take a look at the other societies that were in the town, both big and little. Some of them were as old as Buczacz, some were founded more recently, and some we have no idea of when they came about, or who founded them, or for what purpose. Some served to advance Torah and some to promote good deeds.

I shall begin with those that pertained to Torah. First and foremost was the ḥevrah mishnayot, the Mishnah study society. When the town was founded, or possibly when it was resettled after the pogroms of 1648, the practice was instituted to study every day between Minḥah and Maariv a whole chapter of Mishnah or two individual mishnayot with the commentary of R. Ovadiah Bartenura and, if possible, that of Tosafot Yom Tov. It is said that initially there was an explicit directive that no one should leave for work in the morning without studying a mishnah or two, and if he was not trained in Torah he should hear the text read aloud by the Mishnah reciter. In the old beit midrash there was a particular person who every day at the end of the morning prayers got up and recited a chapter of Mishnah.

A second group, no less important as far as Torah was concerned, was the ḥevrah Shas, the Talmud study society. Its luminaries took it upon themselves to each complete one tractate of the Talmud over the course of a year, and thus the entire Talmud was studied annually.

Third among these groups was the Alshikh Society. Its members gathered on Friday evenings after dinner to study together the weekly Torah portion with the Alshikh's commentary. At first it had many members, but when the Akedah Society got started, most of them joined the group to study the commentary titled *Akedat Yitzḥak*. This branched out into a maḥzor study group that met before each festival to study the commentaries on the piyyutim, so that a person would know what he was saying in the service. This included Rosh Hashanah and Yom Kippur, for which preparatory study began on the fifteenth day of the month of Av.

A fourth Torah group was the Talmud Torah Society. It promoted the teaching of Torah. Its members realized no benefit from it in this world but in the world to come their reward for supporting it was incalculable. They paid melamdim to teach the children of the poor, for it is from them that Torah will spring. Initially all the children were brought to one melamed, but when it became clear that some families were embarrassed at having their children learning in a school for paupers, the children of the poor were farmed out to various other melamdim in the town, each child according to his capability.

Having enumerated the societies that involved Torah, let me now list those that promoted good deeds, first the ones that were established for the general good, then those that were set up to serve the particular needs of Buczacz.

The principal one was a society called Pat Le'orḥim, Food for Transients. A poor person passing through our town, when he was about to set out on his way, would be given food to take with him. The person in charge of this society was an old melamed who suffered from consumption and was not able to operate his own school house. If the poor transient was a woman, the melamed's wife gave her the food. She also went around on Fridays to all the homes collecting bread, assisted by a few righteous women.

A second such society was called Eruv Tavshilin. If the second day of a festival fell on a Friday, a member appointed for that day would go out to the nearby villages and remind the people there to make sure they put aside the food they had cooked for the Sabbath. They did this because those people had little knowledge of Torah and were very involved in their business dealings with the gentiles and so were liable to forget the mitzvah of eruv tavshilin.

A third such society was Esther's Turn, which was composed of young men dispatched on Purim to go out and read the Megillah. Only a few townsfolk benefited from it, mostly the sick and the aged, who were unable to walk to the synagogue for the reading of the Megillah, and the maidservants of the rich, who were busy with cooking and baking. The boys would come and read it to them with the full cantillation. They did this without any thought of getting paid and they set up no collection boxes. They did accept whatever baked goods the various homes could offer.

There used to be a society in town, as there were in most communities in Poland, called the Society for Ransoming Captives. It was the largest of all the societies, but when the Polish Commonwealth ended, it ceased operating, and even though the Austrian Empire was no less harsh toward the Jews, the noblemen no longer imprisoned Jewish tax collectors who failed to pay the taxes on time, and so there was no longer any need to ransom captives. In addition, R. Yisrael Shlomo, who was held in high esteem by the gentiles, was an effective advocate for the Jews of the villages. Whenever there was trouble he interceded on their behalf with the authorities, and his words had effect. The Polish officials were also eager to accede to his wishes because they often needed him to advocate for them with the Austrians. On many occasions, the Poles paid no attention to Austrian laws and conducted their affairs as they had before Austria took over Poland. They thus incurred the wrath of the Austrian authorities and sought out R. Yisrael Shlomo to set things right for them.

Having now enumerated those societies that worked for the general good, let me now list the ones that benefited many people in our town.

The Hakhnasat Kallah Society, the Society for Dowering Brides. The name speaks for itself.

The Time to Be Born Society, for birthing mothers. Righteous women came to poor women giving birth and fed them, assisted them with money, and provided them with medications and diapers for the newborn. This society had its own special Sabbath, the Sabbath when the weekly Torah portion Shemot was read, for it contains in the first chapters of the book of Exodus the passage "When you deliver the Hebrew women giving birth." Those who were called up to the Torah pledged to contribute eighteen coins; some pledged to give forty-four, the numerical value of the Hebrew word *yeled* ("child"); and some pledged fifty-two, the value of the word *ben* ("son"). I heard tell that the Parnas R. Yisrael Shlomo, of blessed memory, would donate 279 coins each year, the numerical value of the words *ben zakhar* ("male son").

The Clothing the Naked Society, whose members went around to the homes of the wealthy and collected clothing and shoes for orphaned boys and girls and the poor. This society too had its own special Sabbath when people would pledge to donate to it. At first this was the Sabbath when the Torah portion "Ki Tavo" was read, for it contains the passage "The clothes on your back did not wear out, nor did the sandals on your feet." Later on the society's special Sabbath was moved back a week, when the preceding Torah portion "Ki Tetzeh" was read. That Sabbath was said to be better for honoring a society that "clothes the naked" because it contains the verse "A man shall not wear woman's clothing," and reading that remedied what some of the uneducated did when they dressed up like women on Purim.

The Righteous Lodging Society, for when someone took sick, each member of this society had to stay with that person for one night.

The Hidden Poor Society helped poor people who came from good families who were ashamed to go around begging. The members of this society went to them and gave them what they needed.

The Society for the Support of the Downtrodden, whose name speaks for itself.

The R. Meir Ba'al Haness Charity. Some say that this was something new and unprecedented and was founded by the first students of the Ba'al Shem Tov. Everyone agrees, however, that it was a significant corrective because it provided assistance to the poor of the land of Israel who subsisted only on what the Diaspora sent them. Several people from our town live in the land of the living, the Holy Land, and it is for that reason that I include this society among those that benefit our town.

The Sekhvi Vina Society. This was founded by craftsmen in town in order to provide hens for the kapparot ritual to those who could not afford to buy them.

The Kiddush Levanah Society. The members of this society made lanterns which they brought to illuminate the ceremony of sanctifying the new moon.

The Wine for Kiddush and Havdalah Society. This society distributed wine for kiddush and havdalah to synagogues and batei midrash. It was founded because of the frequent quarrels that broke out over who would have the privilege of performing that mitzvah. Along came a clever man who created a society to which all who were anxious to do this mitzvah could make a weekly donation, and the funds would be used to buy raisins to make wine. This did not end the quarrels, for there were still arguments over just who would make the wine. Eventually the matter was determined by a lottery, and this led to the creation of the Lottery Society. Now any mitzvah that people were so eager to carry out that they got into arguments over it, this one saying, "I should get to do it!" and that one saying, "No, I deserve to do it!" was put into the hands of the society which arranged a lottery to decide the matter.

The Arrival on Time Society. On Friday afternoons, its members would go to the outlying areas of the town to see whether the wagon drivers had returned from their travels before the onset of the Sabbath.

All these societies were as nothing compared to the ḥevrah kadisha. Not everyone who wanted to be a member of it was accepted; special pleading was necessary. Proof of this is the unsuccessful application of R. Yisrael Avraham, one of the richest men in Buczacz, who, with his own money, built a synagogue in his courtyard. He got in only through the assistance of R. Yisrael Shlomo.

After he was accepted into the burial society, R. Yisrael Avraham made a sumptuous feast for all the members. This was an annual event, but all prior such feasts were nothing compared with the one he made. From the conclusion of the evening service after the seventh day of Adar until morning prayers the next day, the prodigious consumption of food and drink went on without interruption. There are still elders in Buczacz who, when they come to tell of that feast, cover their mouths to keep from laughing, but the giggles that do get out tell more than what was held back. To wit, when the revelers stood up to start the morning service, they all had to lean against the wall, and the standing prayer had to be recited sitting down.

That night, while R. Yisrael Avraham was sitting at the feast he made for the burial society, amid the meat and the fish and the braided ḥallot, the wine, the whiskey and the mead and all the other delicacies, something happened at his home. The doors were broken through, the house was entered, and everything of gold and silver, as well as the money and the cash box and the security deposits of gentile officials, were taken. Even the golden earrings that his regal wife was wearing were removed from her ears and taken. When she raised her voice to scream for help, one of the robbers gagged her with a handkerchief, and in a gentile language told her, "*Cicho bestia!*," meaning, "Shut up, you animal," or I'll strangle you. The lady recognized the voice as Yekele's.

The people in town did not believe that Yekele could be one of the robbers. They knew he was a lout, but that he was a robber or someone ready to kill—that was impossible for anyone to believe. It was out of respect for the standing of R. Yisrael's wife, who insisted that it was Yekele who threatened her and said what he said, that the town leaders agreed to go and ask him. When they looked for him and could not find him, it occurred to one of the gravediggers that during the whole time of the feast he did not see Yekele. At that, his friends, too, realized that they also had not seen him at the feast. It was puzzling. One does not give up a chance to attend a feast worthy of King Solomon, one which he spends a year anticipating. So there must have been some reason why he was not there. They began to inquire whether there might be someone who was not one of the gravediggers or the servants or the officers or leaders of the society who could say they saw him. They became even more perplexed, and as perplexity grew, so did suspicion, especially since everyone knew that R. Yisrael Avraham's wife was a lady of standing, and if she said it was Yekele's voice, then the possibility was real. True, a woman's testimony is by Jewish law not accepted, but still the matter needed to be investigated. Very soon there was no one in town who had any doubt that Yekele was involved with the robbers.

R. Yisrael Shlomo sent the town police out to go and look for Yekele. They searched without success. After two days he showed up of his own accord, and it was apparent that he was ill, his face all scratched up, and his whole body bruised. He was brought to the council house and interrogated as to his whereabouts, but he could give no clear answer. When they pressed him, he became insolent with the magistrates, calling them shills for R. Yisrael Shlomo. "I am not afraid of you or of him," he told them.

His relatives came and asked him to stop being stubborn and answer the questions that he was being asked, though they had not yet told him what he was suspected of doing. After much pleading, he answered them as follows. "I was very upset that everyone was talking about the feast that R. Yisrael Avraham was making for the burial society. I knew a nobleman in a certain village who had in his cellar mead that had been aged for a hundred years. I went to buy a cask of it from him so I could show the members of the society that my wine was better than anything R. Yisrael would serve. On my way back to town, I sampled some of that mead, and that led me to take a little more. I kept on tasting and drinking until the whole cask was empty and I fell asleep. I was awakened by some gentiles who prodded me with their plowing tools and injured me." Yekele did not yet know of what he was suspected. He thought they had wanted him at the feast so he could serve the leaders of the society, and since he was not there, R. Yisrael Shlomo was looking to have him punished. That is why he called the magistrates shills of R. Yisrael Shlomo.

After they informed him what he was suspected of and he made no effort to explain himself, they brought him bound in iron shackles to the prison where he was put under guard and treated with the full force of the law. Yekele was still holding on to the idea that sometime before tomorrow he would be freed. But he did say "God help R. Yisrael Shlomo. I swear he will not leave my hands alive."

Word of all this reached R. Yisrael Shlomo, and it was apparent to everyone that he was scared. He moved quickly to bring the matter to the attention of the regional judges, and he was not satisfied until they condemned Yekele to the gallows.

R. Yisrael Shlomo then sent to Czernowitz for a hangman who was the son of the famous hangman appointed by the Emperor Joseph. He was famous because the rope he placed around the neck of the condemned never broke even once during his entire career.

Yekele still believed that all this was being done in order to strike fear in him and that today or tomorrow he would be released. Everyone in town thought likewise. But when it was reported that a hangman had arrived in town, several leading figures assembled, led by our excellent and righteous master and teacher. They said to him, "God forbid that we suspect your Excellency of wanting to destroy one of Israel, but tormenting him is still a grave sin." R. Yisrael Shlomo sighed and replied, "What can I do? The matter is now out of my hands and there is nothing more to be done. I am not the judge or the one in charge or the one giving orders, and besides, the law of the land is the law." They then went and petitioned the officials. But the officials paid them no heed because from the day R. Yisrael Shlomo was appointed the town's parnas any matter pertaining to the Jewish community or to a Jewish person went through Israel Salomon Behrmann, whom they esteemed and whose wishes they followed. Unhappy and dissatisfied, the petitioners sought out the judges. The judges reprimanded them severely and told them, "If you say one more word we will charge you with trying to influence a judge and will punish you to the full extent of the law."

Meanwhile the hangman from Czernowitz arrived in the town of Buczacz. R. Yisrael Shlomo arranged for him to stay at the home of a woman, now a widow, who, when she was a young lady, had worked in his house. The woman reported that her lodger was a short, muscular man with a thick, long mustache who spoke German, and who every time he opened a flask to pour himself a drink that smelled like whiskey, would, before putting his lips to the cup, lift up his mustache to the left of his nose. She further reported that every night he would pace around his room muttering words in languages she had never heard.

In any event, a place for the gallows was found on a hill called the Basztę, or fortress. A proclamation went out to the noblemen and noblewomen and the lords and ladies in all localities that on such-and-such day of such-and-such month at such-and-such hour in such-and-such place a Jew would be executed. And from all those localities, all the noblemen and noblewomen and lords and ladies of all ranks came, everyone dressed in finery as if for a festival, to witness something they had never seen before.

The judges sent a delegation to Yekele in prison to tell him to prepare himself for death. But Yekele still clung to the belief that this was all one big comedy and it was all being done to scare him. They asked him what he wanted before he died, for they had a law that stipulated that before execution the condemned person was to be given anything he wanted except to be spared from death or to have someone else killed in his place. Yekele answered that since he had been sitting in one place for several weeks, his bones were numb and he wanted to ride a horse. A riding horse was promptly brought and guards were placed around him so he would not escape. Yekele mounted the horse and merrily rode out. When he saw a throng of lords and ladies rushing from all directions to witness an execution, he joked to them saying, "You need not hurry as long as I am here. It won't happen without me!"

After he had ridden about to his satisfaction, he was brought before the gallows and hoisted up onto a wooden platform. As he was led to the noose, the official standing next to him said, "Confess now in the name of the God of Israel!" It was said that that official was a Jew who had renounced his faith. His spirit now aroused, Yekele began to recount one after another all the sins he had committed. But the robbery in the house of R. Yisrael Avraham, he said, was not of his doing. As everyone stood waiting to see if he would recant, he repeated his claim. "That sin I did not commit" he said. The hangman coiled the noose around his neck and did what he did. And even now the rope did not break.

A few days later, an order came from the Emperor absolving the condemned man of any punishment. By the time it arrived the sentence had been carried out and the case was closed.

On the day that Yekele was taken out to be executed, all the God-fearing people of Buczacz went out into the fields and forests outside of town. They walked about the whole day weeping and crying. From time to time, they spread out their hands in the direction of the town saying, "Our hands did not shed this blood."

I take leave now of the horrific deeds that were done in the house of Israel. For even if this narrator's intentions are positive, what he writes still contains a drop of criticism that can moisten a parched field and allow thorns and thistles to sprout and wound Israel. Happy is he who restrains himself while telling his story even if he intends to show that the evil deeds that were done were truly evil.

Translated by James S. Diamond
with Jeffrey Saks

The Earliest Ḥasidim

Even before our rabbi, the Da'at Kedoshim, arrived in our city, there were hasidim who had exchanged the Ashkenazic prayer rite for the Sephardic one. Above the Great Synagogue, on the path to the mountain stands a small house that was known as the room of the hasidim. The common people called it the little shul of the clowns, that is, the prayer house of clowns. For the earliest hasidim were strange in their prayer, strange in their clothing and strange in many other ways as well. How were they strange in prayer? They clapped their hands, stamped their feet, and moaned with their mouths. And how were they strange in their clothing? On weekdays most people wear whatever comes to hand, and on the Sabbath, cotton caftan, as long as it is clean. Meanwhile, they wear white on the Sabbath, which is the dress of the separatist hasidim, except on Yom Kippur, when we are all commanded to wear white, following the example of the ministering angels. And in other ways? In all synagogues the elders sit facing the congregants, who are seated in rows facing the holy ark. In a ḥasidic congregation the prayer room was set up like a home, tables extended across the length of the room with benches crowded up against them. People sat facing each other like those attending an intimate dinner. All of Israel pray with awe and respect, comfortably and calmly, but these people jump around during their prayer, making odd gestures and mixing strange languages into that of prayer. All of Israel pray in the early morning, but they dally, performing unnecessary preparations—immersing themselves in the mikveh, smoking pipes, telling miracle tales and doing other things that are not supported by Torah—missing the statutory time for prayer. Don't be astonished that a holy place was called the clowns' room, for the venom spewed by sectarians of Shabbatai Zvi was still sometimes present in our land, and those who guarded the faith of Israel were suspicious of any small change lest it came from this sect. Buczacz was especially strict because Jacob Frank had come from its ranks. So when Buczacz saw people who differed in their prayer, their dress, and in other ways, they were suspicious, and suspicion leads where it leads.

Others say that it was the hasidim themselves who called it the clowns' room. It's possible. As the ḥasidim spread, so the number of their rebbe's increased; and as the rebbes increased so did the divisions among the ḥasidim. Each ḥasid who dedicated himself to a rebbe discredited that of his fellow. When they realized they could no longer pray together, they divided, and each small group built its own place, named for its rebbe. Those who could not do so because of poverty or because they could not form a minyan, joined some other group. So Ḥasidism spread out from the room of the hasidim, and all that remained was the Sephardic prayer rite and the lax times of prayer. It wasn't long before frivolous people who didn't refrain from talking during the prayers and Torah reading, or from ridiculing the details of ritual law gathered there. And more than anything, they made fun of the hasidim and their rebbes, not because they hated hasidim, but because they loved mockery. The hasidim began to call them clowns and the place they worshipped the clowns' room. But even there, there were some who were filled with piety, Torah and good deeds. They stayed because they did not want to abandon that place where their ancestors had prayed. When someone said to them, "Look who you're praying with!" they answered, "Rather than concerning oneself with whom one prays, one would do better to be concerned with before Whom one prays!"

Translated by Herbert Levine and Reena Spicehandler

In a Single Moment

In the town of Buczacz, where all fine, upstanding Buczaczers come from, there lived a certain man by the name of Avraham David. Avraham David did not stand out among his fellow townspeople. He was like all the other people of Buczacz. He would go to the beit midrash every morning and evening and say all his prayers with the congregation. And if he happened to be among the first ten men needed to make a minyan, he would be pleased with himself all day long, for however early in the morning one gets up to pray, ten others always seem to have preceded him. Like everyone, he would recite, each day, a chapter of the Mishnah, study a page of the Gemara, and read two or three chapters of Scripture. Should he come across a verse he did not understand, he would consult the commentary of Rashi, may his memory be a blessing, or those of the *Metzudot*, or sometimes even the *Mikraot Gedolot*, to see what the great scholars had to say. After completing his morning Torah study, he would turn to works of edification, such as the books of moral instruction that set a person on the right path. If he chanced upon a virtue that was within his grasp, he would embrace it and add it to his other virtues. When it came to charity, if he found a penny in his pocket, he would give it away; and if he did not find one, he would borrow one from his neighbor and contribute it, the way his neighbor would, when necessary, borrow from him in order to contribute.

When one attains a certain virtue, many others come in its wake. Since there is nothing remarkable about that, I shall not dwell on it. He was a Buczaczer, Avraham David. One of us. Neither better nor worse than the rest. Cut from the Buczacz mold. A Buczaczer like all Buczaczers.

What I have said about Avraham David could be said of his wife as well. Husband and wife were alike. He was like the other men of the town, and she was like the other women. Sarah Raḥel was her name. Her original given name was Sarah, but the name Raḥel was added on to lend her the attributes of the saintly, blind Raḥel Leah, who distinguished herself by the help she gave to poor brides. Since the added name fell into disuse, I shall call her Sarah and not Sarah Raḥel.

Now that I have spoken about Sarah's name, I shall speak about Avraham David's as well. Avraham David was not named for our teacher the Tzaddik of Buczacz, as most of the men of the town were, because he was born while the tzaddik was still living. Rather, he was given a combination of two names: Avraham, for a good man who departed for the next world as a result of the rampages of the monastery students; and David for David Prager, a relative on his mother's side, one of the leading citizens of Buczacz, who had authority over the Lvov district.

As I said, Sarah was like the other women of Buczacz. Neither better nor worse. A woman like all the rest. At dawn, she straightened up and prepared breakfast: on winter days, a stew of beets, cabbage, potatoes in fat, and other things one brings up from the cellar; and on summer days, the foods that the beloved warmth bestows on us: fruits and grains and buttermilk and cheese and radishes and onions and squash and lettuce and all the other vegetables commonly found in Buczacz. It is not like other places, where people avoid various vegetables, such as lettuce, for fear of worms, such that it is not to be seen on people's plates except on Passover nights. But the Torah says, *As with the green grasses, I have given you all of these*—meaning that vegetables take precedence over all other foods. Having prepared the meal and set the table for her husband and son, she would go off to the shop.

I have now mentioned the son in passing; later, I shall have more to say about him. And while father and son are sitting in the study house engaged in Torah and communal prayer, she sits in the shop praying alone, not getting up from her prayers until customers arrive. If a customer is perceptive, he lets her add a psalm or two to her prayers, that is, he tells her that he will be back in a little while, so that she can satisfy her soul with a few additional hymns, and if she wants to, she can add the verses recited at the end of the Book of Psalms, too. She does her mending and that of her husband and son in bed at night. Buczaczers do not fill their drawers with clothes, which bring only dust, moths, and bother, put an end to harmony, and provoke resentment. As has been said, a poor man sits and fumes, What? Am I not as good as so-and-so, who busies himself collecting clothing, while I go naked and barefoot, with nothing to cover myself?

But since they are particular about not going out in torn raiment, the women all wake up before dawn, take every garment that needs mending, and mend it in bed to the light of the candles that their husbands and sons have lit in order to continue studying Torah. And the benefit they derive from the light of Torah study they give back with the lamp of good deeds, that is, they light oil lamps in the synagogues and study houses.

I have mentioned the shop, and so I should speak of the merchandise, too. It was leather, such as is used to make shoes, and hides, such as are used to make fur coats. In winter, when people need both boots and warm outerwear, Avraham David would spend a lot of time in the shop, sitting there all day and into the night. In summer, when there is not much demand for shoes and none at all for fur coats, he would let his wife take care of business inside while he dealt with the workers who treated the hides against moths and while he bargained with hunters and other gentiles who had animal skins to sell, stretching the leather over boards until he could get it to the tanner. Then he would go into the beit midrash and dip into a book, according to how much time he had, his frame of mind, and which book came to hand. Although study houses have many books, there are also many students, so that one cannot always study the book he wants, someone else having beaten him to it.

I have spoken of Avraham David and his wife Sarah and how they made a living. About whom have I not yet spoken? Their son. So now I will leave the father and mother in order to tell about him.

The tender darling of his father and mother Menaḥem was. None of the children born to them after him survived, but what the Holy One, blessed be He, took from them He repaid them many times over in their son Menaḥem. He brought pleasure, his learning brought delight, his thinking was sound, and his mind was clear. He was diligent and grew in knowledge accordingly. Even in Buczacz—a place where Torah reigned supreme, a town that produced Torah scholars renowned throughout the country, such that the great rabbis of Lemberg would all hire tutors from there for their sons, who, in turn, then became sages by virtue of the Torah scholarship of Buczacz—even in Buczacz, Menaḥem stood out. He became proficient in half the order of Mo'ed, most of Nashim, and all of Nezikin, and he could read even the little-studied tractates fluently.

A young man who has knowledge of Torah also has knowledge of God, enough to observe His statutes and commandments, including the commandment to honor one's father and mother. Why do I mention honoring one's father and mother? Because there are some Torah prodigies who feel themselves superior to their parents and sometimes allow themselves to be lax in observing this commandment. Hence I want to let you know that Menaḥem was not like that and that he treated the will of his parents like the will of his Father in heaven, which must be obeyed without reservation. And when did he observe the commandment to honor his father and mother? During the six work days, the son did not see his mother at all, for he would be in the beit midrash morning, noon, and night, while she was at the shop. And on the Sabbath, all creation and all creatures become as one, so that, of their own accord, the mother's will and the son's become as one. But it was in his diligent study of Torah, which is Israel's honor, that of men and women alike, that he observed the commandment of honoring one's parents.

2

The time had come for Menaḥem to marry and have children. Why had he not married? Because of the matchmakers. If one of them proposed a match, another would come along with a better one, so that the parents were confused and did not know whom to choose. And were it not proclaimed on high that so-and-so would marry so-and-so, the young men of Israel would remain bachelors, especially the more gifted ones, for the more one excels, the more he is pursued and the more the matchmakers interfere and slow things down. And it is all for the sake of money, the matchmakers' fee, the one and a half or two percent of the dowry that goes to them. And because they are after money, the boys' parents, too, become greedy. So powerful is greed that even those who devote themselves to Torah study use it as a device to marry off their sons for money. Happy is he who can overcome greed, for money is the root of most troubles. And where do the rest come from? In case you do not know, I will tell you: from pride and false pretenses. Yet these, too, are because of money, for whoever has it attracts flatterers and sycophants who would rather honor him than honor God-fearing Torah scholars. And because he regards himself as high and mighty, his judgment gets clouded, and he foolishly believes all the praise showered on him until he begins to think himself wise and superior and becomes arrogant and opinionated. Heeding him is bad, for it means succumbing to the influence of money, while ignoring him leads to quarreling, strife, and sacrilege. Well, this is not what I wanted to speak about, nor is it the place to dwell on it. But the commandment to be truthful applies everywhere, at all times, in all matters.

At one time, every father would marry off his sons and daughters by means of the Torah. How so? If he was a learned and wealthy man, he would go into the beit midrash and say, "To whomever can explain such-and-such passage from Maimonides, or resolve such-and-such textual difficulty, I will give my daughter's hand in marriage as well as a dowry of so-and-so many Rhenish florins, in addition to regular meals." And if he was very wealthy and very learned, he would go to the fair of the Four Lands and say, "If someone can explain such-and-such, I shall give my daughter to his son, along with so-and-so many jars of gold dinars." If he was not learned, he would go to the rabbi of his town and say, "Rabbi, I have a daughter, a good, modest girl, and I want to marry her to someone devoted to Torah." The rabbi would size up the man's worth in terms of his lineage and his wealth—that is, how much he gave to the poor and how much to redeem captives—and provide him with a groom for his daughter. If he was neither learned nor well-to-do but had other virtues in which the holy people of Israel excel, those virtues would earn him kindness, and his daughters would be taken as brides. If he was poor and lived off charity, pious women would marry off his daughters, for in every town there was a fund to assist poor brides, and not even the poorest girl would go unmarried. But over the generations, as people became corrupt and began to think about money, they came to attach a monetary motive to every religious act, until such acts were completely subordinated to financial considerations. There was a proliferation of matchmakers of the kind who do not think about whether a particular girl is suited to a particular boy but rather about how much money the girl's father will allocate to her and how large a fee he himself can get for his matchmaking services. As I said, it was because of the matchmakers that Menaḥem had remained single.

But let us turn our attention from the past to what is yet to come.

3

On one of those summer days when business is slow and the shopkeepers idle, especially those who deal in winter merchandise—like Avraham David the leather merchant, for there are no customers for leather in hot weather, nor do the gentiles bring hides to sell because they are busy with their fields and gardens—on one such day Sarah sat alone in the shop knitting a white sock. At the same time, the Master of All Thoughts was knitting thoughts together for her from His endless store. When those thoughts were good, she would pray that they be fulfilled, and when they were not, the All Merciful would banish them and give her lovely, pleasant ones instead. But since divine judgment hangs over us, even when a person diverts himself with good thoughts his soul remains glum. So it was with Sarah, who diverted herself with pleasant reveries, but her spirits remained downcast. And as her spirits were downcast, so was her face.

Avraham David came in and saw her. He asked, Are you sad?

No, she answered.

Ah, but you are, he said. Has something bad befallen you, God forbid?

Nothing bad, nothing at all, she answered.

May it ever be so, Avraham David said. Relieved, he sat down in front of her and looked at the sock she was holding. She glanced up and saw a look of amusement on his face.

Why are you laughing? she asked.

Unless you have skipped an eyelet in your knitting, he said, I see no reason to be sad. Or perhaps you've forgotten that today is the Fifteenth of Av and recited the Prayer of Supplication?

She gave forth a sigh that began in sorrow and ended in hesitation, like one who knows he should be happy but is not—because his joy is incomplete, because it is mixed with sorrow, because he has been disappointed, because things he had hoped for never came to pass.

"How could I forget that today is the Fifteenth of Av?" Sarah said. "Why, it is Menaḥem's birthday!"

"If so," Avraham David replied, "the question remains: if you know that today is Menaḥem's birthday, how can you be sad?"

"It is because today is his birthday that I am downcast," said Sarah, "for he has turned fifteen and is still unmarried."

Avraham David sighed and said, "You have reminded me of my own distress, for I, too, am concerned about this. What do you think we should do?"

Sarah looked at her husband and said, "How can I answer such a question? If I knew what to do, would I wait for you to ask?"

They fell silent and said nothing. She then began speaking again. "I remember that when you were our son's age, your father had already married you off, and Menaḥem had been born." Sarah grimaced, as if trying to suppress a laugh. Avraham David gave her a benevolent look.

"You look at me like someone wondering whether he has gotten a bad deal," Sarah said. "In business, there is no going back. Once you have bought the merchandise, you are stuck with it."

"May we live to 120," Avraham David replied, "and continue together into the next world." Sarah said, "Milovan, the one whose nose was cut off, was here. He brought a sack-full of roots. Here it is, in the corner by the door. I was too preoccupied to ask him anything, but he said he had brought them to use with hides. Sheepskins, he said. I wonder what dry roots have to do with hides."

"That gentile was quite right," said Avraham David. "They are for tanning hides, which is why they are called tanning roots, and they are especially good for sheepskin. You boil the roots in water, and they produce a foam. After the mixture stops boiling, you put the sheepskin into it and soak it. It comes clean, the leather becomes soft, and the wool turns white, like newborn fleece. I assume that Heretzki is too lazy to have already begun tanning the hides I gave him. I will go take him some of these roots."

"When are you going?" Sarah asked.

"The sooner the better," Avraham David answered. "Why do you ask?"

"Maybe you should take Menaḥem along. The boy has had no fresh air since the first day of the Shavuot. I keep thinking: the boy sits in the beit midrash and never gets outdoors except to go there and back. Maybe it would be good for him to do some walking. How far is it from here to Pidlesh? Half again as far as one is permitted to walk on the Sabbath? That far from here to there and that far again on the way back? Even if it is a bit more than that, the walk would be worthwhile."

Avraham David weighed whether it would be a good idea to interrupt his son's studies for a little fresh air. His wife said, "I can see you do not like my suggestion."

"On the contrary," he said. "Today is the Fifteenth of Av, and starting on the Fifteenth of Av one must study at night as well. Let him stretch his legs first."

Puzzled, Sarah said, "You say one must begin to study at night, but what has Menaḥem been doing at night until now, sitting idle? Has he not been spending all his evenings in the beit midrash?

"I was only referring to other people," said Avraham David. "With Menaḥem, every hour of the day is devoted to the Torah. Now you say I should go to the beit midrash and take Menaḥem out. If you insist, I won't refuse."

"As long as you keep an eye on him and make sure he does not overexert himself or walk in the heat of the sun."

Said Avraham David to his wife, Sarah, "Do not concern yourself either with overexertion or with the sun. The Talmud states plainly that a scholar should not overexert himself, and as for the sun, it is said that 'beginning with the Fifteenth of Av, the sun's rays grow weaker.' "

Sarah got up, reached into a niche in the wall, and took out a wicker basket in which she hid her keys, her siddur, and her book of women's prayers. She took from it a honey roll, the kind that is dry outside and moist within, that is full of honey but appears to be a mere roll, the Buczacz roll that leaves everyone who eats it licking his fingers and marveling at how dry it is, for it is so sweet that it seems to be made entirely of honey. Sarah had wrapped the roll in paper, the sort of paper they used to make in Buczacz, smooth and black on one side and rough on the other, good for wrapping various kinds of food, especially things that tend to crumble, for it keeps them from doing so. She set the roll on the table before her husband, saying, "If Menaḥem should feel faint, you can reinvigorate him with this." Avraham David took the roll and tucked it into his cloak, kissed the mezuzah, and went to fetch his son from the study house.

4

He found his son standing and perusing a volume of Gemara, looking briefly in one place, then another. The father was both happy and unhappy. For if he summoned his son to come with him, he would not be interrupting his study, because he was not studying. But by the same token, he was unhappy that the lad was standing there and not studying.

Following the rule that one does not enter a beit midrash for selfish reasons, and if one must enter to call someone he does so briefly, he took a volume of Gemara and sat down to read. It was the tractate Ta'anit, which he had started to study during the first nine days of Av in order to celebrate finishing it by eating meat but which he had not finished, because the many troubles mentioned in the tractate made the idea of indulging in meat repugnant. And so, to avoid the temptation of eating meat, he had left off studying just before the end of the tractate and never finished it. Now that the nine days were over, and eating meat was permitted, he resumed where he had left off.

When one studies a page of Gemara, his soul expands, all the more so when he has been denying himself such study, all the more so when he has broken off studying at a point where the Temple is mentioned and Israel are happily ensconced in their land, such as the last passage in the tractate Ta'anit: "There were no better days for Israel than the Fifteenth of Av and the Day of Atonement, etc., etc., when the daughters of Israel would go out to dance in the vineyards and say, 'Lift your gaze, young man, and see what you have to choose from.' " And we are taught there that "whoever had no wife went there," and so on.

Avraham David lifted his gaze and looked at his son. It was his birthday, his fifteenth, and he had still not married him off. Why? The reason doesn't matter. It was something that should have been done and had not been. He turned away from his son and looked again into the Gemara. But as he was looking into it, his thoughts returned to his son. I have been given a fitting sign concerning my son, he said to himself. Where from? From the saying, "Lift your gaze, young man."

"What are you studying?" he said to his son.

"I want to review the tractate Kiddushin, and I am checking the discussions there to see if I have forgotten any of them."

"Good for you, my son" said Avraham David. "Torah is acquired not only by adding to one's knowledge but also by reviewing things one already knows. The commandment to speak of the Torah refers to things of which one knows enough to speak. I once knew an elderly scholar who had studied the entire Talmud from beginning to end several times. He said he had completed it three times, but others said eight, and it is the last statement that is decisive. Yet he had not lied, for three is part of eight. After the eighth time, he went back to the tractate Berakhot and studied it eight more times. At a meal he made to celebrate completing the tractate eight times, he said to us, The first time, one learns and understands. The second time, he learns but thinks, I was fooling myself to think that I understood, for I understand nothing. The third time, he understands and doesn't understand. The fourth time, he understands what he did not understand and doesn't understand what he understood. And on and on in this fashion. And if he works very hard and goes back over the text so many times that he loses track, and if he has help from on high, he begins to understand. And this is the beginning of wisdom. My son, I have not told you who that old man was. He was your grandfather. And I have told you all this, not to make you proud of your ancestry, for if one is to take pride it should be me and not you, for my father was a scholar, and your father, in comparison to his, is like a novice compared to a rabbi. Rather, what I was describing to you is the way of Torah, the way Torah is acquired. I see that you are not actually engaged in study, so if I interrupt you there is no need to worry about wasting time best spent on the study of Torah. And so I want to tell you something."

He paused for a moment and thought, How marvelous that I stopped at the passage, "Lift your gaze," while my son Menaḥem stopped in the tractate Kiddushin. The words of the sages are beloved, not only because they are sweet but because they reveal to man what is to his benefit.

He took heart and began speaking warmly to his son. He told him he was going to see Heretzki, in Pidlesh, to bring him roots for tanning sheepskin, and that his mother had said, "Stop at the beit midrash on your way, in case Menaḥem would like to go along."

"Mother said to stop at the beit midrash in case I wanted to accompany you, and you did come to get me, which means you are in agreement, and so I will have to concur with you and fulfill what you have said."

He kissed the volume of Gemara, put it back on the shelf, and got up to leave. And just as Menaḥem had done, so did Avraham David. It was an established rule in our old study house, accepted by all the study houses in Buczacz, that each book had a fixed place in the bookcase. One could take out a book and study it to his heart's content, but when he finished he had to return it to its place out of respect for the book and consideration for other people; so that if someone were to need a book and not find it in its proper place, he would know that someone else was reading it and not waste time looking for it.

After putting their books back, they sat down briefly, to avoid giving the appearance of leaving the study house in haste. Then they kissed the mezuzah and left.

5

By the Sabbath following the Ninth of Av, which that year came only two days later, Buczacz had already cast off its mourning garb. By the Fifteenth of Av, the town looked positively festive. Do not be surprised at this, for in addition to being done mourning for Jerusalem, the town had set up several wedding canopies, and when there is a wedding in a town, there is joy there. Making matches between people is difficult. When a man is fortunate enough to marry off a son, and all the more so a daughter, it is a source of great happiness for him, his loved ones, and the whole town. While the Temple still stood, and no one thought of money but only of finding a God-fearing woman, her husband's pride, there was great joy on that day. Why? Because it was a great day for Israel, for many Jews married off their daughters on that day, as we learn at the end of the tractate Ta'anit: "There were no better days for Israel than the Fifteenth of Av and the Day of Atonement, ... when the daughters of Israel would go out to dance in the vineyards and say, 'Lift your gaze, young man, and see what you have to choose from.' " In our time, when our City has been destroyed, when we are in exile and dishonor, and people think only of money, but not every father has money to give his daughter—how much more joyful now shall be one who marries his daughter off. Likewise his loved ones and fellow townspeople.

There is no rejoicing, however exalted, that does not call for some material expression, even the joy of matrimony—on which the world depends for survival and through which all the commandments can be fulfilled, for if a man marries and begets sons and daughters, he sustains the world, and all the Torah's commandments are fulfilled—even this joy requires material expression, be it in noisy feasts or the sound of fiddles, lyres, drums, and flutes. Thus, here, they baked egg breads and cooked meat and fish, until their aroma spread throughout the town, and the musicians oiled and tuned their instruments. Likewise, the other things that accompany a joyous occasion, new clothes and the like, were readied.

No sooner had Avraham David and his son gone out than they ran into the men who hold up wedding canopies. Zalman the Tall, who helped the important shamashim, was walking bent over, carrying the poles, followed by Meir Yonah, the shamash of the main synagogue, who carried the canopy itself. Meir Yonah took small steps, stopping with each step to inspect his coat and make sure nothing had sullied it. The years he had devoted to his sacred vocation had taught him to maintain his dignity, and he took particular care with the coat, which he had received from his grandfather, who, in turn, had gotten it from his father, a secretary of the Council of the Four Lands. The coat was still intact and spotless, though faded with age.

When Menaḥem saw the shamash and his helper carrying the canopy and the poles, he said to his father, "All the weddings in town must be finished."

"What makes you say so, my son?" replied his father.

"I see," he said, "that they are already putting the canopy back in the synagogue, which means they no longer need it today."

"The fact that the canopy is being returned to the synagogue proves nothing," said his father, "for if the musicians are still tuning their instruments it means a new celebration is in the works, and I hear the sound of instruments."

"Then why are they returning the canopy to the synagogue?" Menaḥem asked.

Said his father, "So that the celebrations are not clustered together, prompting Satan to say, 'Jerusalem has been destroyed, but they are still celebrating without letup.' That is why they pause between weddings and return the canopy to its place, then take it out again. I see you have stopped. Are you having trouble walking?"

"I was trying to think of a support in the Talmud for what you said, and I did not notice that I had stopped."

Meir Yonah glanced at Menaḥem. He stopped short, and his face lit up, like someone who has run into a familiar friend. "Why, this is Menaḥem!" he said aloud in a melodious voice. "It has only been two years since he began to put on tefilin. Is that not so, Mr. Avraham David?"

Meir Yonah called Zalman over and handed him the canopy. He took out a tin of snuff, tapped it, and offered it to Avraham David. Avraham David took a pinch, as did Meir Yonah, and they stood there together. With them stood Menaḥem and Zalman, Menaḥem alongside his father and Zalman behind Meir Yonah, gazing at the latter's fur hat, which on Meir Yonah's head looked like a rich man's shtreimel.

Changing his tone, Meir Yonah said, "The day Menaḥem first put on tefilin sticks in my mind because of two things. One is the book by R. Ḥayyim, of blessed memory, who served several communities in Wallachia and toward the end of his life went to the Holy Land. It was on the day Menaḥem began to don tefilin that the book was brought to the old beit midrash. They opened it and found an argument against the opinion of the great authority the author of *Nodah Biyehudah*, may the memory of the righteous be a blessing, challenging the view of the leading rabbis of that time that a certain mystical formula should be recited before putting on tefilin. He had written, referring to the divinely prescribed paths, that "the righteous can walk on them, while ḥasidim stumble on them." And having mentioned the mystical formula, they mentioned another one that scribes used to recite before preparing their parchment, against the opinion of our great teacher the Neta Sha'ashuim, may the memory of the righteous be a blessing. A respected person from Stanislav reported hearing that the elderly rabbi of Stanislav, may the memory of the righteous be a blessing, had said, 'I am surprised that the rabbi of Buczacz raised an objection in his book. After all, our teacher R. Meshulam, may the memory of the righteous be a blessing, said there was no doubt about the matter.' But the rabbi of Stanislav did not remember where our teacher R. Meshulam had found proof for his ruling, because the rabbi of Stanislav had grown old, and his mind was not too clear. Old R. Shemayah, may he rest in peace, heard this and said, 'Do not believe any of this hearsay that has been reported in the name of our teacher R. Meshulam concerning our great master the Neta Sha'ashuim, for when our teacher R. Meshulam left this province for another one, all the important people here went to him and said, "O our master, our mainstay, lamp of Israel, light of the Torah, to whom do you entrust us?" Said he to them, "R. Hershele Kara, the rabbi of Buczacz, is an unquestioned authority, *a gekoviter moire horo'o*." And in the end, they said, in R. Meshulam's name, such and such a thing concerning our teacher the Neta Sha'ashuim.' After this happened, he said over and over again, 'Master of the Universe, I would rather suffer all the afflictions of old age than have you deprive me of the power of speech, so that I could not put to rest the far-fetched rumors that have started to spread concerning our true teachers, may their memory be a blessing.'"

Menaḥem wanted to review what the sages had said concerning the recitation of the mystical formula. Meir Yonah closed his eyes, the way someone turns away from something that is unimportant for the moment to look at something important. With eyes closed, he turned to the father and son and asked in a singsong manner, "What about the case of donning a prayer shawl? I heard something nice today from R. Yankele, may he live and be well. After leaving his father-in-law's table, Yankele had looked for a rabbinic position, but that generation was graced with scholars the way emperors' crowns are studded with gems and pearls. Even small towns that were little more than villages merited the presence of outstanding learned men. So it was hard to find a rabbinic post. Said R. Yankele, 'I shall go to Lemberg to see the sage the Yeshuot Yaakov. He has authority over many communities; perhaps he can find one for me.' So he went there, to the rabbi of Lemberg. That sage made it a practice to ask you for a novel interpretation you had come up with in your study or to tell you about a novel interpretation he himself had come up with, for he would have such new insights every day. In the event that he did not have one, he would take someone else's insight and give it a completely new twist. 'Tell me something,' he said, and R. Yankele did so. The rabbi of Lemberg could see that he was a clear thinker, well spoken and sharply focused. And that is no small thing, for excessive cleverness can carry one away on endless tangents. Said he, 'Tell me something else.' And he, the Yeshuot Yaakov, would also give him his own original interpretations. This went on day after day. R. Yankele's money ran out, and he could no longer pay his way back home. The sage said to him, 'Until such time as the Good Lord provides you with a rabbinical post, stay with me and study with R. Hershele, the son of my son R. Mordechai Ze'ev, may his memory be a blessing.' R. Yankele liked this idea and studied with R. Hershele for the next thirteen years. He began to come up with novel interpretations, like the one he had expounded the day he first donned tefilin and like the one printed in his name at the end of *Yeshuot Yaakov*. Here I come to the end of the story. The day he began to don tefilin was also the day he first donned a prayer shawl, and that is not done until one marries."

Meir Yonah turned back to Menaḥem and said, "I saw that you wanted to review for us the halakhic arguments in which the town elders were engaged on the day you became bar mitzvah. Since you have such a good memory, perhaps you can recall the 'All Merciful' passages chanted by R. Netanel on the day you were circumcised! Heaven forfend that in praising the old cantor, I should imply criticism of the new one. Still, one never hears such beautiful 'All Merciful' passages from the lips of the new cantor. If your father makes haste and marries you off, you can enjoy hearing the old cantor's voice again before he emigrates to the Land of Israel."

Avraham David asked Meir Yonah, "Who is the fellow getting married today?" Said Meir Yonah, "I am not surprised that you do not know him. How could anyone know all the strangers who have descended on our town since the fire? When people heard that Buczacz was impoverished and could not afford to rebuild, they came running to buy up the empty lots. Now they have made themselves at home here as if this were their ancestral turf. Oh, what money can do! The money of people of means will wipe out Buczacz yet. And so you ask who that bridegroom is. Had you asked me about the bride, I would have said, 'a fair and comely bride.' But since you ask about the groom, I shall tell you exactly who he is. A lucky man he is to have been matched up with such a woman. He is a widower with children to care for, and he has a connection with the gentile authorities. Ever since the day the town burned down and its rich people were wiped out, anyone of means who offers to lend money to the gentry gains access to the higher ups. As for the bride's father, who does not know him? He is R. Moshe Ta'anit, the son of Raḥel Leah the Pious's daughter, a God-fearing man, devoted to Torah, who lacks nothing but a bit of luck. If only someone could bring you back to life, O saintly Raḥel Leah, for you devoted your whole life to providing for poor brides, and now your daughter's son has given his daughter in marriage to... to ... *achoo!* What do you think of my snuff? Zalman, where are you? Wouldn't you like some snuff? Now where did I put it?"

Avraham David looked to see whether his son was paying attention to what Meir Yonah was saying. Even a young man who devotes himself day after day to Torah, never looking up from his studies, should sometimes listen to what clever people have to say, because such talk broadens the mind and opens the heart.

Eyes shut, Meir Yonah reached out to take hold of the cloth of the bridal canopy, saying, "We've got to go. The time has come. A wedding is a wedding."

He and his helper set off to bring the canopy to the bride and groom, and Avraham David set off with his son to deliver the roots for tanning lambskins.

6

Menaḥem would walk with eyes downcast, as young Jewish men do. More than their study of Torah uplifts them, their modesty makes them lower their gaze. The exaltation of Torah can sometimes lead to haughtiness. That is why one who is wise and sensible keeps his eyes on the ground. Just as this land, the treasure trove of kings, is nothing but dust, so, too, a man: however full he is of Torah, his end is dust. Avraham David, on the other hand, would look this way and that as he walked, as shopkeepers do, being used to looking around for customers. For the burden of making a living in this difficult time makes them insecure, and even the most innocent of believers looks apprehensively to the future.

"The musicians have already come out to serenade the bride and groom," said Avraham David to his son, "and if I am not mistaken, Zalman the Tall has already gone to R. Yekele's door to summon him to perform the ceremony. Meir Yonah once told us a nice story he had heard from R. Yekele."

Said Menaḥem, "If R. Yekele is being called to perform the ceremony, it means our Master, the rabbi, will not be doing it. He has not been seen since he returned here. And I cannot say I saw him even before he left town."

"The ten men Mikhl Ber chose to pray with our Master in his home do see him," Avraham David said. "He is weary from traveling and so never leaves his house. The trip our Master made from Kamenetz to Buczacz is enough to wear out even someone who is used to traveling. How much more so scholars who do not travel."

Avraham David took his son by the hand, and together they climbed over a pile of dirt and brick shards that remained from the fire. He looked to see if he had not overtaxed the boy and said, "Our Master did not have to leave Buczacz. Even though the town had been destroyed by fire and its houses stood empty, they could still have found a place for our Master to live. But seeing that the noise of digging and building would distract him from his Torah studies, he was persuaded by a delegation from Kamenetz to accept the rabbinical post there. Can you make it over this pile?"

Menaḥem climbed over the heap and said, "Here, I've done it."

Avraham David returned to his subject. "Our Master did not need to leave Kamenetz either. He was well respected there, treated as well as the ḥasidim treat their rebbes. Why, then, did he come back to Buczacz? Some say it was because of the harsh decrees—the governor there forbade the erection of sukkot for the festival—while others say it was simply that he missed our town. For there is a bond between Buczacz and its citizens, such that anyone who leaves longs for it and returns if he can. His wife, too, said as much: 'All the time I lived in Kamenetz, I longed for Buczacz.' I don't know any parallel, a town from which, if you leave it, you can only stay away for a short time. All those who have left and come back say that at first they were glad to get away but that after a while they remembered Buczacz and felt pangs of longing, to the point where the entire world was not worth a single square yard of Buczacz to them. Thus we can understand why our Master came back. But why look for explanations? It is enough that he did."

The Buczaczers love nothing more than talking about Buczacz, and the essence of the town is its distinguished scholars, those who made Buczacz what it was, who made it world-famous, to the point where Buczacz even began to recognize its own worth. Consequently, do not be surprised if, when a Buczaczer mentions one of the town's great scholars, he goes on and on, saying things that everyone knows and yet is astonished to hear again. That is what makes us love beautiful things: they have a perennial appeal, and hearing about them a second and third time can be even better than the first. The first time you hear it but not all of it. When you hear it again you savor every detail. Thus, when Avraham David spoke about our Master, the distinguished Av Beit Din, he would go on and on about things we already knew, but both the speaker and the listener felt as if they were only now hearing the real gist of it for the first time.

What did Avraham David tell about? First, he spoke about our Master, the Ḥesed leAvraham, who was appointed rabbi of the town of Zboriv when he was only sixteen. "And if Zboriv surprises you, consider

Tisminitz, which appointed our Master, R. Meshulam, to a rabbinical post when he was not yet seventeen, and Tisminitz is, after all, a big town full of great scholars to which many other towns look for authority. Even Stanislav, which is beginning to develop as an important center, has subordinated itself to Tisminitz. But do not be surprised by either Zboriv or Tisminitz. Those communities chose well, and so it is their names that are associated with most of the great scholars. Take the case of our Master, R. Meshulam: he was born in Buczacz, raised in Buczacz, and learned Torah in Buczacz, yet he is not referred to as R. Meshulam of Buczacz but rather R. Meshulam of Tisminitz. Likewise, R. Ḥayyim, who towards the end of his life went to the Land of Israel, was born in a village adjacent to Buczacz, raised in Buczacz, and taught Torah in Buczacz; yet he is not called R. Ḥayyim of Buczacz but rather by the names of the towns where he served as a rabbi."

Avraham David continued, "Now that I've told you about two things that only seem surprising, I'll add a third that might surprise you but should not. Do you know when R. Leibush Te'omim, who served as a rabbi in Brody during the time of R. Zalman Margulies, was first accepted as a rabbi? They made him the rabbi of the town of Lizhensk when he was only thirteen. To make sure you do not think that was merely a slip of the tongue, I'll repeat it: R. Leibush Te'omim was only thirteen when they made him the rabbi of Lizhensk. It seems surprising: how can a thirteen-year-old boy be given rabbinical authority to teach, judge, and lead a community? But in fact there's nothing surprising in this, for at thirteen one is considered an adult in all respects. Needless to say, he was already married, too, like R. Hershele the grandson of the Yeshuot Yaakov, about whom we have heard that the day he began donning tefilin he also began to don the talit, and donning the talit is not customary in these parts until one gets married."

Walking along and telling stories this way, they did not notice the difficulty of the journey or the other travelers who passed by or anything else, be it in town or country, until they got to the Heretzki home in Pidlesh.

Heretzki was a worthy gentile. Being a Ruthenian, he was treated by the Poles like an animal, whereas the Jews treated him like a human being and did not humiliate him gratuitously. Heretzki greeted them warmly and showered them with gratitude for coming to visit him. Having reassured them of his affections with words, he ran out to his garden to fetch fruit for them. The gentiles around Buczacz are clever: they know that when a Jew eats fruit he says a benediction over it, and the benedictions of the Jews make fields and gardens flourish. They said the benediction thanking God for the fruit of trees and also the benediction for the first fruit of the season; for among the fruits were some that had ripened during the Three Weeks of mourning, and they had not yet tasted them.

Heretzki's sons and daughters came to look at the Jews, who would open every cherry before eating it, and if they found a worm inside, they would throw it away. Avraham David reached into his pocket to give them the roll that Sarah had sent along for Menaḥem, but he did not give it to them. And it is a good thing he did not give it to them, as we shall soon see. What did he give them? Money to buy provisions for the journey, which could be divided among them.

After reciting the benediction for a light repast, Avraham David put a finger to the wind to see where a chill might come from. He then sat his son down in the shade of an apple tree and went with Heretzki to see the sheepskins he had given him to tan.

Sitting under the apple tree, Menaḥem went over in his mind some of the beautiful things that were said regarding apples. Just then the tree's fruit gave forth its fragrance, as did the fruits of the other trees and the grasses and shrubs. And as they exuded their fragrance they also yielded a profusion of sights so lovely that no description could come close to doing them justice. Menaḥem sat gazing and marveling at what he saw: the earth and sky, the birds in the air, and even the air itself, which is invisible but which the soul senses as if it had substance. Likewise, the light coming through the branches of the tree and the blades of grass in the field, from which they took on a new radiance that changed from one moment to the next. The effect of these things was peace and tranquility. And from one moment to the next, each of these, the air and the light, each dancing and setting the rest to dancing, would intertwine, pull apart, come back together, and merge, continuously yielding new and unprecedented forms of light and air.

Meanwhile, Avraham David was standing with Heretzki over a pile of large branches laden with hides. He looked them over and fingered them and then gave Heretzki the roots he had gotten from Milovan, explaining how to soak them, how much water to use, and the rest.

Heretzki stood there, listening attentively to every word Avraham David said, nodding agreement but thinking to himself, If Vrum Duvit wants it that way, so be it, but it doesn't have to be so, for it is better for the hides to be treated in a different way, and if I do it the way I want, I will not tell him I didn't do it the way he wanted but rather the way I wanted. And if he says, "You see, Heretzki, I told you the hides needed to be treated in such and such a way, and it is because you did just as I told you that they have come out looking so good, even better than I expected"—I will not tell him what I did. I will not say, "No, sir, it is precisely because I did *not* do as you told me, not at all, that the hides have come out looking as good as they do, because I did it in such and such a way instead, the way the hides themselves want to be treated, and that is why that have come out looking good."

When they were finished with the hides, Avraham David looked up at the sky to see if it was going to rain, for of all the varieties of water in the world, rainwater is the best for washing.

The sky was clear, without a trace of a cloud, as is usually the case just after the fast of the Ninth of Av. Concerning the clear skies following the Ninth of Av, the Buczaczers would say, "*Hark, the archangels cry aloud, the angels of peace weep bitterly*—it is the tears of the angels that have cleared the sky." But on the festival when one is eager to fulfill the commandment to erect a sukkah, the sky is not like this.

Avraham David returned to his son and said, "I have done what I came to do, so we can go back to town."

Menaḥem got up, trying to disengage his mind from everything he had seen and enjoyed. Such worldly pleasures as the sight of gardens and fields may not be sinful, but they can take over one's mind. So one needs to be drawn away from them by one means or another. Otherwise, one can be seduced by them. They may not be the least bit sinful, but it is not good to dwell on them. For something that does not entail wrongdoing may still be dangerous, inasmuch as the attraction to it can distract one from fulfilling his sacred duties.

They took leave of the gentile and his family, Avraham David with words of peace and friendship, Menaḥem, who did not understand their language, with nothing more than a nod. And the gentile did not detain them, for the day was almost over, and they were hurrying to the synagogue to pray with all the other Jews. He walked them as far as the crossroads, and then to the long bridge over the Strypa, for the Strypa bridge marked the entrance to the town.

When they got to the riverbank, Heretzki waded in up to his knees, then bid them farewell with bows, blessings, and thanks to them and to their wife and mother Sorki. Sorki is Sarah. And why did he call her Sorki? Because gentiles have a way of mispronouncing every Hebrew word they utter. For out of love for Israel, the Holy One, blessed be He, gave the holy tongue to us and no one else, and thus it is that whenever a word of the holy tongue passes the lips of a non-Jew he garbles it. And to what end? That Israel, the people closest to Him, might excel in the use of the language in which were given the Torah, the Prophets, and the Writings and in which the Holy One, may He be blessed, praised, and exalted, addresses those who revere Him. But in the time to come, the gentiles will all speak the holy tongue, as it is written, *For then I will make the peoples pure of speech, so that they all invoke the Lord by name.*

7

They walked across the long bridge over the Strypa. Its body hung in the air, while its legs went down into the water. It gave off a smell of tar and was black as tar, too. And though it was long and wide, and carriages and wagons could traverse it, it groaned under the feet of everyone who went by, like someone carrying a heavy burden—this despite the fact that since the fire the Buczaczers had grown thin and were nothing but skin and bones.

They made their way among the mud huts that poked up out of the ground and stuck out between the melon patches. Most hugged the ground, but some seemed to have been put up like the stakes that hold up sunflowers, which crane their necks to gaze up at the sun. They had thatched roofs that had turned black and walls of clay, with straw protruding everywhere. In one place they bulged, while in another they had caved in. Some houses had chimneys on the roof and some didn't but rather had an opening above the door to let the smoke out. Originally, there had been no glass in the windows, only pig bladders stretched across them that admitted light. After the fire, they had found panes of glass in the town dump, which they took and put in their windows. They had found other paraphernalia strewn about the town, some of no obvious use, some that did not mind being reshaped to serve the needs of new owners. Baskets of steaming dung sat fermenting outside their windows and giving off a stench, the liquids seeping out and forming puddles, into which other things flowed. The stench was moderated somewhat by the aroma of roasted corn, together with the smoke of the wood burned for the roasting, all spreading out and mingling with the smells of the fields, the fruit trees, the cowshed, and the cheese.

Avraham David pointed out a picket fence to his son. Looking at it, Menaḥem saw, hanging on each stave, inverted clay jars and tin cans, their mouths downward and their bottoms toward the sun. And he saw his father studying them. Avraham David then broke his reverie and said, "Here lived Yaakov Yehoshua the dairyman. Before the fire, he used to bring us milk. We had been elementary-school pupils together, studying the same talmudic texts. He had a quick mind and a good memory, unmatched by any other boy in the school. He had only to look at a page of Gemara to know it by heart. I recall that when we finished studying the eighth chapter of Ḥullin, he recited the whole thing, word for word, from memory. Having this talent, he gave way to pride, which is one of the bad attributes; for the very thing that gives a person the feeling of superiority over everyone also makes everyone hate him. We had another friend, the son of the meat-tax collector and grandson of Feivush the candle-tax collector, whose mother used to spread fat on both sides of his bread. He said, 'You see this fellow who is proficient in the laws of meat falling into milk? I bet if you put milk and meat in front of him he would not know which was which, for this good-for-nothing pauper has never seen either a scrap of meat or drop of milk in his father's house.' When Yaakov Yehoshua heard this he blushed, then turned pale, but said nothing. We kept quiet too, although we were angry that he had embarrassed our friend. The next day, Yaakov Yehoshua did not come to school. When he had been absent three days, I went to his house but did not find him, for he had hired himself out to a certain dairyman. A while later, I saw him walking along carrying two jugs of milk. 'Yaakov Yehoshua,' I said, 'the Gemara awaits your return.' I saw tears in his eyes. Later, when both of us had settled down, I went to see him and asked him to deliver milk to us. This he did until his cows perished in the town fire. I heard that just as the fire was breaking out he was on his way into the cowshed, to the cows. Seeing the fire, he left them and ran to save what he could, but he neglected to lock the door behind him, and the cows came after him. They went into the fire and burned to death. Now I hear he has bought another cow and gone back to selling milk. I must talk to your mother about asking him to deliver milk to us again."

Pointing out another place, Avraham David said, "Do you see that ruin, my son? It was the home of Raḥel Leah the Pious. As long as it stood, it was referred to as the House of Light, because anyone who entered it with a dark expression on his face would come out glowing. Even people with daughters who were hard to marry off would be helped by this saintly woman to do so. I did not know her; your mother, who was named in her memory, is exactly my age. But your grandmother knew her and used to tell the following story. There was a group of jokesters in town who used to get together every Saturday night in the women's section of the burned-out synagogue, where they would sit around hatching practical jokes to be played on various people, good and bad alike. Among them was a fellow of twenty who had already been matched with the daughter of a high-class family. As they sat and joked, his said to his friends, 'I wonder why we never thought of that blind woman Raḥel Leah.' Some of them had heard of her and were shocked. 'Watch what you say,' they said. Others said, 'If you're so brave, why not prove it?' 'I will,' he replied. Some of them could not believe he would actually pull a prank on that pious woman, while others were afraid he would and warned him against it. He went to her house, pretending to be a woman and speaking in a high voice. He did not have to dress up as a woman, because she was blind. He said to her, 'Woe is me, good, dear, pious, and learned lady. I have gone grey, and I am still without a mate.' She turned her blind eyes toward him and said, 'Yes, your hair is grey.' He began shaking inexplicably. 'Finding a match for you is not going to be easy,' she went on, 'but do not despair. The Lord, blessed be He, will help you, in His mercy.' He laughed in her face and left. When he got back to town, they could not recognize him, for every last hair on his head and even his newly sprouted beard had turned completely white. When they heard what he had done, no father would give him his daughter's hand in marriage. No amount of money would sway them, and if the pious woman had not made a match for him with a poor, crippled orphan, older than himself, he would have rotted a bachelor."

Avraham David placed three fingertips of his left hand on his lips and whispered verse 7 of Psalm 68, a verse that every father who has a son past puberty should remember, because it has power over the pack of demons known as the Rebellious Ones, who conspire to send the young men of Israel who have never tasted sin out into a desolate wilderness, God forbid. The verse also contains a request and a prayer that the young men be found a home, as Scripture says:

God restores the lonely to their homes,
Sets free the imprisoned, safe and sound,
While the rebellious must live in a parched land.

For when David saw that Saul had sent couriers to take Mikhal away from him, he grew faint and composed this verse, along with the rest of the psalm.

Avraham David gestured toward a small reddish-colored cow that had poked its nose into the ruin. Said he to his son, "I wonder if this might not be Milovan's cow! The animal knows where to pasture. It leaves the ashes and is drawn to the grass that grows among the ruins of the saintly woman's house. Milovan, too, knows that no mishap will ever occur in connection with that house, even in its ruins, so he lets his cow roam there unguarded."

Avraham David stood there leaning on his walking stick, gazing at the ruin, and sighing, "Since the day the Temple was destroyed, there has been a harsh decree that the houses of the righteous, too, shall be destroyed. I learned from what Meir Yonah said that that pious woman's grandson scraped the bottom of the barrel to find a match for his daughter. Let us go to her wedding and conclude this day with nuptial joy."

8

They passed from the outskirts of the town into the town proper. They came to the little houses that are nothing like farmhouses except for the kosher animals kept there, along with cats. The latter like to live with Jews, because the Jews take pity on them and do not keep dogs. You also find there piles of wooden beams and timber, plaster, asphalt, tar and kerosene, which contribute to the livelihood of some of the householders.

Having passed the cemetery, they came to the place where the pallbearers would change places, because of a certain incident. (I will not relate it here but elsewhere.) At last they found themselves among people, among the old houses built after the previous fire that had not been destroyed by this one. These houses were not tall, so that if a goat decided to climb onto the roof of one of them it could easily do so. They had little windows, like the lanterns of small children, and old ladies sat in their doorways mending clothes or sorting peas. Nearby, on the earthen porch that protruded from each house, sat old men, their heads resting on their canes, dozing. Every so often they would wake up, raise their heads, and say, "What?"—like someone who is called and answers, "Here I am." And once they had bestirred themselves, they would tell each other stories from childhood, when the great sage the Neta Sha'ashuim was still alive and people would come to him from far and wide with questions, particularly questions regarding agunot, women who could not remarry. For in former generations there were many women—mostly young, actually just children—whose husbands had suddenly disappeared.

Here they encountered passersby, some coming back from the city, some on their way there. Those returning from the city were laden with all kinds of merchandise they had bought there, and those going to the city were dressed like a bridegroom on his way to the wedding canopy. They inquired of each other's health and traded stories, until at last they parted company and went on.

From this point on, they could go no more than three or four steps without encountering a passerby. When they had gone to Pidlesh there was no one out and about, but when they got back there were more people in the town. On their way to Pidlesh, the musicians had been tuning their instruments, and one could hear singing. On their way back, the musical instruments had been silenced.

Most of the day had already passed, the sun was declining, and it was not clear whether the summer days were on their way out or on their way in. Even Menaḥem, who was not used to walking, did not find the way strenuous, because the air was fresh and comfortable for walking and because his father's pleasant conversation made the journey seem short.

Most of the day was already gone, the sun was declining, and it was not clear whether the summer days were on their way out or on their way in. But anyone can see that the end of the summer is not the same as the beginning. There was no difference between the Ten Commandments on the first set of tablets, given on Shavuot, and the second set, given on Yom Kippur. But between Passover and Shavuot the days grow longer, and the heart rejoices, while before Yom Kippur the days are short, and one worries when he will find time to repent. Now the first set of tablets were broken, but the second set will last forever, and originally it was ordained that the days before Yom Kippur be joyful. In fact, while the Temple still stood there was great joy in the world, but since the Holy Temple was destroyed there is no joy except in repentance and good deeds.

They had already passed old houses built after the first fire and spared by the last. Inside the town now, they found themselves among the heaps of dust and ashes and the charred beams that remained from the big, substantial homes. Though the fire had thoroughly scorched them, the rain and snow had cleansed them of the smell of smoke. Still, they had not dispelled the fear that the ruins of burnt houses inspire in those who contemplate them. Here, Avraham David left off telling pleasant stories that gladden the heart and arouse the soul to follow in the footsteps of the righteous and imitate their actions.

They caught sight of one ruin that suddenly appeared through the window of another. Looking at both of them, Avraham David said, "These are the ruins of the new tax collector's house, and the others are the ruins of the previous tax collector's, that of Feivush the candle-tax collector and his family. In all its history, Buczacz has never witnessed a hatred to compare with that of the two tax-collectors for each other.

But along came the fire and made them brothers in distress. You look one way and see the ruins of one house, the other way the ruins of the other. I have heard that they made up and worked together collecting the tariff on meat. The cat and the mouse made a party with the milk of some unlucky fellow. Now, just try to eat the tiniest morsel, and the two of them will yank it out of your throat."

Avraham David went on pointing out the ruins, not yet cleared, that lay among the houses newly built since the fire. He told one story after another. This was the home of a rich man named so-and-so, and that was the home of another rich man named such-and-such. This was the home of someone who was not rich but gave generously to charity. He paused in the middle of his narrative to point out a particularly impressive ruin. "Here," said Avraham David to his son, "stood the home of Shabtai the salt merchant, whom people called Shepsl the Sabbath Observer, for he was known for his great devotion to the seventh day. No sooner had one Sabbath ended than he began to fret about how he would observe the next. Even now, people wonder how someone so punctilious about observing the Sabbath could lose his home to fire, and they pin the blame on his neighbors, who must not have been as zealous about it as he was. For a person can become entangled in his neighbors' sins. Now listen to this, my son. The ruin you see here is of the study house I mentioned. It was filled with astute, learned men, as well as the prominent and wealthy, but for the sin of levity committed by their children, the beit midrash and all their homes burned down, so that, like the rest of the town, they were left with nothing but a crust of bread. All of them, exalted and humble alike, *have embraced refuse heaps*. Overnight, they lost everything they had and were reduced to poverty, may God have mercy on us all."

He went on talking about the high and mighty who had suddenly lost all their property, down to their last crust of bread, may we be spared the like. The very same thing had happened in the first fire, in the days of the tzaddik, may his merit protect us, who wrote about it in the letter he gave the emissaries of Buczacz who went out to solicit donations from Jewish communities all over. "I recall that when I was a teenager, my father, may he rest in peace, wanting to teach me the use of elevated language, asked some important people he knew for a copy of that letter, and I remember reading there: '*When the Lord overturned the city, when the Lord unleashed His wrath upon us, a storm whirled forth and fire lashed out*, leveling the town *to its very foundations* and *consuming its palaces,* so that many householders lost everything, *their property stripped to the ground,* and *they barely escaped with their lives.*' "

9

Avraham David looked to see if his son had picked up the references in his words. Suddenly, his ears were assaulted by a barrage of strange sounds. He listened, dumbfounded. "I hear screaming," he said. He paused for a moment, then said, "It seems to be coming from the courtyard of the Great Synagogue." Again he paused and said, "I do not like the sound of this."

They climbed over ruins left from the fire, skirted one that had collapsed, passed through an open colonnade that remained from a mansion that had been the pride of Buczacz, and entered the desolate, broken-down courtyard of a house of prayer known as the Synagogue of Gems. It was called that because everyone who prayed there was a brilliant Torah scholar, brilliant like a precious stone. They resumed walking, from one heap of rubble to another, one collapsed building to another, one ruin to another, until they came to the courtyard of the Great Synagogue. They could hear that it was from there that the screams were coming.

Avraham David stood there in astonishment. And no wonder, for the screaming was coming from the same Great Synagogue courtyard where the canopy had been set up for R. Moshe Ta'anit's daughter. And never, since the day Buczacz was founded, had such a hue and cry been heard, much less such abuse and vilification, much less such curses, much less at a wedding. And what a wedding! The wedding of the daughter of R. Moshe Ta'anit, the son of the daughter of Raḥel Leah the Pious!

Avraham David stood still, as if the commotion were his own doing. For so it is with good people that if they see something untoward they assume it is they themselves who are at fault. He stood motionless, looking but seeing nothing, like a man who, in his amazement, looks but does not see, contemplates but does not comprehend.

Yonah, the nephew of the shamash Meir Yonah, came toward him. He saw Avraham David standing there and gave him a look that said, "If you open your mouth and ask me, I shall not hesitate to tell you."

Avraham David sensed this and asked, "What is going on here?"

"An uproar," he answered.

"An uproar?"

"A hullabaloo," he said.

"A hullabaloo?"

"An outcry," he said.

"Right you are," he said. "I hear crying. But what brought it on? "

"I could ask you the same question. You tell me: where does a man born to a Jewish woman get such cruelty?"

"About whom are you asking?"

"About whom? Why, the king!"

Avraham David was flabbergasted. We had known that Meir Yonah was a bit crazy, because when his mother had been pregnant with him there was a student rampage of the monastery students, and the fetus in her belly was jarred and brain-injured; but we had not realized that he had been so badly affected until he spoke aloud of the king's cruelty.

"Father," said Menaḥem, "he is referring to the bridegroom. Has it not been said that a bridegroom is like a king?"

Said Meir Yonah to Menaḥem, "Of one such as you it is said, *Who is like the wise, who knows the meaning of things?* For you knew how to explain my words to your father. As long as Buczacz has been Buczacz, no one has been as cruel to a daughter of Israel as this bridegroom to his bride. The wedding canopy is ready, the marriage contract has been prepared, and R. Yekele has been standing here for some two hours, ready to take out his handkerchief for the symbolic transfer. And who is holding up the wedding? The groom himself. He has been shouting, 'I shall not go under the canopy until the entire dowry promised by the bride's father has been deposited in my hand, every last penny of it, every last cent! Should he withhold a single penny,' says he, 'I shall turn my back on him, and he *shall not see my face*.' Such lofty language has Buczacz been privileged to hear! Oh woe that we have come to this. That which the author of Lamentations bewailed concerning Zion has befallen us. *Hear us, O our God, for we have been shamed, and Your tabernacle has been consumed by fire. Why should the canopy be destroyed?* And whereas it was promised that Zion would be rebuilt and re-established, who will rebuild and reestablish Buczacz? The cheese lovers in Yaslowitz The madmen in Potik? The dead of Monasterzyska? The geese of Pidayets? All those outsiders, who have spread throughout Buczacz, are nothing but a curse on the town. If Jews could do so, I would post guards all around to prevent any outsider from entering Buczacz unless he has been examined seven times over."

"And what does the father of the bride have to say?" Avraham David asked Meir Yonah.

Replied Meir Yonah, " 'With the inspiration of Moshe,' he says the customary thing, R. Moshe does: 'When I am doing better,' says he, 'when I am doing better I shall give it.' And R. Moshe can be relied on to keep his word. Of what case are we speaking? Where there is money. But where there is none, there is none. 'When a charitable person has nothing, he is despised by every good-for-nothing.' Or as R. Yoel the Jester put it so well, 'If there's nary a penny, only heaven helps any.'"

So Avraham David asked, "What do other people say?"

Said Meir Yonah, "What can they say? They make a fist and threaten to turn him over to the king's army if he doesn't return to the wedding canopy forthwith, that is to say, they will tell the mayor to turn him over to the king's army. All well and good, but it is a hollow threat, for he can threaten us with the very same thing. He says, 'Before you turn me over to the king's army I'll turn over your sons and sons-in-law.' And that has to be taken seriously, because he has the ear of the gentile officials, and he hobnobs with them. Ever since the town burned down and the well-to-do townspeople lost everything they had, the officials no longer listen to them. With you and me it is different. 'People only get close to someone in order to benefit from him,' and what benefit is to be had from the poor? When the town changed, so did the attitude of the officials. Alas, Master of the Universe, the three weeks commemorating the conquest of Jerusalem have passed, and the seven weeks of consolation have begun, yet there is still no sign of comfort. I think I hear cries of 'Water! Water!,' but perhaps it's just my imagination. Since the fire, I hear 'Water! Water!' unceasingly. Maybe someone is really shouting it."

He caught sight of Zalman leading R. Yekele back home. "What is going on, Zalman?" he said.

"The groom left, and the bride fainted," Zalman replied.

Said Meir Yonah, "If it weren't the Fifteenth of Av, when the bride's pre-nuptial fast is suspended anyway, I would still rule that this bride should be permitted to break her fast. Am I not right, Rabbi?"

R. Yekele nodded and leaned on Zalman, for his legs had grown heavy from all the walking.

"I shall go see what is happening there," said Meir Yonah.

10

Said Avraham David to his son, "The Talmud teaches that 'one may win a place in eternity in a single moment.' If you were to marry this girl, you would restore her soul. Menaḥem, my son, there is no greater precept than that of saving the life of a fellow Jew. And in this case you would be saving three lives: the girl's, her mother's, and her father's."

"Perhaps we should tell Mother," said Menaḥem.

"Of course we will," said Avraham David, "and we must also write a wedding contract. Meanwhile, the poor girl lies as good as dead, and if you tarry, her soul may, God forbid, leave her body. The story is told," Avraham David went on, "of a man who was walking through the marketplace with his daughter. 'I am thirsty, Father,' she said to him. 'Wait a bit,' he said. 'But I am thirsty,' she replied. 'Wait a little while,' he said. And she died."

"Does that not appear in the Jerusalem Talmud, Father? " Menaḥem asked.

"Most likely," Avraham David replied.

"It is in the tractate Yoma of the Jerusalem Talmud."

"Very likely," answered his father.

Menaḥem then began to recite almost word for word the text from the Jerusalem Talmud.

"If he had not lingered, she would not have died," said Avraham David. "The Torah did not command us to delay a wedding for one's mother's sake, my son, but it did command us to save human life. When an opportunity presents itself to fulfill one of the commandments, you must not pass it up. I do not think we should send for your mother, for if we wait for her to get here, we shall prolong the risk. But if you marry the girl right away, you will restore her soul."

The father then took his son to the place where the bride was stretched out as if dead. He pointed to her and said, "She is the one."

Menaḥem studied her for a moment and said to his father, "Do you have in mind the statement in the Talmud that 'a man may not marry a woman until he has seen her'? I have now done that."

The father's love for his son was aroused and redoubled, as happens when God-fearing people see their children eagerly fulfilling the commandments. I am certain that with God's mercy this match will be successful, he said to himself. And to his son he said, "Did you not say we should let your mother know? Now I, too, am inclined to do that. If your mother does not come of her own accord, we must summon her."

One could hear certain things being said. Some who heard could not believe their ears, while others heard and became very angry, for they imagined evil people were amusing themselves at the poor bride's expense. In a time when the power of evil is dominant and growing, one can imagine that everyone has bad intentions. It was bad enough that they had turned the poor girl's wedding canopy into a house of mourning; now they were joking about it to boot. It was especially infuriating that Menaḥem's name was being mentioned together with hers, for over and above the frivolity, this showed contempt for the Torah—that the name of one immersed in Torah should be turned into a joke. Wealthy, important people fought with each other to shower dowry money on Menaḥem, saying he was marrying someone without a penny to her name.

But Buczacz being Buczacz, not all the local people could laugh at one of their own who had fallen on hard times, not even to themselves, not even as a Purim jest, and especially not at a bride whose wedding canopy had been turned into a house of mourning. Still, it was hard to credit the rumor: could a young man devoted to Torah study, from a good family, the grandson of a great Torah scholar who had studied the Talmud from beginning to end eight times—could one such as he be interested in marrying the daughter of Moshe Ta'anit, who, in addition to her being poor, came laden with shame?

The simple truth opens one's eyes and finds a way into one's ears. While one group fumed and the other joked, the sun of truth shone and set things aright. All the inhabitants of Buczacz saw and recognized that it was true. Menaḥem, the son of Avraham David and grandson of R. Yosef the Diligent, was sincerely resolved to go under the bridal canopy with the daughter of R. Moshe Ta'anit, paying no heed to her poverty or to the disgrace that worthless fellow, incited by Satan, had caused her. For neither the latter nor his father nor his grandfather had been born in Buczacz. Rather, when the fire ruined the householders of the town, leaving them without the resources to rebuild, he came from wherever it was he came from, bought a plot of land on which sat a burned-out house, made himself a Buczacz householder, and went after the daughters of the most prominent citizens looking for a Buczacz-born wife. But what he sought was not what heaven had decreed. The Eternal took pity on Buczacz, preventing improper outsiders from latching onto the daughters of the town.

And once the truth came to light and the rumor proved correct, Buczacz beamed with pleasure, its day of lament converted into a day of festivity, its sorrow into gladness, until the town resounded with joy from one end to the other. Could it have been the fact that the town had been emptied by the fire of most of its buildings that allowed the sound to fill it as it did? No, it was the joy itself, growing as it spread outward from the courtyard of the Great Synagogue, where a resplendent new wedding canopy now stood on new poles, in the sweet sunlight of Menaḥem Av, the month that begins with mourning and ends with consolation.

The sound of rejoicing revived the bride. Some say she awoke of her own accord, while others say people whispered in her ear to awaken her. She opened her lovely eyes and looked around. They shone radiantly, and everyone saw how lovely and fair she was. The women all marveled at her beauty, while the men looked at her and said "a fair and comely bride." The pious and God-fearing do not make a habit of looking at women, but some hold that it is permitted to gaze at a bride on her wedding day, and not only at her clothing, in order to endear her, by their admiration, to her husband. So they allowed themselves to look at her.

Here it would be appropriate to mention a custom similar to that instituted by our Master, the learned Av Beit Din. R. Moshe Isserles wrote in his commentary on the *Shulḥan Arukh*, Even Ha'ezer 31, that "it is customary to cover the face of the bride at the time of the wedding ceremony." When this was done, our Master, the learned Av Beit Din, would make a practice of telling the shamash to *uncover* her face a bit so that the witnesses to the ceremony would recognize her and be certain whom the groom was marrying. When our Master came here and instructed people to do this, the Buczaczers were skeptical. But he was only following the Torah, as he explained later in his book *Ḥesed leAvraham*. Our Master had in mind the witnesses, while everyone else saw it as a way to endear the bride to her husband.

The bride was still weak, for since that morning she had eaten nothing but a snack, and now that it was nearly the end of the day she was faint with hunger. But take note that at every turn a Jew is governed by divine providence. And even if one forgets that, the providential eye of God, be He blessed, watches over him. When Avraham David was with Heretzki in Pidlesh and wanted to give Heretzki's sons the roll Sarah had given him for Menaḥem, the roll hid in the folds of his pocket, and he could not find it. Why? Because it was not intended for them. Now that Avraham David was standing before the bride, he reached into his pocket and took out the roll. Could there not have been a hole in his pocket through which the roll could have fallen out? Whoever thinks so does not know Sarah, who leaves nothing unmended that needs mending. Rather, the roll had been covered up before, and now it was uncovered, because the time had come to give it to the person for whom it was meant—not the one Sarah had intended it for, and not the one to whom Avraham David later wanted to give it, but the one for whom divine providence intended it.

So Avraham David took out the roll his wife Sarah had given him for Menaḥem, so that if Menaḥem grew faint with hunger there would be food ready to revive him. The bride took the roll, turned away, and began eating.

Meanwhile, the atmosphere became more and more joyous and the sounds of rejoicing more and more audible. Every real thing makes a sound, especially rejoicing, which has numerous sounds. For every sound gives rise to another, as anyone who has been privileged to experience even a bit of joy knows.

11

At that moment, Sarah was sitting in the store, as usual. The noise reached her, and she looked up from the book of women's prayers she was reading. When she was alone in the shop she invariably held a sock and knitting needles in her hands and read from the prayer book. The prayer she was reading at that moment was a supplication for a match for her son. Sarah prayed that the blessed Lord would, in His mercy, provide her son with a mate.

Now come and see how merciful and kind is the Blessed One. Even as she was saying her prayer, the Holy One, blessed be He, was already providing the boy with a match, the marriage contract was already being written, the witnesses were being lined up, the wedding canopy was being tied to its poles, and people were on their way to fetch the bride and groom to bring them to the ceremony. Nor was there any argument about the amount of the dowry or about clothing to be provided or about gifts or contributions or other such things that normally hold up a wedding, but rather all was done gladly, whole-heartedly, and generously. It has been said that "there is no marriage contract that does not provoke a quarrel"—but those who said it also said there is no rule without an exception.

So the noise reached Sarah and seized her. She put down the sock, the knitting needles, and the prayer book and went out to ask what the commotion was about. She saw that everyone, men and women alike, was leaving his or her shop and running off. Standing there, she asked where everyone was running. "Oh, Sarah," they answered, "what a happy occasion, what a happy occasion!" She understood that Buczacz had cause for rejoicing, but she did not know what it was.

How great is the power of joy. It fills the heart of the celebrant without his even being aware of it and without his even knowing why he should be joyful. Sarah, in this case, did not know what the celebration was about, but she rejoiced. The rejoicing sprouted legs and ran to the place towards which all were running, the courtyard of the Great Synagogue, the place where the wedding canopy was unfurled in all its splendor, the place where her son Menaḥem was about to be married, and everyone present was as joyful as if it were his own private celebration. As Sarah approached the synagogue courtyard people crowded around her, shouting, "Mazal tov, Sarah, mazal tov to the new mother-in-law!"

As loudly as she could, Sarah asked, "Why do you call me mother-in-law?" She asked over and over. They might or might not have answered, because it was impossible to hear anything. The sound of the rejoicing drowned out all other sounds, so great was the joy at that moment. Even before the fire, there had never been such a celebration in Buczacz. Why do I mention the fire? Because it is customary to mention a happy occasion before a sad one. That is why I said that even before the fire there had not been such a big celebration. And you should know that, great as this celebration was, no cause for sorrow followed it. For the celebration of the fulfillment of a commandment is not like other happy occasions, when people celebrate just for the sake of celebrating.

I am leaving aside thoughts and reflections that would slow down the story, in favor of recounting the events and circumstances in full detail. Thus, as everyone surrounded Sarah and said, "Mazal tov, Sarah, mazal tov to the new mother-in-law!" and as she asked over and over, "Why do you call me mother-in-law?" two joyful women began dancing in front of her, stamping their feet, nodding their heads, and curtseying in the way one does before princesses and countesses, all with gladness of body and soul, love, brotherliness, friendship, peace, and good will, in honor of a Jewish woman who had given birth to a son destined for the study of Torah, marriage, and good deeds, one who had been kind to a Jewish maiden whose wedding canopy had been turned into a house of mourning, who had changed her sorrow into joy.

When the other women saw what the two were doing, they, too, got up, put their hands on their hips, and danced, until the very ground under their feet was dancing. Do you think I am exaggerating when I say the ground danced? No, it actually did. Do you think it danced more easily because it was denuded of houses? In fact, there were still the ruins of houses there, and these, too, danced. And those women who had forgotten how to dance with their feet did so with their hands, tapping their fingers so as to enliven the dancing. Do you think Sarah was unhappy because everyone was rejoicing and she did not know the reason? On the contrary, she was as happy as any of them. That is the power of true joy. Fortunate is he who is privileged to experience it; even without knowing what it is about, he can rejoice. So great is the power of joy, you see, that since the day Buczacz was founded there had never been a mother who went to her son's wedding in everyday clothes, but Sarah went in her shop clothes, and in spite of this her joy was uninterrupted and undiminished, even when Disha, the wife of R. Moshe Ta'anit and mother of the bride, came over and embraced her and kissed her and called her "mother-in-law" dressed in Sabbath finery and decked out in a fancy head-scarf and shawl, while Sarah was wearing nothing but her shop clothes. I could reinforce the point, if you wish, by citing the power of the commandments, which enable one to set aside all apparent satisfactions and rejoice in doing what is ordained. And if you must know, I will tell you that Sarah had already cast an approving eye on the daughter of R. Moshe Ta'anit, and had the matchmakers not matched her with someone else, she would have asked to have the girl marry her son. Now that He who makes matches and whose matches always succeed had matched the girl with her son Menaḥem, it was a great source of joy. And that is not to take away from the merit of the father and the son: she did it in her thoughts and they in their actions.

12

At that hour, our Master, the learned Av Beit Din, had just awakened from an afternoon nap. Weary from the journey from Kamenetz-Podolsk to Buczacz, he had allowed himself, after lunch, to lie down fully dressed on a bench and doze a bit before saying the afternoon prayer.

He rinsed his hands, picked up his pipe, and went over to the window. Actually, he had intended to sit down and read through some of the letters that came to him from far and wide, which afterward were collected into his great work, the volumes of responsa titled *Ḥesed leAvraham,* first and second editions. But he was drawn to the window, curious to know what Buczacz was up to.

Looking out, he saw signs of the rejoicing. A man came by, and the rabbi rapped on the window and beckoned to him. As the man was coming in, the elderly R. Netanel entered, too—the same R. Netanel, the Master of Melodies, who was a pillar of public worship, representing Buczacz before the Almighty, lifting the prayers of Israel to Him who dwells amidst Israel's praises, and who himself would merit the elevation of going up to the Land of Israel, from which all prayers ascend to Him who hears the prayers of each and every Jew. R. Netanel had come for two reasons: to greet our Master, the learned Av Beit Din, who had just returned from a journey; and to take leave of him before departing for the Holy Land. For R. Netanel was preparing to go up to the Holy Land, to refresh his spirits with its air and to find repose in its dust. R. Netanel was walking unnaturally briskly, not the way the elderly usually do, so briskly that he came in before the man to whom the rabbi had called. You may be surprised at this, but I am not, for whoever attains the wisdom to go up to the Land of Israel should wind up his affairs quickly. Divine judgment hangs over Israel, and Satan follows closely at one's heels, especially in the case of one who undertakes to fulfill the commandment to go up to the Land of Israel, which is equivalent in importance to all the other commandments in the Torah put together. For such a person, numerous obstacles arise, as we have seen in the case of many great and good Jews who were about to go up but did not do so. Why? Because obstacles present themselves, but also because the Land itself is particular, and when it senses that one has even the slightest ulterior motive or hesitation, it immediately closes itself to him and does not allow him to enter its gates.

So R. Netanel, the Master of Melodies, came in to see our Master, greeted him and was greeted by him. Our Master knew that the man was about to leave for the Land of Israel, that, even if he were to have second thoughts, he would be compelled to go. Why? Because a new ḥazzan had already been appointed in his place and had already assumed that role. So whether he wanted to or not, he had to go to the Land of Israel. Our Master motioned to him to sit down, and he took a chair. He groaned deeply, like a ḥazzan who is clearing his throat before starting to chant a prayer, and said, "I feel privileged to see the rabbi's face before departing for the Land of Israel."

"Since we are talking about the Land of Israel," said the rabbi, "let us say a bit about the birds there." He began to discourse about birds that had recently appeared in Russia and Austria, Greek chickens they were called, which were presumed to be kosher as they had three signs of purity: a gizzard, an exposed crop, and an extra toe. They resembled our chickens, except they were peculiarly tall and broad and had long legs. This is not the place to dwell on such things, but since our Master, the learned Av Beit Din, had been asked about them by the rabbis of Safed, the poultry eaten in the Holy Land being somewhat different from that eaten here, he wanted to explain his opinion to the ḥazzan who was going up to the Holy Land, a learned, God-fearing old man, experienced at repeating things word for word. For if our Master were to leave something unexplained in his letter to Safed, R. Netanel could be brought in to explain it.

Now take note how wise a wise person can be. Even though our Master meant to speak of the Law, he was alluding to something else. Before the Temple was destroyed, birds began to migrate away from the Land of Israel, but now that we are approaching the Redemption, various birds have appeared there that have not been seen since fifty-two years before the Destruction.

As our Master was explaining his lenient ruling, his pure mind was distracted by the roar of rejoicing that filled the air. "What is all this joyful shouting about?" he asked R. Netanel. He told him. He sat there astonished for a few minutes, then stood up and went over to his wife, the righteous, respected Rebbetzin Fruma, and said to her, "Have you heard? It is not for nothing that we have been pining all along for Buczacz. Tell me: is there a town anywhere like Buczacz, and are there people anywhere who are as kind as the Buczaczers?"

13

While our Master was standing with the rebbetzin, Mikhl Ber, the shamash of the old synagogue, arrived. Everyone thought our Master was fond of Mikhl Ber because he would round up a private prayer quorum for him every day and because he was one of those quiet people who don't trouble others with a lot of talk. But if so, how would you explain his fondness for him from the very beginning, when our Master used to say all his prayers in the synagogue? Rather, our Master was fond of Mikhl Ber because he was clever and because he had known our great teacher the distinguished Neta Sha'ashuim, and he would entertain our Master, the learned Av Beit Din, with tales and sayings he had heard from that sage, whose wise leadership was unparalleled in his generation and who knew how to stand his ground with everyone, be they rabbis or elders of the community or householders or simply bothersome people who would harass the rabbi with worthless original interpretations.

Mikhl Ber began in the language of Scripture: "*Like the heavens in their height, like the earth in its depth is the mind of kings unfathomable.* Whom do I have mind by citing this verse? Why, our Master, may he live and be well. Perhaps our Master has thought of going to the wedding of Avraham David, the leather merchant, in order to honor those who do kindness? If so, I have come to accompany him and protect him from the crowd, who will press forward to greet their rabbi." Our Master answered in the language of wisdom, the language of the author of *Beḥinat Olam,* saying, "*Like the heavens in their height, like the earth in its depth, is the wisely generous person unfathomable.* In fact, it had not occurred to me to go owing to other things on my mind and, even more, to weariness from my arduous journey. But now that you have, in your thoughtfulness, come here, I shall disregard my fatigue and go with you. We ought to rejoice in the happiness of kind and generous people."

Mikhl Ber straightaway ordered that a dignified coat and shtreimel be brought for the rabbi. The latter put on the dignified coat and the dignified shtreimel. Mikhl Ber than took the rabbi's cane and gave it to him. It was a cane he had gotten from his grandfather R. Yaakov of Lisa. I could tell you a lot about the rabbi's cane, but since our Master did not like to take time for stories that have no halakhic import, I shall not take time for them either.

Our Master took the cane and went off to the wedding of Menaḥem, son of Avraham David, son of R. Yosef the Diligent, who was marrying the daughter of R. Moshe Ta'anit, the grandson of Raḥel Leah the Pious. The aphorism "the reward of a good deed is a good deed"—meaning that the good deed is repaid by a resultant good deed—applies well to her. All her life, that pious woman worked to make sure girls got married, never neglecting poor brides in Buczacz, whom she helped to reach the wedding canopy. As a result, she merited her poor grandson marrying off his daughter to a bridegroom who didn't care about her background but took her as she was, without a dowry and without dickering over the clothing to be provided. And what a bridegroom he was, one whom even the most distinguished citizens would be proud to have as a son-in-law.

So our Master left his house and made his way to the place of the celebration. Walking on his right was the elderly ḥazzan R. Netanel, the Master of Melodies, our community's prayer leader, and on his left was Mikhl Ber, the shamash of our old synagogue, the cleverest of shamashim. And old men and boys without number joined our Master's entourage, all wishing to welcome him back from Russia. Why, then, did I mention the elderly ḥazzan, if all Buczacz was there? To tell you that he sang the invocation "Who is mighty above all? Who is blessed above all?," which it is customary to sing at weddings. And this was the last thing R. Netanel, the Master of Melodies, sang in Buczacz before going up to the Holy Land. May it be His will that we all rejoice in the gladness of the Land of Israel, speedily and soon, amen.

Wherever you see the greatness of our Master you will also see the humility of Buczacz. For no one in Buczacz said that our rabbi had to return because he missed the town; rather, they said he had to come back because of the harsh decrees in Russia. And when our Master was offered the honor of presiding over the wedding ceremony, he said, "Isn't R. Yekele the halakhic authority here?" But R. Yekele had gone home because of pain in his legs, for he had stood for several hours on account of the uproar that worthless fellow had caused and had to lie down, shoes off, in bed. This was something he never did on weekdays, when, normally, if he wanted to rest in the middle of the day, he would stretch out on a bench with his shoes on.

Consequently, our Master, the esteemed Av Beit Din, presided himself over Menaḥem's nuptials, and Menaḥem was privileged to see him up close, something he had yearned to do, for when our Master left for Kamenetz, Menaḥem was still a little boy, and when he returned he never appeared in public. And when the bride stood under the wedding canopy with her face covered—it being customary to cover the bride's face—Meir Yonah, at our Master's behest, uncovered her face a bit. Then everyone could see the bride's face, just as she was, fair and comely through and through.

To backtrack a bit, they did not get to the wedding canopy until the entire town had assembled there, all joyful and glad. For the joy of good people makes good people rejoice, and who could compare with the people of Buczacz in goodness, and what can compare with the good deed of marrying a woman for the sake of heaven? All those who marry for the sake of heaven are granted sons who are devoted to Torah. Thus it was that all the sons and grandsons of Menaḥem, son of Avraham David, were devoted to the study of Torah and obedient to the Torah, among them scholars of halakhah, *well-known in the gates*—until the enemy came and wiped them all out.

They were wiped out, but the mercies of Him who is to be blessed were not. For every good deed bears fruit, which, in turn, bears more fruit. And if the Almighty grants me life and strength and tranquility, I shall relate some of the good deeds that the good among the people of Israel did when the Holy One, blessed be He, was good to Israel, and Israel was beloved of the Holy One.

Translated by Michael Swirsky

The Frogs

1

There was a family in our town who were called the Frogs. Even those of its members who were rich could not escape this moniker. So accustomed were people to using it that even a gentile, when he would converse with one of them, would address him formally as "Mr. Frog," or, in the case of a woman, "Madame Frog." They simply thought that it was their family name and not a slur.

At first, I thought they were called Frogs because that was what they resembled, perhaps because they were raucous and croaked like frogs, or because they walked in the hippety-hop way frogs jump in the marshes. One of them once came up to me and told me his family are called frogs because their ancestors were great cantors who melodiously graced the podium with their vocal cords at all the services—weekdays, Sabbaths, festivals, the Days of Awe, both at Shaḥarit and Musaf. This is in line with what the *Yalkut* notes: when King David finished composing the Book of Psalms, he boasted to the Holy One, blessed be He, "Master of the Universe! Is there anything in the world that lifts up its voice in song like me?"—upon which a frog appeared before him and said, "Do not be so proud of yourself. I sing more than you do."

Later, when I had attained some understanding of bygone times and studied the past and genealogies and family trees, I came to see that it was not because of what I thought about them or because of the literal meaning of the word that this family was called the Frogs, but because of something that happened.

2

It once came about in our town that the fishermen raised the price of fish beyond what they were worth, and the poor stopped buying them for their Sabbath meals. They were distressed at this curtailment of their ability to enjoy the Sabbath. They went to our Master, the esteemed R. Avraham Te'omim, of blessed memory, and told him that if he would not issue an injunction forbidding anyone in town from buying fish for the Sabbath until the price came down, they would not be able to enhance their Sabbath pleasure by serving fish. Such a prohibition was once issued by the holy community of Nikolsburg. The gentile fishermen there banded together and raised the price of fish when they saw that the Jews would buy it regardless of how expensive it was. The community reached a consensus that no one would buy fish for two months and their rabbi, the venerable R. Menaḥem Mendel Krochmal, of blessed memory, agreed with them.

But our Master, R. Avraham, could find no conclusive grounds for issuing a decree prohibiting the whole town from buying fish for the Sabbath, for there were after all rich people in town, and one could not deny them the chance to perform the mitzvah of enhancing their Sabbath simply because the poor could not afford to do so. One does not tell someone to transgress so that another person may benefit. The fact is that to embellish the performance of a mitzvah one may spend up to a third more than its original cost. Thus if someone takes upon himself a certain mitzvah and then sees the chance to do it in a finer way, one takes pains to get him to put out the money for it up to a third more than it would have originally cost him to fulfill it. Therefore, the rich do not sin when they eat fish in honor of the Sabbath; as long as its price does not rise by more than a third, we do not require them to forego that pleasure on account of the poor who have no such obligation.

Yet even though our Master, of blessed memory, did not compel the rich to stop buying fish, he and his household were strict with themselves in this regard—and our Master was a wealthy man. He even waived his rabbinic salary for his services to the community, as I have related elsewhere. But he went even further. He convened the leaders of the community, the upper crust and the wealthy and told them, "I have not forbidden you from buying fish for the Sabbath, but it would nevertheless be appropriate if each of you would do like everyone else in town and not have fish for the Sabbath." They agreed and acted accordingly.

3

The idea was that if the fishermen would see that no one was buying fish for the Sabbath, they would lower the price. When two Sabbaths passed and the price did not come down, everyone was puzzled. They noticed that the fishermen were casting their nets as usual, and, since no one goes to such efforts in vain, they concluded that not only gentiles were buying fish but the Jews were as well.

An investigation into the matter revealed that there was one house in town where the smell of fish was always present, not only on Sabbath eves but even during the week. Whose house was it? Karpl Shlein's, the son of the elderly Fishl Shlein, who was the father-in-law of Fishl Hecht. Now although no explicit ban was placed on anyone buying fish, the town accepted the prohibition. The Magen Avraham had ruled on this matter when he wrote that no one should buy fish until the price was lowered, and anyone who did so would only strengthen the hands of the fishermen and thereby keep others who could not afford it from enjoying fish on the Sabbath.

People were willing to give Karpl the benefit of the doubt. They explained that he was weak; that he had been a spoiled child; that he was used to eating delicacies; that he was a slave to his appetite and if he did not eat what he craved, he would fall dangerously ill, like the case the Jerusalem Talmud reports of a poor man who was accustomed to eating a daily meal of plump hens with fine wine. One day, they gave him beef and he died. If that happened to a poor man who ate what others gave him, all the more could it happen to a rich man, the son of a rich man and the father-in-law of a rich man, whose food was his own.

When a third Sabbath passed and then a fourth and the fishermen had not lowered the price, people began to get angry at Karpl. They said that though he may have been using his weakness as an excuse to allow himself to be insensitive to the public's suffering, still he really ought to suppress his appetite a bit and not consume so much fish. But the fact was that not a day passed when the aroma of fish being fried and cooked and marinated did not waft from his house. How far ought a person go to indulge his appetite? What the townspeople did not know was that R. Karpl was buying fish not only for himself but for them and for others, too.

What is meant by "for them and for others, too"? At that time Karpl had arranged a match for his son with a girl from another town. He told no one in Buczacz that he had done so, for Karpl was experienced in having his matches go awry. The year before he had made a match, and people cast aspersions about him to the prospective father-in-law. Then, when the food had been cooked and the wine poured and the groom's clothes were folded and packed in a trunk, the prospective father-in-law cancelled the match. So now, having found a mate for his son, he made all preparations in secret so that no one would come and spoil it all again for him. Now just as a rich man has many admirers, so does he have many enemies. They envy him his wealth, and that envy drives their desire to do him harm. That is how it is with money: it appears to be a boon to those who have it but in actuality it is harmful to them.

The clothes, then, were ready. What else needed to be done? The food and drink had to be prepared. R. Karpl did this under wraps, thinking the whole time that no one on the outside had any idea of what was going on inside the house. What R. Karpl did not know was that smells can be detected. It was the fish themselves that made their presence known. R. Karpl thought that if they were brought to him covertly no one in town would know about them, but it turned that the fish themselves spread the word. The aromas of their being cooked and fried and roasted and marinated all wafted out of the house daily and tattled on Karpl, making public what he was doing.

4

The people went back to our Master, the esteemed chief of the beit din, and informed him about this. They entreated him again to issue an explicit prohibition against buying fish. If he would do that, they said, no one would dare break the law. He replied, "As much as I have looked into it, I could find no definitive argument for issuing a ruling prohibiting the rich from buying fish for the Sabbath. You already know what I told them, and they are obeying me. If anyone is disregarding my instructions, I cannot change the law just because of him." The impoverished townsfolk left in dejection, and as for R. Karpl, he was quite pleased with himself.

R. Karpl was a wealthy man and not without a measure of astuteness. He was also held to be something of a Torah scholar. When the community selected a delegation to receive our Master when he came to town to assume his rabbinical duties, R. Karpl was among those chosen. Initially he visited the rabbi regularly and regaled him with the ḥidushim he had come up with in his Torah study, which included regular lessons in Talmud with the commentaries of Rashi and Tosafot, and the commentary of Ramban on the Torah. After a time, however, he stayed away from the rabbi's house because of the furor over interest rates. The practice in Buczacz was to lend money to the governmental officials at 22 percent. The rabbi was satisfied to do so at 12 percent, and sometimes at 8 percent, and R. Karpl was unhappy with him for that. Had the rabbi prohibited outright the purchase of fish, R. Karpl would have complied. But, R. Karpl thought to himself, since he had not issued such a decree, why should I be obligated to be stricter with myself than what the law allows? Were any grounds for a prohibition, the rabbi would have issued one. R. Karpl found one other way to get fish without contravening communal practice. Since the fishmongers had no Jewish customers, they sold to R. Karpl cheaply, and no one could say it was forbidden to buy cheaply. And since he was buying for a wedding feast, he made purchases daily. He found yet another reason to buy fish: it would recoup money from a gentile. This was because R. Karpl would loan money to one Petro, who was known as the dean of the fishermen, and when the Jews stopped buying fish, Petro began to fall behind in repaying his debt, thus jeopardizing R. Karpl's money. R. Karpl then got Petro to agree to provide him with fish in lieu of the debt.

5

While the townsfolk were sitting with the rabbi to complain about R. Karpl, Mikhl Ber the shamash showed up. He had served two world renowned scholars, the venerable Neta Sha'ashuim, of blessed memory, and his son-in-law, the venerable Da'at Kedoshim. In his latter years, he was part of the household of our Master, the venerable Ḥesed leAvraham, of blessed memory.

Mikhl Ber was an elderly man and shrewd, wise and practiced in the ways of the world. He knew how to counter the poor and the rich alike, the scholars and the common folk, hasidim and maskilim. Many things were said of him, some nice, some witty and cutting. When I have a chance, I will relate them. Before he came to our town, he served as a teacher's assistant in the academy that Yossel, son of Todros, otherwise known as Yosef Perl, set up in Tarnopol. Mikhl Ber spent a lot of time with the maskilim and learned a few of their ways. Occasionally, he would do things that people mocked. The testimony he gave to the beit din in the case of the individual who embezzled money from his youngest son, whose mother had willed him all her property, is well known. I omit the details here in order to protect the honor of the families involved.

At the very hour that the townsfolk were discussing the matter of R. Karpl and his fish with the rabbi, along came Mikhl Ber. When the dispirited townsfolk had gone, our Master said to him, "I have nothing but praise for the good people of Buczacz. They accept suffering without complaining. When I was a rabbi in Kamenetz-Podolsk, people would come to me no matter what the problem was, and demand 'Rabbi, pray for a miracle for us!' It didn't matter if the suffering involved was public or private, they wanted miracles. There was no lack of troubles in Russia, but miracles never happened. But tell me, what are you so concerned about, Mikhl Ber?"

Mikhl Ber replied, "I am thinking about Karpl. He sees everyone depriving themselves of having fish and he has no compunction about buying some for himself every day."

The rabbi said, "So what do you have to say about that?"

Replied Mikhl, "Well, maybe even here we need a miracle."

"A miracle here?"

"A miracle however it may come." The rabbi was silent and said no more. We do not know if this was because miracles are not an everyday occurrence or because he did not think that that particular situation required one.

6

Immediately after the evening service, Mikhl Ber lit his big lantern, which they called "The Eye of Leviathan" because on the nights of Seliḥot it lit up the dark streets of Buczacz like that monster's eyes lit up the Great Sea. It was made of shiny brass and had six balloon-like windows with a candle of either wax or tallow stuck in the middle, and above the candle on all sides were smoke holes. In addition to the lantern, he took with him a second candle, the way someone setting out on a long journey carries a spare candle. Then, cane in hand, he left the town. Presently, he encountered a man who asked him, "Where is Mikhl Ber headed?"

He replied, "I assume that you are not the only one asking this question. But look, I'm a frail man and I do not have the strength to talk a lot. Do me a favor and come tomorrow to the beit midrash and I will answer all of you together."

Then another person came upon him and inquired likewise. Mikhl Ber said to him, "I have already been asked this question. And now, since I'm in a hurry, please go and find those who have already asked and they'll tell you."

Thus did he get rid of such nuisances, and soon he reached the river.

The dean of the fishermen, Petro, saw a lantern approaching. He went to see who it was and found Mikhl Ber the shamash. He ran toward him and cried joyously, "Guests! Guests!" Though there was only one person, he spoke of him in the plural so as to heighten his respect for the guest.

7

Petro brought Mikhl Ber into his house and found a choice place for him to sit. He took a choice fish that he had roasted for himself in oil on the fire, and a cabbage leaf. He placed the fish upon the cabbage leaf, set it before the guest, and clucked, "Enjoy, your Honor. It's worth taking a bite of it."

Mikhl Ber peered at him once, twice, and sighed. Petro heard the sigh and was puzzled. He had never heard a Jew sigh like that before a meal. If a Jew were to sigh, it would be during the meal, while eating and drinking, for Jews know that they are not worthy to enjoy what God has created in His world. That is why they sigh when they are served good food. But this fellow here sighs before he has even tasted a thing.

Petro said to him, "Pan Mikhl, why do you sigh?"

He replied, "How can I not sigh when I see how lightly you take me? Had you served me a roasted frog and told me to eat it, I would be no more surprised at you."

The gentile looked at him and said, "Pan Mikhl, what are you talking about? I serve you a fish and you say frog. Dig your nails into it and take a bite of it and I'll run and bring some whiskey and you can make a blessing on it for me and the fish and God the Master."

Mikhl Ber said to him, "Have you ever heard the sound of a shofar?"

"What do you think, just because I'm a gentile I don't know what a shofar is?"

"Well, if you know, then I don't have to go into details."

Petro looked at him and said, "By the life of the Lord God whom I love, I do not know what you're saying. A shofar? Isn't it too early to make yourself sad? According to my reckoning that sad month when you blow the horn has not yet arrived. You are so quiet, Pan Mikhl. Has Petro lost his standing with you? Have you already forgotten that day when Havrila the drunkard got his friends together when they were all liquored up and they went and opened all the vats of whiskey of the Jewish merchants that you sold him before Passover? After the holiday there was hardly a drop left for you. I took my boys and we went and broke every bone in their bodies. They all have mementos of what my good fellows did to them. One of them still limps, one has a broken arm, one lost an eye, one had his nose flattened, and one is a cripple. Do you think my boys and I went to that trouble for Messrs. Feivush, Eisen, Montag, Karpl Shlein, and the other stinking leeches, may their mothers devour them? I did it for you, Pan Mikhl, for the love I have for you, because I knew that you were the middleman between the rabbi and Havrila in the sale of the ḥametz. And now that you have something to say, you clam up. Put your lantern on the table, take your time, and tell your buddy Petro about that shofar you mentioned."

8

Petro took the lantern out of Mikhl Ber's hands, put it on the table, and fixed his eyes upon Mikhl Ber. Mikhl Ber looked around to make sure no one was listening, and said to him, "If you know what a shofar is, then I can tell you that our rabbi has ordered that they should go through every town with a shofar and proclaim that whoever so much as tastes fish will not have the merit of partaking in feast of the Leviathan in Paradise. Do you know what the Leviathan is? You do not know. So let me tell you."

He began to tell him about all the good things that await Israel in the world to come. "They will eat and drink and savor the meat of Leviathan, who is so huge a fish that the whole river Jordan empties into his mouth the way a person guzzles down a glass of whiskey. That is why the Holy One, blessed be He, had to kill the Leviathan, for otherwise it would drink the world dry. Then when he killed it, he salted it to preserve it for the righteous who will in the future inhabit Paradise. Its flesh tastes better than any meat in the world and it combines the flavors of every fish in the oceans, rivers, lakes and streams. If you like carp, that's what it tastes like; if you like hake, that's what it tastes like; if you like salmon or trout, that's what it tastes like. What's best, though, is that all those tastes are blended together, something that does not happen with any other food in the world, each of which has its own individual taste. But why do we need to go into details? The Holy One, blessed be He, knows what is best for the righteous and that is why He has kept the Leviathan hidden away. The Leviathan is to all other fish as a fish is to a frog. As a fish to a frog I say, and that's the absolute truth."

Thus did Mikhl Ber continue to expound until the gentile's mouth watered from desire for a piece of Leviathan. Had he wanted to, Mikhl Ber could have converted him on the spot. But Mikhl Ber had another purpose in mind. As he continued talking he told Petro that the rabbi had made it forbidden for any Jew to buy fish, and whoever would not obey would not be able to participate in the feast of Leviathan.

The gentile's face grew pale and he began to scratch his head. He started musing aloud. "Hmm. What is Karpl going to do? He has ordered twelve baskets of fish for the wedding feast he's making for his son." Mikhl Ber pretended not to hear.

Petro said to him, "Tell me, Pan Mikhl, Shlein, may his mother devour him, the son of Fishko, may his soul rot, has ordered twelve baskets of fish from me."

"Well, if he ordered them, so be it. If he ever pays you, only the fish will know."

Petro sat there puzzled. "How can this be? Karpl Shlein is a very wealthy man. He has lots of money. Last Sunday in church the priest said in his sermon that from what the Jew Shlein earns in a month from the whiskey that the Christians drink, you could make a new roof for the church. And here you come and upset me by telling me that my fish are lost. You're tying a bear to my nose and making me dance to its movements."

Mikhl Ber rested his head on his walking stick like someone about to doze off.

Petro continued, "I know you're as smart as any rabbi, and if you say something it's true. But what you've said now makes no sense to me. I give him fish and he pays me no money. Are twelve baskets of fish nothing?"

To this, Mikhl Ber replied, "Well, you could argue that as long as fish were permitted to be eaten, they were worth money. But now that they're prohibited, they're as forbidden to Jews as frogs. And if you ask me, I'd say that sometimes frogs are better than fish. The proof is that in Egypt the Egyptians suffered a plague of frogs, not fish.

9

Petro sat there stunned. After a while, he said, "Pan Mikhl, tell me yourself if Karpl is not worse than a bandit. He orders twelve baskets of fish and I send out my boys to the river and give them a good thrashing and tell them that if they come back empty handed they'll go to sleep on an empty stomach. They spend nights in the water, and all that for what? So that that leech Karpl, may his mother devour him, shall not be lacking fish at his table. And in the end he doesn't pay me. He does not pay me! What does your Torah say about that? And what does your rabbi say about that?"

Said Mikhl Ber, "You should excuse me but you have a *goyische kop*. I have already told you that our rabbi has issued a ban on fish, which are to the Jews like frogs, forbidden in the same way. Like frogs Petro, except that fish are food and frogs—God knows why they were created. I have explained all this to you quite clearly and I don't think I need to add even a croak more. What do you want? That I should tell you, for example, to fill your baskets with frogs and send them to Karpl? Advice like that you won't hear from me. Karpl is a Jew, and you, even though you are honest with me, you are a gentile. I must tell you that I have to be very particular with you. You make me say everything twice. I'm beginning to hear frogs croaking in my head. Frogs fish, fish frogs. And as far as getting paid goes, what difference does it make if it's fish or frogs?"

At this Petro began banging on his knees in anger until he jumped up in pain. He started to swear at himself and at the whole world for trying to make a fool of him. He wound up vowing that he would not rest until he did what he would do. Mikhl Ber shrugged and said, "What do I care what you do? Do what you want. I was on my way to see how nicely the willows were growing and if they would be kosher for the Sukkot festival. But you interrupted me in this mitzvah and you've come and dragged an old Jew like me into a room full of icons that have cast a spell on me and forced me to tell a secret that it is forbidden to reveal. But this I can say to you: I fear that the waters of the Strypa will pay no attention to you because you are transgressing the word of the rabbi and are bringing fish to Karpl. One can only hope that all the fish in the Strypa should not become frogs."

10

Petro swore that he would do what he would do. But since he didn't know what he would do, his anger burned inside him because he saw himself as weak and unable to defend himself at a time when people were conspiring to cheat him. It was not enough to be losing income from his fish but the fish themselves were angry at him for providing them to Karpl when he knew that he was going against the order of the Jews' rabbi forbidding them from buying fish. Petro was skeptical of Mikhl Ber's conjecture that the fish might turn into frogs. But he was worried they might hide from his nets and trawling lines, as happened with a fisherman who caught a fish and cut off its tail and threw it back into the river. When the other fish saw that they had been treated with such contempt, they imposed a ban on his nets and trawling lines. So not only might he not be able to produce the twelve baskets of fish that he had to send to Karpl, but he would also have to pay him a penalty for failing to deliver them. The scent of the fish he had served to the guest now wafted up into his nostrils. Petro cried out in anger, "That old man cheated me! He didn't eat it because he was afraid of the ban. He didn't eat it because he didn't cook it himself. I know these Jews. They're all swindlers. And that Karpl, may his mother devour him, is the biggest swindler of them all. He orders fish and he has no intention of paying." So angry was Petro that he forgot to go down to the Strypa to supervise his workers. He sat and ran his fingernails over the fish that by now had cooled and lost its flavor, so he could not enjoy it. As if it too were part of the retaliation the fish would exact from him because of Karpl.

Petro sat there, his thoughts flitting around inside him like frogs. Twelve baskets of fish he ordered, this Karpl. It was not enough that he bought them on credit with the interest I owe him compounding, but he ordered more when he had no intention of paying because he could say that, well, since Jews are forbidden to eat fish, he does not have to pay. If they're forbidden to you, then why do you eat them? Why do my boys have to stand in the water and toil for you while you lie in bed with pillows and quilts? Fish I'll bring him? A good punch I'll bring him, one he'll feel till his grave.

When Petro's workers saw that their boss was not keeping an eye on them, they made no effort to go out to the best fishing places. Instead they let their nets lie slack. The fish themselves then arrived at a logical deduction: if the fishermen, whose job it is to go out and catch us, are not doing so, then we, who are not obligated to be caught, certainly do not have to run into their nets. Thus when the time came for them to be full, the nets lay empty.

11

Is it possible in Buczacz for a person to do anything without someone seeing? Certainly not during the daytime when all eyes are open to observe what is going on. But not even at night, for then all the batei midrash are full of old men and young sitting and learning, some until midnight, some even later. Even those who do not study Torah regularly rise for tikkun ḥatzot. So there really is no hour in Buczacz when eyes are not open to notice if anything untoward is going on. How then can one speak of a time when no one sees a thing? It's like this: when a person wants to commit a sin, Satan blinds him and he thinks that everyone else's eyes are closed. He then goes and does what his heart desires and he thinks that no one is watching. That is what R. Karpl thought when he kept his activities from public view. When all the streets were quiet Karpl would tell his son to go to the fisherman. The son would go there and wait for him, take the fish from him and go and put them in the cellar until the time came to cook them. Thus it was on that night. Before he went to sleep R. Karpl instructed his son to go out and get the fish.

The young man went out and waited in front of Petro's house. His legs became jellylike as sleep overtook him. He struggled to stay on his feet until Petro's boys would come with the fish. It was a Thursday night, and on the Sabbath, the last one before the wedding, when the bridegroom would be called up to the Torah, his father was going to make an ample kiddush in his honor, and the fish needed to be prepared, because his father wanted to serve them to the guests at the reception.

The bridegroom-to-be stood there, half awake, half asleep. He propped himself up against the wall and closed his eyes. He saw himself swimming in a great river many times larger than the Strypa, and he heard the fish singing, as we learn in *Perek Shirah*:

> The fish say: "The voice of the Lord is over the waters,
> The God of glory thunders;
> The Lord over the mighty waters.

He cocked his ear to listen and was baffled: not a word of that verse could be heard. He cocked his ear again and heard himself saying:

> I have come to my garden,
> My own, my bride,
> I have plucked my myrrh and spice.

Another voice answered:

> I was asleep,
> But my heart was wakeful…
> I had taken off my robe.

His fiancée saw him and said, "Worry not. What you have heard is from the ḥasidic tradition of prayer. If you want the Ashkenazic version according to your family's traditions, move to the other side." He cocked his ear to the other side and heard them saying: "Blessed be His name, whose glorious kingdom is forever and ever."

Now he was even more baffled because this was the song that the frogs sing, and if so, then how could it be uttered by the fish? He wanted to ask his fiancée but she saw some gentiles coming and fled. He too wanted to flee but they came and beat him up. He awoke and asked, "Why are you beating me?"

They answered, "We have brought fish for your father. Quick, come and take them." He thought to himself, they're rushing me for my own good. The night is gone and the shamash is about to go out and wake people up for prayer. He hustled to take the baskets of fish and brought them down to the cellar. He sent the boys away and went into his house and lay down in bed. He closed his eyes and pretended to sleep as he looked for his fiancée. Then he fell asleep.

Now why did Petro send Karpl twelve baskets of fish? Had he not sworn that he would not send him so much as the scale of one of them? Moreover, where did he get twelve full baskets of fish? The fishermen had not gone out to catch any. Before we clear this matter up it would be best to return to R. Karpl, for when we see what happened with him everything will be explained.

12

It is the custom in our region on the Sabbath before a wedding, when the bridegroom is called up to the Torah, for the father to make a big kiddush reception for all his admirers, friends, and the whole congregation. Hosts who are poor bring whiskey and crackers baked with peppers and onions; those well off supply whiskey, raisin wine, various baked goods, eggs with radishes and onions, and chopped liver with onions; the wealthy provide whiskey, raisin wine, grape wine, meat, fish and other delicacies, along with sweet and stuffed kugels. When fish became too expensive and everyone stopped buying it, everyone got used to doing without it even on Sabbaths before a wedding. R. Karpl, however, stood out in this regard; he was set to serve fish to his guests. He wanted to placate them with the very item for which they were angry at him. For after all, a convivial feast with food aplenty will mitigate anger and bring people together, and there was no one in Buczacz who needed to mitigate people's anger more than R. Karpl. So he went and ordered twelve baskets of fish so they could eat as much of a food they craved after not having had even a taste of it for many Sabbaths.

After ordering such and such a number of baskets of fish, R. Karpl secured the services of several accomplished chefs and cooks who were connoisseurs of every manner in which fish can be prepared—with onions and peppers, with sugar and honey, in vinegar garnished with laurel leaves, or simply roasted.

The large brass pots were taken down from the walls. They were hung there as decoration, now they were about to be used. Up until now, their tops faced the wall and their bottoms faced the house; today their tops looked to the fish as they waited to be cooked. On Friday morning, when R. Karpl returned from prayers, the chefs were already standing in readiness to begin their labors. He gave them their instructions and they in turn did the same to the cooks. They tied on their aprons, picked up the sharpened knives, and got ready to slice the fish.

13

The fire burned and the wood crackled within it, indicating that it was ready to receive R. Karpl's fish. As it burned, the fire looked over at the shining pots and the shining pots looked over at the fire. On the outside the pots were golden and gleaming, on the inside like fish scales, and in between the fire and the pots the glint of the sharp knives flashed. The kitchen was filled with hustle and bustle. The center of activity was R. Karpl who was scurrying here and there checking the onions and the peppers and the vinegar, and sampling the sugar and the honey and so on. A lot was going on which I will not go into in order to make this point: R. Karpl did not engage half a dozen cooks because he was expecting a bunch of ravenous guests; he did so because it was a son he was marrying off and not a daughter. And not to a poor family but to a wealthy one, and there was no question that the father of the bride would make more than ample preparations. Why, then, was R. Karpl going all out? Because the morning after the wedding, the bride's family would be coming to greet the parents of the groom, and it would be good if they could see what the groom's side were capable of doing.

So as the fire crackled and the pots were foaming and the knives standing at the ready, someone went down to the cellar and carried up the baskets of fish that had been put there the previous night. One basket was brought up, then another, and then yet another, until after several trips up and down all the baskets were in the kitchen.

As R. Karpl was about to open a basket, he began praising Petro for being a very businesslike gentile. You ask him to send you twelve baskets of fish and he sends them. Not only that, he added, but you can count on him to send you the very best fish. At that he grew boastful and he motioned to the chefs and cooks to come and look. They gathered around him, looking on the way those who are buying etrogs watch as the etrog vendor opens the box. Boastfully, he said to them, "Get ready to see fish the likes of which you've never seen before."

They all nodded at him the way servants look at their masters. "We are ready to see whatever R. Karpl, long life to him, wishes to show us." R. Karpl waited a moment, smiled, and said, "I know you're all anxious to see, but I like to be patient. But since today is Friday, and we have to move quickly because the Sabbath is coming, I will open it right now."

He grabbed hold of a knife and started cutting all around. The string snapped and the basket opened. When it opened, R. Karpl was astonished. He was astonished not only at this first basket but at the second and the third and the fourth and at all of them. Why? So as not to tell about each individual basket, I lump them all together and you will see that it was not for nothing that R. Karpl was astonished. You will also understand what I meant when I said that in knowing what happened with R. Karpl, you will also realize that Petro kept the oath he made not to send him as much as the scale of one fish. Ah, but in fact Petro had sent something, and had he sent fish, R. Karpl would not have been astonished. But what did he send? He sent frogs. Not one basket or two but twelve baskets, and every single one of them was filled with frogs.

14

So there was R. Karpl, his frogs croaking away in the baskets and his anger croaking away within him. He kicked at a basket and all the frogs promptly scattered. Some expired on the spot, and those that did not began hopping around, some on R. Karpl's shoes and some all over the place. In his attempt to get away from them he crashed into a basket and overturned it, and all the frogs inside fell out. Those that did not expire on the spot caught their breath and started hopping about in all directions. He tried to take refuge from them and wound up stepping on them and squashing them. The same thing happened to his wife and to the bridegroom. While he was looking to be rescued from the frogs, the head chef came over demanding that he and his colleagues be paid, in the midst of which they all came up to him clamoring for their fee. R. Karpl shouted, "Scum! You want to be paid for your troubles? The only trouble you took was to enjoy my distress."

They said to him, "We will not move from here until you pay us."

"You want your pay? Here, take the frogs."

"You take the frogs and eat them to your heart's content. We want our money."

"Money for what? For witnessing my downfall? For witnessing my embarrassment?"

"If the fish turned themselves into frogs, take *them* to court. Meanwhile, give us our money!" They screamed at him, he screamed at them, and the racket could be heard outside on the street. Passersby gathered and heard everything.

What possessed the frogs to give their lives for the troubles of Buczacz? They took their cue from the frogs of Egypt. They reasoned: If it was said of the frogs of the Nile, where no Tashlikh prayer was said or willow sprigs were gathered for the Hoshanas, that "they will come into your houses, your ovens and your kneading bowls," we frogs of

Buczacz, where Tashlikh is recited at the Strypa and willow sprigs are gathered there, all the more so.

By the time people left R. Karpl's house, the whole town knew that the fish Karpl bought turned themselves into frogs.

Buczacz was astounded. Some saw the whole thing as testimony to the power of Rabbi Avraham. Even though he had not explicitly forbidden fish, he did call for people to cease and desist from buying them. Others attributed what happened to Mikhl Ber. He had said that even in this situation a miracle was needed, and a miracle did in fact occur, because Karpl ordered fish and found frogs. Those who ascribed it to the power of Rabbi Avraham said it really testified to the power of Torah; those who attributed it to Mikhl Ber concluded that astute people are beloved in heaven, for their wishes are fulfilled.

Having commended Mikhl Ber, let us now praise Buczacz. Though it hungered for fish and longed to have it at kiddush on Sabbath mornings, it was not angry at the frogs for what they did to them. On the contrary, Buczacz lauded them for laying down their lives for its travails.

15

Things that were not meant to be food, even if you think well of them, eventually are forgotten. Thus it was with the frogs. After a while, they were forgotten. They were barely mentioned, if at all. People stopped talking about them and turned their attention to Petro's part in the whole episode. This too they dropped in favor of talking about R. Karpl and how he had fish regularly during the whole time the town was abstaining from them even on the Sabbath.

The frogs were thus about to be cast into oblivion. But the Holy One, blessed be He, does not dismiss the reward of those of his creatures who do mitzvot in this world. Whenever R. Karpl was talked about, the whole story of the frogs was brought up, to the point where you could not talk about one without mentioning the other, until it became unclear who was primary and who was secondary: the frogs or R. Karpl? And it was not just R. Karpl who was always associated with the episode of the frogs; so, too, were his wife, his sons and daughters, his in-laws, and his grandchildren.

The good people of Buczacz like things stated succinctly, as you can see from how I have told this story. I shall therefore be brief about a matter on which most would wax verbose. The townsfolk stopped using the name of every person in R. Karpl's family. This applied to the men and the women and included the name they were called in the cradle and the name they were given at their circumcision. Instead, every single one of them was called by one name: Frog. And you know the people of Buczacz: they always follow the usage of their forebears. And so, because their forebears called all members of Karpl's family Frogs, for that reason all their descendents were called Frogs. If any of them are still living, the moniker still sticks. My hunch is that those of them who don't go to services or are never called up to the Torah never get to hear or know their real name. As for the women, they are indeed to be pitied.

A story should always be taken at its face value, to be sure. But still it has implications. Here the implication is that when the community is in distress, it is improper for someone to remain aloof from it. Even if he has grounds for exempting himself, a self-respecting Jew should always be at one with the community. Even when it comes to food.

Translated by James S. Diamond
with Jeffrey Saks

The Strypa River flowing through Buczacz

Pisces

Prologue

Seeing that most people do not know the story of Fishl Karp, or they may know part of it but not all of it, or they may know the story in a general way—and indeed, there is no greater enemy to wisdom than superficial knowledge—I have taken it upon myself to recount things exactly as they happened.

I know that I myself have not managed to verify all the details or to reconcile everything, and, needless to say, others would have told it better than I. But I say that full detail is not the main thing, nor is beauty, nor the reconciling of inessential matters. The main thing is truth. In that sense every word spoken here is true.

1. A Solid Citizen

Fishl Karp was a householder. Householders like him are not found in every generation, nor in every place. Tall was he, and as his height, so was his breadth. That is, his height equaled his circumference. Of similar amplitude were his limbs. His neck was fat, and, as they say among us in Buczacz, it measured up to the forearm of Eglon, the king of Moab. This, apart from his belly, which was a creature by itself. Such a belly is not to be found in our generation, but even in Fishl's generation, it was numbered among the city's novelties.

Two merchants once came from Lemberg to Buczacz to buy groats, and Fishl Karp happened upon them. They looked at him and said, Even among the gizzard eaters and mead drinkers in Lemberg, a belly like that would command respect. It was ample, like a cauldron for cooking prune jam. Not for nothing was it said that his double chins compared to his belly like a bird's gullet to its body, and his double chins were fat like a goose before Ḥanukkah. Hence he honored his belly and cared for it and saw that it lacked for nothing. Be it meat and fish, let there be meat and fish; be it gravy and groats, let there be gravy and groats; and if you want a prune compote, let there be a prune compote, aside from carrot wrapped in tripe stuffed with flour and toasted with fat and raisins, not to mention the dishes that come before the meal.

Ordinarily, people eat soup before meat and meat before prunes and carrots. Fishl Karp would eat the meat before the soup and the carrots and prunes before the sauce, so that if the messiah should come, he could give him what he was eating and not deprive his belly. Otherwise, while all the Jews were taking joy in the messiah, his belly would be miserable and sad. If things were thus during the six days of the week, on Sabbaths and festivals it was even more so. What Reb Fishl ate at the optional fourth meal of R. Ḥidka would be enough for ten Jews for an entire Sabbath, and what he used to eat on the eve of Yom Kippur would be enough for anyone for all the three festivals. Even those holidays that are not mentioned in the Torah but which were ordained by Ezra and his court he honored with food and drink, as well as all the other special days when it is one's religious duty to eat a copious meal.

To make them noteworthy, he would prolong his meals until midnight and, in the same manner, would prolong the banquet to bid farewell to the Sabbath Queen. For a person has a bone called *luz* which enjoys no food except at the banquet for the departure of the Sabbath, and from that bone the Holy One, blessed be He, will make the entire body sprout in the world to come. Fishl intended to provide it with much pleasure so it would remember him in the afterlife when there will be Leviathan and wild ox.

The child is father to the man. Even as a lad, it was evident that he would be a man of substance. It once happened that a certain man observed a yahrzeit. After prayers, he gave out cakes and brandy, for in those days, some people had already taken up the ḥasidic custom of bringing cakes and brandy to the house of prayer on the occasion of a yahrzeit to drink to the living and to bless the dead for the ascent of his soul. Fishl saw an old man slice a piece and abandon the rest. He was astonished. The old man said to him, What are you looking at me for? He said to him, I am observing the little slice that is wobbling between your gums and not getting any smaller. He said to him, And you would swallow a slice like that in the wink of an eye? He said to him, Even if they gave me all the cakes, I would not leave a single crumb.

The old man's son heard this. He grabbed Fishl by the ear and said to him, Here, the cakes are yours if you eat them in front of us, but if you leave even one of them, you must stretch yourself out upon the table and receive forty lashes plus one. He listened and agreed.

Twenty-four cakes there were, each as thick as the nose of the official who collects excise taxes on taverns. They were in three layers and kneaded with eggs, and Fishl ate them all. Finally, for fear of even numbers, he ate yet another. The next day, he bet a man who held a yahrzeit that he could drink a jug of brandy without a morsel of food. He downed it all and quaffed another cupful for good measure, and no change was noticeable in his face.

On Sabbaths and festivals, Fishl used to pray with the first minyan; but on ordinary days, he would pray with the second or third, and sometimes he prayed by himself. For on Sabbaths and festivals, a man's table is set and a feast is ready for him when he returns home. His plate and cup greet him, one with food and one with drink. But on ordinary days, many things delay a man before he stands up to pray. For the market swarms with a multitude of fowl, and the butcher shop is full of meat. Sometimes on his way to synagogue, a gentile man or woman would meet him bearing good things to eat. Such was Fishl Karp's custom: he would take his stick in his right hand and his talit and tefilin in his left, and he would cross the market and peer into the butcher shop, sending his eyes in front of him. He might see a fat hen, a fine piece of meat, a fruit worthy of a blessing, or a vegetable that would be good to add to his meal, and he would purchase them, before anyone else preempted him. If his talit and tefilin bag was large enough, he would secrete them there and bring them home after his prayer, and if there were too many things for his talit and tefilin bag to hold, he would send them off with someone else, such as a little orphan boy who had come to say kaddish or anyone else who was at hand to run his errand.

2. A Fish He Found

One day Fishl arose early, as was his wont on the six days of the week. He boiled a kettle and drank hot tea with honey. He filled his pipe with tobacco and saw to his bodily needs. Afterward, he peeked into the cupboard, where all sorts of victuals lay ready, and in his thoughts he tasted their flavors and in his mind he exchanged one food for another and one drink for another, since not all times and not all tastes are equal. You hunger for one thing, and something else comes and appeals to your palate. The manna that fell from heaven for the Israelites had all the tastes in the world. If they wished, it tasted like bread or like honey or like oil. Our foods, alas, have merely the memory of taste.

Once he had made up his mind about what he would eat after prayers—what first, what last, and what in the middle—he took his talit and tefilin bag and went to pray. His talit and tefilin bag was not made of satin nor of the leather of an unborn animal. Rather, it was made from the skin of a calf, from which he had not removed even enough to make a little strap for lashes on the eve of Yom Kippur. This was the calf that Fishl consumed at a single meal before he was required to report to the army officials who had come to take able-bodied men to military service. For by then, the custom had been abolished by which one could redeem oneself from the king's service by hiring one soul for another. Instead, anyone found worthy was taken to serve the king. Some Jewish lads would starve themselves so as not to be fit to serve the king. Fishl was a fleshy man and said, Even if I sit and fast for a whole year, I will still be fitter than five men together, so why should I deprive my soul? I would do better to eat a lot and drink a lot and treat myself well and put on a lot of weight, for they account ample flesh a flaw. And because a miracle happened for him on account of the calf that he ate, in that he fell sick and they excused him from the king's army, he made a bag out of its skin for his talit and tefilin.

Fishl gathered himself up to go to the house of prayer. As he left, he said, I will not linger there long, to announce that he did not have it in mind to prolong his prayers, so that they would hurry and prepare his morning meal, so that upon his return, he would find his table laid and he start his meal without delay. Finally, he kissed the mezuzah, thinking:

Something new has just become clear to me. If you eat some fruit preserves before going to sleep and kiss the mezuzah in the morning, you can find a bit of sweetness on it.

He said, I will not linger long, and Hentshi Rekhil, his wife, knew that he was just talking nonsense because even if he intended to return immediately, he would not, since it was his practice on the way to the house of prayer to stroll through the market and look into the butcher shop and to go out to the crossroads and meet the gentile men and women who brought poultry and vegetables to town. So it was on that day. He set out for the house of prayer, but his feet brought him to the center of town to see the foodstuffs with which the villagers supplied the town.

He met a fisherman with his net coming from the Strypa. He was stooped under the weight of the net, and the net was shaking itself and its bearer. Fishl looked and saw a fish quivering there in the net. In all his days, Fishl had never seen such a large fish. When his eyes settled down after seeing the new sight, his soul began to quiver with desire to enjoy a meal made from the fish. So great was his appetite that he didn't ask how such a stupendous fish had found its way into waters that do not produce large fish. What did Fishl say when he saw the fish? He said, "The Leviathan knows that Fishl Karp loves large fish and sent him what he loves." Though he had still not made up his mind how he would eat it, whether stewed or grilled or fried or pickled, in his thoughts he gathered together all the tastes that the white flesh of that pike was likely to give him.

Fishl's lips quivered with hunger, like a mullet with its many scales and fins. His eyes dimmed, and he did not see the fish. As the saying goes in Buczacz: One sees the Purim goodies but not their sender.

The fisherman saw a Jew staring at the fish without saying a thing. He took his mind off him and went on his way.

Fishl was alarmed and raised his voice in a shout, Hey, fellow, where to? The fisherman replied, To sell the fish. He said to him, And I, am I nothing? He said to him, If you want to buy, buy. He said to him, How much? He answered, This much. He said to him, And if I give you so much, will you write your will and die?

Fishl knew that the fish was worth twice what the fisherman asked, but if you can lower the price, you lower it. In short, the one swore he would not reduce the price by even a farthing, and the other swore that he would not pay half a farthing more. One swore by his God and all his saints, and the other swore on his own head. One raised, the other lowered; one added, and the other subtracted. Finally they came to terms. Fishl opened his purse and got his bargain.

The fisherman went on his way and Fishl stood there, devouring the fish alive. Not that he ate it alive, but he was like a man who sees a fat goose and says, "On your life, I'd swallow you just as you are." Though Fishl was used to fish, such an enormous one had never come into his hands. Even though they bring fish from all the great rivers, from the Dniester and from the Danube, a fish this big had never appeared in our city, or if it had, someone else had beaten him to it.

He looked at the fish again, and then at his own belly, at his belly and at the fish, and he said to them, "You see, you gluttons, what is waiting for you. Right after we finish morning prayers we'll sit down together and eat." He raised his eyes upward, thinking to himself: The Holy One, blessed be He, knows that in the whole city there is no one who makes as many blessings over food as Fishl. When they make their blessings, they bless on the measure of an olive or an egg, but when I make a blessing, it is over a satisfying meal. So may it be Thy will that there's a bridegroom or the father of a child about to be circumcised in the synagogue, so we will not be delayed by saying the prayers for divine mercy.

One good idea brings another. From thoughts of the prayers for mercy he turned his mind to the entire service, when it is long and when it is short, when one recites many verses and when one recites fewer. He began to be amazed at the wisdom of Moses, our teacher, who arranged everything in a timely fashion. You find that on Yom Kippur, when it is forbidden to eat and drink, you spend all day in prayer. So it is with the other fasts: since there is no eating and drinking, one recites many penitential prayers. But on the eve of Yom Kippur, when you are commanded to eat and drink, you don't say the prayers for mercy, you don't add the passage "He shall answer you on this day of affliction," and you skip the Psalm of Thanks. The same holds true for the day before Passover, when you give a banquet to honor the completion of a tractate, and you eat a lot of cakes and biscuits left over from Purim. True, a slight difficulty is presented by the Fast of Esther on the day before Purim, a day of baking and cooking, a day when savory odors waft from oven and range. Yet if you only delve deeply into the matter, you find that even the Fast of Esther has something good about it, for by starving yourself during the fast, you double your pleasure in the food and drink taken after the fast, just as meat eaten on Sabbath during the nine days of mourning preceding the Ninth of Av gives double pleasure. So why does the eve of Yom Kippur come before the day? So that a man will prepare himself for it with food and drink.

What good thoughts would Fishl Karp have savored in his heart were it not for that fish. Consider the matter: the very same fish that taught him the ways of the world put an end to his thoughts. Why? Because not all views are the same. The man thought: I will bring him to make a fish meal for me. And the fish wondered: How long will I be stuck in this man's hands? The man stroked its fins and savored the taste of fish, and the fish grew angry like a bird in a hunter's hands. The man was at peace, the fish at war. At last the fish tightened all its scales like a suit of mail and lifted one of its fins, nearly slipping out of Fishl Karp's hands.

Fishl noticed and said, If that is how you are, I will show you that I am no worse than you. He pressed his two hands together, clamping the fish between them. Its scales stood still as its fins opened, and its eyes were about to pop out when they saw the extent of human wickedness. Fishl looked at the fish and said, You evil scaly thing, now you know that Fishl is not one of those self-righteous folk who pretend to be merciful while they are waving about a rooster that is going to be slaughtered for Yom Kippur.

Though he had reason to be angry at the fish, he dismissed all resentment toward it. On the contrary, he looked at it benevolently and spoke nicely to it. He said to it, "Now that you have left off your wild ways, I will treat you well in return and conceal you from people's view, so they will not give you the evil eye. For there's nothing harder to eat than the evil eye. As my grandmother used to say, 'A stranger's eye on food is like bones on a full stomach.' You might say that a man is valued according to the foods and beverages that come to his table. But you should know that just as people honor the rich for their money, although they lock it away from others, so it is with food and drink. If you have them, you'd better not show yourself at mealtime or display what you are preparing for dinner." Another reason why Fishl promised to hide the fish from people's view was because in those days Buczacz had forsworn the eating of fish. Since the fishermen had raised the price of fish, the entire city was refusing to buy fish, even for the Sabbath, except for one family that didn't share in the public grief, as I have told you elsewhere. Therefore he comforted the fish, saying he would hide it from public resentment. Just as he was about to keep his promise, he found it hard to do so. Why? Because he couldn't find any place to hide the fish. He thought to hide it between his belly and his clothing, like a smuggler, but because of all the pains they take to make a living they are skinny and can do so, whereas his belly was so ample that it would not tolerate any external addition. He thought to stuff the fish against his chest, but his double chin wouldn't permit it. He looked at the fish like a man asking advice of a friend. The fish, which was mute by nature, was all the more mute at that time because of its sorrows, and it did not answer him. Were it not for his talit and tefilin bag, Fishl could not have kept his promise, and people would have given the fish the evil eye.

As I have said, his talit and tefilin bag was made of the skin of an entire calf, and to my eye it resembled those musical instruments that the musician inflates to make a sound. But while the instrument makes a sound and does not absorb anything, the bag is silent and accepts whatever you put into it. Were that not so, how could he put in it meat and fish and fruit and vegetables and sometimes even a pair of pigeons or a hen or a goose that he purchased on his way to synagogue? At any rate, that sack had never in all its days seen a creature as rebellious as that scaly, finny one. When the fish was only a year old, its length was already close to that of Fishl's arm, and since then it had further increased itself by a third and half a third.

The talit and tefilin huddled together and acted hospitably, as did the prayer book. Fishl shoved the fish in among them and the bag stretched itself to receive the fish. The fish, which was weak because of the change in place, the rigors of travel, and Fishl's manhandling, accepted its torments in silence and did not say: *The place is narrow for me.* But unwittingly it took revenge against Fishl, since it was very heavy and hard for Fishl to carry.

3. A Man's Emissary

Fishl got himself to the synagogue and found that even the latest service was over. He said to himself: It would be worth knowing what breakfast was waiting for them, putting them in such a hurry to pray. Now I will pray without a minyan and I will not hear Kedushah and Barekhu. In any event he did not pin the blame on the fish or say to it: You are the one that made me late for public prayer and deprived my soul of Kedushah and Barekhu and the privilege of responding Amen. On the contrary, he thought well of the fish. He would make such a breakfast meal out of it that even the books that heap condemnation on eating and drinking would sing its praises. Since he always took great care to eat breakfast, a meal that the sages praise extravagantly, humility gripped him. He said, "It makes no difference to the fish who hands it over to be cooked, whether it is me or someone else."

He found Bezalel Moshe, the son of Israel Noah the House Painter, who, as was his habit, was sitting in the synagogue. The house painter had been killed when he fell from the church roof while he was repairing one of their statues, and broke his neck, and his only son, Bezalel Moshe, was left an orphan. The shamash of the synagogue took him to the synagogue and found a few householders who took it upon themselves to give him food, each on a different day of the week. He used to live in the synagogue and eat day by day with different householders. Whatever he lacked in food, the shamash supplied, and what the shamash lacked, he supplied with his own hands. For he would make mizraḥim, plaques for the eastern wall of the home, indicating the direction in which one prays, and rotating plaques for counting the Omer, and he would draw letters and drawings for the cloths that girls embroider to cover ḥallot and matzot. He also made playing cards for Ḥanukkah and, by contrast, for Christmas Eve, when it is forbidden to study Torah, and in payment he would take a penny or a farthing or something to eat. Even the tombstone engraver would use him occasionally to draw the hands of Aaron the Priest on the stone, or a pitcher for a Levite, twins for someone born under the sign of Gemini, or fish for someone born under Pisces. Bezalel Moshe would draw on the stone in ink, and the engraver would engrave it on the monument.

At that moment, Bezalel Moshe was sitting in the corner behind the pulpit, next to the holy ark, a spot hidden from all eyes. He was busy making a mizraḥ and was in the midst of the sign of Pisces. Said Fishl, He's sitting there like someone who got a saucer of jam and hides so he will not have to share with others. Fishl inspected the beasts and animals and fowl and fish that the orphan had drawn. Fishl was astonished that this poor son of poor folk had it in him to draw offhandedly what the Holy One, blessed be He, had taken six days to create. And I—Fishl went on to reflect—and I, if I have to sign my name, I distrust my fingers all day. Fishl chirped with his lips, "Pish, pish, pish, as though to say: Miracle of miracles I see here. The orphan heard and was startled. He covered the mizraḥ with his hands.

Said Fishl to Bezalel Moshe, "What are you sitting around for, you idler? On a sheet of paper that size we could write the names of all the weekly portions of the Torah to track the compound interest on each and every portion. Show me what you have heaped together here. What is that, the fruits of the tree in the Garden? Do not be afraid that I will take one to eat. They are not even worth sending to the judge and the ḥazzan as Purim gifts. And what is this? The sign of Pisces? Fish, you call those miserable things?" He extended his finger toward the two fish that were drawn on the mizraḥ, the head of one against the tail of the other, and the fins of one against the fins of the other. Great sadness bubbled up from the eyes, as if they didn't know that Pisces was the constellation of Adar, the month in which we are meant to rejoice. Fishl laughed and said, "You call those fish? If you want to see what a fish is, I will show you."

He took his talit and tefilin bag and removed the fish, saying, "I reckon that in your prayer book you will not find a blessing for a fish like this! From now on, picture to yourself how lovely it will be, stewed or roasted or fried or pickled. Now take it to Hentshi Rekhil my wife and tell her, 'Reb Fishl desires a fish meal.' You can count on her to catch the hint, and I promise you that before I finish my prayers, the meal will be ready."

Bezalel Moshe looked at the fish, which was quivering in Fishl's hands the way his father Israel Noah had quivered after falling from the church roof. At that moment, the fish mustered its last strength and tried to escape from the hands of that human being, who was torturing him with words as harsh as wormwood. Fishl grasped him powerfully and said, "You are shivering, you are cold, a chill has gripped you. I will send you to my house right away, and Hentshi Rekhil my wife will make a fire and warm up a hot drink for you, and she will feed you onions and peppers to warm you up and abate the chill."

The fish closed its eyes in grief, and at that moment they showed it the death that was awaiting it. Then it sang a dirge for itself. If we translate its words to our language, this is approximately what they said:

Not in mighty waters did I end my allotted days;
Nor in ancient rivers shall I wend my destined ways;
In a wicked man's hand I perish indeed;
Though I offer much prayer, he will not heed.

After the fish vomited out the last remnant of its strength, Fishl laid it on the reading table and removed his prayer things from the bag. He picked up the fish and stuffed it back into the bag. The fish, whose strength was gone and who was already half dead, submitted to suffering in silence and offered no protest against Fishl, Fishl opened his talit and tefilin bag again, to show his face to the fish before sending it away. He laughed to himself contentedly and said, "I shall recite some of your praises to your face. You are fit for me and worthy to be eaten by me. Karpl Shlein and Fishl Fisher and, need it be said, Fishl Hecht, the half-brother of Fishl Fishman can all envy us."

After giving praise to the fish, he said to the orphan, "How many feet do you have, all in all? Two? If so, pick up both of them at once and run swiftly to tell Hentshi Rekhil my wife what I told you, that is, 'Reb

Fishl, long may he live, desires a meal of fish. Hurry and cook the fish and make him tasty victuals such as he loves.'"

Bezalel Moshe gazed at him and asked permission to conceal the mizraḥ first. Fishl laughed and said, "Fool, what are you scared of? Not even a mouse would nibble at it, but if you wish, hide it then and hurry, for Reb Fishl craves the taste of this fish."

Bezalel Moshe put away the mizraḥ and the tools of his trade, and took the fish, which was ensconced in Fishl's talit and tefilin bag, for Fishl had emptied the bag and stuffed in the fish.

The fish lay in the bag and its soul yearned to die, for it had come to loathe this world to which no creature comes but to die. Even if it has brought forth great things, its end is death. And how did the fish cogitate, since it was already dead? It was dead, let us say, but its torments were still alive.

Were it not for the fish's ignominious end, it would be worth recounting all its deeds and celebrating each and every detail. Now that it has plunged to the deepest abyss, it is enough for me to recall some of its deeds and to include the deeds of its fathers and also what befell it before reaching Fishl Karp. And do not be surprised that I do not call it by name. It had no name, since no fish is called by a given name, due to the great honor they accord to the Leviathan, their king. Moreover, until the time the Talmud was written, no species of fish even had a general name. This should be evident, for when the Bible speaks of fish, it never mentions the species.

4. Lords of the Water

His fathers and his fathers' fathers were among those venerable fish whose lineage extended back to the fish who were with Jonah in the belly of the Great Fish, and since their souls clung to Jonah's prayer in the belly of the Great Fish, they followed him until the Great Fish vomited him forth, as ordered by the Holy One, blessed be He. Hence there is no doubt that Jonah prayed inside the belly of the Great Fish, contrary to those commentators whose forced interpretation maintains that Jonah did not pray until after he went forth on dry land, since it is written, "And he prayed, et cetera, from the belly of the fish," and not "*in* the belly of the fish."

How did the fish come to our rivers, which are far from the place where Jonah was? But where was Jonah's prayer offered? Was it not in the place where the sea joins the river, as he said, "And Thou didst cast me into the deep, in the heart of the seas, and the river surrounded me."

These fish left the sea and came to the river and tossed in the fresh water from river to river, sometimes willingly and sometimes unwillingly. There are no bounds to the rivers they crossed and no end to the waters they swam in, nor is there any measure to the roiling water they passed through at peril of their lives, nor is there a limit to the snares and nets that caught them. Finally, they came to the least of our waters, the River Dniester, which traverses the lands of His Majesty the Emperor, as did the members of the Kiknish family, who came from the seed of Jonah the Prophet, as their name indicates. For Kiknish comes from *kikayon,* the Hebrew word for "gourd," which is the gourd that the Lord appointed for Jonah to shade him from the sun. I do not know if there are still any members of the Kiknish family alive, but some of them are buried in the Lemberg cemetery.

Nonetheless, it is fitting that you know that what was once accepted as undeniable truth has now come to be challenged. And some people already say that these are legends and that the lineage of this fish is made up. Not that the fish is not the son of its ancestors, but that they are not the sons of their ancestors—meaning those ancestors from whom they claim descent, that is, the fish who were with Jonah in the belly of the Great Fish. And by now every schoolboy is scornful. Using ichthyological terminology, they claim that the descendants of all the fish that were with Jonah in the belly of the Great Fish have become extinct, and that not one of them remains. So that anyone who says that he comes from the belly of Jonah's fish is an imposter. But I say, if we do not have ancestral honor here, we have honor itself. And if you wish to know what that is, I shall tell you in a manner comprehensible to human understanding, just as the early sages put human words in the mouths of beasts and animals and birds. True, they were great sages, and all their deeds were done for the sake of wisdom and morality, and to endow the simple with insight, on the strength of the verse "Who teaches us by the beasts of the earth." But for me, who have not even come so far as the pupil of their pupils, things as they were are enough.

In its youth, when it was still a light greenish color, the fish had already made a name for itself among the lords of the waters. Fish both great and small were in awe of it. Before it reached them, they glided toward it and entered its mouth alive. Fish that float on their bellies and those that swim on their ribs, left-handed ones and right-handed ones—they all came on their own to be his food. Not to mention snouty fish and those with eyes in their heads. Our fish, whose heart was close to its cheeks, let no rings be put through its gills and opened its mouth to dine upon them. Indeed, never in our lives have we heard that a fish like this one was to be found in our rivers, but because of its power and might, the others exaggerated, saying that even the fish in the sea were its subjects.

Cruising mighty waters, dreaded by fin and scale,
Here minnows gulping and there large fish devouring,
When it holidayed, ah, then did its foes all quail.
When it sallied forth with legions noble, scouring

The enemy's scales. Then did they savage and blast
The vanquished adversaries' heads. One day, it called
For banquet and gluttony, then declared a fast.
Sometimes it did fierce battle, other times it brawled.

Now it crammed its huge mouth with seaweed's denizens,
Now it bloodied streams but swam not all the long day.
Now it tripped and capered with the Leviathan's
Daughters, now like a groom, having with them its way.

Here passed it hours in banqueting and pleasure,
Dining with counselors, the shellfish sagacious,
Now crowning players and singers at leisure,
Discharging advisors when feeling pugnacious.

Every white-fleshed fish to its pointed teeth fell prey,
Until done eating, never calling for a pause,

Ruthless, killing whatever swam into its way,
In secret and in public view, by its own laws.

Its dread voice withered the Dniester's watery flora,
Earning it a blessing from everybody's mouth.
For it saved the carp from Sodom and Gomorrah.
You know that carp are lazy fish and quite uncouth.

Hounding and hunting them without surcease, it saved
Them from death by indolence. Hardly lovable,
We might well say—as of those whose life's path is paved
With splendid fortune—that all it lacked was trouble.

After traversing the Dniester and surveying its length and breadth, the fish wanted to see the rest of the waters and to know its relatives, for there is no river in Europe without members of this fish's tribe. This is not a matter of merit or of blame but simply the way things work out, sometimes one way, sometimes another.

Thus, after surveying the Dniester, the fish betook itself to the place where the Strypa falls into the Dniester. It did not stop and return to the waters of the Dniester but rather, it said, I shall go and see what there is in the Strypa.

We cannot know whether this took place in the Strypa at the village of Khutzin or in the Strypa at the village of Kishilivitz. In any event, the fish did not remain there. For it coasted with its fins all the way to the Strypa of Buczacz, that is, Buczacz that sits upon the River Strypa.

It arrived at Buczacz and said, Here I shall dwell, for this is my desire. The other fish of the Strypa saw it and were alarmed. Never in their lives had they seen such a large fish. They erred in thinking that it came from the seed of Leviathan, from those who were born before the Holy One, blessed be He, castrated it and killed the female and salted it away for the righteous in the future. Some paid tribute to the fish and brought it presents. There were so many presents that the waters of the Strypa began to empty of fish. Though we are not dealing with history, this most likely transpired in the year 5623 or 5624, for in those years the fishermen raised the price of fish exorbitantly, and the whole city came to the head of the rabbinical court and asked him to ostracize anyone who bought fish until the fishermen lowered the price.

Thus the fish swam in the waters of the Strypa, and all the fish of the Strypa in Buczacz accepted its dominion over them and paid it ransom for their lives, one delivering its brother, another handing over its friend, and yet another, its relative.

With high hand did it rule in the Strypa's waters,
Eating every fish, the parents, sons, and daughters,
Serene, consuming water folk, it put on flesh,
A delight to the eye, comely, speedy, and fresh.

Everyone scurried like slaves to do its bidding;
Before it knew, its will was done. So, from eating
And drinking in excess its will was lost. The fish
Believed that everything they told it was his wish.

As its willpower faded, so increased its fame:
All the Strypa's wisdom was spoken in its name.

The fish lived in the lap of luxury and lacked for nothing. One day, it rained. Even though fish are raised in water, they greet a drop that falls from above as thirstily as though they had never tasted water in their life. Our fish, too, floated up to snatch a drop.

After slaking its thirst from the upper water, which is the best water, for it irrigates and quenches and enriches the body and gives it purity, the fish lay contentedly with its fins relaxed, like a fish with a mind in repose.

At that moment those who sought its favor stood and pointed to it with their fins, swishing their scales. If I may transpose their gestures to human language, this is approximately what they said: "It sees what is between the upper and the lower waters and apprehends the higher wisdom from which all other wisdom derives."

5. A Day of Grief

People have a saying that it is good to fish in muddied waters. That day the water of all the rivers and streams and lakes was turbulent because of the rainwater, which drew with it tangled weeds, dirt, and mud puddles. All the fishermen went out and set traps in the great and small rivers, in the brooks, the ponds, and lakes, in the Weichsel and the Dniester Rivers and in the Prut, the Bug, the San, and in the Donets and the Podhortsa and in the Strypa River, and in all the rivers of their countries and towns. In the Strypa at Buczacz, too, the fishermen let down their nets, even though at that time none of the Jews would leap to buy fish, except for one man. Since we have already mentioned him elsewhere, we shall not mention him again.

Thus a fisherman cast his net in the waters of the Strypa. Our fish had never seen a net of that kind, for in its home waters, that is, the Dniester, the fishermen's nets are different from those in the Strypa. Every river follows its own custom.

The fish glided up toward the net and wondered: If this is a mountain, since when has a mountain grown up here? The fish had happened by there many times and had never seen a mountain. And if it is a reef, when was it brought here, and who made it full of holes? Or perhaps it is a kind of animal, and these holes are its eyes. If so, what is it, so full of eyes? Perish the thought that it might be the Angel of Death, whom everyone dreads. The fish, too, began to feel dread, and it raised one of its fins to flee. Once it saw that no one was in pursuit, it said, "Not even the Angel of Death wants to kill me." Once its terror departed, the fish returned to find out who that creature was and what it was doing here.

It backwatered with one of its fins and began paddling toward the thing that seemed to it like a mountain, a reef, or a living creature. Not even in its imagination did the fish envision what it really was.

The other fish saw it running toward the net. Fear fell upon them, and they panicked, since of those who enter that net, none returns. They wanted to shout, "Stay away! Keep your distance from the snare!" Terror froze their tongues in their mouths. They did not lose their panic until it gave way to wonder: did the fish not know that was the evil snare in which fish are seized? But in their innocence some of them believed that the fish was such a great hero that even a snare was child's play for it. They began to glory in its heroism and to scorn the snare, since they had a hero who was not frightened of it. They still called the net a snare, that is, a fishhook that is nothing more than a needle, an expression used by King Solomon, may he rest in peace, when he sought to portray human weakness, as he said, "For a man cannot know his time, as fish are enmeshed in an evil snare," and so on. While some fish were praising the fish's heroism, others sought to warn it: "Pick up your fins and flee for your life, for if you draw close sudden disaster will befall you." They held a council and agreed unanimously to rid themselves of this fish completely. They played dumb and told it nothing. Those who did not shut their mouth in great joy on seeing a murderer's impending disaster embraced a language of flattery and lies, and told it things that in our tongue go approximately as follows: "Our lord, you are worthy to make yourself a greater palace than that, but this is a time of distress, for the people of Buczacz have forsworn all pleasure from fish, and they will not even buy a fish for the Sabbath." The fish was seduced into thinking that they had prepared a palace in its honor. It flashed its scales to them and opened its eyes as though to say, "Let us go and see." Some of them began to be remorseful and reflective: "Alas, what have we done? It will see immediately that we wanted evil to befall it, and it will take its revenge upon us." But the fish had already been fated to die. Its foolishness trapped it, and it entered the palace, that is, the net.

The fisherman's hand began to be pulled downward. The fisherman was used to the small fish of the Strypa at Buczacz, and he thought it was not a fish tugging at him and his net but a corpse, a bastard's corpse. He cursed all the wanton women who endanger his nets with the infants they throw into the river. He wanted to leave the net in the river, so that if the baby were still living, it would die a long death and exact its torments from its mother. His hand began to tire and was pulled downward. He gathered that the corpse was conspiring to pull him into the river. He quickly drew in his net.

Our fish felt itself being pulled up. It began to wonder: Is this not the ascent of the soul? Since nothing like this had ever happened to it in its life, and all its life it was used to having everything its way, our fish came to the conclusion that this was the ascent of the soul that all the righteous gloried in. It began to see itself as righteous, in addition to all the praises that had been offered it from the day it had begun to rule over the tides of the Strypa, and it was angry at its ministers and servants for not calling it righteous.

Even if we had no books of moral teachings, we could learn the nature of temporary success from that fish. It was a great creature whose dread oppressed all the creatures in the Strypa, who were all prepared to render up the souls of their brothers and relatives to it, and there was no end to the words of flattery they would utter. Suddenly, disaster befell it, and after that, no one could be found to stand by it in its troubles, not even to console it, not even insincerely. At that time all the swamp fish raised their voices and began to mock it, saying, "They are raising you up in order to crown you king on high, just as you ruled as a king below." Come see these tiny ones, about whom the Talmud says, "Eating the small things reduces a man," who had never opened their mouths in their lives, and who saw themselves only as food for the big ones, and whom the big ones took note of only for a snack. Suddenly they became heroes and mocked the fish to its face. Of this type of thing, I say, with a slight change in the wording to satisfy the demands of the present subject, what they said in the Talmud: "Everything on dry land is also in the water."

6. Ascent That Is Descent

The fisherman drew in his net and found a big fish. He had not seen its like in the waters of the Strypa in his entire life. It was huge in flesh and fat, and its fins were crimson with blood, and its scales glistened like fine silver. The fisherman began to think well of himself and see himself as a wise man and hero. But what can wisdom and heroism offer if they are not accompanied by wealth?

At that time in Buczacz, people refrained from buying fish, even for the Sabbath, which one is commanded to make pleasant with fish. And why did Buczacz refrain from buying fish even for the Sabbath? Because the fishermen had raised the prices higher than their due. Even though the eminent rabbi, the head of the court, had not declared a ban upon fish, everyone refrained from buying fish, except for one man, as I have recounted elsewhere.

The fisherman began to grumble about the fish that had come his way when people were not jumping to buy fish. If it had come in normal times, he would have made a good name for himself and made money and drawn girls' hearts after him. Now it was doubtful whether he would find a customer aside from the priest, who paid with words and not with coin.

The fisherman reflected about what to do, but he came to no thought leading to action. The fish's lodging in the net was hard for it. It began to flop around and to tug the net. The fisherman was afraid the fish would escape. He ran and fetched a basin and filled it with water and took the fish out of the net and placed it in the basin.

The fish was consigned to the basin. Never in its life had it been relegated to such a narrow place, and never in its life had its thoughts been so expansive. Needless to say, not when it was a king and exempt from thinking, for it is the way with kings that their ministers think for them, but even before being crowned it had not been used to thinking. Now, confined in the basin, it was thinking, and the world grew ever smaller: In the days of my forefathers, fish swam in the sea, then in the big rivers which spread out over every land, and then in the Strypa, which is called a river only in honor of Buczacz, and finally the world has been reduced to a basin of water.

Come and see how great the power of thought is. Not only does one thought lead to another, but it also passes from creature to creature. You see, while the fish was in the basin of water, gathering up its entire world in its thoughts, the fisherman laid himself down on his sack and his straw, wanting only to sleep, but thoughts came and visited him. As I have said, the fish was thinking about seas and rivers, about its forefathers and itself, and the fisherman was thinking about the Jews and the fish and himself. God may have graced him and sent him a fish worth a lot of money, but what did the Jews do? They stopped eating fish even on their Sabbath, when they are commanded to do so. And were it not for the pact the Jews had made among themselves not to buy fish, he would have sold the fish to a Jew and drunk wine and offered others a drink and hired a musician to play. The girls would have heard and come out to dance with him. He would have chosen one of the pretty ones and done with her what his heart desired. When he thought about what the Jews had done to him, rage blazed within him. He rolled on his bed and could not fall asleep. He rose and poured a full bottle into his mouth. When the bottle was empty, he threw it against the wall. The bottle broke and its fragments rang like church bells. The priest heard and said, "Thus they ring the bells for a priest who has died. Therefore I am dead, and I have to prepare a death banquet." And because it was Lent, when it is forbidden to eat meat, he sent to the fisherman to have him bring him the fish. The fisherman was sad. Every single one of the fish's scales is worth a penny—why must he part with it for nothing? He pounded his head against the table and wept. The innkeeper saw and asked him, "Why are you weeping?" The fisherman kicked his belly and scolded, saying to him, "Jew, don't stick your tongue into things between me and the Church. If you don't shut up, I will say that your wine is mixed with Christian women's blood, that you pierce the nipples of their breasts and kill their children and throw them into the river, and they get into my nets and ruin them." The innkeeper was alarmed and frightened. He began to console him with a bottle as big as the wall. The wine entered and softened his heart. He revealed his trouble. The innkeeper said to him, "It is a difficult problem. If the priest has asked you for the fish, you cannot put him off with a scale or two. I have an idea." But he did not need the Jew's advice, for meanwhile another Jew had come along and bought the fish.

7. Damp Thoughts

In the morning, the fisherman removed the fish from the basin and put it back in his net, for if people see a fish in a net, they believe there was no delay from the moment it came from the river, and they are fonder of nothing more than a fish that comes right from the place where it lives to the market.

When the fish saw itself lying in the net, it mistakenly thought that the fisherman intended to return it to the river. This is the mistake that most people make, for the greater the trouble is, the more they think erroneously that salvation will arise from it.

The fisherman's thoughts were unlike those of the fish. The fish thought it would be returned to the place where it lived, while the fisherman desired its price. One looked forward to salvation, and the other despaired of salvation. One looked forward to salvation because it had been removed from the basin, and the other despaired of salvation because of the Jews who had conspired not to buy fish. But what was in store for them was unlike the thoughts of both fish and fisherman. You see, as they reached town, there came toward them a certain fleshy man with his bag and put out his hand to the net and took the fish and stuffed it into his bag. Not only was the bag smaller than the basin, but it was also wiped dry of all the moisture.

The one for whom a miracle occurs does not always recognize its miraculousness. If instead of Fishl Karp there had come someone who puts on two pair of tefilin or someone whose bag was full of those writings by which one seeks to approach our Father in heaven, such as *Ḥok LeYisrael* or *Ḥovot HaLevavot* or *Reshit Ḥokhmah,* it would have been more crowded.

The fish extended one of its fins and bumped into a tefilah. I do not know whether it was for the head or for the arm, and what I do not know, I do not say. It also banged its mouth on the prayer book. If the fisherman had been in the place of the fish, he would have hollered, "What do you want from me? Am I a Jew? Am I required to pray and wear tefilin?" But the fish shut its mouth and kept silent.

It shut its mouth but not its thoughts. What were its thoughts at that moment? That fleshy man bought me with scales of silver. If I make a reckoning, my silver scales are more numerous than the scales of silver he gave to the one who delivered me into his hands, and, needless to say, mine are finer. Thus, what made the one deliver me to the other? Perhaps because I am heavy to carry. If so, if I had deprived my soul of good, would that have improved anything? One way or another, it makes no difference in whose hands I am. Neither one intends to return me to the place where I live, but one gives me water for my thirst and the other does not even give me a drop of water.

Having touched upon Reb Fishl with the tip of its thoughts, the fish's mind now wandered from him to Reb Fishl's nation. Damp were its thoughts, and most of them nonsensical. If I were to reproduce them, they would be approximately thus:

The Jews are like fish and they are unlike fish. They are like fish in that they eat fish as fish do, and they are unlike fish since fish eat fish at every meal, and Jews—if they wish, they eat fish, and if they wish, they do not eat fish. It is difficult for the Jews to eat fish, for they have to take great pains before they bring the fish to their mouths. They rise early to go to market, and each grabs the fish out of the other's hands. One shouts out, "In honor of the Sabbath." The other taunts him, saying, "Do not say that it is in honor of the Sabbath. Say that it is in honor of your belly." In the end, they take it and cut it and salt it like those who prepare salt fish, and they light a fire under it. Finally, they eat it, some with their fingers and some with a pronged stick. And their pleasure is not complete, for they are afraid lest a bone catch in their throat. Whereas fish need nothing but their mouth. The Holy One, blessed be He, loves fish more than Jews, for the Jews weary themselves with every single fish, but while the fish swims in the water, the Holy One, blessed be He, sends it a fish that enters its mouth on its own. You know that this is true, for when you find a fish inside a fish, how else could it come to lie in a fish's stomach with the head of one toward the other's tail? Why is that? Because it enters the other's mouth headfirst, and if it had been fleeing, you would find its tail facing the other fish's tail.

The fish recalled times when it was in the water, and many good fish used to swim up and enter its mouth, and it would eat and drink all the delicacies of the rivers and streams and lakes, and the other fish all flattered it and were anxious to do its will. So our fish never imagined that the world was likely to change until it entered the net, which it had been seduced into believing was good for it. Those who had said that they themselves had been created only for our fish were the first to lead it to ugly death, beginning with imprisonment and ending with fire and salt and pepper and onions, and after all of those troubles it would not have the privilege of a watery grave. What would be done to it? It was to be buried in the bellies of human creatures. Wealthy men drink wine after the burial and poor men drink brandy after the burial, avoiding mention of water, in which the fish had lived. They drink to each other's life and are not fearful of dishonoring the dead.

The fish set its death before its eyes, no longer knowing whether or not it desired life. The image of its ministers and workers came to the fish's mind in its grief. Then it despised its world and began to spit in disgust. Were it not for the life force, which did not abandon the fish, it would have spit out the remnant of its life.

Little by little, its salivation ceased, as did all its thoughts. Its thoughts ceased, but its torments did not cease. Finally its thoughts returned and traded places with its torments, and its torments with its thoughts. This is something the mind cannot grasp. The fish lay there as though inanimate, and it is in the nature of an inanimate object not to have thoughts, yet here its thoughts raced about and created torments. It girded up the remnant of its strength and drew its eyes into its head, gathering up scraps of thoughts and reflecting: Perhaps this is the gathering up spoken of in connection with fish: "And even the fish of the sea will be gathered up." Because the fish was kosher, the heavens had mercy upon it, and its spirit was gathered up with a verse from the Prophets.

8. Between One Fish and Another

At the moment when the fish began to depart from the world, Bezalel Moshe was dragging his feet with difficulty because of the weight of his burden and the weight of his thoughts. While he was sitting in the synagogue his heart had been one, bent upon the work of making a lovely mizraḥ. Once he went outside, his heart become two. Thinking about the mizraḥ, he remembered his hunger. Thinking about food, he remembered the mizraḥ.

He nodded his head to himself and said: What is the use of thinking about a mizraḥ if the mizraḥ is in the synagogue and I am outside, and what is the use of thinking about eating if I don't have a slice of bread to sate my hunger? The fish is heavy. Who knows how much it weighs? Certainly the soul of a great tzaddik has been reincarnated in it.

He went and sat by the side of the road to rest from the effort of carrying the fish. He put down the talit and tefilin bag, which had become the temporary home of the fish, and he sat, weary of his burden, weary of hunger, and weary of being a poor orphan. If people wished, they gave him food; if they did not wish, they did not. And if he had something to eat, rather than satisfying him, the food only made him hungry, for he feared lest the next day his soul should languish from hunger and ask to depart, and no one would think of inviting him to a meal or of giving him a penny to buy bread. Maybe that is the meaning of the verse "For the earth was full of knowledge"—in the future everyone would be of the same mind, so that if one person asks for bread, the other gives it to him. Bezalel Moshe knew there was no knowledge but the knowledge of Torah and that there was no bread but the bread of Torah. However, a hungry man removes Scripture from its literal meaning and interprets "bread" as meaning actual bread. The greatness of bread is that even saints who fast constantly cannot live without eating. Some break their fasts on the Sabbath, on festivals, and on days when one is not supposed to fast, and from fast to fast they break their fast with a banquet for the fulfillment of a commandment, such as serving as the godfather at a circumcision. Whereas he fasted without fasting, for even when he fasted all day long, the fast did not count, since he did not fast of his own free will, but rather because he had nothing to eat. Were it not for the drawings that he drew, he would have seemed to himself like a beast whose only thoughts were about eating and drinking.

He began to be ashamed of his thoughts and tried to repress them. When he saw that they were stronger than he, he began to lose himself in them. Since he could not draw food to satisfy himself, though he knew some people can do that, his mind took leave of him and journeyed off to those who eat their fill and do not refrain from eating fish, not even on a weekday, not even when people seek to boycott them. In normal times everyone is used to eating fish, everyone but him, for in his life he had never seen a living fish nor even a cooked fish, except for those in old holiday prayer books next to the prayers for dew and rain. These had provided him with a model to draw fish on the mizraḥ and had given Fishl Karp reason to open his mouth and laugh at them.

He began comparing one form to another, that is, the fish he had drawn to the fish he was bringing to Fishl's wife. He admitted without shame that Fishl's was handsomer than those he himself had drawn. In what way? This is impossible to portray in words something that needs a visual demonstration. He looked all about. He saw no one. He put his hand into the fish's dwelling and removed the fish. He picked it up and looked at it. I would be surprised if any fish eater in the world ever looked at a fish the way that orphan did at this time. His eyes began to grow ever larger to encompass the fish, its fins, its scales, and even its head—it and its eyes, which its Creator had made to see the world with.

The fish began to shed one form and don another, until it left behind the image of the fish that Fishl had bought for a tidy sum and began to resemble the fish that had been in the will of the Holy One, blessed be He, to create when He created the fish. But He had not created it. He had left it to artists to draw. And since this is one of those wonders that we are not permitted to interpret, I shall be brief.

9. Torments of the Will

When an artist wants to draw a form, he detaches his eyes from everything else in the world aside from what he wishes to draw. Immediately everything departs except that very form. And since it regards itself as unique in the world, it stretches and expands until it fills the entire world. So was it with that fish. When Bezalel Moshe set his mind to drawing it, it began to enlarge and expand to fill the entire world. Bezalel Moshe saw this, and a chill seized him. His heart began to flutter and his fingers trembled, as it is with artists who quiver with torments of the will and desire to recount the deeds of the Holy One, blessed be He, each in his own way—the writer with his pen and the painter with his brush. Paper he had none. Now picture to yourselves a world whose essence had been blotted out because a single form was floating in space and occupying all of existence, and there was not a piece of paper to draw on. At that moment Bezalel Moshe felt similar to that mute cantor whose heart was stirred to sing a melody. He opened his mouth and moved his lips until his cheeks crumpled and shattered from his torments. The mute cantor was given the inner sensation of a melody and denied its expression with his voice, whereas Bezalel Moshe was capable of drawing, but he was denied paper. His eyes expanded like nets fish are caught in and like ornamental mirrors into which one gazes. The form of the fish came and settled there, taking on an extra portion of life—more than the fish possessed while it was alive. Bezalel Moshe fumbled in his pockets again. He found no paper, but he did find a piece of black chalk. Feeling the chalk, he looked at the fish. The fish too looked at him. That is, its form rose up and gripped him.

He grasped the chalk and kneaded it with his fingers, like someone who kneads wax with his fingers, which is useful for memory. He looked at the fish and he looked at the chalk. A model for drawing was there. There was chalk for drawing. What was lacking? Paper to draw on. The torments of his will intensified. He looked at the fish again and said to it, "If I want to draw you, I can only shed my skin and draw on my skin." He could have drawn on the fish's skin, just as Yitzḥak Kumer drew on Balak's skin, but Balak was a dog, whose skin absorbs color, which is not true of a damp creature full of moisture, where the color spreads in the moisture and will not register a form.

Bezalel Moshe yielded and returned the fish to the bag. He was about to walk to Fishl's wife, for the time had already come to prepare the fish for the meal.

Without doubt Bezalel Moshe would have brought the fish to make a meal of it, were it not that the fish was destined for greater things. What greater things? Why use words if you can see with your own eyes?

Now when Bezalel Moshe put the fish into the talit and tefilin bag, his hand happened upon a tefilah for the head. He saw the tefilah and was surprised. What was that tefilah doing here? One cannot say that it had remained in the bag with Fishl's knowledge, for what would Fishl do without a tefilah for the head? One cannot say that it had remained in the bag without Fishl's knowledge, for does a man who has a head remove his tefilin in order to pray and take the one for the arm but not the one for the head? You must conclude that Fishl had another. But if so, what was this one doing here? He had found a flaw in it and ceased using it, and perhaps the parchment with the verses had even been taken out, and there was only an empty case here.

Had Bezalel Moshe known that it was a kosher tefilah, he would have kissed it and run to the synagogue and given it to Reb Fishl, and Reb Fishl would have placed it on his head and prayed and finished his prayer and returned home to eat breakfast and examine his accounts and lend to borrowers in their hour of need and eat the day's dinner and lay himself upon his bed and sleep until the fourth meal and eat and attend afternoon and evening prayers and return and eat the evening meal and gratify the Holy One, blessed be He, with blessings for pleasures and with the grace after meals. But now, since Bezalel Moshe did not know that the tefilah was kosher, he did not run to the synagogue and did not return the tefilah to Reb Fishl, and Reb Fishl was prevented from praying and from eating his fill, and so on.

And why was the head tefilah left in the bag? Because of Reb Fishl's craving for a fish dish. When he sent the fish to his wife and cleared out his talit and tefilin bag, he did not take care about what he removed, and the head tefilah had been left there. And what caused Bezalel Moshe to suppose that it was flawed? Because the straps were dirty, like the cords used to tie up chicken legs, and they were tattered, and the paint on them had crackled, for it is a commandment revealed to Moses on Mount Sinai that the straps of tefilin must be black. The tefilah itself was wrinkled and colored like a goose's bill. The rim was broken and it was coated with a finger's thickness of grease.

Bezalel Moshe said to the fish, "Since a cat, which is not a kosher animal, had the merit of wearing tefilin, you, who are kosher, and who are a Sabbath dish, and who are perhaps even the reincarnated soul of a saint—so much the more so are you worthy of the commandment of wearing tefilin. But what can I do? Your Creator did not create you with a head for wearing tefilin, for your head is narrow and long, like that of a goose. In any event, I will tie the tefilah on you with its straps, and if you don't take your mind off the tefilah, you shall be garbed in splendor."

What was that story about the cat and the tefilin which Bezalel Moshe mentioned to the fish? If you do not know, I shall tell you.

At that time, all of Galicia was in an uproar about a certain Enlightener of the age who wanted to get rid of his wife, but she refused to accept a bill of divorce. He went and took a cat and placed his head tefilah on it. The woman's father saw what sort of a man he was and forced his daughter to accept her bill of divorce.

Thus a head that was not required to wear tefilin merited tefilin, and Reb Fishl, who was required to wear tefilin, was kept from the commandment of tefilin. Why? Because he had not been careful to make certain that his tefilin were tidy and that their straps were black. For had he made sure that they were tidy and that the straps were black, the orphan would not have been sure that he had found a flawed tefilah, and he would have run to return it to Reb Fishl, and Reb Fishl would have prayed and returned home and eaten breakfast and sat and examined the accounts of his loans and he would have made loans to merchants in their hour of need, and he who needed to be repaid would have been repaid, and thus a religious duty would have been done, for it is said that the payment of a debt is a religious duty.

10. The Form of a Man

While the fish was being ornamented with the head tefilah, Fishl was looking for his head tefilah and not finding it. That is the essence of the story, and the entire story is as follows. After sending the fish to his wife and preparing himself to pray, he filled his pipe with tobacco and saw to his bodily needs. He stayed there as long as he stayed and washed his hands to recite the blessing one recites after using the toilet, and then he went to wrap himself in his talit and tefilin and pray. His thoughts began to race about within him. One said: Good-for-nothing, again you have forfeited the Kedushah and Barekhu. And one said: Since you are praying by yourself, you are the master of your own prayers, and you are not dependent on the prayer leader, who waits for the old men who take a long time to recite the Shema and the Eighteen Benedictions. Since Fishl did not like the thoughts that were racing about, he removed his mind from them to make room for the prayer itself. He said: Well, while I pray, Hentshi Rekhil will be preparing the fish, and if she has not managed to prepare it for the morning meal, I shall be content with those things that open up the gut, and I shall eat the fish at noon. All of those foods came and settled in his mouth. He hurriedly shook out his talit and placed it on his shoulder and examined the fringes and wrapped himself in it and recited the blessing and recited all the appropriate verses in the prayer book. Then he reached out his arm and took the hand tefilah and placed it correctly on his upper arm, on the distended flesh over the bone, which was swollen because of all the fat, until a good part of the tefilah sank into it. I do not know whether he was accustomed to bind the strap around his arm seven times or nine times, and what I do not know, I do not say. Then he reached out his hand for the head tefilah and did not find it. And why did he not find it? Because it was bound around the fish's head. He sought and searched and groped, and there was nothing he did not look under. But he did not find it. He stooped to look under his belly. Perhaps it had fallen on the floor. And even though had it fallen on the floor he would have to fast all that day—and what a day, a fish day like this he still bent over to the floor and did not find it.

Reb Fishl stood alone in the synagogue, wrapped in his talit and adorned with his arm tefilah, and he shouted, "Nu, nu!" That is, "Give me a head tefilah." But there was no one there to hear him shouting. Had the orphan been in the synagogue, he would have heard and brought him a head tefilah, and Fishl would have recited the blessing for tefilin and prayed, and so on. Since he had sent the fish with the orphan, Reb Fishl was alone in the synagogue, and even if he shouted all day, his shouts would not be heard. When would they be heard? In any event not before afternoon prayers. Since it was a ḥasidic synagogue, they recited afternoon prayers late, just before the stars came out.

A thought occurred to him, and he opened the box under the reading stand, for men who come to pray every day customarily leave their talitot and tefilin in the synagogue. He found a torn prayer book and tattered tzitzit and the case of an arm tefilah and an old calendar and a broken shofar and the letter *heh* made of tin that is hung up for a firstborn who is not yet redeemed, and a scribe's pen. But tefilin were not to be found. And why didn't he find any? Because people had stopped leaving their talitot and tefilin in the synagogue. Why? Because of a drunken shamash in the town who had been discharged. He had looked for a teaching job and found none. He used to take talitot and tefilin, and sell them cheaply to people from the villages, and he would drink up the profits in brandy. Now, picture this: a man has recited the blessing for the arm tefilah but has no head tefilah. Talking is forbidden between putting on the arm tefilah and the head one, and he could not find a head tefilah. Even had he stood there all day, the day would not have stood still, and there was reason to fear the time for prayer might pass.

He rummaged through the box under the table and found what he found: ritual articles that were no longer fit for use. But what he wanted, he did not find. Now you see how expert a person must be in the necessary religious rules. For had Fishl known, he would have followed the rule for someone who only has a single tefilah: he puts it on and blesses it, since each tefilah is a separate commandment in itself. This is the law when a person is under duress: if he can only put on one, he puts on the one he can.

At that moment, while Reb Fishl's world was falling in on him, Bezalel Moshe was sitting in the shade of a tree and playing with the fish and with the tefilah on the fish's head. To avoid dishonoring the dead, I shall not repeat all the words that Bezalel Moshe said to the fish, such as, "Brow that never wore tefilin," and the like. Finally he changed his mind and said to the fish, "Now we shall remove the tefilah from your head, so that Satan will not come and accuse those Jews who sin with their bodies. For you are not commanded to put on tefilin but do so, and they, who are commanded, do not put on tefilin."

As he touched the fish to remove the tefilah from its head, his fingers began to tremble again with desire to draw, like all artists whose hands are eager to work. For if they have succeeded in making one form, they wish to make another lovelier still. And if they have not succeeded, they are even more avid to do so, as many as seven times, a hundred times, a thousand times. As you know, Bezalel Moshe had drawn the sign of Pisces that day, and it had not come out well, because he had never seen a fish in his life. Now that a fish had been shown to him, his soul truly yearned to draw a fish. Out of desire for action his fingers trembled, nor did he take note of the nature of the fish, for it is not the way of fish to absorb color.

He passed the piece of chalk across the fish's skin the way artists do before they draw. They mark a kind of guideline, and that line shows them what to do. Thus Bezalel Moshe drew a line and went back and drew another line, and between one line and another the form of Reb Fishl Karp emerged, until the image of the fish was effaced beneath that of Reb Fishl Karp. And this is something quite unusual, for Reb Fishl's head was thick and round, and the head of that fish was long and narrow like the head of a goose.

And how did Bezalel Moshe come to draw the form of a man, when he had intended to draw the form of a fish? When he reached out his hand to draw, the form of the fish was transmuted into the form of Reb Fishl, and the form of Reb Fishl was transmuted into the form of the fish, and he drew the form of Reb Fishl on the fish's skin. Strange are the ways of artists, for when the spirit throbs within them, their being is negated and they are acted upon. They are directed by the spirit, which obeys the commandment of the God of all spirit and flesh. And why was Reb Fishl transformed into a fish? Because he was a lover of fish.

11. Between an Arm Tefilah and a Head Tefilah

I return to Fishl Karp—not to the Fishl Karp whom the artist drew, but to the Fishl Karp whom his Maker created.

Even before the time came to eat, his mind was driven to distraction by hunger. This is a virtue of man over fish. A fish can subsist without eating for up to a thousand days. A man can remain without eating no longer than twelve days. And Reb Fishl Karp not even a single day.

Bezalel Moshe heard the sound of passersby. He was frightened lest they ask him, "What is that in your hand?" And that they would see what he had done and tell Reb Fishl, and Reb Fishl would scold him, and everyone would say that Reb Fishl was saintly, for it is the way of the world that if a householder scolds a poor orphan, everyone joins in scolding him. He quickly concealed the fish and directed his feet toward Reb Fishl's house.

If the passersby had not interrupted him, he would have removed the head tefilah from the fish and erased the picture of Reb Fishl he had drawn on the fish's skin. Since the passersby did interrupt him, he did not manage to do even one of the things he ought to have done. He neither removed the tefilah nor erased the picture of Reb Fishl from the fish's skin, and he trusted that the tefilah would fall off the fish's head by itself. As for the picture, he expected that moisture would ooze out of the fish's damp skin and erase it.

Bezalel Moshe arrived at Hentshi Rekhil's and handed her Reb Fishl's talit and tefilin bag. And in the bag lay the fish, glory bound to its head and the face of the fish like that of Reb Fishl. Hentshi Rekhil was of her husband's mind. She comprehended that if Fishl had sent her his talit and tefilin bag, certainly something important to eat was concealed within it. The smell of the fish came and told her, You are not mistaken. She quickly took it and hid it so that her neighbors would not notice what had been brought her, and she sent the bearer off without any food, letting him go off far hungrier than when he set out on Reb Fishl's errand.

The orphan left Reb Fishl's house hungry, and his hunger walked with him. It would have been good had Reb Fishl's wife given him some food, which he would have eaten, and then he would have returned to the synagogue and saved Reb Fishl from hunger. But she dismissed the errand boy without food. And since hunger plagued him, he wanted to eat, for he had long since learned that if you put off hunger, it grows ever more importunate.

He had a penny which he had received in payment for drawing a memorial dedication for the abandoned woman's orphan daughter. He had written her relatives' dates of death in her prayer book. He had kept the penny in his pocket to buy paper or paints or red ink. Now that hunger seized him, he put his victuals before his art.

He went to buy bread. A peddler appeared with baskets of fruit. The orphan thought to himself: Half the summer has already passed, and I still haven't tasted a fruit. I will buy myself a few cherries. He bought a penny's worth of cherries and went out of the city, sat under a tree, and ate the cherries and threw the stones at the birds, watching to see how they flew. He forgot Reb Fishl and the fish and delighted his eyes with the birds' flight. He began to perfume their flying with the verse *As the birds fly,* to the melody of R. Netanel the Cantor. His heart filled with the force of the melody, and he began to think of the power granted to human beings. Some are given a melodious voice, like R. Netanel, who stirred people's heart with love of the Lord when he opened his mouth in song, and some are given power in their fingers to make skilled handiwork, like Israel Noah, his father. R. Netanel had the merit of emigrating to the Land of Israel, and Israel Noah his father had enjoyed no such merit but had fallen from the church roof and died. Some people say that the non-kosher wine that he had been given made him fall down and die, and others say he went out to work without eating first, because they had finished all the bread in his home, and hunger had seized him, and he had collapsed and died.

His father's death oppressed his heart, and he was sad. The birds came, and with their flight they carried his mind away from its gloom. He looked at the way the birds fly and sing and how they trace shapes in the sky with their flight. Although the shapes were not visible, nevertheless they were engraved before his eyes and upon his heart. The birds are beloved, since the power to fly is given to them. If the power to fly were given to man, his father would not have died. Now that he was dead, other artisans had come and painted the walls of the Great Synagogue.

The orphan set aside his grief over his father for grief over the Great Synagogue. Ugly drawings had been imposed upon its walls. Far worse were those that had been imposed upon the Tailors' Synagogue, where they had heaped up pictures of birds that did not even look like a likeness. If the painters had raised their eyes upward, they would have seen what a bird was. If so, why did the people of Buczacz praise the artists and their paintings? Because the people of Buczacz walk stooped over all their lives and never raise their eyes above their heads, and they do not see the creatures of the Holy One, blessed be He, except for the fleas in their felt boots. Therefore those drawings look pretty to them. But I shall show them how the creatures of the Holy One, blessed be He, look and how it is fitting to draw them.

From the birds in the sky he returned to the fish he had drawn. At that moment he was grateful to Fishl Karp, without whom he would not have seen the form of a fish. From now on, said the orphan to himself, if I come to draw the sign of Pisces, I will not look in old festival prayer books, but I will draw as my eyes instruct me.

At that moment there was no one happier in Buczacz than Bezalel Moshe, the orphan, and no one in Buczacz was sadder than Reb Fishl, the moneylender. This is indeed a wonder: here is a poor person without enough food for a single meal, and here is a rich man who could have held banquets and celebrations all his life with the interest on his interest. The one was happy because of the birds in the sky, and the other was grieved because of his fish, which he was kept from eating.

Fishl saw there was no point in standing in the synagogue and shouting "Nu, nu" when there was no one to hear his "nu, nus." The thought came to him that perhaps he had left the head tefilah in his talit and tefilin bag when he had sent off the fish. Without further delay he removed his talit and covered the arm tefilah with the sleeve of his garment and rushed home. He already visualized himself with the head tefilah adorning his head, praying swiftly and washing his hands for a meal. He swallowed his saliva and planned to double each of his steps and not to delay for anything in the world.

I, too, shall do as Fishl did and I shall not tarry until I reach the end of the story. For everything that has a beginning has an end. Happy is he whose end is finer than his beginning. Here, with the story of Fishl, though its beginning is apparently fine, its end is certainly not fine. If you wish to know, here it is before you.

12. The Thoughts of a Hungry Man

Indeed, Fishl charged his legs according to the saying taught in the midrash: The belly charges the legs. However, our sages of blessed memory meant that by the power of eating the body has the power to charge its legs, whereas I interpret the teaching thus: Because he craved food, he found the power in his legs to bear the charge of his belly.

Thus Fishl hurried and did not tarry. He did not tarry, but the fortune of his meal tarried. He was not delayed; others delayed him. Where did they delay him? Close to his home, right next to the door of his house. So many people were there that he could not find the door. What did all of those people want at his house, and why had they gathered there, and why were they noisy and turbulent, and what caused them to besiege his house? Go and ask them when you are forbidden to speak, because you are in between the head and arm tefilin. As much as his soul clamors to know, no one tells him. Of such a situation it is fitting to say: There is no servant woman who has not got six mouths. Yet when you want to hear something, there is not one mouth to tell you.

He had a little girl whom he loved more than all of his other daughters, and she loved him too. She saw her father. She came and rose up on her tiptoes and wrapped his neck in her two arms and said, "Oy, Papa, oy, Papa." He could no longer restrain himself and asked her, "Why has the whole town gathered in front of our house?" The girl repeated, "Oy, Papa, don't you know?" And she said no more. Being small, she believed that her father knew everything and that he had asked in order to test her. If it is something that everyone knows, does her father not know more than they? She answered him in kind, "Papa, don't you know?" Fishl saw that the world was conspiring against him, and even the daughter of his old age, whose voice chattered on and on without stopping, would not tell him. Nor were his astonishments finished yet. While he was aching to know what had happened, he heard people saying, "He did well to lie down and die. In any event, he must be buried." Fishl understood that someone had died, but he was puzzled about why they said he had done well. Is death a fine thing? There is nothing better for a man than to eat and drink, and if one is dead, not only does one neither eat nor drink, but one becomes food for maggots. He stooped in sadness and lowered his eyes to the earth. The earth raised itself up and whispered to him, "Now you are treading upon me with your feet. Tomorrow I shall cover you." It also whispered, "You may believe that I am sad because of you. I am sad for those who will bear your coffin, who will have to carry such a big-bellied man as you."

As he looked at the earth, he saw that the earth was dry. He began to converse with himself. He said, If a man dies, the neighbors pour out their water, and here, besides sewage, there is no sign that they have poured out water. Little by little his mind reached the truth—that no person had died here. When his mind reached that truth, it did not know what to do with it. For if no person had died, why must there be a burial? But they had explicitly said that he must be buried. And if there is no dead person, why need there be a burial? One way or another, did they not say that he had laid himself down and died?

Had Fishl been full, he would not have wasted time with such thoughts, but he would have entered his house, washed his hands, and sat down to eat, and after the meal he would have wiped his mouth and said, "What is that rumor that I heard, that someone died there? Who died?" Now that he was weak from hunger he turned his thoughts to death. He thought again: Since they mentioned burial, that means there is a dead person there. If so, if there is a dead person there, why isn't the shamash calling, Come out and accompany the dead? His thoughts began to devolve from person to person. He was alarmed lest someone who owed him money had died.

The thoughts that did him ill now turned kinder to him, for the idea came to mind that no person had died, for had a person died, they would have poured out water, and the shamash would be summoning people to the funeral. If so, what had died? A firstborn beast had died, which had to be buried, as is the law for a firstborn animal that dies. In any event, Fishl was somewhat puzzled as to why it had died at his house and not elsewhere. In any event, it had done a good deed in dying, for the city was released from its mischief. That it died at his house was a coincidence.

Although Fishl said that it was by chance, his mind was nevertheless disturbed, lest the animal had purposely chosen to die at his house, as in the story of the ewe and the old man.

What is the story of the ewe and the old man? It happened in our city that when the flock went out to graze every day, one ewe would leave the rest and go and stand before a certain house and bleat. One day the owner of the house fell ill. The ewe came and bleated. Every day its voice was thin, but this day its voice was strong. Every day its voice was short, and this day its voice was long. People saw that the patient's face was changing because of his great suffering, for his heart was tormenting him because of his misdeeds, and his torments were etching themselves in his face. They believed that his face had changed because of his pains, and were he to sleep without disturbance, his torments would abate. They went out to drive away the ewe, but it would not move. They hit it with a stick, and it would not move. That day a ḥasidic miracle man came to town. He heard and said, "You are struggling to drive it away in vain." "Why?" He said, "I shall tell you a story. There were two friends in the town. One fell ill and was about to die. At the time of his death he deposited a purse full of coins in his friend's hands and said to him, 'My daughter is young and does not know how to keep money. Keep these coins for her until she reaches maturity. And when she finds a good match, give her the coins as a dowry.' One man took the coins and the other turned his face to the wall and died. The orphan girl was close to maturity, and the holder of the deposit did not deliver the coins to her, but he buried them for himself under the threshold of his house. He said, 'No one was present when the coins were transferred. If I don't deliver them to the dead man's daughter, no one will claim them.' No one was present when the orphan girl's coins were transferred. Just a creature of the Holy One, blessed be He, was present to see and to hear. It was a ewe from the flock. And when the orphan girl reached maturity, the ewe pitied her and came to bleat and remind the man that the time had come for him to keep his word to his dead friend and return the money that the orphan girl's father had deposited with him for a dowry. As long as he doesn't return the orphan girl's money, the ewe will not leave the threshold of his house." They went and asked the dying man, "The money that your friend deposited with you—where is it?" He did not manage to tell them before he died. And the ewe died too. They sought to remove its body from the house, but they could not. The miracle worker said to them, "Dig beneath it and remove it with the earth." They dug and found a purse full of coins. They went and handed the coins over to the rabbi for the orphan girl. The ewe relinquished its place and they buried it.

Fishl began to fear that the ram had died in front of his house to remind him of some sin. He scrutinized his deeds and could find nothing in himself except that once he had lent someone money in his hour of need and he had forgotten to remind him that the loan was subject to the permitted form of interest. He began to add up how much interest he had received. His presence of mind returned immediately, and he cleared a way for himself to his house.

13. A Homily on Reincarnation and the Conclusion

Upon entering his house, he saw a kind of dirty creature that gave off the smell of a fish lying on the floor, and on it was some object that would not have been recognizable as a tefilah were it not for its straps. Fishl shouted a great shout, "Oy, my fish!" He shouted a second shout, "Oy, my tefilah!"

The fish was squashed and spotted. Fishl's face, which Bezalel Moshe had drawn with chalk on the fish's skin, had already been effaced by the damp skin and nothing remained of it but the dirtiest dirt. Stranger than that was the tefilah. Until it landed on the fish's head, it had been yellow. Once it had sat on the fish's head, the color of the chalk with which Bezalel Moshe had drawn Fishl's face had clung to it and blackened it.

Before Fishl was freed of one fear, he saw that his head tefilah had been thrown down on the ground. Grief seized him, and he feared that the fish, in revenge, had thrown his head tefilah on the ground to force him to fast until after evening prayers to delay his enjoyment. He grew furious at that ingrate: had he not bought the fish from the fisherman, it would have descended into the priest's belly without a benediction. In his great anger a fit of apoplexy gripped him.

After stripping off his clothes and letting his blood, they found the arm tefilah on his upper arm and stood in astonishment. Could it be that a man with a brain in his skull would put on the arm tefilah but not the head tefilah? Before they could resolve the matter of Fishl, they were perplexed by the matter of the fish. For never in their lives had they heard that you could catch tefilin-laying fish in the Strypa, and even the most absolute of fish eaters in Buczacz said, "Never in our lives have we seen a fish crowned with tefilin."

There was in our city a society of inquisitive people called the Sons of Chance, because they used to say that everything happened by chance. For example, if Reuben ate bread, it was by chance that Reuben had found bread to eat—otherwise why is it that others seek bread but do not find it? Thus it was by chance that the fish found a tefilah. How? For example, a Jew had fallen into the river, and his tefilin tumbled out of his baggage, and the head tefilah caught on the fish's head. No chance event transcends its simple meaning; it is a happenstance like any other.

However, you would do well to know that opposing them there was an elite circle in our city concerned with the wisdom of truth; some of its members met during the ten fateful days between Rosh Hashanah and Yom Kippur, and others regularly after midnight penitential prayers, both in deepest seclusion. They heard the story of the fish and said what they said, but they, too—that is, the sages of truth—failed to discover the truth. However, from their words we have learned some of the secrets of Creation, including information about the reincarnation of souls. Some of what the mind can grasp, I shall reveal to you.

We have learned in mystical works that there are seventy souls, which are reincarnated in several animals, and they are called the Sign of the Lion, the Sign of the Ox, the Sign of the Eagle, the Sign of the Virgin, the Sign of the Scorpion, the Sign of the Ram. For we have found that the Twelve Tribes are compared to animals: Judah to the Lion—*A lion's cub is Judah*; Joseph to the firstborn ox; Issachar to a strong ass; *Dan shall be a serpent*; *Benjamin is a ravenous wolf*. Clearly, the whole secret of reincarnation is that the evil impulse alters everyone according to his deeds, and some are like a lion, a serpent, a donkey.

If so, why are saintly people reincarnated as fish? Because a fish's entire life is in water, and water is a place of purification. When they are removed from the water, their life ceases. Similarly, the righteous live all their lives in purity. Furthermore, the eyes of the saintly are open to their deeds just like fish, which have no lids on their eyes, which are always open; and through the merit of the righteous the Eye on high is ever open upon us for good. Also, the righteous are scrupulous not to be gripped by sins, but we are like fish caught in a net. Another thing: the righteous always pour out their hearts in repentance like water before the Lord, which is how the Targum translated the verse "And they drew water and poured it out."

We have also learned which are the fish in which the souls of the righteous are reincarnated; and what is the fate of those who make a show of righteousness but are not righteous; whether they are also reincarnated as fish; and what is the fate of those whom the world sees as righteous but are neither righteous nor evil.

Know that there are three classes: one consists of utter saints; one of those who pretend to be righteous and are neither righteous nor wicked; and one of the utterly wicked who pretend to be saintly. Absolute saints are reincarnated as kosher fish. The righteous who are neither saintly nor wicked are reincarnated as fish whose kashrut is debatable, for in some places they are permitted and in some places they are absolutely forbidden. And those who pretend to be righteous and are utterly wicked are reincarnated as non-kosher fish, since they are many and multiply and are fruitful like the fish, and they send forth progeny who are similar to them. Therefore the non-kosher fish are more plentiful than the kosher ones. They—that is, those evildoers whose countenance is saintly—are acolytes of Dagon, the Philistine god, who from his waist down was in the form of a fish and from his waist up was in the form of a man. Job prayed concerning them: *Let them curse it who curse the day, who are ready to rouse the Leviathan,* which Rashi of blessed memory interpreted to mean: "To be childless in their joining together, to isolate their company from the society of man and wife, with no children."

We have other dread and marvelous secrets such as the reason why a fish has the merit of being eaten on the Sabbath and festivals. Moreover, there is a fish that has the merit of being eaten on the eve of Yom Kippur and a fish that is eaten at the Purim banquet, and there is a fish that is placed on the table of absolute saints, and there is a fish that descends into the belly of the utterly wicked. That is why some are cooked in vinegar and, in contrast, some are cooked in sugar. And also why it is that there is a fish we eat on the first day of a festival and one that we eat on the second day. Most profound are these matters, and I shall reveal only the tiniest bit here: a righteous man who possesses the sanctity of the Land of Israel has the merit of being reincarnated as a fish that we eat on the first day of a festival, and the soul of a righteous man who does not possess the sanctity of the Land of Israel is reincarnated in a fish that we eat on the second day. This is the secret of the saying of the rabbis of blessed memory: the second day compared to the first day is like an ordinary day.

Why did they not ask Fishl what the reason was for his wearing the arm tefilah and why his head tefilah was on the fish? In truth, they did ask him, but just as a fish does not answer, so, too, Fishl did not answer, because his tongue, may the Merciful One preserve us, was taken from him and he became mute.

I do not know the end of the fish. Fishl's end was thus: from then on he grew ever weaker until he died. But some say this is not so, that he regained his vigor, and that he even grew stronger, but on the Sabbath of Ḥanukkah, which was also the New Moon, between one kugel and another, he suffered a stroke once again and gave up the ghost. I do not know whether he died between the Sabbath kugel and the Ḥanukkah kugel, or whether he died between the Ḥanukkah kugel and the New Moon kugel. And, as you know, what is not clear to me, I do not say.

After he died his daughters built a great monument on his tomb, to honor the man lying beneath it. Since Fishl's Hebrew name was Ephraim, who was blessed with the verse *And they shall abound like fish*—the fish who are fruitful and multiply, and the evil eye has no power over them—and since he was born in Adar, the month of the constellation Pisces, the stone carver carved a pair of fish on his grave. Such fine-looking fish you will not find on the graves of other Fishls or others born in the month of Adar, because the stone carver used the orphan Bezalel Moshe to draw the form of the fish on the stone before carving them. Since before they carve letters or forms, stone carvers customarily draw them on the stone, and since Bezalel Moshe became a specialist in the form of fish, having examined so intently that fish which Fishl had sent with him, he drew the fish well.

Years went by and the monument sank into the earth. Not only do the living finish beneath the earth, so, too, do the dead, and so, too, the things we fashion in their memory. Some people have the merit of having their monuments stand for one generation, and other monuments stand for two. In the end they gradually sink until they are swallowed in the earth. So, too, Fishl Karp's monument sank and was swallowed in the earth, but its tip did not sink. One can still see a pair of fish there. In another city people would say that a fish is buried there, and they would make up alarming stories, such as that once, while a fish was being prepared for the Sabbath, it raised its head and called out, *Remember the Sabbath day and keep it holy*. So it was known that the soul of a Sabbath observer had been reincarnated in it, and the rabbi ordered it to be buried in the cemetery. In Buczacz, people would not tell such a story. Just as Buczacz is full of Torah, so, too, is it full of wisdom, and it does not like wonder tales that are not consistent with nature. Buczacz likes things as they really happen, and just as they happened, so does Buczacz tell them.

And since I was born in Buczacz and raised in Buczacz, mine are the ways of Buczacz, and I tell nothing but the truth. For I say that nothing is finer than truth, since aside from being beautiful in itself, it also teaches men wisdom. What does the story of Fishl Karp teach? That if you are going to pray, do not set your eyes upon meat and fish and other delicacies, but let your path be holy. Lest you say that Fishl is one matter and you are another, He knows that if you are not avid in the pursuit of meat and fish, you are avid for other things.

The question of which is better is still open. We recite a blessing on fish and meat, both before and after eating them. Which of your other desires merits a blessing? May all our actions be for a blessing.

Translated by Jeffrey M. Green

In the Nighttime of Exile

After world war i ended, a small remnant of the people of Buczacz returned to the city. They found their houses destroyed and their stores vandalized. There were houses whose original location was unrecognizable. Because they loved their birthplace and because they saw that no good had come to them in the places to which they had wandered, they began to prepare themselves for returning and resettling. With difficulty and pain they again secured their place. Austria had been replaced by Poland, whose rulers were harsh masters. Because they did not know how to conduct themselves with reason, they ruled with angry cruelty; they knew nothing of mercy, they only understood harsh decrees. They afflicted the Jews in every way that they could, until the Jews despised their lives.

Despite this, the Jews held on with all their strength in the city where their fathers had dwelt for eight hundred years, and they would not give up their place. The Jews of Buczacz were joined by others from the surrounding villages; their homes and land had been stolen by their neighbors, who gave them no opportunity to rebuild their lives. Great poverty descended on the city; there were fewer and fewer opportunities to make a living. People did not know what they would eat or what they would feed their small children. There was not a day on which there was not some new decree that nipped at the Jews' heels. The old took comfort in the fact that they would soon die and not much longer have to endure their afflictions; they would be buried in the city where their ancestors were buried. The young looked toward the four corners of the earth for a place where they would be allowed to live. And the fewest of these few prepared to emigrate to the Land of Israel in order to work its land and to establish for themselves and their descendants a haven where they could be free of the yoke of Exile, which has been Israel's burden since the day it left its land. Meanwhile, each saw himself living in the land of his birth as but a guest for the night.

Translated by Herbert Levine and Reena Spicehandler

Annotations

Original publication data for each story appears below in the individual headings. An asterisk (*) indicates that the Hebrew version of the story was only originally published posthumously in the 1973 first edition of 'Ir u-Melo'ah. *In most cases those stories that had been published in various periodicals during Agnon's life were subsequently revised by him, and were anthologized in* 'Ir u-Melo'ah *by Emunah Agnon Yaron at her father's instruction. A dagger (†) indicates that we have anthologized a previously published translation (although in such cases the translations have been revised and annotated for this edition).*

1. *The Sign*

"HaSiman"; orig. pub. as a fragment in 1944 (*Moznayim* 18 [Iyar 5744]), later expanded to its current length and published in Agnon's 1962 collection *HaAish vehaEtzim* and appended to the 1973 edition of *'Ir u-Melo'ah* by Agnon's daughter Emunah Yaron. For its role as a "consecration story" and its placement here at the opening of *A City in Its Fullness*, see Alan Mintz's foreword to this volume. † The translation originally appeared in *Response* 19 (1973) and subsequently in *A Book That Was Lost* (Toby Press).

1. Disturbances of 1929 / Widespread Arab uprisings against Jewish settlement during which Agnon's home in Talpiyot was ransacked.
4. I shall bear you on the wings of eagles and bring you unto Me / Exodus 19:4.
4. There shall be seven full weeks / Numbers 23:15.

5. And Moses declared the festivals of the Lord / Numbers 23:44, usually recited before the Amidah on holiday eve, but apparently not according to the custom of this synagogue.
5. Because of you, the soul liveth / Genesis 12:13.
6. Brings her bread from afar / Proverbs 31:14.
7. The heavens are the heavens… / Psalms 115:16.
8. Moment when the sky splits open / Mystical idea that the heavens open up at midnight on night of Shavuot.
10. Vigil of Shavuot night / Tikkun Leil Shavuot; it is customary to stay awake and study Torah throughout the night of Shavuot.
10. Solomon Ibn Gabirol / (ca. 1020-ca. 1057), one of the greatest Spanish Hebrew poets, who drew on a wide knowledge of biblical Hebrew and Arabic poetry. The book of hymns referred to are his Azharot, versifications of the 613 commandments composed for Shavuot.
11. Poor captive girl / Allegorical figure for the people of Israel in exile; in the boy's literalizing imagination, she is a real person.
12. Germany / An autobiographical reference to the years Agnon spent in Germany between 1912 and 1924.
14. Heralding voice / Balfour Declaration of November 2, 1917, announcing British support for a Jewish national homeland.
15. The neighborhood was finally built / The southern Jerusalem suburb of Talpiyot, where Agnon built his home.
17. Tremors of 1927 / Devastating earthquake of July 11, 1927, centered in Jericho, causing widespread regional damage, including to Agnon's home in central Jerusalem, after which he relocated to Talpiyot.
18. No man knoweth its value / Job 28:13.
19. We cannot go up and be seen there / From the Additional Service (Musaf) on festivals.
20. Naḥman of Breslov / (1772-1811), ḥasidic Tzaddik who became known for mystical teachings and enigmatic tales. The teaching concerning "jumping over" appears in *Ḥayye Moharan* II, p. 19a (#85, alt. ver. #522).
24. Shevet Yehudah / "Scepter of Judah," an account of the persecutions of Spanish Jews written in the first half of the sixteenth century.
24. Small Yom Kippur / The eve of the New Moon is observed in some communities as a time for prayer, repentance, and fasting, thus the name Yom Kippur Katan, the Small Day of Atonement.

25. May God give strength to His people... / Psalms 29:11.
25. Trees of life / The wooden dowels around which the Torah scroll is wound.
28. At the dawn I seek Thee... / Opening line to liturgical poem by Ibn Gabirol, translated by Nina Davis as "A Song of Redemption" in Joseph Friedlander, ed., *The Standard Book of Jewish Verse* (1917), and available online at bartleby.com.

31. *Buczacz*

*"*Buczacz*"; † translation originally published in *A Book That Was Lost* (Toby Press).

32. Month of Iyar / Hebrew month corresponding to the end of April-beginning of May.
32. Rites of Sukkot / The waving of the "four species" as part of the Sukkot prayers; cf. Lev. 23:40.
32. Booths / The sukkot (huts), temporary outdoor dwellings for the Sukkot holiday; cf. Lev. 23:42.
34. Rhinelanders / First mention *en passant* of the geographic origins of Buczacz Jewry; subsequently, it becomes apparent that (at least according to legend) their arrival predates the Crusades.
34. The whole land / Cf. Genesis 34:10.
34. Three festivals / Passover, Shavuot, and Sukkot.
34. Simḥat Torah / Festival at the conclusion of Sukkot marked by the conclusion of the yearly cycle of Torah reading.
35. Weekday when the Torah is read / Monday and Thursday mornings.
35. Barekhu and Kedushah / Highlights of the communal prayers that can be recited only in the presence of a minyan (prayer quorum of ten men).
36. Ritual bath / Mikveh; specially constructed ritual bath for immersion to remove levels of ritual impurity, especially by women at the conclusion of the menstrual cycle. The construction of a mikveh is one of the marks of having a permanent Jewish community.
37. Worms, Mainz, Speyer / Major Jewish communities of the Rhineland, decimated during the Crusades.
37. Khmelnitski / Leader of the pogroms that swept eastern European Jewry in 1648-49.
37. The Enemy / Nazi Germany.

40. *The Great Synagogue*

"Beit HaKeneset HaGadol"; in it earliest iteration this story appeared in an anthology published by the newspaper *HaTekufah* entitled *Polin* (Warsaw: Shteibel Publishers, 1919); subsequently in *HaPoel HaTzair* (July 10, 1925) and in a volume *Polin: Sippurei Aggadot* (Tel Aviv: Hedim, 1925).

40. *The Brilliant Chandelier*

"HaNivreshet HaMeluteshet"; orig. pub. in *Measef: Divrei Sifrut, Bikoret veHagut* 5-6 (1965-66), ed. B. Benshalom and Y. Cohen.

44. *The Tale of the Menorah*

"Ma'aseh HaMenorah"; orig. pub. in *Atirot: Rivaon LeNoar* (Winter 1957), and subsequently in *Measef: Divrei Sifrut, Bikoret veHagut* 5-6 (1965-66), ed. B. Benshalom and Y. Cohen; † translation originally appeared in *A Book That Was Lost* (Toby Press).

In the Hebrew title, "*Ma'aseh HaMenorah*" (taken from Numbers 8:4), *ma'aseh* denotes a historical occurrence, not a fictional story; *menorah* refers not to the Hanukkah lamp but to the seven-branched candelabrum that stood before the Holy of Holies in the Jerusalem Temple.

44. Bestowed wisdom / Cf. I Kings 5:26.
45. I am unworthy of the least of all your kindnesses / Genesis 32:11.
45. Great Synagogue / Built in 1728.
45. Forbidden to make a vessel identical to one that had been in the Temple / Rosh Hashanah 24a-b.
46. Memorial prayer / Yizkor; recited on Yom Kippur as well as on Passover, Shavuot, and Sukkot.
47. Seliḥot / Special midnight penitential prayers recited in the days leading up to Rosh Hashanah and through Yom Kippur.
48. Twentieth of Sivan / Special memorial day for the victims of the Khmelnitski pogroms of 1648–49; the date (usually falling in June) specifically marks the destruction of the Jewish community of Nemirov, on June 10, 1648, the bloodiest day of the pogroms, in which more than 6,000 Jews were slaughtered, according to some accounts.
48. A new generation arose that did not know / Cf. Exodus 1:8.
49. Sometime later, Poland was conquered / The first partition of Poland occurred in 1772.

49. Blood libels / From the early Middle Ages through modern times, false accusations that Jews murdered Christian children (often in order to use their blood for Passover baking or other such rituals), leading to trials and massacres of Jews.
50. "My Sabbath" / Agnon story found in his Hebrew collection *Elu veElu* (pp. 275–77 in the 1998 Schocken edition; forthcoming in English in *Forevermore* from Toby Press). In the story, Yisrael the Metalworker is imprisoned for counterfeiting seven copper pennies to buy food for the Sabbath; while in jail, a mysterious stranger, later revealed to be the spirit of the Sabbath itself, secretly brings Yisrael's wife seven coins every Friday for her to support herself and buy food for the Holy Day.
51. Wage a war on behalf of their nation / Occurred in 1795, leading to the third and final partition of Poland.
52. Its one head turned to the three branches / Cf. description of the cherubs atop the holy ark; Exod. 25:18-20 and Rashi.
52. Great War / World War I.
53. And the town of Buczacz was also given over to Poland / Following World War I, control of the town went back to Poland; in 1939-41, it was under Russian control, until the Nazi invasion of 1941-44.
54. Note well, and follow the patterns for them that are being shown you on the mountain / Exodus 25:40.
55. Ruthenians / During the early modern era, the term was used primarily to refer to members of Eastern Slavic minorities in the Austro-Hungarian Empire—namely, Ukrainians and Russians.
56. One kingdom comes and another kingdom passes away. But Israel remains forever / Cf. Eccles. 1:4 and Rashi's comment there, which undergirds this story: "*A generation goes and a generation comes:* As much as the wicked man toils and labors to oppress and to rob, he does not outlive his works, for the generation goes and another generation comes and takes all away from his sons, as it is stated (Job 20:10): 'His sons will placate the poor.' *But the earth endures forever:* But who are the ones who endure? The humble and low, who bring themselves down to the earth, as it is stated (Ps. 37:11): 'But the humble shall inherit the earth.' And Midrash Tanḥuma states: All the righteous of Israel are called earth [or land], as it is said (Mal. 3:12): 'for you shall be a desirable land.'"
57. Have pity on Your people / Joel 2:17.
58. How long shall they direct us however they wish? / Cf. Prov. 21:1.

58. ***Until Elijah Comes***

"Ad Sheyavo Eliyahu"; orig. pub. in *Karmelit (Haifa)* 3 (1956-57) and *Haaretz* (September 9, 1963).

In the Talmud, the phrase "let it rest until Elijah comes" is used to describe disagreements that are to be left unresolved. Agnon uses this same verb in his first sentence.

58. Section known as the Curses / Deut. 28:15–68. These sections describe the horrible punishments that will befall Israel if the covenant is betrayed. The story turns on the superstitious belief that the power of the Curses could fall on the person called up to the Torah when they are read.

59. Jewish word for the ascent of my soul / That is, the Mishnah passages or kaddish prayer traditionally recited for the soul of the departed.

61. Bounding chariot / Cf. Naḥum 3:2.

62. Swings a rooster over his head / The kapparot ceremony, practiced by some Jews on the eve of Yom Kippur; swinging something (chicken or money) above one's head is thought to transfer one's sins to the object, which is then donated to the poor.

62. There is no person who does not have his hour… / Avot 4:3.

63. Undertone / Due to the inauspicious content it is customary to chant these passages in an undertone.

64. Sixth Torah honor / The third and sixth Torah reading continue to have special honorific status in many congregations.

65. I was a youth, and now am an old man / A play on Psalms 37: 25: "I have been young, and now am old; yet have I not seen the righteous forsaken, nor his seed begging bread."

66. Pribiluk / A small village near Buczacz.

66. Elijah / Said to preside over the circumcision ceremony where a special chair is left empty for him.

69. The words of your mouth… / Deut. 23:24.

70. Descended from kohanim / The biblical Prophet Elijah was indeed a kohen, descendent of the Temple priests. Customarily, the first aliyah (person called to the Torah reading) is reserved for kohanim; our vagrant, a kohen, cannot receive the honor of the sixth portion.

72. Very good / An allusion to God's blessing of creation, Genesis 2:31.

72. Sleep on Shabbat… / The phrase spelling out the letters of Shabbat forms an acronym for *sheinah be-shabbat ta'anug.*

76. Who gives utterance to the mute / Exodus 4:11.

78. ***The Ḥazzanim***
    * *"HaḤazzanim"*
78. Sabbaths before the New Moon / On the Sabbath before the new moon a special prayer is added just before the Musaf service.
78. Yotzrot / Special piyyutim inserted in the morning service on festivals and special Sabbaths.
78. Twentieth of Sivan / Observed as the collective memorial day for the martyrs of the 1648-49 pogroms.
79. The heavens declare the glory of Lord / Psalm 19.
79. A Song of Ascents / Psalm 122.
80. Hineni prayer / Special petitionary prayer recited by the ḥazzan only in advance of musaf on the High Holy Days.
80. Monasterzyska / A small town west of Buczacz.
80. Soon in our days / Line from the Kedushah prayer recited collectively during the Sabbath morning service.
80. Those who dwell in earthen houses / Medieval piyyut by Solomon Ibn Gabirol.
80. Kerovah / Extended, multi-part piyyut that embellishes the Amidah in the morning service.
81. *Yeven Metzulah* / Firsthand account of the Khmelnitski massacres in 1648-49, written in Hebrew by Nathan Nata Hanover.
85. Ḥametz / Leavened bread required to be searched out by candlelight and destroyed in advance of Passover.
87. Sambatyon River / According to rabbinic literature, a river beyond which the Ten Lost Tribes of Israel were exiled; used as an idiom to signify the boundary of the known world.
87. Tashlikh and the writing of writs of divorce / Tashlikh is a Rosh Hashanah prayer recited by a body of water. A writ of divorce (*get*) must identify the place where the document is issued according to nearby rivers.
92. Nineteen years old / In the original Hebrew version of the story there is an apparent textual problem: Rivkah Henya is "five or six years older" than R. Elya, yet "when he was five or six years old... she was nineteen years old." We speculate that an error in the text rendered "nine" as "nineteen,"

but have translated the story in line with the Hebrew text as published in both editions of the story.

93. *Ḥemdat Yamim* / Kabbalistic work of unknown authorship, first published c. 1731, suspected of containing Sabbatian elements.

94. R. Avraham David / R. Avraham David Wahrman (1771-1840), known as the Tzaddik of Buczacz, where he served as Rabbi from 1814 until his death, author of the halakhic works *Da'at Kedoshim* and *Eshel Avraham*.

96. Whoever finds a wife finds a great good / Prov. 18:22.

98. *The Man Dressed in Linen*

"HaIsh Lavush HaBadim"; serialized in *Haaretz* (September 26, 29, and October 10, 1965), except for the concluding section beginning with chapter 20 which was added to the 1973 edition.

98. Man Dressed in Linen / This pregnant expression means, essentially, an angel. It appears in the Bible first in Ezekiel 9 and 10—describing an angel who performs actions of judgment against Jews on God's behalf; and then in Dan. 10:5, where a man dressed in linen reveals to Daniel the mystery of the end of Israel's exile. More to the point, a "man dressed in linen" appears in the great poem on martyrdom, "Eleh Ezkerah," the recitation of which is an emotional high point of the Ashkenazic Yom Kippur liturgy. In this poem, R. Ishmael ascends to heaven and questions an angel referred to as the Man Dressed in Linen as to whether his martyrdom and that of his comrade R. Simeon ben Gamaliel are indeed God's will. Our story's protagonist, R. Gabriel, is not a messenger from God (i.e., an angel) but a messenger to God from the community. Incidentally, Gabriel is also the name of one of Daniel's angelic informants in Dan. 8:16 and 9:21.

98. Teivah / The ark in which the Torah scroll is housed, but colloquially means the prayer-stand placed before the ark from which the ḥazzan (cantor) leads the prayers. To "go before the teivah" connotes serving as ḥazzan; i.e., leading the prayers.

98. Yahrzeit /Annual commemoration of the death of a close relative. Besides reciting kaddish, a person observing yahrzeit has precedence in serving as prayer leader for weekday services.

99. Seliḥot / Penitential hymns recited at midnight or before dawn on the week before Rosh Hashanah and during the period between Rosh Hashanah and Yom Kippur.

100. Maftir / The last portion of the weekly Sabbath and festival Torah reading. The person called up to the Torah for this final reading also chants the haftarah, the passage from the prophets assigned for that day. In synagogues that do not have a regular ḥazzan, it is common for the person who chants the haftarah to be invited to serve as prayer leader for the remainder of the service.

100. Yekum Purkan, Av Haraḥamim, Ashrei, Yehalelu / Prayers connected with the conclusion of the scriptural readings; when they are finished, the Torah is returned to the ark. The prayer leader, who has been presiding from the table on which the Torah had been unrolled for the reading, now moves to the prayer-stand for the Musaf service, which is preceded by the so-called half-kaddish.

100. Davening / Yiddish word for the ritual recitation of obligatory prayer, usually performed in singsong or actually sung, and accompanied by certain physical gestures. The term is used of an individual worshiper, of a community praying together, and of a prayer leader. We use "to daven" instead of "to pray" because the latter includes personal prayer done in silence, which is not relevant for the story.

100. Prayer leader / The term used here is *sheliaḥ tzibur*, translated as "prayer leader," the generic term for anyone who leads prayers in public; this can be any adult male in good standing with the community who is capable of reciting the prayers correctly. "Ḥazzan," which we translate as "cantor," refers to a prayer leader who is especially designated (and often paid) to lead the prayers every day or on other regular occasions; the latter term also frequently implies a prayer leader who is an accomplished singer, as opposed to merely having a pleasant voice. But there is much inconsistency in the usage of the two terms.

101. Moon... sanctification ritual / This ceremony is performed in sight of the moon during the first part of every lunar month. Part of the ceremony consists of jumping up and down three times; this is what the gabbai's brother-in-law is alluding to in his jocular comment below. The sanctification of the new moon of Tishrei is ordinarily performed at the end of the Yom Kippur fast.

102. Avodah / Description of the Temple service of Yom Kippur that is recited as part of the Musaf service of Yom Kippur. It focuses particularly on the rituals performed by the high priest. It is one of the most distinctive parts of the Yom Kippur service.

102. Hand extended to accept our repentance / An image that occurs in several of the Yom Kippur prayers.
104. Blessing "to dwell in the sukkah" / It is obligatory to live in the sukkah during the seven days of the festival, but an exception is made if the weather is too harsh. Even under harsh conditions, one would try to eat at least enough in the sukkah to justify reciting kiddush and the benediction "to dwell in the sukkah." The blessing may be said only if the sukkah fulfills certain requirements governing its dimensions and construction.
105. Second day of Yom Kippur / The practice of observing a second day of Yom Kippur, by analogy to the other festivals that are observed two days in the Diaspora instead of one, has been observed by ascetics, despite being condemned by many rabbis. Since the second day begins exactly as the first day ends, observing it necessitates fasting on two consecutive days (see Rema, Oraḥ Ḥayyim 624:5). Cf. Agnon's tale "Twofold," forthcoming in *Forevermore* (Toby Press).
106. Did you conduct your business honestly / Shabbat 31a;,one of the questions that each person is asked upon arriving before the heavenly court after death.
108. A person should always depart in an auspicious moment / Pesaḥim 2a and Ta'anit 10b.
108. Your God alone should you fear / Deut. 6:13.
109. He who listens to advice is wise / Prov. 12:15.
109. Those who hope in the Lord… / Isa. 40:31.
110. The earth is the Lord's and the fullness thereof / Psalm 24.
110. Set a table before me / Psalm 23.
110. Who shall ascend unto the mountain / Psalms 24:3.
111. I repay my vow to the Lord / Psalms 116:14, 18.
113. Are you better off being the ḥazzan in a town of two hundred Jews… / Cf. Judg. 18:19.
113. Quorum for grace… / When three men dine together, grace is introduced with a special formula; when ten dine together, the name of God is added to the formula.
114. Torments of the grave / According to tradition, two angels appear to the deceased in the grave and beat him by way of expiating his sins. People who have led especially virtuous lives are thought to be exempt.

114. Council of the Four Lands / Central body of Jewish authority in Poland from 1580 to 1764.
115. R. Moshe of Kraków / R. Moshe Isserles (1530–72), known as Rema; among the most important rabbis in Polish Jewish history, author of the mentioned works, alongside his monumental glosses on the *Shulḥan Arukh*, the work for which he is mainly celebrated today. His *Torat HaOlah* is a detailed survey of the architecture, sacred vessels, and sacrificial service of the Jerusalem Holy Temple.
116. Rashi and Tosafot / R. Solomon ben Isaac of Troyes (1040-1105), known by the acronymic Rashi, composed a universally used commentary on the Talmud. Tosafot are glosses on the Talmud written by his followers. Printed editions of the Talmud include these two commentaries.
116. Ben Sira / Apocryphal work; this passage (3:21-22) is cited often in rabbinic literature. The point here is that the *maḥzor* contains many liturgical poems written in an obscure, allusive style; a cantor, in principle, should refresh his understanding of them each year with the help of commentaries.
117. R. Shakhna... *Mordechai* / Shalom Shakhna (d. 1558) was head of a yeshiva in Lublin. *Mordechai* is a halakhic work by Mordechai ben Hillel Hakohen (ca. 1250–98).
118. R. Amnon of Mainz / Legendary author of the liturgical poem beginning with the words "Let us declare the majestic sanctity" *(Unetane Tokef)*. According to the legend, which is partly told in our story, he recited the poem in the synagogue as he was dying a martyr's death; he later revealed the poem in a dream to R. Kelonymos ben Meshullam (late eleventh century), who gave it circulation. But there is concrete evidence that the poem is considerably older.
118. Geshem / A series of piyyutim praying for rain, forming the most distinctive feature of the Musaf service of Shemini Atzeret and a high point of the festival for a cantor.
119. Heschel of Lublin / Apparently Abraham Joshua Heschel of Kraków (1595–1643), who served as head of the academy in Lublin and later as its chief rabbi before moving on to Kraków.
121. Etrog... valid for waving during the synagogue service but not for the blessing / The rituals performed with the "four species"—etrog, palm frond, myrtle branch, and willow branch—on the seven days of Sukkot involve waving them during certain parts of the synagogue service.

Before they can be used for this purpose, a benediction must be recited over them. It is customary for every individual to say the benediction and wave the four species in the morning, whether or not they attend the synagogue service. Ideally, each person has his own set of the four species, but in places where one of them is hard to obtain, people queue up to use those that are available. The blessing may be recited only if the four species fulfill certain technical criteria for validity.

122. Fifteenth of Shevat / Tu BiShevat is the date (15 Shevat) from which the age of a tree is counted, and therefore is called the New Year of Trees. Sheheḥeyanu ("Who has kept us alive") is the benediction recited when using something new for the first time or when eating a fruit for the first time in the season (among other occasions).
122. Through sloth the ceiling sags… / Ecclesiastes 10:18.
123. Because you did not serve the Lord your God… / Deut. 28:47.
124. Had you deserved it… / Eikhah Rabbah, Petiḥta 19.
124. Pin-money tax / Known in Polish as *szpilowka*, a yearly tax or gift to the wife of the king, count, or other noble-woman, either paid in jewels or money for their acquisition. Called "pin-tax" after origin as gift of pearl hair pin.
125. He who caused the fire will duly pay / Exod. 22:5.
125. Mikołaj Potocki / Polish nobleman (1712–1782), in the 17th and 18th centuries Buczacz belonged to the Potocki family.
126. *Terumat Hadeshen* / Collection of responsa by R. Israel Isserlein (1390–1460).
127. When she was being led to the ḥuppah, a rider came by… / A trope Agnon returned to at various points in his writing, starting from his earliest Yiddish stories. See, e.g., "*Meḥolat Hamavet*" in *Elu veElu* and "*Ḥuppat Dodim*" in *Al Kapot Hamanul.*
128. Why are you weeping… / I Samuel 1:8.
128. God exempts from the commandments… / Avodah Zarah 54a.
128. His mercy extends to all His creatures / Ps. 145:9.
128. I am a stranger and sojourner among you / Genesis 23:4.
130. For God had taken him / Genesis 5:24. The Kedushah is the passage in the liturgy that describes the angels and the people of Israel joining together to recite the Sanctus (Isaiah 6:3). It is often preceded by a series of piyyutim, the last of which is called a silluk (ending poem), which ends with a bridge passage to the Sanctus. "Let us declare the majestic sanctity" is a silluk. The word silluk derives from an Aramaic word meaning "to go up." Agnon certainly has

this meaning in mind, for besides the vision of the worshiper being directed upward to the world of the angels at this point in the service, it is a fitting place for a martyr to offer his prayer (as does R. Amnon in the legend of *Unetane Tokef*) as he ascends from earth to join the heavenly choir.

131. The Mishnah teaches that the early pietists... / Berakhot 5:1.

135. Wealth is no help on a day of anger / Proverbs 11:4.

135. Light is scattered over the righteous... / Psalms 97:11.

138. Two days after the holiday / In chap. 25, the narrator had spoken of the following episode as happening on the day after Simḥat Torah.

139. Many waters cannot extinguish love / Song 8:7.

140. *The Ḥazzanim, Continued*

* *"HaḤazzanim (Hemshekh)"*

140. Maharsha / R. Shmuel Eidels (1555-1631), known by the acronymic Maharsha, was a renowned rabbi famous for his commentary on the Talmud. He served in a variety of communities, with his final post in Ostroh (in today's western Ukraine), where he established a yeshiva.

142. Ḥalitzah / The ceremony of the removal of a shoe in the levirate ritual signifies that the brother of a deceased man is not obligated to marry his late brother's wife (see Deut. 25:5-10).

144. Veshamru / "And you shall observe the Sabbath" (Exodus 31:16), a line from the Sabbath prayer usually recited with great cantorial flourish.

145. Found a wife and a great good / Prov. 18:22.

146. Entice thy husband / Judg. 14:15.

146. Ma'aravot hymn / Piyyutim added to the holiday evening service.

146. Riches profit not on a day of wrath / Prov. 11:4.

146. Ahavah Rabbah / Blessing preceding the recitation of Shema in the morning service, at which point the four fringes of the tzitzit on ones talit are gathered together.

149. By the Rivers of Babylon / Psalm 137, recited in mourning for Jerusalem as a preface to the weekday grace after meals.

151. Tzaddik of Ruzhin / R. Israel Friedman of Ruzhin (1796–1850), a ḥasidic rebbe in Ukraine.

152. "The Sign" / The reference is to depiction of the old ḥazzan in the story "The Sign," which appears as the prefatory selection in this volume.

152. You alone have I singled out... / Amos 3:2.

154. *R. Moshe Aharon the Mead Merchant*
* *"R. Moshe Aharon Mokher Mei HaDevash"*

154. Added name of Moshe / According to tradition that adding a name for one who is seriously ill will serve to deceive the Angel of Death.
154. Sobieski / Jan III Sobieski (1629-1696), from 1674 until his death King of Poland and Grand Duke of Lithuania, famous for his victory over the Turks at the 1683 Battle of Vienna.
155. R. David Ganz / (1541-1613), a Jewish chronicler, mathematician, historian, astronomer and astrologer. His Tzemaḥ David (Prague, 1592) is a work of Jewish and general history. His *Sefer Neḥmad veNa'im* (1759) is a work of mathematics, geography and astronomy (in which he demonstrates knowledge of Copernicus, yet follows the Ptolemaic system), and contains an appended translation into Latin of the introduction and general summary of the work.
157. Maharsha / R. Shmuel Eidels (1555-1631), known by the acronymic Maharsha, was a renowned rabbi famous for his commentary on the Talmud.
160. Balaam's talking ass / Numbers 22.
161. *Days of Awe* / Agnon's anthology of rabbinic sources on Rosh Hashanah and Yom Kippur. This passage appears in Hebrew in *Yamim Noraim* (1998 edition), p. 259 (the abridged English edition, *Days of Awe*, omits this passage).
168. Charlatagne / In Hebrew the doctor's name is Sḥaroni, i.e., "merchandiser," one who sells his "cures" for cash.
172. King is honored in the presence of great numbers / Proverbs 14:28. The decree requiring the unlearned village Jews to spend the Days of Awe in the city brought greater numbers of people together in the Buczacz synagogues, but also enabled them to experience communal prayer, Torah reading, and shofar blowing according to the proper rituals which might not have been attained in the small villages.

175. *The Rabbi Turei Zahav and the Two Porters of Buczacz*
"HaRav Turei Zahav u-Shenei HaSabalim shehayu BeBitczacz"; orig. pub. in a number of locations, undergoing revision and expansion in each printing: *Omer* (October 29, 1937); *Shnaton Bar Ilan* 2 (1964); and *Haaretz* (May 15, 1965).

175. Turei Zahav / R. David Halevi Segal (1586-1676), rabbi in Lemberg from 1653, was one of the great halakhic authorities of Polish Jewry. He was called the *Turei Zahav* (Rows of Gold), abbreviated as *Taz*, after his commentary on the Shulḥan Arukh.
175. Exile brings atonement / Berakhot 56a and Sanhedrin 37b.
177. Section 151 / Taz to Oraḥ Ḥayyim 151:4, in a discussion of the sanctity of the synagogue, and the preference that no other structure be built atop a synagogue, records his comment as quoted in the story about his remorse at having resided above a synagogue, and his sense that the death of his children was a punishment for this laxity.
178. Longer than the earth is its measure, and wider than the sea / Job 11:9.
178. Of the making of many books there is no end / Ecclesiastes 12:12.

181. *A Single Commandment*

"Al Mitzvah Aḥat"; orig. pub. in *Sefer Buczacz* (Tel Aviv: Buczacz Memorial Society and Am Oved, 1956), ed. Yisrael Cohen.

183. Two tables /A reference to wealth and Torah learning (Berakhot 5b). The rabbi is surprised that this simple man knows the talmudic passage.

185. *The Blessing of the Moon*

* *"Birkat HaLevanah"*

The theme of the moon-struck somnambulant girl was treated by Agnon with great effect in his enigmatic novella "Edo and Enam," available in annotated translation in *Two Tales* (The Toby Press, 2014).

185. The sanctification of the moon ceremony / Monthly ritual performed outdoors, most often in the evening following the conclusion of the Sabbath, between the third and fifteenth of each lunar Hebrew month, in which a blessing is recited upon observing the waxing moon, a sign of the renewal of creation and an auspicious sign for future redemption.
185. Ba'al Halevushim / Mordechai Yaffe (1530-1612), the author of a series of commentaries on the Sḥulhan Arukh all entitled with the word *Levush*, thus his rabbinic appellation.

189. *The Market Well*

"Be'er HaShuk"; orig. pub. in *Haaretz* (September 19, 1956).

189. R. Ḥayyim, the author of Be'er Mayim Hayyim / R. Ḥayyim Tyrer (1740-1817) was a kabbalist and ḥasidic rabbi. Born in a small village near Buczacz, he served in a variety of communities before settling in Jerusalem in 1813. His two-volume commentary on the Torah is entitled *Be'er Mayim Ḥayyim* (The Well of Living Water).
190. I am a stranger in the land / Psalms 119:19.

192. *The Great Town Hall*

* *"Beit HaMoetzot HaGadol"*

Although this story was only first published in the 1973 edition of *'Ir u-Melo'ah*, the kernel of the plot—which seems to have been a piece of local Buczacz folklore—was already present in Agnon's very early story, *"Ir HaMetim"* (published in the Lemberg newspaper *HaEt* in 1907).

192. Astonished, struck dumb / Cf. Genesis 24:21.
192. Make a name for himself / Cf. Tower of Babel story, Genesis 11:4.
193. Trembowla / Eastern Galician town about 50 km. northeast of Buczacz.
196. Theodor finished all of his work / Agnon's verb echoes: God's finishing the work of creation (Gen. 2:1); Moses' finishing the work of building the tabernacle (Exod. 39:32); Hiram's completion of the interior of the Temple (1 Kings 7:40, 8:54).
198. First aeroplane that a Jew would make / Otto Lilienthal (1848-1896), German aviation pioneer, known as the Glider King, having been the first person to make well-documented, repeated, successful gliding flights. His book *Birdflight as the Basis of Aviation* served as an important inspiration for the Wright Brothers. Agnon here repeats a well-circulated legend that the Evangelical Lilienthal was a Jew, for which there is no evidence, aside from his very circumstantial Jewish-sounding family name.
198. Servants of the Count Potocki were at their work in the fields / Reminiscent of the Icarus legend as depicted by Ovid in which a "ploughman, shepherd and angler... are astonished and think to see gods approaching them through the aether."
199. Roiling in his blood / Cf. Ezekiel 16:22.

201. *The Partners*

"HaShutafim"; orig. pub. in *Maariv* (September 9, 1963).

211. Two of them walked along together / Echoing Genesis 22:6.

217. A spade to dig with / Avot 4:5; that is, as the rabbi should not profit from his holy work in the rabbinate, the yeast business was given to him to generate income to live by.
218. The wicked may lay it up, but the righteous will wear it / The verse is actually taken from Job 27:17 rather than Psalms.
219. As Rashi had explained about the first man / Rashi to Genesis 2:18.
223. Emanuel Ringelblum / (1900-1944) was a historian, politician, and social worker, known for his *Notes from the Warsaw Ghetto,* and the *Oyneg Shabbos* (Ringelblum) Archives of the Warsaw Ghetto, an immensely important cache of documentary evidence (stored in milk cans) on life inside the Ghetto. In fact, Agnon's tale of his cousin's demise is inaccurate: Ringelblum escaped the Ghetto, but his hiding place was discovered by the Gestapo, and he was killed along with his family and those who were hiding them.

224. *The Water Pit*

* *"Bor HaMayim"*

224. Ashmadai / Demonic character of Jewish folk-legend, mentioned in the Zohar and Talmud (Gittin 68b, et al.).
225. The neighbors poured out their water / Jewish legal codes mention this custom. It appears that water in open containers was thought subject to contamination through the potential incursion of impure or demonic forces.

227. *Feivush Gazlan*

"Feivush Gazlan"; orig. pub. in *Shnaton Davar* 13 (1956).

Gazlan is Hebrew for "robber." When used pejoratively, it denotes a thug or a gangster.

228. Withered or stolen lulav / A lulav that is withered or stolen is ritually invalid (Mishnah Sukkah 3:1 and explanation in Sukkah 30a).
228. Jacob Frank / (1726–91) was the founder and leader of a sect that sought to perpetuate and develop the antinomian and anti-rabbinic teachings and practices of the false messiah Shabbatai Zvi (1626–76). Frank saw himself as Shabbatai Zvi's reincarnation but created his own syncretistic and eccentric blend of Judaism and Christianity. Frank was excommunicated as a heretic by both Jewish and Christian authorities. Agnon's narrator often insists, against much historical evidence, that Frank was born and buried in Buczacz.

229. Candle tax / In 1797, the tolerance tax and the taxes on homes and properties of the Jews in Galicia were repealed; in their place, the idea of a candle tax was broached by one Shlomo Kopler (spelled by Agnon below as Kobler) and encouraged by Naphtali Herz Homberg (1749–1841), a leader of the Haskalah (Jewish Enlightenment) in Galicia. The tax was instituted in 1800. In return, Kopler and his partners, who were less than upstanding individuals, received the franchise for collecting the tax over all of Galicia, and Homberg was rewarded as well. The tax was abolished in 1848.

230. Gentiles might touch the wine and thus render it unfit / As a way of limiting social interactions with non-Jews, talmudic law prohibits drinking wine touched by gentiles, even if otherwise kosher and made by Jews. Esau here is a metonym for a non-Jew, Esau being the eponymous ancestor of the gentiles as his brother Jacob is for the Jews. The point in the story being that the prohibition against drinking this wine was merely academic here: once the drunkard non-Jewish tax authorities spotted the wine, they consumed all there was to be had.

230. Kiddush over whiskey / Magen Avraham is a commentary by R. Abraham Gombiner (Poland, c. 1635–82) on the first part of the Shulḥan Arukh, the authoritative code of Jewish law compiled by Joseph Karo in 1563. See his note to Shulḥan Arukh, Oraḥ Ḥayyim 272:9.

230. Twenty-four chapters / The reference is to the custom of studying during the course of each Sabbath the twenty-four chapters of Mishnah that constitute the tractate Shabbat.

231. Chapter Hanizakin and the midrash on the Book of Lamentations / The Ninth of Av (Tishah b'Av) is a fast day commemorating the destruction of the Temple in Jerusalem (according to tradition both First and Second Temples). Because it is a day of mourning and fasting, only Torah texts can be studied that deal with the destruction. Hanizakin, the fifth chapter of tractate Gittin, includes many legends of the destruction of the Temple, as does the midrash on the Book of Lamentations that is read at the services on that day.

231. Nadvorna / City in eastern Galicia, now southwestern Ukraine, not far from Buczacz.

232. *Sefer Neta Sha'ashuim* / Responsa on the four parts of the *Shulḥan Arukh*, by R. Zvi Hirsh Kara (1740–1814), served as rabbi of Buczacz from 1794 until his death.

232. No harm befalls the righteous / Proverbs 12:21.

232. *Da'at Kedoshim* / Rabbinic work written by R. Abraham David Wahrman (1771–1840), known as the Tzaddik of Buczacz, rabbi of the town from 1814 until his death. Like Kobler, he was born in Nadvorna.

232. *Strasznhiks* / Polish expression for "guards"; it can refer to police, prison officers, royal guards, etc.

233. Hand of Esau… voice of Jacob / Genesis 27:22.

233. Royal army… Jewish community had to supply a quota of men each year / Jewish men were expected to serve in the Austro-Hungarian army. Each Jewish community was given a quota of men to be delivered for conscription, and its officials were charged with selecting and transporting them to the army authorities. This conscription of Jews was different from that instituted in Czarist Russia by Nicholas I from 1827 to 1855, where the prime purpose was to erode Jewish identity and promote assimilation. The Austro-Hungarian Empire simply needed manpower, though the effects on the Jewish conscripts were not too different.

233. Soul for soul, as I have told elsewhere in detail / See the story "Disappeared" elsewhere in this volume.

236. Tzenerena / Seventeenth century collection written in Yiddish of traditional commentary and folklore tied to the weekly Torah readings. It was written for women, who generally did not read Hebrew and were not as well-versed in Bible commentary. Its name comes from the Hebrew *tzena urena* (go forth and see) and is taken from Song of Songs 3:11: "Go forth and see, O daughters of Zion."

237. Shabbat Ḥazon, the Sabbath of the Vision / Named such because at the morning service of the Sabbath closest to Tishah b'Av the dire vision in Isaiah 1 is read, wherein the prophet chastises the people in the most severe terms for their moral failings. The chapter begins with the Hebrew words *Ḥazon Yishayahu ben Amotz* ("The vision of Isaiah son of Amotz").

237. Gnat / Gittin 56b. Two *selas* would be something slightly less than a pound.

237. Sisera / Judges 4:17-22.

237. Nebuchadnezzar / Daniel 4:25-30.

238. Pre-fast meal / When Tishah b'Av falls on the Sabbath, the fast is deferred to Sunday, it being forbidden to fast on the Sabbath (except when Yom Kippur falls on a Saturday).

238. Nine Days / The tradition is to refrain from the pleasure of eating meat during the first nine days of the month of Av, a period of mourning for the destruction of the Temple, which culminates with Tishah b'Av, but on the Sabbath that falls during those nine days, meat is allowed.
238. Shalom Zakhor / Lit., welcoming the male, a festive gathering held on the first Friday night after the birth of a baby boy.
239. King Solomon, peace be upon him... / Midrash Lamentations Rabbah 14.
239. When a wise man contends with a fool / Proverbs 29:9.
239. One who rebukes a buffoon / Lamentations Rabbah 15. The verse is Prov. 9:7.
240. Purposeful labor performed for its own sake / Halakhic category of a purposeful action (*melakhah*) done on the Sabbath not "for its own sake," i.e., for its basic purpose, but to achieve a different end or benefit. In the present context, the act of extinguishing a fire on the Sabbath, though in itself forbidden, would be done to save the life of anyone inside. See Shabbat 94a and commentaries thereon.
240. Injunction not to walk on the Sabbath the way one walks during the week / Shabbat 113b.
240. You shall not hate your brother in your heart / Lev. 19:17.
240. You shall not stand by the blood of your fellow man / Lev. 19:16.
240. Fedor, named for Theodor / See the story "The Great Town Hall."
241. The ways of God are hidden, His thoughts must be very deep / Psalms 92:6.
241. Not immersed in water for three weeks / The three weeks from the seventeenth of the Hebrew month of Tammuz to the ninth of Av, culminating in the fast on that day, are a period of mourning for the Temple during which a traditional Jew will abstain from such physical pleasures.
242. Tashlikh / Lit., casting away; ritual performed on Rosh Hashanah afternoon in which one's sins are symbolically cast away into a naturally flowing body of water.
242. May the Lord increase you and your children / Psalms 115:14.
243. He who utters lies shall not stand firm before my eyes / Psalms 101:7.
245. R. Mendel of Satanov / Menaḥem Mendel Lefin (1749–1826), author of several important work of Musar literature, aimed at providing a behavioral road map to moral and ethical self-perfection.
246. Nothing is as good for digestion as sleep after a meal. Maimonides explains this... / Mishneh Torah, Hilkhot De'ot 4:3, where Maimonides

recommends remaining at rest immediately after eating in order to allow the food to be digested.

246. You have made him little less than divine / Psalms 8:6.

247. Shabbat Naḥamu, the Sabbath of Consolation / First Sabbath after Tishah b'Av, named such because the prophetic reading at the morning service is the message of consolation in Isaiah 40:1–26 that begins with the Hebrew words *naḥamu, naḥamu ami* ("Console, O console My people, says your God").

248. Place where the jokers pray / Pejorative reference to a ḥasidic house of worship.

249. See if there is any pain like mine / Lamentations 1:12.

249. You shall surely provide for him / Deut. 15:14, specifying the treatment of an indentured servant who is freed by his master.

250. Kapparot / Lit., expiations; ceremony performed on the morning of the day before Yom Kippur in which the sins of an individual are symbolically transferred to a live fowl. The fowl—a rooster for a man, a hen for a woman—is swung around the head three times as biblical verses and a formula of vicarious atonement are recited. Money in the amount of the fowl's value is often substituted for the fowl.

251. Numerical reckoning of the word Shabbat / This would work out to 702 fasts because of the gematria value of the Hebrew word Shabbat.

253. *In Search of a Rabbi, or The Governor's Whim*

"HaMevakshim lahem Rav o BaRuaḥ HaMoshel"; orig. serialized in *Haaretz* (September 21, 1960; October 5, 1960; October 12, 1960; and March 3, 1961), except for the concluding section following chap. 17 of the "Water Upon Water" story heading (beginning with "In Poland, there are, thank God, rabbis"), which was only published with the 1973 edition.

253. R. Leibush Auerbach / R. Aryeh Leibush Auerbach (d. 1750), served as Rabbi in Buczacz until 1740.

253. Yeshivah on High / A rabbinic euphemism for heaven; i.e. "after R. Auerbach died."

253. Zabno / Town in contemporary southern Poland, about 430 km. northwest of Buczacz.

254. Maharam Schiff / R. Meir Yaakov HaCohen Schiff (1608-44), Frankfurt, Germany, rabbi and noted Talmudist.

254. Two tables / Wealth and learning (as per Berakhot 5b).
254. Tikkun ḥatzot / Midnight vigil mourning the destruction of the Temple.
255. The second side of folio thirty-three in tractate Niddah / Niddah 33b records that Rav Papa upon visiting a town would visit the local Torah scholar. From the citation to this passage, the Rabbi of Zabno understood that R. Yeruḥam considered him to be the local scholar worthy of visiting upon arrival from out of town.
255. R. Yosei ben Kisma /Avot 6:9.
255. More pride into his heart than the bit that the Sages permit / Sotah 5a: A Torah scholar must have one-eighth of one-eighth measure of arrogance.
256. *Two Tablets of the Covenant / Shenei Luḥot HaBerit* by R. Isaiah Horowitz (1558–1630), known as the Shelah (acronymic of the title of this his most important work).
257. You shall make no graven image / Exodus 20:3.
258. Fast of the twentieth of Sivan / Hebrew date observed by force of custom as a fast commemorating the Khmelnitski Pogroms of 1648-49, in the lands impacted by those tragedies. The "four fasts" are the minor fasts instituted by talmudic decree in connection with the destruction of the Jerusalem Temple.
259. Shas and Poskim / I.e., Talmud and rabbinic codes.
260. A man does not know its value / Job 28:13.
260. Mountains of Darkness / Cf. Tamid 32b, a rabbinic metaphor for the boundaries of Hell.
261. With the humble is wisdom / Proverbs 11:2.
261. There is no man who has no hour… / Avot 4:3.
261. Shmurah matzah / To supervise the harvesting of the wheat for the special Passover matzah.
261. Between strength and wisdom / In his 30s, see Avot 5:21.
262. Pharaoh's dream is one / Exodus 41:25, i.e., it's all the same.
263. Until my bones trembled / Cf. Jeremiah 23:9.
263. 1633 according to the *Tzemaḥ David* / Others give Maharam Schiff's year of death as 1641 or 1644.
265. Four Turim / *Arba'ah Turim* is an important halakhic code, composed by R. Yaakov ben Asher (Cologne, 1270–Toledo, c. 1340).
266. Time is short… / Cf. Avot 2:18.
268. Arise, shine, for your light has come / Isaiah 60:1.

274. *Revealer of Depths* / *Sefer Megaleh Amukot*, by the kabbalist Nathan Neta Spira (Poland, 1586-1633).
274. Elijah binds him up / Kiddushin 70a: In punishment to the husband
274. Great Order of the World / *Seder Olam Rabbah*, second-century ce rabbinic chronology detailing the dates of biblical events from Creation to Alexander the Great's conquest of Persia.
277. The mercy of the wicked is cruel / Proverbs 12:10.
278. He who wishes to eat an animal before its soul has departed / Ḥullin 33a.
278. Rif / R. Isaac Alfasi (Morocco and Spain, 1013–1103), compiler of major halakhic commentary on the Talmud.
279. Esau… Jacob / In the rabbinic metaphor these are stand-ins for Christians and Jews.
279. You made men ride over our heads / Psalms 66:12; the verse continues: "We went through fire and through water, yet You brought us out into a place of abundance."
279. A person should not part from his companion… / Berakhot 31a.
282. Maharsha / R. Shmuel Eidels (1555-1631), known by the acronymic Maharsha, was a renowned rabbi famous for his commentary on the Talmud.
282. Concerning this it is told in the book of the wars of the Lord / Numbers 21:14.
283. Who are these people with you / Cf. Numbers 22:9.
284. Wool… linen / The Torah prohibits wearing garments (or sitting on cushions) containing a mix of these fibers (known as shatnez); see Leviticus 19:19 and Deuteronomy 22:11.
284. Ḥayyim Cohen Rapoport / (1699-1771), Galician rabbi and ardent anti-Sabbatean, from 1740 served as rabbi of Lvov.
287. She is the wife that God has approved / Cf. Genesis 24:44.
288. The splendor of the king is in a great multitude / Proverbs 14:28.
289. Whence will come my aid? / Psalms 121:1.
293. Mar bar Rav Ashi… Sarah bat Tovim / 5th century ce amora (talmudic sage) in Babylonia and head of the academy of Sura; Sarah bat Tovim (or, in Yiddish, Bas-Toyvim), learned woman of the late 17th-early 18th century, author of widely circulated *Tkhines*, Yiddish-language prayer book intended mainly for Jewish women

296. Rabbenu Tam / Jacob ben Meir (1100–1171), known as Rabbenu Tam, was one of the most renowned Ashkenazi rabbis and leading French Tosafists, a leading halakhic authority in his generation, and grandson of Rashi.

296. Great Love / The blessing "Ahavah Rabbah" recited immediately before the morning Shema. Rabbi Mordechai's description of what he hears are all taken from the words of the blessing.

297. Release his soul with the utterance of the word One / The Shema opens with the verse, "Hear, O Israel, the Lord your God, the Lord is One" (Deuteronomy 6:4). Berakhot 61b: "When R. Akiva was taken out for execution, it was the hour for the recital of the Shema, and while they combed his flesh with iron combs, he was accepting upon himself the kingship of heaven... He prolonged the word 'One' until he expired while saying it."

299. Fast of the firstborn / According to custom the firstborn males fast on the day before Passover (marking having been spared in the plague of the firstborn which afflicted the Egyptians). The fast can be avoided by participating in a *siyum*, the celebratory completion of the study of a Talmud tractate.

300. Shelah / Acronym for *Shenei Luḥot HaBerit* by R. Isaiah Horowitz (1558–1630). For the claim that Rashi composed his commentary with holy spirit (i.e., a form a prophecy) see *Shelah* to *Shevuot – Ner Mitzvah* #28.

300. Ba'al Halevushim / Mordechai Yaffe (1530-1612), the author of a series of commentaries on the Sḥulhan Arukh all entitled with the word *Levush*, thus his rabbinic appellation. He makes this point concerning Rashi in his *Levush HaOrah* on Genesis.

304. Reuven and Shimon / These names of biblical sons of Jacob are customarily used in halakhic jurisprudence as placeholder names, equivalent to John Doe and John Roe, for parties in a legal action, case, or discussion.

309. Popiel and Piast / 9th century Polish princes and monarchs.

314. Blessing of dew / Recited on the first day of Passover; i.e., even in spring the world was still snow-covered.

319. Better not to vow than to vow and not to pay / Ecclesiastes 5:4.

323. Curses / Leviticus 26:14-41 or Deuteronomy 28:15-68. These sections describe the horrible punishments that will befall Israel if the covenant is betrayed. See the story "Until Elijah Comes," in which the customs of reading this section in an undertone plays an important role.

324. Reuven sang by himself. He sang, "Blessed be He..." / A variety of Sabbath hymns traditionally sung at the luncheon table.

325. Lamentations / Lamentations 3:37.

325. It is good / Ta'anit 10b: "R. Yehudah said, Rav said that a man must always go out on 'that it is good' and enter on 'that it is good.' " Rashi explains: "That he should wait until there is light, as *And God saw the light that it was good* (Gen. 1:4), and enter on that it was good, in the evening while the sun is shining, for no robbers are present and also so that he will not fall into a pit or a crevice in the city and that they will not accuse him of being a spy or a thief."

325. Melaveh malkah meal / Lit. "escorting the queen"; the post Sabbath meal which symbolically escorts the Sabbath Queen on her departure.

325. Grace after meals with the name of God / If there is a quorum of ten men reciting the grace after meals, the name of God is added to the initial words of the prayer.

328. Bigtan / One of the ministers who plotted to assassinate Ahasuerus, Esther 3:21.

329. Traveler's prayer / A prayer said upon embarking on a journey.

334. Recording the capital and the interest together / A rabbinic device to avoid the prohibition against taking interest on a loan (see Exodus 22:24 and Leviticus 25:35-37).

335. *Porządny człowiek* / An honest man.

335. *Ładny Żyd* / A fine Jew.

335. Vayishlaḥ / The Torah portion beginning, "And [Jacob] sent messengers before him to Esau," Gen. 32:4–36:43. Because the section discusses the epic confrontation between Jacob and Esau (symbols in the rabbinic mind for Judaism and Christianity), it was customary to read this passage before encountering non-Jewish authorities on any official business, based on practice of R. Yehudah Hanasi prior to his travels to Rome (Midrash Rabbah Vayishlaḥ 88:15).

337. Council of the Lands / Alt. Council of the Four Lands; central body of Jewish authority in Poland from 1580 to 1764.

339. Seven attributes that a panel of three judges... / Cf. Maimonides, Hilkhot Sanhedrin 2:7.

339. If a judge has had some benefit... he must be recused / Shulḥan Arukh, Ḥoshen Mishpat 7:12.

340. Great goy / Play on the biblical expression *goy gadol,* a great nation. Shaygetz is a derogatory Yiddish term for a non-Jewish man.

341. Birthday of "that man" / Rabbinic euphemism for Christ; i.e., on Christmas.

342. The widow's rite / *Tikkun almanah*; kabbalistic ritual performed by a widow (or her proxy) prior to re-marrying in an attempt to ward off the bad will of her deceased first husband from interfering with her new marriage.

342. Rashash / R. Shalom Sharabi (1720-1777), Yemenite-born halakhist and kabbalist, served as head of the Beit El kabbalah yeshivah in Jerusalem's Old City.

343. Excommunicate / Shulḥan Arukh, Ḥoshen Mishpat 11:1.

345. Weil… Maharash / R. Yaakov ben Yehudah Weil, known as the Mahariv, 15th century German Talmudist; Maharash, R. Shalom ben Yitzḥak Zekil of Wiener Neustadt in Lower Austria, died c. 1413.

348. Ḥametz that has been kept during Passover / Leavened foodstuffs that have remained in a Jew's possession when they were supposed to have been sold to a gentile or disposed of remain forbidden for Jewish use following Passover.

349. We will do and hear / Exodus 24:7.

352. What is good and what God demands / Micah 6:8.

352. Love work; hate dominion… / Avot 1:10. The Hebrew word *Rabbanut* means "dominion" in the context of the Mishnah; later Hebrew (and in our story's rabbi's reading) it is interpreted as the rabbinate.

352. Better to skin carcasses… / Pesaḥim 113a.

352. Keep a distance from exercising power… / Ovadiah of Bartenura, commentary on Avot 1:10.

353. Keep your way far from her… / Avodah Zarah 17a explicating Proverbs 5:8 and 30:15.

353. R. Yoḥanan said, I remember… / Bava Batra 91b.

354. Nittel-nacht / Yiddish euphemism for Christmas eve, when according to custom Jews refrained from Torah study.

356. River Sambatyon / Agnon has turned the analogy on its head. The legendary Sambatyon is calm on the Sabbath, but the apostate's heart is agitated on the Sabbath.

358. Maharshal / Rabbi Solomon Luria (1510-1573, Poland and Lithuania), leading halakhist.

358. Light shone in the darkness for the righteous / Psalms 112:4.
361. Just as the dead are punished / Berakhot 62a.
362. When a man's ways are pleasing… / Prov. 16:7.
362. The mouse is not the thief, rather the hole is / Gittin 45a.
362. Your destroyers and your ruiners come from you / Isaiah 49:17.
363. He turns them wherever He wishes / Proverbs 21:1.
363. Blessing the sun / A rare blessing recited every twenty-eight years, when the sun returns in its cycle to the place as on the day of creation. The phrase here is used to indicate Yissakhar Ber's longevity.
363. R. Yisrael Ba'al Shem Tov / (c. 1700-1760) founder of Ḥasidut, was attacked and maligned by the rabbinic establishment for the perceived "deviances" in movement he founds.
363. Tablet upon which the whole service of sanctifying the new moon / Recounted, above, in the story "The Blessing of the Moon."
364. Meir Netivim / R. Meir Margaliot (1707-1790), served as rabbi of Yaslowitz, town nearby to Buczacz.
365. Happy is the man whom You choose and bring near / Psalms 65:5.
366. Rema / R. Moshe Isserles (1530–72), known as Rema, among the most important rabbis in Polish Jewish history, author of monumental glosses on the *Shulḥan Arukh*.
366. The law of the kingdom is law / Talmudic principle by which civil law of the host country is binding on the Jew in exile; reference to responsa of Rema #123.
366. First speaker on all occasions / Shabbat 33b. Significantly, this introduces the famous discussion about whether the Romans benefited the Jews in their conquest of the Land of Israel. In that discussion, Rabbi Shimon ben Yoḥai says: "Everything [the Romans] installed, they installed only for themselves. They installed markets to put whores in them. Bathhouses to pamper themselves. Bridges, to take tolls." This radical rejection of Roman rule is consistent with Rabbi Mordechai's opinions and conduct.
366. Tractate Menaḥot / Menaḥot 103b, and Tosafot s.v. Ma'aseh.
367. Fear of God increases days… / Yoma 9a explicating Proverbs 10:27.
367. Martha, the daughter of Boethus / Wealthiest woman in Jerusalem prior to destruction of Second temple; her payment to Jannai is recorded in Yoma 18a.

367. Ḥasidim of Ashkenaz / 12th and 13th century German Jewish pietistic, mystical, and ascetic movement. Not to be confused with the later 18th century ḥasidic movement.
368. R. Zvi Kara / (1740-1814), author of *Neta Sha'ashuim*, rabbi of Buczacz from 1794 until his death. See more on him in the story "In a Single Moment."

369. *Disappeared*
* *"HaNe'elam"*

369. Divided up the Kingdom of Poland / Galicia was part of the Polish Commonwealth until the first Partition of Poland in 1772, when much of it became part of the Austrian empire. The rest of it became Austrian in the Third Partition of Poland, in 1795.
371. And your people are all of them righteous / Isaiah 60:21.
372. Wheat money / Communal funds distributed to the poor to buy wheat to be ground into flour from which Passover matzah was baked. The custom of distributing such funds to the needy goes back to talmudic times.
373. Salt the slaughtered chickens / Salting and soaking of kosher meat, as required by the Torah to remove the forbidden blood, was a time-consuming duty. The mother in the story would buy the slaughtered chickens and prepare them by soaking and salting, or by plucking the feathers, and then sell at a small markup to wealthier women who wanted to "outsource" those onerous tasks.
373. Landesrabbiner / Head rabbi of a district or a province in the countries of Central Europe.
375. A man can surely not redeem his brother… / Psalms 49:8.
375. Master of the universe, Let me perish… / Midrash Deut. Rabbah 7:10.
376. R. Meshulam Igra / (1742–1801), rabbi and halakhist. Born into a distinguished rabbinic family in Buczacz, where he served as rabbi until his appointment in Tisminitz, and later, in 1793, the major Hungarian city of Pressburg.
376. Tisminitz / Today Tysmenytsia, town in western Ukraine, not far from Buczacz.
380. Shakespeare / The reference is to the celebrated German translation of Shakespeare's major works made by August Schlegel and Johann Tieck at the beginning of the nineteenth century. In Germany, their translated versions are regarded as poetically excellent as the original.

381. Dan shall judge his people as one of the tribes of Israel / Genesis 49:16. The verse can also be read with the word Dan not as the subject but as the object: *Dan shall be judged by his people, as one of the tribes of Israel.*
381. Shelah / Acronym for *Shenei Luḥot HaBerit* by R. Isaiah Horowitz (1558–1630), an influential compendium of Jewish practice and mystical teachings.
381. Shatnez / Biblical law (Lev. 19:19 and Deut. 22:5, 9-11) forbids wearing a garment containing a mixture of wool and linen.
383. Tenaim / Lit., "conditions" or "terms," written prenuptial agreement that a couple draws up, stipulating the details and terms of their forthcoming marriage. It is executed at a festive ceremony in advance of the actual wedding. The custom of writing tenaim originated among Ashkenazic Jewry in the Middle Ages.
384. Blessed be the Lord my Rock... / Psalm 144.
388. Taḥanun / Lit. "petition," supplemental petitionary prayer said on weekdays, near the end of the morning and afternoon services.
388. Dan shall be a serpent by the road / Genesis 49:17.
388. O God, remember me... / Midrash Bereshit 97:17, playing off of Judges 16:28 and Jeremiah 15:16.
388. To settle a really difficult problem you need a scholar / Avodah Zarah 50b.
390. Joy to his heart and peace to his soul / Cf. Proverbs 1:2-3.
390. Joseph Perl / (1773–1839) was a key disseminator of the ideas of the Haskalah (the Hebrew Enlightenment) in Galicia. In 1813–15, he edited and published an annual almanac (*Luaḥ Tzir Ne'eman*, Faithful Messenger Calendar), which included not only a calendar of Jewish and gentile holidays and festivals and other useful information but also a substantial section titled *Luaḥ Halev* ("Almanac of the Heart"). The title derived from Prov. 3:3, *Inscribe them upon the tablet of your heart,* and that section, which comprised the majority of the almanac, presented, in a "lucid and fluent" Hebrew, stories from rabbinic literature that served to advance Perl's enlightenment agenda.
391. R. Yossel's book *Faithful Messenger* / A colloquial reference to Joseph (Yosef) Perl, and the aforementioned almanac.
391. Book of Hebrew Letters / The reference is likely to *Mikhtevei Ivrit* (Hebrew Letters, 1847) collected by Meir Halevi Letteris (1800–1871), a poet of the Galician Haskalah and a prolific writer and scholar. He is best known for his edition of the Hebrew Bible.

391. Shalom Hakohen / (1772–1845), Haskalah poet.
391. Most blessed of women in the tent / Judges 5:24.
392. Teḥinah book / Small, pocket-size book of Yiddish prayers written for, and often by, women. The word *teḥinah* (lit., "petition"; pl., Yiddishized as *teḥines*) can refer to such books or to the prayers themselves.
393. They are tiny as peas, and in Dan's case as beans / Presumably, just as when children learn to write, they write the letters much larger than a more skilled hand, so, too, Dan, who was not learned but could write—in his handwriting, each letter sat on the page as large as beans instead of the smaller, more elegant pea-size letters.
393. Shtreimel / Large circular head piece of black velvet surrounded by fur, worn by ḥasidic and other Jews in Galicia and surrounding countries on the Sabbath, holidays, and festive occasions. A spodik is similar to a shtreimel but taller, thinner, and less extravagant.
393. Eastern wall / Place of honor in the synagogue customarily reserved for the rabbi and important people. In the West, at least, it is the place in the synagogue closest to Jerusalem. The ark containing the Torah scrolls is usually situated there, and one faces it when standing in prayer.
400. Jonathan the demon… / Yevamot 122a and Berakhot 18b.
400. God has made one no less than the other / Ecclesiastes 7:14.
402. Agunah / A married woman whose marital status is indeterminate because her husband has either left her, disappeared, or is without agency because of physical or mental illness. If his death could be confirmed or a bill of divorce from the husband would be found or obtained, she would be certified as a widow or a divorcée and be free to remarry. But absent any certifiable confirmation of the termination of the marriage bond and until one is forthcoming, she is, in the eyes of Jewish law, still anchored or chained to her missing husband and is not free to remarry. A remedy for her condition within Jewish law is exceedingly difficult to find and, if available, would involve many halakhic (Jewish legal) complexities and procedures.
403. Moshe Alshikh / (1508–93) was a Bible commentator and homiletician who flourished in Safed. The rabbi brings a quote stringing together Genesis 49:2 and Isaiah 50:1.
408. Count Potocki / Potocki was the name of a prominent aristocratic Polish family that held lands in eastern Galicia, including Buczacz.
414. Hope prolonged creates heartache / Proverbs 13:12.

419. Joseph / A reference to the biblical Joseph in the house of Potiphar (Genesis 39), who did not succumb to the temptations of his master's wife.

427. *Yekele (I)*

* *"Yekele (Nusaḥ Eḥad)"*; this story, and the parallel version that follows, "Yekele (II)," appear to be two different attempts at telling the same story. Neither was published in Agnon's lifetime. From the manuscripts in the Agnon archives of the National Library of Israel it appears that version I of the story likely predates version II, but even this cannot be established with certainty (both merely carry the title Yekele; the styling of the versions as (I) and (II), or more literally in the Hebrew edition: "One Version" and "Another Version," was an editorial decision of Emunah Yaron). It is possible that Agnon always intended to include both versions in the final publication (the choice his daughter made), a kind of "Rashomon"-like attempt to tell one story from different points of view. The incident at the heart of these stories, the execution of an innocent Jew with the assent of the head of the Jewish community, is based on an event which Agnon claimed occurred in Buczacz in 1825, and which he already referred to in a very early story, "*Ir HaMetim*" (published in newspaper *HaEt*, 1907).

428. Seventh of Adar / Jewish tradition ascribes the seventh day of the Hebrew month of Adar as the date of both Moses' birth and death (Rosh Hashanah 11a).

428. Ḥevrah kadisha / The Jewish Burial Society that attends to the details of the funeral and burial. Men attend to men, women to women. The society customarily holds its annual meeting on the seventh of Adar and sponsors a festive banquet for its members, based on the idea that God Himself tended to the burial of Moses upon his death on this day (Deuteronomy 34:6).

428. *Ḥai* / Hebrew word for life, and the numerical value of its two Hebrew letters is eighteen.

430. The voice was the voice of Yekele / Yekele is a Yiddish diminutive for the Hebrew name Yaakov (Jacob), and the reference is to Genesis 27:22, "the voice is the voice of Jacob, but the hands are the hands of Esau."

430. If someone is coming to kill you, rise up and kill him first / Sanhedrin 72a, and several other places in Talmud.

432. Polish Commonwealth / Galicia was part of the Polish Commonwealth until the First Partition of Poland in 1772, when much of it became part of the Austrian Empire.

432. Bulging bellies / Cf. Job 15:27.

432. Hold not a thief in contempt for stealing to appease his hunger / Proverbs 6:30.

432. *Metzudot* / 18th century commentary on the Prophets and the Additional Writings by Rabbi David Altschuler.

433. Czernowitz / Alt. Chernivtsi or Tschernowitz; city in western Ukraine, approximately 125 km. southeast of Buczacz.

435. Our hands did not shed this blood nor did our eyes see it done / Deuteronomy 21:7.

438. *Yekele (II)*

* *"Yekele (Nusaḥ Aḥer)"*; see introductory note to "Yekele (I)," above.

438. The first Yisrael Shlomo, of blessed memory, who we have often mentioned / See Agnon's *Hakhnasat Kallah*, Book I, chapters 11-13, and Book II, chapter 5; in I.M. Lask's English translation ("In order to record the praises of Reb Israel Solomon") as *The Bridal Canopy* (The Toby Press edition, 2015).

439. The greatness of his doings / Cf. Esther 10:2.

440. Ari / R. Isaac Luria (1534–72), one of the key figures in the development of kabbalistic thinking.

440. Bill of divorce / In accordance with Mishnah Yevamot 6:6.

440. It is better to dwell as a duo than to live like a widow / Yevamot 118b, Kiddushin 75a, and elsewhere.

441. *Ḥemdat Yamim* / Published in Izmir, 1731, is an anthology of kabbalistic practices of unknown provenance. It was erroneously regarded as a Sabbatian text. Gershom Scholem writes of it: "[T]his voluminous book remains in my opinion, despite all that strikes us as bizarre, one of the most beautiful and affecting works of Jewish literature (*Major Trends in Jewish Mysticism*, p. 285).

441. Come let us sing unto God / The morning service on Wednesdays concludes with a recitation of Psalm 94 and the first three verses of Psalm 95, which is said in its entirety at the beginning of the service of welcoming the Sabbath on Friday nights; hence its association with and anticipation of the Sabbath.

442. Karpas / Green vegetable dipped in saltwater toward the beginning of the Passover seder.

442. 182 coins… equivalent of that sum is the name "Yaakov" / In the system known as gematria, each letter of the Hebrew alphabet has a numerical value. The four letters of the name Yaakov add up to 182. Yekele is a Yiddish diminutive of Yaakov.

442. The Man of Truth / The reference is to the prophet Elijah likely on the basis of I Kings 17:24, "And the woman said to Elijah, 'Now I know that you are a man of God, and the word of the Lord in your mouth is true.' "

442. You will show truth to Jacob / Micah 7:20.

443. Bartenura… Tosafot Yom Tov / The Bartenura commentary on the Mishnah, composed by R. Ovadiah of Bartenura, Italy, in the 15th century; Tosafot Yom Tov is a 17th century Mishnah commentary by R. Yom Tov Lipmann Heller of Prague and Poland.

444. *Akedat Yitzḥak* / Torah commentary called after the "binding of Isaac" in Genesis 22 was written by Isaac Arama, 15th century Spain.

444. Eruv Tavshilin / Lit., "mixing of cooked dishes." A rabbinic device that allows the preparation of food for a Sabbath that immediately follows a Friday holiday to be prepared on that Friday, despite the general prohibition of performing activities on one holy day for the following day.

446. When you deliver the Hebrew women giving birth / The Torah portion comprises Exodus 1–6:1. The passage is at Exodus 1:16.

446. Ki Tavo / Deut. 29:4. The Torah portion "Ki Tavo" comprises Deut. 26:1–29:8.

446. Ki Tetzeh / Deut. 22:5. The Torah portion "Ki Tetzeh" comprises Deut. 21:10–25:19.

446. R. Meir Ba'al Haness Charity / Lit., "Rabbi Meir the miracle worker." R. Meir (mid-second century CE) was an important rabbinic figure in the mishnaic period who, through a miracle attributed to him (Avodah Zarah 18a-b), became associated with charitable acts. Since the eighteenth century, several charities have operated under his name.

447. Sekhvi Vina / Lit., "discernment to the rooster," after God's question to Job (38:36), "Who put wisdom in the hidden parts? Who gave discernment to the rooster?" The phrase occurs in the first of the preliminary blessings in the morning "Blessed are You… who has given understanding to the rooster to distinguish between day and night."

447. Kapparot / Lit., "expiations" ceremony, performed by observant Jews on the morning of the day before Yom Kippur in which the sins of an individual are symbolically transferred to a live fowl. The fowl—a rooster for a man, a hen for a woman—is swung around the head three times as biblical verses and a formula of vicarious atonement is recited. Money in the amount of the fowl's value is often substituted for the fowl.

447. Kiddush Levanah / Lit., "sanctifying the moon." This is a liturgy, rabbinically prescribed (Sanhedrin 41b–42a), recited in clear moonlight on a night, customarily on a Saturday night after the Sabbath, soon after the appearance of a new moon. The verses chanted express an acknowledgment of the divine presence in the natural universe.

450. To destroy one of Israel / After Mishnah Sanhedrin 4:5.

451. Our hands did not shed this blood / Deuteronomy 21:7.

453. *The Earliest Ḥasidim*

"Ḥasidim Rishonim"; orig. pub. in *Measef: Divrei Sifrut, Bikoret veHagut* 1 (1960), ed. A. Ukhmani and Y. Cohen.

453. *Da'at Kedoshim* / Rabbinic work written by R. Abraham David Wahrman (1771–1840), known as the Tzaddik of Buczacz, rabbi of the town from 1814 until his death.

453. Cotton caftan / The Hebrew text reads "*kaftan shel kitay*," which is nankeen, a type of Chinese cotton. Sailor's pants often made from it. It was a term in Ukrainian and Ukrainian-Polish, which also became a Jewish family name for those who dealt in this merchandise.

454. Shabbatei Zvi… Jacob Frank / Frank (1726–91) was the founder and leader of a sect that sought to perpetuate and develop the antinomian and anti-rabbinic teachings and practices of the false messiah Shabbatai Zvi (1626–76). Frank saw himself as Shabbatei Zvi's reincarnation but created his own syncretistic and eccentric blend of Judaism and Christianity. Frank was excommunicated as a heretic by both Jewish and Christian authorities. Agnon's narrator often insists, against much historical evidence, that Frank was born and buried in Buczacz.

455. *In a Single Moment*

"BeSha'ah Aḥat"; orig. pub. in *Haaretz* (September 16, 1955).

455. The first ten men needed to make a minyan / Berakhot 47b: "A man should always rise early to go to synagogue so that he may have the merit of being counted in the first ten."
456. Avraham David was not named for our teacher the Tzaddik of Buczacz / R. Avraham David Wahrman (1771-1840), known as the Tzaddik of Buczacz, where he served as Rabbi from 1814 until his death, author of the halakhic works *Da'at Kedoshim* and *Eshel Avraham*.
456. While the tzaddik was still living / According to Ashkenazic custom to never name a child for a living person.
456. David Prager / Important lay-leader in Buczacz, central figure in Council of Four Lands, d. 1699.
456. As with the green grasses / Genesis 9:3.
458. The tender darling of his mother and father / Proverbs 4:3.
458. Mo'ed ... Nashim ... Nezikin / Three of the six orders of tractates that make up the Mishnah.
461. The Fifteenth of Av / A festive day when this specific prayer is omitted. The Fifteenth of Av is a minor holiday, which is mentioned in the Mishnah as the beginning of the grape harvest. The Talmud (Ta'anit 30b) mentions an ancient custom of the unmarried girls of Jerusalem dressed in borrowed white garments and went out to dance in the vineyards, attracting the attention of the young men, leading to marriages. The story about a wedding being set on this date is meant to draw the connections back to these sources.
461. Live to 120 / The age at which Moses died, hence the maximum life span one can hope for.
462. As far as one is permitted to walk on the Sabbath / 2,000 cubits past the city limits, or approximately slightly farther than one kilometer.
462. One must study at night as well / Because the days are getting shorter.
463. Beginning with the Fifteenth of Av, the sun's rays grow weaker / Ta'anit 31a.
463. Reached into a niche in the wall / Song 5:4.
463. Eating meat / Otherwise forbidden during the days of mourning preceding the fast of the Ninth of Av.
464. Lift your gaze / Ta'anit 4:8.
464. Whoever had no wife went there / Ta'anit 31a.
464. Berakhot / The first tractate of the Talmud.
464. Kiddushin / Tractate of the Talmud that deals with marriage.

465. Ninth of Av / Fast day commemorating the destruction of the Temples and other disasters in Jewish history.

466. A God-fearing woman, her husband's pride / Proverbs 31:28, 30.

467. Council of the Four Lands / Self-governing body of the Jews in Poland.

467. Put on tefilin / Daily practice begun at age thirteen, upon becoming bar mitzvah.

467. Wallachia / Historic and geographical region of Romania, situated north of the Danube and south of the Southern Carpathians.

468. Mystical formula / Including the words "for the sake of the unification of the Holy One, blessed be He, and His Immanent Presence"; such formulas, based on kabbalistic theosophy, had become part of the liturgy used by the ḥasidim and were strenuously opposed by the Mitnagdim (opponents of ḥasidism).

468. The righteous can walk on them / Hosea. 14:10: "For the paths of the Lord are smooth; the righteous can walk on them, while sinners stumble on them." In an anti-ḥasidic barb, the author of *Nodah BiYehudah* had substituted "pious" (ḥasidim) for sinners. Hearing that ḥasidim had tried to have a printer restore the original wording, the author of *Nodah BiYehudah* is reported to have exclaimed, "I tried to turn sinners into pious Jews, and they are trying to turn pious Jews into sinners!"

468. R. Meshulam / Igra (1742–1801), rabbi and halakhist. Born into a distinguished rabbinic family in Buczacz, where he served as rabbi until departing for Tisminitz, and later, in 1793, for the major Hungarian city of Pressburg.

468. R. Hershele Kara / Alt. Zvi Kara (1740-1814), author of *Neta Sha'ashuim*, rabbi of Buczacz from 1794 until his death.

468. *A gekoviter moire horo'o* / Yiddish phrase in the original, with the same meaning.

470. Descended on our town since the fire / Buczacz suffered a major fire in 1865; the extent of the damage is described in the continuation of the story, which is set in the period following the conflagration, when much of the town remained desolate.

470. A fair and comely bride / Ketubot 16b: "How does one dance before [i.e., sing the praises of] the bride? The School of Shammai says, speak of her as she is, [without exaggeration]. And the School of Hillel says, [every bride should be called] 'a fair and comely bride.' "

472. Ḥesed leAvraham / Responsum of R. Avraham Te'omim (1814–68), who served as rabbi in Buczacz from 1853 until his death.
472. Zboriv / Alt. Zborów; town about 90 km. north of Buczacz.
474. Gave forth its fragrance / Song 1:12.
475. Vrum Duvit / A corruption of the Galician-Jewish pronunciation of Avraham David.
475. Hark, the archangels cry aloud / Isaiah 33:7.
476. For then I will make the peoples ... / Zephaniah 3:9.
481. It was ordained that the days before the Day of Atonement be joyful / Ta'anit 30b.
482. The cat and the mouse made a party with the milk of some unlucky fellow / Sanhedrin 105a, referring to Num. 22:7, where Moab and Midian, bitter enemies, conspire together against Israel.
482. A person can become entangled in his neighbor's sins / Shabbat 55b–56b, which gives examples of "death without sin and suffering without iniquity."
482. Have embraced refuse heaps / Lamentations 4:5.
483. When the Lord overturned the city... and they barely escaped / Gen. 19:21, 25, 29; II Kings 22:13; Jer. 6:11; II Chron. 34:21, 36:16; Deut. 32:22; Hos. 8:14; Amos 1:7, 10; Ps. 137:7; and Jer. 21:9, 23:19, 38:2, and 39:18.
483. I hear screaming / Exodus 32:18.
484. A bridegroom is like a king / Pirke deR. Eliezer 16 records the midrashic equation of a bridegroom with royalty.
484. Who is like the wise, who knows the meaning of things? / Ecclesiastes 8:1.
484. I shall turn my back on him, and he shall not see my face / Exodus 33:23.
485. Hear us, O our God, for we have been shamed / Ps. 79:4, Neh. 3:36.
485. Why should the canopy be destroyed? / II Sam. 20:19.
485. With the inspiration of Moshe / Shabbat 101b, Beitzah 38b, inter alia.
485. People only get close to someone in order to benefit from him / Avot 2:3.
486. One may win a place in eternity in a single moment / Avodah Zarah 10b, 17a, 18a.
487. A man may not marry a woman until he has seen her / Kiddushin 41a.
488. Came laden with shame / lit. "a basket of shame hung on her back"; cf. Yoma 22b.

488. Sun of truth shone and set things aright / Mal. 3:20.

488. Saw and recognized that it was true / From Alenu, a prayer for the End of Days that concludes each service.

488. Its day of lament converted into a day of festivity / Jeremiah 31:13.

488. Sorrow into gladness / Esther 9:22.

488. Menaḥem Av / A common way of referring to the month of Av, especially the remainder of the month following the Fast of 9 Av; the term *menaḥem* meaning "consoling," as well as being the name of our protagonist.

490. There is no marriage contract that does not provoke a quarrel / Shabbat 130a.

494. Birds began to migrate away from the Land of Israel / Jeremiah 4:25, 9:9.

494. Fifty-two years before the Destruction / Shabbat 145b.

495. Like the heavens in their height… unfathomable / Proverbs 25:3.

495. The reward of a good deed is a good deed / Avot 4:2.

496. Wherever you see the greatness… you will also see the humility / Megillah 31a: "Wherever you find [mentioned in the Scripture] the greatness of the Holy One, blessed be He, you also find His humility [mentioned]."

497. Well-known in the gates / Proverbs 31:23; the husband of a "capable wife" is "well-known in the gates" (gathering places) of the city.

498. *The Frogs*

"HaTzfardayim"; orig. pub. in *Haaretz* (April 1, 1956).

498. The *Yalkut* / *Yalkut Shimoni* on Psalms #889. Agnon may be playing off Yitzḥak Isaac Erter's satire *Gilgul haNefesh* (Reincarnation of the Soul), in which a ḥasid is reincarnated first as a frog, and then as a cantor. Erter (1791–1851) was a leading figure of the Jewish Enlightenment in Galicia.

499. R. Avraham Te'omim / (1814–1868) served as rabbi in Buczacz from 1853 until his death. The actual 1864 case of the protest against the rise of Buczacz fish prices is discussed in his responsa *Ḥesed leAvraham* II O.Ḥ., #26.

499. R. Menaḥem Mendel Krochmal / (1600–1661) served as rabbi in Nikolsburg, Moravia (in today's Czech Republic), from 1648 until his death. This case is discussed in his responsa *Tzemaḥ Tzedek*, #28.

499. We do not require them to forego that pleasure on account of the poor / See Bava Kama 9b and *Shulḥan Arukh*, Oraḥ Ḥayyim 656.

499. He even waived his rabbinic salary for his services to the community, as I have related elsewhere / This point is not told explicitly, but the narrator

notes that "all the years, from the time he returned to Buczacz until his death, [R. Avraham] saw himself as a regular member of the community and not as the rabbi of the town" ("HaRav veha'Ir," in *Ir uMelo'ah*, p. 553 [1973 ed.] or p. 569 [1999 ed.]).

500. Not only gentiles were buying fish but the Jews were as well / The 1870 census, with data closest in time to 1864 when this story is set, listed Buczacz with a population of 8,959 people, almost 70 percent of whom were Jewish.

500. Karpl Shlein... Fishl Shlein... Fishl Hecht / These are all fish names in German or Yiddish: karpl is a carp; fishl is fish; hecht is a pike; shlein is a codfish.

500. Magen Avraham / Commentary of R. Avraham Gombiner (1635–82) to the *Shulḥan Arukh*, O.Ḥ. 242:1.

500. Jerusalem Talmud reports of a poor man who was accustomed to eating... / Jerusalem Talmud, Pe'ah 3b, also at Kiddushin 20b.

502. He had served two world renowned scholars... Neta Sha'ashuim... Da'at Kedoshim... Ḥesed leAvraham / Eminent rabbis are often called by the title of their major works, as are these three, all of whom were rabbis who served in Buczacz. *Neta Sha'ashuim* (Plantation of Pleasures) is a work of responsa on the four parts of the *Shulḥan Arukh* by Rabbi Zvi Hirsh Kara (d. 1814). *Sefer Da'at Kedoshim* (Wisdom of the Saints) is a commentary on the laws of slaughtering written by his successor, R. Abraham David Wahrman (1771–1840.) *Ḥesed leAvraham* (Kindness to Abraham) is a collection of responsa on the four parts of the *Shulḥan Arukh* written by the rabbi in this story, R. Avraham ben Zvi Te'omim.

503. Maskilim / Adherents of the Haskalah (the Jewish Enlightenment movement).

503. Yosef Perl / (1773–1839) was a key disseminator of the ideas of the Haskalah (the Jewish Enlightenment) in Galicia.

504. Seliḥot / Penitential prayers recited at midnight or before dawn during the month preceding Rosh Hashanah until Yom Kippur.

505. Pan / Polish for "mister."

505. Havrila / Polish for Gabriel.

505. Vats of whiskey of the Jewish merchants that you sold him before Passover / Permits to sell liquor were awarded by the Crown to Polish agents who would then sublease them to Jewish merchants. Whiskey is liquid

leaven and is thus forbidden to be drunk or even owned by Jews on Passover. The reference here is to the sale to the non-Jew Havrila of all whiskey owned by the wealthy Jews who had won permits before Passover, after which they would buy it back from him.

508. *Goyische kop* / Lit., "brains of a gentile"; Yiddish epithet for obtuseness.

509. When the other fish saw that they had been treated with such contempt, they imposed a ban on his nets and trawling lines / Agnon relates this story in his collection of tales of the Ba'al Shem Tov; see the Hebrew version, "Kevod HaBeriot," in *HaAish vehaEtzim*, p. 157.

509. He didn't eat it because he didn't cook it himself / By rabbinic edict, food cooked by a gentile would be forbidden, regardless of its content.

510. The voice of the Lord is over the waters / Psalms 29:3. *Perek Shirah* (Passages of Praise) is a poem-like collection of biblical and talmudic verses of praise to God placed in the figurative mouths of the heavenly bodies, the elements of the natural world, and the various members of the vegetable, animal, bird, marine, and insect kingdoms. The text appears in authoritative editions of the prayer book but is not part of the liturgy. Author and date are unknown, but the work may go back to talmudic times.

510. I have come to my garden ... / Song of Songs 5:1.

511. I was asleep ... / Song of Songs 5:2-3.

511. Blessed be His name, whose glorious kingdom is forever and ever / A liturgical response recited at various points in the synagogue service, based on Neḥ. 9:5.

511. The song that the frogs sing / *Perek Shirah*, end of chap. 4.

514. Tashlikh prayer was said or willow sprigs / Cf. Mishnah Sukkah 5:4.

514. They will come into your houses, your ovens and your kneading bowls / Exodus 7:28.

518. *Pisces*

"Mazal Dagim"; orig. pub. in *Molad* 91 (January-February 1956). † Translation orig. pub. in *A Book That Was Lost* (Toby Press).

518. Fishl Karp / The Yiddish name Fishl is a diminutive of the Hebrew name Ephraim. The biblical Ephraim was blessed, along with his brother Menasheh, "to multiply abundantly like fishes" (Gen. 48:16). Karp, a Jewish family name, is, of course, a type of fish.

518. Eglon, the king of Moab / Obese oppressor of the Jews, mentioned in Judges 3. When stabbed to death by Ehud, the sword could not be drawn out of his corpulent flesh.

518. Lemberg / Alt. Lvov; major regional center, about 150 kilometers northwest of Buczacz.

519. R. Ḥidka / As opposed to conventional rabbinic opinion, which requires a Jew to eat three meals each Shabbat, R. Ḥidka (as cited in Shabbat 117b) mandated four meals. Scrupulous eaters were stringent to follow his view. Alternatively, the light repast taken following morning Sabbath prayers (colloquially called a "kiddush") was sometimes referred to as the "meal of Rabbi Ḥidka."

519. The banquet to bid farewell to the Sabbath Queen / The so-called melaveh malkah meal is taken on Saturday night to honor the departed Sabbath day (Shabbat 119b). According to Gen. Rabbah 28:3, the legendary *luz* bone receives its sole nourishment from this once-a-week meal, and from this one bone the dead will be revived in the messianic era. Fishl's punctilious observance of the melaveh malkah meal was to ensure that he, too, would be revived at the End of Days so as not to miss out on the promised messianic feast of Leviathan and wild ox (as described in Bava Batra 75a and expanded in the kabbalistic and ḥasidic literature).

520. Fear of even numbers / Talmudic superstition (Pesaḥim 109b ff.) against eating items in even-numbered quantities.

521. Manna / Cf. Exodus 16:4; Yoma 75b describes the taste of manna differed according to the desires of who was eating it.

523. Prayers for divine mercy / Supplementary prayers known as Taḥanun are omitted in the presence of a bridegroom during the seven days of wedding feasts or on the occasion of a circumcision.

524. Meat eaten on Sabbath during the nine days of mourning / In commemoration of the destruction of the Jerusalem temple in 70 ce, eating meat is forbidden during the nine days leading up to the mournful holiday of Tishah b'Av, with the exception of the Sabbath that occurs during that nine-day period.

524. Rooster… slaughtered for Yom Kippur / According to custom a chicken or rooster is waved about the head in the *kapparot* ritual, then slaughtered (and fed to the poor) to both show that one's sins had been symbolically transferred to the bird.

525. Buczacz had forsworn the eating of fish / As outlined in the responsum of R. Avraham Te'omim (1814–68), who served as rabbi in Buczacz from 1853 until his death. The actual 1864 case of the protest against the rise of Buczacz fish prices is discussed in his Ḥesed LeAvraham II O.Ḥ. #26. The family mentioned here who disregarded the ban is the subject of Agnon's parallel story, "The Frogs."
526. The place is narrow for me / Isaiah 49:20.
526. Kedushah and Barekhu / Parts of the prayer service that cannot be said without a minyan (prayer quorum) of ten men.
526. Meal that the sages praise extravagantly / Bava Metzia 107b.
526. Bezalel Moshe / Biblical Bezalel (Exod. 31:1-6) was the principle artisan of the Tabernacle, which was erected in the desert together with Moshe.
526. Mizraḥ / decorative wall-hanging indicating the east, as an indicator for facing direction of Jerusalem during prayer.
527. Compound interest / Fishl, as made explicit by story's end, was a moneylender.
528. Karpl Shlein… Fisher… Hecht… Fishman / All names for fish in Yiddish. Shlein is the protagonist of Agnon's story "The Frogs."
529. Hurry and cook / Cf. Genesis 18:6 and 27:9.
529. And he prayed / Jonah 2:2
530. And Thou didst cast me / Jonah 2:4.
530. Kiknish family / R. Yaakov Kiknish (d. 1630) served as rosh yeshivah in Lemberg, where his gravestone indicates his descent from the prophet Jonah.
530. *Kikayon* (gourd) / Jonah 4:6.
530. Who teaches us by the beasts of the earth / Job 35:11.
532. Here I shall dwell, for this is my desire / Psalms 132:14.
532. Castrated it and killed the female and salted it away / Bava Batra 74b, as cited in Rashi to Gen. 1:21.
533. 5623 or 5624 / 1863-1864 ce.
534. Every river follows its own custom / Ḥullin 18b.
535. For a man cannot know his time / Ecclesiastes 9:12.
536. Eating the small things / Berakhot 44b; in context of general advice about foods the Sages thought unhealthy, a rabbinic taboo against eating things before they had reached full size.
536. Everything on dry land is also in the water / Ḥullin 127a.

536. Ascent that is descent / Ḥasidic concept of the tzaddik's descent into impurity in order to raise himself and his follows to a higher spiritual level.
539. The one for whom a miracle occurs / Niddah 31a.
539. Two pair of tefilin / Some pious individuals wear a second pair of tefilin, whose scrolls are arranged according to a different order, in order to also fulfill the minority rabbinic opinion.
539. *Ḥok LeYisrael* or *Ḥovot HaLevavot* or *Reshit Ḥokhmah* / Popular moralistic books.
539. Deprived my soul of good / Ecclesiastes 4:8.
541. And even the fish of the sea / Hoseah 4:3.
541. Soul of a great tzaddik has been reincarnated / According to ḥasidic folk belief, as described below, that the righteous are reincarnated as fish.
541. For the earth was full of knowledge / Isaiah 31:5.
544. Just as Yitzḥak Kumer drew on Balak's skin / As related in Agnon's epic novel *Only Yesterday*.
545. Cat wearing tefilin / This story reappears in Agnon's *A Simple Story*, chap. 19.
545. Enlightener / Heb., maskil; an adherent of the Haskalah or Jewish Enlightenment movement.
546. Fast all that day / Customary as a remedy for the lamentable act of allowing his tefilin to fall to the floor; Be'er Hetev to Oraḥ Ḥayyim 571:1.
546. Nu, nu / Between placing the arm tefilah and the head tefilah, one is forbidden to speak or otherwise interrupt, thus Fishl (who is stuck halfway through the ritual without a head tefilah) no longer speaks throughout the remainder of the story, only mutely shouting, "Nu, nu!"
547. The letter *heh* made of tin that is hung up for a firstborn / A firstborn male child needs to be symbolically "redeemed" from a priestly *kohen* when thirty-one days old in the *pidyon haben* ritual for the price of five silver coins (Exod. 13:13 and Num. 18:15). During that first month of life, the practice was to hang a sign with the letter *heh*, whose numerical value is five, as a reminder of the five-coin debt to be paid on the thirty-first day.
548. Brow that never wore tefilin / Rosh Hashanah 17a.
550. As the birds fly / Isaiah 31:5.
550. R. Netanel the Cantor / Described above in Agnon's "In a Single Moment," chap. 12.
552. The belly charges the legs / Cf. Gen. Rabbah 70:8.

555. Permitted form of interest / Generally speaking, a Jew is forbidden to make a loan on interest (Exod. 22:24), in the absence of a special rabbinic legal device known as a *heter iskah,* allowing interest payments in certain circumstances.
556. Twelve tribes are compared to animals / Cf. Jacob's blessing in Genesis 49; this passage is adapted from the kabbalistic work *Tikkunei Zohar* 70 (133a).
557. And they drew water and poured it out / I Sam. 7:6.
557. Let them curse it / Job 3:7.
558. The second day compared to the first day / Beitzah 6a.
558. Kugel / Sweet or savory casserole-like Sabbath dish often made of noodles or potatoes. According to folk custom, one kugel is served for each Torah scroll used on that Shabbat (generally only one); on the Sabbath of Hanukkah that coincides with the New Moon, three would be served.
558. And they shall abound like fish / Gen. 48:16; the Hebrew works off a pun between *vayidgu* (abound) and *dag* (fish); additionally, the Hebrew name Ephraim is from a root meaning fruitful or plentiful.
559. Remember the Sabbath day / Exodus 20:8.

560. *In the Nighttime of Exile*

* *"BaLailah shel Galut"*

561. A guest for the night / Phrase taken from Jeremiah 14:8; title of Agnon's 1939 novel set in Buczacz during the interwar period, describing in stark detail the material and spiritual destruction suffered by his hometown. See the most recent edition, *A Guest for the Night* (The Toby Press, 2014).

Appendix

Rabbis of Buczacz

Name	Dates	Dates of Rabbinate	Works and Other Information (* Appears in story in this volume)
Yaakov Eliyahu ben Moshe Meir Mak		From 1648	Fled Sharigrod during 1648 Pogroms.
Elḥanan ben Zev Wolf			*Dat Yekutiel*
Abele ben Elḥanan			Son of *Dat Yekutiel*; son-in-law of parnas of the Council of Four Lands, Zvi ben Shimshon Meisels of Belz.
Moshe			Left Buczacz to serve on Beit Din in his hometown Zhulkva.
Aryeh Leibush ben Mordechai Madrish Auerbach	d. 1750	Until 1740	Left Buczacz to serve in Stanislav (* *In Search of a Rabbi)*
Meir ben Hertz		1765 (?)	In 1765 signed the census of Jews in Buczacz.

Name	Dates	Dates of Rabbinate	Works and Other Information (* Appears in story in this volume)
According to the decree of Josef II from May 27, 1785, the Rabbi of Buczacz serves as the regional rabbi as wellz			
Meshulam Igra	1752-1802	Until 1794	Distinguished talmudist and halakhist, author of many responsa; left Buczacz to serve in Pressburg. *(* Disappeared, In a Single Moment)*
Zvi Hirsch ben Yaakov Kara	1740-1814	1794-1814	*Neta Sha'ashuim* *(* Feivush Gazlan, In Search of a Rabbi, In a Single Moment, The Frogs)*
Avraham David ben Asher Wahrman	1771-1840	1814-1840	Son-in-law of *Neta Sha'ashuim;* served in Yaslowitz prior to Buczacz; author of *Da'at Kedoshim, Eshel Avraham (Buczacz),* and many other works; known as the Buczaczer Tzaddik. *(* The Ḥazzanim, Feivush Gazlan, The Earliest Ḥasidim, In a Single Moment, The Frogs)*
Yisrael Leib Wahrman		From 1840 until at least 1848	Son of the Buczaczer Tzaddik
Avraham David			Grandson of the Buczaczer Tzaddik
Period with no serving rabbik			
Tzadok Reinik		From ? until 1853	
Avraham ben Zvi Hirsch Te'omim	1814-1868	1853-1868	*Ḥesed LeAvraham (* In a Single Moment, The Frogs, Pisces)*
Yaakov Sgan-Cohen		1865	Served as halakhic authority during period that R. Te'omim temporarily departed Buczacz for Kamenetz following the 1865 fire.

Name	Dates	Dates of Rabbinate	Works and Other Information (* Appears in story in this volume)
Shalom Mordechai Ha Cohen Schwadron	1835-1911	1878-1881	Author of halakhic works *Shut Maharsham, Da'at Torah,* and *Mishpat Shalom,* and a 3-volume Torah commentary *Tekhelet Mordechai.* Known as the Gaon of Berezhany, where he served as rabbi prior to his death.
Meir ben Aharon Yehudah Arik	1855-1926	1912-1914	Fled to Vienna during World War I; noted halakhic authority and author of various talmudic and halakhic works.
Shraga Feivel Willig	1870-1941	1935-1941	Served as Av Beit Din before appointment as Rabbi; last Rabbi of Buczacz.

Buczacz – Population Statistics

1765	1,055 Jews (988 adults and 67 children); in nearby villages additional 303 Jews (278 adults and 25 children).
1870	8,959 total population of which 6,077 Jews (67.9%).
1900	11,755 total population of which 6,730 Jews (57.3%).

Source: *Sefer Buczacz* (Tel Aviv: Buczacz Memorial Society and Am Oved, 1956), ed. Yisrael Cohen. Available online at buchach.org

Glossary

Aggadah / Non-legal exegetical texts in the classical rabbinic literature of Judaism, particularly as recorded in the Talmud and Midrash.

Agunah / Halakhic term for a Jewish woman who is “chained” to her married state, unable to obtain a divorce. The classic case of this is a man who has left on a journey and has not returned.

Aliyah (pl. aliyot) / Section of the Torah reading to which a man is called as an honor to recite the blessings. On Shabbat the reading is divided into seven aliyot; during the weekday readings into three.

Av Beit Din / Presiding judge, or head, of a rabbinic court, often the presiding rabbi of the town.

Beit Din / Rabbinic court.

Beit Midrash / Study house; although prayers are also conducted here it is distinct from a synagogue.

Bimah / Lectern at which the Torah is placed during public readings; sometimes the prayer leader conducts the service from here as well.

Council of the Four Lands / Central body of Jewish authority in Poland from 1580 to 1764.

Daven / Yiddish, "to pray."

Gabbai / A volunteer official who oversees the finances of the synagogue and directs allocation of honors.

Gaon / Lit. "Genius"; honorific rabbinic title.

Gehinnom / Gehenna, netherworld, or hell; in rabbinic literature the posthumous destination of the wicked.

Gemara / Component of the Talmud comprising rabbinical analysis of and commentary on the Mishnah; completed around 500 CE.

Haftarah (pl. haftarot) / Passage from the Prophets read in the synagogue after the weekly Torah portion.

Halakhah / Jewish law and jurisprudence; can refer to a specific regulation or ruling, or more generally to the body of Jewish legal thought.

Hallel / Psalms 113-118, recited as a prayer of thanksgiving on holidays.

Ḥametz / Leavened bread or other foodstuffs, forbidden for consumption or ownership during Passover.

Ḥasid (pl. ḥasidim) / Adherent of Ḥasidut, mass eastern European Jewish pietistic and spiritual movement begun in the 17th century by R. Yisrael Ba'al Shem Tov.

Havdalah / Lit. "separation"; ceremony marking the end of Shabbat and holidays, ushering in the new week. The ritual involves lighting a special multi-wick candle, blessing a cup of wine and smelling sweet spices.

Ḥazzan (pl. ḥazzanim) / Prayer leader, cantor; usually refers to a hired town official who is retained to serve as the permanent prayer leader, especially for Shabbat and holidays.

Ḥeder / Traditional Jewish primary school.

Ḥidush (pl. ḥidushim) / Lit. "something new" or an innovation; highly-prized original Torah insight on a classic text.

Ḥumash / The Pentateuch; Bible, often printed with Rashi's commentary.

Kedushah / Lt. "Sanctity"; highlight of the daily communal prayer with a minyan, consists of the public declaration of God's sanctity.

Kiddush / Blessing recited over wine prior to Sabbath and holiday meals to sanctify the holy day; alt. light repast taken following morning Sabbath prayers.

Kittel / White linen robe worn by men as a burial shroud, but also on Yom Kippur and at the Passover seder.

Kloyz / A private house of study, existing separately from the institutions of the community and usually financed by a patron.

Lomdim / Lit. "learners"; class of townsmen who dedicated themselves, at least for a period, to full-time Torah study in the beit midrash. Often supported by communal funds.

Maariv / Evening prayer service.

Maḥzor / Special prayerbook for holiday use.

Maskil / Adherent of the Haskalah (late 18th century European Jewish Enlightenment movement).

Melamed / Lit. "teacher"; either the instructor in the local ḥeder or meant to indicate a private tutor.

Mezuzah / Scroll containing Torah passage written by ritual scribe, and attached to doorways.

Minḥah / Afternoon prayer service.

Minyan (pl. minyanim) / Prayer quorum of 10 adult men.

Mohel / One who performs a circumcision on the eight-day old child.

Musaf / Additional prayer service recited on Sabbath and holidays.

Neilah / Special prayer service for the conclusion of Yom Kippur.

Omer / Period of 7 weeks between Passover and Shavuot. The Torah instructs that each of the 49 days be counted aloud. The first 33 days are observed as a period of mourning.

Parnas / Communal lay leader; usually installed in a position of authority, for a period of time or indefinitely, in deference to his wealth.

Pinkas / Communal register and minute book maintained by most eastern European Jewish communities, containing historical information and demographic data.

Piyyut (pl. piyyutim) / Liturgical poetry.

Ruthenians / During the early modern era, the term was used primarily to refer to members of Eastern Slavic minorities in the Austro-Hungarian Empire—namely, Ukrainians and Russians.

Seliḥot / Penitential prayers recited at midnight or before dawn during the days preceding Rosh Hashanah until Yom Kippur.

Shamash / Sexton of the synagogue and assistant to the rabbi; often a paid official of the community.

Shavuot / Pentecost or Feast of Weeks; holiday marking the giving of the ten Commandments on Mt. Sinai 7 weeks after Passover.

Shulḥan Arukh / Code of Jewish Law; definitive halakhic code by R. Yosef Karo (Safed, 16th century).

Strypa / The river that runs through Buczacz, a tributary of the Dniester River, then in Galicia, today in western Ukraine.

Sukkah / Booths in which meals are eaten during the festival of Sukkot.

Talit / Four-cornered fringed shawl worn by men during morning prayer.

Talmid ḥakham / Torah scholar.

Tashlikh / Rosh Hashanah prayer recited by a body of water, in which ones sins are symbolically cast away.

Tatars / At the time of these stories the term was associated with the Turkic Muslims of Ukraine and Russia.

Tefilin (sing. tefilah) / Phylacteries; set of cube-shaped cases containing Torah texts worn by worshippers on the arm and head as part of morning prayers.

Teivah / The ark in which the Torah scroll is housed, but colloquially means the prayer-stand placed before the ark from which the ḥazzan (cantor) leads the prayers. To "go before the teivah" connotes serving as ḥazzan; i.e., leading the prayers.

Tikkun ḥatzot / Lit. "Midnight Regimen"; prayers of lamentation for the destruction of the Temple recited after midnight by devout Sephardic and ḥasidic Jews.

TISHAH B'AV / 9th day of month of Av; mournful fast day commemorating the destruction of both Jerusalem Temples.

TZADDIK (pl. tzaddikim) / Lit. righteous person; can also specifically refer to the Rebbe, or leader of a hasidic court.

TZITZIT / The rutual knots tied to the four corners of a tallit, or to the so called talit-katan worn under a man's garments.

YAHRZEIT / Anniversary of the death of a family member.

ZEMIROT / Hymns sung at the table during the three Sabbath meals.

ZOHAR / Foundational text of Jewish mysticism (Kabbalah).

Acknowledgements

Our thanks to Cheri Fox, Rabbi Steven Shaw, and Professor Avraham Novershtern and Beth Shalom Aleichem for support in publishing this volume, and to the Jewish Theological Seminary for facilitating the arrangements for this project.

James S. Diamond ז"ל played a pivotal role in the genesis of this project, and we are grateful to his widow Judy for locating the translation drafts Jim was at work on at the time of his tragic death. Our appreciation is extended to the team of translators which completed the task of bringing these stories to the English-reading audience.

For their help with the wide variety of research questions that presented themselves in the course of our work on *A City in Its Fullness*, as well as finessing elements of the translations, we are grateful to the community of Agnon scholars, and especially to: Israel Bartal, Omer Bartov, Haim Be'er, Hillel Halkin, Ariel Hirschfeld, Avraham and Toby Holtz, Elchanan Reiner, Rhonna Weber Rogol, David Roskies, Moshe Rosman, Avi Shmidman, Rafi Weiser, and Hillel Weiss. For help with resource retrieval, our thanks to Yoel Kortik, and for his assistance with Polish phrases and spelling, our appreciation goes to Yoel Chaim Nowicki in Warsaw.

About the Author

S.Y. Agnon (1888-1970) was the central figure of modern Hebrew literature, and the 1966 Nobel Prize laureate for his body of writing. Born in the Galician town of Buczacz (in today's western Ukraine), as Shmuel Yosef Czaczkes, he arrived in 1908 in Jaffa, Ottoman Palestine, where he adopted the penname Agnon and began a meteoric rise as a young writer. Between the years 1912 and 1924 he spent an extended sojourn in Germany, where he married and had two children, and came under the patronage of Shlomo Zalman Schocken and his publishing house, allowing Agnon to dedicate himself completely to his craft. After a house fire in 1924 destroyed his library and the manuscripts of unpublished writings, he returned to Jerusalem where he lived for the remainder of his life. His works deal with the conflict between traditional Jewish life and language and the modern world, and constitute a distillation of millennia of Jewish writing – from the Bible through the rabbinic codes to ḥasidic storytelling – recast into the mold of modern literature.

About the Editors

Alan Mintz is the Chana Kekst Professor of Hebrew Literature at the Jewish Theological Seminary. He is the author of *Ḥurban: Responses to Catastrophe in Hebrew Literature.* With Anne G. Hoffman he edited *A Book That Was Lost and Other Stories by S.Y. Agnon* (Toby Press), and he contributed a critical essay to James S. Diamond's translation of *The Parable and Its Lesson,* a major story take from *A City in Its Fullness.*

Jeffrey Saks is the Series Editor of The S.Y. Agnon Library at The Toby Press, and lectures regularly at the Agnon House in Jerusalem. He is the founding director of ATID – The Academy for Torah Initiatives and Directions in Jewish Education and its WebYeshiva.org program.

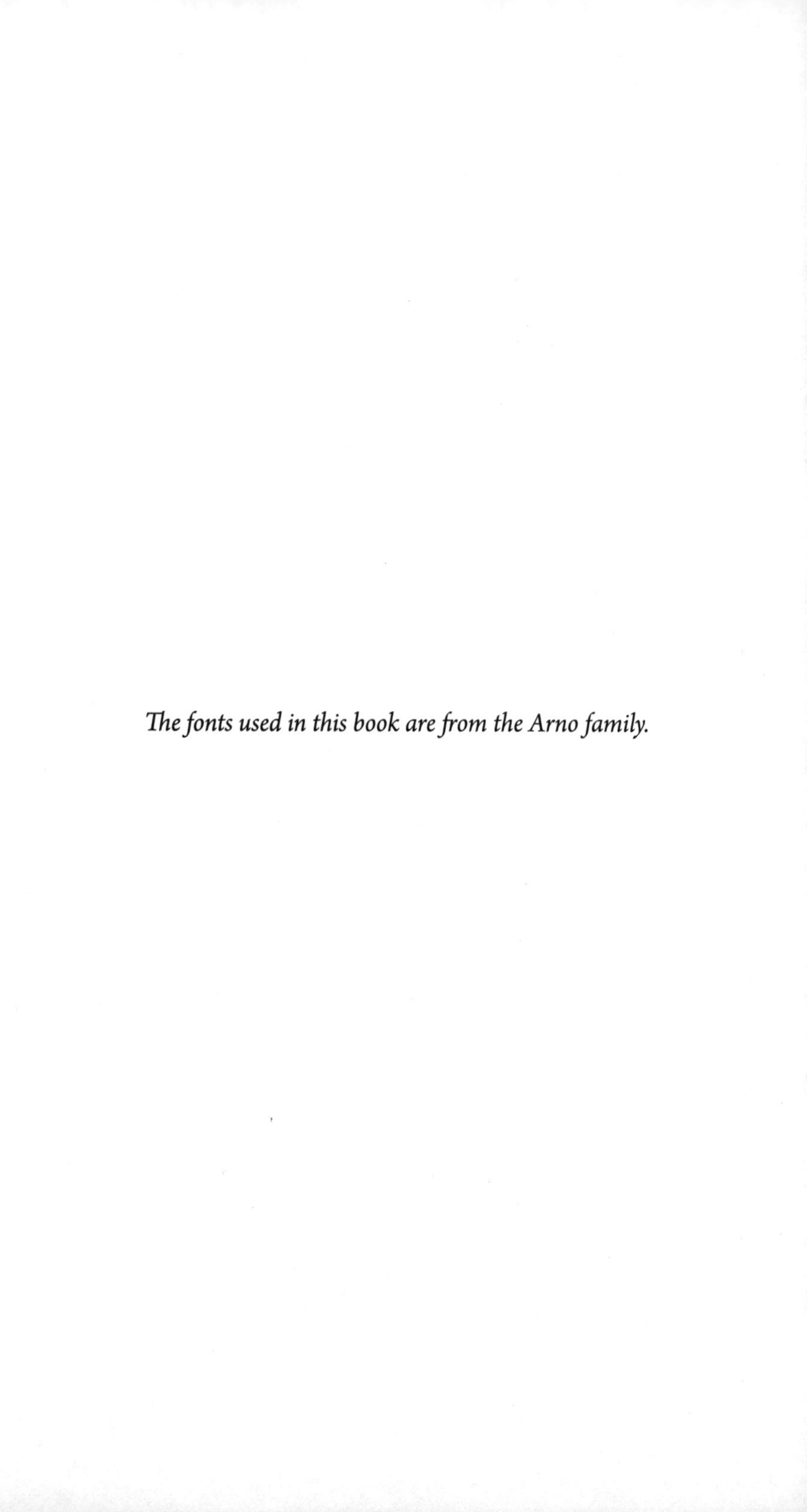

The fonts used in this book are from the Arno family.

The Toby Press publishes fine writing,
available at leading bookstores everywhere.
For more information please visit www.tobypress.com

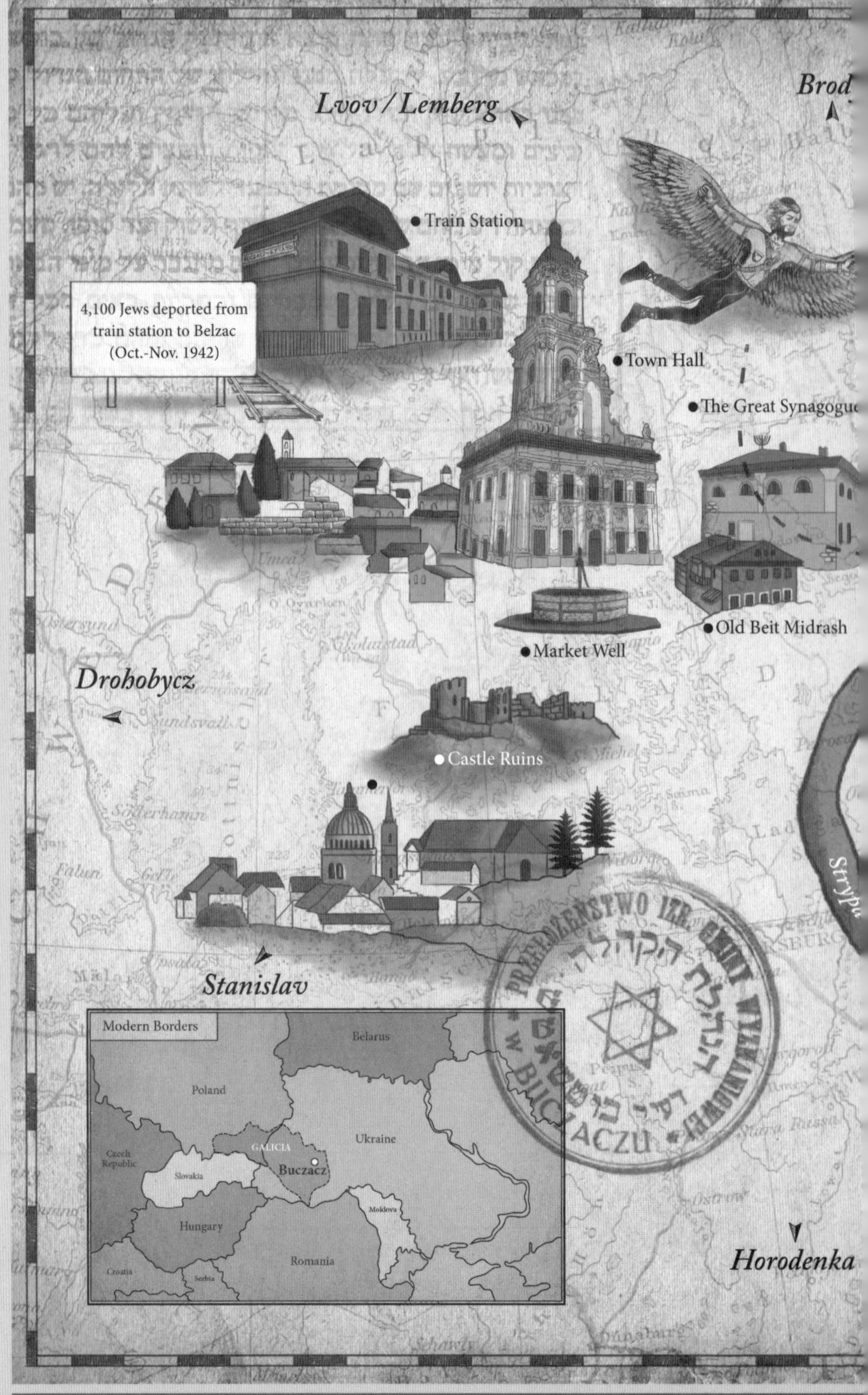

DOWNLOAD A COLOR VERSION AT WWW.KORENPUB.COM/BUCZACZ